Perlmann's Silence

Also by Pascal Mercier

Night Train to Lisbon

Perlmann's Silence

Pascal Mercier

Translated by Shaun Whiteside

Grove Press
New York

First published as *Perlmanns Schweigen* in Germany, in 1995
by Albrecht Knaus

First published in English, in Great Britain in 2011 by Atlantic Books,
an imprint of Atlantic Books Ltd

With the support of the Arts Council of Switzerland Pro Helvetia
swiss arts council
prohelvetia

Printed in the United States of America
Published simultaneously in Canada

ISBN-13: 978-0-8021-1957-5

Grove Press
an imprint of Grove/Atlantic, Inc.
841 Broadway
New York, NY 10003
Distributed by Publishers Group West
www.groveatlantic.com

The others are really others. Others.

I

The Russian Manuscript

1

Philipp Perlmann didn't know how to live in the present. He never had. That morning, though, it was worse than usual. He reluctantly lowered his Russian grammar and looked across to the high windows of the veranda, in which a crooked-growing pine was reflected. It was in there, among the gleaming mahogany tables, that it would happen. They would look at him expectantly as he sat at the front, and then, after a prolonged, unbearable silence and a breathless halting of time, they would know: he had nothing to say.

Ideally, he would have left again immediately, without giving a destination, without an explanation, without an apology. For a moment the impulse to flee was as violent as a physical pain. He snapped the book shut and looked across the blue changing cabins to the bay, which was flooded with the gleaming light of a cloudless October day. Running away: at first it must be wonderful; he imagined it as a quick bold rush, headlong through all feelings of obligation, out into freedom. But his liberation wouldn't last long. His telephone at home would ring again and again, and eventually his secretary would be downstairs pressing the doorbell. He wouldn't be able to go into the street or turn on the light. His apartment would become a prison. Of course, it didn't have to be Frankfurt. He could go somewhere else – Florence, perhaps, or Rome – where no one would be able to find him. But that would turn those cities into hideouts. He would walk through the streets, blind and dumb, before lying in his hotel room and listening to the ticking of his travel alarm clock. And eventually he would have to give himself up. He couldn't disappear for the rest of his life. If only because of Kirsten.

He couldn't come up with a convincing excuse. To give the true reason would be impossible. Even if he could summon the courage, it would sound like a bad joke. It would leave a sense of high-handedness, of wilfulness. The others would feel they were being mocked. Certainly, these people would take control of everything. *But I would be finished. There's no excuse for such things.*

The wonderful light which made the still surface of the water beyond the cabins look like white gold was to blame for everything. Agnes had wanted to capture that light, and that was why he had yielded at last to the urgings of Carlo Angelini. And Perlmann found him unlikeable, this wiry, very alert man with the winning smile that was just a little too practiced. They had met on the edge of a conference in Lugano at the beginning of the previous year, when Perlmann was standing by the window in the corridor long after the session had begun. Angelini had spoken to him and Perlmann had welcomed this excuse not to enter the lobby. They had gone to the caféteria, where Angelini had told him about his job with Olivetti. He was thirty-five, a generation younger than Perlmann. He had taken the offer from Olivetti only two years before, after spending some years as a language assistant at the university. His job was to maintain the company's contacts with the universities, and he was able to do so entirely on his own terms, with a considerable budget at his disposal, because his work fell under the rubric of publicity. They had talked for a while about mechanical translation; it had been a conversation like many others. But all of a sudden Angelini had become very lively and asked him if he felt like setting up a research group on a linguistic theme: a small but intensive matter, a handful of first-class people getting together somewhere nice for a few weeks, all at the company's expense, of course.

Perlmann had felt at the time that the suggestion had come far too quickly. Certainly, Angelini had made it plain that Perlmann wasn't a complete stranger to him, but he had known him for little more than an hour. Perhaps one had to risk such bold gestures in Angelini's line of work. In retrospect, Perlmann felt as if his instincts had been warning him even then. He had reacted to the suggestion without enthusiasm and rather lamely, but he had still observed that, in his view, people from different disciplines ought to be represented in such a group. It had been an offhand remark, not properly thought through, and Perlmann hadn't seriously imagined the project coming to fruition. His impression was that everything had been left sufficiently vague and noncommittal, when he had suddenly dashed to the lecture hall.

Perlmann had forgotten that conversation until a few weeks later when a letter came from Angelini, followed almost immediately by a phone call from Olivetti's headquarters in Ivrea. Perlmann's suggestion, it suddenly appeared, had proved very popular within the company; particularly, of course, with some colleagues from the research department, but it had also been well received by the directors. They were especially charmed by the possibility of being able to promote a project that had something to do with the company's products, while it also went far beyond it, by taking in questions of general interest, of significance to the whole of society, so to speak. He, Angelini, suggested that the encounter should take place the following year in Santa Margherita Ligure, a spa town not far from Rapallo on the Gulf of Tigullio. They had had meetings there on many previous occasions and everything had always gone very well. The best time for the planned undertaking, he said, would be the months of October and November. It was still mild then, but there were hardly any tourists left. There was a quiet, contemplative atmosphere, precisely what was required for a research group. Where everything else was concerned, as the head of the group Perlmann would have an entirely free hand; particularly, of course, in the selection of participants.

Perlmann bit his lip and felt helpless annoyance rising up within him as he thought back to that conversation. He had allowed himself to be taken unawares by the sonorous, confident voice at the other end, and for no reason whatsoever. He owed this man Carlo Angelini nothing at all. At the time he had been glad that the man had helped him to avoid the conference, but he was also a stranger, and his ambitions meant nothing more to Perlmann than the plans of Olivetti as a whole. Certainly, in the conversation he hadn't agreed to do anything. Quite soberly, he could still have said no. But he had missed the crucial moment, the moment when it would have been quite natural to say, 'There has been a misunderstanding. I didn't mean it that way. I'm sorry, but it really doesn't fit in with my other plans. I'm, sure, however, that I have many colleagues who would be more than happy to put your plan into effect. I will think about names.' Instead, he had promised to think about the idea. And instead of simply allowing an appropriate period of time to pass and then declining, he had fetched the map. He and Agnes had sat over it and worked out the places that could be easily reached from there: Pisa, for example, and Florence, but also Bologna, of which they were particularly fond. *Italy in winter*, that was one of Agnes's pet ideas. She had lots of plans for photographs. She might even try color photography, which she usually considered beneath her. *Whatever. At any rate I would like to capture the light of the south, as it is in winter, and this is the opportunity, don't you think? I'll make it sound appetizing to the agency. I'll have to do a bit of persuading, but in the end they'll let me go. Perhaps I could even make a series out of it:* The Wintry Light of the South. *What do you think?* Admittedly, October and November were not exactly winter, but Perlmann didn't want to be pedantic, and some of her enthusiasm had rubbed off on him. It was grotesque, he thought, and pressed his fingertips to his eyes, but at the time he had actually seen himself, above all, in the role of the person who would accompany Agnes on her photographic trip, supported and protected by her ability to conquer the present for both of them. It seemed incredible to him now, but that was how it had been: out of that vision, that daydream, he had finally agreed, had applied for leave from his job and written the first invitations. Ten months later, when Agnes died and everything collapsed, it had been too late to call things off.

Agnes had been right: the blue of the sky was strangely transparent here, as if in addition to the sun there were another, invisible background source of light. It gave the space that arched over the bay a veiled, mysterious depth, a depth that contained a promise. He had first encountered that blue and that light when his parents had driven him to Italy. He had only been thirteen, and had no words for it, but the southern colors had sunk deep within him – how deep he really understood only when

the train came out of the Gotthard tunnel at Göschenen and the world
looked like a picture in tones of grey. Since then the southern light had
been holiday light for him, the light that was life as opposed to work.
The light of the present. But it was a present that always remained only
one possible present, one that one could live if one were not here only
on holiday. Each time he saw it he felt as if this light were only being
shown to him to make him see that he was not living his real, everyday
life in the present. And because it was only ever a holiday light, the sight
of it became interwoven with the sensation of something transient, something that could not be captured and that could also be taken away again
as soon as it came within reach. Increasingly, he had come to see it as a
light of farewell, and sometimes he hated it because it gave him the illusion of a present that perhaps did not exist.

He stared, eyes smarting, at the surface of light now cleaved by a
motorboat. *The crucial thing,* he thought, *would be this: to allow the*
appearance of this light to be everything, the whole of reality, and seek
nothing behind it. To experience the light not as a promise, but as the
redemption of a promise. As something at which one had arrived, not some-
thing that constantly aroused new expectations.

He was further away from that than ever. Against his will, his eyes
slipped once more to the veranda. The gleaming red tables with their
curved legs were arranged in the shape of a horseshoe, and at its head
Signora Morelli had placed a particularly comfortable chair with a high,
carved back. 'Whoever is allowed to sit here must be worthy of it,' she
had said with a smile when showing him the room the previous evening.

For the third time that morning he opened his Russian grammar.
But he couldn't take anything in; it was as if there was no way in from
outside – as if he were suddenly blind to signs and meanings. It had
been like that the previous day on his journey here, a journey that had
become a single tormenting battle against recalcitrance. On the way to
the airport he had envied the people on the tram who weren't carrying
luggage, people with pale, sulky, Monday faces who didn't have to fly
to Genoa right now. Later on, he had wanted to swap places with the
airport staff, and for a long time he watched the passengers, all of them,

who had just landed and who were coming towards him from his plane. They'd put it all behind them. It was a rainy, windy morning, the cars were driving with their lights on, a December mood in mid-October, weather that could have intensified the thrill of anticipation of a flight to the south. But nothing struck him as more desirable than to stay in Frankfurt. He thought of the quiet apartment hung with Agnes's photographs, and what he really wanted to do was shut himself away in there and remain incommunicado for a very long time.

He had been sitting in the waiting room by the gate for a while, when he suddenly went out again and called his secretary. It was a phone call with no discernible purpose; he was repeating things they had discussed many times: what to do about his mail and how else they would stay in touch. Frau Hartwig didn't know what to say, her helplessness was clearly audible. 'Yes, of course, Herr Perlmann, I will do it just as we agreed.' Then he enquired, with sudden impertinence, after her husband and child. That untimely interest wrong-footed her, and there was a long, embarrassed pause before he said, 'All right then,' and she said, 'Yes, bon voyage.' He had been last to board.

On the plane he had struggled with himself. He told himself that while this might indeed have been the dreaded day of his arrival, it was still a day that belonged to him alone, and on which he could do something for himself. He set the Russian grammar down on the empty seat next to him. Then he waited for the magical effect of the plane as it started to move – waited for everything to come into flux in the moment of take-off, for everything to seem lighter. On a day like this you would soon be in the clouds, there were moments that were frightening in spite of one's experience, and then suddenly one emerged into a deep blue, transparent sky, a dome of pure ultramarine, and down below was the dazzlingly bright sea of clouds, from which individual formations loomed, little white mountains with pin-sharp edges, which tended to produce in him the impression of perfect stillness. *I have escaped*, he usually thought, and enjoyed the feeling that everything that had held him trapped until a few moments before was losing its power and falling away silently behind him, and he didn't have to do a thing. Yesterday, however, none of those things had happened, the whole thing had struck him as dull and boring. Forward impulsion with roaring engines, nothing else. Yes, outside it was as it always was, but he felt as if he were in an advertisement for the airline, shown a thousand times and without authenticity, without presence. He pulled the shutter down over the window, chose not to have anything to eat and tried to immerse himself in his grammar. But his usual concentration abandoned him. He stared again and again at the little boxes and exercises, but they simply didn't take. Then, when the plane began its descent, he was as violently startled by the gentle change in the sound of the engine and the feeling in his body as he would have been by the sound of an explosion. So here he was. When someone accidentally bumped into him as they were leaving the plane, he had to close his eyes for a moment and clutch himself before he managed to walk calmly on.

In Genoa the weather had been flat and dead. Grey, dirty-looking cloud banks let through only a dull, uninspiring light. Things were obtrusively only themselves, they had no significance and no lustre. The industrial plants that the airport bus drove past were ugly; there didn't seem to be a single unbroken windowpane, and he wondered how such a run-down terrain could produce all that bright white smoke, which looked poisonous. The few people in the station, it seemed to him, moved wearily in an alien time that flowed with nightmarish slowness. The smoking staff at the ticket counters showed no sign of serving him. Even the taxi driver didn't seem to care much about his fare. Only after he had finished chatting to his colleagues did he bother to ask which way to go. 'The shortest,' Perlmann had said furiously.

Before the plane took off for the return journey, four weeks, five days and three-and-a-half hours would pass. Perlmann stared at the reddish stone tiles of the hotel terrace. It was like a huge mountain range of tenseless time that loomed all the higher the more burning his desire was that things were over. And as the desire became even more violent every time he had it clearly before his eyes, and threatened to grow to infinity overall, Perlmann had a sense that that longed-for moment would never come, because there was no possibility of climbing over all the dead

time that loomed ahead of him like a menacing wall. The only way
out lay in silencing the desire and achieving inner calm. Then the mountain range would remove itself, and once the inner calm was complete,
time would seem like a plane that he would be able to cross effortlessly
to reach that distant moment.

He finally wanted to memorize the various expressions that existed
in Russian for *must*. He ran through the list and immediately forgot
every line. Sitting back in the shade didn't do any good, and it had
nothing to do with the sunglasses, either. And learning foreign languages
was something he had mastered. The only thing, in fact. It was also
the only thing that could really hold his attention. Studying languages,
he had the feeling that his life was advancing and he was developing.
And sometimes, when a foreign sentence, a hitherto inaccessible text,
suddenly opened itself up to him, he felt as if he had snatched a breath
of presence.

It only he could feel that in his academic work as well. It seemed
strange to him, but he no longer knew if it had ever been so. If it had,
it was a long time ago, in a time when he had not yet known the paralysis that had tormented him for so long. By now he had the feeling
that he didn't really know what it was like: doing academic work. It
wasn't writer's block, he was sure of that. He had never experienced it,
and even now he still had the capacity, he could feel it, for fluent, accurate and sometimes brilliant formulations. It was something else, something fundamentally much simpler and at the same time something that
he couldn't have explained, not to himself and even less to other people,
particularly not to his colleagues: he had lost his faith in the importance
of academic work – that belief that impelled him in the past, which
had made daily discipline possible, and the associated failures appear
significant.

It wasn't through a process of reasoning that he had lost this faith,
and the loss did not take the form of an internal discovery. He simply
couldn't find his way back to concentration, to the feeling of exclu-
siveness out of which his academic works had previously arisen. That
did not mean that he would now have declared the unimportance of

his research, or of research in general, as a statement of his world view. Except that he found his way to his desk less often. He spent more and more time looking out of the window. His new chair seemed to become more uncomfortable with each passing month, and the books on the big desktop increasingly struck him as being ungainly objects that disturbed the calming void.

Since this had been the case, he looked upon academic work as if through a wall of glass, which turned him into a mere spectator. Making an academic discovery: he simply had no need for it now. Methodical investigation, analysis and the development of theories, hitherto a constant, a given, self-evident element in his life and in a sense its center of gravity – he had utterly lost interest in it, and so completely that he was no longer sure he understood how it could once have been otherwise. If someone spoke of a new idea, the beginnings of a notion, he could sometimes still listen; but only for a short time, and its elaboration interested him not at all. It felt like wasted time.

Sometimes he tried to convince himself that it had all started on that clear, white, terrible day in January when he had seen Agnes for the last time, so shockingly, so irrevocably still. Then he could have seen himself as someone still in shock, someone only slowly recovering. That would have taken the edge off things.

But it wasn't true. He admitted to himself with amazement and some unease that he had forgotten when exactly it had begun. It had been small changes in his emotional responses to things, which had to do with his profession, emotional nuances, tiny changes of tone which had over months and years added up into something incisive that had one day entered his consciousness with total clarity. The beginning lay at a time when he, seen from outside, was at the peak of his productivity, and it wouldn't have occurred to anyone that something was starting to crumble behind that facade, and silently collapsing.

He had started to forget. Not in such a way that it would have struck anyone else. There were no gaps in the structure of the academic routine. But he noticed increasingly that he was losing track of issues, especially those that weren't yet fully entrenched, and which did not belong to the solid rhetorical stock of the subject – the new and interesting questions, then, which precisely because they were not yet all that well anchored, should have commanded his constant attention. He was, when he happened to flick through his papers, surprised by what he found there, and startled that he had simply forgotten it.

The worst thing was: he was sure that this wasn't a passing thing, a crisis that one knew would pass, even though one couldn't say when and how. It felt threatening, but he knew that what was happening to him was irreversible and inescapable. Behind the feeling of threat, he discovered only gradually, at good moments there was the liberating, almost cheering astonishment over the fact that something was developing within him, something in the center, at the core of his life. But this sensation which glimmered through from time to time did nothing to mitigate his anxiety. To a certain extent there was no contact between the two sensations; they ran unconnectedly side by side. And what struck him about that unsteady and unreliable feeling which he kept trying to grasp was this: he was never sure whether it was a genuine sensation or one that he conjured up within himself and, so to speak, invented in order to have something to cling to when the change that he sensed frightened him too much.

When he looked back at the book and tested himself, he found that he had retained only one Russian word for *must*. He gave up and reached for the other book that he had taken from the room when he had decided to spend his last free hours on the hotel terrace. It was Robert Walser's *Jakob von Gunten*, a book which had suddenly seemed like the ideal companion, as it sat on the shelf the previous morning, even though he hadn't picked it up for many years, and the memory of the titular character and the Institute Benjamenta had become pale and vague. On the journey he had been on the point of opening it, but every time he had felt a strange, inexplicable horror that got in the way of his curiosity. As if the book contained something about him that he would rather not know.

The first sentence took his breath away: *We learn very little here, there is a shortage of teachers, and we boys from the Institute Benjamenta will*

*never come to much, that is, we will all be something very small and subor-
dinate in later life.* As if anaesthetized, Perlmann watched the waiter
bringing a drink on a silver tray to the red-haired man by the pool.
Minutes passed before he found the courage to go on reading, reluctantly and at the same time fascinated by those shattering sentences, the
ghostly lightness of the prose. And then, after a few pages, there came
a passage that felt like a slap in the face: *Herr Benjamenta asked me what
I wanted. I told him shyly that I wanted to be his pupil. At that he fell
silent and read newspapers.*

That last sentence – no, it couldn't be allowed to stand. In all its
innocuousness it was a sentence that could not be borne. Perlmann set
the book aside. The throbbing of his blood subsided only slowly. He
didn't understand why, but young Jakob's story seemed in a sense to
be about himself. All of a sudden he was sure the text that would be
produced if he managed to capture his own distress in sentences would
have a similar tone. They would have to be sentences of equal intensity, and just as incisive, if they really wanted to grab their listeners as
he had done for years when he entered the auditorium.

It wasn't stage fright. It wasn't the fear of suddenly staring into the
audience or straight ahead at the lectern and having forgotten everything. He had suffered from that idea in the past, but it had been over
a long time ago. It was something else, something that he had only
recognized after a long time and with quiet horror: the very precise
feeling that he had nothing to say. Fundamentally, he found it ridiculous walking down the center aisle of the lecture hall under the expectant eyes of the students. With almost every step the sensation grew that
he was stealing their time from them.

Then he opened his notes and began to speak in his practiced, fluent
way. He was well known for being able to speak apparently off the top
of his head. The students liked him, often several of them came up to
the lectern afterwards and wanted to know more. That was particularly
bad. During the lecture the empty space between lectern and desks had
protected him, had acted as a protecting screen behind which he was
able to hide his lack of interest, that stigma. When the students sat in

front of him he felt unprotected, and worried that they might see that he was no longer involved. He took refuge in solicitous eagerness, spoke far too verbosely, filled up another blackboard and promised to bring the appropriate books along the next time. In many cases they were his own, which he pressed into the students' hands like bribes. They felt that they were being taken seriously, understood. A committed professor. They needed to know him personally, and invited him to join them at their table in the pub.

The first non-residential guests arrived for lunch at the hotel. Perlmann picked up his books and went to his room. As he closed the door his eye fell on the notice showing the price list, and he gave a start. The room cost around 300 marks. For a single person, this meant that his stay cost almost 10,000 marks, not including lunch and dinner. Times seven. OK, for Olivetti that was presumably nothing, and Angelini would know what he was doing when he put them up at the most expensive hotel in the town. Perhaps he'd negotiated a discount. But still, Perlmann held his face under the gleaming brass tap and then washed his hands for a long time. If it had been up to him he would never have stayed at a hotel like this, even if money were no issue. He just knew that he didn't belong here. And he began to sweat when he thought of his shabby, black, waxed-cloth notebook that was all he had to give in return, a loose collection of notes that he hadn't even looked at for ages. He felt like a fraudster, almost a thief.

That was the reason why his thoughts of flight, of every variety, included an intention to pay the bill for his room himself. Under the circumstances it would have been a demonstration. The others would have been able to tell that no higher power had forced him to take this step, but that his strange action must have something to do with his attitude towards the group. And he found that uncomfortable: it ran counter to his need to give as little of himself away as possible, and where possible to leave everything in the dark. But he didn't want to be in anyone's debt; at least in that respect he wanted to put things back in order.

Hesitantly, he opened his suitcase and started carefully standing the books up on the desk. It had been hard for him the previous evening when he had finally set about making a selection. Even more clearly than usual he had become aware that he had had no academic intentions for a long time. How, in such a situation, was one to decide what to take along and what not? He had sat there for quite a while, playing with the bold idea of travelling without any textbooks at all, just with his own novels. But however liberating the idea might have been, he couldn't risk it. Just in case they visited him here in the room, he had to construct a facade, a disguise. The important thing was for his distress to remain unnoticed. In the end he had packed a series of books that had turned up over the past few months and remained unread. They were books that anyone working in his field might have bought. He hadn't yet dared to give up such routine purchases, although he was beginning to regret the money – a sensation that startled him, because since his school days it had always been self-evident to him that money spent on books was never money wasted.

The desk was wide enough for the books, and if you pushed them back to the wall, with heavy volumes at the sides, the whole thing was stable, and there was enough room to write. Bringing his computer, the little appliance with the vast storage space for all the unwritten texts, was something he hadn't managed to do; it would have struck him as the height of mendacity. Perlmann set down pencils, a ruler and his best ballpoint pen on the glass desktop, along with a stack of white sheets. Tomorrow morning he would absolutely have to start working. *I have no idea what. But I have to start. At all costs.*

He had been saying that to himself for months. And yet it hadn't happened. Instead he had gone on working on his Russian for many hours a day. That connected him with Agnes. Supported by music that they both loved, he had withdrawn into an inner space in which she, too, sat at the table and quizzed him as usual, laughing as, once again, she understood something more quickly than he did. The specialist literature had been left where it was, and had started piling up on a shelf, within reach and yet never touched, a constant admonition. The language books were almost the only things on the desk. Only when he had colleagues visiting and there was a danger that they would enter his study, did he bring some order into the great chaos of an academic in the midst of his work, with mountains of open books and manuscripts. It was always a struggle between anxiety and self-esteem, and it was always the anxiety that won.

Meanwhile, there had been regular correspondence about the research group. There were enquiries into practical details to be answered, and official confirmations to be written. He had done that in his office at the university. At home there had been nothing to remind him of his inexorably approaching departure, and he had become practiced, almost a virtuoso, at not thinking about it.

For his lectures he had for a long time been using old manuscripts that had become strange to him, and sometimes he had started feeling like his own press spokesman. If an unexpected question came out of the audience and put him in an awkward position, he gave himself a breathing space by saying with deliberate slowness, 'You see, it's like this . . .', or 'That's a good question . . .' These were alienated formulas that he would never have used before, and he hated himself for them. In the seminars he lived from hand to mouth and relied on his memory. He was an experienced player. He thought and reacted quickly, and, if necessary, when he no longer had anything substantial to hand, he could set off a rhetorical firework. Students could still be impressed by such things. In the everyday business of teaching, he thought almost every time he left the practice room, he would retain his disguise.

But this was very different. In less than three hours' time some people would arrive who would not be deceived, people who didn't have to battle with such feelings, ambitious people who were used to the rituals of academic debate and the situation of constant competition. They would be coming with new works of their own, with fat manuscripts, with projects and perspectives, and they brought with them high expectations of the others, and also of him, Philipp Perlmann, the prominent linguist. For this reason they were a threat to him. They became his adversaries, even though they could have had no inkling of the fact. People like them had a very fine sense of everything to do with the social reality of their subject. They registered with seismographic precision if something was wrong. *They will notice I'm no longer involved – that I'm no longer one of them.* And sooner or later in those five weeks it would come out: he of all people, the leader of the group, the conductor of the whole thing, would stand there empty-handed – as if he hadn't done his homework. They would react with disbelief. It would be a quiet scandal. Certainly, a facade of kindness would remain, but it would be a killing kindness, because its beneficiary was certain that it was a mere ritual, which could not attenuate the silent contempt.

It was now just after one. Perlmann felt uneasy; but the idea of sitting downstairs in the elegant dining room eating with silver cutlery was unbearable. And the idea of eating repelled him too. At that moment he felt as if unease and hunger could get as big as they wanted: he would only eat on the homeward flight, at that point in time that was so horrifically far away.

He lay on the bed. Brian Millar was in Rome now. His plane from New York had landed there that morning, and now he was meeting his Italian colleague to discuss the plan for the linguistic encyclopaedia. He wouldn't fly on to Genoa until late afternoon. So there were still a few hours until that encounter. Laura Sand would also be turning up in the late afternoon, because she first had to travel by train from Oxford to London, and was then flying via Milan. It must all have been rather a strain for her, because she had just got back from her animals in Kenya. Would she be true to herself and come here dressed all in black, as she usually did? Adrian von Levetzov had announced his arrival for early afternoon: in his stilted, baroque manner he had written something about a direct flight from Hamburg to Genoa. Frau Hartwig couldn't help laughing at the stark contrast between his elegant writing paper and Achim Ruge's torn-off piece of paper, in which he communicated diagonally across several coffee stains that he had to organize work in his Bochum lab for the time of his absence, and couldn't say whether he would be arriving on Tuesday or Wednesday. When Giorgio Silvestri would be able to leave his clinic in Bologna was uncertain, but at any rate he wanted to try to be here for dinner. After the phone conversation, Perlmann had been uncertain whether he liked Silvestri's smoky voice or not. Angelini's reference to him had been very reticent, and he wasn't entirely sure why he had invited him. Perhaps just because Agnes had said that linguistic disorders in the case of psychoses must surely be interesting.

The first would be Evelyn Mistral. The train from Geneva was to arrive in Genoa at half-past one. He wouldn't regret it, her boss had written to him, when suggesting her in his place, because he himself had to undergo an operation. She was making a name for herself in the field of developmental psychology. The list of her publications was impressive for someone who was only twenty-nine. But the stack of her papers that Frau Hartwig had put on Perlmann's desk had gone unread. All he knew of her was her voice on the telephone, an unexpectedly clear voice with a polished Spanish accent.

Politeness decreed that, as their host, he should wait for them downstairs. But it was another five leaden minutes before he finally got to his feet. When he walked to the chair to fetch his jacket he stumbled over his empty suitcase. He was about to close it and put it away when he noticed Leskov's text half-hidden in a side pocket, a fat typescript in Russian, a bad photocopy in an unusual paper format, folded in at the corners from the journey and otherwise generally crumpled. The text had been enclosed with the letter in which Leskov said that he had not received an exit permit, and couldn't have come in any case, as his mother had suffered a sudden serious illness. The text was about what he was working on at present, he had written, and he hoped that in this way he would be able to stay in academic contact with him. Sending him this text was a piece of flattery, Perlmann had thought. His Russian wasn't nearly good enough to cope with it. He had set it aside and forgotten it. It had only come to hand again when he was packing on Sunday evening. *It's nonsense*, he had thought, but in a way he had liked the idea of having a Russian text with him. It was something exotic and thus intimate, so in the end he had packed it along with his Russian pocket dictionary.

As he held it in his hand now, the text suddenly seemed to him to be something that he could use to distinguish himself from the others, and defend himself. Opening up this text to himself, or at least trying to do so, was at least a plan for the coming weeks. It was something into which he could withdraw in his free time, an internal region that the others could not penetrate, and from which he would defend himself against their expectations; an inner fortress in which he was invulnerable to their judgment. If he stayed in it, and one Russian sentence after the other opened up to him, he might even succeed in wresting a few moments of presence from the mountain range of time. And then, after the remaining thirty-two days, when he was sitting by the aeroplane window again and enjoying the loop in which the plane rose above the sea, he could say that he now spoke Russian much better than before, so that he had not entirely lost that time after all.

Perlmann took the text and the dictionary, and when he went downstairs and nodded to Signora Morelli, his step was lighter than in the days before. He sat down in a wicker chair under the portico by the entrance and looked at the title that Leskov had written by hand in big, carefully drawn letters: O ROLI YAZYKA V FORMIROVANII VOSPOMINANIY. He only needed to use the dictionary once and he had it: ON THE ROLE OF LANGUAGE IN THE FORMATION OF MEMORIES.

That seemed familiar to him. That's right. It had been the subject of their conversation in St Petersburg. He saw himself standing with Vassily Leskov at a window of the Winter Palace and looking out on the frozen Neva. Agnes's death was only two months in the past, and he certainly hadn't felt like going to a conference. But at the time when he had received the invitation, Agnes had been all for it straight away – *Then we can try out our Russian* – and he had gone, because, in spite of the pain it gave him, it made him feel connected to her. After the start of the session he and Leskov had sat in the foyer of the conference building and fallen into conversation; it had, he thought, been much like his meeting with Angelini. Leskov had been far from sympathetic to him at first; a heavy, rather spongy man with coarse features and a bald head, eager to talk to colleagues from the West and therefore solicitous, almost submissive, in his manner. He talked nineteen to the dozen, and Perlmann, who would rather have had his peace, initially found him intrusive and bothersome. But then he had started listening: what this man was saying in sometimes antiquated but almost perfectly correct German about the role of language for experience, above all the experience of time, began to captivate him. He described experiences that had long been familiar to Perlmann, but which he could not have described with such accuracy, such nuance and such coherence as this Russian, who fumbled around constantly in the air with the damp stem of his pipe between his massive fingers. Soon Leskov sensed Perlmann's growing interest. He was pleased with it and suggested showing him some more of the city.

He led him across St Petersburg to the Winter Palace. It was a clear, sunny morning in early March. Perlmann particularly remembered the houses in light, faded ochre, gleaming in the sun: his memory of St Petersburg consisted entirely of that color. Beside him, Leskov showed him lots, explained lots, a man in a worn, green loden coat, with a fur hat and a pipe, advancing with heavy, clumsy footsteps, waving his arms around and snuffling slightly. Perlmann often didn't listen. His thoughts were with Agnes, who had intended time and again to come here to take photographs, ideally in the summer, during the white nights. Sometimes he stopped and tried to see a section of his field of vision through her eyes, her black-and-white eyes, which had only been concerned with light and shade. In this way, he thought now, as he flicked through the text, a curious associative connection had formed between Agnes and this Russian: Leskov as a travel guide on Perlmann's imaginary stroll with Agnes through St Petersburg.

The hours in the Winter Palace and then in the Hermitage collection created a strange intimacy between the two men. Perlmann revealed to his companion, whom he barely knew, that he was in the process of learning Russian, whereupon a beaming smile spread over Leskov's face, and he immediately continued talking in Russian, until he noticed that Perlmann was utterly unable to follow him. Leskov was very familiar with the paintings collected here. He pointed out some things that one might otherwise not have noticed on a first trip, and from time to time he said something simple in Russian, slowly and clearly. Perlmann spent these hours in a mood in which the effect of the paintings and joy of Russian sentences understood mingled with the pain that he would not be able to tell Agnes all this, that he would never be able to tell her anything ever again.

He had resisted the temptation to talk about Agnes while he was in this mood. What business was it of this Russian's? It was only when they looked down at the Winter Place from the Peter and Paul Fortress that he began now, of all times, when their earlier intimacy had fled in the bitterly cold air. It happened against his will, and he was furious when he heard himself, to crown it all, talking about how hard he had found it since then to continue with his academic work. Luckily, Leskov did not understand the full meaning of his words. He replied only that it was quite natural after such a loss, and added almost paternally that it would all come back to him. And then, from their newly revived intimacy, he told him that he had been jailed as a dissident. He didn't say for how long and gave no further details. Perlmann didn't know how to react to this information, and for a moment there was an uncomfortable pause that Leskov finally ended by taking him by the upper arm and suggesting with unfitting, artificial cheerfulness that they should start addressing one another informally. Perlmann was glad that Leskov had to go home soon afterwards, to look after his old mother with whom he lived, and that he didn't invite him along. He had replied to the invitation to Santa Margherita that Perlmann sent him a few weeks later with an exuberant letter: he would apply for an exit permit straight away. And then, three months ago, the depressed missive in which Leskov had declined Perlmann's invitation had arrived attached to this text.

Perlmann understood the first sentence immediately. The second contained two words that he had never encountered before, although, in fact, it was clear what they must mean. The third sentence was opaque to him because of its construction, but he read on, through a series of unfamiliar words and phrases, to the end of the first paragraph. From one sentence to the next he grew more excited, and by now it was like a fever. Without taking his eyes off the page, he looked in his pocket for a sweet. As he did so he touched the pack of cigarettes that he had bought the previous day when he arrived at the airport. He hesitantly set them down on the bistro table beside the dictionary and then picked them up again. He had bought them yesterday as if under a compulsion, and at precisely the moment that he had begun to feel that he had arrived here irrevocably – that there was no longer a gap, either in space or in time, separating him from the start of this stay, and that there was consequently no longer the slenderest possibility that it might not happen. It had felt like a defeat when he had bought the cigarettes, and he had, as he put them in his pocket, had a dull sensation of menacing and inexorable disaster.

It was his old brand, which he had smoked until five years before. The joyful excitement he had felt at his unexpected success in reading Leskov's text faded away and melted with the thrilling fear of the forbidden, when he now, with trembling fingers, put a cigarette between his lips. The dry paper felt ominously familiar. He took his time. He could still stop, he said to himself, heart thumping. But his self-confidence, he felt with alarming clarity, seemed to be leaking away.

He realized that he hadn't got a light, and was relieved by this setback. He took the cigarette out of his mouth and thought of that day on the cliff, in the wind, when they had been on holiday. He and Agnes had looked at each other and then simultaneously thrown their burning cigarettes into the sea, the full packs after them, and laughed at their melodramatic gesture. A common victory, a happy day.

Suddenly, the waiter was standing next to him on the terrace, holding out a burning match. A feeling of defenselessness took hold of him. Things slipped away. He took his first puff in five years and immediately had a coughing fit. The waiter glanced at him with surprise and concern and walked away. The second puff was easier. It still scratched, but it was already a complete puff. Now he smoked in slow, deep puffs, his eyes half-closed. The nicotine began to flow through his body. He sensed a slight dizziness, but at the same time he felt light and a little bit euphoric. Of course, it was a euphoria that went hand in hand with the impression of artificiality, the feeling that this state arose in him without actually belonging to him, without really being his own. And then, all of a sudden, everything collapsed within him, and he felt wretchedly unwell.

He quickly stubbed out the cigarette and walked unsteadily to the pool, where he lay down on a lounger and closed his eyes. He felt exhausted even before anything had begun. After a while he grew calmer. He was relieved that nothing was pulsing and spinning any more, and gradually drifted into half-sleep. He didn't wake up until a very bright voice above him, speaking English with a Spanish accent, said, 'Forgive me for disturbing you, but the waiter told me you were Philipp Perlmann.'

2

She had a radiant smile, the like of which he had never seen, a smile in which her whole personality opened up, a smile that would have broken down anyone's resistance. He sat up and looked into the oval face with its prominent cheekbones, wide-set eyes and broad nose, almost an oriental face. Her blonde hair fell straight down on to a white, crookedly fitting T-shirt; it was uncombed, living hair, a bit like straw.

Perlmann's mouth was dry and he still felt a bit unsteady when he got to his feet and held out his hand.

'You must be Evelyn Mistral,' he said. 'I'm sorry. I must have dozed off for a moment.' *Starting with an apology.*

'Not to worry,' she laughed. 'It's really like being on holiday here.' She pointed to the high facade of the hotel with the painted gables over the windows, the turquoise shutters and the coats of arms in the colors of various nations. 'It's all so terribly smart. I hope they'll let me in with my suitcase!'

It was an ancient, battered black leather case, with light brown edges that were torn in places, and she had stuck a bright red elephant on the middle of the lid. *Kirsten could drag a case like that around with her, too. It would suit her. And generally speaking she somehow reminds me of my daughter, although they don't look at all alike.*

She had come by train, first class, and was impressed in the way a little girl might have been. You feel so important, she said. She had never been treated so well by a conductor. Then she had allowed herself a sumptuous lunch in the dining car. There had been no first-class carriage on the local train from Genoa to Santa Margherita, and it had struck her as quite odd to be suddenly sitting in a shabby, second-class compartment again. How quickly one was corrupted!

Perlmann took the case and accompanied her to reception. She walked lightly in her faded khaki skirt, almost dancing slightly in her flat, bright red patent shoes, and yet there was something hesitant and gawky in her gait. She was greeted by Signora Morelli, who was, as she had been the day before, wearing a dark blue, sporty-looking dress and a burgundy neckerchief, which gave her the appearance of a chief stewardess, an impression reinforced by the fact that she had put her hair up in a rather severe style. When Evelyn Mistral spoke Italian she pronounced the vowels in the Spanish way, short and harsh, in sharp contrast to Signora Morelli's leisurely sing-song. As she checked in, leaning on the desk, her feet played with her red shoes. Sometimes she laughed out loud, and then her voice again had the brightness that Perlmann remembered from their phone call. 'See you later,' she said to him when the porter took the case and walked ahead of her to the elevator.

Perlmann walked slowly back across the expansive terrace to the pool. Now the red-haired man from that morning was back as well. Perlmann replied to his cheerful greeting with a brief wave, and sat down on a lounger on the other side. He abandoned himself to a feeling that was, in fact, merely the absence of anxiety. For the first time since his arrival he wasn't battling against the things around him: the crooked pines that loomed on the coast road; the flags along the balustrade; the waiter's red smoking jacket; the smell of pine resin and the remains of summer heat in the air. Now he was able to see that the grapes on the pergola were turning red. Agnes would have seen that first.

'They've given me a fantastic room,' said Evelyn Mistral, dropping her swimming towel on the lounger next to him. 'Up there. The corner room on the third floor, a double room with antique furniture. I think the desk's made of rosewood. And the view! I've never lived like this. But the price. Don't even think about it! How are you supposed to earn that sort of money? But at least with a desk like that, you have no excuse not to work!'

She had taken off her bathrobe and was standing at the edge of the pool. Her gleaming white one-piece swimsuit set off her brownness, a brown with a yellowish glow. A dive and she was in the water. She stayed under for a long time and then swam back and forth a few times in the big kidney-shaped pool. The water barely sprayed up; the movements of her calm, almost lazy freestyle were elegant and contrasted with her gawky way of walking. From time to time she came over to him and rested her arms on the edge of the pool. 'Why don't you come in? It's wonderful!'

Perlmann closed his eyes and tried to retain that image: the gleaming water and her radiant smile; her wet blonde hair. Even now it was no different: he could never experience the present as it was taking place; he always woke up too late, and then there was only the substitute, the visualization, a field in which he had, out of pure desperation, become a virtuoso.

As unexpectedly as before, when he had given him a light, the waiter was suddenly standing over him, passing him Leskov's text, the dictionary and the cigarettes.

'Someone else would like to sit there,' he said, pointing to the columns. Then he looked in the pocket of his smoking jacket and handed Perlmann a book of matches with the inscription *Grand Hotel Miramare*.

Perlmann set the things down on the floor next to him and looked across to Evelyn Mistral, who was now on her back, letting herself drift with her arms spread wide. Her long hair, which looked brown in the blue water, lay like a chaotic fan around her face. She had closed her eyes, drops of water shimmered on her bright lashes, and when she glided back from a strip of shadow into the sun, her eyelids twitched. As before, when wanting to record an impression, Perlmann lit a cigarette. The inhalation and the sensation of heightened, slightly hurried vividness thus produced created the illusion that he could obtain the impossible through sheer obstinacy: hold the moment until he had managed to open it up and thus give it depth. Again he felt dizzy, but the sensation no longer crossed the boundary into nausea, and when the cigarette was finished he lit another one.

When Evelyn Mistral came out of the water and dried herself, her eye fell on Leskov's text on the ground. 'Oh, you speak Russian,' she said. Then she narrowed her eyes. 'That is Russian, isn't it? I'd love to be able to do that. When did you learn? And how?'

Afterwards, Perlmann couldn't explain why he flinched at that moment, as if he'd been caught doing something forbidden.

'I can't, in fact,' he said, and set down both text and dictionary on the other side of the lounger to make room for her. 'Just a few words. This text here – it's more of a prank that someone took the liberty of playing on me.' *The dictionary was lying with its back to her. She couldn't have seen the dark smudges from all that flicking.*

What other foreign languages did he speak? she asked as she puffed on one of his cigarettes later on.

'I can speak a bit of yours,' he said in Spanish.

'Then you should be more familiar with me,' she laughed. '*Usted* is far too formal. Colleagues don't say that to each other. And in Spain since Franco as a rule we tend to say *tú*.'

After that they stuck with Spanish. Perlmann liked her Spanish voice, particularly the gutturals and the way she turned the *d* at the end of the word into a voiceless sound like the English *th*. It was a long time since he had last spoken Spanish, and he made a lot of mistakes. But he was glad of the language. He hadn't learned anything new in English for years, nothing liberatingly strange in its newness. English no longer gave him the chance to recast himself in a foreign language.

He lost her when he talked about this subject. Her relationship with foreign languages was more serious, more practical. Yes, she enjoyed them, too; but when he talked about the possibility of becoming someone else in a foreign language, even though one was essentially saying the same thing as one said in one's own, she was only a polite listener, and Perlmann felt like a mystic. And when he reflected out loud about whether the Spanish *tú* was more intimate than the English *you* in connection with the first name, or the same, and how both compared to the German *Du* in terms of intimacy, she looked at him with curiosity, but the smile that accompanied her gaze revealed that for her this was more of a game than a serious question. His monologue suddenly struck him as ridiculous, even kitsch, and he abruptly interrupted it to ask her about her work.

What someone can imagine is dependent on what they can say, and the same is true of what they want, she said. In her work with children she concentrated increasingly on this connection between imagination, will and language; on the way in which the internal play with possibilities became more refined and influential as the capacity for linguistic expression developed; and how this refinement of the imagination through language led to an increasingly rich organization of the will.

As she spoke she gripped her tucked-up knees with both hands. Only sometimes, when the wet strands slipped into her face, did she release her interlocking fingers. Her face was very serious and concentrated as she tried to find appropriate words, precise sentences. Perlmann liked her face now, too. But the more she got into her stride, the further away it became. And then when she talked about the chapters of a book that she wanted to present for discussion here, it struck him as very remote and alien. He thought of his shabby, black oilcloth notebook, which he hadn't opened for so long, and it was only with difficulty that he managed to shake off the image of squared pages, yellowed to the point of illegibility. He dreaded the moment when she would ask him about his own work, and for that reason kept asking, apprehensive about the mendaciousness of his zeal, and yet pleased every time she began to respond to yet another question.

When Adrian von Levetzov's name was mentioned, Perlmann gave a start. 'I'd completely forgotten him,' he murmured tonelessly, and he could see from Evelyn Mistral's expression that his face revealed an anxiety that he would gladly have concealed at any cost. He hastily got up from the lounger, went over on one ankle and started hobbling to the entrance. As he passed the waiter, who was clearing a table, he forced himself to walk more calmly, unsure whether it was because of the pain in his ankle or whether it sprang from the desire to battle against anxiety and solicitude.

Von Levetzov was standing at the reception desk talking insistently, and in terrible tourist Italian, to Signora Morelli, who replied to him with a motionless face and in perfect English.

'If the sun disturbs you, sir,' she was just saying with a coolness that Perlmann envied, 'you need only draw the curtains. We cannot easily alter the location of the hotel, now, can we? We do not, I fear, have a larger desk. But I'm sure we can find an additional side table.'

Von Levetzov's face was pinched and slightly reddened when he looked over at the door. 'Ah, Perlmann, at last,' he said, struggling to rein in his irritation. 'I thought you weren't going to welcome me at all.'

'Please do forgive me,' Perlmann said breathlessly. 'I was at the pool with Evelyn Mistral, and completely forgot the time.' *Why am I constantly apologizing? And to cap it all that sounded almost like a budding romance. One should meet such a man in a quite different way. One should be much more, obliging, but cool. I'll never learn.*

'Well, you're here now,' said von Levetzov, and it sounded as if Perlmann were a pupil who had turned up late or a tardy assistant who was being forgiven. 'I'm just trying to explain to these people that I need more room to work, more surface area. Above all, I need a table for my calculator alone. And then the sun. I tried it out just after I got here. There are problems with the screen. You must have noticed that yourself.'

Perlmann didn't look at him as he nodded. Consequently, his lie felt more like an insignificant movement. He turned to Signora Morelli, whom he hadn't liked at all at first when he had arrived the day before, but whose brittleness had made her more congenial to him each time he had seen her since. An additional table would, as she had said, be found for the signore, and, if he insisted, his room would be rearranged: the desk could be put against the back wall, which the sun didn't reach. He could even be offered a different room, facing the rear and very shady, but perhaps a bit small for such a long stay.

Perlmann spoke Italian with her, and he spoke more quickly than his ability actually allowed him to. After the conversation by the pool the Spanish words sometimes came to him rather than the Italian, but he went on and on talking, even when the question of the room had long been resolved, so that Signora Morelli looked embarrassedly across to Adrian von Levetzov, who was irritably waggling a hotel prospectus. She couldn't tell that Perlmann's talking was a demonstration, a show for this man in the dark blue, almost black suit with the waistcoat and the gold watch chain. *Whatever may happen over the next few weeks, I can do that better than he can.*

'I didn't know your command of Italian was so good,' von Levetzov said acidly, immediately changing the subject by pointing out of the door to the bay, where the light was already starting to break, producing a reddish glow. 'I myself prefer the Anglo-Saxon to the Latin world, and, in fact, I prefer English parklands to Mediterranean idylls. But I am forced to admit that it is quite charming here. I am also, of course, looking forward to my academic dispute with you, my dear Perlmann. Recently, sad to say, I have not got around to pursuing your latest works. The last thing I heard was your report at our conference a year ago. My book created quite a considerable stir, discussion forums, lectures, you know all that. But in the coming weeks I can catch up on my Perlmann reading. You know how highly I esteem you, even if we have opposing views. I'm very excited to hear your latest ideas. I shall take my time and I will be all ears.'

It sounded like a threat to Perlmann, and he froze. For someone like him, who carried a facade around with him, and trembled behind it, waiting to be unmasked, this elegant man with the smooth black hair and the rimless glasses was a great danger. The biggest, leaving Millar aside. He talked like a character out of Thomas Mann, and the first time students heard him there were grins and giggles. But only at the outset. He was feared as an obsessive worker who couldn't understand that other people needed a break from time to time. When he talked, as he had just been doing, about himself, it sounded like clumsy boasting. But although he was vain and mannered, he was by no means snobbish, but rather a man who lived in a modest apartment full of books and was entirely absorbed in his subject, to which he contributed more than most of the others. From time to time he was seen at the Hamburg Opera, only ever at Mozart and always alone. There were rumours about a brief liaison with an actress, and about alcohol. No one knew anything precise.

*

Evelyn Mistral's hair was tousled from rubbing when she entered the lobby with her swimming towel around her shoulders. For Perlmann, the radiant presence of her laughter had disappeared into the far distance. The presence of Adrian von Levetzov, and his last words above all, had interposed themselves between him and that laughter like frosted glass. The hour by the pool was by now nothing but a lovely deception, a Fata Morgana. He was relieved that she had rolled up Leskov's text and passed the dictionary up to him with its reverse side up. He took both of them in one hand, which he then hid behind his back.

Tall von Levetzov bowed down to little Evelyn Mistral, took her hand as if to kiss it and said in exaggerated Oxford English that he very much regretted the fact that her teacher hadn't been able to come as he was, of course, irreplaceable. He seemed not to notice that her narrow mouth twitched at his tactlessness, and announced with a glance at the clock that he had to make a few phone calls, while his colleagues in Germany were still in the office. Then he hurried upstairs, always taking two steps at a time; as he did so his watch chain bounced up and down, emphasizing the grotesque contrast between the forced youthfulness of his movements and his old-fashioned appearance.

When Evelyn Mistral had disappeared in the elevator, Perlmann stood motionless for a while and stared at the bright stripe that the afternoon sun cast on the marble floor of the lobby. She was more than twenty years younger than him, and yet the face with which she had watched von Levetzov's departure had expressed a confidence and an effortless detachment of which he could only dream. *It's unfair*, he thought repeatedly, as he hobbled back to his lounger to fetch his cigarettes. And every time that sentence was swamped by a wave of diffuse and directionless resentment, he rejected it as ludicrous nonsense.

Laura Sand was not due to arrive before five o'clock. Perlmann went up to the room. When he slumped on the bed, he felt as if the whole supply of solitude that he had brought here with him had already been completely used up by these two encounters, and he was assailed by a feeling of defenselessness.

What bothered him most when he visualized what had happened was the way he had rushed all the way along the terrace to the reception to greet von Levetzov. He could see himself: a gaunt man in a dark blue polo shirt and light-colored trousers, with short, black hair and a pale face behind his black horn-rimmed glasses, a man hurrying to be of service. And alongside that image, another image of solicitude appeared: the memory of his father when he was called to the telephone. It was the picture of a harmless, banal situation, and yet one of the worst mental images that he had brought from home. His father walked with oppressive haste and a facial expression that suggested it was a matter of life and death. On no account could anyone address him when he was walking like this; he walked in a way that caused one involuntarily to catch one's breath. His face always seemed to have turned red, and to be covered with a film of sweat, glistening. He walked bent forward, at the service of everyone who paid him the honor of calling him on the telephone. The caller must not be kept waiting. By the very fact of calling, this caller had acquired the right to have him, his father, entirely at his command. As the callee, at that moment his father had no life of his own, no time of his own and no needs of his own that a caller would have had to take into account. He was unconditionally available, all the time, on call.

It had taken Perlmann some time to work out that for ages this image had shaped his relationship with the outside world, the world of other people. You had to be at the service of that world, you depended on the mercy of its acknowledgement. But at the same time neither he nor his father could have been described as submissive characters. No, that wasn't it. It was the pure anxiety that this solicitude provoked; a constant fear of the consequences it might have if you let others feel that one had desires of one's own, which were in contact with theirs, even if it only meant that the others had to wait for a while. The idea of these serious consequences was far from clear; the closer you looked, the more their content evaporated. But that didn't change anything about the choking, suffocating power that that anxiety held over you. Once Perlmann had heard a doctor making a phone call during hospital hours.

He had come out with some quite unremarkable sentences: 'No, that's impossible right now. I'm busy . . . I understand. Then you'll just have to call again later on.' The doctor had said these sentences in a friendly but firm tone that clearly delineated him from the person at the other end, and he had said them with an effortless self-evidence that had practically hypnotized Perlmann. It had been like a revelation: saying sentences like that in that tone – that was what you had to be able to do. You had to be able to say them without your heart thumping, without any inner agitation or even just stress, quite calmly and without having to think about them any further. On that occasion, when the door of the hospital had closed behind him and he had gone out into the street, he had known that a lack of solicitude would henceforth be the most important ideal of his life.

When he thought of the veranda, of the gleaming tables and the high, carved armchair at the head, he sensed that he had never been as far from that ideal as he was now. When von Levetzov had spoken to him in his unusual way a little while before, he had felt as if he was at a school desk, as helpless and hopeless as a pupil at the Institute Benjamenta. Every word had been able to penetrate him unhindered, and it seemed to Perlmann that he had no way of preventing words from flourishing inside him like malignant tumours.

Starting more or less with von Levetzov's reference to that conference the previous year, Perlmann had assumed that he would be an ordinary participant when he had agreed, nothing more. He hadn't been to conferences for a long time, and had seen this one as a good opportunity to show himself and to secure with a few skilful questions the general opinion that he was quite on top of things. To some extent he wanted to work on his disguise. It was a shock when he received the printed program two weeks before the agreed date and saw that he was presented as the main speaker, alongside a very vague and general title that someone had cobbled together for him out of a superficial knowledge of his work. In a mixture of fury and panic he picked up the phone, but as soon as he heard it ringing at the other end he hung up. He couldn't give himself away. A man like him, an authority in his field, couldn't lose face because

of such a misunderstanding. However, if the opportunity presented itself
he could make a barbed remark on the subject. But someone like Philipp
Perlmann actually needed to have a lecture ready at all times. He couldn't
phone up and just say, 'It's a misunderstanding. I have nothing to say
at the moment. Please pass that on.' *But really, why not?* Agnes asked
when she saw the way he was sitting at his desk. After that question he
felt very alone. For a while he considered phoning in sick at the last
moment. In the end he delivered a lecture that summed up what he had
published over the last few years. Not a bad text, he thought, reading
it through beforehand. But when he left the lectern to polite applause,
he would really have liked to take the shortest way to the station, even
though the conference lasted another two days. At dinner von Levetzov
had sat down next to him. 'A lecture of familiar clarity,' he had said
with a smile that wasn't unfriendly or malicious, yet which had had the
effect of a pinprick on Perlmann, 'but it was more of a look back at the
past, wasn't it, or have you simply ignored the new?'

A moment before, down in the lobby, von Levetzov had called that
lecture a *report*. Nothing escaped him, that keen-minded man with his
phenomenal memory, and he weighed his words very carefully. He had
mastered the game like very few others. It had been almost impossible
not to invite von Levetzov. Perlmann stepped to the window and looked
out at the bay. The setting sun shone through a fine grey bank of
clouds and gave the water the color of platinum. Lights were already
going on one by one over by Sestri Levante. Only a few seconds had
passed since the first cigarette, and already he was smoking as if he had
never stopped. It hurt when he became aware of it. He felt as if he
was crossing out the last five years, and he had the feeling that he was
betraying Agnes.

He thought of the other four colleagues that he still had to welcome,
and planned to be laconic. Not unfriendly, not even cool, but laconic,
with a certain terseness in his words. He usually said too much, even
though he didn't feel like talking, and they were explanations that
often sounded like explanations, like justifications that no one had
asked for. Also, he often expressed too much sympathy with other

people, sympathy that wasn't expected and perhaps not even wished for. Then he came across as intrusive, which was anathema to him. It was like an addiction.

He reached for Leskov's text. The first sentences in the second paragraph resisted his efforts, and several times he vacillated between the various meanings that the dictionary gave for a word; several appeared possible, yet none seemed really to fit. But afterwards things became more transparent and he understood one sentence or another without inwardly faltering in the slightest. The excitement that he had felt before, when reading the first paragraph, returned. These were not, as they had always been in the past, sentences in an exercise book, which weren't there because someone wanted to say something particular in precisely this way, but because the reader was to be presented with a new variant of grammar or expression. Here the language was not a subject, but a medium, and the author simply assumed that the reader was a master of that medium. So you were being treated quite differently, as an adult, so to speak, as a Russian-speaker, in fact. It was like joining the real Russian world, like a reward for all that effort with your grammar book.

Perlmann was euphoric. He walked up and down a few times, then leaned far back in the armchair and folded his arms behind his head. For the first time since his arrival he felt secure and sure of himself. He understood Russian. *I'm someone of whom you can say: he reads Russian. If only I could share that with Agnes. Then it would be a presence.* He dialled Kirsten's number in Konstanz, but no one picked up. She was probably in a lecture or a seminar.

It wasn't the first time that Perlmann had crossed this point with a language. But this time it was different. The cheering experience was, it seemed to him, more intense than usual. Perhaps it was down to the fact that it had been so difficult for a long time and he had secretly expected never to get that far. Or else it was something to do with the Cyrillic letters, which still looked mysterious to him even though he had known them for almost two years. He looked at the typescript and repeated a game that he enjoyed afresh every time he played it: he studied the writing first with the eyes of someone who couldn't read the letters, for whom they were merely an ornament. Then he let his eyes somehow tip over into the gaze of someone who doesn't stop with the appearance of the script but, guided unnoticeably by his perfect familiarity with them, presses on directly to the meaning of what is written. *It's barely believable*, he said to himself then, *but I can really do it.*

He went on reading now, breathlessly and always fearing that the first two paragraphs might have been an exception, and he was about to capsize and would have to go back to texts that treated him like a schoolboy again. But although his little Langenscheidt dictionary failed him now and again, he managed, and he was so enthralled that he heard the noises in the next room only after some delay. It sounded as if someone were pushing something heavy against the door; then there came the sound of men's voices, the rattle of keys, the door snapping shut, footsteps fading away.

Only now did it become clear to Perlmann that he had assumed – had, in fact, taken it as his due – that there should be no one staying in the room next to him. As if the whole world had to know and respect the fact that he was a person who needed a lot of empty space around him. The new guest cleared his throat, then sniffed loudly, and at last he blew his nose with three long trumpet blasts. Perlmann gave a start: the walls were so thin, the building so badly soundproofed. He tried to find his way back to his cheerful excitement of a few moments before, but it had been displaced by a feeling of oppression, almost panic, and when he spent a while looking in vain for an expression in the dictionary, he discovered that the cause had been a simple reading error. His irritation grew from one minute to the next, and when something fell over with a loud crash in the next room, he lost control, stormed out and thundered with his fist on the door of the neighboring room.

The man who opened it was Achim Ruge. Perlmann felt the blood rising to his face.

'Oh, it's you,' he stammered and offered him his hand.

Ruge pointed at the open hard-shell suitcase, which had fallen so that the clothes now lay scattered on the floor and the alarm clock was wedged between a pair of shoes.

'And I took such trouble packing,' he grinned, 'much more than usual. And it's a new suitcase, too.'

He was wearing a brownish suit which was too short in the sleeves, and looked like a farmer's Sunday suit, and an open white shirt that looked like something left over from the Sixties. But what chiefly captivated the eye was his big round head, which was almost completely bald. *A bullet would bounce off his skull*, Perlmann thought every time he saw him. The fact that there was something grotesque about Ruge's head, something of a living death's head, was down to his glasses, glasses with a yellowish frame of gloomy transparency that was as unmodern, as inelegant as if someone had done everything within their power to create the epitome of an anti-fashion frame. The impression was reinforced by the fact that one earpiece had been repaired with fine wire, the end of which stuck out and threatened to tear open Ruge's temple at any moment.

The organization of the laboratory had gone faster than expected after all, he reported in his broad Swabian accent. Perlmann had forgotten how close his *ä* was to his *e*. Ruge had travelled through the night and hardly slept, because in the full second-class compartment lying down had been unimaginable.

'It didn't occur to me,' he grinned when Perlmann asked him why he hadn't flown or at least travelled first class.

As Ruge walked over to his suitcase to fetch an offprint that he had brought specially for him, Perlmann saw that the room was arranged as a mirror image of his own. This meant that the two desks stood exactly opposite one another, as in a piece with two pianos, except that there was a wall in between. That idea momentarily unsettled Perlmann. With dry words of thanks he took delivery of the thick offprint, which was actually a small book, and disappeared to his room where, without thinking anything about it, he chained the door.

It was now half-past five, and the dusk was sinking surprisingly quickly, almost headlong, on to the bay. The coast by Sestri Levante had become a flickering strip of light, and now the hotel lamps were coming on, each one four white spheres in an irregular arrangement. At midday Perlmann had cursed the southern light because it promised him a present that could never be reached. Now that it made way for darkness and was overlaid with the glow of artificial light, he could hardly expect to see it again. As clumsy as someone constantly running behind himself, only now did he miss its hypnotic power, which made one forget and which took away the past along with its heaviness, just as the need to plan anything burned away to nothing. With the dusk, the muted colors and the magic of the lamplight, his inner space filled once more with all the images that he feared one minute before feeling nothing but weariness the next, and a longing for the strength that could wipe out everything.

The figure that crept backwards out of the taxi, doing battle with two enormous camera bags, which became caught on the seat and then in the door, could only be Laura Sand. She asked the driver who set her suitcase down on the steps to hold her cigarette while she looked for money in the pocket of her long black coat. Then she heaved the case up one step at a time and, with her other arm, caught the camera bags when they threatened to hit the banisters.

Perlmann rushed out and realized too late that he had left his key in the room. Feeling a sharp pain in his leg, he went over on his ankle and came hobbling, face distorted with pain, into the lobby where Laura Sand was stubbing her cigarette out in the ashtray on the reception desk.

He had forgotten the extent to which she could fill a whole room with her white face, her mockingly pouting lips and the shadow of rage in her almost black eyes. He had remembered above all the dense ponytail of deep black hair which fell unevenly to her shoulders on either side of a muddled parting. Even now, as she held out her slender hand with a smile, there was a sceptical sharpness in her eye, further emphasized by the fact that she always held her head tilted slightly to the side. For a moment he compared her face with that of Signora Morelli, who was just taking charge of her Australian passport: the Italian face now looked merely like a pleasant but pale background.

Laura Sand laid her black leather suitcase, which was scattered with faded, battered and torn stickers of foreign cities and rare animals, flat on the floor, opened the zip and dragged from a tangle of underwear, books and rolls of films, an olive-green travelling typewriter. She'd been writing on it for almost twenty years, she said, not least in the Steppes and the jungle. Twice the machine had been taken apart completely and reassembled. Only yesterday her daughter had swept it from the table during one of her fits of aerobics, and now the carriage didn't work properly. It urgently needed to be repaired.

'I can't think without that damned thing,' she said in a broad Australian accent, and with a strange fury that looked almost comical because it wasn't aimed at anyone and seemed to be her second nature.

'No problem,' said Giovanni, when Signora Morelli had translated. He had just arrived to join the nightshift, and had put even more pomade in his hair than the previous evening, when he had got badly on Perlmann's nerves with his slow-wittedness commentaries. He knew someone who could fix it in the blink of an eye, Giovanni said. He couldn't take his eyes off Laura Sand's face, and instead of ringing for the porter, still wearing his coat he picked up her suitcase and walked ahead of her to the elevator.

When the chambermaid who had opened his door for him had gone, Perlmann picked up Leskov's text again. Now that it would be an hour at most till Brian Millar arrived, it was particularly important to build a protective wall of understood Russian sentences around him. The more sentences he could pile up, the less the man with the red shimmer in his dark hair could do to him.

But Perlmann couldn't manage to translate even a single sentence. Like yesterday on the plane he was paralyzed by a kind of seeing blindness, and when finally he managed to read the words correctly, his memory played one trick on him after another. He felt anxiety welling up within him like a poison, which, released in the depths, was forcing its way relentlessly to the surface. While he stood by the window in the dark and smoked, he called Evelyn Mistral's laughter to his aid, and then Laura Sand's furious gaze. But he was unsure whether those two faces would be any use against Millar, and his anxiety wouldn't go away.

And, in fact, there wasn't the slightest reason to be anxious. All right, they hadn't liked each other from the start. But that episode in Boston had been really quite trivial; practically childish, and not something to explain hostility.

Millar had travelled with his girlfriend Sheila, a beauty with long blonde hair and a very short skirt. He was extremely proud of her and treated her like a jealously protected property. The colleagues bowed and scraped around her and wooed with her in the most ludicrous fashion. Perlmann didn't do a thing. During breaks in the conference and sometimes even during the lectures he withdrew into a quiet corner of the building and read a paperback of short stories. Sheila often strolled, bored, down the corridors, smoking. When she approached Perlmann she cast him a curious glance and went on walking. On the third day of the conference she sat down next to him and asked him what he was always reading. Wouldn't she much rather have been somewhere else? he asked her after a while. The question caught her off guard, they started laughing, and suddenly there was a familiarity between them whose charm lay in the fact that it was gauzy and without any history. They walked together to the caféteria, still joking, because Sheila liked his dry, melancholy humor. When she found what he said particularly funny, she put her arm around his shoulder. Her head was close to his. Her hair brushed his cheek. He felt her breath and smelled her perfume. He turned his head, and just at that moment Millar, coming from the session with his colleagues, entered the caféteria. He saw them in this attitude of intimacy, Perlmann with his face bright red. Millar left his colleagues standing, came rapidly over and took Sheila by the arm, as if he wanted to confront her and regain possession of her. She defended herself. There was almost a scene. All under the curious eyes of the colleagues who were still streaming in. Perlmann did nothing, just went on holding his tray, and was unable to suppress a smile of amusement that didn't escape Millar.

In the afternoon it was Perlmann's turn to deliver his lecture. Millar was sitting in the front row with Sheila. Perlmann saw her gleaming stockings and metal stilettos. He made a stupid mistake in a formula at the board. It was quite a trivial mistake, and basically it was of no importance whatsoever for the rest of his thought process. Millar's hand shot up in the air, even before the chairman had finished his introductory words to the discussion. With understatement bolstered by sarcasm, he pointed out the mistake. Perlmann panicked, improved things for the worse and wiped out the correct part of the formula. Millar crossed his legs, folded his arms in front of his chest and tilted his head to one side. 'No, you see, you should have left that part as it was,' he said with slow complacency and a malicious smile. At last the grey-haired chairman, an authority in his subject, intervened in a calm voice. Perlmann regained his sense of security, steadily wiped the whole formula out and without hesitation wrote down the right one. Then he walked slowly back to the lectern, drew the microphone to him with theatrical care and asked, looking down at Millar, 'Happy now?' He managed a tone and a facial expression that turned the mood in the lobby in his favor, because quiet laughter could be heard. Sheila turned her head towards Millar and looked at him with curious and malicious glee. He darted her a poisonous glare in return.

The next morning, when Perlmann entered the hotel foyer with the case in his hand, Millar and Sheila had just gone out through the revolving door. Sheila glanced back and saw him. Millar was already opening the door of the taxi and turning impatiently towards Sheila when she called something out to him, turned round and slipped back into the revolving door. For a few moments she was trapped in it, because on the other side an elderly couple – she with a thick fur coat and a hatbox – were wedged in the door, and only with some pushing and shoving did it start moving again. Sheila tottered up to Perlmann and pressed a kiss on his cheek with comically parted lips. Then she was back at the door, turned round and waved with ironic daintiness. The others watched and laughed. One of his colleagues pointed to his cheek, which must have borne the impression of Sheila's violet lips. Sheila saw it through the glass of the door and smiled, her tongue between her teeth. Millar still stood icy-faced, holding the taxi door. Sheila got in and pulled down her short skirt.

Ruge and von Levetzov, at the first letter of enquiry, had immediately asked whether Millar was to be invited. Maybe they would have come even without him. But Perlmann simply couldn't think of an excuse not to invite this man, Brian Millar, whose name was on everyone's lips.

He turned the light on and went into the shower. At home he never showered during the day. But now everything was to be rinsed away so that he could meet the man with the alert expression afresh and without embarrassment. Like yesterday evening and that morning, he showered for a very long time. *You'd almost think I had a cleanliness fixation.* He tried to persuade himself that all that water could make the afternoon's clumsiness and solicitude disappear. The coming dinner, he said to himself, was the actual beginning. Everything before that was mere chance and didn't count.

When he had shaken the water out of his ears and heard the telephone, he immediately thought it must have been ringing for ages. He ran dripping through the room. As he reached for the receiver, he looked at his wet footprints on the pigeon-blue carpet and felt a desperate annoyance with his subservience, which mocked all his good intentions, rising up within him.

'Hi, Phil,' was all the voice said. Perlmann recognized it immediately. The two syllables were enough to remind him what he had tried without great success to explain to Agnes after he got back from Boston: the voice formed the words in a completely undetached way. Its tone didn't just show that this was the speaker's mother tongue; the tone wasn't only an expression of the self-evidence with which the language was at the speaker's disposal. There was more at stake: the tone contained – and even Agnes's frown could not shake his conviction about this – the message that this was the only language that truly deserved to be taken seriously. *Self-righteous, you understand, his penetratingly sonorous voice is self-righteous. He speaks as if the others were to blame and very much to be pitied for the fact that they, too, don't speak East Coast American, this Yankee language. This self-righteousness, this sonorous arrogance, that was what drove me up the wall.*

'Hi, Brian,' said Perlmann, 'how are you?'

'Oh, fine,' said the voice, and now Perlmann was once again quite sure that what he had said to Agnes was the precise truth.

'By the way, Phil,' the voice went on, and now this American mania for shortened first names was getting on Perlmann's nerves again, 'apparently my room's right next to yours.'

Perlmann saw Ruge's desk in front of him, right up against his own, and he felt as if the two walls of his room were being pushed closer and closer together until they crushed him.

'How nice,' he heard himself saying and had a feeling that with those empty words he was sealing his own defeat. He had never, even when standing naked, felt so exposed.

'Me, too,' he said at last, when Millar stressed how much he was looking forward to seeing him later over dinner.

Big puddles of water had formed around his feet, and were spreading outwards. He was shivering, and went back into the shower. It was quite clear, he thought, as he let the water run over his face: he couldn't stay in his room. And the new room had to be far away, on another floor and if possible in the other wing of the hotel.

But what explanation should he give to Signora Morelli when making his request? And how could he prevent Ruge and Millar from taking it personally when he moved out? He would have to destroy something that would make the room uninhabitable and couldn't be quickly repaired. Maybe rip the telephone from the wall and claim he had tripped over the wire. But a telephone connection could be quickly mended, far too quickly. Or do something with the television aerial and say he'd accidentally bashed it with the chest of drawers. But even a television socket could be easily changed. There wasn't anything that could be broken in the bathroom without making it look deliberate. Pouring something on the carpet, like a whole pot of coffee. But you didn't ask for a different room because of a stain on the carpet, least of all if you'd made it yourself.

Achim Ruge blew his nose and trumpeted even more loudly than he had in the afternoon. Shortly afterwards the sound of piano music came from Millar's room. Bach. Trembling with irritation, Perlmann tried to find the station on the bedside-table radio. Nothing. Millar must have brought a radio-cassette recorder with him.

He listened reluctantly. He didn't know this composition. He had never had a memory for Bach. He wouldn't have dared to say it in the Conservatoire, but he found most of Bach's piano music monotonous and boring. Secretly, he had often thought, Bela Szabo had felt the same. Otherwise he would, like the other teachers, have insisted on Perlmann playing at least a minimum of Bach.

Perlmann picked up his Russian grammar. Leskov's text, he felt, was going to defeat him again now. But he could at least memorize the Russian entry for *must*. Then he would have something, a tiny bit of progress, that he could cling to when he came down to dinner later on. He walked back and forth with the open book in his hand and spoke the words more loudly than usual, to assert himself against Millar's Bach and Ruge's repeated nose-blowing.

Shortly before eight Perlmann stood at the window in his grey flannel trousers and dark blue blazer, watching people coming up the steps from outside, to eat in the famous restaurant of the Miramare. Break a window-pane. That could be explained by clumsiness, and would be a reason to change rooms, now that the nights were growing rather cool. But even a windowpane was quickly replaced. *Run away. Simply run away. Down the steps to the shoreline promenade, around the rocky outcrop over there, out of vision, and then keep going, keep on going.* He clenched his fists in his pockets until the nails cut into the palms of his hands. On the way to the door he stopped and repeated the entry for *must* twice. It took. *Now the important thing to be is laconic*, he thought as he pulled the door shut, *not unfriendly, but laconic.*

On the stairs he was horrified to realize that it was already half-past eight, and he was late for the first communal dinner. Still hobbling slightly, he entered the elegant dining room with the glittering candelabras. Now that he saw his colleagues sitting at a big, round table, it was clear to him that he had no idea what official words of greeting he was going to say.

3

Millar looked at the clock and rose to his feet, although admittedly without coming towards him. He was wearing grey trousers and a dark blue double-breasted jacket, a thin-striped shirt and a navy-blue tie, with a stylized anchor embroidered on it in golden yellow thread. His appearance and his stiff posture recalled those of a naval officer, an impression reinforced by the fact that his angular face with its thrusting chin was as tanned as if he had been at sea for weeks. As he stood there by the table with his broad shoulders, while his colleagues had stayed in their seats, he looked like the man in charge of everything, who had risen to greet a latecomer.

'Good to see you, Phil,' he said with a smile that revealed his big, white teeth. His handshake was so brief and powerful that a sensation of complete passivity arose in Perlmann.

'Yes,' he murmured, annoyed at his idiotic reaction. As before, in Boston, it was the steel-blue eyes behind the flashing glasses that made him shrink inwardly to a schoolboy, a little squirt who was oppressively aware that he still had to prove himself to the teacher. Millar had just had a night flight and a working session with his Italian colleagues, and those eyes still looked as rested, alert and calm as if he had just got up. *Fit*, Perlmann thought, and saw the laughing face of Agnes when he gave free rein to his unfounded hatred for the word once again.

While the others were already sitting by their empty plates, Perlmann hastily wolfed down his soup. He was glad that a seat for Giorgio Silvestri had been left free between him and Millar. There was still some unpleasantness with Millar, he suddenly felt quite clearly: some shortcoming that he couldn't call to mind. Only when he heard von Levetzov thanking Millar for a text he had sent him did he remember the package with the four offprints that had arrived from New York in August, bearing the stamp FIRST CLASS MAIL, which always made Perlmann think of diplomatic mail that had found its way to him by mistake.

The package had been on his desk when he had visited the office in the afternoon (after Frau Hartwig had gone home), aimlessly, just to check that he still belonged to the university. At home he had immediately stuffed the things in the cupboard, from which a mountain of offprints always stared at him, some of which regularly fell on the floor. At first, as outside lecturer and then as lecturer, he had responded to every offprint with a letter that was often as long as a review. A considerable correspondence had come into being, because he had never known when such an exchange of letters was over, and he hadn't been able to bring himself to make the other person's letter the last. The others felt that they were being taken seriously, even flattered. It represented an opportunity for them to go on commenting upon their work, and Perlmann often found in a subsequent offprint that this new work could be traced back to a particularly stimulating correspondence with him. A lot of time had passed on each occasion, and he felt like his correspondent's training partner, both self-appointed and somehow conscripted, while he wasn't advancing his own career. Then, with his commitments as professor, these extensive exchanges had put too much of a strain on his time. He had not found a middle way, and from one day to the next he had simply stopped replying.

He himself had never sent out offprints; it was only in response to an enquiry that his secretary had ever taken one from the stack. He had never been able to believe – really believe – that other people wanted to read what he wrote. The thought that someone might engage with his work was embarrassing to him. And that sensation was, paradoxically, run through with an indifference that amounted to something like sacrilege, because it called the entire academic world into question. It wasn't arrogance, he was quite sure of that. And the fact that other people plainly read his things and his reputation was growing did not alter that feeling in the slightest. Every time he opened the cupboard the mountain of unread material that tumbled out at him felt like a time bomb, even if he couldn't have said what the explosion would consist of.

'I haven't had a chance to congratulate you on your prize,' von Levetzov said to Perlmann when the waiter had cleared the soup plates. It sounded, Perlmann thought, as if he had taken a very long run-up to this remark, a run-up that had begun upstairs in his room, or perhaps even on the journey. Von Levertzov fanned away the smoke that drifted up to him from Laura Sand, and then turned to Evelyn Mistral. 'You must be aware that our friend here recently won a prize that represents the greatest acknowledgement for academic achievements that exists in our country. It's almost a little Nobel Prize.'

'Well . . .' Millar interjected.

'No, no,' von Levertzov continued, and after he had sought vainly for a sign of confirmation in Ruge's face, he added with a smug smile. 'One sometimes wonders a little who is going to get the prize, but I am certain that in this case the decision was justified.'

Perlmann gripped his glass with both hands and studied the ripples in the mineral water with as much concentration as if he had been observing the outcome of an experiment in the laboratory. He had done the same at the award ceremony, when his achievements were being celebrated in a speech. Two weeks after Agnes's death he had sat under candelabras there, too, emotionally dead and deaf to everything, glad that no speech was expected on his part.

It's bound to be your turn soon. The sentence had already formed within Perlmann; but then, to his surprise, he managed not to say it out loud. A small, a tiny step in the direction of the ideal of non-subservience. Suddenly he felt better, and his voice sounded almost cheerful as he said to Evelyn Mistral, 'There's always something random about such decisions. I'm sure it's the same in Spain, isn't it?'

It was exactly the same, she said. To put it mildly. What annoyed her most was that awards were often given to professors who had basically stopped working a long time ago, who lived off their past merits and lazed about in the safeguarding of reputations earned many years ago.

'You would be horrified, Philipp, if you saw that. These are people who have stopped achieving anything at all!'

On her forehead, right above her nose, a faint red stripe had formed. Perlmann had heard a familiarity in her tone, and the tension between that intimacy and her fury, which cut into him like a big, sharp knife, was almost unbearable. *Why did I even think she was different? Because of the red elephant?*

He was glad of the fuss that von Levetzov made about the food to show that he was a gourmet. He took the silence that fell a moment later, and in which all that could be heard was the clatter of cutlery and the voices from neighboring tables, as a sign that from now on he was not the center of attention.

'By the way, Phil,' Millar said into the silence, 'that business with the prize doesn't surprise me at all. The day before I left I was staying with Bill in Princeton – you know Bill Saunders – and he was telling me that you'll soon be receiving an invitation for a guest semester. They already know what you're doing,' he added with a smile in which, it seemed to Perlmann, the customary reverence for Princeton was mixed with a doubt, held at bay with difficulty and nonetheless enjoyed, about the wisdom of this very special decision.

Even though he was holding his fish knife with grim desperation, as about to cut a piece of stubborn, stringy meat, Perlmann was proud that he managed not to look at Millar. *Say nothing. Keep silent.*

'Bill was, incidentally, a bit cross that you didn't invite him, too,' Millar said at last, and because his voice contained a hint of irritation at Perlmann's lack of reaction, it sounded almost as if he himself were Bill Saunders complaining.

'Oh, really?' said Perlmann, and looked at Millar for a moment. He was pleased about the mildly ironic tone that he had managed, and now he looked again at Millar, for longer this time, and quite calmly. *His eyes aren't steel-blue, but porcelain-blue.* In Millar's grin, he thought, there was a hint of insecurity, and the fact that he now started talking briskly and loquaciously about Princeton in general seemed to confirm that impression. But rather than a feeling of triumph, a vacuum suddenly appeared inside Perlmann, and then the sensations of a fugitive suddenly crashed in on him. *Why won't they just leave me in peace?* As he removed fish bones in slow motion, he fought the impulse to stand up and run away. With relief he joined in just as Millar's language was beginning to make him furious once again. He greedily immersed himself in his fury.

Millar let himself tumble into his sentences, particularly his idiomatic, colloquial turns of phrase with a delight that Perlmann found repellent. *Wallowing. He's actually wallowing in his language.* Perlmann hated dialects, and he hated them because they were often spoken like that, with the same trampling presumption with which Millar spoke his Yankee American. Worst of all was the north German dialect that he had grown up with. That his parents had finally grown very remote from him had a great deal to do with it. The older they grew, the more defiantly they insisted on speaking to him in Platt, and the more clearly he sensed that defiance, the more resolutely he spoke in High German to them. It had been a mute battle with words. You couldn't talk about it. What use would it have been to say to them that their faces were becoming more and more rigid and dogmatic, and that that had much to do with the fact that they were increasingly led simply by the phrases and metaphors of the dialect, and by the prejudices that were crystallized in it?

The man with the rolled-up jacket sleeves, the open-necked shirt and the pale, unshaven face who was now looking round in the doorway and then coming towards them must have been Giorgio Silvestri. When Perlmann shook his hand and saw the relaxed, ironic alertness in his dark eyes, very different from Millar's, the alertness of a cat about to pounce, he was immediately won over by him. He felt as if in the form of this thin, frail-looking Italian, who appeared to be scruffy until you took a closer look at his clothes, someone had arrived who could help him. And then when the first thing he did was to light a Gauloise and blow the smoke into Millar's face, Perlmann was quite sure of things. Only the fact that he replied to Evelyn Mistral's greeting in fluent, unaccented Spanish and thus merited her radiant laughter, was slightly disturbing.

His English was no less fluent, although accented. Addressed on the subject by Laura Sand, who was staring at him unwaveringly, Silvestri talked about the two years that he had spent working on a psychiatric ward in Oakland near San Francisco.

'*East* Oakland,' he said, turning to Millar, and went on when he saw Millar's sour, frowning smile. 'After that I had enough. Not of the patients, who still write to me. But of the merciless, in fact one would have to say barbaric American health system.'

Millar avoided the renewed cloud of smoke as if it were poison gas.

'Well,' he said at last, suppressed what was on the tip of his tongue and devoted himself to his dessert.

Silvestri ordered from the waiter, who started treating him as an old acquaintance as soon as he heard his Florentine accent, a special dessert and a triple espresso. Perlmann made a joke about it, and that was when it happened: he was giving in to his need for contact.

For years he had battled against that habit of touching people, particularly when he had just met them, when he addressed a charming joke or a personal remark to them. As he was now doing with Silvestri, he rested his hand on their forearm, and when standing up he would often enough find himself suddenly putting an arm around their shoulders. There were people who saw this simply as evidence of an outgoing, lovable nature, and others who found his behavior disagreeable. His need for physical contact did not differentiate between men and women, and in the case of women there were often misunderstandings. The presence of Agnes had helped, but not always, and when she had witnessed the event, one had been able to tell from her face how puzzling and even weird she found it that he, who preferred to sit on the edge of big, empty squares, had this particular tic. It was no less puzzling to him, and each time it happened he felt the compulsion as a crack running right through him.

It was von Levetzov's idea to go across, after dinner, to the drawing room where the ochre-colored armchairs stood. Brian Millar, who came last because he had been inspecting the little room with the round, green-baize-covered gaming tables, stopped and then walked over to the grand piano.

'A Grotrian-Steinweg,' he said, 'I would prefer this to any Steinway.' He played a few notes and then closed the lid again. 'Another time,' he smiled when von Levetzov encouraged him to play something.

Perlmann felt his breathing suddenly becoming more difficult. *So he can do that too.* He asked the waiter who brought the drinks to open a window.

Von Levetzov raised his glass. 'As no one else is doing so, I would like to greet everyone and raise a toast to our favorable collaboration,' he said with a sideways glance at Perlmann, who felt the sweat of his hands mixing with the condensation on the glass. 'So we will be working up there,' he went on, pointing at the door of the veranda, which was reached by a flight of three steps. 'A perfect room for our purposes. I took a picture of it before. Veranda Marconi, it is called, after Guglielmo Marconi, a pioneer of radio technology, as the plaque outside says.'

Perlmann, who hadn't noticed the plaque, looked down at his new shoes, which hurt him. The painful pinch that would always be associated with confirmation and hard church pews merged with the hot sensation of shame about his forgotten welcome speech and a looming, helpless vexation with von Levetzov's behavior as travel guide.

'Now we're just waiting for Vassily Leskov,' said Laura Sand, and Perlmann felt as if she had been reading his thoughts and was trying, by changing the subject like this, to prevent the others from rising to their feet to catch sight of the veranda. 'When's he coming? And more particularly, who is he?'

He was a linguistic psychologist without tenure at a university, Perlmann said. Teaching commissions only every now and again. How he kept his head financially above water, he couldn't say. What was impressive was how good Leskov was at describing things, much better than most of the other people working in the field. It made one realize the extent to which, before any kind of theory, the important thing was to describe our experiences very precisely with language. Admittedly, his work was a kind of old-fashioned, introspective psychology, which didn't get you anywhere these days. But that was precisely what he, Perlmann, had found interesting in their conversation in St Petersburg.

'So you speak Russian, too?' von Levetzov asked irritably. Perlmann wasn't prepared for the question, but he didn't hesitate for a moment.

'No, no,' he said, and immediately managed a regretful smile, 'not a word. But he can speak perfect German. His grandmother was German and only ever spoke to him in her mother tongue when he lived with her after his father's death. His English was a bit clumsy, he told me; but he would certainly have managed here.'

Perlmann had no idea why he had lied, and he couldn't quite believe how unerringly he had done it. Evelyn Mistral, to whom he glanced across only hesitantly, was watching him with a face that was thoughtful and roguish by turns. *Now we're accomplices*, he thought, and didn't know whether he was pleased about it or whether his new feeling of vulnerability had predominated.

'Unfortunately, his exit permit was refused,' he concluded, and reached for the cigarettes with a relief that surprised him.

'Let's take another look at the veranda,' said Achim Ruge, when the conversation about conditions in the former Soviet Union had run aground and Millar looked at his watch with a yawn.

Perlmann was last to go up the three steps. *What will it be like when I come down them that day?*

Ruge had sat down at the front in the high-backed chair whose embroidered upholstery looked like Gobelins. 'If someone sitting here has nothing to say it's his own fault,' he said with a gurgling laugh, prompting general laughter. Perlmann pretended to study the tasselled coats of arms that ran along the wall.

'So what do you have to say about language, Achim?' he heard Evelyn Mistral asking, trying to imitate a strict teacher. 'Or have you forgotten to do your homework?'

More laughter. Only Laura Sand didn't join in, but investigated the old chest in the corner. Now the others were outdoing one another with caricatures of a cross-examination, and with mounting enjoyment Ruge was playing the devious idiot who hides behind a facade of intimidation. Perlmann's heart thumped in his throat. When Silvestri made a dry remark and then, with a swift movement of his tongue, made his cigarette disappear into his mouth, Evelyn Mistral's bright voice cracked with laughter. Perlmann didn't wait to hear what Millar, who was just getting a breath of fresh air, would say. As if anaesthetized he left, asked Giovanni for the key to his room and hobbled hastily, toes aching, upstairs.

He put on the chain, took off his painful shoes in the dark and fell back on the bed. Immediately the sentences started circling in his head, sentences spoken over dinner and on the veranda a moment before, sentences about the prize, about Princeton, about lazy Spanish professors, about forgotten homework. They kept returning, those sentences, as persistent as an echo that refused to die away or come to an end.

Perlmann was all too familiar with these tormenting circles of sentences, that compulsion to cling to sentences that had been uttered, and every time he was sucked into that wake, he felt as if he had spent the bulk of his life listening like this to sentences that had injured or frightened him. Agnes had suffered from the fact that he would sometimes turn up days, even weeks later with such a sentence and lend it a weight, a drama it had never had – just because he had been chewing away at it for so long, on walks or during hours of sleeplessness. Often she could hardly remember having said anything of the kind. That, in turn, struck him as mockery and made him helplessly furious. He was embittered. He had felt abandoned by everybody and crept away. Agnes told him how dangerous this memory for sentences was, how inhibited it could make you, so that you no longer dared to say anything spontaneous, if the thing you had said was then placed on the scales and later held up in front of you like a crime. He had seen that. This time the insight had helped. But the next time he had fallen right into the trap all over again.

He sat up and turned on the light. Tomorrow morning, at the first work session in the veranda, he would have to act as director. He would have to do that with skill and understanding, to see to it that his own contribution was made as late as possible. To do that, he needed a clear and rested mind. But with the darkness the sentences would come back, too.

He went to the bathroom and saw in front of him the long look that the doctor had given him before writing out the prescription for twenty strong sleeping tablets. *He's a decent man and a good doctor, but he can't understand someone not being able to sleep, he's not familiar with it.* Perlmann took half a tablet, *certainly no more than that.* Then he set the alarm for seven. The session was due to begin at nine. In the joking banter surrounding this question, Ruge, Millar and von Levetzov had won out over the others, even if it was still, as far as Millar's biological clock was concerned, the middle of the night.

Perlmann turned out the light and waited for the tablets to take effect. Down on the coast road a motorbike passed at full speed. Otherwise it was silent. Suddenly, Ruge blew his nose in the next room: three trumpet blasts. It was as if there were no wall between them. Ruge seemed to fill even Perlmann's room with his physical presence. All of a sudden everything was right in front of Perlmann's eyes again: the mirror-image desk, Ruge sitting at it with his great peasant head and watery grey eyes behind his wired-up glasses, and on the other side Millar with his Bach.

Perlmann got to his feet and put his ear to the wall. Nothing. Back in bed he ran once again through the possible explanations for a change of room: *the bed, my back; they couldn't check that, they would just have to believe me.* He relaxed and felt the first hint of numbness in his lips and fingertips.

Now the sentences couldn't get at him any more. And Ruge could sit at his desk playing the piano as much as he wanted. From tomorrow there would be no one on this side. Ruge shook with laughter, gurgled, burped and had to gasp for air. His grand piano came inexorably closer. It expanded, while Perlmann's piano shrank like melting cellophane. Now it was Millar who was playing. *The Well-Tempered Clavier, I tell you, it's boring, even if you find that shocking.* Millar was standing by the ochre-colored grand piano, and while Evelyn Mistral squeaked with pleasure he bowed uninterruptedly until he was finally interrupted by the ringing of the telephone.

'I just wanted to ask you quickly if you got there all right,' said Kirsten. A thin layer of numbness lay on Perlmann's face, and his tongue was furry and heavy.

'Wait a moment,' he murmured, and walked unsteadily to the bathroom, where he let cold water run over his face. His hand tingled as he picked up the receiver again.

'Sorry if I woke you,' said Kirsten. 'I'm just so used to us calling each other at this time of day.'

'That's OK,' he said, and was glad that it didn't sound too washed-out.

The business with the shared house had sorted itself out nicely, she told him; only one woman was a bit difficult. 'And just imagine: today I signed up for my first presentation. About Faulkner's *The Wild Palms*, the one with the double narrative. And then it turned out that it's my turn in fourteen days' time! I feel quite different when I think about it. I hope you don't have to sit at the front as well!'

Perlmann was monosyllabic, and repeatedly collecting spittle against his dry tongue. Yes, he said at last, everything's fine; the hotel and the weather, too.

'And did you bring your Russian things with you?' she asked.

One half-hour passed after the other, and Perlmann still couldn't get back to sleep. In the middle of a poisoned weariness there was still an island of dry alertness that wouldn't go out. At half-past one he phoned reception and for safety's sake asked to be woken at seven. Then he took the second half of the sleeping pill.

4

He was still enveloped in leaden weariness when his alarm call came, from a long way off, it seemed to him. He mumbled *grazie* and hung up. Immediately afterwards the alarm clock rang. Sitting on the edge of the bed he bent over and covered his face with both hands. He had the feeling of having slept deeply in the sense that a span of total oblivion lay between the current moment and the events of the previous day. Nonetheless, he felt insecure, as if we were walking on very thin ice, and something was pushing against his eyes as if someone had poured lead into his sinuses. He cursed the sleeping pill.

After he had misdialled and ended up talking to the laundry, he ordered coffee from room service. As he was waiting for the waiter, he stood in the cool air by the open window and watched as the lights went off over by Sestri Levante. Again a sunrise without any presence, the usual transparent blue seeping through the fine morning mist, but all as in a film seen too often, and this time separated from him by a wall of weariness and a throbbing headache.

He didn't have the strength to protest when the waiter set a tray with a sumptuous breakfast down on the round table. He hastily gulped down three cups of coffee, took an aspirin and lit a cigarette. After the first few puffs he felt slightly dizzy, but the sensation was much weaker than the day before. Now music came out of Millar's room: Bach. Perlmann went into the shower, where he shivered in spite of the hot water. Afterwards he drank the rest of the coffee. Now the cigarette only tasted bitter. Quarter to eight. From eight the others would be going to breakfast. It was enough if he appeared at about half-past. All of a sudden he didn't know what to do with the time left to him except to wait for Millar to go to breakfast and the music to stop.

He picked up Leskov's text. The first sentence after yesterday's marks was difficult, and Perlmann relied on paper and pencil to make the convoluted construction clear to himself: *I shall demonstrate that and in which sense it is by capturing our memories in words that we create these memories and thus our own experienced past in the first place.* The music stopped, and a moment later Millar's door clicked shut. Perlmann slowly drank the orange juice and ate one croissant, then another one. At breakfast down below he would only need to drink something. His headache was subsiding. He closed his eyes and leaned back in his chair. Creating the past by narrating memory stories – that seemed to be the idea. He excitedly looked in his suitcase for his black notebook. He no longer knew what, but that thought had something to do with his own notes.

The door to Ruge's room clicked shut, and a few moments later Perlmann heard the sound of him blowing his nose, much more muted in the hotel corridor. Suddenly, Perlmann was painfully wide awake: he hadn't prepared a single suggestion for the organization of his work over the coming weeks. He put the black notebook back. He couldn't understand how he could have forgotten it, when he usually prepared everything in minute detail. If he had got up later and gone down to breakfast straight away, it might have occurred to him only when he stepped into the veranda. It was as if the fear split him deep within, and for one fleeting moment he had an idea what it must be like to lose yourself.

He quickly washed his face with cold water, thought for a moment about whether he should order some more coffee, then took his writing pad and pocket diary and sat down at the desk. No, Ruge wasn't sitting opposite him now. And anyway, the wall was a wall and not a two-way mirror. His throbbing headache was back, and while he drew columns for the five weeks, with his other hand he gripped his forehead and pressed it as hard as if he wanted to crush it.

Seven blocks of two days in which they would assemble in the veranda to discuss each other's current work. Three days a week, to have individual conversations or withdraw. That sounded like the correct dosage.

Perlmann marked Monday and Tuesday as well as Thursday and Friday. He himself would take the last block. But even so he was left, he was horrified to see, with only three weeks, and not even a whole three, because the others each needed two or three days to read. He had at all costs to see to it that he made it into the last column, the one that had still been left blank, and in the lower half of it, so that he still had four weeks; that was the absolute minimum. That meant using any explanation to keep two half-weeks free. He looked at his watch: twenty-five to nine. He lit his third last cigarette. *They'll walk out on me during the session.* The minutes passed inconsequentially. *If Leskov had been able to come, the problem would only be half as big.* He would have to be careful that he didn't give himself away with his maneuvering.

When he walked over to his suitcase to get a pullover he saw himself in the high mirror on the wall, in the same trousers and the same shirt as yesterday afternoon. He stopped for a moment, then frantically started changing. As he did so, he was filled with furious shame at his insecurity. Battling tears of fury, he slipped back into the clothes he had just been wearing, put his jumper over his shoulders and walked, pencil and paper in hand, to the door. Before he pulled it shut he saw on the carpet a torn-off button of his fresh shirt, which lay on the crumpled bed. When, happy at the absence of pain in his ankle, he hurried down the purple carpet of the wide staircase, it was two minutes past nine.

All the others were already there, with notepads and manuscripts in front of them. Only Silvestri had brought nothing but an untidily folded newspaper. For Perlmann it was impossible not to sit at the front. It would have looked like a ludicrous refusal that gave the carved armchair a far too great, almost magical significance. So he sat down after a brief hesitation, which he alone perceived, at the head. Through the windows on the other side of the room he could see the blue swimming pool, and behind it, beyond the hotel terrace, the top half of a gas station. At this time of day the parasols had not yet been put up, the loungers were still empty. Only the red-haired man from yesterday was already there, tapping out the music from his headphones on his drawn-up knee.

The phrases of greeting and all other introductory words stuck in Perlmann's throat. He wanted to get straight to business, he said, and immediately started explaining his suggestion for the course of the work. As he spoke he became more secure; what he said sounded practiced and well thought out. Then he went to the board and drew the five columns. The second half of the current and the first half of the fourth week he left blank. Sitting awkwardly, he stiffly wrote his own name beside the Thursday and Friday of the last week. *Only three and a half weeks, then. And if you take in the reading time for the others, it's only three; plus one, two days at most. How am I supposed to do that?*

'Why do you want to keep your contribution from us for so long?' von Levetzov asked with a smile that was supposed to express appreciative interest, but in which there was also a bit of irritating surprise and, it seemed to Perlmann, a hint of suspicion, so faint that it took his special eyes to see it. 'You're one of the main reasons we're here.' Evelyn Mistral smiled at Perlmann and nodded emphatically.

Perlmann felt his stomach contracting as violently as if he were reacting to a searing poison. He tried to breathe calmly, and very slowly put a cigarette between his lips. When his eye fell on Silvestri, he thought of the doctor on the telephone. He held the cigarette in the flame for much longer than necessary and inwardly rehearsed the tone that the doctor had used – the tone of natural delimitation, the non-subservient tone. He took a deep drag and, leaning back, finished the uncomfortably long pause with the words: 'I think the work of each of us is deserving of equal interest, so that the sequence in which we get to it is insignificant. Isn't that right?'

Even before he had finished his sentence he knew that he had got the tone completely wrong. He looked up and looked at von Levetzov with a smile which, he hoped, took something of the edge off the rebuke.

'Certainly, certainly,' von Levetzov said, startled, and added sharply, 'No need to get worked up.'

'Perhaps everyone should give a short account of what their contribution will be about,' said Laura Sand, 'then we'll be more able to judge a sensible sequence.'

At first Perlmann was grateful to her for having saved the situation like that. But a moment later he was filled with panic. He hid his face behind his clasped hands. That would look like he was concentrating. Cold sweat formed on his palms. He closed his eyes and yielded for a while to leaden exhaustion.

But it had been as clear as day that it would come sooner or later. After all, even yesterday, when he was talking to Evelyn Mistral, that question had made him shiver. So why, in the meantime, had he not come up with a clever answer? He would have had to work it out effectively and then memorize it until, at the moment it was needed, he could summon it up as something to be presented with complete equanimity and even, for the brief span of his presentation, believed – a staged self-deception that was available to him as part of his facade. *But now, what I say will be completely random.*

Afterwards, Perlmann couldn't have said what subject Adrian von Levetzov had sketched. While he himself sought feverishly for formulae which he could later cobble together into the appearance of a subject, only the complacent, mannered tone of von Levetzov's English got through to him. It was only towards the end, while von Levetzov was preparing for yet another question from Ruge, that Perlmann started distinguishing individual words. But it was strange: instead of receiving the words in their familiar meaning, and slipping through them to the expressed thought, all he heard was that most of them were foreign words, jargon with its roots in Latin or Greek, which, when linked together, produced a kind of Esperanto. He found these words ridiculous, just silly and then that ghostly insecurity suddenly rose up within him again, the sensation that had for some time made him pick up the dictionary with increasing frequency. Each time he did so the feeling fell from a clear sky that he no longer had the faintest idea of the meaning of a technical term that he had read thousands of times; it had an irritating blurriness that made it look like a wobbly photograph. And yet every time he consulted the dictionary he made the same discovery: he had precisely the correct definition in his head; there was nothing more precise to know. Uncertain whether this discovery reassured him, or whether the insecurity grew because it had needed such a discovery, he put the dictionary back on the shelf. And often, a few days later, he looked up the same word again.

Laura Sand had, when it was her turn, a cigarette between her lips, and tried to keep the smoke from getting in her eyes. Her initial sentences were halting as she looked for something in her papers, and anyone who hadn't known that her books on animal languages were among the very best on the subject would have taken it for a sign of uncertainty. At last she found the piece of paper she had been looking for, let her eyes slide over it, and started talking with great fluency and concentration about the experiments she had performed over the past few months in Kenya. What she said was wonderfully concise and clear, Perlmann thought, and set out in that dark, always slightly irritated voice which, when she wanted to emphasize something, dropped into the broad Australian accent normally concealed behind an unremarkable British English. Like yesterday, when she had arrived, she was entirely dressed in black; the only color about her was the red in the signet ring on the little finger of her right hand.

Again Perlmann hid his face behind his hands and struggled to remember the specialist questions that he had recently examined, *when I was still on top of things*. But nothing came. Only Leskov suddenly appeared in his inner field of vision, Leskov with his big pipe between his bad, brown, tobacco-stained teeth, his massive body sunk in the worn, dirty grey upholstery of the chair in the foyer of the conference building. Perlmann tried not to listen when the vividly remembered figure spoke about how deeply words intervened in experience. He didn't need that image, he said to himself. He really didn't need it at all, because he had the black notebook with his own notes in it. If only he could go quickly upstairs and cast his eye over them.

Giorgio Silvestri held one knee braced against the edge of the table and balanced on the back legs of his chair. He let his left arm dangle backwards, and rested his right on the arm, a cigarette between his long, slender fingers. *Un po' stravagante*, Angelini had called him. When he started speaking now, with a voice that was soft but, in spite of its strong accent, very confident, his white hand tirelessly moved with its cigarette, emphasizing certain things, casting others in doubt or making them seem vague. If one listened to schizophrenic patients, he said, the usual expectations with regard to coherence were disappointed. But the shifts in meaning and instances of conceptual incoherence obeyed a logic; there wasn't mere chaos. He wanted to use his time here to write up his collected clinical material on this thesis. He asked for a late date, as all his work in the hospital had delayed him.

Perlmann picked up the chalk. *He has a sound reason. I don't. And the decent thing would be to offer him the last date. But then I wouldn't even have a whole three weeks, so it's quite impossible.* He put Silvestri's name down for Thursday and Friday of the fourth week. Even before he turned back to the others, he felt Brian Millar's gaze resting on him. Again the American held his arms folded and his head tilted on one side. His thin lips twitched, and Perlmann was sure that the question was about to come. He could have slapped himself for not expecting this.

'Of course you can take the last two days,' he said to Silvestri, and drew an arrow across to the fifth week.

'I'd like to leave it open, if that's OK,' Silvestri said.

So for safety's sake I've got to put myself down for the Thursday of the fourth week. The others have to get my text by the previous Tuesday at the latest. That means I've still got exactly twenty days. Perlmann put a cigarette between his lips when he had sat down. He was horrified to see the hand that held the match trembling, and immediately brought his arm up and held his wrist with the other hand.

Achim Ruge, who was next in line, took out a huge, red-and-white checked handkerchief, clumsily unfolded it, took off his glasses and blew his nose loudly and thoroughly. That suddenly brought the room problem back to Perlmann's consciousness. The thought of it was the last thing he needed now. He pushed it powerfully away from him, but felt an additional anxiety rise up. Ruge took off his jacket and sat there in his ill-cut shirt, with rubber bands on the upper arms to shorten the sleeves. *Stuffy. He's the stuffiest person I know. And he's straight, straight to the bone. Maybe it isn't even the case that I have the most to fear from Millar and von Levetzov. Maybe this Achim Ruge, because of his stuffiness, his straightness, is even more dangerous.* It wasn't unthinkable, Perlmann thought, that von Levetzov would creep away from academia for a while – to a woman, perhaps, or because of an addiction to gambling. Rumours were never entirely a matter of chance. Accordingly, he might not be so hard on Perlmann – at least there would be a certain thoughtfulness about his condemnation. And Millar too had a certain straight quality, but it was the athletic straightness of an American who could some- times go off the rails. Where Sheila was concerned, for example. In the case of Ruge, on the other hand, who knew nothing but his laboratory and his computer, any dropping off was unimaginable, and for that reason his judgment was likely to be ruthless and devastating.

Perlmann tried to protect himself with contempt. He stared at the rubber bands and did everything he could to see Ruge as a stiff who was only worth laughing at. And here he was assisted by Ruge's horrible English accent, which sounded like a caricature. He automatically expected Ruge to make grammatical mistakes. But it didn't happen. On the contrary, Ruge had a perfect command of English, and used words and phrases which Perlmann understood, certainly, but which were not actively at his disposal. His carefully constructed contempt faltered. Ruge's pres- ence seemed even more threatening to him than it had before, and again Perlmann used his hands to erect a shield in front of his eyes.

Before she started talking, Evelyn Mistral put on a pair of glasses with a delicate matte silver frame. She had put up her hair, and in spite of the skewed T-shirt under her cinnamon-colored jacket she looked older than yesterday: *an academic, the red elephant doesn't suit her at all today.* All of a sudden she was quite alien to him – in fact, *as a reader, as a worker, she's an opponent I have to be wary of.* Perlmann tried to hide and made one last desperate attempt to remember a subject that he knew something about. *After her it's my turn.* But then he heard her bright voice, which sounded tense and harassed. Her feet under the table slipped out of her red shoes and back in again. She propped herself with her arms on the table, before changing position again a moment later. Instead of merely outlining her theme she constantly justified her work and talked for longer than necessary. After a while Perlmann felt that her tension had passed into his body, as if he could take it away from her. He thought he had to defend her against the faces of the others, even though there wasn't a hint of criticism to be seen in them, merely a patronizing benevolence.

And then, all of a sudden, she had finished, took her glasses off and leaned back with her arms folded. Perlmann felt as if the veranda were filling up with an intoxicating silence, and time seemed only to want to go on flowing when he had started talking. He felt for his cigarettes, touched the pack and discovered that it was empty. With his hand still on the box his eye drifted above Silvestri's head and out and beyond to the sea, to check that the world, the real world, was much bigger than this hateful room, where he was now encircled by all the people whom he had assembled here only because he had wanted to accompany Agnes on her photographic journey through Italy in winter.

Silvestri grinned, and he picked up his pack of Gauloises and threw it to Perlmann in a high arc all the way across the room. Still half-immersed in his attempt to hide in his own gaze and escape unnoticed into the light, Perlmann raised his arm and confidently caught the box. Even though that confidence seemed to issue not from himself as such, but only from his body, which he had been trying to leave behind as a decoy, it gave him back a little of his confidence. He thanked Silvestri with a nod and put one of the unfiltered cigarettes between his lips. *What I say now will be completely random.*

At the first drag the sharp smoke took his breath away, and he couldn't help coughing. He heard Silvestri laughing. Perlmann hid for a while behind his cough and finally, after wiping his weeping eyes with his handkerchief, looked around.

'I'm working on a text about the connection between language and memory,' he said. He was both relieved and shocked by the calm in his voice. It was something, he went on, that had interested him for many years. Too rarely, he thought, did his discipline investigate how language was interwoven with the various forms of experience. And in this respect it was precisely the experience of time that had received special treatment. It was an unorthodox theme for a linguist, he added with a smile that felt like a strenuous piece of facial gymnastics. But he also understood his stay here as an opportunity to go in alternative directions.

Evelyn Mistral looked at him with radiant eyes, and now, for the first time, Perlmann noticed the green of those eyes, a sea-green with a few splinters of amber set into it. She was pleasantly surprised that he was dealing with something related to her own subject, and Perlmann had to look away to keep, in his deceitfulness, from being exposed to her smiling face any longer.

Less had happened in the faces of the others than he had expected. Millar's head seemed to be a little more bent than usual, but there was no mockery to be discovered in his expression, and in Adrian von Levetzov's dark eyes there was even a gleam of moderate interest.

Laura Sand's suggestion for the sequence of the sessions met with general agreement. The date that Perlmann had fixed for himself was now treated as something quite natural. On that point, of course, von Levetzov avoided Perlmann's eye. Instead he came to see him at the end of the session. He had found his announcement rather surprising, he said. But thinking about it properly he was also a little bit nervous. It must be a lovely feeling, trying out something new. He couldn't wait to hear the result!

Perlmann went to see Maria in the office, and introduced Millar to her. Today, as usual, she was wearing a glittering pullover that matched her hair-do, and as on the first evening Perlmann was captivated by the contrast between the hint of punk that surrounded her and the warm, almost maternal smile with which she addressed people. His two texts would be copied by four o'clock, she assured Millar. A copy would be put in everyone's pigeonhole.

'One text you know already,' Millar said to Perlmann as he left, 'and I'll be keen to hear what you have to say about the other one. You have been subject to severe criticism, I'm afraid. But you know it isn't meant personally.'

5

'It won't be a problem to give you another room,' Signora Morelli said off-handedly after Perlmann had told her – in halting Italian full of mistakes – his story about the bed and the pains in his back. 'At this time of year we are far from full.' She saw his hesitation and paused as she was about to turn towards the key racks.

Then Perlmann summoned all his courage and said firmly, 'I would like the new room to be on the other side of the building. Between empty rooms, if possible.'

The hint of a smile appeared on Signora Morelli's severe face, and her eyes narrowed slightly. She flicked through her papers, took a key from the rack and said, '*Va bene*, try this one.'

When he turned towards her again on the stairs, she was resting both arms on the shelf behind the counter, and was watching him with her head slightly inclined.

The new room was on the top floor of the south wing, far from the others. The corridor was gloomy, because of the three art nouveau lamps in the ceiling only two were lit: the middle one was dark, and the bulbs were broken in the other two. For a moment Perlmann was horrified by the room. It was bigger than the previous one, admittedly, and the ceiling was higher – it was almost a sort of hall – but the stucco on the ceiling was crumbling, the carpet was worn and the big mirror on the wall was half-blind. It also smelled musty, as if it hadn't been aired for years. Only the bathroom had been completely refurbished, with a marble tub and gleaming metal taps. He opened the window and looked down the facade: the room was in the only row without balconies. Over by the swimming pool Giorgio Silvestri had stretched himself out on one of the yellow loungers. He had taken off his shoes and socks, and the open newspaper lay over his face. *Like a tramp. A fearless man, a free man – and my thoughts about him are the purest kitsch.*

Perlmann sat down in the big worn-out red plush wing chair next to the window. He started assessing the room with his eyes, and even before he had finished he liked it. He lay down on the bed. Suddenly it was very easy to relax. The new room allowed him to forget what had happened at the meeting. The honks of a ship's horn and the rattle of a motorboat reached him from far away. He thought about the fact that the two adjacent rooms were empty. Their neighboring rooms, in turn, seemed to be unoccupied as well, and his imagination produced endless series of empty, silent rooms. Then he went to sleep.

It was shortly before three when he woke up shivering and dry-mouthed, at first confused by the surroundings, then relieved. On the way down to his old room he clutched the key like an anchor. Millar's music would no longer trouble him, he thought, as he packed the clothes and books that he would bring upstairs at night when all was quiet.

There was a whole hour before Millar's texts were due to be in their pigeonholes. Perlmann picked up Leskov's paper. Once more he ran through the sentence about the linguistic creation of one's own past. What he had written as a translation in the morning was true. But now the text became very difficult. Leskov introduced the concept of a remembered scene – *vspomnishchaya stsena* – and then seemed to develop the idea that we inevitably project a self-image – *samopredstavlenie* – into such scenes. Perlmann had to look up every second word, and the typescript was slowly obscured by his scribbled translations. It was becoming increasingly clear to him: he had to buy a vocabulary book in which he could write all the new words. In this way he would produce a glossary of academic Russian, a sphere of language that was barely touched upon in the books of exercises. He suddenly felt fine: he had a plan that he was able to pursue in his new, quiet room. It was a working project. At last he was a working man again.

When he walked along the port into town to find a stationery shop, his steps were firm and confident.

It was his first venture into the town, and for a long time it looked as if there wasn't a single shop selling writing equipment. At last, in a dark side street, he found a scruffy little shop selling not only stationery but also magazines and trashy novels, as well as cheap toys and sweets. Still annoyed at having had to search for so long, but now also relieved, he turned the handle with brio and pushed against the locked door with his shoulder and head. Still siesta, even though it was nearly four o'clock. He stopped by the shop window and rubbed his aching forehead. After a while his eye was caught by a big book which was set up behind the dirty pane, surrounded by tinsel and paper chains, like a holy book in a shrine. It was a chronicle of the twentieth century. The front cover was divided into four fields showing world-famous photographs, icons of the century: Marilyn Monroe, standing over the ventilating shaft, holding on to her skirt as it blew up; Elvis Presley in a pale blue glittery suit, bent far back as he played; Neil Armstrong's first footstep on the moon; Jackie Kennedy in Dallas, bending over the assassinated president in the open-topped car. Perlmann felt the pictures drawing him into their spell as if he had never seen them before. The idea of being able to read something about the subjects of these pictures, right now, electrified him, and suddenly nothing seemed more exciting, nothing more important, than to comprehend the century in which he lived from the perspective of pictures like that. Excitedly, he tore open the packet of cigarettes that he had bought on the corner. No, it wasn't like that: it wasn't a matter of understanding a century like a historian. What he wanted was to reappropriate his own life by imagining what had happened in the world outside while he was alive. The idea first came to him there in that dark, deserted alley, smelling a bit of fish and rotten vegetables. He was unsure whether he fully understood what he was thinking, but he was impatient to get started, whatever it might be.

The shop's proprietor, when she finally opened the door to him, was a fat woman with far too many rings on her plump hands. She was at first annoyed by Perlmann's unconcealed impatience. But when he asked for the chronicle, her grumpy attitude gave way to solicitous friendliness. She was taken aback, as if she had never imagined that anyone might actually want to buy that big, unwieldy book, the centerpiece of her display; certainly not someone with an unmistakeably foreign accent, and during the dead time of the Italian siesta. She fetched the heavy volume from the shop window, dusted it down in the open door and handed it to Perlmann with a theatrical gesture: *Ecco!* She wouldn't take anything for the vocabulary notebook – it was gratis. She stuffed the bundle of cash into the pocket of her apron. She was still shaking her head with surprise as she watched him leave from the doorway.

Two streets on, Perlmann saw an unprepossessing sign: TRATTORIA. He parted the glass-bead curtain, walked down the long, gloomy corridor and suddenly found himself in a bright, glass-roofed internal courtyard with dining tables covered by red-and-white checked tablecloths. The room was empty, and Perlmann had to call twice before the proprietor arrived wearing an apron. They themselves had just eaten, he said genially, but Perlmann could still have a minestrone and a plate of pasta. Then, when he brought the food, his wife and daughter appeared as well. Perlmann was itching to read the chronicle, but the family was curious to find out about the man with the big book who plainly lived against the grain of the daily rhythm. In return for their hospitality at such an unusual time, Perlmann told them about the research group. Investigating languages, that was interesting, they thought, and he had to tell them more and more. Sandra in particular, the thirteen-year-old daughter with the long, pitch-black hair, asked question after question, and her parents were visibly proud to have a daughter with such a thirst for knowledge. Talking about these subjects went amazingly well given his poor Italian. Perlmann was pleased with every successful turn of phrase that he wouldn't have thought himself capable of, and this delight at his linguistic success, along with the desire not to disappoint Sandra made him draw a positive, almost enthusiastic picture of what they were doing over at the hotel, which was grotesquely at odds with his internal misery. When the proprietor and his family finally withdrew to leave him to read, in their eyes he was an enviable man who was lucky enough to do exactly what interested him most; the rare case, then, of a man who lived in perfect harmony with himself.

Perlmann opened the book at the year of his high-school graduation. The first controlled nuclear fusion. A come-back for De Gaulle. Boris Pasternak forced to give back the Nobel Prize. There had been elections in Italy. Pope Pius XII had died. The Torre Velasca in Milan had been completed. The Bishop of Prato, who had insulted a couple as *pubblici concubini* and *pubblici peccatori* because they had refused a church wedding, was accused of slander before a court, fined and later, after a rebellion of the church, absolved on the grounds of *insindacabilità dell'atto*.

Perlmann read with his eyes aflame. The texts weren't demanding, and by and large his Italian was up to the task. The whole thing was written in a sensational style and had a tabloid whiff about it, but that didn't bother him. He actually enjoyed it, and the fact that the selection of events was made from the Italian perspective gave the affair an exotic charm. He was boundlessly surprised by his fascination, when he read, for example, that the Hungarian uprising, which had been a great embarrassment to the Italian Communists two years previously, had not lost the Party any votes in the elections. He couldn't understand why he asked Sandra to bring him one espresso after another, while smoking like a chimney. But he enjoyed surprising himself by making an unexpected discovery about himself, which, he felt vaguely, could be the start of something.

The sky over the glass roof was almost black by now, and the ships' lanterns on the walls had been lit for a long time when Perlmann left. On a momentary whim he asked the proprietor to keep the chronicle for him; he would come back to go on reading. As he walked through the quiet alleys to the port, Perlmann had the feeling of having found a place or refuge to which he could retreat when the world of the hotel, of the group, threatened to crush him. And he felt a furtive joy at the thought that none of the others would ever find out about this refuge. But as he was walking along the harbor jetty and turned into the shore road on which the hotel stood, those feelings quickly seeped away, even though he paused several times and tried, eyes closed, to stop them.

And when he stood by the front steps and looked up at the name of the hotel, written in white neon letters on a gleaming blue background, his bad conscience at having frittered away half a day superimposed itself over everything else.

The two texts by Millar which Signora Morelli handed him were a shock. The one that Perlmann had stuffed into the offprints cupboard at home was fifty-nine pages long; the other one sixty-five, with seven pages of notes. When he was flicking through it in the elevator, the last remainder of freedom that he had experienced in the trattoria fled. What remained was a leaden weariness and the sense that it would take him hours to read so much as a single page.

In his room he set the papers aside. There wasn't much time left before dinner. He picked up Leskov's text and wrote down the unfamiliar words that he had looked up so far in his vocabulary book. Several times he paused and stared in cheerful amazement at his Russian handwriting. It was a little clumsy, but correct, and it was Russian without a doubt. The annoying thing was that words appeared in the subsequent sentences that weren't in his pocket dictionary. Nonetheless, he was by and large able to follow Leskov's next step. Self-images, the text argued, were something quite different from the experienced contours of an internal world. Making an image of oneself was a process that required far more articulation than the inner perception, the inner exploration of contours of experience could provide on their own.

He had a nose for striking examples, this Vassily Leskov, and gradually Perlmann developed a feeling for the text. He liked its blunt, unembellished style and its laconic tone. As an author, he thought, Leskov was quite different, much more congenial than usual, and Perlmann noticed how the shapeless, pipe-smoking figure of his memory retreated behind another person who had no appearance, but a voice, and thus a clear and strong identity.

It was twenty to nine when he remembered dinner. He quickly changed, grabbed the shirt with the torn-off button and chose a wide tie to hide the spot. Giovanni at reception grinned when he saw him hurrying down the stairs. It was the grin of someone seeing a late school pupil dashing down an empty corridor to the classroom. Perlmann wanted to slap him, this clueless Italian with his bushy eyebrows and ridiculously long sideburns. The glance Perlmann gave him was so poisonous that Giovanni's grin vanished for a moment.

He didn't want a starter, he told the waiter before sitting down next to Silvestri who, plainly involved in a heated exchange with Brian Millar, had set his knife and fork down in a cross on his plate and lit a cigarette in the middle of the meal. Yes, he was saying, and absently blowing the smoke into Millar's face, Franco Basaglia's experiment in Görz must be deemed a failure. But that was still no proof that the traditional psychiatry of grilles and bolted doors could not be changed; and a malicious tone was entirely inappropriate. At any rate, Basaglia had displayed more sensitivity, commitment and courage than the whole psychiatric establishment, whose inertia was directly proportional to its lack of imagination.

'Have you ever experienced what it's like when someone bolts the door in front of your nose, even though you haven't done anything, as if you're in prison? Have you seen the big keys that are turned in the lock by the wardens with a noise that never seems to stop echoing?' Silvestri's white hand with the cigarette trembled, and a bit of ash fell on the Swiss roll.

'They aren't wardens,' Millar said, struggling to maintain his self-control, 'they're nurses.'

'Wardens is what they called them in Oakland,' Silvestri said urgently. 'The same word that you use for prisons.'

'They're nurses,' Millar repeated, trying to stay calm, and then turned, wine bottle in hand, with a forced smile to Perlmann. 'There are happier subjects. How did you enjoy my new paper?'

Perlmann felt Silvestri's excitement vibrating within himself. He shoved a second piece of meat, far too big, into his mouth and made a gesture of apology as he chewed. 'It's OK,' he said at last and attempted a smile that was supposed to express the fact that he didn't take Millar's criticism of him amiss.

'I understand,' Millar grinned when Perlmann failed to say anything more. 'You can save your reply till tomorrow. I'll look forward to it.'

Back in his room, Perlmann worked out his revulsion with particularly forceful movements and sat down at the desk with forced brio. Millar's papers were, as usually, shatteringly brilliant; one could tell that as soon as one started flicking through them. His subheadings almost always took the form of a question, and his original questions, which had prompted so much research, had made him famous. There was also the fact that his vocabulary was unusually large for an academic author, and he had developed an unmistakeable style, juggling skilfully with the vividness of idiomatic phrases, and didn't shy away from putting a slang expression in the middle of a dry sentence summing up data of some kind, and making it explode like a bomb. There were also people who found Millar's style shrill and vain, but they had always been in a minority, and by now no one dared to say it out loud. Only Achim Ruge, who wrote in a desiccated, legalistic style, had made a remark to that effect at a conference some time before, and it had been passed on in whispers.

Perlmann had no reservations; not a single one. He had started with the newer of the two papers, to put Millar's criticism behind him. He couldn't think of a response. As he sat in front of his empty notepad, pen brandished, a fortissimo sounded from Millar's room every now and again. Millar's criticism was harsh, actually devastating. Perlmann was baffled that it didn't touch him. It was a bit like having a local anaesthetic, and after reading Millar's critical passages he felt almost cheerful.

But then, when he had finished the paper, he was shocked by his indifference. To express reservations, to be able to react to a criticism, you have to have opinions, opinions that can be formulated and stated. And that was exactly what he didn't have. For some time he had been a man without opinions, at least as far as his subject was concerned. He agreed with everything, as long as it wasn't obvious nonsense. It had never been so clear to him as now.

He stepped to the open window. The strip of light at Sestri Levante was now quite regular and still. What had it been like when he still had opinions? Where had they come from? And why had the source dried up? *Can you decide to believe something? Or do opinions just happen to you?*

Ruge's room had been in darkness before, and now the light from Millar's window went out as well. But it was better to wait another half hour before moving. Two days out of thirty-three. So one sixteenth had already gone. It was a sum like the ones he had done at school. And like then it felt peculiar: all of a sudden it seemed like a huge amount. In fact, he thought, it had all gone fairly quickly, and if it went on like that it would soon be over. That there was still fifteen times the same amount of time to come seemed almost trivial. A moment later it seemed like an eternity: once and again and again . . . You had to think of the whole thing like a long-distance runner. You had to concentrate on it and overcome the next, manageable segment.

He furtively opened the door and reassured himself that no one was in the corridor. Then he ran, crouching, to the stairs, his suitcases held just above the ground, and hurried to the top floor, taking the steps two at a time in spite of the heavy luggage. Panting, he set the suitcases down in his new room and hurried back again. Together with his grammar and his dictionary, Millar and Leskov's papers formed a big, shapeless stack, which he covered with his coat. After a searching glance through the room he used the key to avoid the noise of the slamming door.

The ceiling light in the new room cast a cold, diffuse light that recalled a station waiting room. On the other hand, the beam of light from the standard lamp beside the red armchair was warm and clear, an ideal light for reading. Once it was lit, the rest of the expansive room sank into a calming darkness that belonged to him alone. After a while he crossed this darkness to the bathroom and took half a sleeping pill. Until it took effect, he would just manage to scamper through Millar's first text in bed. It was a difficult text with lots of formulae. But for that reason he'd hardly be able to do it tomorrow. Perlmann set his alarm clock for half-past seven. He would, he thought in his half-sleep, have to simulate an opinion for tomorrow's session. It wouldn't be enough to capture it in words; it was a matter of staging the opinion inside oneself as well. Was it possible to do that, fighting against the certainty that one lacked any opinion?

6

The waiter who brought him his coffee the following morning passed no remark about the new room. As he approached the round table beside the red armchair, Perlmann covered Leskov's paper with the hotel brochure and pushed it aside to make space for the tray. He did it with a quick, furtive motion which unsettled him vaguely, but which he immediately forgot.

There was no time now for Millar's first paper, which he hadn't got round to reading the night before, because the five minutes of snoozing that he had allowed himself after the ringing of the alarm clock had turned into half an hour. Perlmann looked again at the passages that Millar quoted from his own writings. He could hardly believe that he himself should have written them. Not because he thought they were bad. But the author of those lines had a grasp of his subject and a firmness of opinion that Perlmann was so unable to remember that he suspected he had not even been present when they were written. That remote, alien author was not a bit closer to him than Millar's academic voice, so that he felt like a referee in a dispute between strangers; a referee whose neutrality went so far that he pursued argument and counter-argument without the slightest desire to become involved himself. Afterwards, when he walked through the lobby, turned into the corridor leading to the lounge and approached the steps to the Marconi Veranda, he was still engaged in a vain attempt to stand up for himself.

Millar began by explaining the theoretical motifs and long-term research interests that had guided him in the present work. After a few sentences he got up and started walking back and forth, his arms folded in front of his chest. He wore dark blue trousers and a short-sleeved white shirt with epaulettes, which had clearly been left in a suitcase for a long time. Although his hair was still damp, it looked oddly dull, and there wasn't a sign of its usual reddish gleam. The manner in which he put his case was like a resolute admiral addressing his men. As he set one well-formed sentence against another in his sonorous voice, he radiated the certainty of someone who knew his own world perfectly and didn't doubt for a moment that he was in precisely the right place in that world – a world in which – as in an officer's mess, there were immutable rules like, for example, the rule that one had to appear on time for breakfast. Perlmann had never been to the Rockefeller University at which Millar worked, but somehow it struck him as quite natural that people who went in and out of it were people like Brian Millar. He looked across to Giorgio Silvestri, who, rocking back and forth on his chair, had almost lost his balance a moment ago and had only managed to keep himself from falling by supporting himself on the window behind him. He would have liked to exchange a glance and a smile with Silvestri, but feared that would betray too much of his desire for complicity against Millar.

Millar sat down and sought Perlmann's eye. But Adrian von Levetzov had been preparing to spring for a long time, and immediately began to speak. Had he not curried favor with Millar, fifteen years his junior, by giving him an apologetic smile – Perlmann would have admired him. His questions and objections all hit home, and Perlmann wished that they had occurred to him, too. But it wasn't the case. *To think of these things you have to be right inside – as I am no longer inside.* He felt a twinge of envy like the ones he had felt often before, as an ambitious student, when someone else was faster at formulating ideas that he should have been capable of producing himself; and for a moment he was annoyed by his former violence towards himself. But then something strange happened: all of a sudden he experienced these sensations as no longer belonging to him, to his present; they were only reminiscences, obsolete emotional reflexes from a time when academic work had not yet become alien to him. He was puzzled to feel the extent to which he had survived himself, and for a while, as silence fell around him, it felt like a great liberation. But then the voices of the others reached him again, and he was horrified to realize how far from them that inner development had taken him, and how menacing it was, particularly in this room, which he had feared since his arrival.

Before Perlmann was able to say something, Achim Ruge intervened in the debate. The contrast with von Levetzov's exaggeratedly obliging manner could not have been greater. As a critic, there was something surly and blustering about him, and if he accompanied a reservation with his gurgling laugh it sounded almost scornful. He treated Millar, his contemporary, like everyone else, not without respect, but entirely without subservience, and nothing intimidated him. When Millar said rather sharply, in response to one of his objections, 'Frankly, Achim, I just don't see that,' Ruge shot back with a grin, 'Yes, I know,' for which he was rewarded with laughter, which Millar endured with a sour smile that was supposed to look sporting.

But it was peculiar, Perlmann thought: coming from Ruge, there was nothing wounding about it at all. One simply couldn't take umbrage at the style of the man with the bald head and the terrible Swabian accent, because through all his bluster his benevolence was discernible; there was a sense that his aggressiveness lacked the faintest trace of spite. Now that his loud nose-blowing had been evaded, and he would no longer have to imagine him sitting opposite him on the other side of the wall, Perlmann could accept this Achim Ruge. And, in fact, it was absurd to assume that his respectability and rectitude made him dangerous.

Laura Sand had put down her pen and was about to say something. But when she saw that everyone's eyes were on Perlmann, she leaned back and reached for a cigarette. Perlmann looked across at Silvestri, but instead of finding support there, his gaze bounced off the tense expectation that lay in the darkly glittering eyes. There was no getting away now. The time had come.

What issued from his mouth were unobjectionable sentences, and their dragging tempo barely differed from the natural expression of reflectiveness. But in Perlmann's head they thundered like hollow, meaningless sequences of sounds that came from somewhere or other and trickled through him like something alien, not unlike the quiet vibrations you feel on a train journey. That perception threatened to silence him before each next syllable, so that he constantly had to give himself a jolt to reach the next sentence – to produce the required minimum of sentences, so to speak. And then, all of a sudden, the internal pressure grew too great, and a quiet explosion followed, giving him a gambler's courage.

'Your critique of my work is the most enlightening, the most insightful thing that I have read in a very long time,' he heard himself saying. 'I find your objections completely convincing, and think they refute the whole of my proposal.' He lapsed into laughter shaped by a feverish feeling of vertigo. 'It's a fabulous experience, being freed from a wrong idea. I can't thank you enough for that! And I actually think your criticism is much more penetrating than you assume.'

And now, suddenly in full command of his powers, he conjured one argument after another from his hat, tearing into everything his name stood for, not resting before every last idea that he had ever come up with was finally swept away. He spoke from a sense of ludic inspiration whose bitterness he alone could taste, and accompanied each rhetorical lunge with a motion of his arm which, like the arc of a sower of seeds, had something at once dismissive and generous about it.

Millar was disconcerted, and the others also looked as if they had stepped through a door and fallen unexpectedly into a void. The first to regain his composure was von Levetzov.

'Remarkable,' he said, and it was apparent that his usual inner attitude towards Perlmann had suddenly ceased to seem appropriate, although he had not yet had time to construct a new one. 'But don't you think you might perhaps be going a little too far?'

And then he began to pick up the pieces and cobble them back together until a large part of Perlmann's previous position was once more intact. Evelyn helped with this, and all at once Ruge's chief concern seemed to be to convict Perlmann of reaching over-hasty conclusions. Everyone seemed relieved that a familiar kind of discussion was gradually resuming. Only every now and again did Perlmann feel a furtive glance upon him.

Millar had shaken off his torpor, and was talking about Perlmann almost as if he were absent. He had no evidence, but Perlmann could have sworn that Millar thought of his earlier remarks as revealing particularly foolhardy sarcasm, and felt he was being teased. Nothing could have been further from the truth. And yet: it would be hard to stop hatred arising between them on the basis of this misunderstanding.

Back in his room, Perlmann felt empty and drained, like an actor after a performance. Would they see it as a mere mood, or had he already turned himself irrevocably into an outsider with his orgy of self-criticism? Then there was the business of his supposed topic, and it wouldn't be long until they discovered that he had switched rooms. What sort of an image would that create in their heads? Perlmann slipped into half-sleep, in which he heard someone knocking at the door, quietly at first, then louder and louder, until it was a hammering that seemed to come from a thousand fists. He pressed himself against the door, barricaded himself in with the wardrobe, and now he could hear the wood splintering under axe-blows. Millar's teeth were first to appear – big, white teeth bursting with health – then the whole Millar in an admiral's uniform, behind him Ruge's giant head, from which his chuckles spilled as though from a doll, and from the darkness of the corridor came Evelyn Mistral's voice, distorted into shrill, vulgar laughter.

Perlmann gave a start, and on his way to the bathroom he put the chain on the door, ashamed of his action. Later he stood by the open window, two steps behind the balustrade, and gazed out into the pouring rain. Without the southern light, the bay looked like an abandoned stage after a performance, or like a fairground in the early morning, when the lights are turned off – so sobering and shabby that one felt cheated and hungover. All of a sudden, on the public part of the beach, one could see above all the rubbish and the dirt, empty bottles and plastic bags, and now it was also striking that the blue changing rooms urgently needed a lick of paint.

He picked up Leskov's paper. He had only retained a few of the words he had copied out, and it was a while before he found his way back into the flow of his thoughts. In his next step Leskov now wanted to show that this kind of articulated self-image, on which our memory is based, can only come about through linguistic contouring, through the telling of stories. This announcement was followed immediately by a paragraph that gave Perlmann the feeling that he didn't speak a word of Russian, so opaque was it even after the second and third reading. He tried to leave the whole passage alone and go on after it. But that didn't work. The paragraph appeared to contain an argument that was the key to everything else, and if one hadn't understood it, that which followed seemed unfounded, almost random. What he really wanted to do was hurl the paper into the corner. But then he resigned himself to being once more nothing but a schoolboy where this piece of writing was concerned, and not a reader with a command of Russian, and he began to dissect the individual sentences as if in a Latin class.

Slowly, half-sentence by half-sentence, the text yielded up its meaning. But at the crux of the argument there was a block of four sentences which remained impenetrable in the face of all his analytical effort and patience. What almost drove Perlmann to despair was the fact that it wasn't as if the words weren't in his dictionary. That was true of two of the words, but they were adjectives that struck him as negligible. All the other unfamiliar words were in the dictionary, but still he couldn't wrestle any meaning from those sentences, let alone anything like a coherent argument. In the face of all experience, however, Perlmann acted as if it could be forced, he walked up and down and repeatedly murmured the four sentences, which he by now knew off by heart, out loud, imploring and gesticulating so that he might have been mistaken for a madman. He only paused when there was a knock at the door.

He quickly stuffed Leskov's paper and the dictionary in the desk drawer, before opening the door, which clattered as it caught in the chain.

'Oh, I'm disturbing you,' said Evelyn Mistral when she saw his face in the chink.

'No, no, wait,' Perlmann said quickly and closed the door to get rid of the chain.

She had learned of his new room number from Signora Morelli after ringing and knocking in vain. Now, with her hands in the pockets of her rust-red jeans, she let her eye wander around the whole of the room and then pounced on the wing chair, into which she proceeded to slump.

The bed was the reason for the change, Perlmann said. He had the usual problem with his back.

'And you like to be on your own,' she said with a quiet twitch at the corners of her mouth, and sank cross-legged slightly deeper into the chair.

Perlmann didn't know whether he was startled by her accuracy or delighted.

'You know,' she said, after asking him for a cigarette, which she then just puffed on, 'I have an eye for these things. My father spent his whole life suffering from claustrophobia, which he kept strictly secret. In the cinema, for example, he always sat on the end seat of an empty row, even if he had to keep standing up to let people past, and he often disappeared through the emergency exit when the cinema got too full. If people were jostling each other on the pavement, he was quite capable of walking out into the traffic. And, of course, he avoided elevators like the plague; he only made an exception for those old ones where you can look through the glass doors and the elevator shaft into the stair-well. The worst thing was that when he was operating he always had the other doctors and nurses around him. On more than one occasion he came close to giving up. But I only understood the full extent of his problem when I found him one night in our huge kitchen, sitting like a pile of misery over a glass of brandy, which he never normally drank. A very good friend, perhaps his best friend, whom he spoke to on the phone at least once a week and who was a great support to him when my mother fell seriously ill, had announced that he was moving from Seville to Salamanca, where our house was. "I felt as if I was petrified," my father said. "I felt as if I was suffocating. I hope José Antonio didn't notice." And then, this a man who wasn't used to alcohol, and who, coming from Valladolid, spoke the most pin-sharp Spanish that you can imagine, started talking in a clumsy, blurred pronunciation, about how we had to move away, possibly to the Far East, to Barcelona, perhaps, or Zaragoza; he didn't even need a job as a surgeon. "You see, otherwise I'm going to lose José Antonio," he said with tears in his eyes. At the same time, he was a very affectionate father. I've never understood how that worked. But since then I've been able to recognize people who need a lot of empty space around them very quickly, and I'm seldom mistaken. Of course, I don't mean you suffer from claustrophobia,' she concluded with a smile.

He could tell her. He could spill all his desperation straight from his soul into her – as if they were sitting together in the big kitchen. Perlmann lit a cigarette and walked to the window for a moment to collect his words.

'But I came about something quite different,' she said, when he turned towards her to speak. 'First of all I wanted to say how impressed I was by the inner freedom with which you talked about your work this morning. I didn't, as you will have noticed afterwards, have the impression that Brian really refuted everything you had to say. But the peace, the delight, in fact, with which you summed up the possibility of general error! How do you do that?'

'Perhaps it's a matter of age,' Perlmann said with a lump in his throat, and could have sunk into the ground over the stupidity of his answer.

'Well, I don't know,' she smiled, unsure how seriously he had meant it. 'At any rate I thought it was great. And the other thing was: I'd like to talk to you about your new topic. I was really excited by what you hinted at yesterday morning, because the influence that linguistic articulation has on memory must be very closely connected with the process of linguistic refinement of the imagination which is the subject of my research. ¿Verdad?'

Perlmann apologized and went to the bathroom, where he ran warm water over his cold hands for several minutes. He had to gain time above all, and then make sure that she did most of the talking. Back in the room he suggested having a coffee at the marina. He liked the light and the smell when the sun broke through after a rain shower, as it was doing now.

She found the idea of remembered scenes into which, even if it wasn't done explicitly, one projected an image of oneself, illuminating, and was beginning to consider how this might relate to scenes from dreams and fantasies. Sometimes she leaned back, arms folded over her head, her eyes gazing through half-closed lids at the sea, and thought out loud about examples. She was so keyed up that she gave a start when the waiter appeared, and knocked a coffee cup out of his hand as her arm came down. Then, when the waiter flirted with her and forgave her everything, Perlmann heard her speaking Italian for the second time. She spoke it as effortlessly as she did Spanish, only the harsh vowels were unusual. Her mother had been Italian, she explained, and both were spoken casually at home.

'Like with Giorgio, except that it was the other way round. We often laughed, because we didn't know which we should apologize for. His suggestion is: until twenty-three minutes past two Spanish, after that Italian,' she laughed.

This interlude had not, as Perlmann had hoped, distracted her from the subject, and now she asked him whether, in the case of memory, he knew a reason why the differentiation of the introduced self-image had to occur in the medium of language. She herself had long been in search of a corresponding explanation for the case of fantasy and will. It wasn't enough for her, she said with a face on which Perlmann suddenly thought he was seeing her matte-silver glasses for the first time, that there was a clear connection between the development of the abilities in question. She wanted something that could make visible a closer, a deeper, connection, so to speak, between the phenomena. Could he help her with that?

Perlmann thought about the four recalcitrant sentences in Leskov's paper. Yes, that was an important question, he said, and turned towards the water. Countless times he had wished he could fall silent for a moment in response to such a question – let it work on him all by itself for a while, without perceiving it as a threat that left one with no other chance but to come up with an answer straight away, or to apologize for being unable to do so. Now, sitting beside this woman, whom he would almost not have dared approach until an hour before, he managed:

no, he was *obliged* to do something that seemed, seen from outside, deceptively similar to the fulfilment of his desire; her question struck him as so threatening that he not only felt a void of ignorance, but also a paralysing horror at the thought that his answer might further contribute to the tissue of lies of his false identity; so he fell silent, in the pose of the thinker. Ashamed, and yet once again with a hint of the gallows humor with which he resisted the horror, he then discovered that it had worked; as if the silence of an unanswered question were the most natural thing in the world, Evelyn Mistral herself began trying out answers to her own question.

Just as the moment approached when he himself would have to speak, von Levetzov and Millar walked past on the other side of the street. Von Levetzov waved and said something to Millar, and before they reached the corner, they both turned round. Evelyn Mistral brushed the hair from her face and smiled wryly when the two men had disappeared. Then she looked at her watch and said she had some more work to do; it was only another two-and-a-half weeks until her seminar, and until then she wanted to work on the two chapters of the book that it would be dealing with.

'Do you think it would be enough if I handed the papers in for copying the Friday before?'

Perlmann nodded.

She was bound to be terribly nervous at the seminar, she said. 'In such illustrious circles!'

Later, almost at the same time as the previous day, when Perlmann parted the glass-bead curtain and stepped into the trattoria, the rain started hammering on the glass roof. The proprietor and his family greeted him like an old friend, brought him bean soup followed by chicken, and when Sandra later set the coffee down in front of him, the proprietor came over and placed the chronicle down in front of him as if it were a ritual that had been practiced for years.

As he ate, Perlmann imagined Evelyn Mistral and Giorgio Silvestri talking, playfully switching languages and joking, and it had given him a stitch. Now he brushed that idea aside, and opened the book at the year when he had broken off his training as a pianist.

In the first days of that year Albert Camus had died in an accident. Perlmann grimly remembered the incomprehension that his own excitement had met with at home. Only years later, when he read *La Peste* all the way through for the first time, did he realize how much incomprehension there had been in his own excitement, and the extent to which the book had also been trendy.

He went on flicking through the pages. With the dropping of the first plutonium bomb in the Sahara, France had joined the nuclear powers. Leonid Brezhnev was the new Soviet president. The success of Fellini's *La dolce vita* in Cannes. Anita Ekberg in the Trevi Fountain. The Israelis abducted Eichmann. That was quite illegal, his father had said. Caryl Chessman was executed in St Quentin's, after the death sentence had been postponed eight times. The Olympic Games in Rome; but it wasn't there that Armin Hary had run the 100 meters, but some time before in Zurich.

For September, the chronicle barely mentioned anything but the Italian medals table. It was in that month that Perlmann had made his decision; on one of the last days, he couldn't remember the exact date. He saw the bare room of the Conservatoire in front of him, and that momentous moment was still very much alive, a good thirty years later, present in all its details, as if it had been stamped in his memory with very great force.

It had been early afternoon on a rainy day, with a light in which time seemed to stand still and yet had no present, or only a dead present. He had been working once again on Chopin's Polonaise in A flat major. It was one of the first piano compositions that he had discovered, and for a long time it had been his favorite piece. By then, however, it was his most hated piece, because it had a terrifying passage that he had never mastered. He had gone through it countless times, finger by finger, but it was as if for some inexplicable reason his motor memory was blocked at that point, so that the orders from the brain to the fingers were not resolute and unambiguous, but hesitant and blurred.

That afternoon, to his surprise, that passage had gone smoothly for the first time ever. He had been glad, but from experience he had also remained sceptical at first. He hurried to repeat his success, and finally to memorize the correct fingering once and for all. It was fine the second and third times, and the fourth time it almost felt like a firmly fixed routine. He had the feeling that he had finally managed it, and went down to the foyer to allow himself a cigarette.

Then, sitting back down at the grand piano, when he tried to put his new-won confidence to the test, he immediately stumbled. He tried it a few more times, but it wouldn't work at all. Then, still sitting at the keyboard, he lit another cigarette, which was completely forbidden, and smoked it calmly to the end, using the box as an ashtray. Then he carefully closed the lid and opened the window. Before he went outside, he looked at the little painting by Paul Klee, which, because it was the only painting, merely served to emphasize the bareness of the room. It was right in the player's eye-line. He would miss it.

It wasn't, Perlmann thought, as if he had simply run out of patience that time. Quite calmly, with no inner turmoil, he had walked along the corridor to Bela Szabo's room, and later up the stairs to the Director. It would also have been misleading to say, he thought, that he had given up his training because of his defeat with the A flat major Polonaise. What happened to him that afternoon was simply that a complicated internal play of forces, which had been under way for many months – determined by very different experiences that he had had of himself as a pianist, and by doubts of very different kinds – reached a standstill in his definitive and irrevocable clarity about the boundaries of his talent. If he said to himself that the decision had been made at that moment, it could only, it seemed to him, mean the arrival of that standstill, the end of his internal uncertainty. Apart from that, there had been no further supplementary internal decision that might have communicated between his inner state and the subsequent external actions.

Bela Szabo had seen his decision as a mistake, or at least as premature. In this he had shared the opinion of Perlmann's parents, who thought it was a shame, and ungrateful of him, too, simply to throw away his artistic future, in which they had invested so much. But he was completely certain and his mind would not be changed. He felt it in his hands, in his arms, and sometimes even as a certainty within his whole body: he would never be anything more than a piano teacher. He was proud of being capable of such a sober insight, and did everything he could not to turn his decision into a drama. Still, a wound had remained, which had never quite healed, and which he perceived as a source of personal insecurity.

For several years after his decision, he had not played a single note or set foot in a concert hall. It was Agnes who had persuaded him to start playing again. They bought a grand piano, and he gradually found his way back into Chopin, who had originally awoken his desire to learn the piano. But he never again attempted the Polonaise in A flat major. After Agnes's death he had avoided the piano altogether. He was afraid that the notes would break through all the dams and he would start playing sentimentally. That was something he couldn't have borne, not even when he was alone.

Perlmann gave Sandra a big tip when she brought him the cigarettes that she had bought in the Piazza Veneto. Then he went on flicking through the book. Khrushchev banging his shoe on the table at the United Nations. Perlmann greedily read the article about Khrushchev's demands and the failure of his trip. And the next two pages, entirely devoted to John F. Kennedy's election as president, he read as if they contained revelations about his own life.

When the restaurant began filling up, he barely noticed, but just changed irritably to the other side of the table, so that he had the wall in front of him. With great attention he read every single name on the list of Kennedy's cabinet, and then it continued into the next year: Gagarin in space; Cuban invasion of the Bay of Pigs; building the Berlin Wall.

Letting his life roll out again, along the history of the world: it was, Perlmann thought, like waking up. With every page the need grew to be sure of all the things that had happened throughout all the years in which he had been chiefly preoccupied with himself – trying to use work to banish his fear of failure in life. In the midst of the chatter and laughter from the other tables he felt as if he had, so to speak, been a prisoner of that effort, and as if he were only now coming back. It was like joining the real world. It could have been a liberating, cheering experience, had it not been for the hotel, less than two kilometers away, with the steps, the painted window frames and the crooked pine trees.

Perlmann looked in horror at his watch: ten past nine. He couldn't turn up to dinner as late as that. Nonetheless, he hurried to pay, and walked quickly back to the hotel, which he entered by the back door for the first time. He had just quietly closed it behind him, when Giovanni came round the corner with a big cardboard box under his arm. '*Buona sera*,' he said genially, and bowed slightly before setting off again. Today Giovanni had his face under control. There was not a hint of yesterday's grin. But Perlmann thought he sensed behind Giovanni's expression the laughter of the servant who has caught his master in some unseemly act.

Perlmann had looked forward to turning into the dimly lit corridor upstairs, and in the middle of it, under the unlit lamp, feeling around for the keyhole. So he had been unpleasantly surprised when all the lamps were lit unusually brightly. With his key in his hand, he paced back and forth, before creeping to the cupboard at the end of the corridor and fetching a ladder. With his handkerchief wrapped around his fingers, he half-unscrewed all nine bulbs so that the lighting was just as it had been before.

Tomorrow would be even more about Millar's first paper than today. Perlmann reluctantly bent down to the round table and flicked through some pages. Then he went to the bathroom and took a sleeping pill from the packet. He broke it in two and, after some hesitation, washed down the biggest part.

When he had given up the Conservatoire, emergency laws had been in place, he thought as he lay in the darkness and listened to the unabated traffic. He had watched the demonstrations from the other side of the street. He felt he should have crossed over. But there were all those people there, and the noisy megaphones, and the rhythmical movement of the crowd, which made one feel one was losing one's own will. And so, till now, he had never made a political commitment, even though on his internal stage he always advocated very clear and often radical positions. Not even Agnes had known that for a while he had been almost as at home in Spanish anarcho-syndicalism as a historian.

That night he woke up three times, and still he couldn't escape the leaden power of that accursed word. It was the word *masterclass*, a word that made both his parents freeze with respect as if it were the name of God. Being accepted into the masterclass run by a big name: in their eyes that was the highest attainment possible, and they had no dearer wish for their own son than such a consecration. In the dream that stayed with him even after he was awake, Perlmann didn't see his parents, and he didn't hear them utter the word either. It was more as if his parents were there, and the word as well, and the word was carved into their devout silence in huge letters of trepidation.

Only when he had spent several minutes under the shower did he feel the scorn that was finally able to break the power of the word.

7

The awkward question that Perlmann posed in the seminar when he could no longer withstand Millar's challenging looks was so hair-raisingly naive that Ruge, von Levetzov and Evelyn Mistral all turned their heads towards him with a jerk. Millar blinked like someone who thinks he has misheard, and tried to gain some time by writing the question down with slow, painterly movements. Then – as if looking through a long contract a final time before signing – he stared for ages at what he had written, before turning to Perlmann. It was the first time that Perlmann had seen Millar looking uncertain – not uncertain about his subject, but in his attitude towards a question which, first of all, came from a man like Perlmann, but which on the other seemed to be of almost idiotic simplicity. He opted for an emphatically modest, emphatically thoughtful tone, and explained once again to Perlmann what must have been clear to anyone who had read his paper attentively. He was visibly uneasy as he did so. He basically couldn't believe that Perlmann had really asked that question, and he was afraid of insulting him by taking the question literally. Twice he seemed to have finished. He looked quizzically at Perlmann, and when Perlmann nodded stiffly and said simply, 'Thank you', Millar added something to his explanation.

The pill, Perlmann thought, *I should just have taken the smaller bit.* He rested his head on his hand so that he could rub his temples without anyone noticing. Perhaps that would help against the thumping heaviness that lay over his eyes like a ring of steel. When he took his hand away, he caught the eye of Evelyn Mistral, who was fighting against

Millar's sceptical face with sentences that were growing faster and faster. He nodded, without knowing what they were talking about. When Millar noticed this agreement, he looked like someone who is now utterly confused. Plainly, Evelyn Mistral's train of thought had nothing to do with the interpretation that he had composed for Perlmann's puzzlingly naive question.

Perlmann poured himself a cup of coffee, and when he reached into his jacket pocket for the matches, he felt the packet of headache pills. Keeping his hand in his pocket, he pressed out two tablets, brought them inconspicuously to his mouth and swallowed them. As if his head had been cleared merely by the act of swallowing, he concentrated on the formulae in Millar's paper. With a jolt that he was able to cushion somewhat at the last moment, he sat bolt upright: a bracket was missing from one of the formulae. Struggling to control his excitement, he topped up his coffee. *Don't make a mistake now.* Methodically, and with painful concentration, he looked through the whole formal part. He could barely believe his eyes: just before the end a quantifier was missing, which not only made the deduction wrong, but actually made the formula nonsensical. His headache had fled, and it was as if his impatient alertness were forcing its way out from within himself and straight onto the paper. He was absolutely sure of his case. Now everything hung on the presentation. With a furtive slowness that he enjoyed more than anything in ages, he lit a cigarette, pushed his chair back and sat down with the paper in his other hand, his legs crossed as if sitting at a pavement café. He saw Millar sitting in the front row of the lecture hall on that earlier occasion, Sheila beside him in her short skirt.

'I see,' Laura Sand said, and leaned back. Millar took off his glasses and rubbed his eyes. It was the first time Perlmann had seen his face without glasses. It was a surprisingly vulnerable face with eyes that had a boyish, almost childlike expression, and for that brief moment, before Millar put his glasses back on, Perlmann wanted to have nothing more to do with his planned attack, but the flash of Millar's glasses had closed once more over his face, which had looked so defenseless a moment before, and Perlmann seized his moment.

'Tell me, Brian,' he began with deceptive mildness, 'isn't there a bracket missing from the fourth formula? Right at the beginning, I mean. Otherwise the domain of quantification is too small.'

Millar darted him a quick glance, pressed his glasses firmly on to his nose and frowned as he flicked through the pages.

'Jenny, Jenny, baby,' he muttered with ostentatious irritation, 'why always the formulae? She's the best secretary in the world,' he added, glancing round at everyone, 'but she has a block with formulae. Many thanks, Phil.'

Perlmann waited for him to make a note. 'One other small thing,' he said in a thick voice. 'As it stands, formula ten makes no sense. The deduction isn't right either.'

His whole chest becoming a soundbox for his heartbeat was something he had never experienced before. Perlmann gripped his knee, tensed his arms and braced himself against the power of his roaring pulse. Millar's brief, slightly flickering glance was unmistakeable: this was too much, particularly when it came from someone capable of asking such a simple question.

'Quite frankly, Phil,' he began imperiously, 'I can't see anything there that isn't completely in order.'

'I can,' said Ruge. He scribbled something on the paper and grinned at Millar. 'There's a quantifier missing in the middle.'

Now von Levetzov too picked up his pen. His face twitched with a mixture of delight and malice. Millar ran his biro along the line and faltered.

'Hang on . . . oh yes, OK, there it is,' he murmured. He added the sign and made another note on his piece of paper. 'Jenny, baby, we're going to have to have a serious talk,' he said as he wrote, and then looked at Perlmann. 'Of course, I'd have spotted it in the galleys. But still, thanks.'

His polite smile was like a contrasting background designed to make his humorless, unforgiving face stand out. *It wasn't Jenny. It wasn't a typo.*

Afterwards, on their way through the drawing room, Millar pushed his way next to Perlmann.

'That question of yours,' he said, 'I have the feeling there was something I didn't understand. Perhaps we should sit down together.'

'Absolutely,' Perlmann replied, and afterwards he had the strange feeling of having said it in a gruff way that was alien to him – almost as if he were Millar.

Was he happy with the new room? Signora Morelli asked him as she handed him the key and the first post from Frau Hartwig.

'Yes, very much so,' he replied. He wished her question had sounded less businesslike; he would have liked his sense of complicity with her, which he had felt the previous day, to have lasted a little longer.

In his post there were two lecture invitations and a request for a reference from a student. Perlmann saw the student in front of him, sitting on the edge of his chair with his hands between his knees, looking at him through his thick glasses. The university courtyard was filled with the sluggish, hot silence of an early August afternoon. For more than two hours he had talked through his unsuccessful homework with him. The boy had filled half an exercise book with jagged, frantic handwriting. Then, in the doorway, after stammering an effusive goodbye, he had suddenly bent double, and it had taken Perlmann a moment to work out that this was a deep bow, a minion from another century taking his leave. Leaning against the closed door he had stood there for a long time and considered his office, which he had now been using for seven years: the beautiful desk, the elegant chair behind it, the lamps, the seating area. All of it far too expensive, he had thought, feeling like an interloper in the office of someone who actually did something.

He rang Frau Hartwig and dictated the reference to her, recommending the student for a grant. When she read the text back to him, he was startled by all his unfounded praise. He didn't dare take it back, and moved on to the letters declining to give the lectures. Yes, he said finally, there was a hint of summer left in the air.

'You can be glad that you're down there,' said Frau Hartwig. 'The first autumn storms have started up here. Some people can't suppress their envious remarks. You can imagine which.'

As soon as he had replaced the receiver, Perlmann sat down in the red armchair and picked up Leskov's paper. But he soon lowered it again. *You are going to write something for Italy, aren't you?* Frau Hartwig had said at the end of July. Perlmann had only nodded and continued with his business at the shelf. She had, incidentally, postponed her holiday, she explained a few days later. To just before Christmas. After that he had only gone to the office when she wasn't there, and left her instructions on tape. In late September she had hesitantly asked if she could take two weeks' holiday, or whether he needed her. 'Just go,' he had replied, and by way of disguise he had turned the relief in his voice into enthusiasm for the island of Elba, with which he associated nothing at all apart from Napoleon.

Now there were several pages in Leskov's paper in which he engaged with the objection that we remember many episodes that we never put in story form. How then could he claim that language played such a key role in the episodic memory?

Leskov's reply was expressed in eccentric terms, Perlmann thought, but basically the elements of his train of thought were familiar to him, and suddenly the translation started going faster than ever. When he grasped a sentence literally at first glance, he felt as if he had at that moment forgotten it was a Russian sentence – it had yielded its meaning to him with so little resistance. With breathless delight he went on reading. The truth of Leskov's thesis was irrelevant; the main thing was comprehension. In fact, he noticed, many of the words he had copied out were now in his head. His confidence was growing from one paragraph to the next, and now all of a sudden he also had an incredibly lucky hand when it came to opening the right pages in the dictionary. It bordered on clairvoyance. When he finally had to turn on the light, he was already on page 20.

He could get cigarettes from the place Sandra had bought them from yesterday. *Sandra. The promised stamps from Germany.* He got Frau Hartwig's envelope out of the waste-paper basket and tore the stamps from it. Then he left the hotel by the rear entrance and set off towards the trattoria.

He was late today, the proprietress joked as she brought him the chronicle. He would have to choose something from the menu. Perlmann opened the book at the year when his father hadn't awoken from his lunchtime nap. The Decca record company had, after listening to demo tapes, reached the view that The Beatles had no future, and turned down the opportunity to produce them. Antonio Segni became Italian president. It was a name that meant nothing to Perlmann, and he read the biographical outline to the smallest detail. Adolf Eichmann was hanged.

His father had lived to hear that. After the report he had turned off the radio in silence, his mother had told him. 'He wasn't a sympathizer, you know that,' she had added. 'It's just that he feels somehow under attack when these things are talked about.' By the graveside she had surprised Perlmann: she, who otherwise wept easily, didn't shed a single tear.

She had surprised him for a second time the following autumn, this time with her interest in the Cuban crisis, of which he would not have thought her capable. She had, he had felt all winter, seemed better than ever. And then, sometime in the spring, her startlingly rapid decline began. Her world shrank to magazine articles about kitschy German musicals, Kennedy in Berlin interested her not at all, and when he dragged her to see *Irma la Douce*, she babbled something about pornography on the way home. When he told her about the death of Édith Piaf, she no longer knew who that was, although she had secretly listened to her chansons for years when his father was sitting in the pub with the other post-office workers. She was unaware of the shooting in Dallas. By day she slept with her mouth open, and from ten o'clock she terrorized the night nurse.

When Perlmann arrived at the hospital on the first day of the New Year someone else was already lying in her bed. No, he didn't want to see her again, he had explained to the nurse, who was alarmed by the edge in his voice. And there had been another faux pas. The graveside ceremony wasn't quite finished when he lit a cigarette in front of everyone. Why had he not managed to turn that precious moment of liberation into a permanent distinction from all the others, a calm lack of subservience, a fearlessness that needed no dramatic gestures? He laughed to himself and at the same time bit his lips when he thought about how he had simply left the relatives standing outside the pub. To the baffled question of why he hadn't stayed at the wake, when he was, after all, paying for it, he had said: 'Chiefly because the word disgusts me.' Then he had disappeared around the corner.

The food over at the hotel probably wasn't as good as its reputation, the proprietor grinned as he walked over to Perlmann's table during a break. Perlmann looked at his watch. Ten past eight. Still enough time. No, it was fine, he said, snapped the chronicle shut and picked up his briefcase. The stamps nearly fell into what was left of his tomato sauce. They were for Sandra, he said, holding them out to the proprietor. No, no, he said, Perlmann must bring them to Sandra in person, or she would be disappointed. And then he led him up the stairs to Sandra's room, which, like the whole apartment, was cramped and full of junk.

Sandra's joy over the stamps was subdued by her difficulties with English. She was in every other respect such a clever child, her mother sobbed, but she just couldn't get to grips with this funny spelling that had so little to do with the pronunciation. And they, her parents, couldn't help. Could he stay for a moment and explain one or the other to her? Otherwise her test on Monday threatened to be a disaster. He just had to look at the last exercise in the book. There was more red ink than blue.

Perlmann stayed till eleven. Sitting on an uncomfortable stool, he went through the two last exercises with Sandra and then explained some grammar to her as well. Often she was close to tears, but in the end she smiled bravely, and he stroked her hair.

Then the proprietor brought him almond tart and a grappa. Time didn't matter any more anyway, and Perlmann read through the year he had begun in the chronicle. The incident in the Gulf of Tonkin. Right, that was the start of the Vietnam War. Khrushchev's fall from power. The death of Palmiro Togliatti, the Communist. Perlmann knew him, but he hadn't known that he had only reluctantly condemned the crimes of Stalin. And last of all Sartre, who had refused the Nobel Prize.

What exactly had been his explanation? The text in the chronicle was confused, and made Sartre sound like a scatterbrain. Perlmann tried out various explanations as he walked across the deserted Piazza Veneto and along the promenade to the hotel.

Giovanni, who had been sitting watching television in the side-room, handed him a paper by Achim Ruge, almost a hundred pages thick, the text for Monday. The others had asked after him several times in the course of the evening, he said. 'Because you weren't at dinner yesterday, either,' he added. Perlmann's hand gripped the paper so convulsively that the top page was pulled out of its staple. Again he wanted to slap the pomaded head with the ridiculous sideburns. He turned away in silence and stepped into the open elevator.

In the corridor, all the bulbs were burning in the lamps. For a moment he was tempted to go and get the ladder, but then he walked into his room and sank on to the bed in the dark. After a while his head was filled again with the images of the new patient in his mother's bed, the startled nurse, the coffin being lowered into the grave.

He went into the bathroom and swallowed the small bit of pill from yesterday. Édith Piaf's real name had been Édith Giovanna Gassion, he thought before drifting into sleep. The individual snowflakes had melted on his mother's coffin. He had found that distasteful. Perhaps the unseemly cigarette had had something to do with it as well.

8

Perlmann slept until late into the morning and then ordered a big breakfast. Over the first cup of coffee he was drawn back into the pull of
translation, and now he found himself captivated not only by the experience of his faster comprehension, but by the ideas he was coming
across in the text.

Leskov now attacked the idea that the narration of remembered scenes
was a simple description of images arising, a linguistic inventory of fixed
material that dictated the logic of narration through its unambiguously
determined contours. That was neither the case with regard to the objective fixed points of a scene nor in the facets of the self-image read into
it. The narration of one's own past was always a fresh undertaking in
which other forces were at work than the intention to call up recorded
material in a detailed manner. There was above all the need to make a
meaningful whole out of the remembered scene and one's own presence within it, and accordingly a lack of meaning was interpreted as an
imperfection of memory.

Perlmann faltered. What was the significance in this instance of *smysl*:
sense? He would have liked to read the answer in an abstract form. But
first there came several pages of examples, and the text became accordingly difficult, because Leskov's descriptions were atmospherically precise,
witty, and every now and again there was a sentence which, Perlmann
assumed, had a poetic brilliance. He would have liked to know whether
a Russian would have seen this as a break with the concise, laconic style
that prevailed elsewhere in the text, or whether a native Russian would
still perceive a unified stylistic form. At any rate, translating became a

strain again at this point; he had to consult his grammar several times, and the limitations of the dictionary were infuriating. He irritably sent the chambermaid away again.

Dusk was already falling over the bay, giving the sea a metallic sheen, when Perlmann finally reached the conclusion drawn from the examples. The strongest power in narrative memory, Leskov wrote, was the desire to understand one's past self through its actions. From this desire one composed past scenes in such a way that one's own actions, and also one's sensations, appeared accessible and reasonable. That didn't mean measuring them against an abstract catalogue of reasonable characteristics. It simply meant this: the narrated past must be comprehensible from the point of view of the present narrator. The narrator would not rest before he could recognize himself in his past self. And that referred not only to questions of intelligence and the purposefulness of his previous action, but above all to its moral aspects. Narrative memory was always also a justification, a piece of inventive apologia.

It was just before half-past seven when Perlmann stopped, exhausted, halfway down page 43. Two dozen pages of the vocabulary notebook were full, and on the right, next to the line that ran down the middle of the page, there were many gaps. Another twenty-five pages. If he got up very early tomorrow he would be able to finish it. And now he wanted to know: that business about the inventive elements in memory was all well and good, but where, in Leskov's essay, was the experienced, sensory content of memory? The last time he saw him, his father had, as always, been wearing his wool felt jacket, and the fact that the color of the wool had alternated between dark olive green and light charcoal, depending on the light, was really not something that he had invented; it bothered him now, in memory, exactly as it had at the time. Or the loud thump with which the frozen lumps of earth had fallen on his mother's coffin: what did Leskov make of that? *Sensory content?* He wrote in the margin.

Before he went to dinner, he flicked absently through Ruge's paper. *If I start on it on Monday, I'll still have fifteen days for my own contribution.* It was only when he reached the stairs that he realized the idea didn't throw him into a panic. He paused. It was as if the thought had occurred in the mind of someone else, someone completely uninvolved, and the weird idea crept over him that he was splitting away from himself.

'I knocked on your door several times yesterday and today, Phil. I wanted to talk about the baffling question you asked me at the session,' Millar said across the length of the table when the waiter had brought the soup. 'And then, when you weren't at dinner, I started to get worried. We all did, by the way.'

Perlmann felt that his fear of Millar was suddenly turning into black humor, accompanied by a pleasing sense of dizziness like the one he always felt when he had his first cigarette of the morning.

'I'm fine,' he said. *Deadpan* was how he would have described his face at that moment.

'I know that now,' said Millar, and lowered his head. 'Evelyn's just told me about the business with the new room.'

Perlmann looked into the sea-green of her eyes. She had her face under control, but her eyes contained a certain roguish laughter that seemed to have its origins right in the dark yellow particles of the iris.

'Yes,' he said. 'The bed. My back. Do you get that, too?'

'No,' replied Millar, 'I don't. Not at all.'

'He just couldn't stand being between us, Brian,' Ruge grinned.

Millar picked up his tone. 'And we're such nice guys, Phil. But seriously: can we make an appointment for tomorrow?'

The panic mustn't show in his voice, and Perlmann ran his fingertips along his forehead, back and forth, and then again.

'I've got a lot going on tomorrow,' he said, and was pleased when he noticed that the quiver in his voice had remained a mere idea. 'I'll let you know some time next week.'

'OK,' Millar drawled, and Perlmann was sure that his drawl expressed a hint of suspicion. Or at least the drawl contained the message that suspicion would be inevitable if the matter were to be postponed again.

Perlmann lifted his plate and tried to get the last bit of soup into his spoon. With this kind of spoon that was something of a feat, and so it was that he didn't notice Carlo Angelini until Silvestri got up to hug him. Angelini darted Perlmann an apologetic grin and walked around the table to greet the ladies first. Finally, he fetched a chair from the next table and sat down beside Perlmann. Unfortunately, he would have to leave again tomorrow morning, he said, but he wanted at least to look in this evening. How was it going?

'*Benissimo*,' said Evelyn Mistral, when Perlmann hesitated. Everything was perfect, Millar agreed, and before von Levetzov could speak, he thanked Angelini on behalf of the group.

Angelini listened to the explanation of how the work had been organized, and then asked about the subjects under discussion.

'I know more or less what you're working on,' he said to Perlmann, who no longer had the faintest idea what he had told him back in Lugano. And then, with a smile that alternated between pride and irony, Angelini announced that the mayor of Santa Margherita was going to hold a reception for them all.

From the corners of his eyes, Perlmann saw Laura Sand pretending to blow her nose to keep from exploding with laughter. Only a small party, Angelini said, and the high point would be the appointment of Perlmann, as leader of the project, as an honorary citizen of the town.

'With a certificate and a medal,' he grinned. 'It will begin on the Monday of the final week, so three weeks the day after tomorrow,' he said after glancing at his pocket diary. 'At eleven o'clock in the morning. Of course, I will be there as well.'

If Silvestri gives a presentation in the fourth week, I will gain a day because of the reception.

'Then you just give your paper on Monday afternoon,' von Levetzov said to Perlmann.

'And, of course, we expect something very special from a newly fledged freeman of the town,' Ruge chuckled.

Angelini invited everyone for a drink in the drawing room. It was puzzling what connected Angelini and Silvestri, Perlmann thought as he walked behind the two of them, and saw them joking like very good friends. Angelini, the Italian yuppie in his elegant suit, who moved in the world of conventions like a fish in water, and Silvestri, this insubordinate, anarchically minded individualist, who happened this evening to be wearing a rumpled black shirt on top of everything. Was it something from their school days? Or because they both came from Florence?

My hatred of conventions, he thought when he heard the fragments that Angelini addressed, in turn, to his colleagues. That hatred had been in Perlmann long before he met Agnes. But it was only because the feeling had found an echo in her that he had become fully aware of it. What Agnes had been most unable to bear was people who not only thought and acted conventionally but felt conventionally as well. People who felt what they thought they ought to feel. Her attempts to capture the subject in photographs were a failure. He heard her dark, sonorous voice, which could sound so brave before sometimes collapsing into the deepest melancholy: *At best you can show what people feel, and not that it would be more authentic to feel differently now. There are no pictures for that.* The hatred of conventional feeling had been a strong bond between them. But it had often alienated her from people they liked. It had, against her will, made her shy of people.

'This might be the moment to play something for us,' von Levetzov said to Millar, pointing to the grand piano with a smile full of flattering respect. *He's treating him like his brilliant star pupil, who has outgrown him through his diverse and towering talents. And he didn't need that. Not him.*

'Oh, yes, that would be super!' exclaimed Evelyn Mistral.

Perlmann was irritated by her girlish enthusiasm and the teenage vocabulary that he had liked so much on her arrival, because it matched the red elephant on her suitcase. In defiance of all reason, he was furious about her enthusiasm, and internally reproached her for it – as if she were obliged to know what a nightmare Millar was gradually becoming to him, and as if she owed him making these sensations her own.

'If you insist,' Millar smiled, and heaved himself out of the deep armchair. On springy steps he walked across to the grand piano, unbuttoned his blazer and straightened the piano stool. He was making, Perlmann thought, the face of someone trying not to look vain, even though he knew that all eyes were upon him.

The movements of his hands were economical, energetic in the powerful chords, but without any effusive artistic gestures, he never lifted his hands more than a few centimeters above the keys. Reluctantly, Perlmann was forced to admit that he liked that. He himself had tried to play that way.

And yet he found Millar's hands repellent. They were, he realized for the first time, hairy all the way down to the joints of his fingers. The thick hair on his arms continued into his hands like fur.

He compared the playing hands with the hands of the four other men. The only disturbing thing about Silvestri's slender, white hands was the yellowish shimmer on the right index and middle fingers. Angelini was holding a cigarette, and one couldn't have seen the nicotine on his tanned fingers in any case. Von Levetzov's hands were folded on his knee, manicured, smooth hands with the first liver spots, on the little finger of his left hand a signet ring with his artistically intertwined initials. Achim Ruge's hands lay on the wide arms of the chair, heavy hands that looked more like those of a manual labourer or a peasant than an academic. Perlmann liked them, just as he had found it easy to like Ruge since changing rooms.

The face that Millar made when playing matched the sober, matter-of-fact movements of his hands. It was an attentive, concentrated face that seemed to show a certain emotion, even though Millar had not made the slightest attempt to comment upon the music or his feelings through facial expressions. *I like that, too, in fact. Why can't I simply take this man Brian Millar as he is? Why do I constantly have to chafe at him?*

Millar was playing Bach. It must have been one of the English Suites, Perlmann thought, but he couldn't have said which one. It was a while before he could identify his strange sensation: it was the absence of any surprise that what Millar was playing was Bach. Fine, the music coming from his room had been Bach as well. But that wasn't it, he thought. He had the impression that it couldn't have been anything but Bach; that where Millar was concerned it could only have been Bach. He thought he knew that if he had been asked before what Millar would play, he would have named Bach without hesitation. Bach and perhaps classical jazz, those were the sounds that suited his incredibly blue eyes in his clear, alert face, and his well-articulated, clear way of thinking, talking and writing.

He played brilliantly, or rather, Perlmann thought after a while, he played *competently*, even if that was an unusual word in this context. Perlmann was immediately prepared to concede that he would have expected nothing less from Millar. But it was more to do with Millar's playing. He noticed it only reluctantly, but Millar played his Bach in a quite particular style; a style, besides, that he had never before encountered in such an extreme form. For a long time Perlmann sought words for it, and finally opted for this formula: the melody had been completely dissolved in structure. He tried to identify two features of his experience that were conjured up by Millar's playing. One perceived the way in which the sequences of notes were spread out over time. The notes, even though they had faded away in the usual sense, in another sense remained where they were, and subsequent notes were added as part of a structure, and thus, from one bar to the next, a kind of architecture came into being, one that was experienced as simultaneity. The leading notes currently sounding were, Perlmann thought, like the moving tip of a piece of chalk writing, the traces of whose past movements were seen as a whole on the board. *But isn't that always the case with melody? Isn't that actually the essence of musical form? How come it sounds like something new and specific in his playing, something special? How does he do that?*

The other effect of Millar's playing was that one couldn't surrender to the heard melody. One couldn't allow oneself to fall into it for as much as a moment; one was kept outside as if by an invisible wall, and that made listening demanding, even though one wasn't really aware of it. Perlmann tried out a series of descriptive words: *austere, brittle, matter-of-fact, cold, intellectual, gothic.* He rejected them all. They were superficial and clichéd. One had to take into account the fact that the special quality of Millar's playing was not simply the expression of a temperament, a character, but that it represented an actual interpretation, an interpretation of Bach's music.

Perlmann hid his right hand under his left and tried to play along with Millar's right hand. As he did so he moved his feet inconspicuously. It was a long time since he had done that. Back then, as a sixth-former, he had gone to practically every concert in which a pianist was involved, and sometimes he had even hitchhiked to Lübeck and Kiel. His favorite concerts were pure piano evenings, when you could concentrate upon the pianist entirely without distraction. At the back, in the cheap seats, you could brazenly close your eyes and try to imitate the hands that were playing at the front. Most of the works that he had the opportunity to hear in this way he was already familiar with. His musical memory was – apart from Bach – excellent. It hadn't been that. *Does Millar know what that is: a frightening passage?*

By now the guests from outside, who had previously been sitting at the dinner table, had arrived in the lounge. The ochre-colored armchairs were all occupied, the door to the bar was open, and the formal clothes contributed to the impression that a little concert was taking place. Millar had now been playing for half an hour, and all of a sudden Perlmann found his Bach flat and boring. He would have loved to run to the trattoria and read in the chronicle what had been going on in the world when he had heard the grey-haired, bent-backed Clara Haskil at one of her last concerts.

Millar, who seemed baffled by the size of the audience behind his back, thanked them for their applause with an athletic bow that reminded Perlmann a little of a salute. The loudest and longest applause came from Adrian von Levetzov, who at first looked as if he was going to get up, but then, after glancing around at the others, remained sitting on the edge of his chair.

'*¡Un extra!*' cried Evelyn Mistral. 'How do you say that in English?'

'Encore,' Millar smiled, and when he saw the others nodding he sat back down at the piano. For a moment he took off his glasses and rubbed the base of his nose with his thumb and forefinger. 'What we will have now,' he then said with complacent thoughtfulness, 'is a precious little piece that hardly anyone plays. For example, it doesn't appear on a single record. It's a little *trouvaille* of my own.'

After only a few bars Perlmann felt a sense of familiarity. With increasing clarity he had the impression that he knew this piece, or rather, he had known it well a long time ago. He closed his eyes and concentrated on the past, for a long time in vain, until it was suddenly quite naturally there. *Hanna's piece, of course. It's Hanna's piece. The one we called the 'ingenuous birthday piece', one of her favorites.*

He immediately saw her before him: Johanna Liebig with the dark strand in her fine, golden hair, which framed an unusually flat face with a very straight nose and a bronzed complexion. You could call it a beautiful face, although you had to be careful not to say it to her. He had always found it a little unapproachable, and had feared the direct gaze from her hazel eyes, which she was able skilfully to deploy. That unapproachability was the reason nothing had ever happened between them. He simply hadn't dared, and suddenly he had realized that it was too late. At the time he hadn't known that there was a time for such things, and that you could miss it, and even today he didn't know whether she'd been waiting for it. Then, after a time when she kept out of his way, they became good friends. They listened to each other's playing and criticized one another, and sometimes they went to concerts together. She was more talented than him, but in her case he hadn't minded. There was no competition between them, on the contrary, he didn't mind her being superior to him, and mothering him slightly, in a mocking way. He only grew furious when she, who was able to take everything more easily, more playfully, accused him of stubbornness. That made him feel helpless, and afterwards he wouldn't say a word; something that happened later with Agnes, when she tried to rage against his ponderous and often humorless manner.

'What I like so much about it,' Hanna had said when she played him the piece for the first time, 'is its simplicity. I would almost say, its touching simplicity.' He had understood immediately, but hadn't been contented with the word. '*Simple* is too pallid,' he had said after a while. '*Ingenuous* would be better, if it didn't have that dismissive aftertaste.' Then they had talked about the word for a long time, and to a certain extent rediscovered it for themselves. By the end the aftertaste had gone, and they merely found it a beautiful word. When he glanced at the score and saw that it was number 930 in the catalogue, he had laughed.

'If you read the number the way the Americans write a date, with the month before the day, you get your birthday!' And so the name had been born: *the ingenuous birthday piece.*

'That was all Bach, of course,' von Levetzov smiled, 'but I can't put my finger on that one at the moment. I know my way around Mozart better.'

'Whereas I don't know my way around anywhere,' Ruge said with his inimitable dryness, receiving ringing laughter in which some of the other hotel guests joined in.

'It was the second and third of the English Suites,' Millar said in his explaining admiral's voice.

'English? Why English?' Laura Sand asked with the sulky, irritable expression that she always wore when she didn't understand something.

The title, Millar explained, crossing his legs, didn't come from Bach himself. There was a copy of the score by Johann Christian Bach, who worked in London, and on it was written, without any further commentary, *faites pour les Anglais.* So people became accustomed to talking about the English Suites.

While Millar was talking, and extravagantly explaining every detail of the story, Perlmann suddenly had the feeling that he had made a discovery: *The will to know something very precisely like that. That's what I've always lacked. I only want to know the outlines of things, and I like it when the lines blur a little. That's why academic research was always alien to me from the outset.*

She would like to hear the encore again, Laura Sand said. 'I like it. It's so . . . ingenuous.'

As Millar was playing, she closed her eyes. Her face was beautiful; Perlmann hadn't noticed that until now. Before, her furious expression with its mocking lips had dominated everything else. He had seen her as intelligent and interesting, as filled with a penetrating alertness, but not as beautiful. Now the long lashes and the almost straight eyebrows gave the white face, which the African sun had clearly been unable to affect, a marble calm. She looked exhausted.

Perlmann held Hanna's face next to it. He didn't know whether to be pleased or troubled that this woman had used, in English, the very word that he and Hanna had used for the piece. Did that violate his past intimacy with Hanna, as expressed in their little naming game?

When she opened her eyes for a moment, Laura Sand must have seen that he was examining her, because an instant later she popped one eye open, and that one-eyed mockery was like a protruding tongue.

The encore had been a little Prelude in G minor, number 902 in the catalogue, Millar replied when von Levetzov asked him.

As with the discovery at the previous day's session, Perlmann involuntarily sat bolt upright. His heart was beating like mad. Had he been mistaken, just because he couldn't tell Bach's pieces apart? Wasn't it the birthday piece? While Millar spoke like an expert about Bach's lesser-known piano music, Perlmann let the piece play out again within him. It was the piece, he was quite sure of it. So was the date he had in his head the wrong one? Was Hanna's birthday the second of September?

After a few quick draws on his cigarette, he remembered: once they had gone to the circus on her birthday. Hanna had been furious that the trapeze act had been performed without a net. She had closed her eyes, and trembled afterwards. A few days later the youngest of the acrobats had fallen to her death, her body lying in the sawdust below. And the circus had always come to Hamburg punctually at the start of the autumn, not at the beginning of September. *Millar is mistaken. Brian Millar, the star who knows everything, has made a mistake. And one that involves something he called a* trouvaille. But be careful – to burst out with it before he had checked it would be too risky. Thirty years had passed, and the memory could play tricks on one. Of course, it was a ridiculously insignificant mistake. It was grotesque to make anything of it. But Perlmann felt it with almost physical certainty: while he was on his hobbyhorse, having to admit this tiny mistake, this utterly inconsequential mistake, would hit Millar in the middle of his vanity, it would hit him even harder than if he had made a mistake in his academic subject. And this time there was no Jenny to blame.

Two mistakes in the formulae, and now this. And it was always Philipp Perlmann who found fault with him. Millar would be fuming, this man who was now whipping his American ankle-boots back and forth, as he explained the difference between piano and harpsichord music to Evelyn Mistral, who was listening to him with an irritatingly devoted expression. *I can't afford to make a mistake. I must call Hanna. Tonight.*

Luckily, the guests from outside – some of them slightly drunk – were so noisy that the group soon dispersed. Angelini, who wanted to go into town with Silvestri, said goodbye. He had been delighted to meet everyone. Had nothing changed about Leskov's refusal? Shame. And that Perlmann's session was going to take place on the Monday of the reception – that was still the case? He absolutely wanted to be there.

'Will you tell me if the date changes?'

Perlmann nodded mutely.

'*Prometti?*'

Again Perlmann nodded.

Angelini put an arm around Silvestri's shoulder. 'He will be the last to give a paper. Don't you think he's too modest?'

Perlmann didn't wait for Silvestri's reaction.

Back in his room, he didn't even take the time to remove his jacket, but sat down on the bed straight away and looked up the international enquiries number. When he had lost touch with Hanna, she had been unmarried, and later someone had told him she was now a piano teacher in Hamburg. There were two Johanna Liebigs in Hamburg. Italian enquiries had no information about professions, so he asked for both numbers. As excited as he might have been before a first date, he lit a cigarette.

The first Johanna Liebig was an old woman who was outraged that someone should disturb her so late at night. Perlmann stammered an apology and put the phone down, disappointed, but secretly pleased about the little delay. The second number rang for a very long time. Then Hanna answered. He recognized her voice straight away.

'Philipp!' she said, much more quickly than he expected. 'Philipp Perlmann! My God, how long is it since we heard from one another! Where on earth are you?'

'Listen,' he said, 'I'm sure you remember the little Bach Prelude, the one that people don't know, and that you played so often. You know, *the ingenuous birthday piece.*'

'Yes, of course. What about it?'

'Could you quickly play it down the phone for me?'

'What – now? I've got guests.'

'Hanna, please, it'll just take three minutes. I need to know whether I've remembered it right. It's important.'

'But why in God's name do you need to know now, in the middle of the night, after . . . wait a moment . . . after thirty years?'

'Please, Hanna. Please.'

'Like in the old days. OK, then,' she said, and after a while in which he heard voices, a door closing and the loud sound of the receiver being put on the piano, came the piece that Millar had played.

'So?' asked Hanna as soon as the last note had faded away.

'I wasn't mistaken. Are you quite sure this is the piece? A hundred per cent? No mistake possible?'

'Philipp! My pupils have to play it. You know how suitable it is.'

'And your birthday is the thirtieth of September? And not the second?'

'It still is. And incidentally that piece, the 902, is in G major.'

'And the piece is from the *Klavierbüchlein* for Wilhelm Friedemann Bach?'

'Yes, Philipp,' said Hanna as if to a troublesome child, 'and it isn't one of the two pieces some people think might have been written by the son, with the father's help.'

'Is it true that the piece hasn't been recorded?'

'No, that isn't true. There's a CD released by CBS. Glenn Gould, in fact.'

'Hanna, you're a marvel! But how will I get hold of it?' Perlmann said out loud.

'I can lend it to you, if that's any use.'

'It'll arrive too late if you send it to me. I need to try to get it here tomorrow.'

'So where are you right now?'

'Near Genoa.'

'Philipp, what on earth's going on? You sound so strange, so . . . stubborn.'

'I need to prove something to someone, and quickly.'

'Are you in some sort of trouble?'

'No, no.'

'You just need to be right?'

'Not that exactly, but not far off.'

'You don't seem to have changed very much.'

'It's a long story, Hanna, I'll explain later.'

They were both silent for a while, until Perlmann asked in a different voice: 'Do you remember: *glass clarity with velvet edges?*'

'Of course I remember. The others laughed at us.'

'Yes. But I've never heard a better formula for Glenn Gould.'

'Neither have I. Do you still play sometimes?'

'No.'

'You're not in a good way, are you?'

'Not especially.'

Gently, as if it were fragile, Perlmann rested the receiver on its cradle. So that was how Hanna remembered him: as someone who always wanted to be right. That hurt, and he thought it was unfair. And yet after a while he admitted to himself that it probably wasn't a coincidence. For example, the conversation from a moment ago: he hadn't asked about her at all; he hadn't asked a single question about her. He had effectively ambushed her with his urge to get one over on Millar, without giving her anything at all by way of explanation. Still, sitting on the edge of the bed, full of exhausted sobriety, he was shocked by the extent of his self-obsession. In the tiny world of this hotel he threatened to lose all sense of proportion.

So it was true that she had become a piano teacher. She had imagined things differently back then. *I'll visit her when I'm home again. In four weeks and one day.*

Hanna had been the only one who had immediately understood his decision and found it correct. She knew the limits of his talent precisely, and she wasn't, like the teachers, under a self-imposed compulsion to believe the student. Not that she said a single word to that effect. Not a single one. When he visited her that day, after he had closed the lid over the keys, she mutely stirred her coffee cup for a while and then asked simply, 'So what do you plan to do now?'

That university studies would take the place of musical training was something as fixed as an axiom. He had to concede that he himself had also acknowledged this axiom, at least in the sense that he had never visibly resisted it. And yet, he thought today, it was not a principle that was the natural, undistorted expression of his feelings at the time, and in that sense his own principle. It had had its origin not within himself, but in his parents. Not so much in what they said – one could have defended oneself against that. What had exerted its unassuming, sly power was the whole way they were, the post-office worker and his ambitious, half-educated wife. She, the daughter of a director of studies, had never been able to cope with the fact that her husband wasn't an academic, so the son had to become what the father was not. And the father, who depended upon her entirely in defiance of his domestic tyranny, had made that ambition her own. The pianist idea had at first made the parents insecure; but then they had started talking about the son as an *artist*, and of course it was much more than if he had just become one of the many academics who, as his mother said, were often rather respectable people. Then, when that flight of fancy had ended prematurely, a few days after the shock and recriminations, praises began to be sung about a solid academic career.

Perlmann could not remember a single conversation in which the pros and cons of university study had been discussed. Calling something so obvious into question was literally unthinkable. The worst thing, he thought, was that the silent power of this premise had paralyzed the imagination, about the very question of what one could do with one's life as a whole – the most important question, then, that anyone ever addressed. When his interest in academia – or what he saw as academia – began to crumble, he had begun to investigate what professions other people were pursuing. He was utterly astonished by all the things there were that he didn't know about, and then he began to irritate Agnes by complaining with childish fury that no one had told him anything about them. At first he fell into romanticizing other professions, above all those that lay far from his own. By now his gaze had become more sober and analytic, and always determined by the same question, namely whether he would have found it easier to experience the present in some other profession.

Tonight Perlmann quarrelled with his dead parents, because he thought there was a clearly visible causal connection between the unshakeable, rigidly dogmatic expectations they had imposed on their only child, and the fatal situation and inner misery in which he found himself at present. Tidal waves of accusation, of reproach, of reckonings of guilt and neglect buried him beneath themselves and dragged him, against all efforts of reason, away with them. When it was approaching two o'clock he took half a sleeping pill. At three he swallowed the other half. He was playing the A flat major Polonaise in front of an audience that seemed to extend infinitely back into the darkness of the hall. He knew he had to concentrate entirely on playing: everything depended upon him making no mistakes. Instead, he stared into the darkness of the hall and looked for Millar. He knew his gleaming glasses were there somewhere, but he couldn't see him anywhere, his eyes streaming with exertion. Then, all of a sudden, Evelyn Mistral's face appeared, with a radiant smile, as if she wanted to ask a question, but now it was Hanna's face that studied him quizzically; it was Hanna's face and also Laura Sand's, mocking and white and still. From the very outset he heard the dangerous passage like a paradoxical, premonitory echo, he knew that he couldn't rely on himself, that it was a matter of chance whether his fingers would do it right or not, whether they would be able to assert themselves against the paralysing influence of fear, his hands were sweating, the sweat was coming more and more, it was getting between his fingers and the keys, his fingers were slipping, now came the passage, he could hear quite loudly what it was supposed to sound like, but he couldn't do anything, his fingers ceased to grip, it was a sensation of boundless impotence, and then he woke up with dry and very cold hands, which he immediately stuffed back under the covers.

9

The effects of the pill lay heavy on his eyes, but he still couldn't get to sleep. While the first, pale light gave the bay an unreal presence, Millar's invisible dream-figure transformed into a real person, to whom he had to prove his superior knowledge of Bach. But how was he to deliver that proof? Getting hold of the score was not a solution; on no account must it look as if he had made a special effort. The crucial thing, if he were to draw Millar's attention to his error, was the incisive casualness of the man who had been familiar with these things for decades. The CD that Hanna had talked about. This would prove that it was a twofold error: it was not only the catalogue number that was incorrect, but the assertion that there was no recording. The story that it was a *trouvaille* thus acquired a ridiculous note in retrospect. Once again Perlmann heard Millar's impossible pronunciation of the French word. You had to think about it for a moment before you understood. But the question about the CD was similar to the one about the score: how come he had it with him? A cassette would be easier to explain; with a Walkman, for example. He couldn't have bought one of those little CD players that cost an absolute fortune. Or could he?

I happened to see it and just picked it up. That had exactly the right casual feeling, Perlmann thought as he shaved. And the sentence, if spoken in the right tone, had an urbane touch about it. The remark also explained why he didn't mention it until the following day. Signora Morelli had already referred to the CD player in the drawing room upon his arrival.

He relaxed, and when he reached for the receiver to order coffee, he suddenly wanted to sit opposite Millar this morning, bolstered by the secret of his plan. On the steps he felt as if his brain were swimming around inside his skull. But somehow it would work. At eight on the dot he walked into the dining room.

Apart from the red-haired man from the pool there wasn't another soul in the room. Perlmann greeted him and sat down in the other corner. He hesitantly ordered breakfast from a waiter he had never seen before. Then Evelyn appeared in the doorway and walked over to him with surprise. She had thrown a pullover over her shoulders, and her hair was tied in a ponytail. No, no, she said, communal breakfast was usually at eight, but for Sunday they'd agreed on nine. But that was too late for her today. She was plainly embarrassed at having to explain to him, the leader of the group. She straightened her cutlery and quickly changed the subject.

'You won't believe this,' she said, 'but the red-haired man's name is John Smith. He comes from Carson City, Nevada. Brian talked to him recently, from one American to another, so to speak. He's filthy rich and he's spending his winter here. "It figures," Brian said to him when he finally told him his name. If Brian despises somebody, he does it with good reason,' she smiled.

'And that must happen quite frequently,' Perlmann couldn't help saying.

Her hand, holding its croissant, stopped mid-movement. 'You don't like him that much, do you?'

Perlmann took a sip of coffee. His brain was swimming. 'I think he's fine,' he said, 'although he doesn't exactly suffer from a lack of self-confidence.'

'That's true. But there is something he can't deal with at all, and that's Laura's kind of irony. He gets completely helpless, and babbles like a little boy. But otherwise he feels he's a match for everything – if I can put it like that.' She gripped her ponytail, and the reddish strip appeared on her forehead. 'Recently, at the session, I was annoyed at the way he treated me. Somehow condescending, I thought. But he played wonderfully last night, didn't you think?'

'Yes . . . yes, I did,' Perlmann said haltingly, as if he had stumbled over a threshold.

Only the hesitation in the movement of her knife revealed that she had noticed his halting attitude. 'I wish I'd learned an instrument,' she said, and only now did she look at him. 'My father urged me to; but at the time I didn't feel like it. Juan, my little brother, did it better than me. He plays the cello. Not especially brilliantly, but he enjoys it.'

And you, do you play an instrument? He had to prevent that question being asked at all cost, so he asked more about Juan and the whole family, including the grandparents. One might have thought he was looking for material for a family saga.

They were in the doorway of the dining room when von Levetzov and Millar came down the stairs. They exchanged a glance that didn't escape Evelyn Mistral. She raised her arm, made a delicate movement with her fingers as if doing a trill on the piano, took Perlmann's arm with a smile and guided him out through the door to the flight of steps. It was only when they reached the promenade that she looked at him, and then they both burst out laughing.

She held his arm as they strolled along the harbor. Walking did Perlmann good, and the pressure above his eyes gradually subsided. Wrapped in the remaining after-effects of the pill, which lay on his eyes like a protective filter, he yielded to his imagination, which told him that he was enjoying this radiant autumn morning with the delicate plume of mist over the smooth, sparkling water. The present was within reach when Evelyn Mistral, who had now shaken her hair free, described Salamanca, and he was quite sure it would be his next travel destination.

They turned the corner and suddenly found themselves standing in front of a church, a bridal couple just coming out. He wished the photographs, the congratulation and the jokes would last much longer, and was disappointed at how quickly everyone suddenly climbed into the cars and drove away, honking jauntily.

Finally, Evelyn Mistral took his arm again and drew him gently away. It was nearly half-past eleven, she said, and she still had lots of plans. 'I'll be back at work two weeks tomorrow!' Maria was already working on her first chapter, but in the second there were still so many gaps and incongruities that it was hopeless. 'And when I think about Brian, Achim and Adrian sitting there . . .'

On the way back Perlmann had the feeling that his swallowing reflex had stopped working, and that he had to replace it every few seconds with an additional, almost already planned action. It didn't mean anything, he said when she asked him why he was so quiet all of a sudden.

Back at the hotel he drew the curtains and lay down in bed. It was baffling, he thought, how little he had internally bridled against all that conventional business outside the church. What had the bride actually looked like? Her features were suddenly strangely blurred, and he tried in vain to give the face back its sharp contours. He fell asleep while doing so.

It was after three o'clock when he woke up. He showered for a long time, ordered coffee and a sandwich, and then sat down to Leskov's paper. He wanted to finish it today. So that he could start on his own contribution tomorrow. He would just drop in very briefly at the trattoria to check on Sandra and reassure her about her test.

Sensory content? It was a while before he understood his marginal note again. Leskov himself now addressed this point, and Perlmann was waiting impatiently for his conclusion. But the paper approached the question indirectly. First of all it discussed the case of remembered emotional qualities. Again the text became very difficult, because now Leskov began to deploy the rich Russian vocabulary for emotions and moods, and the pocket dictionary was not up to these nuances. Irritated, and with a feeling of linguistic imposture, Perlmann inched his way along from one example to the next. The conclusion was concise: if the story of the experienced past is retold, the remembered qualities of the experience also presented themselves in a different way.

Perlmann was annoyed that he couldn't understand the examples in all their depth because of the gaps in his language. It meant that he didn't know what to make of the general assertion. And it was the key to what came next, because now Leskov constructed the case of remembered sensory impressions in analogy with the case of the emotions. The vocabulary for shadings in smell and taste became a problem, and there was much that Perlmann understood only very vaguely.

Could one rewrite a whole world of past sensory impressions in the course of a new narrative memory? He doubted it. What he had felt at the sight of the new patient in his mother's bed might really look different, even in terms of its quality of experience, if the narrative memory were one day to take a different path – if, as Leskov wrote, it were on the one hand to describe larger loops and on the other hand to grow more dense. And something similar might apply to the internal drama that was played out that evening when his father accused him of ingratitude for breaking off his training at the Conservatoire. *It's my life, and mine alone*, Perlmann had replied in a quivering voice before rushing into the night. He couldn't rule out the possibility that different stories could give different shades to the remembered experience of that moment. If, for example, one added the contemporary insight that his life had remained under the diktat of parental expectations, in spite of the touching heroics of his rebellion, his fury at the time still felt quite different from what it might have been in a story of a successful liberation.

To this extent, then, one could follow Leskov. But the color of his father's wool jacket, and the thumps on the coffin? Could that be rewritten? In a separate section Leskov, quoting no source, introduced Marcel Proust. But Perlmann found that less helpful than embarrassing, since it didn't sound as if Leskov knew Proust at first hand.

He turned on the light. Another nine pages. In conclusion, Leskov wrote, he now wanted to address the question of what his previous conclusions meant for the idea of the *osvaivat'* of his own past. The page on which *osvaivat'* should have appeared was missing from the dictionary. Perlmann furiously established that three pages were missing. He flicked to the end and glanced at the last few sentences of the paper. And so, he hoped that he had shown, Leskov concluded, that the ability to narrate and the ability to create a particular, very individual past were in the end one and the same. In this way, language and experienced time were much more closely linked than one might at first imagine. No one – this was the last, rather bombastic sentence – had understood the nature of language if they did not see it as the medium which, above all others, made possible a sophisticated experience of time.

Perlmann set off for the trattoria. When he sat down to these last sentences after taking a break, he would also know, at last, the meaning of *osvaivat'*.

Sandra wasn't there. A child needs to have a bit of a life, too, her mother said, so she had let her go out when her friends had called round. The test – God, yes. '*Che sarà, sarà!*'

Perlmann rested his elbow on the chronicle and smoked. He saw himself lying on his belly in the shade of the hotel garden, with his Latin book in front of his nose. Holidays on the Mediterranean, the first that his parents had been able to afford thanks to a small inheritance from Switzerland; then, seven years after the end of the war, still a sensation. Siesta time. Even his parents had had a lie down for a bit. Some of the hotel guests were dozing in the loungers on the beach. Over there was the sea, glimmering in the midday sun, and that shimmering glare, that was the present, the thing that really mattered. Some children were in the water, splashing each other and shrieking. Back then, of course, at thirteen, he hadn't thought it explicitly but he had behaved and felt as if he had to master all those Latin words and irregular verbs before he would be allowed to go out into that glittering present.

Perlmann opened the chronicle. It must have been in July. He read what it said about politics as if it had happened before he was born, it had so little to do with his life at the time. That applied equally to Eisenhower and King Farukh, and the death of Kurt Schumacher the following month. Benedetto Croce, finally, was something from another world. He only remembered Juan Manuel Fangio, the racing driver, and the day after his return from Italy there had been that radio report on the funeral of Evita Perón. They had sat by the little radio, and the speaker's melodramatic voice, hacked about with atmospheric disturbances, had turned the funeral procession into something mythical, making his mother cry. Was it then that he had started to understand the time difference between continents? Because it was very curious for

hundreds of thousands of people to walk through the Argentinian afternoon late in the evening.

On the day of his visit to the circus with Hanna, the chronicle recorded
only one event: Antonio Segni, who was still Italian prime minister at
the time, set off on a trip to Washington.

A few weeks later the film *The Bridge* by Bernhard Wicki had been
shown. Perlmann was already holding the tickets in his hand when
Hanna had looked in the display case and said no, she simply couldn't
bear to see such pictures. It had been the start of the critical period
between them, and when she had gone running through the foyer of
the Film Palace, her coat billowing around her, it had looked as if she
were running away from him rather than the images.

Sandra's face was hot, her loose hair tousled. She greeted Perlmann
only fleetingly, and the way her exuberance went out at the sight of
him revealed that his presence reminded her of the test, and the fact
that she didn't want to think about it right now. Perlmann paid.

Assimilating, he thought as the hotel came into view: that might be
the meaning of *osvaivat'*. Assimilating your own past through narrative
memory. What could that mean in Leskov's theory? And what else did
it mean?

It was just before three when he had read the paper through to the
end. Exhausted, he stepped to the open window. It was as quiet as the
grave. He felt hungover and, what was worse, robbed of a support. What
should he do now that the task of finishing Leskov's paper no longer
held him up?

What Leskov had written on the last pages, he thought as he got
undressed and slipped under the covers, did not produce a clear, consistent image. First of all there was the idea that appropriation – if that
really was the term – was a form of understanding: one appropriated
one's own past by giving it a meaning. It was the understanding achieved
by narrative memory, Leskov continued, that produced the crucial feeling
of belonging. And accordingly, he interpreted the taste of strangeness
that a past experience might have as a lack in their understanding. It
was through narrative memory, this was his rather pithy conclusion,

that a person first acquired a spiritual identity beyond time. So: without language no spiritual identity.

Perlmann felt drawn to this thought; for several minutes he was enthused by it. Then again he felt uneasy: was there not also mental identity in the sense of an organic structure of feeling around which both a person's actions and his imagination revolved, regardless of whether the structure of sensations was articulated in language or not? But that wasn't the actual problem about Leskov's theory, he thought, while, counter to his habits, he smoked a cigarette in bed. How did the business about appropriation fit with the thesis that remembering was in a certain sense invention? Appropriating – that assumed a given inner space of remembered experience that had to be paced out, so to speak, and conquered. But such a given inner space could, strictly speaking, not exist if past experience, even in its emotional quality, was only created by narration. Or not?

Exhaustion took hold of him, and he buried his head in the pillow. On the desk was Ruge's paper, of which he had read not a word. And at some point in the next few days he would have to go and see Millar, who wanted to talk to him about his idiotic question. For a moment he rested on his elbows and made a frantic attempt to remember. But the question had escaped him, and he fell back on to the pillow.

In Santa Margherita, this little dump, he would hardly be able to get hold of the CD of Bach's lesser-known Preludes. Should he try to do it in Rapallo, or go to Genoa? And how would he find the shop with the biggest range? Did taxi drivers know things like that?

He had taken such trouble with Sandra and now, standing by his table, she looked snootily down at him. And why were the pages of the chronicle suddenly stuck together? Two menacing shadows darkened everything, and when he looked up, Millar and Ruge were standing in front of him. Ruge was bent forwards, holding with his chin and hands on to a tower of paper that could at any time bend in the middle and collapse. Millar's flashing glasses came closer and closer to the chronicle. The word *sneering* shot through Perlmann's head, and in the middle of the desperate attempt to snap the chronicle shut in front of Millar's nose, he woke up and heard the rustle of the rain.

10

As he sat at the front, in his inevitable brown suit with the too-short sleeves, on the ostentatious armchair, Achim Ruge looked like a member of the plebs who had usurped the Kaiser's throne. He had – this was more striking than usual today – a problem with the switch from shortsighted to far-sighted, and constantly put his glasses crooked, making everyone scared that he would injure himself with the wire end that stuck inwards like a thorn. In spite of his bizarre pronunciation, his English was bafflingly fluent, and today, once again, he surprised Perlmann with his rich vocabulary, which made Millar's oral mode of expression sound practically pitiful. Back at Harvard they had smiled at him at first. The peasant boy from the country, from Germany. Then, he delivered his first works on the theory of grammar, supposedly it was a hundred pages long. It went off like a bomb, and Ruge became a star overnight. He stayed three years. Then, when they made him a tempting job offer (the story continued) the American way of life wasn't for him. He wanted to get back to the farm. And this from a boy who had grown up in Böblingen, the son of a tax official.

His paper began with a reference to experiments by Perlmann, which had attracted attention nearly ten years before, because they contradicted a current theory about the linguistic learning process. Perlmann had realized this with horror when he had sat on the edge of the bed, head heavy, quickly flicking through Ruge's text. On the way down to the veranda Perlmann had tried in vain to call to mind the details from back then. It was all so far away. Only the summary that Ruge now repeated brought back the contours. But they were outlines of something that someone had discovered and plainly presented with verve at the time, but who was only coincidentally identical with him, Philipp Perlmann. Nonetheless, those experiments had established his position in the subject for years, and it had been a long time before the others had noticed that he had finally become a theoretical linguist. That this had come about because he didn't like labs, and felt leeched dry after a day of teamwork, they could not know.

The bad thing for Evelyn Mistral's father had been the other doctors and the nurses who stood around him when he was operating. *Yes, exactly*, Perlmann thought now, *exactly*.

It was strange – ironic, in fact, he said to himself as Ruge now explained his own experiments – but back then Perlmann had especially wanted to know something quite precisely, and this desire, atypical of him, had catapulted him into the spotlight. Or was what he had thought on Friday on this chair about his need for blurred lines wrong? Because his later works had been precise as well. Would they have been possible at all if there had not been a will to precision inside him? But those were two different things: the natural need and the learned will.

His writings were well liked among the students, they were well written and transparently constructed. What never came was a big hit like Adrian von Levetzov had had, and Millar with his book two years before. Perlmann was quite sure that the others sometimes wondered what, in the final analysis, his achievement really was. That certainty was always at the forefront of Perlmann's consciousness when he was dealing with colleagues on technical matters. Then he would have an impressive idea and for a while all self-doubt was forgotten: he came up with arguments, observations and suggestions that were somehow original, too. You could see it in the faces of his listeners. He had won them round. A cushion of respect had come into being, and he stayed up half the night to hold on to the feeling. The next morning he was once again nothing but a hard worker wondering what he had achieved.

The next hour was entirely filled with a conversation between Ruge and Laura Sand, who compared her animal experiments, detail by detail, with what had been done in Bochum. To Perlmann's surprise all the

irritation and impatience had fallen away from her, and the concentrated peace and intensity of their analyses had something so hypnotic
about it that from time to time even Ruge forgot to react. For the first
time Giorgio Silvestri took notes. Only once was the atmosphere broken,
when the red-haired American appeared and did his exercises outside
the window. 'John Smith,' said Millar, keeping a straight face. 'From
Carson City, Nevada.' Amidst the laughter Evelyn Mistral glanced at
Perlmann.

The way the academic preoccupation with language sounded this
morning, it was a good thing, thought Perlmann. An interesting thing
that should be encouraged. And then, all of a sudden, he sensed that
he was thinking this thought with a very particular internal attitude:
like someone watching an academic program on television after work,
before switching to sports.

It wasn't really true to say that he was only marginally interested in
language, but he wasn't interested in it in this way. Dissecting, measuring, formalizing language: that basically didn't interest him any more
than chemistry. If languages constantly cast their spell over him, it was
as a medium of experience, and above all as a means of feeling his way
towards the present, which eluded his grasp with such diabolical dexterity.
At the time it had seemed, when he was on the student secretariat, so
natural, so logical, to enrol on the linguistics course. Many of the other
things, like law or physics, ruled themselves out from the outset, so he
didn't even have to think about them. And medicine was out of the
question, too: it meant far too much physical proximity to other people.

He liked languages. *And you have such a* facilité, his mother said,
seeking with her sprinkling of such words to conceal her complete lack
of talent for foreign languages, not least from herself. And besides, there
wasn't a word of truth in it. As with so many other things, the only
thing that he possessed was hard work, endurance and an often blind
constancy of will.

Achim Ruge had taken off his jacket and hung it on the back of the
chair. The two carved claws of the seat-back were wider than the armpits
of the jacket, and stuck so far into the sleeves that they created the

impression of a scarecrow that towered above Ruge's big, bald head. But Perlmann didn't want to be distracted either by that or by the ludicrous rubber bands on Ruge's upper arms. For the first time he thought he understood his own choice of academia. *It was a misunderstanding, nothing more.* And this misunderstanding was fundamentally so simple, he thought, that it took one's breath away: by leaving the Conservatoire he had said farewell to the hope of outwitting the present by playing the piano, and bending it to his will. Because the mere hearing of music would never extend further than to an intensified yearning for the present. And now he threw himself into a preoccupation with language as a medium that was supposed to take the place of music and replace the unfulfilled hopes for the present. These hopes had been so powerful, and so breathless the switch, that he had overlooked one simple fact: language created presence when one allowed oneself to fall into it, when one swam in it and played with it, and not when one dissected it and considered it with the eyes of one seeking for laws, for explanations, systematizations and theories. It was laughably simple, every child knew that. And yet he had confused the two things and had – in love with the impressionist, sensual density of language – devoted himself to an analytical effort that must systematically lead him away from what he was looking for, because it was quite simply defined in a different way.

While Silvestri was reporting on experiments into aphasia and thus provoking a heated debate, Perlmann was in the Auditorium Maximum of Hamburg University, accepting his record of study from the hands of the dean. Whether he really felt, when he saw beneath the photograph and his name the entry *linguistics*, that something was wrong, or whether he had retrospectively read his warning unease into that distant moment, was something that could not be decided. And if one believed Leskov, it was a meaningless question. At any rate it now seemed to him that he had been separated from the crowd of the others in the hall by a fine and unnameable gap that had something to do with the fact that those others had experienced their self-selected membership of a subject with greater enthusiasm. And the longer Perlmann reflected upon this insidious little gap, the more the suspicion germinated within him that his action had even then sprung from a vagueness and a lack of internal definition, on the basis of which indifference towards the whole idea of study and research lay an indifference that it had taken him thirty years to discover and acknowledge.

The departure of the others made him jump; he had been so far away. Didn't he have anything to add? Ruge asked him on the way out. Perlmann was still filled with the insight that he had just gained into the logic of his misunderstanding, and managed a relaxed smile. He had just enjoyed listening for once, he said offhandedly. Otherwise one has to do so much talking.

'Erm . . . well, yes, you're right there,' Ruge laughed, and it seemed to Perlmann as if his laughter was a touch less confident than usual.

Millar was leaning against the reception desk, playing with his room key. Now he walked up to Perlmann. What was happening about their meeting? 'About that question, I mean.'

Perlmann asked Signora Morelli for the key and sought her eyes as if she could help him. The protection given him by his insight of a moment ago seemed to have been blown away.

'I'll give you a call,' he said at last and disappeared so quickly into Maria's office that it bordered on effrontery.

The many bracelets on Maria's wrists clattered with every movement that she made at the computer. Today she had chewing gum in her mouth and, as usual, she breathed out the smoke as she spoke. Perlmann asked her to phone Rapallo about the CD. Laughing, she made the people at the other end look it up, in spite of the fact that it was the beginning of the siesta. Neither of the two music shops there had the CD, but the second offered to order it from Genoa, it would take between one and two days. Perlmann shook his head when she passed on the information, so she ended the phone call, puzzled by his haste. She showed no impatience when Perlmann asked her to try in Genoa. The chewing gum snapped from time to time between her teeth. She knew the big music shop in the city; she had, she said, grown up there. At first they said they didn't have the CD, and judging by Maria's face they doubted whether it existed at all. But then Maria said a few indistinct words, slurred to the point of incomprehensibility, which must have been Genoese dialect, and then she asked them to take a look in the storeroom and amongst the new acquisitions. It took a long time. Perlmann felt uneasy, and he was grateful to Maria when she jokingly said that there must be some really lovely music on it. She was visibly relieved when she was finally able to tell Perlmann that the CD was there. It had come in the last delivery and hadn't yet been properly unpacked. He asked her to see to it that it was set aside for him, and that it should on no account be sold. He would drop by in the course of the afternoon. As he left he would have liked to give Maria an explanatory word, but apart from a repeated *Mille grazie!* nothing came to mind.

He fetched money and credit cards from the room and then walked to the station. There was no point hurrying. He didn't want to find himself, yet again, standing outside a shop closed for siesta. On the platform, where he had to wait for almost an hour, at regular intervals that remained inexplicable, one was assailed by a shrill ringing sound that penetrated one to the marrow. Luckily, the train was almost empty. Perlmann drew the grubby curtain over the window of his compartment and tried to sleep. A week had passed. A fifth. Was that a lot or not much? He wished Silvestri would make up his mind soon about whether he was going to deliver his lecture in the fourth or fifth week. If it was the fifth, Perlmann had only another fifteen days to write a paper. Otherwise it was eighteen days; nineteen, if he postponed the copying until Saturday. Sometimes Maria didn't work on Saturday. Was copying possible anyway? Might she leave him alone with the machine?

Genoa was crammed with cars. All over the place trucks parked in the middle of the street to be unloaded. You sat at a green light, not moving an inch; a concert of car horns, it was hopeless. It was always like this, the taxi driver said calmly, looking at his flustered passenger in the rear-view mirror. Siesta? Yes, sure, but not for delivery men. At least not on Mondays. When they stopped outside the music shop after an eternity, the shop was still in darkness, even though the lunch break had been over for ten minutes, according to the sign on the door. Perlmann dispatched the taxi. Why didn't people stick to what was written down? Why?

And then, as if his desperate irritation had suddenly woken him, it occurred to him that he would have to factor in at least two or three days for Maria to type out his paper. All of his previous calculations had been wrong. He took off his jacket and wiped his sweaty forehead with his handkerchief. In reality it was like this: if Silvestri opted for the fifth week, and if he also wanted to give Maria the Friday, Perlmann had no more than ten days. And if she was willing to write the whole thing out on Monday and Tuesday, that made thirteen, which required his colleagues to read the paper in a single day. On the other hand, if Silvestri made his presentation in the fourth week, that made sixteen days, again assuming that Maria could do it in two days and make the copies on Friday evening before she went away for the weekend. Trembling, Perlmann put his jacket back on and shook himself disgustedly as he felt his shirt sticking to his back.

He had to wait again in the shop because the man Maria had spoken to was late. Under the startled eyes of the salesman Perlmann tore open the wrapper and frantically fumbled around with the double sleeve without managing to get it open. '*Ecco!*' smiled the salesman, flipping it open with a single, easy motion. The second of the two CDs was the right one. Perlmann looked for number 930, put the CD in the CD player and put on the headphones.

It was the piece that Millar had played.

His earlier panic had vanished. But he was disappointed that the feeling of triumph wasn't stronger. That it wasn't, in fact, there at all. Suddenly, the whole action struck him as entirely pointless – childish and pointless. He paid and stepped into the street, weary and ashamed. With a sluggish gait he set off towards the station.

At first it was hard to make out that behind the scaffolding there was a bookshop, which seemed just to have opened. Perlmann turned round and walked into the shop, which had lots of mirrored windows and was fabulously illuminated. With his hands in his pockets he strolled along the tables of bestsellers, past the shelves of literary fiction and back into the languages section.

The big book with the red back and black inscription immediately caught his eye. It was a Russian-English dictionary, and vice versa. The paper was thin and greyish, and when you touched it you were left with a soapy film on your fingers; but the entries for the words were very detailed and in many cases a quarter of a column long. *Osvaivat'.* Perlmann sat down in an elegant but uncomfortable chair and looked up the word. *To assimilate, master; to become familiar with.* He had guessed correctly: what happened in the process of narrative memory was, according to Leskov, that one *mastered* one's own past and thus *brought it closer*; and those were precisely the elements in the term *assimilation. Making it one's own* would be another formulation, he thought. How would one decide between those words if one were to translate the text into English?

He wished he had his vocabulary book with him, then he could fill in the many gaps in it via a detour through English. He looked along the shelf: they didn't have a Russian-German dictionary. But they did have the German-English Langenscheidt that he, too, had at the hotel. *Sich aneignen: to appropriate, to acquire, to adopt.* So *appropriating*, it appeared, was the action of taking things into one's own position, while one needed *acquiring* in the appropriation of knowledge, and *adopting* could mean assimilating an opinion and perhaps also taking up an attitude. He picked up the red dictionary again and looked up *to appropriate: prisvaivat'.* Then *to acquire* and *to adopt: usvaivat'.* Words, then, which were each distinguished only by their prefixes from *osvaivat'.* How precisely could one work out Leskov's choice of words? Permann stepped aside to let a woman with enormous earrings get to the shelf, where she made straight for the little Russian-Italian dictionary. He was tempted to talk to her and draw her into his internal discussion, but she had already turned away with an absent smile and was walking to the cash register. You could not, he thought, appropriate your own past as you could a subject. And not like a piece of knowledge, an opinion or an attitude, either. Did *appropriation* not also mean *recognition*? For *recognizing* the dictionary gave *soznavat'*, which could also mean *realizing*;

for *acknowledging, priznavat'*. Had he not seen one of those words while skimming Leskov's paper?

He looked furtively around and set the dictionary slowly back on the shelf. Again his face was hot in that way that you could see from outside. Agnes had seen that heat, at any rate, when he sat on the floor with mountains of dictionaries, and she hadn't liked that hot face. *You look somehow . . . fanatical*, she had once said, and it had done no good when she had later explained that it had been the wrong word entirely.

He was two streets on when he turned round. He stopped under the scaffolding for a while, teetered on his heels and looked into the gutter, where the remains of an ice-cream wrapper lay in a disgusting brown mush. Then he turned abruptly, went in and got the big red dictionary down from the shelf. As he did so, he saw in the mirror that he was wearing the expression of someone reluctantly performing a secret mission. Credit cards only from 100,000 lire, said the man at the cash register. Perlmann set down next to it the other copy of the Russian-Italian dictionary that the woman had bought before, and now that was enough.

Was *assimilation* really an adequate translation of *osvaivat'*? he asked himself in the train. *Assimilating*, when used about emigrants, for example, meant *adaptation* or *conforming*, which was quite far removed from the idea of appropriation. And *mastering* could, in principle, also mean keeping certain memories at a distance. Given that *usvaivat'* was also to be found in the text, could one acquire something which, like one's own past, already belonged to one? Fine, Leskov might say that before narrative memory it didn't really belong to one . . . And what about *adopting*? Perlmann walked down the associative corridors that led off in his mind from the English word. You could also use it, he thought, when it came to absorbing a piece of culture or a religion. That meant that a certain internal detachment was involved, as when one was acting a part. And wasn't there a hint of fakery and fraud in there as well? Then *adopting* would be impossible as a translation of *usvaivat'* in the sense of appropriation. Or was it? For if narrative memory were a kind of invention . . .

Lots of people boarded the train at Genova Nervi, and the carriage became very noisy. Perlmann had to struggle to concentrate. Appropriating the past: didn't that also mean *standing by it*? And what would be the best English word for that? He lost his thread for a moment, and slipped into an exhaustion that often came upon him when he spent too long sitting on the floor with dictionaries. At Recco Station it occurred to him: *endorsing*. Under the curious glances of the people sitting opposite him he looked it up, balancing the big dictionary on his knees. *Indossirovat'*. But that seemed to be a word that only occurred in a financial context. *Podtverzhdat'* in the sense of *confirming*. Did that word occur in Leskov's text? He looked out the window, past the eyes of the others, into the gloom. *Incorporating something*, it seemed to him, was also part of the meaning of appropriation. But now the train stopped in Santa Margherita.

'One moment, please,' he said afterwards to the taxi driver. He set the dictionaries down on the lid of the trunk and looked up *incorporating. Vkluchat'*. It seemed to him that he had read that. 'I'm in a hurry,' he said to the baffled driver.

In his room he immediately sat down at the desk. He was glad that he hadn't stacked the books up as he had in his first room. In this way he could comfortably set out the material that needed to be translated. Above all, there was enough room for the Russian-English dictionary, which, when it was opened, occupied almost half of the desktop. The other dictionary, the one that the woman with the huge earrings had bought, he pushed into the right-hand corner at the back. He had never seen earrings that size before. He had liked the emerald green with the fine gold edge.

He started where Leskov began to speak about the idea of appropriation. For *osvaivat'* he wrote both *assimilate* and *master*, with a slash between them. It was a much slower process than translating into German. On the other hand, it was much more exciting, and if he managed an English sentence easily he breathed out heavily with joy. Often, on the other hand, easiness didn't come into it. Comprehension was also possible when there were vague edges of meaning. Then, without really noticing, one brought along the great diversity of knowledge that accompanied every word in one's own language, and that knowledge enabled one to fill in the gaps in comprehension when confronted by unfamiliar foreign words. Translation from one foreign language into another, on the other hand, ruthlessly exposed the smallest uncertainty in one's linguistic sensitivity. Of course, that applied particularly to Russian. But Perlmann also quickly got a sense of how great his uncertainty was with regard to certain English expressions, and there were sentences when both sides blurred, it was like an equation with two unknowns. At such points he became aware of how many things he had hitherto simply ignored.

And, nonetheless, from the start it was like a fever that he didn't want to come to an end. He had filled almost two pages, when the word *priznavat'* arrived. He was about to see if there was a translation other than *to acknowledge*, when he remembered dinner. He irritably slipped into his jacket and dashed down the stairs. The waiter was already clearing away the soup plates when Perlmann sat down at the table opposite Millar.

Only now, at the sight of Millar's face, did Perlmann remember the CD. He reached into his jacket pocket and felt the cool plastic of the packaging. He had the sense of touching a relic from some past inner world that looked ridiculous in retrospect. And had Millar's face not shown disapproval of his repeated lateness, he would have let things lie.

'Oh, by the way, Brian,' he began, trying to keep all sense of triumph out of his face, 'that encore you played on Saturday isn't number 902 in the catalogue. It's 930; 902 is in G major.'

He had managed to say it in a relaxed, almost playful manner, and a touch of awareness of how ridiculous the whole business was had made its way into his voice. But now a silence fell upon the room, where the only person who wasn't part of the group was John Smith, and gave the scene an ominous feeling of drama.

Millar straightened his glasses, leaned back and folded his arms over his chest. He stuck out his lower lip for a moment, shook his head barely perceptibly and said with a smile that made his eyes narrow:

'Quite frankly, Phil, I don't think I'm wrong there. I'm pretty familiar with the lesser-known Bach.'

Perlmann took his time. He held Millar's challenging gaze. This one time he found it wonderfully simple. Their eyes locked onto each other. That moment compensated for much, and he savored it. After what was about to come, Millar wouldn't dare to return to the business about his idiotic question.

He took the package containing the two CDs out of his pocket, let his eye rest upon it with theatrical elaborateness, and then pushed it slowly across the undulating tablecloth to Millar. *Laconically. Very laconically.*

'You can see your mistake for yourself. It's a very popular recording, by the way. You can have it.' He was glad that he had said *mistake* and not *error*. It sounded more like school and would hit him harder.

Von Levetzov looked curiously across to Millar and then at Perlmann with a smile that was supposed to indicate that this time he was on his side. *He's an opportunist, a conversational optimist, who always throws in his lot with the stronger battalion.*

Ruge smiled as well, but it was a smile without partisanship. He was simply amused by the matter; he who was always ready to attack in debates, and loved an exchange in which someone stood to win or lose.

Millar had opened the CD case, and shook his head with his lips pursed. 'The label on the CD – that doesn't mean a thing.'

'It's all in the booklet. In the other case.'

Millar contemptuously let the side of the booklet slide along his thumb. 'That would mean that it's a piece from the *Klavierbüchlein,*' he said, and the comedy of his unsuccessful attempt at an umlaut took some of the contemptuous sharpness away from his words. 'And it isn't one of those. I'm absolutely sure of that.' He snapped the case firmly shut and pushed it across to Perlmann, who left it in the middle of the table, right next to the gravy boat.

'Well, Brian,' said Perlmann, and tilted his head to the side as Millar often did, 'we can listen to the piece over there later on.'

'Yes, please,' Laura Sand joined in. 'I love that simple tune.'

If there was anything ironic about her remark, it was only the merest hint. But Millar irritably raised his eyebrows as if someone were mocking him in the most brazen way.

'Well, Phil,' he said, aping Perlmann. 'Liner notes can contain mistakes, can't they? It does happen. Even on CBS. No, no, we would need the score.'

'Which could also be misidentified,' said Silvestri, blowing smoke across the table.

'Well now, Giorgio,' snapped Millar.

'*Buon appetito,*' Silvestri grinned, raising his glass.

Millar stayed out of the rest of the conversation. He stared at the plate in front of him. Only once did he glance past Perlmann into the room, but lowered his head again immediately. Evelyn Mistral giggled, and when the others turned round they saw John Smith raising his glass to Millar.

'By the way, Phil,' Millar said suddenly over coffee, 'how come you happen to have a copy of the record on you?' He rested his chin on his folded hands and looked steadily at Perlmann. 'Sort of a fluke, huh?'

The cool, casual sentence that Perlmann had had ready was gone. There was nothing there but a void, and in it his old fear of Millar. He put another sugar lump in his coffee and stirred it. He saw the ice-cream wrapper in the gutter and the emerald-green earrings. The translation of Leskov's text was waiting for him upstairs. Suddenly, the sentence was there again. He looked up, and it was as if he could feel the collective eyes on his face like the heat of a lamp or the faint sting of a salty breeze.

'I happened to see it and just picked it up,' he said. It didn't sound worldly, more embarrassed and apologetic, and he feared Millar's next remark. Then he heard Laura Sand's dark, throaty laugh.

'A *trouvaille,* in fact,' she said, and gave Millar one of her ironic glances as she stubbed out her cigarette.

There was mute, helpless fury in Millar's face as he folded his napkin. He was the first to rise from the table.

Perlmann took the CD from the table. She would really like to hear it, Laura Sand said with a mocking glance at Millar, who was energetically striding through the door. Perlmann nodded and walked ahead of her. On his way into the lounge he felt as shattered as if he had just been through a long day's competition.

Millar didn't come in until the CD was already playing. The fury in his face had made way for a scornfully cagey expression. With ostentatious boredom he let his eye glide around the whole of the lounge and set his glasses on his head from time to time, so that he could get a better view of something in the far-off corner.

Perlmann was holding the CD booklet in his hand. 'That was number 902 in G major,' he said once the piece was over.

'Oh, I know that piece very well, Phil,' Millar said smugly. 'It is, I fear, number 902a. In G major.'

Perlmann looked at the booklet. '902a is only a third as long. Not quite, even. You'll hear it in a moment. Because this is the piece coming now.'

Millar's face twitched, but he didn't say anything. In the short pause before Hanna's birthday piece Perlmann waved the booklet at him, pointed to a line with his index finger and said, 'Now. Number 930.'

Millar raised his eyebrows as if he didn't understand, and went on surveying the room.

'I should point out the mistake to CBS,' he said when the last note of the record had faded away. 'I could also point out to them that I don't think it's a particularly good recording. Glenn Gould, of course.'

Then, in the foyer, he stepped up beside Perlmann. 'Have you forgotten our appointment?'

'No,' said Perlmann, resisting his blue gaze. 'By no means.'

Afterwards, at the desk, it was immediately clear to him again where he had broken off his trail of thought before: was there another translation for *priznavat'* apart from *to acknowledge*? That was important, because of the inventive components that narrative memory had, according to Leskov. Wouldn't it sound strange to talk about acknowledging one's own inventions? Didn't one tend rather to acknowledge facts?

Before he looked it up he paused, so as to be clear about the strange sensation that accompanied his renewed concentration on Leskov's paper.

He was surprised how quickly and easily he managed to brush aside the battle with Millar in which he had just been involved. Such things usually preoccupied him for an unreasonable length of time, and often one would have said that he was being persecuted by them. It was as if at the sight of Cyrillic script he had gone into a different room within himself, and closed the door behind him. It was wonderful being behind that door, which protected him against everything that raged in him outside it. The thought of what might be going on in him beyond the door, and beyond that in the outside world, could not be suppressed; but it was present only as a faint glimmer in the background, and one could get used to ignoring its occasional flickerings.

Priznavat' could also mean *admit*, and *priznanie* was plainly the classical word for *confession*. Here again Perlmann wrote down all the possibilities. All his fatigue fell from him now; he was busy starting something new and exciting.

Admittedly something – something outside – was still missing to make everything right. It was a while before he hit upon it. Then he fetched the ladder from the end of the corridor and restored the gloomy lighting in the corridor ceiling lamps. Now it was good. Now he could work.

The business about appropriation was still unclear at four o'clock in the morning. Once Leskov used *podtverzhdat'* and three times *vkluchat'*. So there was also an idea involved that one appropriated a piece of the past by making it part of a whole, which was oneself. One brought it, if it had previously been alien, back within this unity.

Apart from the fact that, of course, the idea of wholeness or unity required explanation: what could this process of integration look like if it was supposed to be the case that narration was what created memories in the first place? Was it true to say that the various narratives grew increasingly together, so to speak? *Making something one's own, sich etwas zu eigen machen* – one thought at first of a piece of substance, a solid core that was extended by the new, which had hitherto remained outside. But for Leskov there could no such solid core, a constant that was taken for granted in all narrative appropriation, because what applied to one piece of memory applied to all. If he was ready to claim that a self, a person in the psychological sense of the word, had no solid core and nothing whatsoever in terms of substance, but was a web of stories, constantly growing and subject to a constant process of relayering – a little like a structure of cotton candy at a carnival, except without material? Perlmann grew dizzy at the thought, and excitedly turned his attention to the next paragraph.

It was half-past five when weariness overtook him. Seven of the nine last pages of the text were translated. It was years since he had been so proud of something. And it was, he thought, the first time in ages that he had managed to immerse himself so thoroughly in something.

Since Agnes's death. He took her picture from his wallet. She was reclining on a lounger on the beach, her arms folded over her head, her sunglasses pushed into her chestnut hair. Her water-clear gaze, which had so often given him courage, was directed at him, and it was plain that she had just been mocking his wish to have a color photograph of her.

During that holiday they had learned Cyrillic script and their first Russian words. She had been faster then him. She had done it playfully, while he had as usual worked methodically, almost pedantically. While she was grasping whole words at once, he still had to think about each individual letter.

Perlmann turned off the light. She had driven that stretch of road hundreds of times, briskly and confidently. Until that jinglingly cold morning. She had only wound the window down a chink, and the waving hand in its black glove had looked doll-like and mechanical. They had both laughed, and in the middle of that laugh she had scooted off in her ancient Austin, a racing start down their shovelled driveway. She hadn't driven more than ten minutes to the road through the forest. A film of powdery snow over treacherous black ice, a moment's inattention. The photographic equipment on the back seat had been undamaged.

11

Three hours later, on the veranda, Perlmann struggled to keep his eyes open and poured one cup of coffee after another into himself. Silvestri grinned when he saw him reaching for the pot again, and rubbed his eyes as a sign of sympathy. Ruge was now explaining the part of his text that had nothing to do with Perlmann's experiments. He wore a baggy, roll-neck sweater that hung in untidy folds over the collar of his jacket and made his neck look even shorter than usual. At first Perlmann attributed it to his own weary head, in which there were repeated little absences, but then he became aware that Ruge really had lost his concentration this morning. His presentation was halting and disjointed, and his eyes lacked their usual belligerent, roguish gleam. Increasingly often he ran his hand over his bald head and turned the pages as hesitantly as if he didn't understand a word of what they said. And when he put his glasses on his head, with his sparse ring of grey hair he looked like an old man who was losing his sight. The lack of pleasure that he emanated transmitted itself to the others, too. Not even Millar stepped in when the pauses were drawn out. And for a while the session seemed to be going completely wrong.

In the end it was Evelyn Mistral who saved it. She asked a critical question, and when she saw the others nodding with relief she went on talking and, speaking more and more freely, developed a long train of thought that made the others reach for their pens after a while. The strip of red appeared on her forehead, and her explanatory hand movements were more vivid and expressive than Perlmann had ever seen them before. The nervousness with which she had previously had to battle in this room fell away from her, and only every now and again did she slip her heel from her right shoe. Later, when she became the center of a lively debate, she often tossed her hair to the left as the answers and interjections formed with her, to free her face from the hair that she was wearing loose today. But rather than swinging back, her hair hung in front of her face like an untidy veil, so that when she looked up from her notes only half of her glasses could be seen. Then she blew upwards from the left-hand corner of her mouth, and as that generally didn't do the trick, at last she brushed the straw-blonde strands out of her face with her hand. When the coffee had produced a jittery alertness in him, Perlmann feverishly tried to find a possible way of contributing something to the discussion. But his thoughts were always too slow, and the two conclusions that he attempted were so ineffective that he started to feel like an onlooker. Both times Millar simply went on talking, without even turning to look at him, as if there had just been an irritating noise that he had had to let wash over him.

It had stopped raining, but dark clouds still hung over the bay, and drops fell into the gravel from the white tables on the terrace. The young man with the rucksack and the cape who now entered Perlmann's field of vision had a hesitant gait, and was looking round like someone afraid of being caught doing something forbidden. He looked up at the facade, took a few steps towards the swimming pool, and when he saw that people were sitting on the veranda he walked quickly back to the steps. The gauntness of his build and the way he had held his cigarette reminded Perlmann of something unpleasant, something that had happened during the university holidays, but shortly before he could grasp hold of it, it had disappeared back into his exhaustion.

True, in fact, Millar was saying, this was the ideal opportunity to calmly revisit the various grammatical theories of the past few years and attempt to achieve some kind of balance. Achim and he himself could start work on it tomorrow, and then they could go through things together on Thursday and Friday. Would Adrian mind if his session was moved to the start of next week?

*That means everything's shifting by half a week. That means that my
turn isn't going to come in the fourth week. Which leaves me with fifteen
days, assuming that Thursday and Friday are enough for the copying.* He
thought it was a good idea, Perlmann said when the others looked at
him quizzically.

'Talk about a good idea!' Evelyn Mistral said to him when they were
the last to leave the veranda. 'It gives me half a week extra! Shall we
celebrate in town with a pizza? In spite of the rain?'

He would rather rest for a while, he said; he had slept badly.

'Yes, I can see that,' she said and touched him lightly on the arm.

When he woke up just before four, Perlmann suddenly knew what the
young man in the cape had reminded him of. For the third time Frau
Hartwig had reminded him to answer a letter about his working with an
Israeli colleague; so just before the end of the day he had visited the office
and dictated his refusal. After that he had gone through the rest of his
mail, and because he was busy hurling a book catalogue into the waste-
paper basket, he had almost failed to hear the hesitant, guilty knocking.

It was a student, a gaunt young man with a protruding Adam's apple
and sticking-out ears, holding his hand-rolled cigarette noticeably far
away from himself, as if it disgusted him. In the labyrinthine building
he had lost his bearings, and actually just wanted a lecture list. Perlmann
asked him in and quizzed him for more than half an hour; the boy
didn't know what was happening to him. Perlmann even asked him
about his holiday plans and his financial situation, and suppressed the
question about a girlfriend only at the last moment. Afterwards, he was
shocked by his own lack of detachment. A few days later the boy had
come towards him with his girlfriend on the other side of the road.
Perlmann had given a start when he saw the two of them whispering
and laughing, and had had to warn himself against becoming paranoid.
The girlfriend was very pretty, and the boy had no longer seemed intimidated and helpless. Even his ears didn't seem to stick out so much.
Now Perlmann remembered very clearly what he had thought: *I'm losing
my power of judgment. If I ever had one.*

He showered for a long time to wash away the memory, and then started reading Leskov's paper from the beginning. Now, going through it for the second time, he understood everything much better, and read the first paragraphs astonishingly quickly. The new dictionary was really fabulous; only the greyish paper with its soapy smoothness was still unpleasant to the touch, so that he needed to wash his hands every now and then. The programmatic sentence at the beginning of the text wasn't a problem in English, and it was only in the examples for the concept of a remembered scene that he faltered. His concentration waned, and he started feeling uneasy. *Sandra. The test.* Shortly before eight he crept out of the hotel by the rear entrance and set off towards the trattoria.

The proprietress asked jokingly where he had been yesterday, and then she called for Sandra, who came running over, ponytail bouncing, and put her open exercise book on his plate. There was still a lot of red on the pages, but it had been enough to get her a satisfactory mark – the first in weeks. His meals would be free for the rest of the week, the proprietor said, clapping his heavy hand on his shoulder. And he was to order the most expensive thing on the menu!

Perlmann opened the chronicle at the assassination of Robert Kennedy. That was right: only a few weeks before, while he had been preparing for his doctoral examination, Martin Luther King and Rudi Dutschke had been shot as well. Prague Spring. The student unrests in Paris. From week to week, almost from day to day, the tension between Perlmann's personal concerns about the examination and the assistant's post, and the political developments out in the world had entered his consciousness with ever greater clarity. What was more important? What did *important* mean in this context? And in what sense could one speak of an obligation to participate in the political developments? Was it clear what *participate* meant? For a while he had changed his habits, and read the newspaper before he arrived at his desk in the morning. But it went against his feelings and so, without finding an answer to his questions, he had gone back to his old, reverse rhythm.

It had been on the train to Venice that he had read about the assassination of Robert Kennedy in the newspaper. Perlmann rested his head on his interlocking fingers and thought back to that moment in Mestre when the train turned on to the embankment to Venice. He had stretched his head out into the warm evening and repeated the magic word: *Venice*. Even now the moment was still so vivid that he thought he could see all the other heads and outstretched arms along the train. And then, as they entered the station, he had seen his newspaper on the seat, open at the thalidomide trial. Already clutching his suitcase he had looked once more at the pictures of crippled children. A painful alertness had passed through him as he realized that he was, in his significant irres-olution, the last one standing in the compartment. Since then he had experienced in countless variations that conflict between his own happi-ness and his sympathy for the suffering of others. He had finally left the newspaper where it was, and the terrible pictures of the children had been washed away by the noisy, wonderful hubbub of the station.

The pigeons had brought them together, the pigeons in St Mark's Square. As he stood there with his hands in his pockets, watching them land on the heads and shoulders of the tourists, he, too, had suddenly found himself in the middle of a cloud of flapping animals whose wings smacked along his face and just missed pulling off his glasses. He felt as if he were being ambushed, and he had flailed his arms excitedly around. He had only noticed Agnes, with her big camera in front of her face, when the pigeons had stopped bothering him. Her camera clicked a few more times, and then for the first time he saw her clear, water-bright gaze and her mocking smile, softer and lighter than Laura Sand's, because there was no background of rage.

She had come towards him in her light trousers and ankle-strap sandals. 'I hope you're not cross with me,' she had said, and, as on countless subse-quent occasions, he had been surprised by the darkness in her voice, which didn't match her transparent eyes. 'But it just looked so funny when you were defending yourself there. As if you were fighting a hailstorm or a typhoon. There was a story in the scene. I have to capture things like that. It's like an addiction. If you like, I'll send you a few prints.'

Before he had had a chance to answer she had laughed out loud and pointed to his hair. 'No, don't touch! It's full of pigeon poop!'

When she discovered that his hotel was at the other end of the city, she pulled him with her to the little *albergo* around the corner where she was staying. He had to kneel on a stool, and then, in the cracked and stained washbasin, she had washed his hair. Her gentle, practical manner broke all resistance. She couldn't explain to him why she had spoken to him in German, she said as she rubbed, something about him had just looked that way.

Back in the street she soon said goodbye to him. An appointment with a colleague from the newspaper. He had scribbled his address on a piece of paper, and then she had disappeared into the nearest alleyway. It had all been like a ghost story. He was glad that he hadn't written his newly acquired title of doctor on the paper. And he had no idea what he felt when he sat afterwards in a café in St Mark's Square, listening to music as he spent the little money he had on ridiculously expensive drinks, so that he was left with nothing to pay for dinner. Or rather he did. He knew one thing: he liked the way the episode with that woman had flashed into his life and cut into his present-poor time without either history or aftermath.

His train home left at noon the following day, and as he had only been there for three days he left the hotel early in the morning to see more of the little unspectacular canals and bridges. And then they met for a second time. Agnes was quite different from the day before, much more reserved, and at first he had the feeling that he was just bothering her. But then, looking again and again through her viewfinder, she had started talking about light and shade and the magic of black-and-white photography. He had felt like a blind man learning to see. Afterwards, over coffee that he paid for with the money he had set aside for a sandwich on the train, she wanted to know something about him. Linguist, he said, and before that he'd played the piano. Chopin. 'Yeeesss,' she had said with a nod, her eyes half-closed. And then, once again: 'Yeeesss.'

On the long journey his thoughts had kept returning to that 'Yeeesss'. Had it signified agreement? Agreement with him? Or had his information only confirmed her first impression, which might also have been negative? In all the years that followed he had never asked Agnes; he couldn't say why. That mysterious 'Yeeesss' had also kept him from discussing the business about the thalidomide children, which had suddenly leapt out at him from time to time during those days, when the moment seemed to be perfect.

Which of his fellow passengers had it been who had lent him *L'Espresso?* Perlmann immediately recognized Pier Paolo Pasolini's poem, which the chronicle republished; it was the one that had been in the magazine that day when he was travelling home: *When you fought the policemen yesterday in Valle Giulia / I sympathized with the police / Because the police are sons of the poor, they come from the outskirts, whether urban or rural.* And then he accused the students: *You have the faces of spoiled kids / . . . / You are fearful, insecure, desperate.* Perlmann had been preoccupied with that poem for a long time, because it struck him that there was something in it, and at the same time thinking something like that struck him as an act of disloyalty. He had avoided the countless teach-ins over the years that followed, and had instead, in the silent library reading room, pursued the question of how the peasants of Andalusia had worked out the idea of freedom and self-determination during the Civil War.

By the time Agnes's photographs had arrived, Venice was but a pale memory, and his excitement about the assistant's post kept him on tenterhooks. Never before had he seen such vivid pictures of himself. Or such funny ones. One, in which a girl with Asian features stuck her head at an angle into the picture, even had a certain slapstick quality. And what was incredible: in these black-and-white pictures St Mark's Square was drenched in a light more glowing than he had ever seen in color.

And yet he was startled to the core: the panic that had filled his eyes at his encounter with the pigeons revealed a profound fear of life. *There's a story in the scene*, she had said. He hoped the camera exaggerated. Or else that Agnes didn't see what he saw. Both were unlikely. Weeks passed. In the end she was the one who rang.

The chronicle was already an astonishing potpourri, Perlmann thought. Between an analysis of the way in which the Italian press reacted to the student revolt, and the report on the Soviet troops' invasion of Prague there was a gossipy article about Sophia Loren's latest affair, which was only slightly shorter. The photograph of the diva was in fact slightly bigger than the picture of tanks in Wenceslas Square. He would have liked to go on reading, but he was the last one in the restaurant and the proprietor was yawning as he cleared up. And tomorrow Perlmann wanted to get a good bit further with Leskov's paper.

By now it was a familiar experience, walking across the deserted Piazza Veneto to the hotel. He wondered whether Leskov was really giving an accurate account of the matter of the self-image. His examples, he now noticed, were always about someone making a decision or at least performing a pointed action that was preceded by a process of reflection: a proclamation was signed; the military doctor was duped; a marriage concluded against the will of the parents. That in such cases there was a remembered self with complicated contours that could only be articulated linguistically was clear. But what about when he remembered the pigeons that had besieged him? Agnes might have been right that there was a story to be told about him. But he, the one who was remembering, didn't know it, not even now. All there had been, it seemed to him, was panic and sweat and flapping feathers. And if he read a self-image into that frantic confusion, then that picture consisted of contours of feeling and nothing else. Everything else was impenetrable; that was part of the specific nature of that panic, and also of its power.

A calmer example of his past self, which resisted narrative disclosure, was the very correctly dressed young man from those days who had been irritated by the spinsterish librarian in the reading room, because she had asked him why he wasn't over at the teach-in. And what about that wide-awake moment when his joyful excitement about Venice and his horror at the thalidomide children had collided? Perhaps, he thought, these things would become clearer in Leskov's work if he now exposed what he had skimmed through in an impatient first reading to the precise attention of a translator.

Someone had rung from Germany an hour ago, said Giovanni. As far as he had understood, it had been Perlmann's daughter.

Perlmann immediately called Kirsten.

'You were away for a long time,' she said. 'Do you often go out with your group?'

She was nervous about her presentation. Only one more week. She was desperate about Faulkner's remark that the relationship between the two stories was one of musical counterpoint. From one day to the next she found the various theories about the unity of the whole more and more incomprehensible. She wondered whether, contrary to most interpreters, she should claim that the unity didn't exist at all. Or, at best, only in Faulkner's mind. She didn't have time to write out a whole paper, she would have to make do with detailed notes.

'What do you do if you have a blackout and suddenly don't know what to say?'

'You won't have one,' said Perlmann, and heard how disappointed she was by his silly answer.

12

Wednesday was a radiant late autumn day with a horizon that dissolved into a dreamlike haze. When Perlmann got up from his desk and looked down at the terrace he saw Millar and Ruge, who had sat down to one side at a table full of books and papers preparing the next two sessions. Once he stepped to the window just as John Smith was approaching them with an affable gesture. Millar's reaction was plainly so unfriendly that Smith immediately turned on his heels and trotted over to the pool.

The translation was coming on nicely, and Perlmann was becoming practiced at quickly retreating behind his fortress of dictionaries after looking out of the window. He would have liked to walk over to the window less often; but there wasn't much to be done. When he had finished a paragraph, he picked up the Russian-Italian dictionary as a reward and translated some of Leskov's easier sentences into Italian. Then he imagined sitting in a circular room whose walls were filled to the top with dictionaries. He would walk along these walls and translate more and more new sentences into more and more new languages. There was no reason ever to leave this room, because this was the place where he found his actual will. Here, after more than three decades, he could roll back the misunderstanding that he had become aware of back then in the Auditorium Maximum, without recognizing it or being able to keep it from unfolding.

At noon he went to see Maria in the office and asked her the Italian word for *self-image*. To explain to her that he didn't mean *autoritratto*, *self-portrait*, he sketched out something of Leskov's train of thought.

She was immediately gripped by the subject and kept asking him questions until he had given her an outline of the whole text.

'So *that's* what they're talking about on the veranda!' she said at last, and choked on her smoke. 'I wish I could listen in!'

He hastily turned towards her screen and asked straight away if that way of writing wasn't tiring on the eyes after a while.

Now came the four sentences in Leskov's text that had hitherto been a complete puzzle to him. With the help of the new dictionary they were soon translated. But it was a long time before Perlmann had worked out the concise and awkwardly phrased argument for the necessary linguistic nature of self-images.

Seeing a past action as meaningful meant attributing reasons for it to one's past self. But reasons related to one another as only sentences can. Hence the differentiation of the self-image that bore the memory was possible only through language.

It was a strikingly simple thought, and at first sight it seemed telling. But when Perlmann lay down on his bed to rest, his doubts began to accumulate. Was it true that one considered oneself in the light of one's reasons when one looked back? And what did the internal wrangling which – at least for him – tended to precede an important action, have to do with logical relationships between sentences? Not to mention all the ambiguities and dichotomies that ran through the emotional life, and which one sometimes remembered very clearly. Again he saw himself standing in the empty train compartment, looking at the thalidomide children and then stepping on to the platform, into the echoing voice of the loudspeaker and the unfamiliar smells.

Suddenly, Leskov's train of thought seemed to collapse like a house of cards, and when he began translating again he felt sobriety, almost reluctance. But that passed quickly when he managed some elegant English sentences, and in the course of that afternoon he understood that apart from joy in the sensuality of language there was also something else that drew him irresistibly to translation: one could think without having to believe anything, and one could speak, without having to assert anything. One could deal with language, without having to be concerned about the truth. *For a man with no opinions, like myself, translator or interpreter would have been the ideal profession. The ideal disguise.*

When Perlmann next looked down at Millar and Ruge, von Levetzov was sitting at the table as well. There was a hurricane lamp between the papers, and the waiter was arranging the cable of the standard lamp, which he must just have put there. From time to time, Millar rubbed his bare forearms, before starting to speak again, making energetic gestures. Now Ruge shook his head, picked up a sheet of paper and held it up in front of Millar's nose with two fingers like a search warrant, as the American went on speaking.

At that moment Perlmann knew that he would never, never again, want to take part in a debate. He didn't want to be attacked ever again, and never again did he want to have to defend an opinion that was no more his own than was any other opinion.

Now he couldn't find his way into Leskov's text. The words he had written out over the last hour seemed to be extinguished within his head, and his vocabulary book struck him as the symbol of eternal homework which one would never finish, however long one lived. When he got a Cyrillic letter wrong twice in a row, he realized that he had had enough. He had thought he was on his way to see Maria to ask her about the lovely old fountain that he had stood by for a long time in Genoa two days previously, before he discovered the bookshop in the next street.

But then he found himself in the corridor at the end of which was Evelyn Mistral's room and, after a brief hesitation, he knocked.

She had really organized her room. While up in his own, his unpacked suitcase and the plastic bag of dirty laundry stood under bare walls and his coat lay on his unused bed, here everything was tidy and inhabitable. She had put her second bedside table next to the desk as a storage space, and although there were stacks of paper and books lying around all over the place, it didn't look chaotic. On the walls there were two posters of Rome and Florence and a row of photographs. Push pins weren't permitted, she laughed, but Signora Morelli had allowed her to use them. She stood for a remarkably long time in the corner by the window, and when he looked towards the photograph behind her head she became embarrassed and held her hand over it. It was a picture of her dog Totó.

'And he's been dead for a year,' she said. 'Crazy, isn't it?'

Perlmann sat down at the antique table with the ornate legs, and looked at her across the bunch of flowers. If she had – that night in that huge kitchen in Salamanca – understood her father's problem, then she could understand his misery now; in spite of the silver glasses that lay on an open book on the desk in the beam of light from the lamp. He smiled, and when he then took a deep breath, it was like a long run-up to something risky.

'I recently told you about Juan, my brother,' she said and got up to fetch a letter from her bedside table. 'Now the lunatic writes that he's giving up his studies and going into films. He wants to be a cameraman! He hasn't a hint of training in that direction.' She narrowed her eyes and held the paper far away from herself. 'And then this remark here: "And even if I can only carry the cables for the first few months . . ." *Dios mío*, he's so brilliant, he could have studied law standing on his head!'

'I envy him,' Perlmann heard himself saying, and then again: 'I envy him a lot.'

Puzzled, she folded up the letter. 'That sounds as if you want to run away on the spot.'

Did he see in her smile a willingness to sympathize with such a wish? Or did her reaction to Juan's letter reveal fixed boundaries of understanding? The red elephant on the suitcase: what did it represent?

'Oh, no,' he said, and straightened a flower. 'It's just . . . sometimes I think we don't try nearly enough things out before we settle on one. Out of fear, probably. A fear that can become a prison. Juan doesn't seem like the fearful type.'

'No,' she laughed, 'quite the opposite: sometimes I think he has the soul of a gambler. Then I worry for him, and get annoyed about his irrationality. But basically, I think I love him for it.' She looked at her watch and disappeared into the bathroom to change for dinner.

They were already in the corridor when she stopped and looked at him thoughtfully. 'You are joining us for dinner?'

He hesitated and looked at her uncertainly.

'It would be better,' she said quietly. Then she took him by the waist for a brief moment and pushed him slightly. 'Come *on*,' she laughed, trying to parody Millar's pronunciation, in which an *o* sounded like an *a*.

Her touch a moment ago, he felt, protected him as they entered the dining room, and that protection continued until the waiter cleared away the plates from the starters. Then Millar abruptly turned aside from Laura Sand and looked at him.

'I'm slowly coming to think you would prefer to forget our appointment about your question. Or am I mistaken?'

'Yes, you are,' Perlmann replied, and was glad that he didn't need to say anything further. His reply had sounded firm, and it had even contained a challenge. But it didn't correspond to anything inside him. Inside there was suddenly nothing but a vulnerable void, and it didn't help at all that Evelyn Mistral was sitting next to him.

'Oh, I see,' said Millar, stretching the last syllable out until it sounded grotesque.

It was this melodious sarcasm that tipped the balance. Perlmann felt himself getting hot, and he was fleetingly brushed by a warning sensation, and then the attack that seemed to come from nowhere started moving relentlessly within him.

'By the way, Brian,' he began, and tilted his head involuntarily to the side, 'I was reading a newspaper article about that fellow Chessman, who was gassed in your country in 1960. He was on death row for twelve years. The execution was postponed eight times, always a few hours before the appointed day. I'm sure you know about that?'

Millar wiped his mouth so slowly that the movement looked affected. Laura Sand gave Perlmann a penetrating look.

'Now, Phil,' Millar said at last, 'I was eight years old at the time.'

'But Americans know about these things, don't they?'

'So what?' Millar's voice had become very quiet.

'What? You mean . . .' Giorgio Silvestri joined in.

'No. *Of course* not,' Millar interrupted irritably, 'all that toing and froing was impossible.'

For a moment silence fell around the table; the voices of the few other guests and the muted clatter from the kitchen could be heard. Silvestri twirled a Gauloise between his fingers as if he had just rolled it. He looked at Millar with a dark gleam in his eyes.

'But basically you think it's all right for people to be gassed? Or strapped into the electric chair?'

Millar's cheeks suddenly looked hollow, and it was as if he had blanched under his tan.

'I have no definitive view on the death penalty. But there are points in its favor. And rhetorical tricks won't help you at all.'

Silvestri violently pushed his chair back and had already half-risen to his feet when he calmed himself, picked up his cigarette from the floor and pretended to be examining a wobbly chair leg. There could have been an explosion between the two men at any moment, and the others all seemed to start breathing again when the waiter came in with the main course.

'It's the impersonal, bureaucratic aspect of an execution that makes my blood boil,' Laura Sand said a moment later. 'Quite apart from the terrible details of the killing. I always have the same picture in front of my eyes: two uniformed men with doughy official faces dragging this person, who has done nothing to them, along the corridor and strapping him in. When I see the stupid rectitude of their bootsteps, I always think I'd be capable of shooting at those uniforms,' she said and clenched her fists.

'The state has a monopoly on violence,' von Levetzov broke in.

'Exactly,' said Perlmann, 'that's exactly why you mustn't give it that power.'

'I'm not trying to defend it,' von Levetzov reassured him.

'Anyone who thinks the death penalty worthy of consideration is suffering from an incurable disease: a lack of imagination,' said Silvestri, who had regained control of himself and avoided Millar's eye.

Evelyn Mistral rested her hand on his arm. 'That's what we always said at home, too. Our example was the garrotte, which we had right through to the end of Franco.'

'You probably think you're the only person with an imagination,' Millar said to Silvestri. 'I think that's presumptuous.'

'I feel much the same as Laura,' said Ruge, 'but we must be honest: there was also Höss.'

'And Eichmann,' added von Levetzov.

Perlmann had thought much the same, sitting in the trattoria, and he had felt uncomfortable not knowing what to think about it. Now, when he saw Millar nodding, something within him made up its mind.

'The victims should have gone to Buenos Aires,' he heard himself saying, 'rather than the secret service. And once they got there they should have shot him down. And the same with Höss.'

Millar curled his lips and looked at him. 'I wouldn't have thought, Phil, that you were in favor of lynch law.'

Perlmann felt as if he were stumbling. 'Killing must be based on a personal relationship,' he said quietly, stirring his coffee. 'A hatred for one's tormentor, for example. Otherwise it's perverse.'

In spite of the sleeping pill, Perlmann woke up twice that night and lay awake for a long time. He thought of the vulnerable void that had spread within him after Millar's remark, and the inner violence that had suddenly blazed through that void. He kept thinking about those two things, and no longer understood himself.

It was nearly morning when he found himself back in that circular room full of dictionaries. A calm, milky light fell through the conical glass roof. The room didn't have a door. It didn't need a door. It was silent. It was unreachable, untouchable. It was wonderful. Then the room began turning around him, and with him at the same time. The revolutions became increasingly swift, the bright spines of the books became colorful smears that grew paler and paler until they merged into a paper-thin wall of the palest grey, which only survived for a short time before collapsing under the merciless glow of noon and revealed the view of the bay, which was full of shouting children. He was high above the bay, but that didn't matter, he would just step out into the light, everything was very easy and full of hope, and it was quite incomprehensible why his head should have collided with a diamond-hard, invisible wall. It allowed itself to be touched, that strange wall, but then again it didn't, because the touched resistance could not be distinguished from an unresisting void. He feverishly tried to find a door, but the wall with its unyielding void mercilessly made his damp hands slip, so that he sank to the floor and suddenly felt his pillow growing damp from his tear-wet face.

13

For the two days after that Perlmann tried to be as unnoticeable as possible during the sessions on the veranda. Even though it had been a long time since he had looked at grammatical theory, he was still familiar with the difficulties of the individual proposals, and twice he managed to express objections that surprised and impressed the others, so that even Millar raised his eyebrows and nodded grudgingly. After that, on each occasion he could slip back into the background.

While listening, he had an experience which, he now became aware, had accompanied him for a long time, but which he had never been able to imagine so clearly before: every time a new title was mentioned, or a label for yet another theory, he gave a start, and the complicated Latinate word seemed like an instrument of torture, because his first thought was always: *I don't know and I should know.* But then, when they talked about the theory, he realized time and again that he knew it down to its smallest details. In fact, he knew it at the very moment of horror, one might almost say that this knowledge was part of his horror, and gave it its peculiar coloring. Except that the knowledge had no power of any kind over the horror. And over the years, he thought, the horror at a supposed gap in his knowledge had become a horror at the powerlessness of knowledge. Knowledge was like a wheel rotating at an overheated rate, without moving anything in his soul and without being able to protect him against the iron logic of its experience. Perlmann thought of the sentences of hopelessness that Jakob von Gunten had written down.

After the sessions he slept into the afternoon and then sat down to Leskov's paper. By now he had worked out in English Leskov's theoretical vocabulary. There were some repetitions, and the more abstract passages went relatively smoothly. The only difficult parts were, time and again, the examples with all their sensory details and nuances. Even now he sometimes found himself at a complete loss with them, and in some cases the English text, black with corrections, remained hopelessly wooden and clumsy.

One particularly hard nut to crack lay in the many examples with which Leskov illustrated his argument that narrative memory was unscrupulous when it came to defending the moral integrity of the past self. He cited clinical material that had been assembled by two of the pupils of Luria, the famous Russian neuropsychologist. These consistently concerned people suffering from a moral trauma. The extent of the confabulation and reinterpretation of past actions took one's breath away, and even Leskov himself was plainly struck dumb by them, because he could hardly stop giving examples.

And then came a piece of text describing how some of these people, when their truthful memories were too oppressive to be straightened out, split internally and kept the transgressive self away from the unstained self that was a refined fabrication. Perlmann stayed up half the night polishing these examples. And as he did so he discovered that in his impatient first run-through he had skipped a whole paragraph explaining the idea of these internal separations with reference to the ramification of stories. Leskov, it was clear, was playing here with the many Russian words for the concepts of separation and splitting, and it made Perlmann furious that he simply had no feeling for the nuances and had in the end to level everything out into *splitting* and *fission*. For the first time he found the new dictionary disappointing. *Razdvoit'* was cognate with *dvoinik*, the word for a double or doppelgänger. But what exactly did that kinship mean? Then there was a missing sentence that would have given an example to confirm his suspicion that *razyedinyat'* referred to the separation of people, although that – but even here he wasn't entirely sure – wasn't right for the *severing* given in the dictionary. And it was particularly irritating that the dictionary gave him no help as to whether he could use the obvious word *cracking* without doing violence to the text. When he looked through the English version of this section on Friday before he went to the trattoria, he crossed out the names of Luria's pupils, and adapted the rest of the text accordingly. Who cared about those names anyway?

It was noisy in the trattoria that evening. Some sort of club that the landlord belonged to was celebrating its jubilee, and even Sandra had to help in the restaurant. She had kept the little corner table free for Perlmann, but soon he was joined by an old man with a pipe and a beret. 'Big fat book,' the old man said when Sandra brought Perlmann the chronicle. Then the old man's eyelids closed slowly, and he seemed to go to sleep over his beer.

Perlmann had been surprised when Agnes had suggested getting married on the anniversary of their first meeting in St Mark's Square, the day that she called *the day of the pigeons*. She normally rejected anything that carried a whiff of sentimentality. But he had liked it, and at the register office he had used all his powers of persuasion to make it possible.

Then, when they were waiting for the train to Paris that day, the headlines of the tabloids announced the death of Louis Armstrong, and now it seemed to him that the photograph used back then was exactly the same as the one in the chronicle. Agnes, who affectionately called him *Satchmo*, had been very quiet for a while after that, and when they got home to their first shared apartment, they had listened to the many jazz records that she owned. Their responses had been strangely contrasting: while he started liking these sounds, which had accompanied Agnes for a long time, to her they seemed suddenly alien. He could no longer remember the details, but at the end of their conversations on the subject they had decided to buy a used grand piano on instalments.

At the newspaper stands in Paris, too, Armstrong's death had been the predominant theme. At the corner next to the hotel, even today, there was a kiosk, as he had seen straight away when he had travelled to Paris in the last days of the previous August, because the start of the new school year with its noisy fervour in the playgrounds had thrown him into a panic. But today the kiosk looked quite different from before, when he had gone to fetch the paper every morning for ten days. And the hotel was barely recognizable, too. That had unsettled him. *As if the world's chief task were to serve as a stage for my memory.* He had trudged morosely through the hot streets and wondered what he was doing there in Paris. Everything was different from how he remembered it, and with every discovery of that kind his French got even worse, so that the waiters answered him in English or German. After the second night he had taken the early train home.

The pipe fell out of the old man with the beret's mouth as he slept. He started awake and downed his glass in one. He looked curiously at the picture of Charles Manson being led along a corridor by two prison wardens. His tired face contorted into a grin and then, with the edge of his hand he made the gesture of a throat being slit, accompanied by a click of his tongue.

Perlmann quickly flicked back to the previous year. The picture of a thalidomide child, and next to it a report on the suspension of the trial. Was the report bitterly ironic or not? His Italian wasn't good enough to tell.

The invasion by the Americans of neutral Cambodia and Laos. Perlmann flicked three years ahead: Nobel Prize for Henry Kissinger. That had been a month before Kirsten's birth, when Agnes was finally able to leave the hospital, still weak from the infection. No, Kirsten's leukemia had had nothing to do with that infection, the doctor had reassured them two years later. Frozen with fear, they had spent whole nights wondering whether they should take the risk of chemotherapy, which had only just been developed. For months their fear overshadowed everything else, and the news from the rest of the world bounced off it. Even the last American helicopter lifting off from Saigon left him cold.

Only the death of Dmitri Shostakovich got through to him. It had been incredible to see him come on to the stage in person after the twenty-four Preludes and Fugues, his homage to Bach, had faded away. A man with round, horn-rimmed glasses in his pinched, twitching face, who had on the one hand written this music and on the other been caught up in his love-hate relationship with Stalin. For the first time Hanna had been sitting next to Perlmann at a concert. Her bandaged, blistered hand, which had forced her to take a few days' break from playing, had been in her lap. He had very much liked her simple black dress.

The old man had simply got up and left, without paying. Perlmann paid for him, and there was a debate because the proprietor didn't want to take any money from him except for the beer, because of his extra tuition. 'See you next week!'

Today a crazed motorcyclist was driving around the deserted Piazza Veneto. The roar of the engine could be heard all the way to the hotel.

Giovanni handed Perlmann, along with the key, the four texts that Adrian von Levetzov had distributed for his session on Monday. It was almost 200 pages in all. Perlmann set them on his suitcase and then fetched the ladder to unscrew the lightbulbs in the corridor, which had all been put back in.

14

Waking from a few hours' troubled sleep, at dawn Perlmann sat down to Leskov's text. Now came the sections which were supposed to show that not only the interpretation, but also the experienced quality of remembered feeling depended upon narration. If narrative memory became both more extensive and more dense – this was the thesis – it could be that the coloring and shade of remembered experience changed dramatically. It was, Perlmann thought, clever of Leskov to operate even here with terms like *coloring* and *shade*, which actually belonged in the domain of the sense of sight. He was thus rhetorically preparing the later thought that where the suggestibility of qualities of experience was concerned, sensory impressions behaved no differently from emotions. But was his thesis, in fact, accurate where the emotions were concerned?

It all depended on the examples. During his first attempt, they had defeated him because his pocket dictionary contained only a small part of the vocabulary that Leskov was drawing upon. That problem was solved. But now he discovered once more how uncertain he was, deep down, with the English words. It wasn't crude uncertainty, based on simple gaps in his knowledge. He was familiar with all the English words. But it was as if, when he tried them out, he was on shaky ground that could slip away at any moment – it was a bit like walking on a thin layer of fresh snow over black ice.

That applied particularly to *coloring, shade, tint, tone* and *nuance*. What, for example, would the selection of words be like if it came to describing the colors of autumn leaves? And what about the political hue of a daily newspaper? If one were to slip at this point, Leskov's text could easily be messed up, and even made to look ridiculous. And it was much the same with the naming and description of emotions and moods. *Abandonment* wasn't the same as *loneliness*; *melancholy* and *grief* were not to be confused; *cheerfulness* and *serenity* – what about those? It was, he thought, difficult even in one's mother tongue to distinguish between purely rhetorical variants and tangible emotional differences. And the further removed the foreign language, the less certainty there was in the matter.

But in that case how could one know whether an example really was evidence for Leskov's thesis? And could one honestly expect this area of vocabulary to be clearly transferred from one language to the other? Or was it the case, in the end, that each language categorized the experienced inner world in a slightly different way? And did that support or contradict Leskov's thesis?

Perlmann was torn between the vexing uncertainty that hung over his translation, and the cheering feeling of just having developed a new thought. The hours flew by. Every now and again he walked to the window and looked out on to the bay, which was filled once again with the glowing autumn light, so different from the broken, pallid light that would now be falling on the trees outside his window at home.

Aside from the task of translating: what was the actual substance of Leskov's thesis? Would remembered anxiety really change if the story of Kirsten's leukemia had ended differently? Would not the terrified wait when the young doctor with the horn-rimmed glasses had picked up the final lab report be fixed in his mind forever, just like the thump of the clods of earth on his mother's coffin? And the unforgettable mixture of admiration and trepidation that Shostakovich's appearance had prompted? Were such things not simply part of a solid core of past experience, around which there grew stories that one might rewrite several times in the course of a life, leaving the center of experience itself unchanged?

Trembling with hunger and exhaustion, Perlmann went to the trattoria at about half-past two. The only thing that interested him in the chronicle was the day when his anxiety about Kirsten had come to an end. No other day had embedded itself in his memory with such diamond-hard precision. Not even the day of the pigeons. Agnes had touched his arm when the doctor, holding the lab report, gave them the liberating information. Then they had walked across half the town, showing each other the colors of the gleaming wet autumn leaves, over and over again. For the first time he had cancelled his teaching duties with a lie, and they had gone to Sylt for a week. Those were days full of presence, days of wind and expansiveness and relief.

The fact that the death of Jean Gabin had been in the paper at the time had escaped him. Now that he read the long article in the chronicle Perlmann remembered telling Agnes the story of the film *Le chat*, while they tromped gurglingly through the mudflats. For years, Gabin hadn't exchanged a word with Simone Signoret because she had killed his beloved cat out of jealousy. When they were sitting opposite one another by the fire in the evening, he would hand her a piece of paper that always bore the same words: *le chat*. She put these pieces of paper in a drawer, and one day, when she got clumsy, they all fell on the floor, hundreds of them. Agnes had thought the movie was monstrous, and Perlmann was ashamed, because Gabin's behavior in the film wasn't all that strange to him.

The first time since his arrival, Perlmann felt the need to leave after dinner, and near the hotel he found a small path leading into the hills. As he tapped rhythmically on the stone wall with a stick, he tried out Leskov's theory of the emotions, which he had recalled in the trattoria a short time before. But then he simply yielded to the pride that soon he would really have translated this long Russian text into English. He had another eighteen pages before the conclusion, and seven of those he had recently dealt with, even if there were still minor gaps involving the problem with the concept of appropriation. When the path turned and ran parallel to the slope, he supported himself on the wall and looked down at the town and the sea. *The translation will be ready by the middle of the week.* Then the neat stack of pages would lie on the otherwise empty glass plate of the desk. He had done something he wouldn't have thought himself capable of doing. He felt that he, whenever he thought about this moment, should also really have thought beyond it. But that didn't work. It didn't work.

In the middle of the week, half of his stay was over. And yet from a presentless time the mountain was just as high as it been at the beginning. And it was all much worse than it had been at the start, because the fear that ate like a silent acid into his pride as a translator – and hollowed it out so that it might collapse at any moment – made the mountain look like a gigantic wall that leaned towards him, with every heartbeat a tiny bit more.

'It's basically impossible to capture this light on film,' said Laura Sand, setting her big camera bag down on the wall next to him. 'It's as if a luminous depth is something quite different from the physical radiance to which the film reacts.'

Perlmann had given such a violent start that she rested her hand on his arm, startled, and apologized. It was always the same, she said. David, her husband, often jumped because she was so quiet.

'That's balanced by Sarah's noise! Especially with her bloody aerobics!'

They stayed together until dusk. She didn't really like people watching her take photographs, she said at one point. 'But since it's you . . .'

She taught him how to see. Like Agnes. And yet quite different. Agnes had always talked about light, form and shade, brightness and depth, planes and edges. Listening to her, one might have thought she saw the world as a deserted geometrical structure. And her actual theme was human movement. Not just any movement: moments that point beyond themselves, scenes that concealed a story within themselves and forced the viewer to invent that story. *Narrative photography* she had called it. *You understand: colors would only disturb us, distract us from the essential. It's important for the man on the platform to explode in his movements when he glimpses the woman on the running board. The color of his coat is irrelevant.*

She had had an incredible instinct for the density of moments. And her patience had been incredible, too, when she had waited hours and days for dense scenes, in pubs, at stations, at the beach, once even at a boxing match, which she loathed. When that wait even exceeded her patience, she had been tempted to start smoking again.

Laura Sand's thinking was quite different. She thought in colors and moods, and what she said about them in the course of the morning contrasted so blatantly with her love of black clothes that Perlmann came close several times to talking to her about it. She used only color words that he had never heard before, and when she noticed that he couldn't get over his astonishment, she laughed her throaty laugh and went on: '. . . *medium flesh, canary, rose madder lake, magenta, true blue, sap green, sanguine . . .*'

No, she wasn't interested in people – 'when I'm taking photographs, I mean'. At first, she had only taken landscape shots, and later, in connection with her job, animals had joined them. David had to take the holiday snaps.

'He thinks I'm a misanthrope,' she smiled. And after a pause she added: 'He knows me well. "That's why you leave the monkey talk to other people," he said again recently, "monkeys are far too much like people."'

Impressionist photography, she called her idea.

'Actually impossible. Physical events are far too dense. I've become an expert in filtering things out. My theory is, in fact,' she laughed, 'that it has much more to do with the gaps – the void – than the rest. David and Sarah have been teasing me about it for years, and at David's poker game my theory has turned into the monthly running joke: "So from now on let's build the houses with a load of void, it'll be cheaper." Oh, well. It's a weird theory anyway, and sometimes I don't even understand it myself.'

You wouldn't have to worry, Perlmann thought, about this one delivering the kind of remark that Agnes came out with at the airport that time. Standing on the moving walkway, he had turned round to look at a big poster for Hong Kong, a picture with soft, velvety contours, a dreamy picture. *Nice bit of kitsch*, Agnes had said, *a bit like the way you look at the world.* Then, probably startled by her own slipped-out observation, she had laughingly taken his arm and pressed her head against his shoulder. *Don't be cross*, she had said quietly as she felt how stiffly he was walking on. At passport control he hadn't, as he usually did, turned round again. On his return they both made more of an effort; she was particularly attentive, and talked more than normal. They didn't mention the remark. But for a while he was rather monosyllabic when she showed him her pictures. A thin fissure had remained between them, barely visible and yet never quite forgotten.

It was night by the time they entered the hotel. After Signora Morelli had given them their keys, Perlmann would have liked to voice his feeling that the past few hours had meant something to him. But the few steps to the elevator didn't give him enough time, and when Laura Sand looked quizzically at him, it was as if anything that might have developed into a suitable sentence had been extinguished. He raised his hand with the key, it jingled faintly, and then he went upstairs, alone, and was glad that no one had done anything to change the gloomy lighting of his corridor in the meantime.

It was pure nonsense, he thought under the shower: what was there to make her suspicious? He had asked her whether *severing* was an apt word for the splitting of a personality; then they had talked for a while about *cracking*; in the end she had, with a laugh, explained the Australian phrase *cracking hardy*. Then it had seemed for a moment as if she wanted to ask him the reason for his particular interest in these words, but he had managed to change the subject. No, it really couldn't be said that he had given himself away.

Lying on the bed, he thought again of Agnes and what was special about her photographs. Sometimes she had spent months taking pictures only of the faces of ancient people, it had been like an addiction. The series had been a hit. She had had an eye for details, a gaze, it seemed, that could give a detail a stressed and unusually intense presence – as if it were her gaze that had fetched that detail from the blurry distance of a shadowy, temporal existence into the brightly lit present of solidly outlined forms. How he had envied her that gift!

She had never planned for it, forgetting things, losing her overall vision in her chaotic jumble of notes. Then he was the one who had jumped in to straighten things out. As a result he had become a compulsive planner, a fanatic of the overall vision. That had been the price, the price for her present.

The dining room looked very different this evening. Most of the circular tables had been replaced by a festively decorated dining table, and garlands of colored paper hung from the garlands. It was a wedding dinner, served by two extra waitresses who had been hired specially, as Adrian von Levetzov was able to report.

'Hungry again?' Millar asked, looking at Perlmann with his head inclined and a resigned smile on his lips. Perlmann said nothing, and concentrated on the shellfish starter. The jokes being made at the big table were hard to make out; most of the wedding guests spoke a dialect that he didn't understand.

Now von Levetzov was telling everybody about a book about Henry Kissinger that had been discussed in the *Herald Tribune*.

'That war criminal,' Giorgio Silvestri said tightly. 'He urged Nixon to bomb Cambodia and Laos. They were neutral countries at the time. That man ought to be up before a court.' He looked challengingly across at Millar, who was dissecting his fish. 'Isn't that right, Brian?'

Millar slid his fish knife carefully under the spine, then used his fork to release the whole skeleton before setting it down on the edge of the plate. The corners of his mouth were twitching. He savored the moment. At last he took a sip of wine, dabbed his lips with his napkin and returned Silvestri's impatient gaze with a soft, warm smile that Perlmann had never seen on him before.

'Absolutely correct, Giorgio. That was exactly what I wrote in the college paper at the time. On the first page. After that my parents' check didn't come through for a while.' He narrowed his eyes. 'And it never really sorted itself out.'

It was incredible how quickly Silvestri's face reacted. Barely had there been a hint of surprise and bemusement than his tense and hostile expression collapsed to make way for a grin, which revealed as clearly as in words that he had underestimated Millar. He raised his glass to him. '*Scusi. Salute!*'

It took Perlmann much longer to deal with his surprise. *Millar as a spokesman for the student movement?* He glanced furtively across at Millar, who was now concentrating once more on his fish. Something within him began to move, as slow and creaking as a rusty cog. Perhaps, out of pure fear, Perlmann had got him wrong. Fear was a feeling that degraded other people into mere screens. He was about to declare him a sign of his altered perception, when that silly remark over dinner occurred to him, and he devoted himself once more to the task of removing the head of his fish. It was only when the waiter had cleared away the plates that his irritation had sufficiently faded.

'One question, Brian,' he began, and then set out his uncertainty about the various English words for *color* and *shade*. Once again Millar surprised him. He tried out the different words, some out loud and some again with mute movements of his lips. He was starting to enjoy himself, and when he took a sip of wine it looked as if he were tasting the words along with the wine.

Again Perlmann's feelings pulled and creaked. *Millar, the man from Rockefeller, the intellectual interpreter of Bach, as a sensual man. Sheila.* And then, as suddenly as if he had been struck by lightning, he was filled once more with hatred for this man Brian Millar, who was, by pleasurably weighing up nuances of meaning, contesting the activity on which he, Perlmann, had spent two weeks up in his room defending himself against the others, not least against Millar himself. *And like an idiot I myself have inspired him to do so. Because I thought I had to give him a sign. Solicitous idiot that I am.*

He thanked Millar in the hope of stopping him, but now Laura Sand smilingly reminded Perlmann of their afternoon conversation about other English words. Achim Ruge once again demonstrated his astonishing confidence in English, and all through dessert these things formed the topic of conversation.

'You need this for your paper on language and memory, don't you?' Millar asked at last.

Perlmann felt his hands turning cold. He didn't want to nod at any cost, and yet he nodded.

'I'm really looking forward to it,' Millar said, and through the swelling heat in his face Perlmann could see that he was saying it without suspicion or spite.

'One has the sense that you're working on it day and night. Well, in . . . wait . . . in two weeks we'll be able to read it.'

Before Perlmann followed the others into the drawing room, he went to the toilet and held his face in the water that he held in his cupped hands. *It's only another eleven days. By Thursday morning Maria will have to have the paper.*

'If I play again today, it will have become a ritual,' Millar was saying as Perlmann entered the lounge.

Von Levetzov and Evelyn Mistral clapped. Millar grinned, unbuttoned his blazer and sat down on the piano stool after a hint of a bow. He played preludes and fugues from *The Well-Tempered Clavier*.

For several minutes Perlmann sat there with his eyes closed and drove all his strength inwards to keep the panic from welling up in him like a fountain. *If I'm inside something I can write very quickly. I know that. And things like that don't change. I need a day to get into it. Or two. Then there will be nine days left. Seventy, eighty working hours. I can still do it.*

His spasm eased slightly, the music got through to him, and vaguely, as if from a long way away, there arrived the memory of Bela Szabo wiping the sweat from his face with his handkerchief. Perlmann reached for this hazy image as if for a life-saving instrument, and pulled it to him and stared at it until it became clearer and denser and gradually revealed a whole scene which, in its growing vividness, forced back the flickering fear.

While telling Perlmann the story in a hoarse voice, Szabo had sat doubled up, his elbows propped on his knees, his head in his hands. Shostakovich, who had been sent as a juror to the Bach competition in Leipzig, had spoken to him at the subsequent buffet. Szabo's composition wasn't bad, he had said, it was thoroughly pleasant, and even a bit more. *But not really a creative idea.*

While trucks thundered by outside the Conservatoire Szabo had repeated that sentence over and over again, and in the bitterness of his voice there had been the certainty that he would never be able to forget it. Perlmann had got up and, in spite of the heat, closed the window.

And that time in Leipzig Shostakovich had revealed himself as a complete coward, Szabo had said as he wiped his face with his handkerchief. When he was asked about an unsigned article in *Pravda*, in which Hindemith, Schoenberg and Stravinsky were branded as obscurantists and lackeys of imperialist capitalism, he had, albeit hesitantly, declared his agreement. He couldn't believe his ears, Szabo said, and then Perlmann had seen the blood pulsing in the purple vein of fury that had appeared in his pale, alabaster temple. That kind of cowardice, Szabo had squeezed out, was partly responsible for the bloody crushing of the Hungarian uprising, at the end of which his father had been put against the wall. For perhaps a whole minute Szabo had sat there with his fists clenched. Then he had looked at Perlmann with his watery grey eyes, which were not dissimilar to Achim Ruge's. *Why am I telling you all this?* Then, in English: *Let's get back to work!* When he hated the language.

This evening once again Bach's preludes and fugues had become invisible structures of crystalline architecture – *fine white lines behind the night.* That was the music that had so fascinated Shostakovich in Leipzig at the time that he reacted with his own cycle. Perlmann tried to hear the fugues of both composers side by side. Had he really liked the glass pearling and that special kind of fading that characterized Shostakovich's pieces at that concert? Or had it been Hanna with her bandaged hand who had transfigured everything?

'You looked as if you were very far away, on a different star,' Evelyn Mistral said as they went outside. 'Shall we have another walk tomorrow? Perhaps there'll be another wedding!' Perlmann nodded.

But not really a creative idea. As soon as he had closed the door behind him, Perlmann looked up the Russian term for a *creative idea* and then tried to formulate Shostakovich's whole remark in Russian. He wasn't sure whether the way the Russian words lined up obligingly side by side caught the fluid casualness of the German remark – *nicht wirklich ein Einfall.* And suddenly he felt as if he couldn't speak Russian at all. He stared at the words for a while to make sure that he really could read the Cyrillic script.

Had he himself ever had a truly creative idea? The moon shone into the room. He drew the curtains. Now the darkness was stifling. He opened the curtains again. *Nine days. Ten.* Panic seeped into his agonizing alertness. He went to the bathroom and took a whole sleeping pill.

15

He slept long into Sunday. The room-service waiter who brought him his late breakfast handed him a piece of paper that had been stuck on the door: *So, no 'wedding walk'? If you want to do anything in the afternoon, let me know! Evelyn.*

He liked her careful, forward-leaning handwriting with its rounded connecting lines, and when the waiter had closed the door behind him, he went to the telephone. In the middle of dialling he hung up. *Not with this head, and certainly not in such a jittery state.*

Now, in Leskov's paper, came the pages in which the memory of sensory experience was interpreted as analogous to the memory of emotions. The rich vocabulary for nuances of smell and taste, but also for qualities of sound, was like a thicket that one had to fight one's way through, one step at a time, and once again Perlmann became aware how many nooks there were in English into which he had never yet shone a light. Often he had to pick up his English-German dictionary to know what was being talked about, and a good two dozen points remained where he wrote down an English word without knowing what it meant. *Millar would know.* Then he felt like a machine arranging signs purely according to syntactical rules, without knowing anything about the correspondence of the meanings. That didn't only produce a sense of blindness and helplessness, but also kept him from really entering the slipstream of translation, which could have protected him against the panic that was – now that the numbness of night had faded – forcing its way ever more powerfully into his consciousness.

When he became aware that anxiety could spill over and drag him away at any moment, he stretched out his arm and reached for the Russian-Italian dictionary in the back corner of his desk, as if for an anchor. He was lucky, a series of the words he had failed to understand were made clear to him via this indirect route, and now he threw himself with all his might into the attempt to translate the next few paragraphs directly into Italian.

He deleted the first few lines that he had written right after an English paragraph, and took fresh sheets of paper for the Italian text. The prickly feeling that he always had when he jumped back and forth between two foreign languages slowly appeared. The passages that followed dealt with memories in color, and now he discovered how inexperienced he was in Italian when it came to unusual words for colors. Cheerfully excited, he picked up the red dictionary, in which he found many of the words that Laura Sand had explained to him the previous afternoon. He assembled an English-Italian list of these words, and was irritated that the Russian-Italian dictionary was too limited to fill in all the gaps.

When he looked in his suitcase for new writing paper, he came across the black moleskin notebook with his notes in it. *The only text of my own that I have with me.* In a mixture of curiosity and dread he sat down in the red armchair and began to read:

It cannot be stressed often enough: one grows into the world by repeating words parrot-fashion. These words don't come by themselves; we hear them as parts of judgments, mottos, sentences. For a long time these judgments behave in a similar fashion: we simply parrot them as well. Not unlike the refrain of a children's song. And one must almost describe it as a stroke of luck if one later manages to recognize these insistent, numbing sequences of words for what they are: blind habits.

MESTRE IS UGLY, says the father whenever the topic turns to Venice. VENICE IS A DREAM. MESTRE, ON THE OTHER HAND, IS UGLY. We hear the sentence over and over again; it comes with the regularity of a machine. It's sheer repetition, the click of an automatism, nothing else. And then one repeats the sentence. One has not checked it, not a trace of appropriation. All that's really happening is this: one repeats it; one says it again with increasing routine. That's all. One understands the sentence; it's a sentence in one's mother tongue. Nonetheless, it doesn't express anything that one could call a thought. It is a blindly understood, literally thoughtless sentence.

THE PO VALLEY IS BORING is another of these sentences, this time one from the mother. One says in future: 'If it's night when you're travelling through the Po Valley it doesn't matter; the Po Valley is boring anyway,' and so on. The sentence is no longer available. It's an internal fixed point, a constant, a load-bearer in the construction. It represents a set of points. It makes a track impassable. It obstructs a possibility. It steals a landscape from one, a piece of earth, because it directs one around this area and thus turns them into a white, blind patch on the map of experiences. How many of our familiar sentences behave like the sentences about Mestre and the Po Valley – without our noticing?

The memory of the bare hotel room with the high walls and the ancient fittings in the bathroom forced its way into his consciousness; a memory that Perlmann hadn't touched for years. Even today he wanted nothing to do with it. He turned the page, determined to chase away, by doing so, the distant echo of his former feelings.

And then he was baffled to see that the paper continued in English, with smaller letters and a thinner ballpoint nib. First there came sections in which the theme was picked up from the beginning and modified. The *parroted sentences* were now described as *frozen elements* which, in their treacherous inconspicuousness, kept experiences from being made, and, by being experienced, from changing anything. They had a hypnotic effect, he had noted, and then added that this applied not only to statements like the ones about Mestre and the Po Valley, but also to questions that came like a refrain in every conversation about the future: AND THEN? WHAT DO YOU WANT TO DO AFTER THAT? WHEN WILL YOU BE FINISHED? WHAT'S THE POINT OF ALL THIS?

Linguistic waste was what he had called everything that blocked experience like this, and robbed one of the chance of getting involved in anything new and surprising. *Linguistic waste*, Perlmann repeated to himself, and as he murmured the German word he was pulled into the slipstream of memory and saw himself lying on the bed in the bare room in Mestre, furious about all the linguistic waste that he had discovered far too late within himself, and also furious about himself because he had undertaken that senseless journey for a single sentence.

He had taken a night train to Milan, and then travelled through the Po Valley one grey morning in early October, even though it was a detour. He couldn't remember now what it had looked like. But he very clearly remembered the defiant feeling with which he had pressed his face against the train window so that his fellow-passengers asked several times what he was looking at that was so interesting.

In Mestre he had gone into a hotel opposite the station, where the bellboy had opened up the dance hall of a room. After a few hours of sleep he had gone trotting down insignificant streets in the breaking dawn, until he was completely drenched. Afterwards, in the bathtub, he had felt nothing but emptiness. It was grotesque and bordered on madness: the whole journey, this whole exercise, just to come to terms with that one sentence of his father's. As if he wanted to set up an example to stand in for all the other linguistic waste. Set up for whom? No one saw it; no one was aware of it. On the contrary: he would never be able to tell anyone. He would be laughed at or looked at as if he were out of his mind. Why, then? Would an indifferent shrug not have been much more effective? The worst thing was Agnes wasn't an internal companion. She thought his journey was madness and was furious about his fanaticism. Even the film on television, with his favorite actors, didn't help with his knowledge.

He called home later and was glad that Kirsten answered. Her voice awakened the absurd hope that he might be better understood by her, a sixteen year old.

'What are you actually doing in this . . . what's its name . . . Mestre?' she asked.

After a pause, filled fortunately with hisses and clicks, he asked her how one managed to live in the present.

'What? I can't hear you properly.'

He repeated the question, this time fully aware of how ridiculous it sounded.

'Dad, are you drunk?'

No, there was no need to call Mum, he said: she should just tell her that he had arrived safely.

He no longer had to prove the wrongness of the sentence to himself. It hadn't got in his way for ages. He was ready, without further ado, to imagine Mestre as a flourishing city, something like Kyoto in cherry blossom. He had already thought that at the station in Frankfurt, and for a moment he had considered turning round. But by now he felt it was a question of loss of face, and at the same time he had flinched at the thought that such a thing might suddenly be an issue between them.

Did he still have to prove it to his father? Or was the journey a weird way of working off his fury at mountains of linguistic waste? Standing in for all the sentences? Why was no one else furious about the stifling power of linguistic waste? He had looked round at the station and also in the train – as if you could tell such a thing by looking at someone.

Would he have taken this ludicrous journey if he hadn't had to assert himself against anyone with his lonely rage? Was it, in the end, a journey against Agnes more than anything else?

The question had pursued him when he had trudged across Mestre the following day. It was ridiculous, walking through a town – any town – and constantly asking oneself whether it was beautiful or ugly. *Absurd* didn't cover it, he had thought. And then he suddenly landed in the Piazza Erminio Ferretto, an elongated square with lots of cafés and a great crowd of people smoking and chatting as they enjoyed their holiday. He had liked it there in spite of all the people. He had liked it, Agnes or no Agnes. Then, not far from the square, he found the Galleria Matteotti, a small-town echo of the famous Galleria in Milan. He didn't know whether it was despair or self-irony, but he had paced it out, that insignificant passage, fifty-three comfortable paces it had been. He still remembered that.

In the afternoon, when he was standing outside the *albergo* in Venice where Agnes had washed his hair, it hurt again. The sun broke through when he sat down in that café where she had uttered her mysterious 'Yeeess'. The tourists were taking off their coats and jackets. It didn't keep him there. In the middle of giving his order he apologized to the waiter and walked quickly to the *vaporetto*, which took him to the station. In Mestre he paid the outrageous hotel bill and travelled direct to Milan, where he changed to the night train for Germany.

When he washed his worn-out, unshaven face in the train toilet just before Frankfurt, he was surprised to notice that he was pleased and contented to have made the journey.

'Mestre is beautiful,' he said when Agnes looked at him. 'You should see the Piazza Ferretto! And the Galleria!'

He said it ironically, but she didn't like that shade of irony. She sensed that it concealed an endured loneliness, and that that same loneliness gave him an unpleasant, reckless strength, a strength that could, because it was drenched in pain, drive him to a cruel act of revenge.

Perlmann showered for a long time, and then went on reading. The ballpoint nib changed again, and the handwriting became agitated, as if he had been in a hurry or irritated. *Language as an enemy of imagination.* He couldn't remember this at all. He read it like something written by a stranger, astonished, uncertain and also a bit proud plainly to have had more thoughts over the course of time than he would have imagined himself capable of.

Thinking in sentences – he read – always meant a diminution of possibilities. Not only in the simple sense that the actually thought sentence by both logic and attentiveness ruled out other sentences that could have been thought instead. It was more important that linguistic thought took its initial bearings from the repertoire of familiar, tried-and-tested sentences which expressed a familiar picture of things, which seemed in their familiarity to lack alternatives. This impression, that things could not be seen differently, was the natural enemy of the imagination as the ability to envisage everything quite differently. And now example followed example. At first Perlmann was only full of amazement at the diversity of examples; but insofar as the outlined alternatives to the really existing world became increasingly radical, he recognized the text more and more clearly as his own, because his hatred of empty conventions was expressed more and more flagrantly.

In the next paragraph came observations running in precisely the opposite direction. Sentences as a medium that drove the narrator to more and more new images that could come as a complete surprise to him. *Language and imagination*. Wasn't that Evelyn Mistral's theme, too? Or was it an illusion, prompted by the mere connection between the two words? Perlmann felt his thoughts crumbling, and that slipping sensation merged with a feeling of weakness that came from his empty stomach. He slipped into his jacket and was already in the corridor when he opened the door again and pushed the moleskine notebook under the bed cover. Then he walked a secret path to the trattoria.

Sandra had plainly kicked the duvet on to the floor, and she herself lay fully clothed on the bed, with one knee-sock pulled down to the ankle and her cheek pressed deep into the pillow. He absolutely had to check on her, her parents said as soon as he stepped inside the restaurant. They were more laconic than usual. He had only learned that she had a maths test the next day, and her mother's face revealed that there had been an argument that she now regretted.

Sandra's shining head hung over the edge of the bed and swung slightly with each breath she took. Perlmann looked at her twitching eyelids and the dangling hand with its cheap ring and chewed thumbnail. Once her calm breathing was interrupted by a faint groan. He walked over to the little desk that her father had made and picked up the exercise book that Sandra had set defiantly face down on it. The last two pages were full of furiously crossed-out calculations. He snapped the exercise book shut, and the landlady gave a start when she noticed her anxious expression bouncing off his closed face.

'I just thought . . .' she said faintly as she brought him the chronicle.

The chronicle listed nothing for the days of his senseless, lonely journey to Mestre. Perlmann flicked back: bloodbath in the Square of Heavenly Peace in Peking. He didn't read the column to the end. Against his true emotions, when he paid, and this time the proprietor didn't dare to protest, he managed a conciliatory smile. Then he walked through the unusually warm evening to the harbor and sat down right on the edge of the embankment on a rock, against which the light waves broke.

Thousands of people had been shot, and he had wasted three days of his life on a harmless, ridiculous sentence, that anyone else would have forgotten long ago. He had the feeling of making himself very small and paying for this loss of any sense of proportion by staring, completely motionless, at the fine strips of spume that broke twitching from the night. It was not until he started shivering that he took off his glasses and wiped away the blurring layer of salt.

It was that movement that made him aware that resistance had been stirring in him for some time against his incipient feeling of guilt. It had not been a completely random sentence that he had fought against, but a sentence, *my* sentence, that stood in for all the linguistic waste that could bind and stifle someone's experience. *Sentences as a source of unfreedom.* And the business about proportion, the sense of scale that had to be preserved – that wasn't right either. Not here at any rate. Perlmann would have liked to know where the error was if one thought that the broadening of one's perspective automatically produced the complete unimportance of all things in the forlorn limitedness. But the explanation didn't come. He just knew: it wasn't like that, even when expansion beyond the purely geographical encompass the magnitude of suffering.

With a movement of violent resolution he got up and as he walked slowly to the hotel, he silently battled his inner adversary, who was trying once again to make his sentence about Mestre ridiculous with bloody images from Peking. When the crooked pines of the hotel, the flags and lanterns came into view, he began to sense that if he admitted to that crazy journey, this also had to do with his struggle for self-assertion, which he was tirelessly fighting for over there at the hotel. And as he climbed the steps, that sense turned into a hot, palpitating defiance.

He had crossed the lobby and was on the first flight of stairs when he heard the voices of his colleagues coming from the dining room.

'We'll find out tomorrow!' Millar was saying, and this was followed by Adrian von Levetzov's laughter, accompanied by Evelyn Mistral's bright voice.

Perlmann involuntarily took a step towards the wall, took another two steps and disappeared out of eyeshot. After that he hurried on, and was out of breath by the time he turned into his corridor. The whole corridor was pitch-black; the two lightbulbs must have blown. As he felt around for the lock with his key he was startled at how insecure that harmless darkness made him. Afterwards he stood by the window with his heart thumping, and looked down at an elegant couple who, coming from the restaurant, moved towards the steps with a hint of a tango step, before hopping down, laughing, and disappearing in an Oldtimer with chauffeur.

It was a long time before he had recovered his comforting defiance. At last he took the black notebook out from under the cover and went on reading.

The next few paragraphs described how concise sentences, apparently drawn from a wide overview, could become a prison by cutting off contradictory feelings, and thus causing the internal world to shrink still further. The particularly treacherous thing about this, he noted, was that such sentences had the deceptive sound of superior insight, against which even the author of the sentences was hardly able to defend himself. I NEED A LOT OF ANONYMITY, was one of the examples, and another: I LIKE LISTENING BEST. And a little later: I HAVE DEVELOPED A DREAD OF PEOPLE.

Perlmann vaguely remembered: he had written those lines after a convivial evening with some of Agnes's friends. Because time had seemed too slow and sticky to him, he had talked far too much, not least about himself. Afterwards, in the dark, everything he had said had struck him as entirely wrong, and he had got to his feet again to become clear about his feelings.

He was glad that the next paragraph was about sentences which, rather than adding something, could point the way towards a freedom that had hitherto only been guessed at, by creating a new state within one's inner world, capturing it in words and thus keeping it from slipping away again. BEING ABLE TO SAY NO WITHOUT INNER EFFORT: THAT'S WHAT MATTERS. And a paragraph further on: THE OTHERS ARE REALLY OTHERS. OTHERS. EVEN THE ONES ONE LOVES.

The air that came streaming in when he opened the window suddenly seemed much less warm than before. Over in Sestri Levante a fire raged, looking quite large even from here. Distorted by individual gusts of wind that made the pines down on the terrace bob, the sirens of the fire department echoed across.

All these example sentences, which he had with one exception written down in German, so that they now effectively leapt out at him from the middle of the English text with the intrusive familiarity of the mother tongue – were they actually sentences that applied to him?

He felt as if his inner contours blurred when he tried to look them straight in the eye for an answer to this question, and it passed through his mind that that feeling was like the impression that one had of things when one swam towards them under water. Uncertainly, almost fearfully, he turned the page and found a few very carefully written pages about the connection between language and presence. In a first attempt he had outlined – in different variations – how linguistic expression could give experiences presence and depth by wresting things experienced from fleetingness. And to his surprise he found, placed in parentheses, a digression in which he compared the linguistic and photographic fixing of the present.

Perlmann was amazed at how stubborn and precise his thinking had been in this respect, and at the same time it hurt to feel how clearly he had had Agnes's photographs before his eyes as he wrote. He took off his glasses and rubbed the bridge of his nose.

The young Sicilian in the frayed army coat who had dropped his battered suitcase and coat on the platform, and the bride he was now whirling around in the air. Agnes had shot about twenty pictures of the scene. One was published, in which the young woman, battling dizziness, held her hand in front of her laughing face, which appeared over her husband's shoulder, half of her chin hidden by his raised coat collar. This photograph had earned Agnes a great deal of praise. But at home she had hung another one, which she thought was much better: it captured the swirl at exactly the moment when the spin, supported by flying hair, concealed both faces so that the viewer felt challenged to invent them. *That's what I thought!* Agnes laughed when he expressed his disappointment at the real, very peasant-like face of the bride and invented a different one.

And then that other picture: the gaunt Chinaman, with one hand on the saddle of his bicycle, bending down to his son and offering him his cheek to kiss. The child, a nipper with a baker's boy cap that came down over his ears, held his face up to him and pursed his lips while his eyes, half-covered by the brim of his cap, were caught by something entirely different that must have been somewhere in the direction of the photographer. Agnes had taken the picture in Shanghai, on the trip on which that fellow André Fischer from the agency had accompanied her, about whom she had been so expressively silent.

Perlmann's thoughts sluggishly returned to the present of the hotel room. The fire beyond the bay was now clearly under control. He tore open a new pack of cigarettes and read diametrically opposite views on the next page: the present as something essentially fleeting that could be artificially deep-frozen by linguistic description. This did not establish presence, but created the mere illusion of presence. Real presence, he had noted, arose out of the readiness to yield utterly to the fleetingness of experience. And then, emphasized by their insertion, two German lines that took him completely by surprise him once again: *presence: a perfume, a light, a smile, a relief, a successful sentence, a shimmer under olives.*

That in this way – experimenting with words, images and rhythm – he had occupied himself with his vain search for present, had escaped him entirely. For the duration of two cigarettes he tried in vain to summon up the scene in which these lines had been produced. Suddenly, he took a piece of paper and wrote: *sunk in white oblivion.* As he slowly stubbed out the cigarette until the rest of the tobacco was completely crumbled and the naked filter scoured along the glass of the ashtray, he stared at the words. Then he scrunched up the paper and threw it flatly into the waste-paper basket.

Another one-and-a-half pages; the rest of the notebook was empty pages from which, when he shook them, the wing of a dead fly fell on Leskov's text. A long paragraph and, finally, quite a short one. The long one, written with the same pen as the one before, set out an observation that moved Perlmann as if he were reading it for the very first time: experimenting with sentences was a way of finding out what experiences one really had. Because just having experiences, by experiencing something, did not mean that one had any idea what they were. *Speechlessness as blindness to experience*, he had written in German: *Sprachlosigkeit als Erlebnisblindheit.* Glum because it sounded bombastic, he read on and found an observation that struck him even more: it could happen that one went on thinking in the medium of old and outdated sentences and thus see oneself as someone who still had the old experiences, even though quite new experiences had in the meantime seeped into the old structure, and they would only be able to unfold their transforming power when they were also poured into new sentences.

While Perlmann was pursuing this thought, he suddenly realized the circumstances under which he had written the lines about present, perfume and smiling. It had been a winter evening, and the galleys of the second edition of his last book had been in the beam of light from his desk lamp. At first it had been the content of the text that he hadn't been able to deal with. Then that feeling of staleness had spread to everything else – to paper and print as a whole, to desk lamp, desk and bent backs. The questionable line had carried him out for a moment into a brighter, freer space, the comforting enclave of the imagination. His protest had gone no further than that. *Why not? Why didn't I get up and go?* Perlmann hesitated. He didn't know whether the question had arisen within him only now, or whether it, too, was part of the memory of that moment when the sharp beam of lamplight had seemed like torture.

He read the few sentences of the last paragraph with mounting dread, and all of a sudden his eyes seemed to hurt, so that he would ideally have liked to keep them from looking at the lined paper. *What separates me from my present is like a fine mist, an intangible veil, an invisible wall. They don't put up the slightest resistance. Nothing would shatter if I were to walk through it. Because there is actually nothing at all between me and the world. A single step would be enough. Why didn't I take it long ago?*

His eye still darting over the words, Perlmann started to close the notebook, and he could only catch the final question by tilting his head on one side. Then he stuffed the notebook back in his suitcase and pulled the strap unnecessarily tight.

When he got up, his eye fell on von Levetzov's texts, which were stacked up on the desk. Soon he would be thinking *another nine days* – he felt that extremely clearly, and his heart was already preparing to thump at a faster rate. He hastily reached for a cigarette and stifled the thought with a look of tight concentration at Leskov's text.

Almost another five pages, he saw quickly, dealt with remembered sense-impressions, before the conclusion about the appropriation of the past began. His notes had kept him from finishing today, and then he had wasted hours on his attempt with the Italian version. A twinge of guilt crept over him, but he resisted its burden by convincing himself it was all about the translation and not the fact that he had read nothing at all in preparation for tomorrow's session.

What he sought was something quite particular, while afterwards, waiting for the effect of the sleeping pill, he slipped into half-sleep. He would recognize it straight away; but this abstract impression of particularity was still not enough deliberately to push open the door to the right corridor of memory. Only once he had abandoned his strenuous efforts was it suddenly there: back then, on the first trip to Venice, he had not thought once about his father's sentence concerning Mestre. Amazed, he buried his face in the pillow and let himself slide towards oblivion. At the last moment he gave a start and propped himself up on his elbows, his hands clasped, both thumbs on the base of his nose. Again he struggled with the terrible images from Peking, which made it look like sheer scorn that someone could consider it important whether he had once thought of a particular sentence years before or whether he hadn't. And again that struggle ended in a defiance that became all the more violent the more opaque the problem appeared from the point of view of justification.

Exhausted, he let his head drop back into the pillow, and soon slipped into a dream which consisted only of him, sweating, as if at an exam, looking for the Chinese name of the big square in Peking. His futile search made him so furious that he repeatedly wrote down the spookily intangible word so many times in a squared exercise book until it turned into sentences uttered by his parents, which, in an attempt to cross them through, he thickly underlined. At last he clapped the open exercise book face down on to the table, and was amazed that, although it was clearly Sandra's exercise book, it had a black wax cloth cover.

16

'Signor Perlmann!' Maria stopped him as he dashed through the hall at five past nine the next morning. 'I just wanted to ask when I can start writing out your text. It's like this, you see: now that her old typewriter has been fixed, Signora Sand is giving me nothing more to do, and Evelyn – I mean, Signorina Mistral – has her own computer. Giorgio isn't finished yet, so I thought I would ask you myself. I would have time to do it straight away, and I've been told that it's your turn in ten days from now. Signor Millar has some work for me, too, but, of course, you come first.'

Perlmann closed his eyes for a moment and brought up his other arm when he felt that the stack of von Levetzov's texts was threatening to slip out from under his arm.

'Not for fourteen days,' he said hoarsely. 'My session isn't for fourteen days.'

Maria straightened the yellow silk scarf at the neck of her glittering black pullover and looked at him uncertainly. Perlmann's heart was beating so violently that he had the impression she must be able to hear it.

'I would be happy to let Signor Millar go ahead of me,' he said at last with a smile that felt as alien on his face as he always imagined it must feel when he saw an air steward smiling on a plane.

'*Va bene*,' said Maria hesitantly. He heard no clattering heels on the marble floor when he turned into the corridor to the veranda. She would be watching after him thoughtfully.

Von Levetzov was just putting his watch back into his waistcoat pocket when Perlmann sat down. This man with the smooth, black hair and rimless spectacles, who was wearing a new tie yet again and looked more than ever like a senator out of a picture book, looked so right in the high, carved chair, as if the chair had been made specifically for him.

'We should tell you first of all,' he said, turning to Perlmann, 'that we have decided to have another meeting in the second half of this week. It suddenly struck us as nonsensical to waste the little time that we have. Laura will take over the block of Thursday and Friday; Evelyn will do the start of next week; and then you would be in ten days. In that way there would be a few wild-card days at the end, depending on when Giorgio can sort it out. Only, of course, if that's all right with you,' he added with an expression that betrayed not the slightest sign of suspicion.

Perlmann looked into the distance. Evelyn Mistral's feigned panic looked to him like tasteless clowning, and was at the same time as unreal as the scene on a transfer picture.

'It's OK,' he heard himself saying in a hollow voice.

'Fine,' said von Levetzov, and began to elucidate his texts.

My text has to be in the pigeonholes by Tuesday at the latest. I have to give Maria two days. Friday morning, then. I have to be ready by Thursday night. Only another four days, of which three half-days are down the drain because of the sessions. Which leaves only two-and-a-half days. And the nights. Once in the silence of a single night I wrote out half an essay. Once. A long time ago. Only when he caught the eyes of his colleagues did Perlmann notice that von Levetzov had clearly asked him a question.

'Yes,' he said into the blue, and saw straight away from Ruge's frown that that made no sense as an answer. Cheeks burning, he started flicking through the texts and waited until von Levetzov went on, saying, 'Well, then . . . ?'

For a long time – it might have been two hours – Perlmann didn't hear what was going on around him. He could find only a single way to resist the overwhelming panic. He began to work. Methodically, he began to draw up in his notebook a list of all the themes he had ever worked on. Then he took a new page for each heading and jotted down the associations grouped around it. He marked the relationships of the themes to one another with various kinds of arrows. A structure formed. He slowly grew calmer, and all that remained of his inner tension was a thumping headache. Wrapped up in a cocoon of forced and barely substantial confidence, he suddenly rose to his feet and, ignoring the sudden silence, left the room without looking at anyone.

She always carried aspirin with her, Maria said, and started rummaging in her handbag. When she found nothing, she ran both hands threw her gleaming lacquered hair, disturbing the quiff that had stood out above her forehead like the brim of a hat. Finally, she found the tablets under a pile of paper on the desk and offered Perlmann her glass of mineral water.

She would have his manuscript on Friday morning, he said, as he set the glass back down on the corner of the desk. The cold in his fingers couldn't just come from the glass, he thought, his left hand was cold as well. Could she have it ready by Monday evening?

How long was the text? she asked. The question disconcerted him, and for a moment he felt as if he was stumbling.

'It's just that everyone else's texts are so long,' she smiled apologetically, as the pause got longer and longer.

'Maybe fifty pages,' he said woodenly. Then he thanked her formally for the tablets and left the office.

For a moment he stepped up to the glass front door. The sky of the bay, which looked strangely boring, seemed this morning to be entirely colorless. *Disappear behind the rocky spur.* He didn't want to think it yet again, and forced himself to go back to the veranda.

This time there was no interruption. Laura Sand's alto voice with its smoky petulance flowed on. Perlmann sat down and looked at his notes. Words, nothing but individual words. How could he have thought, before, that this scribble could help him out of his fix? Let alone the fact that he was supposedly working on a text about the connection between language and memory.

Now the others leaned forwards as if in response to a command, and started flicking through von Levetzov's texts. So as not to draw attention to himself, he started flicking, too. But it didn't work: the pages were still charged from copying, and stuck together, so that a heavy clump moved as a whole. Perlmann tried in vain to pull the pages apart, and his thumb, his ugly thumb with the ridiculous grooves on the nail, became bigger and more ugly in front of his aching eyes, as if a merciless magnifying glass were being held over it. Beyond his swelling thumb he caught the amused and sardonic glances of the others, and what he didn't see of those glances he felt.

That he didn't hurl his clumps of paper at the heads of the others, or bang his forehead down on the table top, struck him later as a miracle. At the very last minute something intervened so that he – outwardly untouched – pulled one of the texts apart with a faint electrical crackle, and started making notes in the margin.

But that saving gentleness was only whitewash. At the next break in the discussion Perlmann took the floor, and what he now delivered into an awkward, leaden silence for almost half an hour was a vehement, ruthless denunciation of the whole area of linguistics that von Levetzov stood for – and not only von Levetzov.

After the first, hesitant sentences, during which he had to clear his throat several times, he spoke with a calm and a fluency that startled him, and which strengthened themselves from one moment to the next, so to speak, and the pauses during which he drew on a cigarette further underlined, he thought, the firmness of his conviction. As he spoke he didn't look at anyone, but kept his eye fixed on the reddish, gleaming wood of the conference table, after he had banished his reflection with a sheet of paper right at the beginning.

He had no idea where everything he was saying came from. He had never thought it out in the form of explicit, memorable thoughts, and yet it felt as familiar and natural as a conviction that one has carried around with oneself for half a lifetime. At that moment he was grimly determined to yield to the astonishing process that had got under way, as long as it continued, let the others react how they might. Once he almost lost the thread, because the thought came to him that this could be a rare moment of present – a present, certainly, that had the strange quality of coming to him not from outside, from the world, but rather of being produced from within, creating the impression that time as a whole was not something that made its independent progress outside him, but something internal, an aspect of himself which, according to the amount of freedom he granted it, unfolded into the world in a rich or a parsimonious form. This idea made Perlmann dizzy. He stammered and repeated himself, and only when he had furiously crushed all the marginal thoughts about time did he find his way back to the earlier flow of his speech.

After that he intervened in what he said only in a guiding sense, so that his criticism explicitly and with suicidal sharpness also referred to his own works. He wanted to soften what he sensed was the inevitable impression that he was launching a personal attack on von Levetzov. His words had long ceased to bear any internal connection with von Levetzov, but were directed against Brian Millar, although he did not mention his name a single time. As, staring blindly at the mahogany, he imagined Millar's face, his sentences became more and more strident, his choice of words more and more uncontrolled until it verged on vulgarity. On the edges of his field of vision the world began to blanch and to darken, so that he spoke his annihilating appraisals into a reddish, glowing tunnel from which, as if they were coming simultaneously from within and without, his father's sentence about Mestre and his own sentence about saying now came towards him. Dismayed, he felt things within himself falling into utter disarray, but there was no stopping, he talked and talked, slicing the air with his palm as though bringing down a butcher's axe, until the energy of desperate self-assertion finally gave way to a feeling of exhaustion.

For a while no one spoke. Voices could be heard from the lounge, and from outside came the stuttering of a boat engine that wouldn't quite start. From the corner of his eye Perlmann could uneasily see Laura Sand adding details to the figures in her notebook.

The first eye he caught was Silvestri's. He wore an expression of calm, sad alertness, an expression that he might have used with a confused or weeping patient, free of professional condescension, filled with an inward-turning shadow of solidarity, but also a gaze that concealed a will not to be disconcerted by anything he might encounter.

Perlmann would have liked to cling to that expression, but there were all the others: Achim Ruge, polishing his glasses with a corner of his wool jacket; Evelyn Mistral glancing shyly at him as she played awkwardly with the clasp of her white bracelet; Brian Millar, his arms folded particularly energetically and his head lowered, his eye focused on his fingertips as if he were inspecting his nails. And last of all Adrian von Levetzov, whom Perlmann looked at last, in the certainty that he had just made an enemy. Von Levetzov had taken off his glasses and let them dangle lightly in one hand as he rubbed his eyes with the thumb and index finger of the other. Perlmann had never seen him without his glasses, and was startled by the baggy eyelids that could now be seen. For a few fearful seconds in which hope and fear discolored one another, he waited for his reaction.

And then he was properly put to shame by Adrian von Levetzov, whose patriarchal elegance he had privately mocked and despised. He clumsily put his glasses back on and checked that they were on straight, by running two fingers along the curve of the ear pieces. Then, thoughtfully and gently, he pushed all the papers away from him, leaned right back into the chair and folded his hands over his head – a gesture that Perlmann had never seen him perform before and of which, even though he could not have explained it, he would not have thought him capable.

'Recently, at a conference in London,' he began and, after looking briefly at Perlmann, raised his eye beyond him, as if looking for someone at the pool, 'I went to the theater one evening to see *Macbeth* again. I was alone, and in a strange mood free of self-deception. I immersed myself fully in Shakespeare's wonderful language, and suddenly I had the feeling that there was nothing rewarding to be discovered about language that was not already contained within that experience of immersion. In the minutes leading up to the interval the thought of our profession had something tired, almost ludicrous about it, and I was quite ready to throw off my professional garb like a tired and worn-out skin. I think the two colleagues whom I met in the foyer found me rather strange at that moment. And then, all of a sudden, the whole thing had passed like a ghost, and afterwards in the pub I talked heatedly to my colleagues about a new publication in our field.'

He drew his glance back from the distance and smiled at Perlmann. 'Somehow your . . . outburst of a moment ago reminded me of that,' he said, speaking in German. 'Except: there's nothing I can do about it. I didn't invent our discipline, did I? And it isn't as uninteresting as all that, either; in spite of Shakespeare. Otherwise, I'm sure you wouldn't have called us all here. Would you?'

Perlmann lowered his eyes and gave his head a slight shake, without a clear intention and significance, turning it into an equally slight nod.

The awkward pause was ended by Ruge. 'I didn't know you had a weakness for poetry, Adrian,' he said with a grin, drawing imaginary circles on the table top.

'Neither did I,' Millar cut in, 'and I can't wait to hear about the exciting kind of linguistics that Phil is doubtless going to introduce us to next week.'

Von Levetzov slowly packed his things together, got up and then stopped by the table, his hands on the stack of books and paper. He kept his eye – a searching eye that seemed to spring from an inner circling – fixed on the parquet floor beyond the table's edge. His features, it seemed to Perlmann, had formed into an expression of self-reliance that he had never seen on this man's face before, even Evelyn Mistral gazed at him the way one gazes at someone who is forming a completely independent judgment about something.

'I don't know, Brian,' he said slowly, and the smile with which he now turned to Millar contrasted starkly with his usual solicitousness towards his admired American colleague, 'that may not be Philipp's concern. I could imagine that he's not interested in that at all.'

He darted Perlmann a fleeting glance and then walked to the door with an attitude that suggested he wasn't a part of the group any more.

Perlmann thought about von Levetzov's attitude and his last sentence all afternoon, over and over again. As he did so, he oscillated between the worrying sensation of having completely lost his balance, and the liberating feeling of someone who, by voicing a proscribed opinion with no regard for the consequences, has edged a step closer to himself.

Finally, now, he read all the texts he should already have known that morning. They interested him not in the slightest, those texts which, as always with von Levetzov, were composed with almost baroque care and attention. But he forced himself to read every line. He wanted to be prepared for tomorrow.

Hidden behind that thought, however, he was driven by the wish discreetly to thank the tall northerner – about whom he had plainly been completely mistaken – for his considered reaction. And also for addressing him in German. Recalling that moment now, it seemed to him had never before felt the intimacy of his mother tongue so forcefully and gratefully. From time to time he imagined von Levetzov's face without its glasses, looking strangely naked. *Opera. Always Mozart. Alcohol. An actress.*

Midway through his reading of the third text he suddenly got to his feet, slipped into his jacket and walked down to von Levetzov's room. He had no idea what the apology should sound like, and to gain time he put his ear to the door. Von Levetzov was on the phone, clearly to his secretary.

'Then we'll have to move the whole program,' he was saying. 'Let the contributors know that their times are changing accordingly. All right, so that's that. What about the application to the foundation? Aha . . . yes . . . good. And the galleys?'

Perlmann turned round and went back to his room. Again he called the end of the session to mind: von Levetzov's sentence, his attitude. And now this businesslike voice, the voice of a man merging with his subject. It didn't fit. Not at all.

He dragged himself to the middle of the fourth text, then broke off and went to the trattoria. Even as he parted the glass-bead curtain he sensed that it had been wrong to come here. He could only concentrate on the story of Sandra's test by concentrating very hard, and he immediately forgot it again. *There's still Tuesday, Wednesday and Thursday. One whole day and two half-days. And the nights.*

When the proprietor brought him the chronicle he waved it away at first, but then he took it after all and looked up the summer when he had been given his first professorship. Aldo Moro murdered. Sandro Pertini new president. Death of Pope Paul VI. Bored, he snapped the book shut.

What had been happening in the world back then didn't interest him. He was looking for something quite different, a memory that forced its way to the surface and kept exploding just before it got there. It had something to do with the grand piano and a question asked by five-year-old Kirsten.

Lost. I've lost. That was it: that was what he had thought back then when he set his professorial certificate down on the grand piano and tried to play with leaden fingers. Little Kirsten, clutching her teddy, had clearly been standing in the doorway for a long time before she asked why he was playing so many wrong notes.

Are you sad?

We're going to move, Kitty, to Berlin.

Isn't it nice there?

Yes, child.

So why are you sad?

Dad is sad, she told Agnes, who was breathlessly setting down the shopping bags. *Nonsense,* he said and showed her the letter with a smile. *The Berlin agency is bigger,* she laughed, and gave him a kiss.

When suddenly he hadn't been able to get to grips with the chronicle it was as if a safety net had been taken away. What still supported him was the translation of Leskov's text, he thought on the way back, and hurried to get to his room.

Another five pages on the daring thesis that narrative memory also creates the sensory content of the remembered. Perlmann struggled once again through the thicket of unusual words for sensory nuances, and after three hours he had an English version of the part that he had translated directly into Italian the previous day – with lots of mistakes, he now realized. Immediately after that came the zealous, awkward passage on

Proust. The last page and a half on this subject were easier again in terms of vocabulary; on the other hand, the concluding argument was so incomplete and bizarre that he kept checking whether it might be down to his translation. At last he came to the conclusion that Leskov had simply fudged matters – he had wanted to force through at all costs his exotic thesis of the past as an invention. He seemed to be truly in love with it.

Shortly after midnight Perlmann walked through the clear, cold, starry night to the Piazza Veneto to buy cigarettes. Next came the closing passage about appropriation: nine pages, seven of which he had largely finished, leaving aside the difficulties with the key concept. He wanted to get through it that night, so that he could finish the text in one go on Wednesday. At the same time he felt a suffocating sense of trepidation at the thought of having to set Leskov's text aside and move over entirely to the emptiness in his head. He tore open the packet as soon as it fell from the machine, and then discovered that he hadn't brought any matches. Shivering, he ran back to the hotel.

First of all he addressed himself to the last two pages, for which he still didn't have an English version. Here, in summary, Leskov discussed the creation of the individual past through narration. And again he fudged his way past an unambiguous position by jumping back and forth without comment between quite different words for *create*. He began with *sozdavat'*, then switched to *tvorit'* without explanation. The translation for both in the big dictionary was given as *creating*. The second word applied, judging by the example sentences, to the creation of something from nothing; it was used as if God's Creation were the topic under discussion. The former referred more to artistic or academic creation; creative activity, such as the creation of a character in a novel. A huge difference, Perlmann thought, about which Leskov wasted not a word. Or did it only seem that way to the beginner that he suddenly felt himself once again to be?

Then, all of a sudden, came *izobretat'*, which was given as *inventing*, *devising* and *designing* and thus dealt with inventions, but now in the sense of the creation of a new object – a machine, for example – out of entirely real materials. Cutting one's past to size by means of narration, and thus to a certain extent sculpting oneself as a character – there was a lot in it. But that was something quite different from the thought that one actually invented or even created oneself in remembering narration. But Leskov, Perlmann sensed through all his linguistic doubts, would really have liked to put forward the extreme thesis of invention, and once there was also the word *pridumat'*, which was translated as *thinking up* – as if, for example, one were thinking up an apology.

The last sentence of the text. In English it sounded less bombastic than it did in German, which had to do, above all, with the fact that *essence* had a lighter, more transparent sound than the whispering *Wesen* and – Perlmann supposed – the Russian *sushchnost'*. And that it was essential for language to make the experience of time more diverse – that was a claim that matched many things in his own notes.

Perlmann took his black wax cloth notebook out of his suitcase, and was annoyed to break a fingernail on the straps, which had been stupidly pulled too tight. He read once again what he himself had jotted down about the formulation of memories, and then the passages about language and present. At some points the parallel with Leskov's train of thought was startling. He put the notebook back in his suitcase and left the straps loose.

Outside there was dense fog now. The streetlights could only be seen as a diffuse blur of light, in which approaching billows of vapour disappeared. What on earth had made him defamiliarize his notes with another language? *Can one be afraid of stepping too close to oneself?* Or had another fear been at work: that articulacy in one's mother tongue – and only in it – could change experience, so that the old means of experience, which one must not lose, would suddenly disappear?

Anyway, in English he could read his observations as if someone else had written them, someone who was spiritually akin and yet different to him. He opened the window and felt the cool night air like damp cotton wool on his face. In foreign languages one could feel sheltered just as one did in fog. No attack presented in another language could ever hit him, could penetrate him so thoroughly as an attack in his mother tongue. And his own, most intimate sentences hit him less hard when they were packed in foreign words. Because he also had to protect himself against these sentences, paradoxically. Or was it, in the end, something quite different? Had he been seeking to intensify the intimacy by enjoying the open secret of being the author of these notes?

The preceding, already translated pages about the appropriation of the past remained unclear, however one might twist and turn them. Once again, Perlmann looked up the crucial words, slipped into the example sentences and experimented with every possible combination of translations. For a while, for *osvaivat'* he even considered *confer*, which only came up under *prisvaivat'*; it would be good to harmonize with Leskov's idea of invention. In the end he crossed out all but one of the many alternatives he had jotted down, and was discontent because a feeling of randomness remained.

The light grey of dusk seeped into the fog, and the halos of the streetlights assumed a dazzling white gleam. Perlmann carefully piled up the handwritten pages of the translation. Eighty-seven pages. He also arranged Leskov's text in order, and put it in the bottom laundry drawer. Then he wiped the dust from the table with his handkerchief and emptied the brimming ashtray. The translation was finished. His translation. It was finished. *A relief, a successful sentence.*

Shaking, he ordered coffee and had to clear his throat several times. He was shivering with the heating turned up when he poured coffee into himself later on. From time to time he picked up the translation and flicked through it for a few moments without reading. He wouldn't be able to show it to Agnes. He would never be able to show her anything ever again. At a quarter to nine he bathed his eyes, put von Levetzov's texts under his arm and went downstairs.

17

When the others stepped out on to the veranda and saw Perlmann sitting there already, they interrupted their conversations and, as soon as they sat down, fished busily among their papers. Perlmann just nodded to them briefly and turned the page.

'So, on we go with this strange discipline,' von Levetzov said cheerfully, and summed up the next text in a few sentences.

Perlmann was winning his battle against tiredness. It was a while before he had pulled what he had read the previous afternoon out from among his memories of the night; but then behind its tiredness his brain ran like a well-oiled mechanism, and he managed some contributions that largely determined the course of the session. Von Levetzov asked him several times to repeat his objection, and then took notes. Only Millar looked, while Perlmann was speaking, with ostentatious boredom through the window into the fog. Evelyn Mistral took off her glasses several times and listened to Perlmann with the expression of someone who is glad about someone else's recovery from an illness. Every time he noticed that, he ended his contribution sooner than planned.

'So, Perlmann, still working on your gay science?' von Levetzov joked as he left.

Perlmann went to sleep as soon as he had crept under the covers. Kitty, holding the bear lispingly, asked him only questions that he didn't know the answers to. The only thing he knew was that the grand piano wasn't where it had always been. It wasn't in Berlin either. There were only auditoriums there with masses of students, and when he came home and looked around the rooms for the grand piano, Agnes nodded incessantly and pulled open boxes of material for her own darkroom.

It was already dark when he woke up drenched in sweat. He would ideally have liked to stay in the shower for ever, and kept turning it back on so that the water ran over his face and distorted his view of the future. At last he sat in his dressing gown by the round table and let his eyes slide over the pages of the translation. He had forgotten that there was a whole series of gaps on the first thirty pages. He contentedly noted that the work on the later parts now made the open questions look quite simple. In the end he crossed out the marginal jotting *sensory content?* and made sure that it could no longer be deciphered.

Only the title was still missing. *Formirovanie* was *formation*. So: ON THE ROLE OF LANGUAGE IN THE FORMATION OF MEMORIES. Perlmann hesitated, looked up *Rolle* in his German-English Langenscheidt, and then replaced *role* with *part*. The whole thing sounded wooden, he thought, and also *formation* was actually too weak for the subject if one considered the radical theses of the texts. Had Leskov become frightened by his own courage? If one looked up *formation*, one found *formirovanie* and *obrazovanie* with the note (*creation*). Nonetheless, *creation* was unambiguously *sozdanie* or *tvorenie*; those were the words Leskov should have called upon here. The intricate, programmatic sentence that had caused too much trouble also included *sozdavat'*, after all. Perlmann sat there motionlessly for a while. Then he wrote in capital letters at the top edge: THE PERSONAL PAST AS LINGUISTIC CREATION. There was no room for his name.

To make further amends for yesterday, he set off for the dining room. Maria was still sitting in front of the screen in the office. When Perlmann saw her he stopped, teetered on his heels a few times and then went back up to his room. He irresolutely held the translation in his hands, half rolled it up and then opened it again. In the end he took it with him.

The others were now standing in the hall. He waved to them with the text and stepped into Maria's office.

'I thought you weren't going to give me the text until Friday morning,' said Maria.

'Erm . . . this is . . . this isn't actually it,' stammered Perlmann, feeling his face burning.

'Ah, so this is a different one,' she said. 'How industrious you all are!' She flicked through it and suddenly paused. 'There are a few lines in Italian here! Why did you cross them out?'

'It . . . it was a sort of experiment,' he said quickly with a dismissive gesture.

'When do you need the text by?' she asked as he turned to the door. 'Because of Signor Millar, I mean.'

'There's no rush.'

She fastened the text together with a big paperclip, and held it away from herself. 'Cute title,' she smiled. 'Where do you want your name? Over the title, under it, or only at the end of the text?'

'No name, please.' His *per favore* was out of place; not only was it superfluous, but it sounded suspicious to his ears. 'The text is just for me,' he added stiffly.

She rocked her head as if to say she didn't think it was a good reason. '*Va bene*. As you wish. We can always add it. And what about the other text?' she asked, when his hand was already on the door handle. 'Will I have it by Friday morning?'

'Yes,' he said, without looking at her.

'By the way, Phil,' said Millar as Perlmann dipped his spoon into the soup, 'about Maria: she said she'd have time to type something out for me by Thursday. But I thought it was a misunderstanding. She could hardly have typed your text in two days. And a moment ago I saw you bringing her your text. No problem. Jenny will just have to get down to it as soon as I'm back.'

The soup scalded Perlmann's tongue and throat. 'Erm . . . no, no, you can . . .' he began, and then closed his eyes until the peak of pain had passed. He coughed and wiped the water from his eyes. 'I mean . . . yes, thank you very much.'

Millar looked at him thoughtfully. 'You OK?' Perlmann nodded and had to rub his eyes again.

He was glad that every subsequent mouthful hurt. The pain was something that he could deal with while the others gossiped about a series of colleagues who had recently published something.

'I noticed again today how precisely you read,' von Levetzov suddenly said to him.

Perlmann let the ice cream melt on his tongue and swallowed it in small portions. He had been repelled by the way his mother, after his tonsil operation, had enjoyed playing the role of nurse.

'Yesterday it almost looked as if he hated the whole subject,' Ruge giggled, unashamedly licking the cream from his upper lip.

Perlmann thought of the cramped nursery with its floral wallpaper, and managed a vague smile.

'By the way, there really is another wedding in our church on Sunday,' said Evelyn Mistral when they were going upstairs together afterwards. 'This time I went in. An unusual space. Just chains of colored lights. There's something of the fairy tale about it. Shall we go on Sunday? Now you've finished your text?'

Perlmann said nothing.

'Oh, well, let's see,' she went on and touched his arm. 'You look as if you've been working solidly for the past few days. Get some sleep!'

She had already turned into her corridor when she suddenly came back. 'Maria printed out a copy of my text for you this afternoon. It's in your pigeonhole. Would you tell me what you think of it? Especially the thing we talked about in the café.'

'Yes . . . of course,' said Perlmann and turned round on the stairs.

Only now did he become aware that he hadn't looked in his pigeonhole for days. Giovanni handed him a big stack of things. Laura Sand's texts for Thursday were there as well, and two envelopes from Frau Hartwig.

'A lot to read!' grinned Giovanni, who had been flicking through a magazine. Perlmann walked in silence to the elevator.

As soon as he had set the papers down on his desk the telephone rang.

'Guess what – it worked!' said Kirsten. 'Admittedly, Lasker frowned at first and fiddled with his bow tie even more than usual. Luckily, Martin was there. But then when I plucked apart one after another of those theses of unity, the old man suddenly looked attentive and flicked through the text. I shifted into gear and got cheekier and cheekier. I even attacked the claim that elements of one story are echoed in the other. And at last, even though it wasn't in my notes, I went so far as to say that the romanticism in the two stories was very different. I stumbled a bit there. But in the end there was a lot of applause, and then Lasker said in that grouchy tone of his: "Quite clever, Fräulein Perlmann, quite clever." Incredible: *Fräulein* Perlmann! He's the only one in miles who could still get away with something like that. But the comment, I've learned in the meantime, was huge praise coming from him. Imagine, the great Lasker! Dad, I'm quite high!'

She was talking like a waterfall, and it was only towards the end that he remembered the presentation had been about Faulkner's *The Wild Palms*.

'Aren't you glad?' she asked, when he didn't reply.

'Yes, yes, of course I congratulate you on your success,' he said woodenly, and even before he had finished the sentence he found himself in a strange panic: for the first time in his life he couldn't find the right tone with his daughter.

'That sounded very formal,' she said uncertainly.

'It wasn't meant to be,' he replied and cursed his awkwardness.

She gave an audible jolt and found her way back to her cheerful tone. 'When will you be ready with your presentation? I mean your lecture?'

'The middle of next week.'

'When exactly?'

'Thursday.'

'How long do your sessions actually last?'

'Three or four hours.'

'God, that's twice as long as a seminar. And you have to talk all that time?'

'Well . . .' he said so quietly that she couldn't hear him.

'What did you say?'

'Nothing.'

'Dad?'

'Yes?'

'Is there anything wrong? You sound so far away.'

'Nothing. It's nothing, Kitty.'

'You haven't called me that in ages.'

Perlmann felt his face falling. 'Sleep well,' he said quickly and hung up. Then he buried his head in the pillow. Only after almost an hour did he get undressed and turn out the light.

Tomorrow. I'll have to do it tomorrow. The hours of the next day stretched out in his mind until he saw a long, silent expanse of time ahead of him, turning increasingly into a ramrod straight, wonderfully broad and empty road along which one travelled in shimmering heat towards the blurred outlines of an ochre horizon.

18

Shortly after six he woke with the certainty that he had to travel home straight away and convince himself that not everything he had written so far had been fraudulent. Without showering he slipped into his clothes, made sure that he had passport, money and the key to the apartment, and crept out of his room like a fugitive.

Giovanni had been dozing; now he looked at him like a ghost and misdialled twice before he got through to the taxi company. It was only when he was sitting in the back of the car that Perlmann noticed how exhausted he was. He stretched out against the back of the seat, and after a while he remembered the dream that had held him imperceptibly in its clutches. The most prominent and oppressive thing about it was the rubbing of his sweaty thumb on the little slate with the wooden frame – a movement that stuck to him like a physical stain. Again and again he wiped out his incorrect conversions from Réaumur to Fahrenheit and stared at the blackboard which, from the front row, he could almost have touched with his outstretched arm.

'Who hasn't got an answer?' yelled the man with the bulbous nose and the open-necked shirt. Perlmann kept his hand down and stopped breathing, while his heart beat deafeningly – until it suddenly stopped beating when the man's wrinkled arm entered his field of vision from behind and his short, knobby fingers reached for his empty slate.

Perlmann straightened and asked the driver for a cigarette. What the teacher had drilled into him with a smile of relish had been a proverb. But he couldn't call it to mind.

When he stepped into the airport departure lounge it was a quarter past seven. The first flight to Frankfurt left at a quarter to nine. He bought cigarettes and drank a coffee. Then, as he waited to buy a ticket, he suddenly felt vulnerable because he had nothing to read.

The plane rose into the bright sky, and if you half-closed your eyes, that brilliance merged with the silver gleam of the wing. When the stewardess brought newspapers, Perlmann suddenly felt as if he had woken from the nightmare of the hotel and returned to the normal world. He greedily read the newspaper, and for a while – behind his reading, in a sense – he managed to pretend that it was all over and he was flying home for good. But as soon as the plane dipped into the blanket of clouds, which he noticed only now, this comforting illusion collapsed, and what remained was the thought that he was now wasting the whole last day that he could have spent writing, and that he was wasting it on a trip that couldn't have been more pointless.

The landscape that opened up below the clouds was covered with a blanket of snow. He hadn't expected that, and his first impulse was to want to stop the plane and turn round. He forgot to fasten his seat belt for landing, and was told off by a brusque stewardess. When the engines stopped with a whistle, he would have liked to stay in his seat, as if he had arrived at the tram terminus.

When he passed the shop with the books and magazines in the big hall, his eye fell on the name LESKOV. He gave a start like someone who is suddenly caught in bright spotlights while carrying out some forbidden operation in the dark. The cover was a detail of a painting showing the Palace Quay in St Petersburg, seen from the Peter and Paul Fortress, with the Neva in the foreground. They had stood at the spot chosen by the painter as the most favorable, he and Leskov, and it seemed to Perlmann as if it really must have been precisely the same place. It was there that Perlmann had, against his will, told Leskov about Agnes, while the cold almost took his breath away.

He excitedly opened the book and read the titles of the short stories. *He didn't say a word about this.* Then, holding the book irresolutely in his hand and making his first attempt to get over his surprise, Perlmann finally noticed: the author was, of course, Nikolai Leskov, whose work he had not yet read, but whom he knew as a famous name in Russian literature. Annoyed with himself, he set the book back down. *As if someone whose books are translated and sold here would have Vassily Leskov's material concerns!*

But he wasn't, in fact, annoyed about his thoughtlessness. What enraged him more and more with every step towards the exit was the excitement that he had felt at the sight of the name. As if he had somehow injured Vassily Leskov with his translation. Why had he felt as if he had been caught?

He stepped through the automatic sliding door, out into the bitterly cold air, and almost collided with the dean of his faculty.

'Herr Perlmann! I thought you were in the warm south! And instead here you are wearing your summer clothes in our premature cold snap, and shivering! Has something happened?'

'What could have happened?' Perlmann laughed irritably. 'I just have a small thing to attend to here. I'll be back down there this evening.'

'By the way, there are mutterings about you being invited to Princeton. Allow me to congratulate you. Some of that glory will rub off on the faculty, too!'

'I don't know anything about that,' said Perlmann, and the firmness in his voice gave him back some of his confidence. He shivered.

'You're shivering,' said the dean, 'so I won't keep you. After Christmas I'm sure you'll deliver a full report to the faculty – given that we let you go off in the middle of term. Not everyone looked kindly on that – understandably enough.'

Twice on the journey home the taxi stopped at the lights near a book-shop window. Each time Perlmann's eye was caught by Nikolai Leskov's book, and he boiled with rage as he discovered that he reacted to it as if to a wanted poster of himself. To the driver's annoyance he rolled down the window and deeply inhaled the cold air.

His letterbox was full of junk mail, his freezing apartment smelled musty and strange. For a moment he felt like an intruder who could not touch anything. Then he opened the balcony door and, in his light shoes, took two crunching steps in the snow.

He put on a thick pullover. He didn't turn on the radiators. He couldn't live here now.

He lay on his belly by the open chest and read his writings. He had last lain there on the floor like that as a boy and, through all his trepidation, he enjoyed the unfamiliar posture.

He was amazed at what he read. Boundlessly amazed. Not just by all the things he had once known, thought, discussed. Even his language surprised him, his style, which he liked for a moment and then didn't like at all, and which struck him as strangely alien. He didn't read any single text all the way through, but dug his way frantically through the mountain of his offprints, reading a beginning here, there a conclusion, and sometimes just a few sentences in the middle. What was he looking for? Why had he come here? But it was ludicrous to imagine that he would be able to find out in this way whether he had copied anything. And why that suspicion, which he had previously only felt in a dream? Everything was cited meticulously enough, the bibliographies filled many pages.

He hesitantly lit a cigarette and went into the kitchen to make some coffee. The bread in the bread bin was as hard as a rock. He took the coffee pot into the sitting room. From the sofa, he looked out into the driving snow. The white backdrop was so strange that it was impossible to think it coexisted in time with the bay in front of the hotel. He braced himself against the white wall outside and escaped to the hotel terrace, the crooked pines, the red armchair by the window, the strip of lights at Sestri Levante. But over these images there lay a murky film of anxiety and trepidation, so he cleansed them of everything until they made way for a world full of silent, southern light, in which there was only Evelyn Mistral's radiant laughter, Silvestri's slender white hand with its cigarette, Ruge's cheerful face and Millar's firm handshake. And countless colors, with countless names of colors.

The ring of the telephone made him start. He knocked the coffee pot over with his arm, and watched as if paralyzed as the brown liquid seeped into the pale carpet. After a pause the telephone rang again. It rang for a very long time. He counted, for no reason. On the fourteenth ring he suddenly leapt to his feet. When he picked up the receiver, the line was already dead.

He slowly brought the pot and the cup to the kitchen and rinsed them out. It was just before three. The plane didn't leave until six. He sat down on the edge of the piano stool and lifted the lid of the keyboard. No, it couldn't be the touch, and it didn't seem to be a trick of the pedal, either. How did Millar manage to make those sequences of notes achieve that strange simultaneity of experience? When he closed the lid, he saw the traces of his fingers in the dust and wiped them away.

On the windowsill by the desk there stood a photograph of Agnes, a serious picture, in which she rested her chin on her hand. He avoided her eye and got back to his feet. Something had come between them. She hadn't been ambitious in the conventional sense. Nonetheless, would she have understood what was happening to him down there? And would he have dared to confide in her what he knew about it?

He hesitantly walked across to her room, where it seemed even icier. He let his eye slide over her photographs. It was insane: of course he had always known that they were all black-and-white photographs. He wasn't blind, after all. But only now, it seemed to him, did it really become clear to him what that meant: there were no colors in them. None at all. No *ultramarine*, no *English red*, no *magenta* or *sanguine*.

I've remembered the names. His stomach hurt.

Now his eye fell on the two-volume German-Russian dictionary that Agnes had one day brought home triumphantly after a long search. He looked it up: *crib (homework, answer): spisyvat'. To plagiarize.* He quietly pulled the door, which had been open, shut behind him.

He glanced quickly into Kirsten's room. Only half of her furniture had been there since September. The rest was in Konstanz. She had taken her teddy with her, but not her giraffe. The day she moved out he had gone to the office early, and only come home late at night, after going to the cinema. It wasn't until the next day that he summoned the courage to open the door to her room.

*

Perlmann gave the taxi driver the address of his doctor. Without another prescription he wouldn't have enough sleeping pills. The practice was closed for a holiday, and the locum's receptionist was adamant: no, no prescription or consultation with the doctor, and he was doing house visits until the evening. Perlmann furiously asked the taxi driver to take him to the airport. As he stepped into the departure lounge all that remained of his fury was a feeling of impotence. *I can't possibly ask Silvestri.*

But Nikolai Leskov's short stories really hadn't the slightest thing to do with him, Perlmann said to himself over and over again as he waited by the cash register with the book in his hand. Nonetheless, when he reached the waiting room he immediately opened the book and started excitedly reading it as if it were a secret document. On the way to the plane he held the book in front of his nose and, once he was on board, sat down in the wrong seat at first.

Would the shapeless man in the shabby loden coat have been capable of writing such a book? That snuffling man with the fur cap, the pipe and the brown teeth? Perlmann compared the text with sentences from his translation, laboriously and without the slightest sense how one could answer such a question across the boundaries of literary genres. They were already far above the clouds when he finally managed to shake off this compulsive activity. No sooner had he snapped the book shut and stowed it in the pocket in front of him, than he had completely forgotten what the story was about.

'Not exciting enough?' the fattish man in the seat next to him, reading an cheap novelette, asked him cheerfully.

A last glow of light lay over the dark sea of clouds. Perlmann turned off the reading light and closed his eyes. Yes, that was it: Agnes had looked at him from the photograph as if she guessed his thoughts – even the ones that he himself didn't yet know. He tried to banish that gaze by conjuring up her living face, a laughing face, a face in the wind, bathed in flapping hair. But those memories had no endurance, and soon made way for images from the classroom, in which the man sat at his raised desk, always in the same open-necked shirt, and damply yelled the names of the pupils into the room. And all of a sudden there it was, the proverb: *Honesty is the best policy. Isn't that right, Perlmann?*

Perlmann asked the stewardess for a glass of water and ignored the curious gaze of his neighbor by closing his eyes again. Perhaps he would have got through his Latin and Greek tests even without that little notebook under his desk? But he wouldn't have dared. Because in point of fact he had never found foreign languages easy. There was no question of a particular talent. He wasn't like Luc Sonntag, who would see through the most intricate ablative constructions, even though he was always going around with girls. Perlmann was industrious, and thorough – so thorough that Agnes had often fled from the room because she was afraid of his particular kind of thoroughness. Then he had firmly dug his heels in still further and gone on swotting so that, at some distant point in the future, he could enjoy his new linguistic understanding.

He was good at that, he thought. It was perhaps the only thing he really was good at: with an unimaginable firmness of will, undertaking an effort with a distant goal in mind, for the sake of a future ability that would someday make him happy. He had mastered his renunciation, this deferral of happiness, in a thousand variations, and his gift of invention was inexhaustible when it came to thinking up more and more things that he had to learn in order to be equipped for his future present. And thus he had systematically, and with impeccable thoroughness, cheated himself of his present.

When the plane touched down he had the feeling that a seal was being put on something, even if he couldn't have said what. The fat man next to him turned down the corner of his page and put his book away. 'Bad as that?' he asked with a grin when he saw that Perlmann had deliberately left his book in the seat pocket.

White columns of smoke rose into the night sky from the industrial plants beside the airport. Perlmann trudged heavily across the tarmac towards the red building. When he took his passport from the official's hand the thought suddenly struck him: *I may not get out of here alive.* In the taxi he asked the driver to turn up the music. But from time to time the thought flickered up anyway. As he stepped into the hotel he was grateful for Signora Morelli's crisp '*Buona sera*', and tonight it didn't bother him that someone had once again fixed the lighting in his corridor.

He sat down, exhausted, on the bed and stared for several minutes at the stack of texts by Evelyn Mistral and Laura Sand, and the mail from Frau Hartwig. His exhaustion turned into indifference, and at last all that still interested him was his hunger. He showered quickly and then went down to eat. As quiet as someone who has given up on everything, he shovelled the food into him and answered questions with the mild friendliness of a convalescent.

Later he lay awake for a long time in the darkness without thinking anything. There was nothing left to calculate. He wouldn't have a text to give Maria on Friday. The tension was over. Everything was over. When the effect of the pill flooded through him, he gave up and dropped off.

19

Right from the start, Laura Sand's session went better than all the others. The veranda was in darkness and the projector cast film images on a screen that stood at a slightly crooked angle on a stand. There were quite long sequences of images, in which animals showed behavior that would be hard to see as anything other than symbolic. At short intervals, clouds of cigarette smoke passed through the beam of the projector. Laura Sand's voice was strangely soft, and sometimes that made her seem bashful, so that she threw in the occasional brash remark. There was nothing – that much was quite clear – that she loved as much as these animals. Often she showed a sequence several times to stress an observation or enlarge upon an explanation. But she also repeated sections in which the movements of the animals were simply comical. 'Again!' Ruge cried out at one such point, and to Perlmann's surprise Millar joined in, too: 'Yes! Where's the slow-motion button?'

Perlmann was glad to be able to sit in the dark. After the third aspirin that he put in his mouth with the most economical movements possible, and washed down with coffee, the headaches slowly faded, and he escaped into the wide Steppe landscapes that formed the background of many of the animal scenes. Often Laura Sand hadn't been able to resist the temptation, and had played expertly with the light, until the animals' bodies moved against the light like figures in a shadow play. And sometimes the camera escaped the research discipline, and crept over the empty landscape, which glimmered in boiling midday light. Then Perlmann managed to forget that in exactly a week he would be the one sitting up there at the front.

When the blinds went up and everyone rubbed their eyes in the murky light of a rainy day, it was already past twelve. A debate immediately broke out about the fundamental concepts with which Laura Sand tried to capture what she had observed. Perlmann got involved, too, and defended them even more resolutely than Evelyn Mistral. What he said contradicted everything that he usually claimed in publications, and more than once Millar raised his eyebrows in disbelief. Barely a quarter of Laura Sand's texts had been discussed when it was time for lunch.

'So you had a film show today!' laughed Maria when Perlmann ran into her outside the office. 'By the way, I explicitly told Signor Millar again that your text, as you told me, can wait. But then he didn't want me to type out his things anyway. I didn't understand why.' She smiled coquettishly and glanced at her reflection in the glass door. 'So first of all I went to the hairdresser, and then started on your text, which I some how like – if I may say that. I'll just interrupt it if you bring me the other, urgent text tomorrow. *Va bene?*' Perlmann nodded, and was glad when von Levetzov appeared and dragged him along into the dining room.

'Have you been able to take a look at my synopsis?' Evelyn Mistral asked him over dessert.

'Yes, I have,' Perlmann said, and scraped the last bit of pudding out of the bowl as he racked his brains as to how she had described her problem to him.

'So? You can just tell me if you think it's stupid,' she said with a forced smile.

'No, no, absolutely not. I think the idea of producing the connection through the concept of the ground is a good one.' Even before he had finished the sentence he realized that he was really talking about Leskov's argument, which was contained in those four recalcitrant sentences.

Evelyn Mistral's spoon circled aimlessly in the bowl. 'Oh, right, yes. That could be a thought,' she said at last, glancing at him bashfully.

'I . . . I'll sit down to it again this afternoon,' Perlmann said. 'Time is . . . time is a bit short.'

Something in his quiet voice made her sit up and listen. Her face relaxed. 'Fine,' she said and laid her hand on his arm for a moment.

Afterwards, in the room, Perlmann tried in vain to concentrate on Evelyn Mistral and Laura Sand's papers. He felt obliged to try. If he could have shown tomorrow that he had at least been working in that sense, it would have been some small protection against everything else that was now heading inexorably towards him. But faced with that writing he felt as he had done on his outward-bound flight: as if he were suddenly blind to meanings; the texts couldn't get through to him and flattened out before his eyes into pedantic ornaments.

Over the next few hours he walked slowly and aimlessly through the town. At the stationery shop where he had bought the chronicle the window display had been completely changed. Perlmann was annoyed that this made him lose his sense of equilibrium; but only several streets further on did he manage to shake the whole thing off.

Complete nonsense, he said to himself repeatedly as he became aware of something inside him stubbornly trying to make the chronicle responsible for the dilemma he was in. At the bar of a café, where he drank a coffee, the internal struggle finally stopped. The clouds had parted, the sun glittered in the puddles, and suddenly life seemed to gain pace and color. Perlmann held his face in the dusty beam of sunlight that fell through the narrow glass door. For a moment he felt a forbidden happiness like the one that comes from skipping school, and when the sun disappeared again he clung with all his might to that feeling, although it grew more and more hollow from one moment to the next, and made way for a dull and barely restrained anxiety which suited the gloomy light that now filled the bar again.

For the time being it was only Maria that he would have to say anything to. His colleagues' questions would only start on Monday, and the situation would only come to a definitive head on Wednesday. His anxiety was somewhat assuaged by this thought, and Perlmann continued his aimless walk through little side streets.

He got to the trattoria early. The proprietress brought him the chronicle and told him with delight that Sandra's drawings had been singled out for special praise by the art teacher that morning. Then he had allowed Sandra to travel across to Rapallo with some other children. Perlmann forced out a smile and struggled to stuff into his mouth the spaghetti that he thought was overcooked today. The proprietor's question of where he had been for the past two days annoyed him, and he pretended not to have heard it.

His interest in the chronicle was over now, once and for all, he established as he flicked through its pages. Just as he was about to snap it shut, his eye fell on a painting by Marc Chagall. In the cheap, miniaturized reproduction the blue had lost much of its luminous power. Nonetheless, Perlmann had immediately recognized that it must be Chagall's blue. He fully opened the book again and read the text. There was something about that date; but it escaped his remembering gaze and remained far outside on the periphery of his consciousness, as intangible as the mere memory of a memory. It had had nothing to do with Chagall's colors, of that he was sure. He had avoided that subject for many years, so as not to have to hear Agnes's harsh judgment about it. And, in fact, it seemed to him, it hadn't really been about Chagall at all. Something else was to blame for the fact that he had suddenly felt quite alone. But behind his closed lids nothing appeared that might have explained why his disappointment then seemed so closely connected with his anxiety now.

The memory only came later, when he was sitting in front of the television at the hotel, just as alone and desperate as he had been in the living room after he had called off the lecture. *If you think so*, was the first thing Agnes had said when he had asked her, even though there was no longer any possibility. And when she saw the wounded expression on his face: *Oh, all right then, why not. It can happen to anyone.* But her relaxed tone and dismissive gesture hadn't been able to conceal her disappointment: her husband, a rising star in his subject, hadn't managed to write the lecture that he had been supposed to deliver in the Auditorium Maximum, even though for days he had been sitting over it until late into the night.

But the worst thing was that twelve-year-old Kirsten heard him cancelling down the lecture with a reference to illness. *But you aren't ill at all, Dad. Why did you lie?* That was the only time that he had wished his daughter was far away, and had even hated her for a moment. He had gone into the living room and had, contrary to his custom, closed the door. And then Chagall's death had been announced on the television news. He had stared at the stained-glass window shown in the report with a fervour which was, when he noticed it, so embarrassing to him that he swiftly changed channels.

Perlmann had lost the thread of the film that was playing out in front of him, and turned off the television. That was seven years ago now. And throughout all that time he hadn't thought once about that cancelled lecture. In the nights leading up to his capitulation he had for the first time the very same experience that had paralyzed and frozen him for weeks: the experience of having absolutely nothing to say. It had been such a shock, this sudden experience, that he had had to banish it from his mind. And in that he had been very successful, because he had gone on to write dozens of lectures which had flowed easily and naturally from his pen. And throughout all that time not a single trace of a memory of that failure had crossed his path. Until today, from which perspective that late-March evening appeared as the first, menacing premonition of his present catastrophe.

He took half a sleeping pill, hopped through all the television channels again and then turned out the light. It was not quite true to say that the experience that had been banished back then had never again announced its presence. He thought once more of that moment a year ago, when he had suddenly found himself presented as a main speaker. From the panic that had flared up then there was – it now appeared to him – a hidden experience arc leading six years back to the day of Chagall's death. *And why not?* Agnes had said when he irritably explained to her that he couldn't simply tell the organizers of the conference that he had nothing to say.

Perlmann's thoughts began to blur at the edges. How did Agnes's two reactions – the one a year ago and the one seven years ago – fit together?

He tried to imagine the face that had accompanied the two remarks. But the only face that came was the one in the photograph in Frankfurt, which he had fled yesterday because it knew too much.

Whenever all thinking and wanting began to dissolve and silence could have begun at any moment, he gave a start, and then everything behind his forehead convulsed. The fourth time he turned the light on and washed his face in the bathroom. Then he dialled Kirsten's number. Her drowsy voice sounded annoyed.

'Oh, I'm sorry,' he said, 'I woke you.'

'Oh, it's you, Dad. Just a second.' He heard a wiping sound, then for a while nothing more. Only now did he look at his watch: a quarter to one.

'So, here I am again.' Now her voice sounded fresher. 'Is anything up? Or are you just calling?'

'Erm . . . just calling. That is . . . I wanted to ask you why Agnes . . . why Mum didn't like Chagall's colors.' He cursed himself for ringing her up with a heavy, furry tongue and not at least testing out his voice beforehand.

'What colors?'

He clenched his fist and was tempted simply to hang up. 'The colors in Marc Chagall's paintings.'

'Oh, right. Chagall. You're speaking so indistinctly. Well . . . I don't know . . . funny question. Did she really not like them?'

'No, she didn't. But there's something else, too: do you think she would have understood if I'd had nothing to say?'

'What do you mean, *nothing to say?*'

'If . . . I mean, simply if nothing had occurred to me.'

'About what?'

'About . . . just like that. Nothing had occurred to me. And the others were all waiting.'

'Dad, you're speaking in riddles. What others?'

'Just the others.' He had said it so quietly that he was unsure whether she had heard.

'I haven't the faintest idea what you're talking about. Dad, what's up with you?'

He quickly tried to produce some spit, and let it run over his tongue. 'Nothing, Kirsten. It's nothing. I just wanted to talk to you a bit. Good night now.'

'Erm . . . yes. So, ah . . . good night.'

He went into the bathroom and took another quarter tablet. Luckily, he hadn't asked her if she remembered his cancelled lecture back then. It had been a close thing. He turned on to his belly and pressed his face into the pillow, as if by doing so he could force sleep to come.

20

Laura Sand's second session also started with film images. It was quite different material from the previous day, and in the first half-hour there were occasional sequences in which she'd got the aperture wrong. She cursed at the poor quality of the film, but Perlmann saw immediately that that wasn't the problem. Almost as clearly as if they were images edited in, he saw Agnes coming out of the darkroom in her white apron, furious with herself and as much in need of comfort as a child. Instead of returning to the real film, he stayed with these images and slipped back through the night to the conversation with Kirsten. He had mumbled something about Chagall, and asked her some absurd question about Agnes. The damned pill had immediately obliterated the details. *I've got to give them up. Give them up.* He reached for his mineral water, and when his glass clinked against the coffee pot the others turned their heads. Luckily, Maria had been sitting in front of her screen before. As a result he hadn't had to spool out the prepared sentences, which had sounded even more wooden with each internal run-through.

'*¡Dios mío!*' Evelyn Mistral murmured quietly. Perlmann looked straight ahead. The images that were being shown now were, in fact, breathtakingly beautiful. The glassy light of an early morning over the Steppe turned the contours of the meagre shrubs into mysterious, poetic forms that made the imagination pounce upon them immediately, and the faded yellow of the Steppe, run through with pale grey, lost itself against the rising sun in an apparently endless white depth. The view had so captivated even Laura Sand herself that she had lingered on the same shot until her arms had been trembling with exhaustion.

Now the camera swung slowly to the side, and all of a sudden the Steppe was scattered with the ribcages of dead animals. '*¡Jesús María!*' cried Evelyn Mistral, and then she could be heard gasping, open-mouthed. The camera moved further to the left, then came a cut, and now one saw the edge of a settlement, still in the same dreamy light. The people barely moved. They looked suspiciously or apathetically into the camera. The swollen bellies of children, fully grown bodies so gaunt that their wrists looked like grotesque enlargements. Flies every-where, which the people had given up resisting long ago. The camera slowly crept over the settlement. The pictures were all the same. The camera glided on until the people had disappeared from the picture. For a few seconds once again the beauty of the deserted Steppe, now already in a light that gave a sense of the searing midday heat. Then the film stopped.

For a few moments no one stirred in the dark, the only sound was Laura Sand's chair shifting. Then Evelyn Mistral and Silvestri walked to the window and released the blinds, which snapped up.

'Well,' said Millar in the tone of someone who has just heard some-thing very dubious.

Laura Sand jerked her head up. 'Something wrong?' A lurking harsh-ness quivered in her voice.

'Well, yes,' said Millar. 'Hunger and death as a poetic backdrop – I don't know.'

Laura Sand's face looked even whiter than usual above her black polo neck.

'Nonsense,' she said, squeezing the word out so violently that only the first syllable could really be heard.

'That,' Millar said slowly, lowering his head, 'I can't find.'

Adrian von Levetzov's nervous hand revealed that he couldn't bear the coming argument. 'In which area was it filmed?' he asked with the cheerful interestedness of a member of the educated classes, something to which he would not normally have succumbed.

'The Sahel,' Laura Sand snapped back.

'Indeed,' Millar murmured, 'indeed.'

Giorgio Silvestri blew out his smoke more loudly than necessary. 'The pictures at the end were very impressive,' he said. 'Even if that light – *come dire* – seduces one into oblivion. Or obfuscation. But I would actually like to come back to the subject: the interpretation of the interesting looks that the animals gave each other.'

His voice had had a strange, unassuming authority, Perlmann thought afterwards when the specialist discussion had once again got under way. It was the voice of someone who was used to intervening at the right moment and giving an awkward situation in a conversation a particular turn. That intervention had not been even slightly boss-like, and now the Italian had once again pulled up one knee, and was lolling in his chair like a teenager.

In the rest of her contributions Laura Sand remained cool, and one could sense her restrained fury even when its first explosion had passed. Millar made an effort and disguised his objections in the form of questions. Today, luckily, the words just poured out of Evelyn Mistral any old how, and when she said that the animals were, in her view, exchanging a boisterous linguistic form, which also contained some funny grammatical errors, even Laura Sand couldn't help laughing.

Perlmann said nothing. It was nearly one o'clock and he was internally rehearsing the sentences for Maria; because the idea that he could walk past her unnoticed for a second time, when she was waiting for his paper, was unlikely in the extreme.

He found all this material incredibly exciting, Millar said when Laura Sand looked at her watch and gathered her papers together. So he suggested continuing with the same thing on Monday. He flicked through the texts. 'And on Tuesday. Because there's is a lot I'd still like to know about it, in theoretical terms as well.'

Laura Sand took her time before returning his expectant glance. 'OK,' she said then, and the way she imitated Millar's Yankee accent was a sign that she had accepted his conciliatory offer.

Millar pushed his glasses back on his nose with his index finger. 'Swell.'

She pulled a face at the word. His mouth twitched.

Perlmann calculated feverishly: that meant that the second half of the coming week was taken up with Evelyn Mistral, and it would be his turn on the Monday of the last week. The text would have to be in the pigeonholes by Saturday at the latest. That meant that Maria would have to have it on Wednesday morning – Thursday at the latest. *Five-and-a-half days. That could be enough.* His heart was pounding. Suddenly, everything was open again.

'While we're on the subject,' Silvestri spoke into Perlmann's calculation. 'As far as the last week is concerned I can only do the first half. On Thursday I'm afraid I have to sort a few things out at the hospital.' He looked at Perlmann. 'So I can't be at your session, which will probably happen at the end. But I'll get the text.'

'Of course,' Perlmann said hoarsely. *A week, I've gained a whole week.*

As if numb with relief he walked through the lounge. Maria was waiting for him in the hall. He walked over to her with a presence of mind that later surprised him as much as it repelled him.

'I didn't get around to saying it in the morning. The timetable has changed slightly, and now I'm going to use the opportunity to rework my text again. As things look right now, you won't have to do anything with it until next Friday.'

'I see,' she said, slightly irritated, and ran her hand sideways through her hair so that her earring jangled quietly. 'What should I . . . ? All right, then. I'll just go on typing up your other text. Will that do?'

During Maria's last words Evelyn Mistral had joined them.

'Yes, do that,' said Perlmann, and couldn't help running his tongue over his lips.

'You've been writing a lot recently, haven't you?' Evelyn said to him as they were walking together through the hall. 'And all in secret!'

Perlmann pulled a helpless face and shrugged.

'And now I've gained half a week,' he said. 'Not bad. Although, I'm actually finished and almost a little disappointed having to wait until Thursday. Silly, isn't it? And I've got such stage fright!'

No, said Perlmann, he didn't have time to stroll through town. He had something he wanted to work on. But on Sunday he would be available again, very definitely.

He sat for almost an hour in the red armchair before he worked out what was going on. Before, when he had parted from Evelyn Mistral and gone energetically upstairs, two at a time, he had been glad to enjoy his relief, and at the same time – for the first time in ages – he had once again felt something like buoyancy. In that one week that he suddenly had at his disposal he would surely be able to get something written. But then, when he had lit a cigarette and, to his surprise, rested his feet on the circular table, the relief he had promised himself did not come, and it had not helped at all to predict the unexpected, happy turn of events. He meekly took his feet off the table and sat up straight. And only now did it dawn on him that the cramped weariness that had set in instead of relief was disappointment – disappointment that it wasn't all over yet, and that there was still a long sequence of days to come, in which he would have to live through that tension, that anxiety and above all that lack of belief in himself. He drew the curtains, took a quarter of a sleeping-pill and lay down in bed. Just before he fell asleep there was a knock on the door. He didn't react.

It wasn't, in fact, Chagall's colors that he had been defending in his dream, he thought when he woke up in the gloom and, sitting on the edge of the bed, rubbed his throbbing temples. Admittedly, the painter's name had wandered constantly through his thoughts like a ghost, but what he had cried out – in a hoarse voice and the most indistinct of words, against a wall of incredulity – had been a defense of Laura Sand's poetic images of suffering.

He went into the shower and tried to find the words that had remained only a furious intention in his dream. Words came. He spoke them into the stream of water, choked and then intensified his defense until it became a fiery speech peaking in the claim that only beautiful images could depict suffering for what it was – because beauty was, in fact, truth, and the only truth that could plumb the whole depth of suffering. When he turned off the water and rubbed the taste of chlorine from his face with his towel, he shuddered at his kitsch and was glad for a while to be able to listen to the sober, boring voice of the announcer on the television news.

At dinner, Achim Ruge amazed him. In the middle of the main course, and without interrupting his dissection of his fish, he suddenly said: 'You know, Brian, I really didn't understand what it was that bothered you so much about Laura's film. They're very precise, very eloquent shots – much better than anything you get to see on television on the subject.'

Laura Sand went on eating, without even looking up. Millar lowered his knife and fork, took off his glasses and cleaned them thoroughly.

'Now, Achim,' he said then, 'I see it like this: in this case dreamlike, photographically successful pictures conceal more than they reveal. Beauty, you might say, is lying here. Of course, I don't mean, Laura, that you are lying,' he added quickly, although without getting a glance from her, 'I just mean it in a – how should I say it? – in an objective sense. Truthful pictures of hunger and death don't need to be bad, of course. But they should, I think, be as dry as agency reports. Sober. Completely sober. Certainly not dreamy. And I don't think it's an aesthetic question, it's a moral one. Sorry, but that's how I see it.'

He waited for a reaction from Laura Sand, but again he waited in vain, so that after an apologetic gesture in Ruge's direction he addressed himself to his dinner again.

For a while the only sound was the rattle of cutlery, and the waiter who topped up their wine seemed like an intruder. With all his might Perlmann resisted the feeling that there was something in what Millar had said. He was tempted to adopt the opposite view, and that impulse also had something to do with the fact that Millar's hairy hands got on his nerves, hands that were capable of producing that mysterious simultaneity of sounds in Bach and now manipulated the fish cutlery with the delicacy of a surgeon. But then he thought about the taste of chlorine in the shower and bit his lips.

'I'm not convinced,' Ruge was saying now. 'Taking suffering seriously and allowing oneself to be morally touched by it can't mean denying beauty. Or forbidding it, to a certain extent.'

Laura gave him a glance of agreement.

'Erm . . . no, of course not,' Millar said irritably. 'And that's not what I meant. But that's exactly where there's a contradiction in Laura's film. There's no getting round it.'

'Of course. And nor should there be,' Ruge smiled. 'What concerns me is just this: it's a contradiction that we've got to endure, both here and elsewhere. Endure it, without avoiding it.'

'*Ecco!*' said Silvestri.

Laura Sand leaned back and lit a cigarette. There was a complacent gleam in her furious expression. Perlmann didn't like that gleam. Suddenly, he missed Agnes.

Millar gave Silvestri a contemptuous look. 'I think that's too simple,' he said then, turning to Ruge. 'Cheap – if the word is allowed.'

'Oh, it's allowed, certainly,' replied Ruge. 'But it's wrong, I fear. Because enduring that contradiction – in the sense in which I mean it – that is, on the contrary, extremely difficult. Or expensive,' he added with a grin.

Millar drummed his fingers on the table top. 'I don't think so, Achim . . . Oh, forget it.'

Over dessert and coffee he didn't say a word. Now and again he bit his lips. Perlmann suddenly wasn't sure whether Brian Millar was as tough an opponent as he had previously thought.

Before he went to bed, Perlmann prepared his desk for the following day. He moved the lamp to the side and straightened a stack of blank sheets on the glass, with his writing materials next to them. He went through the books in his suitcase and finally carried three volumes over to the desk. Then he took half a pill. If he was to be able to start writing straight away tomorrow, he would have to sleep well. When the first, familiar signs of numbness set in, he began to compose the structure of his paper. Four subheadings, underlined and with a number in front of them. The four lines were precisely the same length. It looked very neat. It would turn out well.

21

When Kirsten, announced by Giovanni, stood at his door at six o'clock the following morning, Perlmann had to control himself to keep from throwing his arms around her neck.

'Hi, Dad,' she said with a smile in which sheepishness and mockery mixed, and which also contained a confidence that he had never seen in his daughter before. 'You sounded so weird on the phone the day before yesterday that I thought I should check everything was all right.'

She was wearing a long, black coat and light-colored sneakers, and her recalcitrant hair was held together with a lemon-yellow hairband. On the floor next to her was the scuffed red leather travelling bag that Agnes had dragged around with her like a talisman on all her trips.

'Come on, sit down,' he said, and cursed his heavy head and furry tongue. 'How on earth did you get here?'

She had been on the road for fifteen hours from Konstanz, hitching all the way. Six times she had stood by the roadside, and once – at a gas station on the Milan ring road, long after midnight – it had been more than an hour before anyone had picked her up. Perlmann shuddered, but didn't say a word. The best part had been at the beginning, in Switzerland. There, a man had even invited her to dinner before they drove down the Leventina gorge. 'A nice respectable Swiss man with suspenders!' She laughed when she saw his face.

No, she hadn't actually been scared. Well, OK, perhaps a bit when the guy who drove her from Milan to Genoa kept on about her appearance. She'd been annoyed that she didn't speak enough Italian to shut him up. But then he'd let her get into the back to sleep for a while.

And when he insisted on a goodbye kiss – well, yes, apart from the fact that it had scratched a bit and she hadn't liked his smell, it had been quite funny. She had driven the rest of the journey with a dolled-up woman in an open-topped Mercedes, who had talked without interruption about her argument with her husband and paid her, Kirsten, no further attention. Here, in the sleeping town, it had been a long time before she had found someone to show her the way to the hotel.

'But now I'm here and I think it's great that I've done it! You know, Martin was quite cross about me suddenly leaving like that. He actually tried to talk me out of it. But when I was coming out of the student canteen I met Lasker, and when he stopped specially to tell me how perceptive he thought my presentation was, I was so high that I just had to do something crazy. Do you think I could give Martin a quick call and tell him I got here safely?'

Perlmann showed her how to get an outside line, picked up his clothes and went into the bathroom. He took alternate hot and cold showers to drive away the after-effect of the pills, and every now and again he held his tongue under the stream of water.

So in the end she hadn't come because of him, but because she wanted to celebrate her success. He tried to fight against his disappointment with vigorous rubbing. He had never seen her with purple lips before. It was the same purple that Sheila had worn. It emphasized the pout of her lips, which even as a little girl she had refused to accept. The color didn't suit her. Not at all. And then all those rings, at least one on each finger. They were all mixed up, and yet it looked as if she was wearing knuckle-dusters on each hand.

Only now did he notice that his chin hurt because he was convulsively gripping his razor. Once again he bathed his eyes, which looked swollen and unhealthy. Then he slipped into his clothes, leaned against the door with his eyes closed for a moment, and then went back into the room.

Kirsten was still on the phone, and guiltily turned her head when she heard Perlmann. 'See you on Tuesday, then!' she said quickly. 'Yes, I will. See you then. Bye.' She put down the phone. 'I want to be back in time for Lasker's seminar. I thought there might be a night train from Genoa on Monday evening. It doesn't matter if I'm tired at the next session! But . . . umm . . .' she looked at the floor.

'Of course, I'll give you the ticket,' said Perlmann, 'after all, you came here because of me.'

She came up to him and he rested his hands on her shoulders.

'You look tired. And pale,' she said. 'Has something happened? The way you asked about Mum on the phone: I couldn't understand a word.'

'Oh, yes, that.' His tongue was heavy again. 'I don't know . . . I was a bit confused. It doesn't mean anything more than that. And as to what's happened, no, no, nothing particular has happened.'

She looked at him with the concentrated, sceptical look that she had inherited from Agnes. 'But you're not having a particularly great time here, either, are you?'

'Oh, I don't know. It's all a bit exhausting. With all the other colleagues.'

'And it's been less than a year. Sometimes it seems to me as if it can't have been more than a few weeks. You too?'

He felt the burning sensation behind his eyes and pulled her to him for a moment. Then he pushed her away with forced brio. 'Right, so let's find you a room in this place!'

Less than half an hour after she moved into her room, she was back with him, her clothes changed and her hair still damp.

'God, the price of a room like that – it's insane!'

She didn't want to sleep now. She wanted to see the sea at dawn, the terrace, the really fantastic hotel in general.

'And you've got to show me the conference room as well! Have you got a session on Monday? Do you think I could listen?'

Perlmann felt as if his chest was filling with lead. Breakfast first, he finally suggested. As they walked to the elevator, she turned round and looked back down the long corridor.

'Are you all up here?'

'What? Oh, I see. No. Just me, in fact.' He pressed the button for the elevator again.

'And why's that?'

'Why? Umm . . . ah . . . that's more or less coincidence. Lots of the rooms downstairs are being renovated over the winter, and there was some sort of problem with the bed. I'm quite content. It's nice and quiet up here.'

The elevator door opened. 'Aha,' she said and plucked at her yellow sweatshirt with the printed emblem of Rockefeller University. On the way down Perlmann looked with concentration at the jumping illuminated numbers.

It was only a quarter past seven, and the dining room, its lights still lit, was deserted. The waiter struggled to hide his surprise. '*Benvenuta!*' he said with a slight bow when Perlmann explained who Kirsten was.

She ate for two, admired the silver cutlery and the chandeliers and kept pointing enthusiastically at the sea, where the day was breaking, and the faint dawn light was making way for the transparent blue of a cloudless sky.

Perlmann drank only coffee. He would have liked to smoke, but didn't dare. Before, when Giovanni told him he had sent up a signorina who claimed to be his daughter, the first thing he had done was to check whether he had emptied and rinsed out the ashtray. He couldn't tell her now that he was smoking again. He guessed that this half hour, sitting quite alone in the big, snow-white dining room as light filtered increasingly in, so that the chandeliers suddenly were switched off, as if by an invisible hand – that this half hour would be the loveliest moment of her visit, and he wanted to hold on to it for as long as possible.

When she was finished, she took a pack of cigarettes out of her Indian-looking shoulder bag. She sheepishly put one between her lips. 'Only one every now and again. Not like Mum and you before.' Then she rummaged for a red lighter with a fine gold rim and lit her cigarette. Perlmann registered that she was only inhaling it half-heartedly. It was nearly eight o'clock. Soon it would be over, that moment of silent intimacy in the empty dining room.

Millar, Ruge and von Levetzov came in at the same time and stopped, nonplussed, for a moment. Then they approached the table and Perlmann introduced Kirsten. At first she didn't know what was happening when von Levetzov lifted her hand and made as if to kiss it. There was still a confused smile on her face when Millar shook her hand and bowed athletically.

'Good girl!' he said, and pointed to the sweatshirt. 'That's my university!'

'And, of course, he thinks it's the best one,' Ruge said to her in German. 'Only because he doesn't know Bochum!' he added with a giggle. He shook her hand. 'Good morning. When did you get here?'

Perlmann was glad that the women hadn't come yet. When Kirsten had finished her cigarette, he excused himself and they went out to the terrace. Before they reached the veranda Kirsten suddenly stopped and craned her neck.

'That looks like . . . Is that the conference room?'

Perlmann nodded.

She took his hand. 'Come on, you've got to show it to me now.'

Inside, she immediately sat down in the high armchair with the carved back. She compared the elegance of the room with the shabbiness of the practice rooms at the university: here the mahogany tables, there the greyish Formica ones; the gleaming white porcelain ashtrays, as opposed to the cigarette butts floating in the dregs of the cardboard coffee cups; the immaculate, electrically adjustable board behind her, in contrast to the blind boards back home, which constantly got stuck. Then she picked up one of the crystal glasses for the mineral water.

'You know, I had a terribly dry mouth when I was sitting up at the front, at least at first. Luckily, I found a boiled sweet in my jacket. Lasker nearly managed a smile when he saw how bothered I was by the stickiness on my fingers afterwards.'

On the way to the door she tugged on the tassels of the coats of arms and laughed at the clouds of dust. In the doorway she turned round again.

'Incredibly elegant – almost illicit. And then the view out to the pool . . . But the position at the front is the same. Emotionally, I mean. I was worried I might forget everything at the crucial moment. Complete nonsense, of course. But still.' She looked at him. 'You probably can't understand that any more, when it's been routine for so many years. Am I right?'

Perlmann rested his hand on her shoulder and pushed her gently outside.

After a walk along the sea, in the course of which she talked about Martin and stopped from time to time to hold her face in the morning sun, she grew tired and wanted to try and get some sleep. Outside the door to her room she gave him a kiss on the cheek and laughed at the purple print it left.

'See you later? Do you have work to do?'

He raised his hand and quickly turned round.

He stood by the window for hours on end until his back hurt. Now and again he glanced at his desk. *How tidy the desk looks!* she had said before they had gone to breakfast. *As if you'd just finished something.*

The presence of his sleeping daughter. She made everything seem unreal, or rather she created a twofold reality: two levels to a certain extent, between which he swung back and forth at every moment, not knowing which one he belonged to – or wanted to belong to – more. Above all, with Kirsten's arrival time had doubled, two unconnected strands of time passed through him now, both claiming to be actual, real time, the time that mattered. One was the time that Kirsten had brought with her, the time of her weekly seminars, and also the time in which the weeks and months of her acquaintance with Martin were counted. That was the time into which he had threaded himself before, on their walk, to be close to her. Now, standing at the window, he tried again to slip into that time, he searched it for present, a present that could make everything apart from his daughter unimportant and free him of his anxiety. But Kirsten's sleep had, if it hadn't demolished that time, deep-frozen it for a few hours, and the imagined present with her would only be able to turn into a real present at the moment when she opened her eyes down there, on the second floor of the other wing. By now he was entirely back in that other time, the time of the hotel, the time of anxiety, which had gone on ticking with treacherous silence behind the back of Kirsten's time.

Perlmann drew one curtain and lay down on the bed. There were, strictly speaking, not only these two temporal realities, he thought, and was grateful for the soft, velvety sound that his thoughts now assumed. There was, in fact, also the time that belonged to him and Kirsten alone, the time that began with Agnes's death, the time of shared abandonment and grief. That one – Perlmann's hands clawed involuntarily into the cover – Martin had no business with, absolutely no business at all. And before that there was, again, another time in which Herr Wiedemann or Wiedemeier or whatever that young whippersnapper's name was, had no place: the time with Agnes and Kirsten, the time when all three of them had chosen, from mountains of pictures, the photograph of the month and in the end the photograph of the year: family time, so to speak.

Perlmann rubbed his eyes. The serious picture of Agnes on the windowsill appeared, and now he also saw the coffee seeping into the pale carpet. There was also Frankfurt time, the snowed-in time when his letterbox filled up with junk mail and the dean waited for his report. That time had something to do with Kirsten's time in Konstanz, it seemed to him; but now the thoughts became so gentle and pleasantly vague that it would have been a shame to spoil them by concentrating.

When Kirsten woke him with her knocking it was late afternoon. 'I slept like a log!' she said and whirled through the room. 'Will you show me the town now?'

When he came out of the bathroom, she was holding the big Russian-English dictionary, flicking through it and then constantly rubbing her fingers on her jeans.

'That's an amazing thing,' she said. 'Every single turn of phrase explained! I don't think Martin knows that. Except the paper's horrible to the touch. Actually repellent. Where did you get this great tome?'

Perlmann felt as if he were seeing Santa Margherita for the first time. And as if this wasn't the town that had the Marconi Veranda in it. The many squares, arches, alleyways – it was as if they hadn't been there before, and sprang into being under Kirsten's gaze. By the wooden way he stood around when she went up to things to look at details, one might have thought he was bored. In fact, with his eyes often half-closed, he was letting himself fall into the borrowed present of her enthusiasm, feeling like someone looking out at the sea through the barred windows of his cell.

Afterwards, in the café, he was a hair away from succumbing to the overwhelming temptation to tell Kirsten about his desperation. Just before it came to that, he felt the blood pulsing through his whole body. At once disappointed and relieved, he then heard her asking the waiter the way to the toilet, and when she came back with her springy gait and swinging bag, it seemed to him impossible to take the step which, he knew, would have changed so much between them. But his blood pulsed on, so he took out his cigarettes.

She stared at him, thunderstruck.

'You . . . since when have you been smoking again?'

He played it down, spoke with hollow nonchalance about Italy, the cafés and the cigarettes that were simply a part of it. He was revolted by himself, and she didn't believe a word. There was a shadow on her face now. She felt it was like a betrayal of Agnes, a desertion. He was quite sure about that. A burning helplessness took hold of him, and without anticipating it, he started talking about intimacy, about various forms of loyalty, about love and freedom.

'If intimacy has something to do with the harmony of two lives, one might wonder whether it's compatible with the ideal that two people shouldn't curtail each other's freedom,' he concluded.

'Dad,' she said quietly, 'I don't know you like this!'

The shadow had disappeared, making way for a smile full of curious dread. She accepted one of his cigarettes and took out her red lighter.

'Actually, I don't think it's so bad that you're smoking again,' she said. 'At least it means I don't have to apologize!'

Turning the corner of a building on the way back, they were suddenly in front of the trattoria. Perlmann stopped and pushed the flat of his hand between the glass beads of the curtain. Then he slowly drew it back and walked on without a word.

'What was that?' asked Kirsten.

'Nothing. That kind of curtain . . . I like it. There's something . . . something of the fairy tale about it.'

'You're full of surprises today!' she laughed. 'And on the subject of fairy tales: doesn't that white hotel on the hill up there look fantastic? Could we go there tomorrow?'

'The Imperiale. You have expensive tastes,' he laughed, and for a moment he disappeared entirely in her time and forgot that the other time, the time of the veranda, was ruthlessly ticking on.

When he collected her from her room for dinner, he was struck dumb for a moment.

'Smashing,' he said at last, in English, after she had twirled twice on her axis in her glittering black dress, still slightly crumpled in places from the journey. Around her neck she wore a piece of Indian jewellery, and all the rings but one had vanished. When his eye settled in puzzlement on her hands, she winked an eye and grinned.

'You didn't like them, did you?'

'Was it that obvious?'

'I can read you like a book. Always could. Don't you remember?'

He looked at his watch. 'Time to go. Don't forget your bag.'

On the way to the door she looked at herself again in the big, half-blind mirror on the wall and straightened a stocking. *If only she would drop the damned purple*, he thought. And her heels didn't need to be quite so high, either. Just before they left the corridor, he stopped and held her back by the arm.

'I wanted to ask you a favor. Just a small thing.'

'Yes?'

'Brian Millar will probably play in the lounge after dinner. At the grand piano, I mean.' He paused and looked at the floor. 'No one here knows that I play as well. Played. And I'd like it to stay that way. OK?'

She looked at him quizzically and shook her head very slightly.

'But you don't need to hide yourself! I'd like to see if this man Millar plays better than you!'

'Please. I . . . I can't really explain. But that's how I'd like it.'

'If you want, of course,' she said slowly, and played absently with the strap of her bag. 'But . . . there's something up with you. I've been feeling it for some time. Won't you tell me?'

'Come on,' he said, 'or we'll be the last ones in.'

At dinner Perlmann felt as if he were sitting on hot coals. He tried not to look, but his attention was focused entirely on what his daughter was saying, and he twitched at every mistake she made in English. But she did dazzlingly well. She had ended up next to Silvestri, diagonally opposite Millar.

The Italian had – and Perlmann wouldn't have expected it of him – immediately stood up when they stepped to the table, and had straightened Kirsten's chair for her as she sat down. At the sight of this, Ruge's face had twisted into a grin, and Kirsten had blushed slightly under her freckles. When she dared to speak a few words of Italian, Silvestri immediately continued in his mother tongue, until she waved him to stop and he rested his hand, laughing, on her bare arm. And even though she talked mostly to Millar after that, Perlmann was quite sure that she didn't forget Silvestri's presence beside her for a moment.

English and history, she said, when Millar asked her what subjects she was studying. But that might change, she was still only starting. When answering Millar's questions about the details of her study she made more linguistic mistakes than before, and Perlmann had no idea what he was eating.

But then, when the subject turned to Faulkner, and in particular to *The Wild Palms*, it came bubbling out of her almost faultlessly, and he wondered more than once where she got all these obscure words. Her dinner grew cold as she defended her thesis, face glowing, and Millar, who couldn't quite remember the novel and whose argument was surprisingly weak, set down his cutlery several times and grabbed his gleaming glasses. When Kirsten was clearly about to win on points, Perlmann forced himself at least to eat the last mouthful of fillet steak, and thought of his colleague Lasker, who had stayed specifically because of his daughter.

Although he didn't know why, he avoided looking in Evelyn Mistral's direction. But twice he caught her eye, and both times he was confused by the mocking shyness in her green eyes. As if his daughter's presence revealed something about him which, to her annoyance, disturbed her previous feelings.

Laura Sand, on the other hand, listened to the discussion of Faulkner in her sulky way and asked at the end what phase of his life the novel coincided with. Just once, when she thought Perlmann wasn't watching her, her eye slipped over him and betrayed that she too was busy revising her previous image of him.

Over coffee, Silvestri offered Kirsten a Gauloise. Smiling smartly, she bent over his lighter, inhaled the smoke and instantly had a coughing fit. Silvestri's unshaven face pulled into a grin, and he kept his next drag in his lungs for a particularly long time. Kirsten bravely wiped the water from her eyes and carefully took another drag; by now she had her coughing under control. As she added milk and sugar to her coffee, she let the cigarette with its purple stains dangle casually from the corner of her mouth. When Silvestri went on looking teasingly at her, for a moment it looked as if she were going to stick out her tongue at him.

As they left, von Levetzov held the door open for Kirsten and bowed slightly. Perlmann, who was walking behind her, had had enough of seeing his daughter in his colleagues' force field, and really wanted to go upstairs. But now Kirsten was shaking hands with Evelyn Mistral, whose head was tilted sideways almost as much as Millar's usually was, and then the two women walked silently towards the lounge without saying a word to one another.

While Millar was playing, Kirsten kept glancing across to Perlmann, giving him to understand, with the disparaging twitch of her lips that had for a time made Agnes furious, that she couldn't understand why he was hiding in the face of this mediocre performance. And when Millar stood up and closed the lid over the keys, her applause was the shortest and faintest.

But he had been good, rather better than usual, and Perlmann was slightly hurt that his daughter felt the need to cheer him up with her partisan judgment.

. Although few questions were being put to Kirsten now, she looked very excited, turned her head to everyone who spoke and, to Silvestri's delight, smoked one Gauloise after another. When, in passing, someone mentioned Perlmann's imminent invitation to Princeton, she frowned and smiled at him. She was the last to stand when the company broke up.

At the bottom of the stairs Evelyn Mistral walked towards Perlmann, who was with Kirsten.

'Yet again, our wedding stroll comes to nothing,' she said in Spanish, pointedly looking only at him. 'I'm sure you have other plans.'

'Erm . . . I don't know . . . yes, we'll . . . ,' he said, annoyed both by his stammer and by the fact that the Spanish woman, whom he felt he barely recognized at that moment, was so expressively ignoring Kirsten with her eyes.

'You don't need to apologize,' she said with a face that reminded him of a schoolmistress. '¡Buenas noches!'

Halfway up the stairs Kirsten stopped and looked down to the hall, where Evelyn Mistral was standing with Ruge and von Levetzov. 'Did I hear her wrong or did she call you *tú*? I mean, I don't speak Spanish that well, but that's what it sounded like to me.'

Perlmann hadn't known it was so hard to sound casual. 'Oh, that, yes. It's quite customary in Spanish academic circles.'

Before she turned into her corridor, Kirsten stopped again. '*Boda*. What does that mean again?'

This time he managed a natural smile. '*Wedding*.'

The steep wrinkle that he didn't like formed above her nose. 'Wedding?'

'A little joke between us.'

She kicked something imaginary from the carpet, glanced at him briefly and disappeared into the corridor.

22

When Perlmann woke from his light and troubled sleep the next morning, and looked down at the terrace, he saw Kirsten laughing at Silvestri's trick with the swallowed cigarette. They both had cups in front of them, and on the white bistro table there were two blue packs of cigarettes that looked precisely identical. Kirsten's tousled hair fell on her yellow sweatshirt, and now, as she brushed a strand out of her eyes, he saw the big sunglasses that covered half of her face.

In his dream she had been wearing last night's glittering dress, and her piled-up hairdo hadn't suited her at all. Had she really been wearing sunglasses? Perlmann held his face under the jet of water. Or was the feeling that she was strange to him – the feeling that he had constantly battled against – to do with something else? He had been surprised and proud that she could suddenly speak Spanish. But he hadn't really understood what she was saying with her purple mouth as she walked past him down the stairs. His colleagues were waiting for her in the hall, and when she walked up to them, the bright sound of her laughter had made him unsure whether she really was his daughter.

He walked so slowly down the hall that Signora Morelli looked up from her papers behind the reception desk. His daughter seemed to like it here, she said. He nodded, ordered coffee from the waiter who was just coming in, and stepped outside.

Kirsten desperately wanted to go across to Rapallo.

'Do you know,' she asked Silvestri in stumbling Italian, 'whether the building where the two treaties were signed is still standing?'

Perlmann was silent. She was calling the Italian *tu*. And why two treaties?

'I've really got to get some work done,' Silvestri laughed when he saw how disappointed she was that he didn't want to come with her. 'I haven't been as industrious as your father.'

Later, on the ship, Kirsten talked about Silvestri's work in the clinic, and if her voice hadn't been a touch too casual, one might have thought she had known him for years. He had plainly talked to her a lot about his previous work with autistic people, and all of a sudden she also knew about Franco Basaglia, whose boldness she described as if she had been present at his experiment in opening the portals of the institutions. From time to time she drew on an unfiltered Gauloise, and it seemed to Perlmann as if the way in which she plucked crumbs of tobacco from her tongue was copied from the movement of Silvestri's white hand. In ten days, she announced, Giorgio would have to go to Bologna to oversee the start of a new therapeutic plan, and at the same time he would be able to tend to some particularly difficult patients who would otherwise have had to get by without him.

The fact that Kirsten was, behind her big sunglasses, preoccupied with Silvestri's appointment diary, added yet another new time to the many others, and Perlmann was uncertain whether this new time – in which Kirsten was Silvestri's companion – brought his daughter closer to him because it was an Italian time, a time on this side of the Alps, or whether Kirsten, wrapped up in this new time, seemed strange to him, a traitor, even, because it was the time of a person who – unlike Martin beyond the Alps, for example – was waiting for a text from him.

She also knew about the time that Silvestri had spent in Oakland.

'On the subject of America,' she said, 'I think this Princeton business is brilliant! Do you think I could visit you there?' With a strange hesitation, as if she had to struggle to remember him, she added after a pause: 'With Martin. He'd love to see New York!'

The people they asked in Rapallo didn't know whether the historical building was still there. Over lunch Perlmann learned about the treaty between Italy and Yugoslavia that had temporarily made Fiume into an independent state. He was amazed at how much his daughter knew, and how hungry for knowledge she was. *And deep down that's exactly what I never was: hungry for knowledge.*

Within a few minutes the sky had clouded over. In the gloomy, flat light that now fell through the pizzeria windows, Kirsten's enthusiasm suddenly faded, and they looked shyly at one another.

'I'm not taking too much of your time away?' she asked. 'It's your turn on Thursday, isn't it?'

It was hard for Perlmann to admit to himself that he was furious about her tone, which expressed the fact that she now saw every feat that anyone had to perform in the light of her first presentation. He nodded briefly and suggested they leave.

On the journey back they stood in silence at the railing and looked at the foamy crests of the waves forming under a cold wind. Kirsten asked at one point whether she could read what he was going to say here. Perlmann was glad that a gust of wind gave him a moment's pause. Maria had the text at the moment, he said then, and told her who Maria was. For a few frightened minutes he waited for her question about the subject of his talk; but it didn't come. Instead Kirsten said, without looking at him, 'Brian Millar. You don't like him. Do you?'

'Umm . . . he's OK. He strikes me as a bit too . . . self-confident.'

'Cocksure,' she said in English, and looked at him with a smile. 'I can see that.'

As they left the ship she suddenly stopped. 'Is that why you don't want to play the piano? You're not scared of him or anything, are you? I thought he sounded pretty shallow last night, when we were talking about Faulkner.'

Perlmann knocked an empty coke can over the edge of the quay wall with his shoe. 'This just isn't the place for it, I reckon. That's all.'

Now he needed to be alone and started walking at a brisk pace. But when the hotel came into view, Kirsten stopped again.

'And you won't explain that thing about Mum and Chagall? I'm sorry. I'm getting on your nerves. But you're so . . . so down.'

'Come on,' he said. 'It's about to start raining.'

In the hall Silvestri came towards them, the collar of his raincoat turned up and a cigarette in the corner of his mouth. He was going to the cinema, he said with the guilty grin of a schoolboy skiving on his homework. Could she come with him? Kirsten asked, and turned red when she became aware of the impetuousness of her question. Again Perlmann could hardly believe how quickly the Italian was able to react. The only clue that he would rather have gone on his own lay in the fact that his gallantry sounded a little too cheerful.

'*Volentieri; volentierissimo, Signorina,*' he said and offered her his arm.

Perlmann had to turn on the light when he sat down at the desk. Only now, when he saw the skewed pens and the screwed-up paper in the waste-paper basket, did he remember that he had got up in the night and tried to work. It wasn't a very clear memory, and there was something strange and distant about it – as if it hadn't been him at all. He picked up the crumpled paper, only to drop it again after a brief hesitation. Then he started to jot down some keywords. When Kirsten left from Genoa on Monday evening, he would be able to take a taxi quickly back here and start writing straight away. And then he still had three days before he absolutely had to give Maria a text.

The keywords, which stood side by side and on top of one another, refused to turn into sentences, and in the growing carelessness of the writing the lack of belief became increasingly evident. Perlmann ran a bath and sat down in the tub long before it was full. The worst thing was that he wished it was already Monday evening. As he did so he thought constantly about when the film would be over and Kirsten might knock at the door. He added more and more hot water until it was hardly bearable. Then he lay on the bed in his dressing gown, and as the burning of his skin slowly eased, he dozed off.

Something had gone wrong between her and Silvestri. Perlmann could see it at once when he opened the door to Kirsten. There was something defiant in her face, an expression like the one she had worn in the school competition when she had been beaten by her arch-enemy from the same class. She walked up to him and put her arms around his neck. She hadn't done that for years, and Perlmann, who no longer knew how to hug a daughter, held her like a precious, fragile object. When she pulled away he stroked her hair, which smelled of restaurant. She sat down in the red armchair and reached into her jacket for her cigarettes. She looked furiously at the pack of Gauloises that she had fished out, and hurled them towards the waste-paper basket, which she just missed. Perlmann picked up the cigarettes, which had slipped from their wrapping. When he looked up, Kirsten was holding one of her own cigarettes in the flame of the red lighter. Her dark eyes glittered.

'And now I'd like you to take me out, up to the white hotel on the hill,' she said with a purple pout.

It sounded like a sentence from a film, and Perlmann had to suppress a chuckle. He put on his clothes and chose his blazer with the gold buttons. He was glad that it wasn't yet Monday evening. When he came out of the bathroom, she pointed to the page of keywords that still lay on the glass desktop.

'When I get bored in seminars I doodle as well,' she said.

It was only when the taxi turned into the drive of the Imperiale that Perlmann managed to forget that remark.

Kirsten leaned far back in her turquoise plush armchair and looked out into the backdrop of lights in the bay.

'I wish Mum was here, too,' she said into the quiet music that spilled across from the bar into the lounge.

Perlmann choked on his sandwich. So perhaps, after all, she hadn't come to terms with Agnes's death better and faster than he had. And even if she had, it had been silly to resent her for it.

'Yesterday in the café,' she went on, 'you said something about intimacy and freedom. I don't know if I understood.' She paused without looking at him. 'Were you happy with Mum? I mean . . . It was good at home, there were never any arguments. But maybe . . .'

Perlmann closed his eyes. The camera clicked, and Agnes laughed mockingly as he beat his arms around him to drive away the pigeons. Then they were walking together through Hamburg, pointing out the gleaming colors of the wet, glistening autumn leaves to one another, while inside he repeated over and over to himself the doctor's redeeming words about Kirsten's health. In his face he felt the wind over the cliffs of Normandy, and saw Agnes's arm in the yellow windbreaker, slinging the full pack of cigarettes far into the void with a circular motion. And then, as if this new memory had pushed its way darkly over the others without quite erasing them, he felt Agnes's head on his stiff shoulder, after she had made her remark about that dreamy photograph of Hong Kong at the airport.

He opened his eyes and saw that Kirsten was looking at him.

'We were fine. Most of the time we were fine together.'

Her smile at that moment, he thought later, revealed that she was pleased about the confidence in his voice, but unhappy with his choice of words. After all, she had asked about happiness.

She shook her packet of cigarettes and made to go. Following Silvestri's habit of fishing one out with her lips, she paused, started the whole movement from the beginning and then used her fingers, as she normally did.

'You know, Martin's OK. He really is OK.' She paused for too long, sensed it and struggled for words. 'Really, he is. It's just . . . I don't know . . . sometimes he lacks a bit of . . . excitement. Something, you know, like that stupid guy Giorgio . . . that stupid Silvestri . . . or François . . . Oh, forget it.' Turning her head quickly she threw Perlmann a crooked grin and then looked out of the window again.

Perlmann thought of how Agnes had come back from her trip to Shanghai, the one André Fischer had been on. That one present, a little ivory dragon, she had chucked at him halfway across the living room without warning, something she never normally did. And for a few days her other movements had become jauntier than usual, sometimes practically exuberant for no reason. Then things had returned to normal and the quietness that marked their dealings with one another had swallowed up the exuberance.

Perlmann asked how good Martin's Russian was, when Kirsten's silence began to oppress him. He was asking, he said, because she had made that remark the previous day about the big dictionary with the bad paper.

'Oh, not bad, I think. His father, who's a pretty revolting character, by the way, worked in Moscow for a long time, and Martin wanted to match his linguistic abilities. It seems to be the only bond between the two of them.' She clumsily stubbed out her cigarette. 'He is talented. In lots of ways. That's . . . that's not it . . .'

It was long past midnight before they got out of the taxi in front of the Mira. Over the past two hours Kirsten had done almost all of the talking, and he had learned far more about her life than he had for ages. He now knew all about the other members of their shared apartment. He knew Kirsten's travel plans for the coming year, and had joined her in her fury about the sloppiness of the medical insurance she'd taken out for her eczema. But most of all he now knew what her everyday life at university was like. He could even have quoted some of the graffiti that she saw every day. Enthralled, he had absorbed every single detail, and with each new topic he had tried to enjoy the closeness that his daughter sought with him as she went on talking, relaxed and almost dreamily, about the various different atmospheres over Lake Constance. But then she had fallen back into that tone that conveyed her pride for her father, who knew the university much, much better than she did, and for whom all the stories she told him must have been old hat. *Stop, please stop!* he could have cried out to her a dozen times. *I'm not there any more. I haven't been for ages!* Her naivety had become more and more of a torture – as the lounge, with its fin-de-siècle plush charm, became emptier – and had driven him into an icy loneliness in which his temptation the previous day to confide in her all his fear and despair had not once returned.

Before Kirsten entered her corridor, she walked up to Perlmann, wrapped her arms around him and rested her head against his chest.

'We haven't talked like that very often. Maybe never. It was nice. Did you think so, too?'

He nodded mutely. When she looked up and noticed the tears in his eyes, she stroked his cheeks with both hands. And before she disappeared round the corner three steps later, she waved at him, shyly at first, and then with ironic affection.

23

At about half-past eight he picked her up for breakfast. She was dressed as she had been when she arrived, and was wearing all her rings as well. On the other hand her lips were bare, so that you could see the spot where her bottom lip had burst. When she saw Perlmann's expression, she ran her index finger over the spot.

'May I?' she asked, and walked over to the mirror in the bathroom.

The pills. I should have cleared them away. Perlmann walked over to the window, closed his eyes and sought words for a casual, innocuous explanation.

'Tell me,' Kirsten said when she came out of the bathroom. 'Barbiturates – isn't that pretty strong stuff? And pretty dangerous, too? Because of addiction and everything, I mean.'

Perlmann breathed out before he turned round. 'What? Oh, you mean the pills.' He managed a smile. 'Oh, no, the doctor told me not to worry about that. It's all a matter of dosage. And I only need them very rarely, luckily.' Now he hadn't needed his well-chosen words. 'Just now and again, so if there's a night when my back hurts. And there's something that isn't quite right with the bed up here. And before the whole of the next day goes down the drain . . .'

She put one foot on the bedstead and retied her trainer. There was no way of telling whether she believed him.

Silvestri didn't appear in the dining room until five to nine, and only drank coffee. Although he was sitting opposite her, Kirsten tried to ignore him, suddenly bombarding Ruge with questions about his lab in

Bochum. Then, when Silvestri reached for his cigarettes, he sought Kirsten's eye to offer her one. In the end he lit one for himself, glanced at Perlmann and sent the pack sliding jauntily all the way across the table so that it bumped into Kirsten's saucer and made her coffee spill over the edge. Kirsten gave a start, lifted her dripping cup reproachfully for a moment, and then picked up the packet. Only now did she meet Silvestri's eye. For a second Perlmann feared that she would simply push the pack back to him. But then she very slowly fished out a cigarette, put it between her lips and, looking in a completely different direction, stretched out her arm towards Silvestri with a gesture so blasé that it looked as if she had learned it at drama school. With a grin, the Italian dropped his lighter into her open hand from an exaggeratedly high position. There was a quiet metallic sound when it rubbed against all her rings. Without deigning to glance at him, Kirsten held her cigarette into the flame, snapped the lighter shut and set it down in the middle of the table. *'Ecco!'* Silvestri laughed and reached for it. Then Kirsten turned and looked at him and stuck out her tongue.

Perlmann caught a glance from Evelyn Mistral. Her oriental face with its green eyes shot through with amber seemed to come at him from a long way away, and he didn't know whether he was pleased about that, or unhappy.

Laura Sand's third session passed at a more sluggish pace than the previous two. Some films injected a little life into proceedings, raising the question of whether animals understood the meaning of certain signs only in the sense that they reacted appropriately to them, or whether – albeit in a simplified, pallid sense – they attributed to others the intention of giving them a sign. Did animals have anything like a theory about the intellectual lives of their own species?

'But that's blindingly obvious!' Kirsten exploded. 'Of course they have! You can see that in their eyes!'

'The fact is,' Millar cut in, 'that you can't see anything at all in their eyes, and that it's pretty fantastical to assume any such thing. To put it mildly.' He said it in his usual confident, professional tone, and only a hint of irritation revealed that a discussion about Faulkner had taken place.

Perlmann thought about the funny things that Evelyn Mistral had been saying lately about the eloquent facial expressions of animals, and expected her to come to Kirsten's aid. But she didn't say a word, her arms folded over her chest, and even nodded when Millar and Ruge ridiculed a suggestion of goodness that von Levetzov had, in Perlmann's eyes, only made because he wanted to be nice to Kirsten.

Like everyone else, Laura Sand was waiting for Silvestri to join in, since he was known to share Kirsten's spontaneous opinion. But the Italian met this tense expectation with a poker face and picked more crumbs of tobacco from his tongue than were actually there. At last Laura Sand revealed with a twitch of the corners of her mouth that she had understood his refusal, and now developed her own thesis, which wasn't so far removed from Kirsten's feelings. At first Kirsten listened to her with excitement; but when it got technical, she leaned back inconspicuously and looked furtively at her watch.

'I am a bit puzzled, though,' she said to Perlmann later in the hall, though it sounded more intimidated than puzzled, 'about how tough the debate was there. At our seminars it's a lot . . . a lot looser, friendlier. Did you think it was really embarrassing when I burst out with my opinion?'

Perlmann didn't reply, because at that point Maria walked up to them and handed him a printout of Leskov's text, with the pages of his handwritten translation underneath.

'*Eccolo*,' she said. 'It took until now because Signor Millar had some other things to write.'

For the title, printed in an exaggeratedly large, bold font, she had used a sheet of its own. Now she pointed at it and started to remark upon it. With a presence of mind that he didn't experience deep within himself, Perlmann anticipated her and introduced Kirsten. He held the text behind his back with both hands, as he uttered words of praise about Maria which struck him as unbearably hollow. And no sooner had Maria addressed a question to Kirsten than he made an apologetic

gesture, walked over to the reception desk and asked Signora Morelli
to put the stack of paper in his pigeonhole.

'I thought the text was very interesting,' Maria said when she walked
back to them. 'Only the last third, that stuff about appropriation, I
didn't really understand that.'

'Yes, that is a problem,' said Perlmann, and started to turn away.
'And many thanks for your work.'

'You're welcome. And . . . Just a moment . . . We're still on for the
other text on Friday?'

Perlmann felt Kirsten's eyes on his face. When he turned round again,
he had the feeling of moving a heavy, shapeless load. 'Yes,' he said, 'as
agreed.'

He was already holding the dining-room door handle when Kirsten
pointed towards the pigeonholes. 'That's the text for your session on
Thursday, isn't it? Something about linguistic creation. Or did I misread
it? You whisked the pages away so quickly!' she laughed.

'Later,' Perlmann murmured when he saw Ruge and von Levetzov
coming towards them.

'You know,' said Kirsten when they sat down at the table, 'I thought
I might be able to take a copy of the text. To read on the journey. Do
you think I could ask Maria to make another printout for me?'

'Later,' said Perlmann. He hadn't managed to keep his distress and
fury out of his voice. He put his hand on her arm and smiled awkwardly.
'We'll talk about it later. OK?'

It took her ages to freshen herself up for the journey and pack her few
belongings. Perlmann looked apprehensively down at the bay, where
the first dawn was breaking below the gloomy sky. She hadn't said
another word about the text. And that (he knew his daughter far too
well) had nothing to do with the fact that they had all gone on sitting
in the dining room until after three, laughing at the jokes of Achim
Ruge, who had risen to the occasion under Kirsten's admiring gaze.

She would never speak again about that text of her own free will.
She would sooner bite off her tongue. It had always been like that

when he had treated her impatiently about anything. As before, she then tended to put on that pointedly oblivious, uninterested face that conveyed a single unambiguous message: *It's nothing*. Once, when someone in a specialist discussion had put forward the thesis that there was no other form of expressing negative assertions of existence apart from the linguistic, he had said, laughing, 'You don't know my daughter.'

Shortly after Kirsten had gone to her room, he had taken the text from his pigeonhole. He had only looked quickly at the last printed page: thirty-seven pages, it was now. Then he had put the printout in his suitcase and added the handwritten sheets to Leskov's text in the lower clothes drawer. He had phoned Genoa Station and reserved a sleeping compartment. Five minutes later he had phoned again and changed the reservation to a couchette. No, she couldn't tell him with the best will in the world, the irritated woman had said, what connections to Konstanz there would be at six o'clock in the morning in Zurich. Since then he had been standing by the window and, although his back hurt, that seemed to him to be the only position in which he could bear to wait.

She was wearing the black coat again, and holding her red travelling bag when she suddenly appeared at about half-past six. It was as if the question of the text had never come up. He was actually quite nice, stupid Giorgio, she said, but she really couldn't stand his endless mockery. And she certainly knew more about Faulkner than he did. She was wearing make-up again, and the bright-red hairgrip, he thought, didn't match the gleaming, greasy purple of her lips.

They got to the station far too early; the dimly lit platform was still deserted. There was suddenly an embarrassed silence between them. They looked shyly at one another, and then Kirsten began aimlessly rummaging in her travelling bag. Suddenly, the abandoned platform was filled with the shrill ringing that Perlmann already knew. It was a penetrating, endlessly protracted noise that sounded ghostly because it was in the night, even though not the slightest thing was happening.

They both exploded simultaneously into laughter, and Kirsten put her hands over her ears. They hastily left the station and stepped out under the plane trees in front of the exit.

She asked him if he really wanted to ride with her to Genoa when silence threatened to fall once more. That was really awkward. But he insisted on it. So later on they sat opposite one another in the shabby carriage, and Perlmann felt like bursting into tears when he realized that he was searching for topics of conversation as frantically as if she were a total stranger. At last he brought the subject around to Maria's hairdo and asked whether hairspray was the latest thing.

'Have you been living under a rock?' she laughed. 'That's been out for ages. It's like way, way out. No one wears it any more!'

Later she lit her last Gauloise and handed him the red lighter. Before he gave it back, he studied it very precisely, glad to be able to do something to counteract the silence that was threatening to fall once more. On the delicate gold rim the word *Cartier* was engraved in tiny letters. He was about to ask where she had got it, when her facial expression warned him, and he put it in her hand without a word. She turned it between her fingers as she looked out into the night.

'I'll give it to you,' she suddenly said, smiling with relief like someone who has just said a long overdue goodbye. 'Here, take it.'

He hesitantly took it from her. Her lips curled mockingly, then she snapped her fingers. 'Over.' He glanced at it once more and slipped it into his pocket. *François.*

She was temporarily alone in the couchette compartment. That could change in Milan, he thought, and then asked if she had any francs with her. For breakfast in Zurich. She leaned out of the window and stretched out her arm. He took her hand. At the front of the train the conductor started to close the doors.

'You didn't come to breakfast very often at home, either. To Mum's distress.' She sniffed, and now he saw the tears. 'Only on the first day of the holidays, then we always sat together, all morning. That was . . . that was wonderful.' She let go of his hand and wiped her eyes. 'Giorgio told me you never come to breakfast.' The train started moving. She laughed. '*Gli ho detto che ti voglio bene. Giusto?*'

Perlmann nodded and raised his hand to wave. Through his tears he saw Kirsten making a sieve with her hands and calling out something that he didn't understand. He stopped until he was quite sure that he could no longer see the red tail light of the train.

Because Kirsten's ticket had cost more than he had expected, he no longer had enough money for a taxi. He only just caught the last train to Santa Margherita. Now and again on the journey he reached for the red lighter in his pocket and ran through Kirsten's Italian sentence in his mind. In the hotel he threw himself on the bed and let his tears flow freely.

24

At the end of the Tuesday session, Millar suggested talking about Evelyn Mistral's works on Wednesday and Thursday, so that he could travel to Florence on Friday to meet his Italian colleague about the encyclopaedia. For a moment Perlmann felt a helpless fury, because the last free day on which he could have written was being taken from him. But even before Laura Sand gathered her things together and the others got up, that feeling had already collapsed in on itself, making way for a numbing indifference.

It was accompanied by a leaden weariness, which was further diminished by the fact that he was yielding to his compulsive need for sleep more and more often and with increasingly little resistance. If he woke up, the weariness tended to weigh heavier on him than before, and every time he crept under the shower in his clothes, the indifference seemed to become even more encompassing until he felt as if he had, in that short time, forgotten how to feel anything at all. If he ate anything, it happened very mechanically, and where the blindness of sensation was concerned, it was barely distinguishable from the food ingestion of a plant. It was only a matter of time before he ceased that activity, too, he thought, as he slipped once more into a twilight state in which he felt sheltered for a few moments, before the next maelstrom of flitting dream images carried him away.

On Tuesday evening Kirsten rang. He had been right, she said, the compartment had filled up in Milan, and then a real snoring concert had started up, so that she hadn't had a wink. In Zurich she had had to wait for almost two hours for a connection, but breakfast had been fantastic.

'I hope,' she said with anxious hesitation, 'you didn't misunderstand my farewell remark. It wasn't supposed to be an accusation.'

The practice room in the Institute had struck her as even shabbier than usual. 'And those inevitable paper cups! I couldn't help thinking about your crystal glasses!'

Martin? 'Imagine. He was standing at the station just by chance, because he'd worked out the thing with the night train.' She paused. 'When I saw him, I had a guilty conscience. Because . . . well, yeah, because of what I said.'

The seminar session? 'I slept through it with my eyes open! Once, when Lasker mentioned *The Wild Palms*, I couldn't help thinking about my discussion with Millar. God, is that guy pleased with himself! *Cocksure* doesn't begin to cover it!'

Afterwards, Perlmann couldn't get to sleep, and wished his earlier compulsion to rest would return. In the middle of the night he fetched his notes from the suitcase and sat down at the desk. He slowly flicked the pages. No, translating the German examples into English didn't work; they sounded dull, weird and even ridiculous. *Presence: a perfume, a light, a smile* . . . He had already picked up the felt-tip pen to cross out the two lines when he stopped and smoked a cigarette. He left the lines as they were and flicked to the end. *What separates me from my present* . . . Without hesitation he crossed out the whole of the last paragraph. But that wasn't enough for him. He went on blackening the page until the last white dot had disappeared and the whole thing formed a deep black block that left traces on the next page. He waved and blew the page dry, then flicked back to the two indented lines. After a quick look he blackened them out too. For a while he sat motionless in front of the first page. Then, with the felt-tip pen, he drew the heading: MESTRE NON È BRUTTA.

On Wednesday morning on the way to the veranda he went to see Maria in the office and gave her the notes. She laughed at the title. Now the text was ready earlier after all, she said. She still had a whole pile of things to get done today and tomorrow, but she would manage to get it done by Monday, as agreed. Perlmann nodded to everything. He was already in the doorway when he heard her laughing again. She was pointing at the blacked-out closing paragraph. 'Like something in a secret dossier!' she said. 'It really stirs the curiosity!'

It took Evelyn Mistral almost an hour to shake off her nerves. Only then did her frantic play with her glasses stop, and she started sitting comfortably in the big armchair. It was plainly hard for her to believe that Millar and Ruge weren't just being polite, but that they had really liked her paper. But then, when she felt safe, she became more commanding from one minute to the next, delivered a lot that wasn't in the text, and reported on a series of exciting experiments of imagination and will that Millar found really inspiring. The feeling of having succeeded in this illustrious circle was making her increasingly excited. Her face was red and she smoked much more than usual, von Levetzov holding out a burning match to her, always at exactly the right time, with the attentiveness of a trainer. Once when, contrary to her usual habits, she tried to inhale and started coughing, there was laughter which unambiguously expressed the fact that the others accepted her in her accomplishment and were glad of her relief.

Perlmann took the greatest trouble to look interested, and on Wednesday afternoon he finally – constantly struggling against exhaustion – caught up with reading her paper. But everything he said sounded wooden, and even as he spoke all the meaning seemed to drain from his words. In the first third of the text came the passage where Evelyn Mistral spoke about why the differentiation of imagination and will occurred in the medium of language. It wasn't the same reflection as the one in Leskov's work, he noticed straight away. But when he tried to remember Leskov's argument, there was nothing but emptiness. That kind of emptiness, which had something definitive about it, and was quite unlike a temporary gap in the memory, chilled him to the core. He only just managed to fight down the idea that he was on the point of losing his mind.

On Thursday evening he went to the trattoria. He saw that it was on the tip of the proprietor and his wife's tongues to ask him where he had been for the last few days. But after a long, startled look at him they both suppressed their curiosity. Perlmann went to the toilet and looked at his face in the mirror. It wasn't, he thought, any paler than usual. On the contrary, the boat trip with Kirsten had left a hint of a tan. But the color, he saw now, had not been the cause of his hosts' shock. It was the lifelessness of his features that had made them start. His face had something of the exhaustion of a shipwreck about it, something forlorn that gave one the strange idea that its owner had run off and simply left it there. Perlmann attempted a smile, but immediately stopped when he saw how cold and mask-like it looked.

When Sandra came skipping into the almost empty restaurant, her parents glanced at Perlmann to tell her to be quiet. Then he asked the girl to sit down with him and enquired about school. She didn't seem to notice anything special about his face, but was bored by all the questions and relieved when she was allowed to go again. Perlmann left half of his dinner on the plate, mumbled a vague apology and was glad when the glass-bead curtain rattled shut behind him.

For a while he stood in the harbor watching the waves breaking on the concrete blocks in front of the jetty. It wasn't at all true that it was going to happen tomorrow. Tomorrow was, after all, only Friday, the day when he had been supposed to give Maria his text. Assuming that he was going to deliver lectures at his session rather than use handouts, he still had six days to play with. Minus the time for Silvestri's sessions. He took a few deep breaths. Now the important thing was to keep alive the little bit of confidence that still stirred. Five days, that was basically a lot of time. After all, he had experience of writing lectures, a lot of experience. Slowly, as if his confidence might be broken by excessively violent movements, he walked back to the hotel.

When he opened the door to his room, the phone began to ring.

'It's me,' Kirsten said. 'I just wanted to hear quickly how you've been.'

At first Perlmann didn't understand. It was only when Kirsten called 'Hello?' for the second time that he got it: she thought his session had been today. It was out of annoyance at the tone of student camaraderie, which she was using again now, that he hadn't mentioned the postponement to her on Sunday in Rapallo.

'It isn't my turn yet,' he said. 'There was a change to the timetable. I'm not for a week.'

'Oh, so there was no point in me touching wood. Whose turn was it today?'

'Evelyn.'

'Aha.'

There was a pause.

'Is Giorgio still there?'

He laughed, and was surprised. 'Yes, he's still here.'

'Say hello from me. Don't be too friendly, though! And tell him . . . no, leave it.'

Perlmann sat down at the desk and looked at the page of headings, on which he had drawn some figures in the margin. *When I get bored in the seminar, I doodle as well*, she had said. He would probably never know what had happened between her and Silvestri. And he couldn't ask under any circumstances. He had only made that mistake once. He saw her furious face in front of him and heard the joke that Agnes had made about his startled reaction.

At that moment the phone rang again.

'I have to go to Bologna, to the clinic, tonight,' said Silvestri. 'Now of all times, when the boss is away, the other senior doctor is ill and suddenly all hell seems to have broken out.' Perlmann heard him smoking. 'Two patients have . . . run away. They're considered dangerous, and the police are involved.' He coughed. 'I'm sorry to be so unreliable. But I can't just leave the others hanging. My sessions on Monday and Tuesday are out of the window. I assume you yourself will take on these dates.

I'll be coming back, and perhaps I can present something in the second half of the week.' He laughed. 'And if not – academia will have to go on without me!'

Perlmann slowly hung up. His fingers left traces of sweat on the receiver. *Monday. Tomorrow is Friday. And I have nothing. Not a single sentence.* He wiped his hands on his trousers. He shivered. What he did now didn't matter in the slightest. Any movement was just as unfounded and useless as any other. There was now no stopping it.

With dragging steps he walked into the bathroom and took a whole sleeping pill. The water tasted more chlorinated than usual. The taste reminded him of his first swimming lesson in the municipal pool, when he had almost drowned. It was an oppressive memory, but it led away from the present, and he clung to it as the numbness slowly spread within him.

II

The Plan

25

He woke with a headache and a film of sweat on his face. It was a quarter to ten, and the sun shone from a cloudless sky on the mirror-smooth water of the bay. *Today I have to make a decision. Any decision.*

Here in this room, under the eyes of the others, so to speak, he couldn't reach a decision, he thought in the shower. He left the hotel by the rear entrance and had a coffee in a bar on the Piazza Veneto. His headache gradually eased, and he was better able to bear looking out into the radiant autumn day.

There was no point hushing up Silvestri's departure from the others. Over the course of the day they would find out from Signora Morelli, certainly by the time they asked for the texts for the Monday session. And then they would inevitably assume that he, Perlmann, would be giving the next two sessions. *Where are his papers?* he could hear Millar asking. By dinner time Perlmann would have to be able to say that copies were being made. Otherwise he wouldn't be able to show his face.

Down at the jetty, where the liners docked, people were gathering: locals with baskets and bicycles, but also a few tourists with cameras. All of a sudden it seemed to Perlmann that a long boat trip would help him more than anything else to gain clarity, and he put as much emphasis as possible on that thought to drown out his mounting panic.

A boat left for Genoa at eleven. He stood aside from the waiting group. Another quarter of an hour. He smoked impatiently. Now he didn't think he could bear to stay on dry land a moment longer. He finally wanted to set foot on the boat and watch the stretch of water widening between himself and the jetty. At eleven o'clock the ship had still not come into view. He cursed the Italian lack of punctuality.

When he stood at the railing half an hour later, right at the front of the ship, he made an effort to open his senses wide so that their impressions would penetrate him deeply and powerfully, overwhelming and suffocating his despairing thoughts. He had no sunglasses with him. It hurt to look out into the dazzling light, but he narrowed his eyes and tried to take it all in even so. The light broke on the water. Near the bow it was sparkling points, gleaming little stars, further out calm surfaces of white gold and platinum; above it a layer of gauzy mist, and in the distance the glittering surface passed seamlessly into haze that dissolved at the top in a dome of milky blue. He inhaled the heavy, slightly intoxicating smell of seawater in slow, deep draughts, a smell that had repeatedly drawn him to the harbor in Hamburg, even as a child, because it promised an intense and also a completely effortless present.

I must concentrate. When I pass this spot again on the way back, I'll have to know what I'm going to do. He sat down in the shade under the cabin porch. There were only three possibilities. One consisted in presenting nothing at all. No text. No session. That would be a declaration of bankruptcy, which would also alienate the others, because it would come unheralded and without a request for understanding. He had missed that. On the contrary, when asking Millar for information about English words, he had inevitably created the impression of working on a paper. It would be a sudden, speechless bankruptcy, without explanation on his part and without understanding from the others, an abyss of mute embarrassment. And that possibility struck Perlmann as completely unbearable, when he considered how he could announce it. He couldn't simply put a piece of paper in his colleagues' pigeonholes telling them aridly that he would not be providing a contribution, that the sessions assigned to the purpose had been cancelled. Should he add: *because with the best will in the world I haven't been able to think of anything?* They would demand an explanation, either explicitly or through their silence. Or should he admit complete failure over dinner, tap his glass and then, with words upon which the very situation would bestow a dreadful and involuntary solemnity, explain that unfortunately he had absolutely nothing more to say in academic terms? Should he perhaps visit the individual colleagues in their rooms and tell them of his incapacity, six times in a row and then a seventh time on the phone to Angelini, who was so keen to come to his session? Perlmann got a dry mouth and walked quickly back to the bow to let the airstream dispel that thought.

A local family with two children was coming forwards from the rear of the ship. The children threw a ball to each other, and suddenly the peace up here at the front, where only a few tourists had been standing at the railing taking photographs, was over. By the violence of his blazing irritation Perlmann could tell how far off-kilter he was. When the boy missed the ball, which flew overboard, he started screaming as if he were being burned at the stake; his parents could do nothing to calm him down, and Perlmann had to control himself to keep from yelling at him and shaking him till he stopped. He fled to the stern of the ship, but the screaming was even audible there, and the roar of the engine made clear thinking impossible. At last he went to the cabin and drank a lukewarm coffee at the bar.

He could – this was the next possibility – present his notes on language and experience as his contribution. He would have to call Maria from Genoa and ask her to have the paper ready by today, tomorrow lunchtime at the very latest. He could tell her what had happened with Silvestri. And ask her to cross out the heading MESTRE NON È BRUTTA – as the title of a paper that was already extremely questionable, it was an additional and unnecessary provocation.

He went through once more the sentences he had looked at on Monday night; some of them he read out under his voice. This morning he liked them; they struck him as apt and seemed to capture something important that one might easily fail to notice. They were unassuming, precise sentences, he thought. For a while their calm style merged with the peace of the gleaming surface of the water far out, and it didn't seem impossible to him to approach the others with these sentences. But then a tottering old man bumped into him and knocked him against the bar, and suddenly Perlmann's sense of security and the confidence that he had felt in his words just a moment before collapsed all around him. Now they struck him as being as treacherous as mirages, or the wishful thinking one has while half-asleep, and as he poured his slopped coffee from the saucer back into the cup, he said to himself with apprehensive sobriety that this solution was also unthinkable. Quite apart from the fact that it was not a coherent paper, these strange notes would be mocked as impressionistic and anecdotal, as unverifiable, often inconsistent, full of contradictions, in short, as unscientific. The paper would leave people like Millar and Ruge speechless. They saw only the possibility of irony. The most charitable thing would be for them to maintain an expressive silence.

That Perlmann would be left standing there as someone who had abandoned academia, and could henceforth not be relied upon, and that now, of all times, when he had received the prize and the invitation to Princeton was approaching – that wasn't the worst thing about this possibility. What made the thought entirely unbearable was the fact that these notes were far too intimate, and laid him bare before anyone who read them. They had seemed so intimate to him that he had felt more at ease using a foreign language as a protection even from himself. To someone with English as a mother tongue – Millar, for example – that distance did not apply. Perlmann shuddered. And then, suddenly, he had a sense that he understood his dread about his own sentences better than before: many of the notes showed him as a shy and vulnerable child wrestling with experiences it had not understood.

If he presented nothing at all, that would in itself reveal something he would have preferred to keep silent. But it remained global and abstract. It was the confession of an incapacity that remained otherwise in darkness. What he thought and experienced behind it remained unclear, unfamiliar. It was up to him to hide himself away from further insights. His notes, on the other hand, were, it seemed to him, like a window through which one could see right into his innermost depths. To let the others read them would mean obliterating all the boundaries that he had so painstakingly constructed, and it seemed to Perlmann that there was barely any difference between this process and complete annihilation.

The air in the ship's cabin was so thick that it could have been cut with a knife, and Perlmann felt he was suffocating on his own smoke. He stubbed out his cigarette and went quickly outside. He performed a complete tour of the ship, his eyes seeking something that might hold his attention for a moment, for just a few moments which would mean his last small respite, a last opportunity to catch his breath for what was about to come.

He was glad when an elderly, dwarfish man asked him for a light. For a moment he was tempted to escape into a conversation with him, but then he was repelled by the man's permanently open mouth with its swelling, protruding tongue. Perlmann pulled his face into a painful smile and walked back to the front, where he stepped up slowly, almost in slow motion, to the railing, supporting himself on outstretched arms and closed his eyes.

The third possibility was one that he had not, until that moment, dared to capture in an explicit thought. Hitherto it had been present to him only in the form of a dark, impenetrable sensation, from which he had turned hastily away whenever it had appeared on the edge of his consciousness. Because it was a sensation – he felt that very clearly whenever it touched him – that emanated a terrible sense of menace, and merely to pursue its precise content was a sense of danger. And so it seemed to him a tremendous effort. It was a summoning of courage that he thought he felt physically now that he looked this possibility in the face for the first time: the possibility of presenting the translation of Leskov's text as his own.

It was as if a treacherous poison were spreading through him when he allowed this desperate thought to unfold before him in all its clarity. It hurt to experience himself as someone who could in all seriousness consider such a thought. It was a dry pain, free of self-pity, and all the more horrific for that reason. What happened there, he sensed with an alertness in which all self-reassurance burned away, was a deep incision in his life, an irrevocable, incurable break with the past and the start of a new computation of time.

None of his colleagues would be able to discover the deception, even if the Russian text were by some improbable coincidence to fall into their hands. For them a Russian text was nothing more than a closed typeface, an ornament. And besides, none of them knew Leskov. No one knew his address. All they had heard was the name 'St Petersburg'. And last of all, none of them had the slightest reason to make contact with this unknown, obscure Russian, who was a nobody in professional circles, and thus provoke the threat of discovery by Leskov himself. Later, if the works were to be published, Perlmann could withdraw the paper and replace it with one of his own. If necessary he could also delay the printing. He would publish the volume. Aside from his own printout there would be only seven copies of the bogus text, and it would be respected when he expressly asked that the text should not be distributed further, as it was only the first, provisional version, an experiment. If they then heard nothing more about its further development, saw no further versions and instead read an entirely new text by him, the others would at last set the paper aside. It would be forgotten, and grow yellow and dusty on a shelf or in a cupboard, until eventually it fell victim to a clearing operation like the one that everyone undertook sooner or later in their own flood of paper, and was destroyed.

So he could risk it. And from the point of view of scholarly esteem he would be in a much better position than in the two other cases. Admittedly, Leskov's text was wayward and in some places bold; one could even call it eccentric. But in the discussion Perlmann could refer to the literature of memory research which had not been accessible to Leskov himself, and one could also characterize the paper as a conceptual one, a broad-brushstroke outline, and thus basically precisely appropriate to this occasion. Millar and Ruge, this was fairly clear, would screw up their noses at so much speculation. But it was certainly possible that the others would find the text interesting. That much was certainly true of Evelyn Mistral. But even a man like von Levetzov had recently taken notice of the subject. Perlmann, it might appear, was trying something new, something that perhaps was no longer linguistics, but which was imaginative and provocative. Something was happening, developing in Perlmann's work, and secretly they might even be a bit envious of his courage.

Perlmann felt ill, and he threw the cigarette he had just lit into the water. He was relieved that they were now entering Genoa harbor and there were some things to look at: the crew throwing the ropes, the steaming water spraying from the bow and, further away, the big ships and the cranes whose arms glided over the tall stacks of colorful containers. When the family from before was suddenly standing next to him and the children were loudly calling out the things they could see, Perlmann wasn't bothered, quite the contrary. He fled his thoughts and wished he could step outside his innermost depths and lose himself in things, dissolve himself entirely in the stones of the quay wall, in the wooden poles against which the ship was rubbing, in the cobbles of the street, in all the things that were simply just there and entire unto themselves.

There was nothing to keep him on dry land. The lack of any rocking movement gave him a feeling of imprisonment, even though he had the chance of going wherever he wanted in this city on the slope, which in the noon autumn light had something about it of a desert city, something oriental. The ship didn't get back until a quarter past three, but there was a tour of the harbor every hour, and the people for the one o'clock trip were just boarding. Perlmann was glad that it was late in the year and the two seats next to him were free. When he let his arm dangle over the side, he could almost touch the dark green, almost black water. Pools of oil and rubbish drifted past, at the clearer spots one could make out seaweed, and sometimes a rusty chain used to moor a ship.

He gave a start when the loudspeaker was turned on with a click, and an unnecessarily loud woman's voice greeted the passengers, first in Italian, then in English, German, French and Spanish and at last in a language that must have been Japanese. It was idiotic, but he hadn't thought about that, as if he were on a sightseeing boat for the first time in his life. It was going to be an hour of torture: all that information, all those explanations that interested him not in the slightest, and everything in six languages. And he urgently needed to think. Peace and concentration had never been as important as they were now.

The voice from the loudspeaker, shrill and bored, began with details about the size of the harbor and the volume of its goods shipments, then a tape played the same information in the other languages, all women's voices, only the Spanish text was spoken by a man. Perlmann covered his ears, the repetitions were unbearable. That he had been so stupid as to take this trip struck him as a sign that there was no way out of his plight. It was like a harbinger of inescapable doom.

They passed by the first big ships, their curved, black bows loomed far into the air, lifeboats were fastened along the railings, and single sailors waved. Hidden behind another vessel, a black ship's wall suddenly appeared, bearing the word LENINGRAD in white, Cyrillic script. Perlmann turned hot and cold. He gulped and felt everything convulsing inside him. At that moment he desperately wished the letters were completely alien to him, just white lines that provided nothing to read and nothing to understand. That they were so familiar and self-evident to him was a source of unhappiness; the actual reason, it seemed to him, for his desperate situation.

Agnes, he was quite sure, would have advised him to take the first path. Of course, she would have understood that it was unpleasant for him; but she would have seen the whole thing in far less dramatic terms than he did. It was, she might have said, as if she had had to tell the agency: 'Sorry, but over the past few weeks I haven't come up with any usable shots.' That was all, a temporary crisis, no reason to speak of a loss of face.

But Agnes had worked for an agency in which everyone was very cooperative, almost chummy. She hadn't known the academic world, with its atmosphere of competition and mutual suspicion, she had just known it from his stories, and there had often been a bad atmosphere between them when he thought he sensed she was mutely reproaching him for an excessive and disproportionate sensitivity in such matters.

The trip now continued along the quay where the big freighters lay. Between the individual ships one could see the long row of trucks that picked up the goods. This was where the freight was discharged. *Discharged*, he thought to himself, and for a moment he stopped resisting the loudspeaker and concentrated instead on the vocabulary of harbors and ships. He lost himself entirely in the shrill Italian voice and then the others, the taped voices with their sterile tones which, it seemed to him, had not the slightest thing to do with the colorful backdrop outside.

Without really noticing, he began translating from one language to another in his mind. At first he tested how well he could keep up when he translated into German. It became increasingly clear to him that it was a matter of keeping a very particular balance of concentration. One had to look back at the sentence that had just come to an end, and could only begin to form the German sentence when the point of syntactical clarity had been reached in the foreign sentence – no earlier, because otherwise one could find oneself starting on the wrong foot, and end up stumbling. That meant that you inevitably concluded the German sentence after a certain time lag, with a powerful need to put it behind you to have your head free for the next one. So in the second half of the sentence you automatically speeded up, exploiting the routine and self-evidence with which your mother tongue was available to you. That phase could barely hold the attention, because it already had to be deployed entirely upon the new sentence. During that second it was a tightrope act, from which one could fall either of two ways. First of all, it could happen that you had to think for a moment too long about the old sentence, perhaps even that an unfamiliar word would put you in a panic; then you started too late into the process in which you should have been constructing your trained expectations concerning the new sentence, and had to admit that you had missed the new sentence. Or else you were pursued by the fear that that was precisely what could happen; then you risked the danger of letting your eye dart just a bit too far forward, even before the German version of the old sentence had found the point at which it sounded most natural and could be left up to the unconscious concluding process, so then you couldn't conclude the old sentence. The worst case was a combination of the two. Then a kind of paralysis set in: you sensed that you should actually take a quick look back to finish the old sentence correctly, but it was plain that you had arrived too late for the new sentence. You didn't know which was more important, and that doubt meant you lost time, and then you lost control of both sentences, the old one and the new one, and you had to shake off your irritation with your own failure very quickly to catch up with the next sequence of sentences.

That seemed to Perlmann to be the hardest thing: not to succumb to irritation over occasional and inevitable errors. Part of the training of an interpreter, he thought, would be to show no irritation, to reach in a flash and unemotionally the decision that the current sentence was beyond saving, a normal breakdown that should be forgotten straight away. Above all it was a matter of confidence: the certainty that one could depend completely upon one's capacity for concentration. And as long as one maintained and experienced that difficult balance, remaining master of the situation, it was a wonderful feeling that could be quite intoxicating. That feeling would intensify still further, he thought, if one were capable of translating between two foreign languages, two that were as exotic as possible, far removed from the natural self-evidence of one's mother tongue. A diversity in the languages you had mastered, that was freedom, and being able to push your own boundaries far out into the realm of the exotic, that must be a massive intensification of the sense of life, a real rush of freedom.

Perlmann now tried to leap back and forth between the foreign languages that came out of the loudspeaker, and each time he did so he felt clumsy and stupid as he collided against Japanese as if against an impenetrable wall. Then the particular pitch and brightness of the Japanese voice sounded as if the woman were mocking his incomprehension. He liked being able to make the whole effort on the quiet, involving himself only internally, to some extent, without the sound that came when you engaged with the world by speaking. And during a pause from the loudspeaker, when the only sound was the quiet rushing of the water and the puttering of the engine, he knew all of a sudden what he could have been: a long-distance runner through all the languages of the world, with lots of empty space around him, and without the obligation to exchange a single word with people.

He pursued that thought later on, sitting in a shabby bar near the harbor, over a pizza that repelled him. He asked the surprised proprietor for some paper and a pencil and started describing, on a stained waiter's pad, the kind of presence and freedom that arose when one passed through several languages at brief intervals. At first it was an effort, he was tired by the sun and the loudspeaker, and the excessively loud voices still rang in his head. But then he got going. He managed precise and dense descriptions, and he formulated things that he had previously felt only vaguely, but had never grasped in words. Every now and again he glanced southwards. The hotel was over an hour's boat journey away. He grew calm. Here at this wobbly table, from which the paint was flaking, amidst men in vests and dungarees, who probably worked in the harbor, he suddenly felt safe. He managed to stand by the idea that he was someone who was far more interested in sentences like the ones on these little bits of paper than the whole flood of linguistic data and theories.

He asked if he could use the telephone on the bar, and phoned Maria in the hotel. Something in his schedule had changed, he said, and asked whether she couldn't have his paper ready by this evening or at least by tomorrow afternoon.

She would try, she said, but she couldn't promise anything, and in fact it was rather unlikely, because some people from Fiat had just arrived and, of course, she would now have to see to them as well.

He knew it was childish, but he was hurt that Maria had reminded him that there was something else in the world apart from him and his group. Her reaction hadn't been unfriendly, but her voice had been quite businesslike, and that was enough to suggest resentment, mingled with irritation that he hadn't given her his notes to be typed up much sooner.

On the way back clouds rolled in and accumulated quickly, dark mountains with a delicate edge of sunlight. A squally wind announced a storm and soon the sea was like foaming, greenish lead against a dark, slate-grey wall in which flashes of lightning appeared like scribbled lines. When a violent shower began, the people withdrew inside, leaving Perlmann alone outside under the cabin porch.

Again sentences from the notes circled in his head. He tested them, tasted them, attempted a neutral, sober, detached judgment. Instead, he became increasingly insecure, the English language dampened the sentences, made them less brilliant, less pretentious, *but in the end it's all trash anyway.* He pulled the stained pieces of paper from his pocket and read them, as gusts of wind lashed the rain across and drenched him to the skin. When it had finished, he paused for a while and stared out into the sheet lightning. Then slowly, almost softly, he crumpled the pieces of paper and pressed them with both hands into a solid ball. He turned them back and forth in his hands a few more times. Then he threw them out into the sea. The second possibility was eliminated, once and for all.

It was so terribly cramped, this prison of the three possibilities, whose bars he rattled with furious frustration. Again and again he attempted to flee by clinging to the idea of bigger connections, of altered proportions. *It's mad to let myself be so tied up by ludicrous issues of respect within a group of colleagues that all that I remain seems to be entirely insignificant and not even present. And besides; there are disasters, wars, hunger and misery in the world out there, and there are real tragedies and real suffering. Why do I not free myself by simply denying the importance of this tiny, laughable problem? Why don't I just tear down the prison walls by declaring them to be imaginary structures? Who's actually stopping me from doing that?*

But each attempt to take that much-longed-for step into freedom through an altered perspective and a re-evaluation of things proved to be deceptive and without any lasting effect as soon as the image of the loathed hotel re-entered the foreground and, as if it had hypnotic powers, extinguished everything else.

When the Portofino peninsula came into view Perlmann was gripped by panic, a panic that had seemed to have been defeated two hours before in the bar at the harbor. The word PLAGIARISM formed within him; against his will it grew bigger and bigger, it spread within him and filled him with an internal roar. He had never been confronted with the word as he was now, he was discovering it properly now for the first time. It was a terrible word, a word that made him think of the color red, a dark red with a hint of black. It was a gloomy, heavy word with a doom-laden sound; a repellent and unnatural word. It seemed to him like a word that had been deliberately assembled to frighten and torment someone to their very depths by calling up in him the feeling that beneath all the actions of which people were capable there was no crime greater than the one represented by this hateful, angular word.

The only one who could unmask him would be Leskov himself, and he was in St Petersburg, thousands of miles away, without an exit permit and still tied to his sick mother. Better security from the discovery of deception was hard to imagine. But that reflection sounded feeble and papery compared to a mute certainty which made him shiver even more in his wet clothes: committing such a fraud, a theft of thought and writing on that scale would – for someone like himself, to whom words meant so much – inflict a wound that would never heal, a trauma from which he would never be able to recover. In a sense it would be the end of his life. After that the time until death would be something that he could only endure. Occasional forgetfulness and immersion in the everyday would make it a little more bearable, but Perlmann was quite sure that on the whole stretch that still lay before him there wouldn't be a single day when he could keep from thinking about it, and hearing the word PLAGIARISM inside himself.

On the way to the exit he was once again filled with shame that he had allowed this thought so much space, and at the same time he was glad to have looked it openly in the eye, and to have fought it down once and for all.

When he set foot on dry land and set off towards the hotel, he still had no idea what he was going to do.

Back in his room he took off his wet things, showered for a long time and then walked to the open window. The rain had stopped, the storm had headed southwards, and only in the far distance could one still see the occasional flash and hear a faint rumble of thunder. Night was closing in. Perlmann lay down on the bed. He felt exhausted to his very last fibre. It was a vibrating weariness that flowed through him, and yet at the same time his body was tense, and resisted any attempt at relaxation. He felt only one wish: that the tension might collapse in on itself and make way for sleep. But that state persisted, the yearned-for process of metabolism in his brain didn't begin, and after a while he went to the bathroom and took a quarter-tablet.

His face in the mirror had received some color from the boat trip. *Philipp Perlmann, tanned on Italian holiday,* he thought and didn't know what to do with all his despair. With a dull, empty head he smoked two cigarettes, then lay back down again and, after a few tormented minutes in which he tossed back and forth, he slipped into shallow, troubled sleep.

It was ten o'clock at night when he woke up. He immediately noticed that the paralysing apprehension which had held him in its grip during his sleep had passed uninterrupted into his waking state. But it was a while before he had overcome his state of disorientation. *I've got to do something now. It's the last moment. If I don't do anything now, that, too, is a decision. All that I'm left with is a declaration of failure.*

He felt dully that a complicated process of reflection had taken place over the course of the day, a thick net of serpentine, dead-end thoughts. But his head was too heavy for them now. He remembered the boat trip, but that whole day seemed to be far away and unreal. The only clear thought he was able to have was that he now had to go downstairs and hand in a text that could be copied tomorrow morning, while he was still asleep. *Maria. My text isn't ready yet. The people from Fiat.*

As he fumbled with the combination on his suitcase lock, he realized that his fingertips were numb from the sleeping pill. It was by no means a complete numbness. It affected only the outermost layer, and was actually more of a faint tingle, but it gave Perlmann the feeling that contact with the world was being lost; the contact that one needed if one were to maintain control. It was as if a tiny gap had appeared between him and the world, a thin tear through which the world was escaping him. He took his translation of Leskov's paper from his case and walked towards the door. There he turned round, went into the bathroom and swallowed a whole sleeping pill. He took the elevator downstairs.

There was no one at reception, but in the back room Giovanni sat with the television on. Perlmann saw a floodlit football stadium. Giovanni was leaning forward and hastily smoking. Perlmann rang the bell, but it wasn't until the second ring that Giovanni turned his head and hesitantly got to his feet, his eyes still fixed on the game. 'Penalty,' he said apologetically when he saw Perlmann's face.

For a moment Perlmann felt as if he wouldn't be able to open his mouth. Never before had he been so aware that he had a mouth. Giovanni glanced impatiently over his shoulder at the television, where a roar of jubilation was exploding at that moment.

'Six copies,' Perlmann said urgently, 'then please put them in my colleagues' pigeonholes.'

'*Va bene, Signor Perlmann,*' said Giovanni, and accepted the text. As he did so a bit of ash fell from his cigarette on to the immaculate, gleaming white of the title page. It was only by turning away in silence and leaving that Perlmann managed to control himself. When he glanced back he saw Giovanni quickly putting the paper under the counter and disappearing into the back room.

The pills were already taking effect when he hung the DO NOT DISTURB sign on the door. He was grateful when a gentle wave of numbness washed over the sensations that were forcing their way to the surface; sensations of defeat, shame and anxiety, the feeling of falling without knowing when he would land; the certainty that from now on he would never stop falling. Without turning on the light he lay down in bed and was glad that the gap between himself and the world was rapidly growing.

26

I must have been crazy. Completely crazy. All of a sudden Perlmann was gripped by a painful feeling of alertness, an alertness behind his closed eyes, which were steeped in physical drowsiness. It was quarter to eight. Quickly, his movements still uncertain, he pulled his trousers and pullover over his pyjamas and slipped into his shoes with no socks on. *Perhaps the copies won't even be ready yet, in which case I'll simply collect them up again. Nothing has happened yet.*

With jerky movements that betrayed his giddiness, he ran downstairs, nearly falling twice. Just before the last step he came to a standstill, clutching on to the banister with both hands. Millar and von Levetzov were standing down by the desk, taking the texts that Signora Morelli was handing them.

'The paper's still warm,' Millar said with a grin, and ran the pages along his thumb like a pack of cards.

The other copies were still in the pigeonholes. *Minutes, I just got here minutes late, but now I can't go over and demand the text back, it would make me look ridiculous. You can't explain something like that. If only the signora had been less efficient, just this once.*

Perlmann hurried back to his room, his breath catching with each step at the idea of bumping into one of his other colleagues. In the bathroom he rinsed out his mouth and then sat down with a cigarette in the red armchair. He felt dizzy. He had crossed a threshold and would never be able to go back. This fraud – its consequences now unfolding inexorably – was something he would have to live with for ever. The day after tomorrow and the day after that he would sit in the Marconi

Veranda defending a text he had stolen. The hours, the minutes that he spent sitting there in front of the others as an unacknowledged fraud would last for ever, and once his stay here was over it was as a fraudster that he would enter his apartment in Frankfurt. He would look at Agnes's picture and talk to Kirsten, always aware of his deception. Nothing would ever be the same. His plagiarism would now stand for ever between him and the world like a thin glass wall, visible only to him. He would touch objects and people without ever being able to reach them.

Perlmann couldn't stay in this building filled with people who would in the next few hours be following Leskov's thought processes on the assumption that they were his. And he could no longer bear it in this hotel room, for which almost 300 marks a day had been spent for more than four weeks, and in which he had done not a single thing. Apart from a translation, which was now a fraudulent translation.

He didn't shower. He no longer felt he could use the luxurious bathroom for longer than was absolutely necessary. After he had got properly dressed, he would have liked to order another coffee to fight the after-effects of the tablet, which could no longer protect him against anything, and only lay on his eyes like a continuous pressure, so that he constantly felt the need to close them. But he didn't even want to appear in front of the waiter, and room service was one of the things to which he no longer had any right in future.

He left the hotel by the rear entrance and stepped out into a cloudless, radiant autumn day. As quickly as he could, he walked to the spur of rock behind which the road to Portofino disappeared, almost running the last few yards before he was out of view of the hotel. *But they have no idea. Nevertheless, I have to disappear from their field of vision.* He didn't dare lean against the railing around the corner. He must have looked like a holidaymaker, a spa patient enjoying a wonderful Italian autumn morning. So he smoked his cigarette upright and stiff, one hand in his trouser pocket. He had to walk, keep on going; walking made it almost bearable. His stomach hurt. He hadn't eaten a thing since the few mouthfuls of pizza in Genoa yesterday, and now the cigarettes.

He found it hard to remember exactly what it had been like last night. The most difficult thing was the attempt to recall the internal *Gestalt* of that moment when he had taken Leskov's paper out of the suitcase and gone to the door. It had happened during those few seconds. Something had been set in motion that could not now be stopped, a sequence of events that dragged him with it to the end, from the fatal motion of the arm with which he had handed the text to Giovanni, to the strenuous movement of his mouth, with which he had given the disastrous instruction to copy and distribute. Now that he thought back to it with his eyes closed, it struck him as less his own action than something that had come over him, that had simply happened to him; or if it were an action, then it was the action of a sleepwalker. For a moment this thought brought him relief, and his step became a little lighter.

But that didn't last for long. There was – and there was no getting around it – something in the structure of his own thoughts and feelings that had activated this quite particular sequence of movements, and not another. On the ship yesterday it had looked like a balance of reasons. The three possibilities of action had balanced one another out precisely; all three seemed equally inconceivable, and that was where the agony had lain. During his troubled sleep it must have been working away inside him, a power play must have taken place, and in the end something, perhaps just a tiny preponderance or sensation, must have tipped the scales.

Although the sun shone directly down on him, Perlmann buttoned up his jacket. The thought that he was someone in whom – without his noticing it or being able to do anything about it – fraud had taken the upper hand, chilled him. The only thing he had with which to counter this fact, so that it did not crush him entirely, was an explanation for those internal events. His fear of personal revelation – of standing there without any means of distancing himself from other people – must have been far greater than he had previously assumed, greater even than his conscious awareness. Plainly it was so powerful that the two other possibilities must – somewhere deep within him, and without his assistance – have vanished, and no option remained but to hide behind Leskov's text, which was to protect him against the other two alternatives. In this way, without his being aware of it, the paradoxical will had arisen in him to achieve his delineation, his defense against others, through an instrument that did not belong to him, something that was not his.

That explanation couldn't mitigate anything, or prettify it. But it did represent an insight that gave him back a scrap of inner freedom, the freedom of the perceiver.

Over the mirror-smooth, dazzling water lay a film of delicate mist, just like yesterday, when he had stood at the front of the ship and tried to open up his senses to this gleaming present. But eons lay between yesterday and today. Yesterday his gaze upon the surfaces of the purest brilliance had still been a gaze into an open future. Its openness had tormented him, because each of the possible paths upon which he could enter it had seemed threatening. But in spite of everything it had been an open future, there had been ramifications of action and, consequently, there had still been hope, or at least the freedom of uncertainty. Now everything, uncertainty and hope, was destroyed, the future was no longer a space of possibilities, but just a cramped, undeviating stretch of time on which he would have to live through the unalterable consequences of his deception. In that all-deciding moment, when he handed Leskov's text across the counter and uttered those doom-laden words, he had robbed himself for ever of an open future and thus, perhaps, of any hope that he might find his way back to his present.

The gleaming surface of the water, the white depth of the horizon, the vault of translucent azure, cut through by the silver trail of a rising aeroplane – it had all retreated to an unattainable distance, inaccessible to his experience. When one had done the kind of thing that he had done, one could no longer look outside. Joy and beauty, even a moment of happiness, were no longer possible. The price of deception was blindness. What you were left with was the option of huddling up inside and letting the maelstrom of guilt and lack of present wash over you. The outside world was nothing now but a backdrop, a backdrop tormenting in its beauty, a torture.

Perlmann was glad that it was a long way to Portofino. He had found
a rhythm of walking through which pain and despair held one another
in suspension. It was an unstable equilibrium, and when he had at one
point to stop and let a group of scouts pass him in single file, the sensations tumbled in upon him; he was defenselessly delivered over to them,
and only after a few minutes of renewed walking had he managed to
detach himself from them to any extent. The rhythmical movement and
the after-effect of the sleeping pills merged into a state in which, with
half-closed eyes directed at the tarmac, he occasionally managed to think
nothing at all.

Into such a phase of inner emptiness fell the sudden suspicion that
his earlier explanation for his nocturnal action was not at all true. *The
truth is that I wanted to put it behind me as quickly as possible, whatever
it might be, so that I could go on sleeping.* Waking at ten, he hadn't so
much as thought about the possibility of handing in nothing at all and
standing there empty-handed in front of everyone, and that was, of
course, no accident. To that extent there was a degree of truth in the
explanation that assumed a decision-making process, however unconscious it might be. But there could be no question of making a decision between his own notes and Leskov's paper. What had happened
was something far simpler, more banal: he had picked up Leskov's text
because it was to hand, because all he had to do was open the suitcase.
Finding out whether Maria, contrary to expectation, had finished typing
out his own paper had been too much for him at that point. He had
wanted nothing else but to lie down as soon as possible and yield to
the persistent effect of the pills. There might also have been the fact,
he thought, biting his lip, that he had avoided a question concerning
Maria, because a childish sense of hurt at her businesslike remark on
the phone still lingered. At any rate, he said to himself with embittered,
self-destructive violence, he had basically been quite glad that the arrival
of the people from Fiat had effectively removed that possibility.

Perlmann was startled by the banality of this explanation; by the fact
that in a matter upon which so much depended he had allowed himself
to be motivated by something so primitive as a need for sleep – and

self-induced sleep at that. *The pills. They made the decision.* He wasn't sure whether that wasn't, in the end, even worse than if it had been an unconscious but still genuine decision to commit fraud. Because what struck him now, while he blindly walked, as the truth, meant only that he had in that unhappy moment lost himself as a decision-maker, as a subject of his actions.

Perlmann only became aware that he had arrived in Portofino when he found himself in the square where the buses turned to make the journey back. He was puzzled to be here now. He had no business here in Portofino, where he was stuck as if in a cul-de-sac. He wanted above all to stay in motion, to hold his inner misery in check, he was afraid of coming to a standstill and being delivered over to his tormenting sensations with no possibility of defending himself. He took the street along which the tourists would stream down to the water during the holiday season. At this time of year most of the shops were closed. The radiant weather and the dead impression that the place created did not suit one another. Most of the restaurants around the little marina were shut as well. Outside the last café down at the quay he sat down at a bistro table and ordered coffee and cigarettes from an old and sulky waiter who didn't deign to look at him.

It was his first coffee that morning, and he greedily drank two cups. Again he became aware of his stomach and choked down two dried-up rolls that he had fetched from the counter inside. With his eyes closed, he listened to the quiet sound of the boats bumping gently against one another. For a few minutes, in a state between half-sleep and voluntary activity of the imagination, he managed to create the illusion of being on holiday: a man who could afford to drink coffee on a beautiful November morning in the famous town of Portofino; unattached, a free man who was able to go off travelling while others had to work; someone who could make his own choices and wasn't accountable to anyone. But then he suddenly became aware once more of his actual situation. He was a fraud – an undiscovered fraud, admittedly, but a fraud nonetheless. And now Portofino seemed like a trap.

He could no longer bear it. He called for the waiter, looked in vain for him in the empty bar, and then, because he couldn't find anything smaller, left far too large a bill beside his cup and walked quickly back to the main street. He bought a ticket from the driver of the waiting bus, who was standing outside and smoking, and took a seat at the back. He was the only passenger. When the driver stamped out his cigarette and sat down at the steering wheel, Perlmann jumped out at the last moment. Astonished, the driver watched him in the rear-view mirror, then set off.

Perlmann didn't want to go back, and he wanted to sleep. He was tempted just to lie down on the bench by the bus stop, but that was too public. A hotel. He counted his money. It would only be enough, if at all, for a very cheap room. He was relieved to have a goal for a moment, and walked through the narrow alleyways of the town. Many hotels had closed for the winter, and of the ones that were open, even the shabbiest-looking dives were more than he could afford.

At last he found a room in an *albergo* that opened up on to a narrow alley full of garbage bins. The landlord – a squat, fat man with a moustache and suspenders – studied him with a suspicious and contemptuous look: a man without luggage and without much money, wanting a room at half-past eleven in the morning. Perlmann had to haggle. He only wanted the room for a few hours. OK, until five o'clock, discount, cash in advance.

He took off the grubby cover and lay down on the bed with his hands folded behind his head. The ceiling, its plaster crumbling, was covered with yellow and brown water stains; cobwebs had formed in the corners, and in the middle hung an ugly lamp of yellow plastic that was supposed to imitate amber.

Self-defense, he thought: couldn't one regard what he had done as a form of self-defense? Powerless to do anything about it, he had lost his academic discipline, which had won him respect and a social position, and now he had been pushed against the wall by the expectations of others, demanding constant new achievements and threatening to withdraw their respect, and he had been forced to defend himself. And the only way he had managed to do that was through Leskov's text. You could see that as a defense of his own life. It had not happened casually or for the sake of some cheap advantage, but simply in order to avert something that would have amounted to his professional and, in the end, his personal annihilation. Self-defense, in fact.

OK, if you were going to be literal about it, you might describe what he was doing as plagiarism. At that moment the others were holding in their hands a text which, even though his name wasn't on it, they assumed was his text, even though he had only translated it and not written it himself. But that way of looking at things was fundamentally superficial, and didn't do justice to the real process. Because he hadn't translated the text just like that, without any internal involvement or intellectual engagement, as a professional translator in an agency might have done. Piece by piece he had allowed Leskov's thought-processes to pass through his mind. He had repeatedly measured it against examples from his own memory, and in the end, to mention only this, he had actually spent many hours, whole days, in fact, on his attempt to structure Leskov's fragmentary reflections into a consistent theory of appropriation. So one couldn't really say that the text that had been distributed contained nothing of his own thoughts.

And that wasn't all – it wasn't even the crucial thing, he thought. There was something else, too, which made it seem unfair and actually incorrect to speak in terms of a theft of ideas. It was the fact that he had always immediately – once linguistic problems had been swept aside – recognized Leskov's thoughts as his own. As he thought this, Perlmann saw before him Millar's face with its flashing spectacles, and he heard his scornful voice; no words, just his scornful voice. The face and the voice came closer and closer. They oppressed him. They threatened to crush him. He had to defend himself. He got up, sat on the edge of the bed and lit a cigarette. You couldn't prove something like that to anybody, and you wouldn't ever be able to express it to anyone without making yourself ridiculous. Nonetheless, it remained the case: Leskov described experiences with language and memory all of which he, Perlmann, had had himself, and the intellectual outline that he came up with was such that with each individual step Perlmann had once again had the impression: *I have often had that thought myself, really precisely the same one.* Admittedly, he hadn't sat down and written it out; the corresponding sentences from his pen did not exist. But he certainly could have done. He saw himself at his desk in Frankfurt, writing out, word for word, the text with which Leskov, to some extent by chance, had anticipated his own ideas. Nobody could say that he had passed off as his own thoughts that were alien to him.

He walked to the window and gave a start. On the other side of the narrow alley, exactly opposite his window and no more than six feet away from him, an old woman with a black headscarf and a toothless mouth leaned out of the window and grinned at him from a wrinkled face with a protruding chin. Next to her on the window-ledge there cowered a scrawny cat, the dividing-line between its orange and white fur running crookedly down its whole face and giving it an ugly, malevolent expression. Perlmann quickly drew the heavy, greasy curtains and lay back down on the bed. The hint of self-respect that he had managed to regain in his internal monologue a few moments before had been destroyed by the sight of the old woman and the cat, which now seemed to him like sly and menacing grotesques. Once again he felt like a cheap fraudster, lying in a shabby, dark hotel room in a trashy and abandoned tourist flophouse.

Only gradually did he find his way back to the two thought processes that he had begun to work out yesterday on the ship, still shocked at the time, and filled with shame to have found himself thinking any such thing. First of all, it was more or less impossible that one of his colleagues here could ever establish a connection with the unknown Leskov in faraway St Petersburg that might constitute a threat to him. And secondly, the seven copies of the translation, the seven manifestations and material proofs of his deception that existed would eventually be forgotten and finally destroyed. And with the disappearance of the paper from the world, his deception would also be extirpated and removed from the world – it would be just as if it had never happened.

Perlmann sensed that there was a daring leap somewhere in that thought, a transition that wasn't quite flawless. But he didn't want to look any closer. He wanted to look forward to the point in the future when the world, as far as his integrity was concerned, would be exactly as it had been before his deception. Once again he sat down on the edge of the bed and smoked hastily, his body tensed, as if by doing so he could impel time to reach that far off point of innocence more quickly.

Perlmann imagined how the destruction of the paper and the writing might come about. It seemed to him that his thoughts became more correct and compelling the more he succeeded in imagining the process down to its smallest details. Millar's copy, for example, would one day end up in one of the gleaming black garbage bags on a street in New York. The text might even be destroyed inside the bag, by some sort of leaking liquid, for example, but certainly by rain on a garbage dump, Perlmann could actually hear the pattering sound. The idea that appealed to him most was the inky letters running, undoing the baleful, guilt-ridden arrangement of the lines. Or else the text would go up in flames in a refuse incinerating plant. One day – in a few months, a year, perhaps, or two – this unfortunate text, this sequence of signs, this pattern of molecules would no longer exist in the world. All that would remain would be traces of memory in his colleagues' heads. But they would become increasingly vague. All that would be left in the end would be a rough idea of the subject. The memory would fade especially quickly in the heads of his most dangerous opponents, Millar and Ruge, because they would regard it as overblown anyway, a piece of writing without sharp intellectual outlines that didn't deserve to be remembered with any precision.

Perlmann grew calmer and lay down again. Now his earlier reflections regained their effect, and he drew up a little list in his mind, a crib sheet containing the points that he could always run his eyes over to ease his sensations of anxiety and guilt: (1) it was self-defense; (2) Leskov's thoughts were also his own; and (3) after some time everything would be just as it had been before. Perlmann repeatedly ran through these points in alternating sequence; at first he thought about the order of priority, but then the inner list became increasingly mechanical, a mere ritual of self-reassurance, and in the end he finally fell asleep over it.

It was a long time before he heard fists on the door and the unpleasant, barking voice of the landlord calling to him that it was time to go. He put his glasses on and looked at his watch. Just after four. His rage was as violent as an exploding flame. He opened the door a chink and yelled in the landlord's face that he had paid until five o'clock. Later, in the cramped bathroom, which was only lit by a gloomy bulb, and which smelled of chlorine and drains, the hysterical sound in his voice a moment before struck him as unpleasant, and when he saw his hands trembling under the tap he looked away.

Nonetheless, he was glad to have been so furious. Being furious meant experiencing oneself as someone who had the right to take offence at someone, to accuse someone else of something, and that, in turn, meant granting oneself a right to existence, a right that had seemed to him this morning, when he had gone running straight for the cliff, to have been deleted or erased. He showered. Here in this hole, where the shower produced only a few thin streams of water, because most of the holes in the shower-rose were furred up, that was fine, particularly because it gave out only cold water. He rubbed himself for a long time with a tatty, threadbare towel, and then reluctantly pulled his sweat-drenched shirt back on.

The window opposite was closed now. He opened the curtains and aired the smoky room. The narrow strip of sky that could be seen from this alley was dark grey and dominated by a light that recalled an early December twilight. He stood with his back to the window, smoking, and enjoyed insisting on his right to stay in the room until five o'clock. At five on the dot he went down and, without bothering to glance at the landlord, he threw the key on the counter so violently that it fell on the other side.

Perlmann was hungry – for the first time in ages, it seemed to him. The next bus back didn't leave until half-past six. He didn't have enough money for a taxi. He didn't even have enough for the stall where he could eat a pizza standing up. After some searching he managed to buy half a loaf and a piece of cheese. He walked past the unlit, deserted souvenir shops to the harbor and sat down on a cold stone on the jetty. The grey of the water passed uninterrupted into the grey of the sky. That morning's café was lit, but empty.

He collected all his forces into a single inner point and imagined himself stepping into the dining room over at the hotel in two hours' time, sitting down and, over dinner, reacting to the first comments on Leskov's text. For the sake of caution he immediately forced himself to think about the list of exculpating perspectives that he had worked upon in his gloomy hotel room, and to his great relief he found that panic didn't come. Instead, he was filled with apprehension, the apprehension of someone who had a long and unpleasant journey ahead of him, which would require all his strength and all his alertness. He would get through it, he thought, if he bore this one thing in mind: *They didn't know. They would never find out.*

The worst thing was the sessions on the veranda, where his text – Leskov's text – would be discussed. But those meetings consisted of a limited number of hours and minutes. They would pass, however, and then there would only be another three days before it was all over and the others left.

Most of the bread and the cheese Perlmann threw into a rubbish bin as he walked down the main street, which was like a ghost town, to the bus. It was lucky that he had crossed out the names of Luria's pupils, he thought as the bus set off. They could have made people suspicious. Luria himself was a different matter. Everyone knew him.

In the middle of the journey, where the coast road was particularly narrow, the other bus came towards them. There was a slight crunching sound. The driver cursed, and then the two buses stood side by side for several minutes, only inches apart. Neither of the drivers seemed to want to accept responsibility for what happened next.

Perlmann was sitting by a window towards the middle of the bus. The people on the other bus gaped across. From the dim interior they all seemed to be staring at him. With every passing moment their faces grew more scornful. He felt as if he were in a pillory: a fraudster being displayed to others as a warning. A little boy pointed at him, his index finger flattened against the window. He laughed, revealing a big gap in his teeth that looked diabolical to Perlmann. *But I'm not a criminal.* He didn't know how he would survive the next second, and was afraid he would succumb to a fit of hysteria. He closed his eyes, but he could still feel the eyes of the others all focused on him. He saw the image of people who had been arrested, pulling their jackets over their heads when they had to run the gauntlet of photographers. He thought convulsively of his list, and imagined it as a white sheet of paper on which the three headings stood in printed letters, one above the other: SELF-DEFENSE; OWN THOUGHTS; ANNIHILATION. He didn't open his eyes again until the driver put his foot down.

On the rest of the journey he sat quite still, quite motionless, as if that was what he had to do to keep from panicking.

27

He was relieved that no one was standing behind the reception desk when he stepped into the hotel lobby. Sticking from his pigeonhole was Leskov's text, the fatal stack of papers that he had at this very spot, twenty-one hours ago, handed to a distracted, impatient Giovanni. The others had collected their copies, but there was still one in Silvestri's box. Perlmann quickly went round the counter and took the sheets from his own pigeonhole. He was tempted to take Silvestri's copy as well, and had already begun to stretch out his arm out when he heard a noise in the next room and quickly withdrew.

On the stairs, walking ahead of a group of people in evening dress, von Levetzov was coming towards him. Before von Levetzov could say anything, Perlmann raised his rolled-up manuscript a little bit high, said hello and slipped past the people, taking two steps at a time, relieved that the group which was now once again occupying the whole width of the stairs, was between them. *It wouldn't have done any good if I had taken Silvestri's copy away*, he thought as he turned into his corridor. *It would probably only have led to confusion. Perhaps even provoked suspicion. You can make copies of copies. And more from those. Thousands of them. Hundreds of thousands.*

In his room he went first to his cupboard and shoved the text in the top laundry drawer among his shirts. Then he looked round. The contrast between the cramped room that afternoon and this great space was overwhelming. He felt as if he had spent days in that gloomy, musty den. He waited anxiously for the luxury of the room to seem once more like something forbidden, something he was no longer permitted. But that feeling didn't come, and after a while he turned on the gleaming, decorated brass tap and ran a bath.

It was nearly eight o'clock, and he was amazed at how calmly he was approaching the moment in which he would confront his colleagues for the first time as an undiscovered fraudster. It was only when he was sitting in the marble tub that he understood that this peace was the indifference of complete mental exhaustion. After two days of wandering around, of hopelessness and despair, all that remained within him was a dull void.

That void, which bordered on insensitivity, persisted as he slowly went down the stairs, and he carried it before him like a protective shield as he stepped into the full dining room with the Saturday evening guests, and sat down at the table next to Evelyn Mistral, grateful that the other chair next to him was free because of Silvestri's absence.

The others were already at work on their starters. The conversation in which Millar, Ruge and Laura Sand had plainly been involved broke off, and the subsequent silence, broken by the sounds of cutlery and laughter from the next table, sounded to Perlmann's ears like amazed startled observation: he's come to dinner again for the first time in four days, and even then he's late. Without looking at anyone Perlmann started to eat his avocado. It tasted of nothing; the white, floury flesh was just like any random substance in his mouth. He prepared himself to look at them, and each time he dug his spoon into the pale-green flesh with a twist of his hand, it was as if that moment were being delayed for ever.

At last he raised his head and looked at the others, one after the other, trying not to make the sequence seem too mechanical. Their eyes, which must have been resting on him for quite some time, seemed to reach him only now, and the important thing was to resist their gaze, protected by the certainty that they couldn't read his thoughts. *They don't know. They will never find out.* He felt his pulse quickening when he looked at Millar, who raised his eyebrows in ironic resignation; he had to meet his gaze for a moment, lest he avert his eyes too early, like an admission of guilt.

But overall it was easier than he had expected, and after a jokey remark from Laura Sand about his long absence, conversation resumed. The everyday nature of the topics gave Perlmann the sense of being safe with his dangerous secret; but it also clearly showed him how alone he was with the drama of his experiences over the past few days, and the degree of isolation he would have to maintain if his deception was to remain undiscovered.

No one said a word about the text they had received from him. He didn't need to invoke a single one of the reactions that he had assembled on the jetty at Portofino and later on the bus. He must be mad after all, but there was no denying that even though he was pleased about it, he was somehow hurt as well. They can't have been painfully touched by Leskov's text either. What hurt him most – and again he was aware of the absurdity of the sensation – was that even Evelyn Mistral, sitting next to him, didn't make a single remark about the text, even though it had many points in common with her own subject. When their eyes met he could discern no disapproval, but her smile was fainter than usual, as if she were afraid of hurting him.

During the main course, which he shovelled mechanically into himself with his eye focused on his plate, he defended Leskov's text in his mind. He tried himself out as a particularly strict reader and as a mocking critic. But even then, he thought, one could not ignore the substance and originality of this outline, and by the time dessert arrived he was so absorbed in the defense of the text that he almost regretted having to wait until Monday morning to defend it publicly. A faint feeling of dizziness and a heat in his face warned him not to be driven any further in that direction. But then his furious doggedness passed. He lit a cigarette and turned to Evelyn Mistral to talk to her about the text.

At that moment the waiter's black arm appeared with the silver tray, on which there lay a telegram.

'For you, *Dottore*,' said the waiter when Perlmann turned his head towards him. 'It just arrived.'

Kirsten, he thought suddenly, *Kirsten has had an accident*, and that thought suddenly filled him so completely that all the things that had preoccupied and tormented him over the last few days and hours seemed to have been erased. With trembling fingers he tore open the telegram and unfolded the sheet. He took in the text with a single glance: *Arriving Monday Genoa 15.05 Alitalia 00432. Grateful to be picked up. Vassily Leskov.*

For one or two seconds he didn't understand. The message was too unexpected and too far away from the thought about Kirsten that had wiped everything out for a moment. Then, when the meaning of the words on the glued white strip seeped into his consciousness, the world around him became colorless and quiet, and time froze. All his strength fled, and he felt the weight of his body as never before. *So that's what it feels like when everything's over*, he thought, and after a while a further thought formed in the hollow, dull interior of his mind: *I've been waiting for this for years.*

He must have sat there motionless for a long time, because when Evelyn Mistral pushed an ashtray under his hand and he looked up, he saw a long piece of white ash fall from the cigarette. She was looking at him with an expression of uncertain concern, when she pointed at the telegram and asked, 'Bad news?'

For a moment Perlmann was tempted to tell that open face, that bright, warm voice everything, regardless of the consequences. And if, when she pushed the ashtray at him, she had touched him with her hand, he thought later, that was actually what would have happened. So unbearable was the feeling of isolation that spread within him like an ice-cold poison.

But then, for the first time since the waiter had held out the silver tray in front of him, he saw the expressions on the faces of the others. They weren't mistrustful expressions, faces that displayed suspicious feelings. Rather they were mild expressions, with a hint of curiosity. Not unfriendly faces, on the contrary, even Millar's eyes seemed to hold a willingness to be sympathetic. And yet they were eyes that were all directed at him, as they had been before on that bus. Perlmann felt nausea welling up within him, he got to his feet, stuffed the telegram into his jacket pocket and ran out across the lobby to the toilet, where he closed himself in and threw up in quick, violent spasms.

When his retching ebbed and only trickles of burning gastric acid ran from his mouth and nose, he went out to the wash basin, rinsed his mouth and wiped his face with his handkerchief. The expensive wash basins of gleaming marble, the fashionable faux-antique taps of flashing brass and the huge mirrored wall were at that point unbearable. He avoided catching his own eye, and locked himself in a stall again to have a think.

Going back to the table was unimaginable. Admittedly, it would look very peculiar to the others, and border on impertinence if he didn't come back after his abrupt departure. The most varied conjectures would be made about the apparently dramatic content of the telegram. But now that complete social ostracism lay ahead this was no longer of any importance. The only unpleasant thing was – and on the edge of his consciousness Perlmann was amazed that such a thing could preoccupy him at such a moment – that his cigarettes and the red lighter that Kirsten had given him in the train were still over there on the table.

His thoughts went no further than these banal reflections. There was an impenetrable grey wall there, and a curious feeling of inanition. Never in his whole life had it been more important to think and plan clearly. But he faced this task like someone who had never come into contact with such intellectual activities; like someone who hadn't even mastered the ABC of any sort of planning that extended beyond the next moment. Body and emotion had reacted immediately; thought, on the other hand, was sluggish and wouldn't move from the spot. He felt how hard it was. Sitting on the toilet seat, he stared at the white door in front of his nose and registered that there was no graffiti on it. He felt the burning aftertaste of vomit on his gums and crumpled up the wet handkerchief in his fist. When two men came in and went on talking in Italian at the urinal, he involuntarily made his breathing very shallow and didn't move. He could only grasp a single thought, and it repeated itself at increasingly short intervals, like an accelerating echo: *A day and a half. I have a day and a half left.*

28

When the two men had gone, Perlmann left the stall, checked through a chink in the door that none of his colleagues was in the hall, and hurried back up to his room. Sitting on the edge of the bed he reread the crumpled telegram. Leskov had sent it. He could see on the white strip at the top right: yesterday afternoon just before four o'clock in St Petersburg. The other details, recorded in a code, were not quite clear to him. But plainly the message had been transmitted via Milan and Genoa to Santa Margherita, and had arrived shortly after half-past seven. *If the connection had been quicker and the telegram had been brought to me before Signora Morelli started copying this morning, I wouldn't have become a fraudster, and wouldn't now face professional annihilation.* He took another good look: it was three minutes to four when the message had been dispatched in St Petersburg. Perlmann's ship had been supposed to set off from Genoa at a quarter past three, but in the end it had been almost half-past. Three minutes to four – the storm had already been raging. *By then it was already clear that he would come. It was already clear. It was already a fact.*

That Leskov was stuck in St Petersburg because his exit permit had been refused and his mother was sick had been axiomatic in all of Perlmann's calculations. These two independent obstacles had given him the impression that they were insurmountable, so that he hadn't even begun to consider the possibility of Leskov's arrival. And now, through some unexpected concatenation of circumstances, Leskov had been able to free himself after all, and everything was collapsing. And yet the information in Leskov's letters had sounded so definitive, so immutable.

Perlmann's emptied stomach convulsed painfully. He went to the bathroom and slowly drank a glass of lukewarm water. As he did so his eye fell on the pack of sleeping pills. He knew precisely how many were left. Nonetheless, he took the box over to the red armchair and checked: seven. *That's not enough, not even with alcohol. If my doctor hadn't recently been on holiday, I'd have had enough by now and I'd be able to do it.* He went to the window, opened it and stopped, as he usually did, two steps behind the balustrade. Slowly and deeply he breathed in the cool night air, and felt his stomach cramp slowly easing as a slight dizziness set in. He heard cars pulling up down below, voices moving across the terrace to the flight of steps, laughter, the Saturday evening outside guests driving off.

He took two paces, held on to the balustrade with both hands and looked down the wall of the house. The only row of windows without the obstacle of a balcony. He would crash against light-brown marble. He wouldn't do it now, of course, not till after midnight or in the early hours of the morning when everyone was asleep. To be quite sure, he would have to jump head-first, and it would take three or four endless, terrible seconds before his head touched the stone. He closed the window and leaned his head against his hands, which were clamped around the handle of the window. For a moment everything went black.

When he straightened up again, there was a knock at the door. The thought of having to talk to someone now, even just a few words through the door, threw him into a panic. He had never before felt so exposed and defenseless. He had nothing to offer the presence of someone else at that moment, and even that presence, he felt, would crush him. And even so, he was pleased at the knocking, which freed him from the frozen solitude of the last few minutes. Halfway to the door he turned round and fetched the pack of sleeping pills, which he stuffed with cold fingers into his sponge bag in the bathroom before opening the door.

It was Evelyn Mistral, bringing him his cigarettes and the red lighter.

'We were worried when you didn't come back,' she said with an uncertain, inquisitive look. 'Bad news?' Then her eyes narrowed a little, and she added more quietly: 'You look like you've seen a ghost.'

He stared at her straw-colored hair, her oval face, its complexion looking even darker than usual in the faint lighting of the corridor, and at the skewed T-shirt that she wore under her broad-shouldered raw silk jacket. The temptation to ask her in and, in the intimacy of his room, far from the eyes of the others, to confess everything, was as overwhelming and physically tangible as a wave crashing over him. He lowered his head and pressed a hand against his forehead, just above his closed eyes.

'Everything is all right,' he said in English when he looked at her again.

He saw immediately that her face assumed a hurt and embarrassed expression. It was the first time since their initial conversation by the pool that he had refused the special intimacy of Spanish, which they had always spoken when they were alone. And even though he hadn't addressed her directly, it was as if he had now destroyed the closeness and the magic that her Spanish *tú* had held for him. It hurt like a farewell, and pain mingled with despair that he would never be able to explain to her that it had arisen out of a helpless attempt to protect himself.

'And thank you,' he said, pointing at the cigarettes as he reached for the door handle.

'Yes, all right. Good night, then,' she said quietly, and left without looking at him again. Perlmann threw himself on the bed, buried his head in the pillow, and after a while he subsided into a series of slow, dry sobs.

When Perlmann sat back up and went to the bathroom to wash his face, he felt the cold, desperate strength of a person who has just burned all his bridges. He lit a cigarette and all of a sudden he was capable of clearly and methodically thinking about his situation. He banished from his consciousness the image of his head smashing on the marble, shattering and being crushed to a pulp as he now, more coolly this time and with a synoptic view, considered putting an end to his life.

What would such a deed look like to the others? From Monday evening onwards – when the truth came to light, after Leskov had seen the text that had been handed out – as far as the others were concerned Perlmann would simply be a craven fraudster lacking the courage to even come clean to them. Dead, Perlmann would no longer have the chance to explain anything, referring to his distress and explaining to one or other of them – perhaps even to Leskov himself – his strong feeling that the text contained so many thoughts that were also his own that in a sense it was also his text. His deception would be subjected to the simplest and most superficial interpretation, and he would no longer be there to mitigate the judgment and make it more sophisticated. No one would take the trouble to pursue it, but the suspicion would spread that Philipp Perlmann, the prize winner with the invitation to Princeton, might have copied the work of others before, although perhaps not so brazenly as he had this final time.

Perlmann tried to adopt the view that this might all be a matter of complete indifference to him: as long as he was in the world and experiencing something, the time had not yet come; and when it did, he would not be there to endure it. He was unable to find an error in his reasoning on this point, but, confusingly, regardless of its simplicity and transparency, it struck him as fallacious, almost insidious, and so unconvincing that it immediately eluded him again as soon as he ceased to grasp it by concentrating on it particularly hard.

The idea that certain people might henceforth see him merely as an audacious trickster, a cheap fraudster, was easy to bear. Angelini's opinion, for example, left Perlmann cold. And, in fact, he didn't care too much about Ruge either, he reflected with a certain surprise. Even though Perlmann had by now become quite fond of Ruge, he had for four weeks been afraid of him, this respectable man with the chuckling laugh, in which Perlmann hadn't been able to keep from hearing a dangerous self-righteousness, often against his better judgment. But now, when fear should have overwhelmed him, the big bald head with the watery grey eyes behind the broken glasses seemed merely alien and distant and had nothing to do with him. The fact that Ruge had defended Laura Sand's beautiful images of suffering barely did anything to change that.

A more difficult case was Adrian von Levetzov, whom Perlmann had come to revere, even with all his affectation. Outwardly, he would join in with the chorus of outrage; that was the game. But Perlmann hoped – and thought it possible – that von Levetzov might secretly bring him a certain understanding and even a certain sympathy. What had von Levetzov said to Millar at the end of that session? *I could imagine that he's not concerned with it at all.* Once again, Perlmann imagined von Levetzov's tall figure, leaving the veranda with that strange posture of his. No, von Levetzov's judgment was not a matter of indifference to him.

Giorgio Silvestri, Perlmann was quite sure, would not condemn him, and he trusted him to guess at his distress. Laura Sand: in her ironic, defensive way she liked him. And there had been that afternoon of many colors. If he was correct in his impression that she had very quickly seen through him, she would not be terribly surprised, and would receive the news as something that fitted effortlessly into her gloomy picture of human cohabitation. Far from judging him, she would be annoyed that he had allowed the silly academic world to acquire such power over him.

Evelyn Mistral would be terrible. He thought back to the times when she had spoken furiously about Spanish colleagues who didn't take their work seriously, and as he did so he always saw her with her delicate, matte-silver glasses and her hair piled up. She would inevitably be torn between the undaunted, slightly naive earnestness that sustained her in her work, and the friendly, unphysically affectionate feelings that she brought to him. Now she would inevitably see those feelings as something that he had obtained by false pretences. They would disintegrate and assume the color of contempt and revulsion. In his mind's eye he saw her again, turning sightlessly away after his snub, as she had done before. He couldn't think of her face when she found out.

What about Leskov himself? What would you feel about a person who has stolen a text you are proud of? Fury? Contempt? Or would you be capable of some generosity if you learned the price the thief had paid in the end? Perlmann realized how little he knew Leskov the man, how vague a sense he had of his innermost character, as opposed to Leskov the writer. He felt vague relief shading into indifference. Leskov's judgement was not what mattered in the end.

He didn't dare to think of Millar's reaction, half-averting his inner eye. It was unbearable to imagine the complacency that this self-righteous Yank, with his blue, unchangingly alert gaze, would feel. *Somehow I'm not terribly surprised*, he might say, tilting his head to the left, all the way to the shoulder, with an emphatically diffident smile. A throbbing wave of hatred washed over Perlmann and seemed to force its way into every cell of his body, and for a while he felt nauseous again. Submerged in that hatred he saw, as clearly as in a hallucination, Millar's hairy hands in front of him, gliding over the keyboard of the grand piano.

But worst of all was the thought of Kirsten. It was a relief to feel how much more important his daughter was to him than anything else, and how even his hatred of Millar paled when she appeared before him. That gave him a feeling that he hadn't lost his sense of proportion entirely. But it was, then, all the more shocking to imagine what would happen when she found out. Dad was a fraud, using someone else's words because he could no longer come up with anything himself. She might somehow be able to understand that nothing further had occurred to him. She had sensed something on her visit, and she would explain it with reference to Agnes's death. But that he hadn't had the honesty or the courage to admit it openly, that she wouldn't understand. Like her mother, she didn't know the milieu, and above all she could have no idea that he wasn't standing there empty-handed because of Agnes's death, but because of another loss, one that was in a sense much greater, and which was so difficult to describe and, in fact, impossible to explain. But equally, she couldn't know that he could not have experienced a confession of his present inability as something which was unpleasant, embarrassing, but still something for which one might seek understanding in view of a personal tragedy such as his own; that he would rather have had to experience it as a public admission of a more substantial bankruptcy which applied to him as a whole person, and that for that reason a declaration of failure had been unthinkable. He thought of her standing outside the door early in the morning in her long black coat. He saw her mocking, embarrassed smile and heard her say *Hi, Dad*. Once again he felt the warm, dry hand with all the rings on it, the hand that she had stretched out of the train window to him. *Gli ho detto che ti voglio bene. Giusto?*

He looked over to the window. *No. No.*

After an exhausted pause, in which he slumped back on his pillow, he sensed with quivering alertness that the thoughts he was about to have were terrifying, and would change him for ever. It seemed to him that they were coming from far away, from somewhere unknown, and that they were coming towards him like waves, getting bigger and bigger until they finally crashed over. He pressed his ice-cold palms against his forehead, as if by doing so he might drive the thoughts away. But they came inexorably nearer. They were stronger than he was, and in his powerlessness he felt that they were going to break his resistance.

He switched on the television. There were films on most of the channels, and right now he wanted nothing to do with made-up stories, conflicts and feelings. He immediately flicked on from talk shows as well; never before had the views of strangers been of so little consequence to him. At last he found a news program. That was what he needed now: objective, real events, excerpts from the world in which something important, something of real significance was happening, ideally dramatic events which, because their scope went far beyond individual lives, could help him escape the prison of his own thoughts, which referred entirely to him. He wanted each news item to be like a bridge by which he could reach the real world, in which the nightmare that held him prisoner in this room would be dispelled, revealed as merely a horrendous hallucination. He stared at the images until his eyes were streaming, he wanted to lose himself entirely in the events out there in the world; the further away the scene of a news item, the easier it seemed to him to remove himself in it all by himself. He envied the people in the news stories, they weren't him, and with a feeling of shame that he didn't want to examine any further, he noticed that he particularly envied the disaster victims. He envied them their tangible misfortune. He even wished he could swap places with the soldiers who lay wounded on stretchers.

He turned off the sound and let the images run on mutely. Was it imaginable that Leskov would remain silent – out of gratitude for the invitation, and perhaps also in memory of the Hermitage?

But even then: it would be unbearable to know he was in Leskov's debt for all time. Leskov wouldn't blackmail him, Perlmann was sure of that. But the knowledge that he would henceforth be for ever vulnerable to blackmail would be enough to paralyze him completely. Just imagine: him, Perlmann, sitting at the head of the table in the veranda, elucidating and defending the text, while Leskov sat somewhere at the back in his shabby clothes, drawing on his pipe, roguishly contented, possibly asking questions and raising objections for his own macabre entertainment, all with a deadly serious expression. Perlmann felt the cold sweat on his hands when he rested his burning face on them.

And then their intimate relationship: Leskov's paternal tone might not, objectively speaking, change at all. But from now on he, Perlmann, would always hear a menacing undertone, a nuance that stripped him of every possibility of defending himself. He would have to remain silent. He would be like a lackey if so much as a single word on the subject were mentioned.

Perlmann started to hate this man Vassily Leskov. It was a quite different hatred from his hatred of Millar. His hatred of Millar had to do with what Millar had said and done. It had its origin in things that had happened between them. Millar was actively involved in its genesis and, as a result, Perlmann's hatred was rooted in the man himself. He hated Leskov, on the other hand, even though this Russian, at that moment innocently packing his suitcase, hadn't done the slightest thing. So, on closer inspection, the feeling of hatred which seemed to be targeted at Leskov in fact slipped off him and fell back on Perlmann, who was aware of the shabbiness of his feeling, but was unable to resist it.

He turned the sound back up on the television, annoyed that the report on an earthquake was coming to an end. Sport and fashion – those weren't images capable of freeing him; rather they seemed to mock him. He could have slapped the bright and cheerful faces of the presenters and gave a start when he became aware of his absurd hysteria. He was relieved when the weather-map appeared; the detached perspective of the satellite image did him good. He had never studied a weather report with such keen attention. He eagerly studied the tip of the pointer as it went from place to place – all places that he contemplated with yearning simply because they were somewhere else.

When the forecast for the following day began, he found himself in a state of rapidly mounting panic. The broadcast would soon be over, and then he would be overpowered by thoughts that would turn him into a different, ugly person, cold and alien to himself. He clung to the forecast for Italy. When the camera pulled back and the presenters' desk became smaller and smaller, he stayed there, eyes straining, to the very last picture and the last note of the signature tune.

The advertisements leapt out shrilly at him, and he immediately turned off the television. But the empty, dark screen, his bedside lamp reflected in it, left him defenseless against himself, and he turned it back on. He hopped desperately from channel to channel, trying frantically to numb himself with erotic images, and even the attempt to slip into the excitement of a car chase with wailing sirens and gunfire was doomed to failure. His flight from his own thoughts was over. They had caught up with him, and forced their way violently into his consciousness. He tapped the keys of the remote control ever more quickly and desperately, the individual channels pursued one another and flashed up only briefly, then at last he turned off the television.

He went into the bathroom and took the pack of sleeping pills from his sponge bag. Two of those tablets would be enough to erase all thoughts for a while. He already had the pills on his tongue and could taste their bitterness, promising oblivion, when he lowered his glass of water. It was mad, now of all times, when everything was at stake, to yield to anaesthesia, not knowing how long it would be until his head was clear enough again to think in practical terms. He set the damp pills down on the shelf, drank the glass dry and then walked very slowly, head lowered, back to the red armchair, like someone whose time has run out once and for all, and who must at last give himself up. He set the red lighter, which he was already holding, carefully back down on the table and lit the cigarette with a hotel match. He inhaled the smoke more deeply than usual and breathed it very slowly out. He waited until the very last moment before breathing in. Then he began.

It would have to look like an accident. An accident that had happened somewhere between the airport and the hotel. An accident that happened in Perlmann's presence, and one to which he could testify. There was basically only a single possibility: it would have to be an accident in a car that he rented at the airport.

A rental car just for Leskov? Someone might ask if that was necessary, whether a taxi wouldn't have done. After all, everyone else had arrived by normal means of transport. But there were possible explanations: Perlmann held this man, Leskov, in even greater esteem than they had previously supposed, clearly in a personal sense as well. Or: he wanted to make a special gesture to a Russian who was travelling from St Petersburg and who had never been in the West before. Or: the expenses budget that Angelini had set aside was so generous that it was easily affordable. And besides, after a fatal accident no one would utter such a question. By no means, he could be sure of this, was the rental car on its own a cause for suspicion.

But how would he do it, from the technical point of view? Stage an accident in such a way that Leskov would be killed while he himself was unharmed – that was practically impossible. Other people must on no account be drawn into sympathy with him, that much was clear. He didn't need to think about it for a second. And driving into a tree at the roadside, a lamppost or a rock – the outcome could never be calculated with any certainty. Only one thing came into question, in fact, and Perlmann found it very strange how quickly, almost automatically he hit upon the idea: he would have to stop right above a steep cliff – in the mountains or on a rocky bit of coastline – get out and send the car rolling over the edge with Leskov inside. In his mind's eye he saw the slowly rolling car, inside it Leskov's massive form, his horrified face, his mouth widening to a scream; the car would tip over and plunge into the depths before going up in flames or sinking into the sea. Perlmann pressed his thumb and forefinger to his eyes to banish the details of the picture, and it was a while before he could go on thinking.

It would have to happen in a rest area, a spot where the ground fell away in a rocky plunge. How would he stop? He could change to neutral and put on the handbrake. After getting out he would have to bend and reach inside, press in the button on the handbrake, pull up the lever and let it go. To pull it up, he thought, he would have to hold his arm, or his forearm at least, more or less parallel with the lever, or else it wouldn't release, and that would mean that he would have to lean very far in towards Leskov, his victim. Perhaps he could do it if he supported himself on the driver's seat with his left hand; but perhaps he would also have to use his right knee as well. It depended how wide the car was. At any rate, and this was the worst thing about the idea, he would come very close to Leskov's body again, and if he bent his arm clumsily or lost his balance as he supported himself, he might even touch him. He didn't need to look at him, he could violently narrow his field of vision and stare hard at the handbrake. Once he had the lever in his hand he could close his eyes. But that moment of unseeing physical closeness, which would be so entirely different from physical closeness on the journey, would be terrible. And absolutely unbearable was the idea that Leskov might see through his intention, and that there would be a fight, in the course of which they might plunge together.

He had to do it without the handbrake, just with the gears. Leave him in the car when he stopped it, get out and then, in a flash, lean in to knock it out. It would take one or two seconds. And to do that he wouldn't have to support himself, or only on the steering wheel, in which case he wouldn't go near the passenger seat. Would Leskov pull up the handbrake when he felt the car rolling? He couldn't drive: Perlmann now remembered him saying dryly that his income would never stretch to a car. But actually, every passenger knew that there was a handbrake and where it was. On the other hand, Perlmann's attack would strike like lightning from a clear sky. And even if Leskov wasn't looking out of the window at that moment, and saw Perlmann's movement quite clearly, he wouldn't be able to grasp the situation quickly enough; the truth would be too unexpected and too monstrous. He would be confused by the rapid movement and horrified by the rolling, and probably paralyzed by both. But Perlmann couldn't rely on it. He would have to prevent Leskov from defending himself in any way by driving close to the cliff edge, so close that the front wheels protruded beyond it as they pulled up, and the car's center of gravity lay irrevocably beyond the edge in the air. Leskov might say something anxious as they drove so close to the abyss. But Perlmann would no longer need to react to it. He would concentrate entirely on what he needed to do, and a few seconds later it would all be over.

Police. He would have to call the carabinieri. He hadn't thought about that for a moment until now. In the world of Perlmann's thoughts over the past hour only Leskov had existed, and his colleagues in the background, and the dawning awareness that the planned accident also affected the rest of the world to some extent, the public world of laws and courts, and newspapers, bathed everything in a harsh, icy light. Perlmann took off his shoes, sat down at the head of the bed with his knees drawn up, and pulled the blanket up to his chin. That position was something unfamiliar, something alien that made him realize how far removed he was from himself already.

Whether he hadn't left the car in gear when he stopped, that would be the first question. Of course he had, he would reply. How else could he have got out? Besides, after thirty years of driving experience, you would do that automatically at such a spot. It would have to sound irritable, cranky. Leskov must accidentally have knocked it into neutral when, wide as he was, he bent over to reach for something. At the very same moment as he, Perlmann, turned round and, with his hand still on the zip of his trousers, noted that the car was rolling forwards, Leskov's head had appeared behind the glass. Perlmann, of course, had started running, although with a feeling that it was all in vain, but the car had tipped over before he could reach the spot.

They wouldn't be able to prove anything, nothing at all. They could reproach him for not having pulled on the handbrake, because such clumsiness on the part of the passenger was always a possibility. But that was a rebuke for lack of care. It couldn't be turned into an accusation of murder by negligence. Criminal prosecution would only be a possibility if someone stood up and said: 'Signor Perlmann, you are a liar. The truth is that you reached into the car again after you got out and took the car out of gear yourself, and that means murder.' But that would remain an unfounded accusation that no examining magistrate and no state prosecutor could put into effect. Because it mustn't be forgotten: *There wasn't a single visible motive.* If questioned, his colleagues would be able to report nothing but the great regard – reverence, in fact – with which Perlmann had always spoken of Leskov.

Or would suspicion sprout within the group? Would the telegram and Perlmann's rather striking reaction to it become connected with the accident? Would Evelyn Mistral remember his corpse-white face?

But even if one put the two things side by side in one's mind: even discreetly one couldn't make anything of them. Because once again it was true that there wasn't the merest hint of a motive as far as the others were concerned. They couldn't know anything about the poison of deception that pulsed within him.

Even so, at the scene of the crime he would have to avoid anything that could give rise to suspicion. Perlmann became aware of his stomach and, shivering, pulled the blanket still further up. First of all, the place in question would have to look like a spot where it would seem natural to stop in order, as he would say, to step outside for a moment. But it couldn't just be any old lay-by where one didn't obstruct the traffic. It would have to be a place that invited one to park facing the abyss; ideally a place with a beautiful view. 'I parked like that quite automatically,' he would say. 'It was the best way of viewing the panorama.'

And then there was the question of terrain. If it were tarmac, brake marks wouldn't be an issue. With soil, gravel or sand, on the other hand, he would have to be careful. Just by the edge of the cliff, where he would really stop, there could be no skid marks, because that was where the car, according to his story, had started rolling without a driver. A little way back from there, on the other hand, at the place where he had supposedly been standing, there would have to be the usual brake marks. That made the sequence of movements clear: he would have to leave the road and drive in a circle until the hood was at right angles to the edge of the cliff. Then, at a natural distance from the edge, he would brake until the car was at a standstill and turn off the engine, before rolling very gently to the abyss, quickly tapping the brake pedal in such a way that no skid marks were produced.

Under the blanket, Perlmann involuntarily made the corresponding movements: putting down the clutch with his left foot, pumping quickly and very, very gently with his right – it could really only be the hint of a push – and at last, along with the last touch on the brake, carefully letting off the clutch, so that it too didn't produce a skid mark. Perlmann, who had leaned forward as he concentrated on these delicate movements, sank back again. He was as exhausted as if he had just made a gigantic physical exertion, and for a while there was nothing inside him but an oppressive, baleful void.

He gave a start. Witnesses. Of course there must be no witnesses. Before he made the crucial, fatal movement and knocked the car out of gear, he would have to straighten up and make sure by looking along the road in both directions that no one was coming. If a car was in view, he would have to wait. They would be agonizingly slow, those last seconds of Vassily Leskov's life. Perlmann would have to assume an innocuous pose. He could put a cigarette in his mouth and then throw it away as soon as the car was out of view. He didn't dare to think that Leskov might get out while this was happening, or that another car might stop next to them. What happened then would be almost unbearable: sequences of movements and an exchange of words, whole scenes, in fact, with a ghostly lack of presence, because in his eyes the only reason for them to take place was so that they would, in a sense, clear themselves out of the way and thus free up a segment of time in which the murder could actually take place.

The road would have to be remote; a quiet stretch that hardly anyone would be driving along on a November day. There would be a certain degree of surprise that he had not driven Leskov – who had already travelled from St Petersburg – to the hotel by the quickest route to the hotel, along the highway. But Perlmann could say that Leskov was more excited than tired from his journey, and had suggested a detour. No one could accuse Perlmann of lying and, without any other causes for suspicion, nor would anyone want to.

He needed a map. They would have one at reception. Perlmann looked at his watch: a quarter to eleven. Giovanni would be on duty again, and that was fine by him: the more unsympathetic and indifferent the person he asked (indirectly) to help him with his murder plan, the better. He threw back the blanket, slipped into his shoes and was almost at the door when he stopped, then hesitantly came back and sat down on the arm of the red armchair. So far he had only developed his plan in his mind, silently, under the blanket. Now he was about to take the first step to implementing it. A murderer preparing for his deed. The icy feeling of self-alienation that surrounded this thought was numbing, and for a while Perlmann lingered motionlessly in nameless despair.

Then, when he put a cigarette between his lips, he avoided looking at the red lighter and picked up the hotel matchbook again. He needed to recall to mind the reasons that compelled him to this terrible plan, and assure himself of their constraining character. But every attempt at concentration ran immediately aground, and all that remained was the dull, rather abstract conviction that there was no going back – a conviction that had the aftertaste of being forced, but which was nonetheless firm for that. At last he stubbed out his half-smoked cigarette and walked to the door with movements that felt lumbering and mechanical.

As he looked down into the hall from the last landing, for one oppressive moment he had the idea that he would soon stand facing Leskov. He took a deep breath, closed his eyes and held the air in his lungs as if its painful pressure might crush the ghostly vision from within. Then he walked to the reception desk, which was unmanned.

Only now did he hear the music coming from the drawing room. Saturday evening: Millar was playing. As always it was Bach, the Overture in the French Style, which Hanna had once played for the sixtieth or seventieth birthday of an adored aunt. Perlmann felt as if he were a quite unreal life-form, a creature from an alien star that had strayed to this world, in which everything was happening as it usually did, and in which no one took note of the internal events that were driving him inexorably towards the abyss. He hiccuped, and the helpless yelp that seemed so loud in the empty hall reinforced the sensation that he was now in the charge of forces over which he no longer had any control.

He didn't dare strike the silver bell, and he was just about to put an end to this waiting, which felt like an anticipated humiliation, and go back to his room, when Signora Morelli came out of the corridor that led across to the drawing room. After glancing at Perlmann's face she quickened her steps, and almost ran the rest of the way until she was behind the counter.

'The music,' she said apologetically. 'Signor Millar plays wonderfully.' In her smile there lay unspoken surprise that he, too, was not over with the others, and at the same time the awareness that she wasn't keen to know why.

'I need a map of this area,' Perlmann said, and because he didn't respond to her remark in any way, but convulsively concentrated on completing his sentence without yelping, it sounded overbearing, and he was startled by his tone. 'A large-scale map,' he added. He wanted the second part to sound friendlier and appropriate to a request, but the last word was distorted by a ridiculous yelp.

Signora Morelli went into the back room, looked in various drawers and at last returned with a road map of Liguria.

'*Ecco!*' she said and added, after a pause, during which Perlmann was shaken by another eruption, 'They say it's going to be sunny tomorrow.'

Perlmann took the map, thanked her silently and went to the elevator. The sliding door closed on one of Millar's massive chords.

The coast road, he thought as he sat on the bed with the map spread out in front of him, was out of the question. Certainly, you could tell from the twists and turns that there were sections of steep coast, or at least with sheer drops. But roads like that were generally cut tight into the rock and had no rest areas quite deep enough. They were also generally secured with wide guard rails. And last of all, this was the road that connected the big coastal towns like Recco and Rapallo: on a Monday afternoon between four and five, the rush hour, they would be far too busy.

He would have to take the mountain road and leave Genoa in the direction of Molassana. After that there were several possibilities. Perhaps the loop that started at Bargagli and ended near Lumarzo would be a suitable spot. It was plainly bendy, and marked entirely in green, which meant it was a mountain road with a special view. There were probably viewpoints along it like the one he needed. Unless the guard rails thwarted his plans. But then he could try one of the small roads marked in red, on which one left the main road and drove down along a series of twists and turns towards the coast, via Uscio, for example. And if he found nothing there either, he could try the stretch that branched off just after Molassana and led up via Davagna to the Passo di Scoffera.

When the image of a narrow mountain pass rose up in him, leading past black slate walls gleaming with moisture into dark, low clouds, Perlmann gave a start. While studying the map he had for a while been nothing but head, a cold, calculating intelligence unconnected to the other parts of himself. Now the image of the gloomy mountain pass filled him with horror and despair. His empty stomach convulsed and he sensed the sharp, sour smell that vomit had left in his nose.

He stepped to the closed window and looked out without seeing anything. Could he live with this deed – with the image of the car tipping over the edge, with the memory of Leskov's scream forcing its way through the open car door, with the noise of the impact and the explosion that would come after it?

He wouldn't be able to stand the sober, brightly lit awareness of having committed a crime, he was sure of that. What he had to do was this: persuade himself, day by day, that it was an accident; overlay the clear, precise memory of the real crime with fantasy images of an accident, constantly adding new ones, and doing that so stubbornly and for so long that the original, traumatic images would remain for ever in the background and the fantasy images would take root as if they were the true memories. It was a matter of laying one thin layer of self-persuasion on the other until a new, solid conviction came about, whose blind firmness he no longer needed to worry about on a daily basis. Could that be done? Was such a methodical construction of a self-deception, so planned a construction of a life-lie possible? Once more, he thought, a very particular kind of lack of presence would be produced, one with which he was not yet familiar: the lack of presence of the lie – a state in which the presence was absent because a fundamental truth, a defining reality of one's own life was denied.

The phone rang. Even though Perlmann had set it to the quietest volume, the ring seemed shrill and penetrating; the whole world seemed to be jumping at him through that sound. *Kirsten.* He walked over to the bedside table, slowly extended his hand and let it rest on the receiver. The desire to listen to her clear voice and carefree tone was overwhelming, like a burning pain. But he drew his hand back, sat down on the edge of the bed and rested his head on his fists. Beside him, he could see through his closed lids, lay the open map with the route of the crime. The ringing wouldn't stop. Perlmann put his hands over his ears, but in vain, because now he could hear the sound in his imagination.

In the silence that finally fell, he picked up the red lighter. *Killing must be based on a personal relationship; otherwise it's perverse.* All of a sudden his trains of thought over the past few hours seemed unreal, practically grotesque. Murdering Leskov was completely out of the question. Because even if he managed to weave himself into an effective self-deception: at his first meeting with Kirsten, at their first exchange of glances, their first touch, the whole structure of lies within him would collapse like a house of cards. Then he would stand before her in the glowing white consciousness of being a murderer.

Involuntarily, he rose to his feet to stifle that unbearable idea with a movement. He took a cigarette and opened the window. He felt boundless relief at the fact that the thoughts of murder fell away from him like a bad dream, and after a while he started to notice the lights outside. He greedily absorbed them with his eyes, each individual one of them. When he had absorbed the night-time scenery and calmed down, he lit the cigarette with Kirsten's lighter, which gave a quiet click.

During the first few drags he managed to concentrate entirely on the idea that he wasn't going to be a murderer now, and he experienced a kind of presence, the presence of a great relief. But that whole state, he felt very clearly, had something provisional about it, something of a mere intake of breath, to some extent it took place in a parenthesis that consisted in the oppressive question of what in the world he was to do now that the possibility of murder had been ruled out. When he felt that he couldn't hold off that question for much longer, he went into the bathroom and swallowed the two still slightly damp sleeping pills. The map that he folded up and laid on the round table was already a prop from a long-forgotten drama of the imagination.

When he turned out the light, the tablets were starting to take effect. His left foot pressed on the clutch, his right made cautious braking movements. Over those convulsive motions, against which he fought in vain, he went to sleep.

The handbrake was as firm as if it were cemented in. He had to creep further into the car, supporting himself with one knee on the driver's seat; but the lever wouldn't move a millimeter, not even when he tried to pull it up with both hands. The button that was supposed to release it wouldn't move either, it felt as if it were made of stone. Then suddenly there was no button, and the pressure of his thumb disappeared into the void. It all took seconds, and his pulse was racing. Now sweat-drenched, rough hands grabbed him by the arm. There was a struggle. Leskov was as strong as a bear, but otherwise he was a faceless opponent. Suddenly, the car started rolling – actually it was more of a slide, the horror of which lay in its silence. The battle was done, and they tipped over into blind white, as if in slow motion.

Then again he felt his right hand knocking out the gear. He made that quick, violent movement over and over again. It was as if he were nothing but that arm and that hand. Again the car began to roll, then Leskov pulled up the handbrake; the crunching noise had an endless echo that seemed to fill the whole parking lot and the whole gorge. This time he had a face, a face with wide-open, fearful eyes that turned into a triumphant face with a look of contempt. Leskov's face jerked close to him and became a close-up; in the end it was a face with a wide, curling moustache that quickly turned into a grimace of scorn.

29

When Perlmann awoke, drenched in sweat and still quite dazed, it was half-past eight, and the sun shone from a cloudless sky as it had done on the previous two days, so that behind his numbness he managed to think for a tiny moment that it was only Friday morning and everything was still all right. Once it had slipped away, the illusion could not be repeated, and he walked slowly and unsteadily to the bathroom. Yesterday, showering had seemed to him like something that was no longer the fraudster's due. This morning, after a night in which quite other things had passed through his mind, that feeling seemed obsolete, almost laughable. Under all that water the numbness fled, and the returning dream images gradually lost their power.

Nothing has happened yet, he thought again and again. *I still have thirty hours left.* His hunger repelled him. He really didn't want to eat anything ever again. But that vexatious feeling had to be removed, so he ordered breakfast, even though the idea of meeting a waiter now was disagreeable. As he mechanically stuffed croissants down himself and drank cup after cup of coffee, it slowly dawned on him that there was one additional possibility he hadn't thought of in the course of the previous night. He could stage a car accident in which he killed himself and dragged Leskov to his death as well.

Initially, he didn't dare imagine how that might happen in any detail; at first the important thing was to resist the thought in its abstract form. He felt his breath racing, and saw his hand trembling slightly as he lit a cigarette. And yet he was amazed how little resistance that new thought encountered within him. It was, after all, a murder. But that struck him as oddly irrelevant. The main thing was that everything then would be darkness and total silence. He smoked in long, deep drags as he plunged into that idea. The longer he lingered with it, the more drawn into it he became. All the weariness that had grown within him over the past few days seemed quite naturally to have been invested in that imagined silence. And not only that: suddenly he felt as if all he had done during those months since Agnes's death was wait for that silence to arrive. Certainly, there was a murder bound up with it. But the thought of Leskov remained pallid, the after-effect of the pills paralyzed his imagination, and behind Perlmann's heavy lids one single thought formed over and over again: *I will not have to live with this murder for so much as a second. So not for a second of my life will I be a murderer.* He felt that this was a piece of sophistry, an outrageous false conclusion, but he didn't have the will to disentangle it, and clung to the truth that those two sentences bore on their surface.

He wrote a circular in which he informed his colleagues that Vassily had plainly found a way to come here, at least for a few days, and that he would be arriving tomorrow afternoon. So the first session on his, Perlmann's, text would not, as planned, take place on Monday afternoon after the reception at the town hall, but not until Tuesday morning, as he intended to collect Leskov from the airport on Monday. He wrote quickly and without hesitation, and afterwards, when he put his money and credit cards in his pocket, and the road map in his jacket and went downstairs, he was both pleased and horrified by the businesslike manner, the cold-bloodedness, even, that had taken hold of him.

He asked Signora Morelli to copy the circular and put it in the pigeon-holes. Then he told her of Leskov's imminent arrival and reserved a room for him, spelling out his name. Finally, he asked her to call for a taxi.

On that sunny, warm morning they were all sitting on the terrace. Perlmann put on his sunglasses, greeted them with a curt wave and without slowing his pace, and walked down the steps. He had just – he thought as he waited by the road – felt strangely unassailable when, a bit like a ghost, he had walked like the others. Admittedly, he had avoided looking at Evelyn Mistral. But that, it seemed to him then, had actually been unnecessary; because from now on she was far away from him, in another time. That, in fact, was what made him so calm and unassailable: by deciding to drive to his death he had stepped out of the usual time that one shared with others, and in which one was entwined with them, and was now moving in a private time of his own, in which the clocks moved identically, but which otherwise ran unconnectedly alongside the other time. *Only now that I have left the time of the others have I succeeded in delineating myself from them. That is the price.*

The new time, he thought in the taxi, was more abstract than the other one, and more static. It didn't flow, but consisted in an arid succession of moments which one had to live through, or rather, deal with. A lack of present, he was puzzled to note as he looked out through the open car window at the smooth, gleaming water, was suddenly no longer a problem. In the new time, which would last until some point tomorrow afternoon, before disappearing from the world along with his consciousness, present did not exist even as a possibility, so that one couldn't miss it either. All that existed now was this: coolly calculating and sticking to his schedule in the planning and execution of his intention. Perlmann wound up the window, asked the driver to turn off the radio and leaned back in the tatty seat whose broken springs stuck into his back. He didn't open his eyes until the taxi stopped under the yellowed plane trees in front of the station.

On Monday evening, when he had waited with Kirsten on the platform, he had been thankful of that meaningless, shrill ringing noise. It had freed them both for a while from the embarrassment of being together in silence. In his mind's eye Perlmann saw Kirsten's liberated laughter as she held her hands over her eyes. Today the penetrating, endless sound rendered him defenseless, and he went back outside to the plane trees.

He would leave a piece of paper with Kirsten's phone number on the desk, so that they didn't need to rummage for it in his belongings. That was quite natural. After all, Kirsten hadn't been in Konstanz for as much as three months. Which of his colleagues would call her? In all likelihood von Levetzov would take on the task. Such bad tidings were, if possible, best passed on in the mother tongue, and Ruge would take a backseat. But how would his colleagues find out in the first place?

The carabinieri would have to find something in Perlmann's wallet to show that he had been staying at the Miramare. Unless the car went up in flames. It was the first time that Perlmann thought of the possibility of burning to death at the wheel, and he started perspiring with terror at the idea that the flames might engulf him when he wasn't even dead, perhaps only unconscious. He was relieved that the sound of the arriving train tore him away from that idea.

The rhythmical knocking of the wheels did him good; it gave him the feeling that everything was still in suspension. He was free and could at any time revoke his desperate decision. He would have loved to be carried along by that knocking for ever, and was annoyed that he had taken a slow train that stopped at every station. When the knocking started again after a halt, and grew faster again, he managed to escape for a few minutes into the thought that things weren't that bad, it was just a text, after all, a few written pages – that couldn't possibly be a reason to put a violent end to everything. But then, when the train stopped again, he was seized once more with horror at the idea of having to live through the discovery of his plagiarism and the ostracism that it would entail, minute by minute, hour by hour, until the end of his life. When an old woman in a black crocheted headscarf sat down opposite him in Nervi, made a friendly remark and gave him a maternal smile, he got up without a word and went to another compartment where the seats were free.

The worst of it was that because it was supposed to look like an accident he couldn't sort anything out before his death. There were people he would have liked to say something to. Kirsten above all, even though the right sentences wouldn't come to mind. He would have liked to see Hanna again, too. He owed her an explanation for that sudden ghostly phone call in which he hadn't asked her a single thing about her own life. He tried to imagine what she must look like now. He saw that flat face in front of him, framed in her blonde hair with the single dark strand, but her face remained frozen in the past, and refused to develop through the three decades that had passed in the meantime.

He would have liked to walk through his bright Frankfurt apartment again, sit down at his desk for one last time and look, for one last time, at Agnes's photographs. And then his diaries. He wished he still had the chance to destroy them. This way, Kirsten would find them now. He tried in vain to remember what was actually in them. He fervently hoped he was mistaken, but when he stepped on to the platform in Genoa, he had the oppressive feeling that he was leaving behind a big pile of kitsch.

He went out into the station portico, had to put off a number of taxi drivers and finally found a quiet corner. He would take the smallest car they had, one with a short hood and no crumple zones. So that it would happen quickly and he could be sure that it would work. Suddenly, he felt he was having an attack of diarrhea and ran to the toilet. It was a false alarm. His heart was pounding in his throat when he went back to the car rental company's counter. He stopped in a corner and forced himself to breathe calmly. Renting the car, in itself, didn't force him into anything. He could always bring it back as if nothing had happened. He had to utter that thought out loud to himself a few times, slowly and with great concentration, before he managed to contain his excitement, and he had a sense that he could be sure of his voice.

The counters of all three companies were closed. He hadn't expected that, and he hadn't noticed before, even though they were all right in front of his nose as he stepped out. For a few minutes he just stood there, his hands in his trouser pockets, and gazed into the void. Then he slowly walked over to the timetable and checked when the next train left for Santa Margherita. On the way to the platform he paused abruptly, bit his lip and then walked back to the taxis.

'Here you are, after all,' grinned the driver he had turned away before. Perlmann slammed the car door shut. 'To the airport,' he said in a tone that made the driver turn round and look at him in amazement before he drove off.

'I'm sorry, Signore,' said the Avis lady, with bright make-up and a red dress, 'but we just have one car free, a big Lancia. All the others are out until the middle of the week. There's a big industrial fair in the city.'

'If that's the case,' Perlmann said irritably, fighting down his mounting hysteria, 'then why is your counter at the station closed, and why are the other companies here closed as well?'

'That, Signore, I can't tell you,' the hostess snapped back and turned her attention to her computer.

Perlmann looked at his watch: half-past eleven. In five hours it would be dusk, and it could take a long time before he had found a suitable location.

'All right, I'll take it,' he said.

The hostess took her time before starting to fill in the form. How long did he want to rent the car for?

The question took Perlmann aback, as if he had been asked something obscene. That he was being asked for information that extended beyond his death and was hence without any significance for him once again made him keenly aware how deep the gulf had become between his private time, which was about to come to an end, and public time, the time of contracts and money, that would go on for ever.

'For two days,' he said hoarsely.

Would he be bringing it back tomorrow evening?

It was far too long before he finally, without any reason and with the feeling of saying something completely random, opted for a 'yes', and the hostess was visibly surprised at how little this customer, who had seemed so arrogant only a few moments before, seemed to know about his own plans.

What insurance did he want to take out? Did he want to include fully comprehensive cover?

'The usual,' Perlmann said tonelessly.

'I'm sorry?' the hostess asked, not trying to conceal her impatience.

'The usual,' Perlmann repeated with forced firmness, and had the feeling that she must be able to see how his face was burning. In the worst case, then, the police would be able to get to the hotel via his licence and Avis, he thought, when the hostess finally entered his local address.

As he walked towards the exit he stopped in front of the monitor showing the arriving flights. The last one currently on the list was coming from Paris and was supposed to be landing at five to three. It didn't matter in the slightest, he said to himself, where Leskov's flight came from. There was, of course, no direct flight to here, but it really couldn't have mattered less where Leskov changed. And the plane that he took tomorrow wouldn't necessarily be a daily flight. Nonetheless, Perlmann stopped, smoked, and stared fixedly at the flickering screen. And when he had stamped out his second cigarette and looked up again, the flight was there: AZ 00423, 15.05 from Frankfurt.

For a moment Perlmann saw Leskov flailing and snorting his way through Frankfurt Airport in the threadbare loden coat that he had worn before. It was childish and, in his situation, grotesque, Perlmann thought, but the possibility of Leskov changing at his, Perlmann's, airport enraged him, and he felt as if Leskov were violating his personal sphere. Irritated, he dismissed the image and went outside to the parking lot.

30

As he got into the long, dark-blue limousine, his eye immediately fell on the handbrake. In this car it was unusually far over towards the passenger seat. So, he would inevitably have to touch Leskov's broad body when he freed the lever over the abyss. It gave him a feeling of helplessness that this idea held him prisoner for a moment, even though it was obsolete and no longer had any practical significance. In the end he managed to shake it off, and he unfolded the map.

For a frontal collision with a truck in which no one else would come to any harm, the coast road was out of the question. Heavy trucks would be unlikely to drive there, and it was also true that at the time in question there would be far too much traffic. For this plan the only possible road was the one via Molassana to Chiávari. He would have to assume that trucks drove there on Monday afternoons. It was disagreeable to him that his terrible scheme depended on other people and their temporal plans. Immediately, before it disappeared in darkness and silence, his own time would have to cross the time of others. When he set the map down on the seat beside him and lit a cigarette, Perlmann was overcome with nausea at the unbridled self-involvement expressed in such thoughts.

The handbrake was pulled up tight, and was only released the third time he pushed the button. *As if in a dream*, he thought, as he steered the car uncertainly out of the car park. He drove like a beginner, and very soon he had hit the curb and cut off someone's right of way.

Judging by the map, the turn-off to Molassana was to the east of the center, so he drove first along the industrial plants and then the harbor, down a deserted road with dilapidated houses, dead construction sites and mountains of rubble. In spite of the radiant weather it was an oppressive backdrop, and he drove so quickly over the uneven cobbles and the many potholes that several times the steering wheel was knocked out of his hand. He saw no signs for the center, and when it was all becoming impossible he discovered that he was already on the way to Genova Nervi. He started sweating and took off his jacket. It wasn't that bad, after all. He had just lost a quarter of an hour, twenty minutes at most. He turned and took the next road that led into a residential district. 'Straight ahead,' said the sulky gas station attendant when Perlmann asked the way.

Immediately, it seemed to him, he found himself in one of the squares that he had passed – it was an eternity ago – on the way to the record shop. He hesitantly drove on, turned at random into the next street, had to do a loop because of the one-way system and ended up in the same square. The city center was curiously quiet this Sunday, there was no sign of the industrial fair, and he had to chase after the few passers-by to ask them the way.

'Keep going along the river,' an old man told him at last, dressed in his Sunday best and creeping past the dark shop windows with his walking stick. Only now did Perlmann see the river on the map. Annoyed with himself, he drove in the direction indicated. At a bus terminal he asked a driver.

'Molassana is a well-known part of Genoa, a suburb; nobody needs a road sign,' the driver replied to Perlmann's reproachful remark, looking at him as if he had lost his marbles.

Behind the wheel, Perlmann cursed the misleading representation on the map, and only calmed down when he crossed the river, where there was in fact a road sign. He had just put his foot down on the accelerator when he braked and turned off to the right. *I can't get lost tomorrow. That would be hell.* For a while he tried to reconstruct the direct route here in his head, cutting out the various diversions. But it didn't work. The toing and froing had been too confusing. Five past one. *He'll be landing in exactly twenty-six hours.* He took a few hasty drags, threw the cigarette out the window and drove back to the port road.

Driving back to Molassana, he stopped repeatedly and memorized the crucial spots. First of all there were the two ironmongers' shops, which were precisely identical: the same size, both on a corner, both with rusty shutters. If you turned by the first, the one-way system forced you back to the port, while a similarly inconspicuous turning near the second led towards the center. *On no account turn at the first.* Next he had to be careful that at the square where the building with the portico stood he didn't – as he had before – follow the tram tracks to the right, but take the bend to the left. At the construction site with the diversion he got lost twice: you had to turn off immediately past the bakery to get back to the main road. And finally, the place with all the bus stops was critical: you couldn't follow the three-lane road into the underpass; you had to keep to the left and keep going along the cobbles at a sharp angle to the main arterial road. It was still a rather roundabout route, he thought. Probably there was a simpler one, but he couldn't lose any more time.

At two o'clock he was back at the river, where he had turned. On the almost empty street he drove far too quickly. He was afraid of reaching a spot where it could be done, but even worse was the uncertainty, and it became more unbearable with every kilometer that didn't match his requirements. He might have to wait longer for a truck. At the spot in question there had to be a rest area where he could park beside the road. He would have to be able to see the truck coming from a long way off, so that there was enough time to drive off, speed up and pull the car over to the left at the last moment. And it would have to be impossible for the driver to swerve. Ideally, there would be a cliff on his side of the road.

On the steep piece of road before the tunnel which cut off the loop into the mountains and formed the apex of the stretch, there was just such a point. Perlmann stopped, his heart thumping. No, this wouldn't do, he thought, as he dried his moist hands with the towel. Having the long, stable hood between himself and the truck, everything depended on high speed, and even with this car he couldn't achieve that on the mountain. Besides, the truck's brakes could be damaged by the impact, and then, with the wreck of the Lancia in front of it, it would roll down with mounting speed and unforeseeable consequences.

After the tunnel there were a few spots which might have been possible in terms of the course of the road. But in those there were houses with people who leaned, gawking, in the windows. There would also be people like that tomorrow, and it would be impossible to do it in front of them. There were too many houses generally; one village followed on from the other. And everywhere there were people in the windows, hundreds of them, it seemed to Perlmann. This wasn't how he had imagined it. On the map there was no sign of these hamlets.

He had already covered far more than half of the stretch when a piece of road that was the right length appeared: straight and at a slight slope, with a supporting wall on the other side. At the exact spot where he expected the collision to occur there was a road sign, black on white: PIAN DEI RATTI. At the end, where the truck would appear around the bend, there was a house, but the shutters were closed and it looked uninhabited. At the bend around which he came himself, there was a workshop for the cutting and grinding of slate slabs. People would be working there tomorrow. Perlmann drove to the spot where the trees meant that he couldn't be seen from the workshop. The rest of the stretch was still long enough. Only stopping was a problem. On the right there was a sheer drop to the river, and in spite of the damaged crash barrier he could only get about half of the big car on to the narrow strip of grass. Nonetheless, he thought, it could be done here. But he would have to fix in his mind the features leading up to that spot so that he didn't miss it tomorrow.

He turned and drove to the next road sign: so the name of the village was PIANA. After the road sign came a biggish, abandoned-looking factory building, then two well-tended houses and behind them, at the start of the bend, three pines with a big poster for Renault customer services. When he passed the poster, he was already in the bend with the workshop. He could see the sign that said PIAN DEI RATTI, and then it was only another fifty meters.

He wanted to drive down that stretch of road very slowly to etch it in his memory as sharply and in as detailed a way as possible. But a car with a bridal couple and a tail of rattling tins was hooting behind him like crazy, so that afterwards he had the impression that he couldn't rely on his memory. He drove back, turned in the factory yard and repeated the whole thing. But it felt as if his memory was simply refusing to absorb the images. It was as if he was jinxed: every time he read the words PIAN DEI RATTI again, it was as if what he had just seen had been erased.

He needed more advance warning time and more pointers. Sweating, he drove two villages back, staring at the signs until his eyes hurt: tomorrow he would pass first MONLEONE and then PIANEZZA, which turned directly into PIANA. Then the pines and the poster, and finally PIAN DEI RATTI.

He stopped at the spot in question, exhausted, and lit a cigarette. When he looked forwards to gauge the distance again, he saw that a shutter had been pulled up at the house on the bend. Again he began to sweat. Had he ignored that before? Or had someone come home in the meantime? He put his glasses on his head, but still couldn't make out whether someone was standing at the window. Perhaps the people were just away today, and tomorrow, when he came round the bend with Leskov, they would be leaning in the window. They would see the Lancia stopping at this unnatural spot, for who knows how long, and dashing off exactly as a truck came from down below. And they would see the car suddenly being pulled off the road. In his mind, Perlmann took up position there at the window: to any observer it would look intentional. There was no doubt about it.

It was hard to keep in check his annoyance with the futility of the last half hour. But he made an effort and went on driving with calm control. Twenty minutes later the elegant villas of Chiávari came into view, and he hadn't seen a single suitable spot: either the road had too many twists and turns or you couldn't stop; or there were houses, time and again there were houses. Perlmann drove to the first parking lot on the edge of Chiávari and got out. Half-past three. His stomach was cramped with hunger and tension. He took the few steps to the nearest bar, ate a sandwich and asked the surprised waitress for a large glass of lukewarm water.

The tunnel. I've got to do it in the tunnel. The thought came to him after he had stood there for a while with his head completely empty, and had plainly even ignored the request for a light that had been uttered right next to him. He hastily laid some money on the counter, ran to the car and drove off. *I didn't notice, but the tunnel must have passing places where you can stop; all tunnels have them, it's the law,* he thought again and again as he drove back at breakneck speed. PIAN DEI RATTI. He slowed down, turned round and looked up at the house: everything unchanged, a single shutter pulled up. At the last ascent, where the road widened, he drove at over seventy and only stopped at the entrance to the tunnel. Yes, there were several passing places on both sides, he saw that straight away.

Back outside, he drove on another stretch, and only turned then. Here, too, he wanted to memorize the things that announced the spot. But it was actually quite easy: first of all there was a sign showing that the road climbed towards Piacenza on the left, and on the right on to Chiávari and then, just before the tunnel, came the crossing with the individual arrows. Perlmann drove on to the patch of gravel to the right before the tunnel entrance and turned off the engine.

At the touch of a button the tinted window slid down with a quiet hum. He rested his elbow on the frame and lit a cigarette. When he had quite recovered after a brief pause for exhaustion, he stubbed out the cigarette and took his arm off the window frame. Here, outside the tunnel of death, his comfortable, sloppy attitude struck him as obscene. It was a feeling like the one yesterday morning on the handrail behind the rocky spur. *Except now everything's worse, much worse.* Now all of a sudden he no longer knew what to do with his hands. Finally, he pressed them between his knees and, crouching there, stared for a moment beyond the steering wheel, into the tunnel.

It was long enough, perhaps two kilometers. Of course, he couldn't begin his approach out there. If you stood on this patch of gravel, you couldn't see far enough in, and if you wanted to improve your view, you had to adopt an unnatural and conspicuous position, halfway into the road. It could take quite a long time tomorrow, and hereabouts there were also houses where people would lean out their windows and watch the expensive limousine. Perlmann felt generally drawn to the tunnel because it meant that everything – the waiting as well as the collision – could happen in secret.

He drove in and stopped on the bright mud with which the first passing place was covered. Now he could see to the end of the tunnel, and in the side-view mirror, without conspicuously having to turn his head, establish whether the road was clear behind him. There was comfortable room here for a second car. Tomorrow he would have to stop in such a way that no one would think of stopping and offering him help. The best thing to do would be to park at an angle to the mud-pile with the shovel sticking in it. He could only hope that the police didn't come by. At that thought he gave a start and went on driving. He didn't dare turn into the tunnel, but drove out and then back to the patch of gravel. As before, he crouched down and rested his forehead on the steering wheel.

The first thing he would see of the truck would be its lights, bigger than those of a passenger vehicle, and fixed higher up. He wouldn't set off until the driver's cab was clearly visible, so that he could be sure that it was a big, stable vehicle. Ideally, it would one of those American trucks that were proper great fortresses. What he would have to do, down to the individual movements, was much less clear than he had previously assumed. In order to ensure that they were both killed, he would have to hit the truck head-on. In order to do that, he would have to switch to the opposite lane early and completely, as if he were trying to overtake. But that would make it clear to anyone who saw it – at least to the truck driver – that it was intentional. And, of course, during those horrifying seconds in which the front of the truck came hurtling towards them, Leskov would recognize that he had a murderer beside him, a murderer and a suicide. He might grab the wheel, and there would be a struggle, a struggle with an uncertain outcome. *Again, as if in a dream.*

On the other hand, if he pulled the wheel round just before the collision, if he did it a moment too late the truck's bumper would only hit the left-hand side of the Lancia. He might be killed, but Leskov would stay alive, and perhaps be able to testify to attempted murder. If, on the other hand, Perlmann did it a bit sooner, so that the whole length of the Lancia ended up in the opposite lane, diagonally in front of the truck, the right fender and then the right door would be crushed. Leskov would be killed and pressed against him. His fat body would be the protective shield that saved his life and so, buried under Leskov's corpse, he would feel the truck shoving the crumpled Lancia in front of it for a while, before coming to a standstill with a snort of its hydraulic brakes.

Perlmann was shocked by the macabre precision of his fantasy. He tried to resist the pull of the imagined details and turned on the radio to break the power of his visions. When that didn't help, he got out and walked mechanically up and down on the gravel, sometimes stopping at the edge, staring blankly at the rubble and blowing his cold hands.

If only he knew what the traffic here was like on working days. The fact that there were only a few cars on the road today – and so far not a single truck – didn't mean anything. What if there were traffic jams tomorrow, so that it couldn't be accomplished without putting other people's lives at risk? *But this is the only possibility. And I can't give it all up. I can't walk into the university every day as an unmasked fraudster, an ostracized man.*

Twenty to five. It was still light down at the coast, but here in the valley it was already starting to darken. They would be here tomorrow around about now. By the time Leskov had got through customs with his luggage it could easily be as late as half-past three. They could drive more briskly than today; there was nothing more to be sought and memorized, and in Genoa there would be far more traffic than today. He had seen that when he was buying his CDs. It would hardly be possible to get here in less than an hour. A shocking, endless hour, during which he would have to talk to Leskov as if everything was fine and he was delighted by his arrival. Before pelting, foot to the floor, into the glowing white headlights of a truck.

More traffic could also be a help, he thought, back behind the wheel. Rather than just driving along the line that you make when overtaking, he could make it look as if he had really been overtaking. That often happened: someone swerving and colliding head-on with the vehicle coming in the opposite direction. To make it believable, the driver of the swerving car would have to have his vision of the oncoming traffic obscured. As the traffic in this instance was a big truck, there couldn't be a car in front of him. He would have to be driving behind another truck or a bus, then pull out of its wake and on to the other side, at full speed and at precisely the moment when the truck in question appeared. The whole thing would have to be calculated in such a way that the truck or bus driving ahead, if it were to remain unaffected, was already past the oncoming vehicle when the collision took place. No, it couldn't be a bus, at least not one with passengers. *So that's the last thing I'm going to do in my life: gauge the speed of physical bodies moving towards one another.*

He rejected this plan as well. Too many things had to come together: a suitable oncoming truck; another one that he could drive behind for a moment; and an otherwise empty tunnel. This arrangement was far too unlikely; he couldn't rely on it. There was also the fact that no one actually overtook in a tunnel with oncoming traffic; the double line in the middle of a tunnel was respected even by people who otherwise drove recklessly. It wouldn't prove anything, but people would still be amazed that Perlmann had been driving like a hooligan.

As at the station three hours previously, he was overpowered for a moment by a numbing indifference. He was tempted simply to drive to the hotel and – without thinking about anything any more – go to bed. In the middle of this weary indifference, which made the world retreat by a few steps and covered it in dull grey, a truck emerged from the tunnel. In an instant Perlmann was wide awake, got out of the car and, resting on the open door, stared spellbound at the vehicle; it was carrying a load of gravel, water trickling from its platform. The front bumper hung down on one side and was fastened provisionally with a piece of rope. It was as if he were hypnotized by the sight of it, and didn't see the driver waving to him as he drove past. Then he watched after the damp trail and tried to become aware of the perception that was beginning to torment him. *The gas tank.* On this rickety old truck it was right at the front – the filler neck was just past the front wheel – and it had looked as if the tank behind the wheel was even further forwards. A vehicle like that would immediately go up in flames; it would be certain death for the driver.

It had been at the harbor, on Friday, when he had seen all the trucks waiting for the unloaded goods. It must have been around the spot where he had seen the freshly laid tarmac leading to the harbor area. There he could check that in modern vehicles the tank was set further back and better protected. But he couldn't leave this place before he was completely clear about the whole progress of the faked accident, the last movements that he would execute in his life. He got back into the car, slid the window closed and switched on the air heater. He quickly turned off the music on the radio when he felt the tears coming. Someone planning the things that he was had forfeited the right to music, and also to tears.

He stared out into the dusk, where the contrast in light between the inside of the tunnel and the world outside was slowly weakening. Yes, that was it: at first he would drive quite normally towards the approaching truck and then, still two or three hundred meters away from it, start to careen inside the empty tunnel, so that the driver and the police would have to assume there was suddenly something wrong with his steering wheel. Regardless of whether the driver tried to avoid him, or whether he simply braked: with a last swerve he would aim the Lancia straight at the truck's radiator. The autopsy would eliminate a suspicion of alcohol.

But in this variant, too, wouldn't Leskov grab the wheel? Was that something a person who didn't drive himself would do? He would do it when he recognized Perlmann's intention; it would be like a reflex. But he wouldn't do it if Perlmann acted as if the steering had failed – if he behaved as if he were convulsively trying to bring the car under control. He would have to underline it with a desperate remark, with a curse. He ran through a few in his mind. *So the last scene of my life will be theater, a cheap deception, a farce.* At this thought he had the impression for a moment that the worst thing about his plan was not its recklessness and its cold ruthlessness, not even its brutality, but the terrible shabbiness of its treatment of a man who had been in prison, who had had to live in much harsher conditions than he did, and who was now, for the first time and with great expectations, travelling to meet admiring colleagues in the West.

Perlmann wished he could do it right now and get the whole thing over with. But first of all there was dinner to get through, and this time it wouldn't be enough just to let it wash over him in silence. Because of the reception tomorrow, Angelini would be there, too. They would talk about Leskov, and now that his arrival was imminent the others would want to know more than they had before, when the only issue was his refusal. Perlmann would have to provide information in a natural, unforced way, because this was a conversation that the others would remember when news of the accident came in. The impression he left behind would have to be such that every individual, if he were to secretly suspect, would say to himself: *No, that's impossible. He couldn't have talked about Leskov like that yesterday evening.*

And then the ceremony in the town hall at which Perlmann – on his way to a terrible deed – would be made an honorary citizen of the town. He would be deluged with quivering rage, mixed with nausea, a rage directed at Carlo Angelini, who had caught him unawares and thus brought him to a state of fatal affliction, and who had now, to crown it all, organized this ludicrous ritual, this empty shell of exaggerated politeness, this conventional nothingness. Perlmann saw him in his mind's eye, the slim Italian in the tailored jacket, his tie in a skilfully loose knot. Angelini's whole manner and appearance, which Perlmann had secretly envied, now struck him as smarmy, pomaded and repellent. He gripped the steering wheel hard and banged his forehead against it until his own hooting brought him back to his senses.

The click of the seatbelt as it shut was already a memory, and he already had his hand on the ignition key when it occurred to him. *The seatbelt. I must make Leskov's belt unusable.* He released his own belt, turned on the light in the car and leaned over the passenger seat to get a look at the little box containing the roll of the belt. The only inconspicuous manipulation would be to block the narrow slit through which the strap ran. He took a handful of Italian coins out of his jacket pocket. The 100 lire pieces were the most suitable. But they only seemed to jam between the belt and the side of the box; if you pulled on the belt, they either came out at the same time or, more often, slipped into the box. Perlmann's movements became increasingly frantic. He wasted coin after coin and at last, helplessly and slipping away from himself like an addict, he pushed in all the coins that had seemed unsuitable from the outset. All the coins in the box made it rattle a bit when he tugged on the belt: but the strap still passed unobstructed through the slit.

Perlmann sat up, rested his head on the headrest and forced himself to be calm by breathing slowly. In his seat pocket he felt the wallet in which he still carried around his German money, even though he had often planned to leave it behind. He took it out. The two five mark pieces felt fatter and more massive than the Italian money, and when he tried one of them out it fitted more firmly, and resisted an initial pull. But at the second, rather more energetic tug it, too, fell into the box on to the other coins with a quiet chink.

When Perlmann reached into his jacket pocket for the lighter, he felt one last remaining coin. It was a thin 200 lire piece. He took the cigarette out of his mouth and set the half-blackened brass coin on top of the second five mark piece. The two coins couldn't be pressed into the slit at the same time by hand, but it was a close thing. Perlmann got out and searched through the tools in the belt. Then he opened the passenger door, set the two coins on the slit with his right thumb and ring finger, and with his index and middle fingers held the tip of a screwdriver over them, carefully tapping it in with an adjustable wrench. Light blows had no effect, but when he tapped harder the screwdriver slipped off, and at one point the brass coin almost fell into the slit. Once, when he sat up and stretched his aching back, Perlmann was passed by a cyclist in worker's clothes and a peaked cap, holding a pick over his shoulder. '*Buona sera,*' he said with a curious expression. '*Buona sera*,' Perlmann wanted to reply, but afterwards he wasn't sure if he had actually uttered it, or only thought it.

A moment later, when the screwdriver slipped again and scratched the black plastic box, he lost his nerve and the next time he struck it with all his might. When the screwdriver squashed the tip of his ring finger and slit it open, he dropped everything, stuck his finger in his mouth and hopped up and down with pain. After a while he wrapped his handkerchief around his finger and gave it one last try. The two coins caught, and now, carefully, millimeter by millimeter, he hammered them in. Once there was a groaning sound as if the box were about to explode. But it held and, at last, the belt was blocked. Perlmann sat down and tried it out. The curves of the two coins remained visible. He couldn't get them any further in. Otherwise they would slide in with the others. If Leskov looked carefully when he noticed that the belt was jammed, he could, with a shake of his head, say something about vandalism.

First he had borrowed the map, then rented the car, and now this. He was getting deeper and deeper into the realization of his plan. His actions were gradually becoming more deliberate, his reflections more ingenious, his traces clearer. And even so, he thought as he packed the tools away, it all felt like an inward-rotating spiral that was constricting itself around him all by itself and without his help, and would in the end strangle him with his own crime.

With his hand still on the lid of the trunk, he saw a woman on the other side of the crossing opening a grocer's shop and turning on the light. He ran over and walked into the shop. The old woman's white hair was so fine and sparse that she looked almost bald. Her in-turned lips and jutting chin reminded him of the toothless old woman at the window in Portofino.

'Closed,' she said, pushing her pointed chin even further forward.

'Just one question,' Perlmann said.

She looked at him suspiciously.

'Do lots of trucks come along here?'

'What?'

'Lots of trucks. Is there a lot of traffic? Through the tunnel, I mean.'

'Not today,' she grinned, showing her single stump of tooth.

'On working days, I mean.'

'Well, sometimes more, sometimes less.'

'What does it depend on?' Perlmann put his hands in his pockets so that he could clench his fists.

'I don't know. There's more going on in the summer.'

'But are there trucks at this time of day?'

'Of course there are. They make one hell of a noise. And they stink. But why do you want to know?'

'We're making a film, and it has to have trucks in it,' Perlmann said. He had no idea where that came from, but the information came without hesitation.

'A film? In our village?' She gave a croaking laugh and pushed the rolled tip of her tongue between her lips.

'And what about the time of day? When does the traffic ease off in the evening?'

'You want to know very precisely, don't you?' she said and now made a curious face as if she were trying to believe the story about the film. 'Nothing comes down from Piacenza after four. And from Chiávari through the tunnel – well, from half-past four there aren't as many, *c'è meno*.' And then, suddenly quite enraged, she added: 'Knocking off – these days they knock off at five in the evening!'

'So not many trucks come through after half-past four?'

'That's what I said.'

Perlmann was tempted to repeat the question, however pointless it was. But he didn't dare.

'A real film, eh?' she said when he was saying goodbye.

He felt he was about to suffocate in there, and just nodded.

'As if!' she murmured.

She watched after him as he walked back to the car. He was glad it was now too dark for her to make out the details of the car. When he turned round and set off towards Genoa she was still standing in the doorway.

31

Customs control at Genoa Airport wasn't much to worry about, he thought, and shifted down, having been an inch away from causing a collision on a tight bend. His calculation had been too generous. If the flight was on time, Leskov could be out by a quarter to three, and then they would arrive when there were still trucks on the road. If his estimate for tomorrow's journey, which stretched into the rush hour, was remotely accurate, he would have to be careful that Leskov didn't notice his haste and ask about it.

And, generally speaking, how was he going to explain to Leskov that they were taking neither the coast road nor the highway, but driving through this bleak, grey valley, in which there was absolutely nothing to see? Perlmann stopped when it struck him as boiling hot. But not a single excuse occurred to him that would have sounded even halfway plausible. No thoughts came at all. The last few hours had leached him out completely. His finger hurt. And how would the others explain the strange route? His colleagues? Kirsten? The police? He drove on. *I've still got twenty-one hours, after all.*

Even before he could begin to get his bearings, he reached an area at the harbor that was veiled in dense fog, cut through with beams of cold, rust-red light from the high harbor floodlights. It was impossible to see three feet ahead, and his own headlights made everything even worse. He got out of the car. Apart from the sound of the water it was completely silent. He had no idea how to find the parking lot, but in his exhaustion he was grateful for the fog, and went deeper and deeper into it.

Suddenly, a gap opened up, and between two swathes of fog he saw, a few hundred yards away, the row of trucks that he remembered from the ship. He turned up the collar of his jacket and stamped on, shivering. He only saw the bars when they appeared right in front of his face. They were part of a metal fence that ran on rails and clearly surrounded the whole truck lot. It must have been eight or nine feet high. For a while Perlmann stood there dejectedly and smoked. Then he threw away the fog-damped cigarette, which tasted horrible, and started climbing.

It was difficult. The meshes of the fence were tight and barely provided purchase for the tips of his feet, and his hands – he could only really use the right one – threatened to slip from the damp wire when he loosened his grip because it was so painful. At last he managed to grasp the top bar, and after a quick pause for breath, in which he hung from the fence like a sack, and felt the wetness penetrating his trousers, he managed to hoist himself up. When he drew up his second leg, his trousers caught on a screw. There was a long tear along his thigh. The sound of the tearing fabric seemed to echo across the whole of the harbor. When he reached the bottom Perlmann had the feeling of having done something completely senseless, and only his sore hands and a desperate defiance kept him from immediately climbing all the way back up again.

With his arms outstretched like a blind man, he walked slowly towards the trucks. The first thing he touched was a headlight. Then he felt for the bumper and ran his hand along it, from left to right and back again. He took off his fogged glasses and brought his eyes very close to it, felt the metal and the hard rubber covering, tested its height and compared it in his mind with the hood of the Lancia. He gripped the massive metal supports that held the whole thing together, and rattled them in a desperate awareness of how ridiculous he was being. Then he ran his hand along the length of the truck in search of the filler neck for the gas tank. He eventually found it on the other side, after half-creeping under the loading platform. The tank was in the middle, and there was a wide gap between the tank and the driver's cab. Exhausted, he leaned on the bumper, looked at his hands, smeared with oil and damp rust, and removed the dirty handkerchief from the wound, in mute despair over the bitter thought that such solicitude towards himself had now become superfluous.

For a while the image of the rickety truck with the loose bumper seemed to have been vanquished, and he was ready to head back. But then he was drawn on towards the next truck, which he examined with the same precision, after he had established that it was of a quite different type. The third truck bore a construction made of two powerful metal bars, making it look like a vehicle that had been designed to crush anything that entered its path. Perlmann saw it driving towards a red-brick wall and, with playful ease, smashing through it as if it were a cardboard film set. He took a few steps back into the reddish fog and then walked slowly to the front of the truck, thinking about the steering wheel, with his foot on the accelerator.

He was shivering, his clothes were damp, and his leg in his ragged trousers was icy cold. His nose was running, and it didn't help at all when he cleaned it with the last clean tip of his handkerchief. Afterwards, as he was walking to the next truck, it started running again. The urge to keep on going intensified as his sense of the absurdity of his actions grew. By now he was too tired to search all the trucks for their gas tanks. His examinations became increasingly rudimentary, and at last he was merely feeling his way along the bumpers. At first he did so by bringing his narrowed eyes up to them, his useless glasses in his left hand, and comparing a new type of bumper with the ones he was already familiar with. Later, when he had long since lost count of the trucks, he ran his hand only lightly over the damp metal. More and more rarely he stopped, and at last he fell into a trot with an arm that hopped from bumper to bumper, a bit like on the way to school when he had ran his hands, interrupted by the gaps for the house doorways, over the iron fences of his Hamburg district.

It was only when he had briefly touched the last truck that he turned around. The fog was now as dense as an enveloping cloth that one might bump one's face into. He would have liked to touch the truck with the huge metal bar one last time. But the fog had stripped him of all feeling for distance, and when, for a moment, blind behind his misted-up glasses, he seemed to lose the ground beneath his feet, he was no longer sure whether that truck even existed.

He slipped off twice before – bent double, head down – hanging over the fence again. He had thrown away the repellent handkerchief that repelled him, his injured finger stung, and his nose was running so violently that now, disgustedly, he blew his nose with his bare hand. At last he simply let himself fall, and was glad that it didn't hurt more than it did.

He was worried that he wouldn't find his car. But suddenly, without transition, the foggy cloth was gone. He was standing in a star-bright night, and saw the Lancia straight away. At first he hesitated to sit on the elegant, immaculate upholstery in his damp and dirty clothes. Then he swallowed a few times, slipped, exhausted, behind the wheel and switched the heating to its highest setting. A quarter past seven. *In twenty hours he will be waiting for his luggage behind customs control. Or else he will just be stepping out, and he will see me.*

After Santa Margherita, Perlmann took the highway and didn't worry about speed limits. He wanted to get out of his clothes and into the shower. *Physical needs remain the same; they're stronger than anything else.* The high speed helped him to think of nothing. It was ten past eight when he parked the Lancia by the filling station next to the hotel. Before he walked to the steps, he glanced back. The tires were covered with pale mud.

32

In the hall he ran straight into his colleagues, who were standing outside the dining room with Angelini. They looked at him with a mixture of puzzlement and shock.

'What have you done to yourself?' asked von Levetzov, pointing to Perlmann's trouser leg, where the frayed triangle of torn fabric hung and flapped each time he moved.

'I was helping someone with a breakdown, and had to creep under the car,' Perlmann said without hesitating, 'and I got caught on something.' He had no idea where the sentence came from; it was as if there were an invisible ventriloquist standing next to him.

'I didn't know you could do things like that,' Millar said with his head tilted, and it was clear how reluctant he was to revise his image.

'Oh, sure,' Perlmann smiled, and felt relieved that he was once again master of his utterances. 'I know a bit about cars.'

Never before in his life had he lied so unconcernedly, so brazenly. An impetuous feeling of freedom spread within him, a feeling of playful boundlessness in the face of a running clock. Now he was ready to invent everything about himself, any story was fine, the bolder the better.

'I used to be a good rally driver, in fact, and when you do that you pick up a whole lot of technical knowledge,' he added, and ostentatiously set off upstairs, two steps at a time.

The artificial high spirits that he had managed to preserve while hastily showering and changing were further reinforced when he elaborated his story about the breakdown over dinner and, as the driver of the car in question, invented a woman to whom he attributed the qualities of a local television presenter. Casually, as if it were barely worth mentioning, he wove in the rental car and a trip into the mountains. His story, backed up with dramatic hand movements that were quite alien to him, also prompted the others to tell anecdotes. There was a great deal of laughter. Perlmann laughed most of all. He drank glass after glass and plunged himself with all his might into a desperate exuberance. He became aware that his laughter constantly had to overleap the obstacle of the soul when it became something that could be felt as a distinct tug of his facial muscles, a mechanical process that made him feel unpleasantly hot. For a few black and icy minutes he felt like a sophisticated doll, a dead man pretending to the others, by laughing, that he is alive. Then he asked the waiter to top up his glass and went on drinking and laughing until he had found his way back to his old mood, which was a bit like invisibly warped glass that would shatter into a thousand pieces if the play of forces were to get out of kilter.

Laura Sand seemed to have been watching him for quite a long time when he caught her thoughtful eye. He turned round, waved to the waiter and asked for some more bread. *No, she can't possibly have seen through me. She might find me a bit strange this evening, and perhaps tomorrow evening when it all comes out she'll think about it. But even she doesn't know anything that could establish a connection between the two things. Absolutely nothing at all.*

'It's very gratifying that Signor Leskov can come for a few days after all,' Angelini said beside him, adding, after an expressive pause, 'I found out from the others.'

Under normal circumstances Perlmann would have fallen into the trap, and would have solicitously produced an explanation for his omission. Now nothing meant less to him than the fact that he had forgotten to leave Angelini a message.

'Didn't you get my message?' he asked in a cool, almost indifferent tone, and took a sip of wine.

'No,' said Angelini, now very obliging again, 'but now I know, and I'll see to it that he gets some cash when he arrives. Things are a bit different for people in his situation. By the way,' he continued quietly in Italian, resting his hand on Perlmann's arm, 'at the reception I was given Giorgio's copy of your paper, and I had a read of it in my room. I'm very excited to hear what your colleagues will have to say about this unusual work. But, of course, you'll be able to defend yourself.'

'Of course,' said Perlmann, turning his head towards the waiter who brought him his coffee. While he thanked him extravagantly, as if he had just received an enormous present, all the ghostly serenity vanished from him, and he no longer knew how he would bear to stay at this table for even a minute longer.

The questions about Leskov, which came as expected, he answered curtly, hoping no one would notice how often he was drawing on his cigarette and reaching for his empty coffee cup because he feared his voice would fail him.

As he left he turned round again. So this was where his last supper had taken place. He must have stood there for a long time, because Evelyn Mistral, who held the door open for him, leaned, waiting, against it with arms folded and legs crossed, looking at him as one looks at someone whose thoughts one doesn't want to disturb.

'*Gracias*,' he said hoarsely and walked quickly past.

The room was spinning as Perlmann slumped fully dressed on to the bed. Against his better judgment, he was seized with fear that the effect of the alcohol might not have faded by tomorrow, when it mattered. And that fear was mixed with a sensation that he didn't recognize straight away: a guilty conscience. Not because of his planned deed, but because he had got drunk on the last evening of his life. It was a struggle to think about it, because at the same time he had to battle against a lurking feeling of nausea. And when he finally knew what it was, the discovery intensified his despair still further. Because it meant that a perverse shift of values had taken place within him: he found it reprehensible that while awaiting death he hadn't shown the required sobriety and alertness; he reproached himself like someone awaiting death, who has to remain entirely alert. But he had already separated the monstrous, criminal aspect of his plan so completely from himself – or else he had got so used to it in the course of a day – that it was no longer the object of a suicide attempt, and, even now, as he internally brought it up, it made no waves in his conscience, not even when he reproached himself for this cold and repellent fact and watched with a shudder as the rebuke for his insensitivity slipped silently away.

When this spiral of self-observation merged with the renewed circling of the room, he could bear it no longer and showered in cold water until his teeth chattered. Then, under the covers, he felt better. He got up again, mechanically put a bandage on his stinging, bloodstained finger and took a fresh handkerchief to bed to staunch the renewed running of his nose once and for all. The room was no longer spinning, and nausea gave way to weariness, which came as a relief. Only his blood pulsed loudly. He listened to it pounding and slipped into half-sleep, from which the ceiling light finally woke him.

It was half-past eleven. His head was clear again. He sat down at his desk and wrote Kirsten's phone number in big, emphatic letters on a piece of paper, and beneath it her full name and Konstanz address.

There was no point in calling her. He didn't know what he could have said. He couldn't even think of the usual things they said to one another.

He sat on the bed and dialled her number. She answered only with the word 'Kirsten'. There was still a chuckle in her voice; she clearly had visitors, and had just been enjoying a jocular conversation.

Perlmann put the phone down. He tried to remember the last thing she had said when she had called three days before. It had been something cheerful and boisterous; that was it, to send her greetings to Silvestri. *But don't be too friendly!*

Her studies were paid for, and the money would last some time afterwards. He knew that without thinking. Nonetheless, Perlmann went through the sums again: the savings books, the few shares, the life insurance on which Agnes had insisted.

Agnes. He turned out the light. She, whose thinking had always been rather sharper than his, would have advised him to just come clean that he had nothing to say right now. Recently, on the ship, Perlmann had been profoundly convinced that such advice could only come from someone who didn't know the world of the university, which is why it had struck him as worthless. Now, just before the end, it struck him as the best advice.

The deception would have stood between them for ever, he thought. But it wasn't impossible that she might somehow have been able to understand him. She, too, might have been able to see it as a kind of self-defense. And she would have found it idiotic that he had had suicidal thoughts after Leskov's telegram. She would have seen it as a typically pig-headed male overreaction; but she wouldn't have condemned him for it. On the other hand, that he was capable of hatching this villainous murder plot – that would have prompted only horror and revulsion in her; she would have flinched from him, and looked at him in disbelief, as if he were a monster.

He turned on the light. Suddenly, he was far from certain that he knew what Agnes's response would really be. He took her picture out of his wallet. In his misery, would he have confided in her? Would she have been able to protect him from disaster? How had she actually reacted when he had repeatedly hinted to her that his profession was slipping away from him? Had it ever been clear to her how much he had had to fight to assert himself internally against the expectations of others? He increasingly had the impression of not having known her very well, above all where her perception of him was concerned. At last, when he held the picture out at arm's length, he had a feeling of complete strangeness, and he thought he was sure that she couldn't have helped him. He was saying goodbye to her for the second time. It was much worse than it had been by the graveside.

In the dark room, lit only by a faint glow of cold moonlight, Perlmann leaned upright against the wall at the head of the bed. Really lying down, snuggling up and pulling the covers over his ears – with a plan like the one he had in his head, that was impossible. *Sleep well, to be fit for your journey into death.* He shuddered when those words formed within him, and reached for a cigarette to chase them away. If he wanted to avoid any kind of tastelessness, it was, strictly speaking, impossible, he reflected, to do anything except what the implementation of his terrible plan urgently demanded. Everything else was scorn, cynicism, even if it wasn't intended that way and he alone could see it.

He didn't really know why, but that seemed above all to apply to reading, to the desire to immerse oneself in a book. What he really wanted to do was open Robert Walser's novel again. He wished he could touch it at least. But even that was too much. Books were now forbidden objects. He felt as if that bitter thought had severed his last connections with the world. There on the bed, in his uncomfortable posture – in which his back and neck were beginning to hurt – he felt as if he were on an island, cut off from everything, and with nothing left to do but sit still until the time came.

He started recapitulating the route through Genoa. On the right, the industrial plants with the white smoke, then the harbor cranes. On no account turn at the first ironmonger's shop. But careful: when it appeared, it meant there was less than 300 meters to go. At the columns, don't follow the tram tracks, but turn left. The place with the dug-up road and the diversion where he had twice got lost, was particularly tricky because the passing street formed such a natural, almost mandatory bend that you saw the turn-off with the diversion sign – which was, further-more, half-hidden by a protruding building – too late, and then you found yourself in a maze of one-way streets, from which you only found your way out with great difficulty. When you came to the square you had to keep to the right to let the others past, and then what you had to do was catch sight of the bakery in the yellow building in good time and brake, even though it didn't look at all like a turn-off. And last of all there was the bus collection point. Keep left so that the flow of traffic didn't force you into the underpass – that was particularly important tomorrow, at the start of the rush hour.

Otherwise not much could happen, he said to himself. Then it occurred to him that he no longer knew whether he was supposed to take the second or third turn-off at the big square with the column. That was something he hadn't explicitly memorized. Presumably because it seemed unambiguous. But was it? He started sweating, and for a while he thought of driving there straight away and checking. But after three days and nights – in which one anxiety had come in hot pursuit of the other – that last shock, even if it was comparatively mild, was just too much. All emotion was extinguished in Perlmann, and without being aware of it he slipped under the bedcovers.

It was perhaps the hundredth coin that slipped out and fell through the slit into the box. The belt should really have been jammed from below by all the metal ages ago, but it ran as quickly and smoothly as a fan belt, and cut his finger so that he couldn't use that hand to keep from falling into the red fog from the top of the fence. His leg was stiff and numb with cold, and he limped as, sniffing continuously, he ran his hand over the endless bumpers, which at first felt deceptively solid, before they suddenly buckled as if they were made of damp cardboard. With arms blindly outstretched he touched the radiator grille, which parted silently when he drove at it with the accelerator to the floor. He dashed inside and drove through unresisting red cotton wool, in which the Lancia could no longer be steered at all; it ran as if on rails, and turning the steering wheel had absolutely no effect. But then the cotton wool had disappeared, and the car careened along wavy lines through the tunnel. Like a bumper car at a carnival, it crashed against the planks to left and right and then he heard and felt with horror his own bumper scraping along the tarmac, he saw a rain of sparks getting higher and denser, he wanted to stop, but the car was speeding up all by itself and dashing straight towards the huge, full-beam headlights of all the trucks that came hurtling towards him in a single wide line without the tiniest space between them. He threw his arms in front of his head, waited for the collision and was woken by the deafening silence that came instead.

33

He just lay there only until his heartbeats had grown fainter. This time waking from a nightmare was quite different from usual, because the relief of the first few seconds was swept away by the intruding certainty that a scene similar to the last one would be repeated in reality in only a few hours. Before that thought could fully develop its paralysing effect, Perlmann turned on the light and got out of bed. The alarm clock said just after six and he mechanically calculated the number of remaining hours. He hesitated outside the shower and stared into the void, then briefly let cold water run over his skin. As he rubbed himself dry he felt his scalp twitching, but then put the shampoo back again. No time for that. In his dressing gown he called down for coffee and insisted to the sleepy kitchen-maid that it was all he wanted for breakfast.

Then he sat down at the desk. Perlmann's mind was dominated by a numb, glassy alertness that left all inner turmoil behind. He started the last preparations, concentrated and methodical, as if he were planning a course of lectures or a long journey.

He would have to commit the murder in the best clothes he had with him; in his dark grey flannel trousers and his blazer with the gold buttons, and the black shoes that he hadn't worn since the first evening. Because coming back to the hotel and getting changed after the reception was out of the question. *Dress more comfortably for the murder.* The thought sent the blood rushing to his face. He violently bit his lip and, filled with revulsion, drove the words from his consciousness. Then he put on his grey trousers and a white shirt, hung his blazer on the wardrobe door and set out his dark blue tie with the red pattern.

It wasn't just reading, eating and grooming that had become impossible, he thought, as the waiter had pulled the door closed behind him. Even greeting someone, thanking him and responding to a smile were things that now, in the most loathsome way, felt dishonest, cynical, obscene. He pushed the milk and sugar aside when he poured himself a cup of coffee on the desk. Smoking was the only thing that was different: the stinging on his tongue and the occasional tightening in his lungs sat well with fear and destruction.

From the hotel folder he took a business card with the address, wrote his name on it and put it in his wallet with his passport. The gas tank was more than half full, he thought and, by pressing thumb and forefinger on his eyeballs, he dispelled the image of flames. The parking ticket at the airport and possibly in front of the town hall, the highway toll, one or two coffees. Otherwise there was nothing for which he would need money now. He put a few small notes in an inside pocket of his suitcase along with his traveller's checks. It was a strange discovery that he was making about himself: ideally, he wouldn't be carrying a single coin on him when he started the car for the last time.

Next he looked all through the case. He stuffed his pyjamas in the plastic bag with the dirty laundry and tied it shut. But the bag wouldn't leave him in peace. He took his reference books out of his suitcase and stuffed in the bag. He would throw it away on the journey.

For a while he looked down at the reference books that lay scattered on the bed. Then he started piling them up on the desk.

Outside the day was slowly breaking. *He'll already be airborne by now.* Perlmann took the Russian text and the handwritten translation out of the bottom laundry drawer. He stuffed the pages with the unfamiliar format and the badly copied Cyrillic letters in with his laundry bag in the suitcase. He held the translation irresolutely in his hand and then sat down on the bed. They assumed that he had written this text, they knew that he preferred to write by hand, so it would be the most natural thing if the handwritten version were found. He flicked through the thick pile of pages. Were corrections made during the translation process not different in kind to those made when actually writing? There were, for example, the many points where several variants of a word or a sentence were separated from one another by slashes, and in the end he had crossed them all out but one. Perhaps they would assume that he had been uncertain about his English in each case; or else they would see him as a fanatical stylist. But if someone looked closely and thought about it, it might seem curious – particularly as there were no intellectual corrections of any kind, which would have revealed themselves in deleted paragraphs, major additions and transpositions.

It was too dangerous. He would have to take this stack of papers with him and throw them away on the journey. Admittedly, most people who started with a handwritten version had a sentimental attachment to the text, but he also knew others who threw their manuscripts away when the computer printout was available. He also squashed that paper into the suitcase with the laundry. As he did so part of it came away, got caught in the Russian pages, something tore, and the sound of the tearing paper worked like a triggering signal on his emotions, or a catalyst. An impotent fury broke out of him. Blind with tears, he reached into the mass of paper as if into a mass of dough. He crumpled and tore the pages. He thumped them with his fists until he was out of breath and wheezing, with his face bright red and a face twitching like mad.

He washed his face, and after drinking a cup of his now cold coffee in small, slow sips, and smoking a cigarette at the open window, he was able to go on. The other thing he would have to get rid of was the vocabulary notebook. He picked it up and, like an exhausted body dipping briefly in and out of sleep in defiance of the will, even though there was nothing he could do about it, Perlmann's soul grabbed a breathing space by making him forget his situation and giving free rein to curiosity. With one hand he covered over the English columns and tested how many words he knew by heart; then he did the same thing in the other direction. Only after a few minutes did the awareness of his situation catch up with him. He felt as if he had been caught and, after two vain attempts, tore the vocabulary notebook through the middle before stuffing it in his suitcase along with the other waste paper.

The three dictionaries and the Russian grammar, scattered with crossings-out and cross-references. They would – if they were found here – prompt astonishment, because he wasn't supposed to speak a word of Russian. But that wasn't suspicious in itself; it could be seen as modesty, coquetry or simply as a whim. Evelyn Mistral would think back to the time she had surprised him at the swimming pool with the Russian text, and how he had cast her a conspiratorial glance over dinner when he had lied. But without any further knowledge that couldn't turn into deliberate suspicion; the mere fact that Leskov, the man who had died with him in the accident, was a Russian, would have to remain unconnected with the dictionaries even for her.

On the other hand, why did Perlmann have these dictionaries here – especially when the Russian-English one was such a tome – if there were no Russian texts to be seen far and wide?

Perlmann no longer knew which suspicion was likely and which was not. He stopped surmising and suddenly knew only this: he didn't want to leave any Cyrillic letters behind, not a single one. No one must associate him with the Russian language, and if there were any memories of that connection, they must fade as quickly as possible. His eye ran back and forth among the four books and the stuffed suitcase – then, on the spur of the moment, he turned the case upside down and tipped its contents on to the bed. The torn and crumpled pages piled up into a mountain on top of the laundry bag, and some of the sheets sailed to the floor. He packed the books into the suitcase, put on his usual jacket and went down to the rear entrance. The door was still locked. With a resoluteness that cancelled out any other feelings, he crossed the hall, nodded to Giovanni, who was on the phone, and went down the steps to the gas station parking lot.

Screened by the open lid of the trunk he stowed the books under the panel that covered the spare wheel. For a moment he was worried that the panel wouldn't fit properly because of the thick dictionary, and was wobbling slightly; then he interrupted himself abruptly and walked quickly back through the hotel hall to the elevator. As he was waiting, Ruge and von Levetzov came downstairs on their way to breakfast. They were surprised to see him so early, and cast a quizzical glance at the suitcase.

'See you later,' Perlmann said firmly, and disappeared into the elevator.

Upstairs he stuffed the laundry and the paper back into his suitcase and fetched the printout of the translation out from under the shirts in the top clothes drawer. Where should he put it? The most natural place would be the desk. But there was a sensation in the way that revealed itself to him only gradually: he didn't want the eyes of anyone who came in – whether it be his colleagues, the hotel staff or the police – to fall on the fateful text before anything else. It wouldn't be able to tell them anything, nothing at all; they could read it a thousand times and stare at it for as long as they liked. And yet he didn't want this pile of pages, which made him a murderer and drove him to his own death, to lie conspicuously on the glass desktop – even though each of the others had identical copies.

He didn't want that to happen, not least because of Kirsten. The fraudulent text mustn't be the first thing she found when she came to collect his things. It wouldn't tell her anything either. Or Martin. But if it was lying on the desk, she would immediately pick it up. *The last thing Dad wrote.* She would recognize the title and remember the upset there had been a week before, when he had reacted so impatiently to her idea of reading it on the journey. The idea was unbearable. Perlmann looked around the room. At last he put the text in the desk drawer under the phone book.

It would soon be half-past eight. He had stopped calculating. Now he had a keen sense of how much time he still had left. For several minutes he thought of nothing at all, just looked out into the still pale sunlight over the bay. He wished he knew how to do that: take your leave of a place to go to your death. He thought that everything he saw would now have to have a special quality. It would have to be clearer and calmer, because at that moment you no longer projected anything on to things – because you no longer cast an emotional shadow yourself, to darken your view. Because by deciding to die, you had withdrawn completely from the world. Its entanglements had lost their power over you. You stood next to them. You could see them all quite undistorted. That brought you as close as possible to the vantage point of eternity. That was what you gained if you were prepared to put everything at stake.

But after a while he admitted to himself that he experienced nothing of the sort. He stood by the open window, as always two steps back from the balustrade. Outside the bay lay in fine morning mist; the noise of traffic, a ship's siren, a knot of phlegm in his throat from all the smoking. Nothing else.

He put on his tie, slipped into his blazer and then sat down, his suitcase by his side, in the red armchair, to wait. Leaving a place, but still having to wait, like you did before. At such moments, he thought, it had often seemed as if he, too, could achieve a present. You had a piece of time ahead of you – two hours, perhaps – in which you didn't need to do anything. You had the excuse of enforced waiting, and could yield entirely to the sensation of inner freedom that unfolded when you simply let that time elapse with full consciousness. In that state he had always imagined what it would be like to live here and experience the present; and he had done exactly that when he had left home by plane. The imagination then effortlessly brought about what seemed otherwise unattainable: by sketching out the image of a lived present, it also gave the very moment of sketching the quality of the present. It was fragile, this present, and it needed practice to deal with it. At the moment, in fact, at which one actually began to live at that place, even if only in the airport, if one then promised to help someone – keeping an eye on their suitcase, for example, or changing money for them – at that moment the present would be over. It was a present beside the suitcase, and everything depended upon not the slightest obligation, not even a conversation, penetrating or even touching the ring of detachedness, of utterly detached waiting. And because that repeatedly threatened to happen through the way in which people approached him, he had restlessly shifted from seat to seat with his suitcase in the departure hall.

Now that he had only a few hours left to live, everything was different. The delicate operation of finding one's way through an imagined present into the real one could only happen if one had an open future ahead of one, into which one could recast oneself. But he knew all about a stiflingly cramped and inexorably shrinking future. He could have written down the whole sequence of events still to come, to the smallest detail, so the hour left until his departure was nothing but an abstract, pallid piece of time, marked by an unshakeable, unswayable dimension of the physical world in which one could observe how the sun rose, and in which one could count how often someone beeped their horn down on the coast road.

It isn't boredom, for God's sake; no, it can't be boredom. And it wasn't, he thought with relief. It was quite different from being in bed, back then, with camomile tea, poultices and yet again the same picture book. Because what made this waiting here so terribly lifeless wasn't a hindrance, a limitation, a lack of opportunity. It was an inner rigidity that he was trying without success to loosen, until he understood at last that it was the only thing that protected him from the horror which was – silent, high and blinding – hurtling towards him from the tunnel.

Eventually, he got up, fetched two packs of cigarettes from the cupboard and put them in his pocket. Later he went into the bathroom and washed his hands. As he dried them, he paused all of a sudden, and began to pull his wedding ring from his right hand. In spite of the soap that he used, it was difficult and painful. He turned the ring irresolutely around between his fingers, then put it in the suitcase with his valuables. Kirsten would find it, and he was sure her thoughts would turn to Evelyn Mistral. That wasn't something he didn't care about; but he felt the thought of others losing its influence hour by hour, and now he was plainly freeing himself from his daughter as well.

Just before half-past ten he carried the suitcase to the door. Then he went slowly through the room. He stopped before the desk and shifted the piece of paper with Kirsten's phone number to the middle of the glass plate. After scrutinizing it for a moment he pushed it into the lower right, then the top corner. He fetched the red lighter from the round table and set it down next to it. He had already turned to the door, when he turned round, put the lighter back on the round table and shoved it with a finger until its position looked random enough.

From the door he glanced once again through the room. Only then did he notice the white paper edge peeping out from under the overhanging bedcover. It was a torn and crumpled page of the Russian text. Perlmann threw up the cover, fell on his knees and checked everything. Again and again his eye ran over the whole surface under the bed, as if a new sheet might suddenly materialize. At last he pulled the cover over, stuffed the sheet into the suitcase and waited until his pulse had calmed down. Then he went out without looking back.

34

In the hall Brian Millar came up to him, having just finished a conversation with Signora Morelli. He was wearing his dark blue double-breasted suit and the tie with the embroidered anchor. His face and movements bore an organizer's zeal.

'Have you thought of leaving a copy of your text in Leskov's pigeon-hole?' he asked, with his eyebrows raised, and in the reproachful tone of someone who is sure of getting a negative reply.

Perlmann was bracing himself, as usual, to struggle against his fear of Millar. But now, all of a sudden, there was something of the detachment from things for which he had previously waited in vain. For three or four seconds he managed not to react at all, and to stare past Millar to the door. He enjoyed the absence of any kind of fear and any temptation to solicitude. Then he looked into those blue eyes, which already contained a hint of irritation, waited for another two or three seconds and then said with cool indifference, 'No, that hadn't occurred to me.'

'That's what I thought,' said Millar, in a voice in which Perlmann thought he heard a trace of puzzlement and even uncertainty. Perlmann had never responded to him like that in the whole four weeks.

'I gave Signora Morelli my own copy of the text so that she could do it. It'll be nicer if Leskov has the text given to him as soon as he arrives. A question of style.'

'OK,' said Perlmann. He left Millar standing there and walked to the counter, where he handed Signora Morelli the key to his room. He was the only one who noticed that the gesture was performed more slowly and deliberately than usual, because before it was concluded the phone rang.

He stopped on the terrace of the steps and put on his sunglasses. No more fear of Millar, and a lack of the subservience that he usually struggled to conquer – so that was what he had gained by deciding to die. He lit a cigarette and walked slowly over to the Lancia. He wanted to savor the experience he had just had. He set the suitcase down on the back seat and then sat still behind the wheel for a while.

It was a moment of presence – or it could have been if it had belonged to a life with a future, a life with expectations, hopes and plans. Here at this gas station, with his hand on the ignition, with which he would later carry out his crime, Perlmann understood for the first time how completely the capacity for internal delineation from other people was dependent upon the experience of presence. With an exaggerated sense of clarity that almost made him dizzy, he understood that his repeatedly failed attempts at delineation and the constantly retreating present were two facets of a single difficulty which ran like a thread through his life and had turned him into a person who, even in the quietest phases of his life – and even without his really noticing – was always out of breath. And with the same clarity he saw that the thought of imminent death made delineation possible and thus created the precondition for an experienced present, but at the same time robbed him of the future and created the awareness of a guilt in which all experience was frozen.

As he drove out into the coast road, the others were all coming down the steps. Only Angelini was not among them.

'Perlmann!' called von Levetzov, who was wearing, with his dark suit, a grey waistcoat that gave him a distinguished appearance.

Perlmann had automatically looked over at him, and now it was impossible simply to go on driving. He stopped.

'Nice car,' said Millar, running his fingertips over the gleaming fender. Ignoring the honking cars, he walked around the car with the face of an expert, and then looked at Perlmann with an expression in which surprise, curiosity and acknowledgement flowed into one another. *Now this murder weapon, which was forced upon me because of the industrial fair, also turns me into a man of style.*

'The dirt on the tires doesn't fit, though,' grinned Ruge, who was wearing his brown suit with an open shirt even for this occasion. He got into the back.

'It's fine,' he said, as Perlmann prepared to move the suitcase and put it in the trunk. 'It's even quite comfortable,' he added, and rested his elbow on it. *Nothing would happen, even if he looked in. He can't speak Russian. No one here can speak Russian.*

When Millar and von Levetzov had got in as well, Perlmann automatically fastened his seatbelt and started the engine. The click of the belt as it fastened made Millar, who was sitting next to him, reach for his own. He tugged twice, and when the belt didn't yield, he half-turned on his seat and tugged with both hands. Perlmann held his breath. He became aware of his injured finger and noticed that his other hand, which was moving the gearstick back and forth in neutral, was drenched in sweat.

'It's just for this short journey,' von Levetzov said behind him, as Millar was about to rest on his knee to take a better look.

Before Perlmann turned the corner, he cast one last glance in the rear-view mirror at the hated hotel, and the crooked pine that loomed out over the road. Then he drove past the two women, who had chosen to go on foot. Evelyn Mistral was wearing a white pleated skirt that swung with each step she took, and a red jacket whose collar she had turned up, making her blonde hair curve outwards. When she waved to him with a radiant smile, Perlmann closed his eyes and almost knocked down a cyclist who had suddenly darted from the pavement on to the road. In the few minutes since the gas station all his detachment and clarity, which had seemed so stable, so definitive, had fled, and he felt claustrophobic in the full car, his body convulsed, and he drove as awkwardly as a learner.

Millar and Ruge talked about the safety standards of cars, about crumple zones, yielding steering-columns that broke in a head-on collision, and about the airbag system. Ruge drove a Volvo, Millar a Saab.

'I've just been reading a report on this car,' said Millar, giving Perlmann a sideways look. 'It seems to be the safest Italian thing on the market.'

'Really?' Perlmann murmured hoarsely, and returned Millar's glance slightly too late.

Outside the town house he drove past several parking spaces that the others pointed out, because he was afraid they might be just too tight for the Lancia. He didn't want to embarrass himself when parking this unusually large car. *As if that still mattered.* Amidst the baffled silence of the others, he turned into a side street, where all the parking spaces were free. He had already got out when von Levetzov looked again through the half-closed car door.

'That's odd,' he said, 'the box for the belt is all scratched.' Then he pushed the door shut.

Millar, who had jauntily slammed the door already, and was walking towards a shop window, turned round. But before his hand reached the handle, Perlmann had already activated the central locking and slipped the key into his trouser pocket.

In the square in front of the town hall, Angelini, who had picked up the two women on the way, was just getting out of his red Alfa Romeo. He was wearing a respectable grey suit with wide lapels and a little badge, and a pink shirt with a blue tie. He took the cigarette out of the corner of his mouth and said something about the figure on the ivy-covered monument, a man with folded arms, his head thoughtfully inclined and a scroll in his hand. Perlmann didn't hear a single word that was said. He just glanced towards Angelini when he noticed the Italian repeatedly trying to catch his eye.

He had thought he knew everything there was to know about the torment of the lack of presence. Now he noticed that it had intensified still further. While Angelini's voice reached him as if from a long way away, the present withdrew from everything that surrounded him. It fled from things, leaving behind a world that seemed to him like a lifeless papier mâché backdrop in which all movements seemed as aimless and artificial as those of figures on a church tower clock. He was glad at last to walk towards the building with the faded yellow facade, the green shutters and the two palm trees outside the door, and regain a little reality by virtue of his own movements.

*

There was no one there to welcome them. The doors to the council hall and the mayor's office were locked. In the first-floor corridor, from which one could look down into the dusty stairwell and the hall with the flaking plaster, clerks walked past, smoking and chatting, paying the waiting group not the slightest attention, and disappeared into various rooms.

While the others rocked embarrassedly on their heels, or walked over to the glass display case, Laura Sand enjoyed the situation. Her face bore an expression of mocking contentment. She strolled along the corridor in her black corduroy trousers and elegant light-grey jacket, and at last said with amusement to Perlmann that they were all slightly too elegantly dressed. Angelini, who had looked as if he were sitting on hot coals the whole time, jerked his head round when he heard her remark. With the icy face of a superior, he stubbed out the cigarette that he had just lit on the tiled floor, and stepped into the nearest office without knocking.

When he came out, he was followed by a slim, pale man with black horn-rimmed glasses, who looked and behaved like the caricature of a subservient office worker in a film. After trying out two wrong keys, he finally opened the door of the mayor's office and let them in.

The room was dominated by a black, carved desk and a chair which, with its decorations and high back, looked like a church pew. Behind it, stretched between two engraved silver staffs, was the flag of Santa Margherita, two yellow lions on a green-and-white background. Beside the Italian flag in the corner was the picture of the President of the Republic. With a tortured smile that couldn't conceal his annoyance, Perlmann made a host's gesture and invited them to sit down on the red leather benches with the gold knobs. Then he went outside.

Everyone was laughing at a remark that Ruge had made about the thick layer of dust on the desk, when the Mayor came bursting in. With his belly, his greasy hair and his moustache, he reminded Perlmann of the landlord in Portofino. Puffing, he apologized for his lateness and darted Angelini, who was closing the door, an embarrassed glance. Then he set down the shallow box and a roll of paper on the desk, and as the swirled-up dust settled, he awkwardly pulled some sheets of paper from his jacket pocket.

It was a great honor and a special joy, he began, to welcome Professore Philipp Peremann and his group to the town.

'Per*l*mann,' hissed Angelini from the bench, '*con l.*'

'*Scusi,*' said the Mayor and shook his head as he looked at his text, which plainly contained a typo. He asked Perlmann to join him by the desk, shook hands with him and then went on reading out the prepared English text, his free hand repeatedly pulling up his trousers, which constantly threatened to slip beneath his belly.

Perlmann looked sideways at the Mayor's sweaty face, his badly shaven throat and his dirty shirt collar. Before, when he had entered the hall and accidentally touched Evelyn Mistral's hand as she held the door out to him, he had thought he would need all his remaining strength of will to resist the overwhelming urge to flee from one second to the next. Meanwhile, the odd, even grotesque course of the reception had put him in a state of cheerful, almost exuberant indifference, which he wanted to maintain for as long as possible, even though it felt unpleasantly artificial, as if a drug were responsible for it. He had to be careful, he thought, not to do anything impossible right now, like this, for example: walking right up to the Mayor and, with a loud '*Permesso!*', straightening his crooked tie.

He kept his eyes lowered to the desk, on which, as in a church, beams of dusty sunlight fell through the high windows. Only once did he raise his head. Then his eye fell on Millar, who had turned away slightly and was looking out of the window. At first Perlmann couldn't believe it. He examined his feelings again, but his hatred of Brian Millar had vanished. It was simply no longer there. It had vanished like a nightmare. And when he followed his eye-line and saw that Millar was looking at a huge balloon painted with a pouting woman's mouth in gaudy purple, which was drifting sluggishly over the monument, he thought of Sheila's kiss, and all of a sudden he liked the handsome American with his naive self-confidence and the unusual red shimmer in his dark hair.

When their eyes met, Perlmann smiled at him. Millar hesitated, then his face darkened, and he irritably raised his eyebrows. He seemed to think Perlmann was making fun of him. But then he saw that Perlmann's persistent smile was a different smile, not an ironic or a hostile one. He blinked two or three times, reached for his glasses and made a first, still cautious attempt to smile back. As he did so there was still scepticism in his face, and only after a further hesitation did his features fall into a relaxed, casual smile that turned into a broad, warm grin that Perlmann had never seen on his face before. *He's glad, too, just as glad as I am. Was that hatred necessary?*

Perlmann only noticed that the Mayor had stopped talking when he pointedly cleared his throat. From the box he had taken a gold medal that hung from a strip of fabric in the colors of the town's coat of arms. Now, with an expression of ridiculous solemnity, he stepped up to Perlmann, who bent far forwards to avoid contact with his belly. The Mayor put the strip of fabric over Perlmann's head and then handed him the unrolled certificate declaring him to be a freeman of the town. Then he shook his hand endlessly, coming out with the usual phrases in Italian. To Perlmann's annoyance, Angelini now started clapping and went on sedulously clapping until the others joined in, timidly and plainly embarrassed by so much empty convention. But for a while Perlmann maintained his feeling of relief at having shed his hatred of Millar. He delivered a brief speech of thanks, and even managed a joke. That sense of relief, and the hint of presence that it contained washed everything else away. He swapped a smile with Evelyn Mistral, and for a moment it seemed as if everything was fine again. As incredible as it seemed to him later in the car, he quite simply forgot that in less than four hours he would murder somebody and end his own life.

The town's visitor's book was bound in red leather, and the two lions from the coat of arms were stamped on it in fine black lines. The Mayor had taken it out of his desk, and now asked them all to approach and write in it. Perlmann was the first to sit on the high-backed chair, shifted it closer to the desk and drew the open book to him. He automatically reached into the left side of his blazer, but he had no pen. He tried again on the right, and was about to voice his request, when he was handed a fountain pen from above. When he looked up along his arm, the only person he could see at first was von Levetzov; but then he suddenly became aware that they were all standing around the desk in a semi-circle, looking down at him. And as he unscrewed the pen, he discovered that some clerks had now come into the room as well, and were watching him from the second row.

At that moment everything that he had been able to maintain since the beginning of the reception collapsed within him. He felt himself freezing at the focus of all those eyes. His nose started running. The hand holding the pen felt numb with cold, and when he was about to start writing he saw to his indescribable horror that it was trembling as if he had a violent case of the shivers. For two or three seconds he tried in vain to calm his hand by pressing his forearm against the edge of the table. Then he set the quivering fountain pen down next to the book with a quiet clatter and took his handkerchief out of his trouser pocket. As he blew his nose he closed his eyes and tried to relax while breathing out. As he did so, he felt as if his nose-blowing, which was subject only to his own will, after all, would never stop, it was like the beginning of an endless nose-blowing compulsion through which time stretched until it seemed almost to stand still.

Doggedly, as if wresting the movement from alien powers, at last he stuffed the handkerchief back in his pocket, where he clenched his hand into a fist to check that it belonged to him again. Then he braced himself, picked up the pen with a flying motion and guided it as quickly as he could over the paper, only writing the *P* out properly, just hinting at the *e* and levelling out the remaining letters in a single line which, from pressure on the nib, showed a fine white line in the middle. It wasn't his signature. It wasn't even like it. In fact, it wasn't actually a possible signature for his name, because it didn't even contain the suggestion of an elevation for the *l*. He also saw, as he automatically screwed the top of the fountain pen back on, that it was curiously crooked and began far too low on the fresh page. And on such an occasion, he thought as he got up, of course one signed one's full name. He forgot to give the pen back to von Levetzov, but just left it there and, without looking at anyone, withdrew to the corner beside the door where, under the surprised eyes of the clerks, he lit a cigarette.

When the prosecco was handed out, his colleagues came over to study the medal at close quarters. Not a word was said about his trembling hand, and he couldn't discover anything special in their expressions, either. The ribbon with the medal wandered from neck to neck, the jokes about the whole ceremony became more and more silly and frivolous, and at one point Millar clapped Perlmann on the shoulder with a laugh. Perlmann made an effort not to draw attention to himself, and laughed along. It was a laugh with no inner echo, a laugh with a run-up, a kind of facial gymnastics. He was glad that Ruge outdid a joke that had just been made, turned on his side and pretended to double up with laughter. As he straightened up, he wiped away the tears, interrupting himself with a feigned burst of laughter.

When the merriment finally faded away, they noticed with some embarrassment that both the Mayor and Angelini had already left. Apart from them, there were only two clerks in the room, talking about something with empty glasses in their hands.

Perlmann looked at the clock above the door: twenty past twelve. *He'll be in Frankfurt now.* His nose started running again. His handkerchief fell on the gleaming parquet, and when he straightened up again, everything went black for a second. He was already at the stairs behind the others when Laura Sand touched his arm and, with a mocking smile, handed him his forgotten certificate. As they went downstairs together, she said abruptly, without looking at him: 'You're not terribly well, are you?'

It was the first time she had said anything so personal to him, and never before had he heard such warmth in her smoky voice. He braced himself against tears, and crushed the certificate in the middle as he did so. He swallowed twice, glanced at her quickly and swallowed again.

'I'm OK,' he said more quietly than he had planned, and added in a louder voice: 'I slept really badly.'

'See you later,' she said as they parted in the hall. He watched after her as she opened the heavy door, leaned against it and lit a cigarette with her big lighter before stepping out into the square. He was relieved that he had resisted the massive temptation to confide in her. At the same time, though, he had the feeling that he had just wasted his last chance.

He hurried into the toilet, which was actually meant only for council employees. It wasn't diarrhoea, it was, once again, that deceptive sensation in his abdomen. Nonetheless, he sat there for a while with his head in his hands, thinking about nothing. He didn't get back up until he finally started feeling cold. It was as arduous as if he were made of lead.

Evelyn Mistral was waiting outside the door.

'You're going to the airport now, aren't you?' she asked in Spanish. There was a hint of shyness in her face, but above all the hope that the last few days' estrangement was in the past.

'*Sí*,' said Perlmann, and felt his throat tightening as he waited for what was to come.

'Would you mind if I came too? The weather's so lovely! And that fantastic car! I thought we might take the coast road. How long is it until Leskov's arrival?'

Perlmann stood there motionless for a moment and gazed into the void, as if the idea that questions needed answers were completely new to him. Then, with the awkwardness of someone intellectually backward, he looked at his watch and said in a monotonous, absent voice, 'Another two hours at least.'

As she waited for Perlmann to go, Evelyn Mistral stuck her hands in the pockets of her jacket, crossed her legs and slipped one foot half out of her shoe. After a pause that seemed to last an eternity, she looked up from the cobbles.

'Forget it,' she said, glancing at him through half-closed eyes, and turned to leave.

'*No, por favor, no*,' said Perlmann hastily, grabbing her by the arm and dragging her across the road, forcing a beeping car to screech to a halt.

Once they were on the other side she pulled gently away and looked at him uncertainly.

'¿*Seguro?*'

Perlmann just nodded and walked ahead of her into the side street. *Even now I'm not capable of drawing a boundary around myself and saying no. Not even now, when everything depends on it.*

He had just opened the door, and Evelyn Mistral was already holding the door handle when she slapped her forehead with the palm of her hand.

'Oh, damn!' she exclaimed. 'I can't. I've got to wait for this stupid phone call from Geneva!' And then she told Perlmann over the car roof about her annoyance concerning the failed financing of a project.

Then, when he sat in the car and looked at her in the rear-view mirror, he saw her turning round again before she went around the corner, and brushing the hair out of her face. As soon as she had disappeared his whole body started trembling. This time it was much more violent than it had been when he was signing his name, and he was quite sure that it would never stop.

35

Just before the highway access road near Rapallo he found a skip where he didn't feel he was being watched. It had taken him almost three-quarters of an hour to get there. Because almost as soon as he had left the side street near the town hall, he had got into a series of traffic hold-ups caused by delivery vans, which, as before in Genoa, stopped brazenly in the middle of the street to unload their goods. All of his desperation had turned into a boundless, crazed fury with the drivers of those vans, who, when they had closed the empty van at the back, walked with maddening slowness to the front, often exchanging a few words with an acquaintance before finally driving off. Sweating, Perlmann had lowered the window, but then closed it again straight away, because he couldn't bear the furious beeping of the cars in the line. He had slung his tie, along with the medal and the certificate, on to the back seat. Again and again he had forced himself to envisage what would have happened if Evelyn had forgotten that phone call. But a paralysing fatigue in his head had made every attempt to imagine it fizzle out.

Now he set down the suitcase and pushed the heavy lid of the skip back with both hands. He was greeted by a pungent smell of rotting vegetables. The container was half-full of brown, almost black cabbage that gave off warm, stinking fumes. Perlmann opened the case and looked round. He couldn't have cared less whether the woman at the wheel of the approaching car saw him or not. Nonetheless, he let her drive past before he tipped the laundry bag and the two dangerous texts on to the cabbage. Then, holding his nose, he watched with fascination as the sheets absorbed the dark goo that had formed between the cabbages. It was more or less how he had imagined the future destruction of the fraudulent text when he was lying in bed in Portofino. What had tormented him then now struck him as a mere bagatelle, barely worth mentioning, and he would have given anything to turn back the time of those forty-eight hours.

He took the four books out of the trunk. First he threw the yellow Langenscheidt on to the stinking cabbage. It landed with a sluggish gurgle. Next, the Russian-Italian dictionary. Perlmann gave a start when the dark juice spurted up. Then came the big red dictionary. It landed half-open on the brown pulp, and the greyish paper immediately began to corrugate. He hesitated longest over the grammar. He opened it up and flicked through it. There were various layers of meticulous marginal notes, progressive residues of ownership, apparent from the various different kinds of ink. Contemplating them from a certain internal distance, with eyes half-closed, it was as if one were looking down a long corridor of memory, far into one's own past. What he was holding here in his hand, he thought, was one of the most real, the most authentic things that had ever existed in his life. At home, on Agnes's bookshelves, which were still completely untouched, there was the same grammar. When Perlmann realized how senseless it was to cling to those thoughts, he snapped the book shut with forced determination and threw it in. Even before he heard the dull thud of its impact, he had already turned away.

He put the empty suitcase back down on the back seat. The medal and the certificate. He was already holding them and stepping towards the skip when he paused. *No, of course not. They will have to be found in the car.* He sat down at the wheel.

All the tunnels on the stretch of road were torture. He hadn't felt like that yesterday in the dark, but now in every pair of lights coming out of the tunnel in the opposite lane, he saw a truck. He was glad of the dusty bushes and the two crash barriers between the lanes. Nonetheless, his heart thumped as he entered each tunnel. For a brief moment he wished the two lanes, even up on the mountain where he would be

driving along with Leskov, went down two different tunnels. It wasn't
a wish that turned into a thought, and it didn't leave a trace in his
memory.

As he got out at the airport he noticed that his blazer was soaking
and stuck to the leather seat. He locked the car and had already taken
a few steps when he turned round and walked back to the car. It would
be better to release the handbrake now. Afterwards, Leskov's leg would
be there. It was the last time, he thought, as he pressed the lever down.

When, stepping into the arrivals hall, his eye fell on the digital clock
on the wall, it still showed 14:00. But a brief moment later, before he
had even looked away, the display changed to 14:01. The number 01
and the perception of its silent appearance acted on Perlmann like a
signal: the time remaining to him now could already be expressed in
minutes. He felt his blood thumping, and the cheerful exclamations of
the arriving passengers and waiting children now reached him as if from
a long way away as he stared at the clock until it was five past two.
Then he set his watch. He could do nothing to resist the complete senselessness of the action.

The flight from Frankfurt had been showing on the monitor for a
long time, and also on the black display panel. Perlmann leaned against
a pillar, automatically lit the last cigarette from that pack and threw the
box into the garbage bin next to him. He would have liked to do more
with the passing minutes than stare at the black rubber surface of the
floor, but nothing moved in his head now. It was as if his thoughts had
dried up, and he even seemed to have lost his capacity to pay attention.
Only his body was there, clumsy and repellent. His scalp itched. He
scratched himself bloody and then automatically brushed the dandruff
from his blazer. The shoes that he had barely worn pinched, and when
he bent down to tie them more tightly, his ice-cold nose started running.

And then, all of a sudden, his thoughts began chasing one another.
The others had seen his trembling hand in the town hall, and they
would think about it when they found out about the accident. He saw
Ruge in front of him, putting his mended glasses on top of his head
and thoughtfully studying the empty suitcase at the site of the accident.

It would become known that Leskov wasn't belted in, and then von Levetzov and Millar would look at each other in silence. They would find it strange that Perlmann had practically no money on him, and had left his credit cards in the trunk. *And the five mark piece, for God's sake! It will give me away. The car has barely been driven, and I'm probably the only German who has had it.* Perlmann felt the blind impulse to run out to the car, but the next thought was already there: *The shovel. Why was there a shovel in the pile of mud? What will I do if someone's working at that very spot?* That thought was swept away by another: *Kirsten. She'll wonder where the Russian books are. Particularly the big one with the nasty paper that Martin doesn't know. She won't let the matter lie. She's wilful and she can be stubborn. She'll ask the others, each one of them individually , and that mystery will be associated in their minds with other peculiarities, like the curious route.* And then one last thought fell within the tension of that flight of thought, and it made Perlmann freeze: *The old woman. If she sees a photograph of the dead men in the local press she'll talk. It was idiotic, simply crazy, to talk to her and draw attention to myself, not least with that half-witted idea of a film. Hopefully, I won't be recognizable afterwards.*

Perlmann couldn't bear standing around any longer, and walked towards the departure lounge. Before he stepped onto the moving walkway he glanced at the display panel. IN RITARDO, it now said by the flight from Frankfurt. *From half-past four there's not so much, c'è meno,* he heard the old woman saying and saw her tooth-stump in his mind's eye. He ran up the steps to the Alitalia counter.

'Only about another quarter of an hour,' the hostess said in response to his question, startled by his agitation.

I can catch up. So, another three-quarters of an hour. He walked over to the seats, where he had waited in the early morning nearly fourteen days before, and had felt defenseless without a book. But the memory was unbearable, and at last he went to the bar and ordered an espresso.

Beside him, someone unfolded a newspaper. Perlmann read the headlines and looked at the photographs. On the front page was a picture showing a blanket of smog over Milan, and on the last page there was a snapshot of a beauty contest. Behind him, a woman with a very clear voice burst into loud laughter and then called, '*Ancora!*' He turned round and saw her companion, a man with a long, white scarf and the appearance of a film star, going a little way into the room, then turning round and standing still for a moment, as if preparing for the long jump. Then, with a blasé expression on his face, the man took several deliberate shuffling steps and all of a sudden, switching his movements at lightning speed, he turned his feet outwards and walked frantically on the inside of his shoes, sticking his tongue in his cheek to give himself a cockeyed expression. The sight was so funny that all the people at the bar, including the waiter, roared with laughter.

And then something happened that Perlmann wouldn't have thought possible: the humorous aspect of it all took hold of him as well; something erupted inside him and he laughed a loud and liberated laugh – not a forced, hysterical laugh like the one last night at dinner, and not a fake laugh like just now at the town hall, but a laugh that brought him deceptively close to the present: it seemed as if he could reach out and touch it with his hands. That laugh acted like a rapid erosion of the cramped and callused framework of emotion, on which the decision to kill and to die had been constructed; the whole internal structure collapsed, and at that moment he saw the whole murderous plan as something very alien and remote, abstruse and practically ridiculous.

He was hoping for a repeat performance, but by now the man, still wearing an idiot's expression, was lying in the woman's arms, leaning against her so heavily, with feigned inertness, that for a moment she lost her balance and knocked Perlmann with her shoulder. He caught her apologetic smile, smelt her perfume and looked past her shiny black hair through the big glass windows of the hall into the distance where, in a rectangle formed of roofs and poles, a plane with gleaming wings was at that moment rising. He hadn't known that such a thing existed: a will to live that could flow through one as hot and stupefying as a drug. He ordered a second espresso, put in two, three spoons of sugar and let the little sips melt away on his tongue. Then he ate a slice of panettone, then another and, with yet another espresso, a third. He took off his blazer, hung it over his shoulder on a finger, and rested his arm with his cigarette on the counter. He liked the hard, bright *e* that the woman next to him was using, and as he waited repeatedly for that sound, he began to wonder where he could fly to. *When does your next flight leave? Where to? Anywhere.*

When the woman with the comedian had left and the waiter behind the counter snapped at the service staff, everything shattered. It disappeared like a mirage, as if it had never existed, and all that remained was a coffee-induced quiver. Perlmann looked at the clock: ten past three. He walked slowly back to the arrivals hall. These were the last minutes of his life when he could be alone with himself. In spite of the sultry air in the building he was shivering. And what if it wasn't even this Monday? There hadn't been a date in the telegram. But he had given Leskov the group's dates. And today was the last possible Monday.

The monitor showed Leskov's flight as having already landed. Perlmann got a stomach cramp. He positioned himself right at the back of the group of waiting people. He didn't know what to do with his hands. At last he pressed them to his painful stomach and rubbed it. As he did so, he ran through the route once more. Not till the second ironmonger's shop. Don't follow the tram tracks. First right at the bakery. Before the underpass keep left. At the square with the column it was the third rather than the fourth turn-off. His hands were ice-cold in spite of the rubbing. His sweat-drenched shirt was cold and sticky, too. *If only they hadn't gone to the Hermitage.* He wished Leskov hadn't suggested, back there on the bank of the Neva, that they call each other by their Christian names.

He reached for the matches in his jacket pocket and found his parking ticket. And then he realized that he had only a few coins, and not a single bill. He looked at the coins: 600 lire. *I can't get out of here,* he thought. *I can't pay the parking fee.* Then he saw Leskov.

36

He was wearing the same worn-out loden coat as the last time, and looked even broader and more shapeless than Perlmann remembered. In one hand he was carrying a big, antediluvian-looking suitcase of a pallid, stained brown that made it look as if it were made of cardboard. The other hand held a small suitcase with an outside pocket. Leskov stopped and looked uncertainly around through his thick glasses, bent slightly forward because of his heavy case. Perlmann felt as if he were shivering with cold when he saw him standing like that. Over the past few weeks Leskov had been the invisible author of a text, a voice without physical presence, which Perlmann had liked and admired more and more as the translation had progressed, and with whose haunting tone he had temporarily been able to identify. Now he stood there, a lost-looking man with an untidy, sweaty fringe of hair around his bald pate, and greying stubble, and with the tip of his tongue wedged between his teeth in tense expectation. Perlmann found him repellent. There was also something ludicrously dramatic about the sight of him. But those feelings did nothing to mitigate the thought that swept over him, that that physically present man over there who now, rather than putting down his suitcase, was standing there, legs apart, shifting his weight, was the man he was to kill.

Perlmann pushed his way through the group of waiting people, and then walked stiffly towards Leskov, his hands in his trouser pockets. When Leskov saw him, his whole face lit up. He set down his luggage and spread his arms. Earlier than necessary, Perlmann took his right hand out of his pocket and took his last steps with his arm outstretched.

His face was devoid of feeling, and refused to obey him. The only thing he was able to muster was a gaze aimed rigidly at the open collar of Leskov's red-and-blue checked shirt. Leskov ignored the outstretched hand, grabbed him by the shoulders with both hands and wrapped him silently in his arms, burying Perlmann's formal 'Hello' beneath him.

He smelled of sickly sweet tobacco and sweat. Perlmann stiffened when Leskov pressed him firmly to him, and wished he could shrink away quite quickly. But Leskov mustn't notice that he was disgusted by him, so Perlmann hesitantly put his arms around him and hugged him briefly and lightly. When he tried to break away from the embrace, Leskov went on holding him tight, and Perlmann felt like shoving him away with all his strength. At last Leskov let go, too, and now, with a guilty conscience, Perlmann gripped him by the upper arms and moved his hands up and down, as if stroking him. It was a mechanical gesture, hollow and empty, and yet it was a mockery, Perlmann felt, and wanted to sink into the ground.

'Philipp,' said Leskov, pausing dramatically, 'it's wonderful to see you again! Fantastic! You can't imagine how glad I am!'

'Yes,' was all that Perlmann could force out. He could only endure Leskov's gaze for one or two seconds, then he bent industriously for the suitcase and, in his nameless trepidation, it all seemed entirely unreal to him, as if it were not really happening; as if it were just a possibility, a scene in his imagination.

'Wait, please,' said Leskov when Perlmann hurried ahead with the suitcase as if they had to catch a waiting train. 'I would like to change some money.' He awkwardly took his wallet from his back pocket and pulled out a fifty dollar note. 'I haven't got much,' he said with an embarrassed smile, 'but I quickly managed to rustle this together and would like to change it straight away.'

In his obsessively detailed fantasy, Perlmann had imagined everything in the tiniest detail. He had tried to calculate every individual step, to master every factor so as to leave as little as possible to chance. There was only one thing he hadn't thought about: that Leskov was a flesh-and-blood human being with his own will and pride. In Perlmann's fantasy, Leskov had been a figure with a particular appearance, with a past and, of course, with a scholarly voice; also a figure which, in quite general and abstract terms, behaved like a human being in such a way that it could broadly be predicted – but again, merely a figure that could be shoved back and forth by the imagination, a creature without the particular, surprising and stubborn desires and preferences that constituted the resistance, independence and autonomy of a human being.

Very slowly Perlmann set the suitcase down, breathed out and stayed bent for longer than usual, his eyes closed. It was a good thing that he was facing the door and Leskov couldn't see his face. By the time he stood up and turned round, Perlmann had regained his composure. Over by the bureau de change the fourth traveller was about to join the line. But it wasn't just a waste of time. Much worse was the fact that the changing of money was preparation for an open, expectant future, which, for Leskov, who had followed Perlmann's eye and was already taking his first step, would last no more than a single hour.

'That isn't necessary,' said Perlmann, and he was relieved that only the first word had sounded hoarse. 'There are expenses waiting at the hotel.'

Leskov hesitated and looked down at the bill. 'I like to have my own money,' he said with an apologetic smile that also contained a hint of firmness. 'And it won't take long,' he added, pointing to the first of the four travellers, who was just leaving the counter.

'But it really isn't necessary,' Perlmann repeated with uncontrolled sharpness. 'And anyway, they can change money at exactly the same rate in the hotel,' he added in a conciliatory voice and made a gesture that dismissed everything as barely worth mentioning. Then, without waiting for any further reaction from Leskov, he took the case and went through the door, which, without turning round, he held open for Leskov until he had no option but to follow him.

Only now, when he saw the kiosk with the cash desk, did Perlmann remember his parking fee. *What an idiot I am. Then at least he would have had some money.* He walked to the counter and pushed the parking ticket under the sliding window. Inside, deafening rock music came from a transistor radio. A man with a red peaked cap looked at him vacantly and waited.

'How much?' yelled Perlmann and bent down to the opening.

Without turning his head, the man pointed to the display: *1000 L.* Perlmann pretended to look for his wallet, reached into both sides of his blazer, then tapped his pockets and finally pulled out the 600 lire note, which he pushed at the man.

'That's all I have on me,' he shouted, his lips right next to the glass. 'I've forgotten my wallet.'

The man with the red cap had now half-closed his eyes, and pointed again at the display, no longer moving his whole arm, just making an infuriatingly abrupt, jerky motion from the wrist.

When Perlmann felt his face turning red with annoyance, and he sat up without having the faintest idea what to do now, Leskov touched his arm and held out, with a grin that revealed a small triumph, a 2,000 lire note in front of his nose, mended in the middle with Sellotape. 'A souvenir that my brother-in-law gave me.'

Without a word, Perlmann took the note and waited, bobbing impatiently up and down, until the man with the cap, who was now whistling along with the tune, pushed his change towards him. He held the 1,600 lire out to Leskov. 'Thank you very much,' he said stiffly, 'the rest later.' He had been late this afternoon, and in his haste he had left his wallet in the hotel.

But Leskov waved the money away. Plainly it was hardly worth anything, he laughed.

As Perlmann put the bags in the trunk and straightened the panel that covered the spare wheel, which had slipped a little from where the books had been taken out, Leskov took off his coat and looked round. The light, he said, holding his hand as a screen over his eyes, he had never seen such a light before. '*Kakoi svet!*' As a student he had once been in the south, in Gruzia, but that was a long time ago, and he didn't think the light had been as intense there.

'Not as *siyayushcy*. It hadn't illuminated itself so powerfully as it does here. But at the same time this light here isn't . . . what do you say, harsh?'

'Yes,' said Perlmann, turning the two cases round again for no reason.

Now Leskov stared across to the purple mountains and the brown haze, which looked like a sandstorm.

'As it lies there in this light,' he said dreamily, '*Genuya* has something about it of an oriental city, a city in the desert.'

Perlmann had known that the coming hour would be difficult. Terribly difficult. More difficult than anything ever before. And that it would seem endless to him. He had told himself that repeatedly yesterday, and had tried to arm himself. And yet, he now thought as he got in, he had had no idea how great the pain would be. First the macabre irony that he was dependent on Leskov's money to be able to embark on the fatal, murderous journey. Then Leskov's precise perception of the southern light and his joy. And now this statement about the city, which was exactly what he had thought himself when he had seen Genoa from the ship on Friday. The harmony of their perceptions abolished the distance that Leskov's repellent appearance had helped to create, and when he stuck the key in the ignition Perlmann had to tell himself inwardly to be able to continue: *He alone would unmask me. Through him I would become an ostracized man, an outcast. There is no other solution. I've thought about it long enough.*

As he turned on the ignition the clock lit up: twenty to four. Puffing, Leskov sank into his seat and rested his hands in his lap. He showed no intention of fastening his seatbelt, but sat on the elegant, light-grey leather upholstery as if in an armchair in a club. Perlmann felt himself looking at him, and couldn't help turning his head as well. It would have been the moment to say how lovely it was that he had been able to come after all, before adding, 'Tell me!' Instead, Perlmann turned his eyes away again. For a fraction of a second he felt an impulse to reach for the seatbelt, but stayed his hand, which had been moving to the left instead of forwards to the ignition, just in time. *Don't do that now, or he'll try it as well.* Relieved that he had noticed in time, Perlmann gripped the ignition key and turned it. Immediately a high, penetrating sound rang out, which acted on Perlmann like an electric shock and for a moment disconcerted him completely. *The unfastened belt signal. Of course, they have that in cars like this. Oh my God, I'll have to do it with this terrible noise going on.* His sleeve caught on the light-switch before he finally turned off the ignition again. Moving as economically as he could muster, he pulled the belt across his body and very carefully snapped it shut. He did so with the gentleness of someone who doesn't want to wake a child. For one terrified moment he waited.

'Incredible, this light,' said Leskov.

Perlmann set off as if they were sitting in a porcelain box. After a while he really put his foot down.

Yes, said Leskov, it had all come as quite a surprise. His mother had died ten days before, not entirely unexpectedly after her illness, but much more quickly than might have been supposed. Larissa, his sister, who had come from Moscow, had urged him, when he had mentioned Perlmann's invitation, to reapply for his exit permit. That urging, he added, probably had something to do with Larissa's bad conscience: since she had moved to Moscow after her marriage, he had had to look after his mother all by himself.

In Perlmann's imagination, the man next to him had been someone who looked after his mother, but who otherwise stood all on his own and had no one else who would miss him. Everything that Leskov said about his sister now, awkwardly and in a loving voice, tightened Perlmann's throat. With each new character trait that became visible in Larissa, the invisible rope tightened further. Slowly and inconspicuously, he took a deep breath and tried to free himself by directing his attention at objects by the side of the road which had no significance for his driving.

The traffic grew denser, and two motorcycles that overtook him dangerously, and which he had to avoid, helped him to ignore the words beside him. Leskov had no sense whatsoever that someone behind a steering wheel had to pay attention to the traffic, and talked nineteen to the dozen. And then the rusty shutters of the first ironmonger's shop had come into view. Perlmann felt his back and neck tensing up. *Absolutely not the first one.* With cold hands he strengthened his grip on the steering wheel and stared straight ahead with great concentration so as not to miss the second.

Something was wrong. He didn't remember the long red building ahead of him. He broke into a sweat. He looked over to the shutters, then turned round and looked back. For one breathless moment he didn't know what was going on. Then he understood: he'd been waiting for lowered shutters. The image of the rusty surfaces was fixed in his expectation, and had been uninfluenced by the fact that the other shops were open today. But the first ironmonger's was also open; there were no shutters; the whole street corner looked completely different as a result, so, without noticing anything, he had driven to the second shop, whose shutters were still lowered.

He thrust his foot down on the brake, pulled the wheel round and turned off before the shutters. Tires screeched behind him and in the opposite lane, and the driver of the car he had narrowly missed tapped his forehead. Perlmann stopped and reached for a cigarette. 'I'm sorry,' he said and closed his eyes as he filled his lungs.

Now Leskov moved with a groan and looked for the seatbelt. Perlmann froze.

'That belt is broken,' he said blankly, and then, when Leskov started tugging on the strap, he repeated more loudly than necessary, 'The belt on your side is broken.'

Leskov turned heavily back towards him and looked at him calmly. 'You're pale,' he said in a paternal voice. 'I noticed that before. Is something wrong?'

'No, no,' Perlmann said hastily and turned the engine back on. 'I just don't feel that great today. But let's change the subject: what was the story with your exit permit?'

In spite of the political upheavals at the very top of the country, everything was pretty much as it had always been in large parts of the administration, Leskov reported, falling back into his seat as Perlmann went on driving slowly and felt his pulse calming down.

'You've still got the same people sitting at the same desks. And there are still blacklists,' he said with a sobriety that expressed both experience and suffering. It would be a while before the new laws guaranteeing the freedom to travel came into force. So he had reapplied with no illusions. This time he had done so via the dean of the university, and that seemed to have worked, even though he had not previously thought of him as a powerful man. At any rate, a phone call had come early on Friday morning: he could collect his passport along with the permit. Leskov took out an army-grey oilcloth wallet, pulled his passport from it and looked at the permit stamp.

'They've given me exactly a week,' he said bitterly. 'Not a day longer. I have to be back in Moscow on Sunday evening.' He took out a pipe and tamped it laboriously.

By now they had passed the spot where the car had to leave the tram rails. Perlmann had done it right. Things had only got awkward when a tram coming in the opposite direction, obstructed by a turning car, had meant that he had had to stop all the traffic behind him for a few moments.

Now came the first diversion sign. Perlmann was relieved that the traffic was flowing here, too. He thought about the bakery in the yellow building, followed the column of cars around the bend by the big hotel, and suddenly found himself in the middle of a traffic jam; there was lots of hooting, and some drivers had already got out and were drumming impatiently on the roofs of their cars. According to Perlmann's watch it was one minute after four. *She didn't say there weren't any trucks at all after half-past four, just that there weren't as many:* c'è meno. *There could still be a few.*

Leskov had discovered the electric window winder, and was as delighted as a child. All in all, he said, this was a dream of a car. Perlmann abruptly changed the subject and asked him about his flight.

Organizing it had been a bit of a drama, Leskov said with a laugh, and while Perlmann stared ahead at the dashboard, where the minutes were ticking away, Leskov told him how he had to borrow money from friends, how it had taken hours, and how he had flown to Moscow yesterday, where he had spent the night with Larissa's family.

'I've hardly slept,' he said, 'I was so excited. It's my first trip to the West.' And after a pause. 'I can't actually remember what happened on

Saturday. Oh yes, of course, Yuri came by. You know, with the fifty dollars. Years ago he was allowed to visit his dying father in America. He was the one who welcomed me outside the prison gate that time. And now . . . how can I put it? You know, he just wholeheartedly granted me this trip. Really granted it to me. People just say that kind of thing. But with Yuri it's something else. He's the only person who really knows what it means to me to be able to come here. Here, to the Mediterranean. The Riviera.'

A policeman with a radio came around the corner and walked along the queue of cars that was moving at a walking pace. Perlmann gave a start, and when the policeman, a giant with long sideburns, suddenly stopped, looked at the Lancia and then walked straight over to him, his heart pounded and his mouth turned dry. The giant gestured to him to lower his window. Twice Perlmann pressed the wrong button with his damp fingers, and he felt that as long as he had lived, no face had ever come as close to him as this big, dark face behind the glass.

'Your lights are on,' the giant said in a friendly voice.

'Oh, yes, *mille grazie*,' Perlmann stammered solicitously.

A moment later the traffic started flowing again. The turn-off by the bakery wasn't a problem, because another policeman was pointing the way to the line of traffic, and, of course, the third turn-off was at the big square with the column.

Perlmann relaxed. For a few moments he enjoyed the feeling, and leaned back in his seat. Then he started. It was a sensation like twitching awake from half-sleep from no outward cause: how could he relax, when he was driving to his death?

While Leskov was talking about the delays and the chaos at Moscow Airport and blowing clouds of his sickly sweet tobacco towards the windscreen, the underpass came into view. Perlmann was about to get into the left-hand lane, when a Jaguar came hurtling up from behind and forced him back. He came very close to losing his nerve. Suddenly, all his anxiety and despair discharged themselves, flowing into a boiling-hot, overwhelming desire to pull the steering wheel round and crash with all his might into that dark-red, gleaming bodywork. *For God's sake, let's not have an accident now.* The warning came from a long way away, and its power seemed to be hampered by that distance, but Perlmann clung firmly to it with what remained of his will and braked hard, so that Leskov tipped forward again, and when the Jaguar was past, just before the concrete plinth that marked the start of the underpass, Perlmann slipped across on to the cobblestones. He immediately put his foot on the accelerator again and asked Leskov, whose hand was now on the door handle, what changing at Frankfurt had been like.

Difficult, he said. And he'd got lost. 'There are these endless corridors. You have the feeling you're never going to arrive.'

'I know the airport,' said Perlmann. He no longer had the strength to conceal his irritation.

It was twenty past four when they reached the river and drove through Molassana. *Half-past four, that was just an approximate time, it could vary, and besides, it's the start of the week, perhaps the carriers are more active then.*

When the climb began, Leskov asked, after a pause, when they were going to get to the coast road. 'There is one, isn't there?'

Perlmann took the cigarette lighter, which had just clicked, out of its holder and held it to the tobacco for a long time. As he put it back in, he slowly blew the smoke out through his nose.

'Yes,' he said with a calm that had an underlying vibration, 'there is a coast road. But it's closed at the moment because of a serious accident. The report was on the radio. So I'm driving around the back, through the mountains.'

His words came fluently. They sounded a bit as if he were reading them out. Now he simply summoned them up from his memory after formulating them over and over again on the way to the airport, making sure that they sounded neither noticeably curt nor unnecessarily long.

'Ah,' said Leskov, disappointed. 'And the highway? A moment ago we drove past some green signs that said Autostrada.'

'The traffic's terrible at this time of day,' Perlmann said and breathed quietly. It was over now. It was twenty-eight minutes past four.

Trucks were still coming towards them. Perlmann started staring at their bumpers. When they drove past, he quickly turned his head and looked for the gas tank. Unable to resist, he slipped further and further into the state of mind in which he had run his hand along the damp bumpers the previous evening, in the red fog of the harbor, and, after a while, he felt last night's dream images forcing their way into his consciousness.

'Have you had a chance to take a look at my paper?' Leskov asked all of a sudden. His voice had changed. It contained a note of anxious expectation, bordering on submissiveness.

Perlmann wasn't prepared for the question. It was unbearable, absolutely impossible, in fact, to talk to Leskov about that disastrous text, which had destroyed everything, and which would in a few minutes kill them both. It was a thought so unendurable, so far beyond his powers, that Perlmann crouched behind the wheel as if paralyzed, and glared through the red of the fog in his imagination at the bumper of the next truck that was coming towards them, high and white. *In a few minutes it will all be over.* He clung to that desperate thought as – the truck had passed them – he sat up again in his seat and said, 'I started it, but couldn't get beyond the first few sentences. I had to set the paper aside. It's still too hard for me. Maybe I'll try again later.'

'But then you won't be reading that first version, but the new one,' said Leskov, whose voice seemed to have regained some of its self-confidence. 'I've fundamentally reworked the text over the past few months. It's much better now. It's actually a totally new paper. When I cast my eye over the first version recently, it struck me as terribly primitive and confused. I can throw that one away now! I'm just glad I didn't hand in that text. The new paper is the best, the most self-contained that I've ever managed to write. One should be careful with the word *original*: but I think there are a few things about it that really are original. At any rate I have the feeling that it's come entirely from myself. I'm really a little bit proud of it. And I also hope that this work will finally get me a post. There is one free at the moment, as a matter of fact.' He had the text with him, and would report on it to the group. Unfortunately, he had only his hand-written version, which was far too confusing to be copied, and unreadable to anyone else. As soon as he had transcribed it, he would send Perlmann a copy straight away. 'I'm quite sure,' he said with playful impudence, touching

Perlmann on the arm, 'that you'll understand this paper. If you just take the time!'

Perlmann felt ill, and his stomach cramp had returned. Again he had that sensation of diarrhea. He switched gear. His body had reacted faster than his mind. Only now, in fact, did he begin to grasp the nature of the shock that Leskov's words had provoked in him: if the car didn't burn up completely, the text in question, back in the trunk, would survive the collision. It would be found, and then there was the possibility that the deception would be discovered – with all the consequences that that might have, not least for the explanation of the apparent accident. Even the changes in the second version could not keep that from happening. Certainly, he said to himself once again, no one in the hotel spoke Russian. But if the belongings of the deceased were in the hotel after they had been identified, it was quite possible that both texts, the Russian and the English, would end up in the same room, perhaps even on the same table, side by side, page by page. And the mere possibility, the mere thought, that someone with a command of both languages might approach that table brought him out in a cold sweat.

Before they reached the tunnel there was another gas station. Perlmann would have to get rid of Leskov's manuscript there; sheltered by the open lid of the trunk he would quickly have to take it out of the suitcase, hide it behind something and drive on straight away.

'I've just got to check the tires for a second,' he said as the gas station came into view.

He stopped next to the air-pump, opened the trunk from inside the car and quickly walked to the back. The straps of Leskov's suitcase were already untied when he felt the car rocking and looked up over the lid of the trunk. Leskov was heaving himself, panting, out of the car. He had to hold on to the frame with both hands and pull himself up. The car door banged against the plinth. Perlmann quickly closed the lid and bent to the air-pressure gauge.

'I've been sitting down all day, and the seats on the plane were so cramped,' Leskov said with a yawn. 'I just need to have a bit of a stretch for a moment.'

Perlmann unscrewed the cap of the valve on the wheel and pretended to measure the air pressure. His fury at this shapeless Russian, who was unashamedly making the most unappetizing noises as he did his exercises, was turning into hatred. That hatred would be helpful later on, he reflected. He loathed himself for that thought, and that made his hatred still more violent. He switched his attention to the other back wheel. Leskov was just bending forward, and stretching his wide rear end towards him, a grotesque and revolting sight. No, Perlmann couldn't depend on the exercises taking long enough, particularly since he would now have to go back to the front, to his seat, to open the trunk for a second time. He put the pressure-gauge back on its holder and sat down behind the wheel. There he collapsed and was prepared to drive to the hotel and simply let things take their course. Exhaustedly, he closed his eyes. Sleeping, sleeping for a long time, until everything was over, his unmasking, the shame, everything.

Leskov's head appeared in the open passenger door. 'Do you think there's a toilet here?' he asked uncertainly.

'No idea,' Perlmann said flatly. Leskov seemed to have expected Perlmann to come with him to find out. Now he walked alone to the pump attendant and gesticulated. Perlmann was reaching for the lever that opened the trunk, and was sitting with his feet on the cobbles, ready to move. But the pump attendant shook his head, once, then again.

Leskov came waddling back to the car. He glanced at the back seat. 'There's a medal there. With a ribbon. As if someone's received an honor of some kind. May I know what it means?'

Why didn't I think of that? I could have put the thing in the suitcase. 'What? Oh, that. No idea. Someone must have left it behind.' It hadn't been hard to give his voice a tone of indifference. Exhaustion had accomplished that all by itself.

'The roll next to it looks almost like a certificate. Shall we take a look?'

Perlmann gulped. 'I'd like to get on now,' he said impatiently.

A shadow flitted across Leskov's face. 'Of course.' He wedged himself on to the seat. One of his suspenders caught on the door handle. 'How far is it?'

'Not far now,' said Perlmann, and his voice had stopped obeying him.

37

The clock showed six minutes to five when Perlmann drove back to the road with his headlights on. Clouds had rolled in, the last rays of sunlight from the sea giving them a purple sheen. There was a strange, hostile twilight. He drove slowly, at barely forty, and kept to the right.

'Is something wrong?' Leskov asked after a while.

Perlmann didn't reply, but stared straight ahead at the bend, where a huge truck appeared with its headlights on full. He shielded his eyes with his hand and waited until it had passed. Then he stopped the Lancia and pressed the lever that opened the trunk, and it was only by a reflex that he was able to prevent a passing car from brushing his opened door. As he hurried to the back, Perlmann inwardly braced himself for the furious beeping and the flashing headlights, opened the trunk quite high and pulled open the zip of Leskov's suitcase. It was stuffed full of paper. How was he supposed to fish the crucial, dangerous text out of this jumble? In feverish haste, he rummaged among the papers, all Russian texts, some of them typed, most of them hand-written. What was he supposed to do? He was at his wits' end. He tore open the zip for the outside pocket. It contained a single manuscript, a fat pile of pale yellow pages, held together with a red rubber band. He pulled it out. The rubber band got stuck on the zip and broke. This was the text, the heading in careful, almost calligraphic letters: O ROLI YAZYKA V FORMIROVANII VOSPOMINANIY. So he hadn't changed the title. With trembling fingers Perlmann closed both zips and refastened the straps. Then he bent down – ignoring the insults of a driver who couldn't overtake because of the oncoming traffic – right down to the road and laid the pile of papers under the exhaust. He slammed the trunk shut and got in.

'Problem with the tires again,' he said, without turning his head towards the passenger seat. Now it was important that Leskov didn't look into the side-view mirror. 'They grow a famous wine over there on the right,' he said, and set off with a jolt, his eyes on the rear-view mirror.

The text, which existed only in this single copy, the version that Leskov was so proud of, and which was to help him with his professional advancement, the work of months, flew apart, the yellow pages whirled up and gleamed in the headlights of the other cars, then they danced and sailed into the darkness of the side embankment. The cars behind him tried to dodge the flapping pages as if they were heavier than they were, and the next car that came along seemed to have driven precisely over the rest of the stack of papers, because once again there was a cloud of pages. Then they drove round the bend, and the pages disappeared from Perlmann's field of vision. Leskov had put his thick glasses on his head, and was still looking up the slope on the left.

'Not much to be seen now,' he said.

It can only be another three or four bends. All of a sudden Perlmann no longer knew whether to accelerate or change down. It was just turning four minutes past five. Yesterday, outside the tunnel, when he should really have done it straight away, his remaining time had seemed like an obstacle, a medium that he had to wade heavily through, minute after minute. And even in the town hall, every movement had struck him as something that one had to accomplish against the resistance of sluggish time. Then, on the way here, it had been the other way round: time had run ahead of him, the minutes elapsed at a furious pace, it had been a race against the clock, against the figures on the digital display on the dashboard, which were changing far too quickly. Now, just as he was counting the remaining bends, Perlmann felt something changing, moving, shifting in his innermost depths: even now he wanted to stop time, and with all his might; but it wasn't like before, because at the same time he also wanted to stop the road, which was rolling away backwards behind him, where he would never see it again. He didn't want to reach the tunnel either in time or in space. The time on the whole journey had been precious already, because after half-past four there wouldn't be as much traffic – *c'è meno*. But now that same time was suddenly precious in a quite different, more extended sense. It forced its way into Perlmann's consciousness as the last brief stretch of his life, as a comprehensible series of minutes ticking ruthlessly and inexorably away, bringing the final darkness and the final silence closer.

Just behind them a huge truck flashed its lights, and now Perlmann heard the hard and threatening noise of its diesel engine. He gave a start, but it was a strange, unfamiliar kind of start, because it immediately opened itself up to the hot, surging, almost pleasant desire that the truck might simply drive over them and extinguish them with its light, its noise and all its tons. He accelerated, took the next bend and saw the sign with the arrows to Piacenza and Chiávari. In the rear-view mirror the high front of the truck came quickly closer. He heard the driver speeding up and changing gear. Now they were on the crossing and could see the tunnel, the truck roared and sped up for the straight stretch through the mountain. Perlmann put his foot on the accelerator, drove far to the right on to the patch of gravel and skidded to a stop.

'There really is something up with you,' Leskov said, bending over and resting his hand on his arm. 'Are you unwell?'

Perlmann smelled the tobacco and the sweat. 'I just felt dizzy for a moment,' he said. 'I'll be OK soon.' He put a cigarette between his lips and reached for the matches in his jacket pocket, because he didn't know how he would survive the idle seconds that the lighter would take.

'You shouldn't do that,' said Leskov, who had just put out his pipe with his tobacco-yellowed thumb and lowered the window.

Perlmann paused in the middle of the lighting motion, closed his eyes for a moment and then got silently out of the car. He walked to the side of the road, lit the cigarette and looked into the tunnel. The shovel wasn't there any more, but the pile of mud still was. Only single cars came from the opposite direction. He looked at his watch: thirteen minutes past five. Nonetheless, there had been that truck before. Why shouldn't there be others?

Now he had to make up his mind. He had to choose between murder and death, or life as someone experiencing his professional decline, the public shredding of his reputation. If he went on driving through the tunnel now, past the pale mud and out into the other night at the other end, Leskov would find out an hour later. The others would find out at dinner, and he wouldn't be able to appear in front of them any more, and from them it would spread in circles, wider and wider circles, until the last of his colleagues knew. *And Kirsten would have to watch as well. Kirsten, to whom I could never explain it.*

Perlmann had been looking at the ground in front of him, and only now did he see the truck coming towards him in the tunnel. He immediately dropped the cigarette and turned towards the car. Leskov had got out, and was standing with his legs spread and his back to him at the edge of the patch of gravel. *It wouldn't have been enough anyway.* Again he lit a cigarette. It was the second-to-last. His eyes slowly wandered around. The toothless old woman's grocer's shop was lit with a dim light. To the west a last strip of light in the reddish sky. *The last light.*

Leskov was sitting in the car again, looking across at him. Unusually, Perlmann smoked the cigarette down to the filter. The hot smoke stung his lungs, and now he had a nicotine taste on his tongue that he didn't like. He felt as if all the strength was about to leave his body. Stiffly, head lowered, he walked over to the car, got in and fastened his belt.

'Sorry about before,' said Leskov. 'I didn't mean to patronize you.'

'Don't worry,' Perlmann said quietly and started the engine. He drove in a big arc on the patch of gravel and then drove the car on to the empty road. For a moment he just let the car freewheel. Then he put his foot down and drove into the tunnel. He looked up at the bright curve of the tunnel entrance, and when it drew over him he felt as if he were leaving the world.

Just before the first rest area he clutched his brow, braked and drove on to the muddy ground. Without pulling up the handbrake he stopped right in the middle between the two ends of the crash barriers. He undid his seatbelt and threw both hands to his face.

'I'm dizzy again,' he said through his hands. Leskov touched him gently on the arm and said nothing. Only after a long pause, during which Perlmann stared ahead into the tunnel through his fingers, did Leskov ask, 'Do you think you can make it to the hotel?'

At that moment the blue, rotating light of a police car appeared in the side-view mirror. The car had already passed him when it braked abruptly and reversed with a screech along a slightly wavy line. The passenger got out, put on his cap and bent down to Perlmann's window.

'You can't park here,' he said brusquely. 'It's just for emergencies.'

'I suddenly felt . . . ill. I had to stop,' Perlmann said with a dry mouth. He had forgotten the Italian word for *dizzy*, and made two mistakes in that single sentence.

'Foreigner?' asked the policeman, taking a few steps forward and looking at the numberplate. 'Rental car?'

'Yes,' said Perlmann and gulped.

'Do you need help? Shall we call an ambulance?'

'No, no,' Perlmann said hastily. 'Thank you very much, but it's fine now.'

'But then you'll have to drive on,' said the policeman, and looked at him thoughtfully for a moment. 'There's a parking lot just beyond the tunnel.' Then he tapped his cap and straightened up.

'*Va bene*,' said Perlmann. Apart from that he did nothing.

In the time it took the policeman to reach his car, Perlmann perceived this event as a salvation. He was very close to throwing up, just so that he wouldn't have to bear the terrible tension any more. These policemen would keep him from becoming a murderer. All he needed to do now was turn the key in the ignition, put the car in gear and drive to the hotel with Leskov. That was all.

But the image of the hated hotel that now appeared in his mind kept him from doing so. He saw himself next to Leskov, dragging his stained suitcase, going up the steps and stepping up to the reception desk, from which the fraudulent text, which Millar had made him put there, protruded from Leskov's pigeonhole. Again he hid his face in his hands.

Now he could only hope that the carabinieri didn't do what policemen would do at home: wait until he actually drove on.

'What did he want?' asked Leskov.

Perlmann said nothing.

The policeman took off his cap and got into the car. He hadn't looked back. The car stayed where it was. The driver would now be watching them in the rear-view mirror. Now the passenger lit a cigarette, blew the smoke out of the window, laid his arm on the frame; they both laughed, and then the car lurched off. *They will testify that I was feeling ill. That's good.* It was twenty to six.

As long as the policemen were within view, there was somewhere for the eye to rest. When the tail lights disappeared into the night, the tunnel was quiet and deserted. Perlmann would have liked to light his last cigarette. He had a craving for one like never before. But he couldn't risk it. He didn't want to do it with a cigarette in his hand. From the corners of his eyes he saw Leskov's massive legs in their brown trousers, the ankle-high boots with the thick soles and the hands folded in his lap with the yellow thumb and the black under the nails. The span of time in which two people can sit side by side in a stationary car was already long past. Perlmann tried convulsively to do the impossible: the absolute unrelatedness of two people who were sitting a few inches apart. He felt Leskov looking at him, and closed his eyes. His scalp twitched and his nose started running. He was glad to be able to do something, and reached for the handkerchief with his ice-cold hand.

'You think about Agnes a lot, don't you?' Leskov said into the silence.

Through all the coldness and fear a terrible fury flamed up, a rage at the emphatically mild, almost tender tone that Leskov had used; the sort of tone one adopted with children or sick people. But more than that it was a fury at the fact that this fat, repellent person next to him, whose fault it all was, dared to talk about Agnes at all, and took it upon himself to touch that open wound and thus to touch Perlmann in his innermost depths. And it was also a fury with himself, over the fact that he had given that part of himself away for no reason that time, in the icy air of St Petersburg. This fury acted as if he were in the middle of life and not on its outermost edge. It crashed in and flowed through him as if there were no tunnel full of fatal silence and white-hot lights in the high, thundering front of a truck. It was such a violent fury that it left him dazed. Perlmann buried his face in his handkerchief, and now his fury discharged itself into his nose-blowing. He went on blowing his nose even though his whole handkerchief had been damp with snot for ages and repelled him. One pant came more violently than another. The preparation for each was even bigger than the last, but all in vain. His nose went on running. Fresh mucus kept coming from somewhere, and more and more. It flowed. It streamed. Perlmann pressed and pressed and only paused when the moisture in his cold nose suddenly turned warm and his handkerchief turned red. As he held the handkerchief away from him and looked with surprise at the blood, it dripped from his nose, and when he looked down at himself, his white shirt and the light-grey leather upholstery between his legs were covered with bloodstains. He stared, motionless, at those stains, which were still spreading at their edges. It was as if he were hypnotized by them and forgot to keep the handkerchief to his nose, so that the blood went on dripping, fast and constant.

That was the reason he felt it so late. It was a light, choppy vibration of the ground that conveyed itself straight to the car and his body. Still captivated by the sight of the blood, Perlmann glanced quickly forwards over the steering wheel, and then he saw the two bright orange lights flashing at short intervals. A giant bulldozer was already quite a long way into the tunnel, moving towards them rather jerkily on caterpillar tracks as big as tank treads. The two flashing lights were attached to two poles sticking out at the sides, and provided the visual limitation of the machine, which kept quite close to the crash barrier and still extended some way beyond the middle strip. It took two or three seconds before Perlmann had torn himself away from the bloodstains and the sight of the oversized shovel of the bulldozer: a slightly curved, high wall with prongs at the sides. But then he reacted in a flash. He dropped his handkerchief, put his foot on the clutch and turned the key in the ignition. The penetrating whistle assailed him. He had forgotten it, and gave a start just as he had the first time. Again he turned the key, a crunching noise, because of the whistle he hadn't heard that the quiet engine had already sprung into life.

The Lancia, *the safest Italian car*, accelerated with silky smoothness, but Perlmann pulled out all the gears so that the engine screamed. The blood flowed warmly down his lips and chin. The whistling was maddening. He looked rigidly straight ahead, his arms outstretched. Just under a kilometer: now he saw, in the narrow, yellow driver's cab, a lanky man in blue workmen's overalls with a beret. The curved wall covered with pale earth was high. *It's high enough. Nothing will happen to him.* So now the time had come. The last few seconds of his life – *and even now no presence*. He was driving at over a hundred now – that would be enough. His head emptied completely. All his plans for careening and pretending the steering wheel wasn't working were forgotten. All he knew now was that he had to pull the steering wheel to the left at the right time, but not too soon because of Leskov. Now he heard the clattering engine of the bulldozer, the vibration of the ground merged with the sensation of speed, and that insane whistling noise and Leskov's fearful voice, and then all of a sudden it was perfectly silent. It all happened soundlessly as if in cotton wool and snow. Less than 100 meters: *the glasses* – he pulled them from his face. Now he had to do it – *now*. He pressed himself into his seat, closed his eyes and took his sweat-drenched hands off the wheel.

Beside him, only inches from the car window, there was a red flash. He opened his eyes. They were past, but everything was blurred. The lines were broken, as if under water. He pushed his hand against the wheel. The car veered to the left. Perlmann pulled it back and over-steered. The right fender crashed against the guard rail. The whole length of the car scraped along the metal. It was a deafening crunch. Now he heard that whistling noise again. He pulled the car to the left, into the middle of the tunnel, but now two headlights came towards him out of the dark, each one of them like a tattered bundle of gleaming crystals, shifting blurrily towards one another. Perlmann pulled to the right: again it crashed and crunched. In the midst of it all was that mad whistling, but he kept the wheel turned firmly to the right. The approaching car was past. Another crunch, then they were outside in the dark. Perlmann drove blindly to the right, put both feet on the pedals. The car slewed round, then only slid and, finally, after an eternity, it came to a standstill by a pile of rubble.

At first Perlmann was merely grateful that the whistling had stopped. He felt his blood thumping from his head all the way down to his feet; his veins seemed to be about to burst. Then, after a delay of almost half a minute, he started shuddering. It wasn't just trembling or shivering, but an uncontrollable, violent twitching of his limbs the like of which he had never experienced before. To stop his arms from drumming against the steering wheel, he rested them on his thighs. Now he sensed that his trousers, too, were covered with blood, and that his nose was still bleeding, more violently than before. He bent for his handkerchief, which was down by the pedals. The blood on the cloth was mixed with dirt. A drop of blood fell on the lapel of his blazer when he sat up, rested his head against the headrest and pressed the handkerchief under his nose with a trembling hand.

'Take mine,' said Leskov, who had turned in his seat and held a crumpled handkerchief in front of his face. It was the first thing he had said since they had come to a halt. Perlmann had no idea what Leskov was thinking at that moment, or what his face was like. But he was astonished by the calm, matter-of-fact tone of his voice. He would not have thought him capable of it, having seen him looking around so anxiously at the airport. Perlmann was revolted by the handkerchief, which smelled of sickly tobacco. 'No, thanks,' he said and got out.

He held his head tilted far back as he walked past the old tires and the rubble. Slowly and deeply he breathed in the cold night air. His nosebleed was subsiding, and his shivering was gradually easing, only every now and again there was a spasm of twitching. He stopped at the side of the road and put the last cigarette between his lips, but for fear of his nosebleed starting up again he didn't dare light it. In the windows down at the road that he had pelted up the previous day, a light was burning. He saw shadows moving. *I haven't become a murderer.*

'The right headlight's broken,' Leskov said two steps behind him, 'and there are nasty scrapes.' Now he rested his hand on Perlmann's shoulder.

'But otherwise not much has happened. Just body damage. It was a horrible shock, though. And without a belt.'

Again Perlmann started shuddering, more weakly than before, but unmistakably.

'You're trembling like an ashpen-leaf,' said Leskov. 'That's what you say, isn't it?'

The linguistic mistake and the innocent question that followed it brought tears to Perlmann's eyes, he didn't know why.

'Aspen-leaf,' he finally managed to say, and attempted a smile. 'It just came over me when I saw the bulldozer,' he added after a pause. 'I'm sorry.'

'Came . . . over . . . you?' asked Leskov, clearly enunciating the individual words and placing them side by side like someone who had never heard them in that sequence before.

Perlmann felt his intestines. He gulped and looked into Leskov's eyes. No, it wasn't the biting sarcasm it had sounded like at first. It was merely linguistic curiosity. Perlmann's alarm gave way to irritation.

'Panic,' he said tightly. 'I panicked when I saw that monster. I had to get past it as quickly as possible.'

'But why?'

'I don't know,' Perlmann said bluntly. 'It's always been like that.' He lit the cigarette.

'And what about the glasses?'

No, it didn't sound suspicious. There was real sympathy in the question, which simply overlooked Perlmann's coarseness.

'I felt dizzy again, so I involuntarily grabbed my head and pulled them off by mistake.'

There was nothing new. Over the last few days he had got to know himself as a talented, cold-blooded liar. Not as someone who reached for a necessary lie from time to time, but as someone who lied confidently and as a matter of routine.

Perlmann looked silently and fleetingly at the damage to the car as something that affected him not in the slightest. What bothered him were the bloodstains on the pale leather. He moistened the last clean tip of his handkerchief and rubbed, but it only made it worse. Leskov was fumbling around with his seatbelt when Perlmann sat down at the wheel. At one point Leskov gave it a quick, strong tug. In the dark, Perlmann held his breath until he realized: *It doesn't matter now.* The two coins held.

Leskov was silent as they drove on, and when Perlmann at one point glanced at him his eyes were closed. The silent figure in the dark struck him as the embodiment of suspicion. *No, he's not suspicious. Because he doesn't know the motive. In as little as an hour that could be different.* Perlmann would park at the gas station near the hotel, and perhaps have to answer a question about the damaged car, then up the steps, the veranda on the left, greeting from Signora Morelli, who would hand the text to Leskov. Leskov would rest for a bit, then Perlmann would have to introduce him at dinner. There would be the usual ritual greetings, the clichés, the conventional smiles, elegant, smooth words from Angelini, and then, back in the room, Leskov would make his discovery. He would reach into the outside pocket of his suitcase to confirm the monstrous discovery – horror – and then, once the first paralysis was past, it would dawn on him and he would know everything. Or else Leskov would be too tired this evening; then it would happen tomorrow morning when he, Perlmann, was sitting at the front on the veranda. Or else Leskov would be so curious that in spite of the long journey he would start reading immediately, perhaps even in the elevator. They would step towards one another under the chandeliers in the elegant dining room, and then . . . At that point Perlmann's imagination failed. The images collapsed, and inside him it turned grey, dark grey, but above all opaque, impenetrable and gloomy, numbingly gloomy.

He knew he didn't have the strength to endure it. *Pian dei Ratti.* It ran through his head. *Pianezza, Piana, Pian dei Ratti.* Those names, black text on a white ground, were bound up with trepidation and haste, and they echoed within him a thousand times over. There was no one at the slate works at that time of day, and in the dark the people were no longer leaning in the windows. And it wouldn't matter if there were people up in the house by the bend. He hesitated. It was very questionable whether another truck would come along. It was twenty past six by now. But that wasn't it. Perlmann felt that he no longer had the strength to try again. He could no longer summon the will, and if he tried to force himself to believe that he had it, it felt like a will that was hollow inside and could at any moment, at the slightest resistance, collapse in on itself.

They were now past Lumarzo, and soon the first of the two roads would branch off, leading straight down to the coast and skipping yesterday's route to Chiávari. Perlmann slowed down when the sign came into view.

'So has your own contribution been discussed already?' asked Leskov when Perlmann had turned on the indicator.

At first Perlmann couldn't find his voice. 'No,' he finally managed to say, and it was almost a croak. He slowed down still further until they were rolling only very gently.

'Oh, then I'm lucky.'

Right by the turn-off, in the middle of the opposite lane, Perlmann tapped on the brake, and for the duration of a breath they stood quite still. Then he turned off the indicator, put his foot on the accelerator and drove on towards Chiávari. He didn't reply to Leskov's question. He could assume that Perlmann hadn't heard it, because he was dealing with the turn-off, or that he was wondering how to describe his subject as simply as possible.

'Is it something formal, technical?' Leskov asked.

'No,' Perlmann said quietly.

'I'm glad of that. At least I'm looking forward to it. When's the session?'

'Tomorrow morning.'

'It's as if you'd just been waiting for me,' Leskov laughed.

I've got to tell him. Now. Here. Perlmann had no idea how Leskov would react to this confession. There was this almost paternal relationship that he had with this man, who was practically his own age. Would those feelings come into it? Of course, the information would shock him. *But perhaps he'll be able to see it as self-defense if I explain to him how it came to this.* And clearly he hadn't forgotten the misfortune with

Agnes. What had prompted a blind, intoxicating fury was now suddenly a hope, a straw that Perlmann clung to. Perhaps Leskov could see the deception as the deed of a person who had completely lost his equilibrium as the result of overwhelming grief and was no longer himself.

Perhaps, though, and this was far more likely, Leskov would be so dismayed that Perlmann couldn't possibly ask him to keep the matter quiet. He would need time to grasp the full significance of the confession; only gradually would it become clear to him how monstrous Perlmann's revelation was. Perlmann, the one who had issued the invitation, had shamelessly exploited the refusal of an exit permit, Leskov's lack of political freedom, and his connection with his mother, which was a moral obligation. Perlmann had also exploited his trust, which had led Leskov to hand over his first draft, an unfinished and, to that extent, intimate text, unprotected. His colleagues were now holding in their hands that provisional, rough text, which was unorthodox and might scandalize. It was awkward enough appearing with such a text. Leskov would feel unmasked, even if he conceded to Perlmann's request and didn't come forward as the author.

'Has a time been fixed for the session with my contribution?' asked Leskov.

'Thursday,' said Perlmann, and that day seemed to him to be infinitely far away. It was a day he could no longer imagine reaching, a day that might have appeared on the calendar and might exist theoretically, so to speak, but an unreal day without morning, noon and evening, a day that he would never experience.

Perlmann's request would mean asking Leskov to stand up and say that he had no lecture to deliver – the clueless Russian who had been invited out of sympathy with his political situation, as development aid. It meant, Leskov would say, that the second version in the trunk, the one he had brought with him, was useless. He couldn't either. Generally speaking, he couldn't present any of his ideas, nothing of the whole of his recent work. Otherwise it would seem as if he were the one who was copying Perlmann and simply hanging on to his theme. It would at least be screamingly obvious that the two men were writing about similar questions in a very similar, unorthodox way. Suspicion would be inevitable and, of course, the question of originality would be resolved to the disadvantage of him, the obscure Russian. It wouldn't occur to anyone that it was the other way round, particularly since Perlmann, as it appeared at the time, was able to present a proper text, while Leskov would at best be able to quote verbally from his work.

'You know, I've got this idea that you can appropriate your own past through narration,' Leskov said out of the middle of his thoughts. 'In the new version, this idea in particular has become much clearer. It took me a long time. And at the same time, in fact, I want to say that remembering is in a sense inventing.' He laughed. 'That must sound a little bit crazy to you, hearing it out of the blue like this. But in the text I develop it step by step. And just assume, hypothetically, that there's something in it: then, of course, I'm immediately left with the question of what appropriation could mean with reference to one's own inventions. In the first version, the one that you have, that's still quite unclear. But now I think I have the solution. It's rather a complicated story, and I'm glad that I managed to capture it on paper before I set off.'

Osvaivat'. Appropriation. So that's true. The thought ran through Perlmann's head without his intervention. It felt strange, and cut off from everything else. Or rather it didn't feel like anything at all. It wasn't really present as a thought of his own. It was more as if he were thinking someone else's thought. As if someone else were now thinking that thought.

Leskov took out the handkerchief that he had previously offered to Perlmann and laboriously blew his nose. 'And I had almost forgotten the text. It was still a bit too soon to drive to the airport, and I took another look at it and made a few notes. Then there's this phone call that I get really excited about, not least because of the post I'm hoping for. It goes on and on, and suddenly I'm short of time. I pick up the two cases and walk to the door, still filled with rage, and it's only when I see the open outside pocket on the suitcase that it occurs to me. I'd have been left standing there like a bit of an idiot.'

I should tell him about the text on the road. Because if he discovered the loss, he would immediately put two and two together: that strange stop in the middle of the road, and after that the tires had barely been mentioned. His fury would be boundless: once, of course, because of the destruction of his paper, and then over the fact that Perlmann, the coward, hadn't even had the courage to tell the whole truth. And that rage might loosen his tongue.

Now came the turn-off to Uscio, and then down to the sea at Recco. Perlmann stopped. 'I've got to stretch my legs for a moment,' he said.

If he took the turn-off, there was no second chance: it wasn't a road for big trucks. Then he would walk up the steps beside Leskov, and the disaster would take its course. Then there was no longer anything that could stop it. If he drove straight ahead, in ten minutes they would be in Pian dei Ratti. Perlmann stood there motionlessly, his hand on his trouser-zip by way of disguise. He couldn't deliver his confession, with its lengthy explanation, at the steering wheel. At some point he would have to look Leskov in his bright, grey eyes and tell him that he had destroyed his text. The text he had put everything into. The text that had helped him win his post. That he had simply set it down in the road under the exhaust like a pile of rubbish, of filth.

It was impossible.

Pian dei Ratti. The factory, the pines, the Renault poster. Wait for the front of the truck with the big lights. Sit next to Leskov again, silent and mute. Drive off once more, the whistling noise again and the feeling about the glasses.

It was impossible.

Perlmann got in and drove on towards Uscio and Recco. He drove fast on the almost deserted road, just fast enough for Leskov not to protest. Perlmann didn't want another thought ever to pass through his head ever again. The Lancia took the many bends effortlessly. Only once, on a sharp curve to the right, did it sound as if the tires were touching the crushed metal.

'I expected us to get to the hotel more quickly,' Leskov said at one point. 'What time is dinner?'

In Recco, when they turned into the alleyway leading to the coast road, it was just before seven. Perlmann stopped at a gas station. 'Just a moment,' he said and disappeared into the toilet, where the stench of urine took his breath away. He propped himself on the washbasin and threw up. But hardly anything came, apart from mucus and gastric acid; in the end it was nothing but dry retching. The face in the mirror was as white as a ghost. Under his nose and on his chin there was dried, almost black blood. His hair on his forehead was damp with sweat. He shovelled cold water into his face and then rubbed it dry with the sleeve of his jacket.

He would have to behave towards this Russian, who repelled him and whose paternal tone he found unbearable, as one does towards a father confessor, with the hope of absolution. And Perlmann would be in his thrall for ever, for good or ill. It was inconceivable.

But then there was this calculation: it was no longer possible that his deception would remain undiscovered. There was nothing more, absolutely nothing, that Perlmann could have done to deflect the exposure. So there was only the question of how many people would find out – whether the discovery would stop with Leskov, or reach everyone else. And looking at it quite soberly everything argued for at least making the attempt. He no longer had anything to lose.

A fat man came in. Perlmann gave a start. For a moment he thought it was Leskov. He couldn't meet him at the moment. He wasn't ready yet. He didn't want it to be a confession in a stinking toilet. He locked himself in a stall. He wanted to sit down and rest his head in his hands, but it was a squat toilet, so all he could do was lean against the door, his forehead and nose pressed hard against the greasy plastic.

It wasn't true that he had nothing to lose. But it was a while before Perlmann could summon the necessary concentration. The crux of it was this: if he didn't confess to the murder plan straight away – and that was simply unthinkable – he had no plausible explanation for getting rid of the second version. That wouldn't matter in the slightest if Leskov acknowledged the English text as his own. So what had he imagined he would achieve by getting rid of it? *You should have got rid of me at the same time,* Leskov could say. The separating wall that might still exist between that remark and the apprehension of the truth would be extremely thin, and could at any moment collapse if Leskov thought again about the tunnel.

And then Perlmann suddenly had the vision of Leskov, now in command of all moral authority, telling him to turn round and collect the crushed and scattered pages. He saw himself creeping around in the dark on the embankment, and scurrying back and forth across the carriageway in front of beeping cars with flashing headlights.

Battling against the sharp stench of urine, he breathed in deeply and then very slowly out. A confession was impossible. It was impossible.

'This is how I've always imagined the Riviera by night,' said Leskov as he looked down on Recco and later on Rapallo. 'Exactly like this. It's fantastic!'

Perlmann didn't look. He stared at the road, lit by the one-sided beam of light. He drove, and with each passing meter he concentrated only on the fact that he was driving. Although his gums still stung from the gastric acid, he would have given anything for a cigarette. But the 1,600 lire – *his money* – hadn't been enough to buy a pack. Right at the back of his consciousness, with dull indifference, he registered that his thinking had been correct: for the first plan – the car rolling over the edge – the coast road would have been out of the question.

'Who's going to be presenting the final paper this week?' asked Leskov as the lights of Santa Margherita came into view.

Once again, one last time on this journey, Perlmann gave a start. Over the last four tormented, breathless hours he had managed not to address Leskov directly, and avoided using the familiar *you*. It had been difficult at times, and had involved all kinds of linguistic somersaults. There must be a sentence, he thought, that would do it. But his brain couldn't do it any more, so he said it: '*You. Du.*'

They turned the corner. The crooked pine. The streetlamps. The neon sign. The painted window frames. The flags. There were lights on in Millar's, Ruge's and Evelyn Mistral's rooms. Perlmann drove up to the gas station parking lot. It was closed. So no questions about the body damage. When he lifted Leskov's suitcase out of the trunk, he saw a bit of the red rubber band that had got stuck in the zip of the outside pocket. 'Along here,' he said and, as if he were Leskov's servant, he picked up a case in each hand.

38

What happened then was something that Perlmann had seen in his mind's eye so many times that it was more or less exhausted from being imagined. Now that it was actually taking place it was just a scene that had been rehearsed ad nauseam – flat, papery and without the reality of experience; the only real thing was the angular wooden handle on Leskov's suitcase, which was cutting into his hand. But there was no relief associated with that unreality. On the contrary, the sensation of waste and death that clung to the walk up the steps was, as Perlmann knew, an expression of the utmost horror. His gait was more sluggish than the luggage called for, and his body felt like that of a puppet, each movement of which had to be put individually into action. It took him a huge effort of will to impel that body step by step closer to the front door.

As he entered the portico, he noticed that Leskov was no longer following him. He was standing at the top of the steps, looking up at the illuminated facade of the hotel.

'Fantastic!' he called breathlessly to Perlmann and, with his arm, his coat hanging over it, made a gesture that encompassed the whole hotel. Then he turned round, supported himself on the balustrade and looked out on the nocturnal view of the bay.

Perlmann set the luggage down. Waiting for Leskov was unbearable. Admittedly, it meant that the moment of his exposure was momentarily deferred. But this waiting was worse than any other waiting, worse even than the waiting at the airport a short time before. There it had been a waiting at the end of which he himself would assume control – bloody, murderous control, admittedly, but at least he could do something; it was down to him what would happen next and when. Now, on the other hand, there was nothing more he could do. He was no longer an active participant in the events that would follow. Now he was only their victim, their plaything. He had to wait impotently until Leskov condescended to emerge from his absorption to take delivery of the text that spelled the end for Perlmann. And Perlmann had to linger in that waiting, regardless of whether it lasted hours, days or years. His humiliation was his own responsibility, and his alone. But that insight was unbearable. He couldn't stay on his own with it for more than a brief moment. He would explode if he locked himself away in it entirely, in line with the terrible logic of the matter. He needed some exoneration, someone who could bear at least a portion of the guilt, so this feeling of humiliation struck in blind hatred at Leskov, who came now, at last, a dreamy and enthusiastic expression on his spongy face.

He touched Perlmann on the arm. 'I'll never forget,' he said, 'that you invited me to this divine place.'

The lobby was empty as they walked across the gleaming marble floor to the reception. Perlmann saw the text from a long way off. There was only a single pigeonhole with a pile of papers sticking out of it. And now his anxiety returned to its usual form of expression: he felt his heart thumping all the way to his throat. There was no one behind the counter. *I'll just go and grab the text.* The thought overwhelmed him. It allowed no other thoughts, no reflection and no contradiction. He quickly walked around the counter and took the text from the pigeonhole. He was about to roll it up to hide it from Leskov, when Signora Morelli appeared behind him: 'Sorry, Signor Perlmann, for keeping you waiting.'

Perlmann froze. The force of the thought that had made him take the text had to fade away before he could react.

'Oh, I must have given you a start,' said Signora Morelli. 'I didn't mean to.' And now, as Perlmann turned to face her, she saw the blood on his clothes. '*Dio mio!*' she exclaimed and threw her hand to her mouth. 'What's happened?'

Perlmann looked down at himself, as if trying to recall something long forgotten. 'Oh, that,' he said as if Signora Morelli had grotesquely lost all sense of proportion, 'that was just a bit of a nosebleed.' He rolled the text up tightly, as if he were about to stuff it into a pneumatic post system. 'I . . . I was just about to give Signor Leskov the text.' Standing next to her, he made a gesture of introduction. 'This is Professor Vassily Leskov, the man I told you about,' he said in English.

'*Benvenuto!*' she smiled, blankly shaking the hand that Leskov held out to her across the counter.

As Perlmann, still clutching the text, walked around the counter and back to Leskov, he had the feeling that his alert reaction had used up the very last remnants of his strength. He would never again be capable of an alert reaction, never. *And why all that effort at concealment? As soon as he starts reading the text upstairs, it will all be over in a few minutes anyway. And on top of everything, here I am handing him the text myself.*

Signora Morelli had pushed a pad of registration forms towards Leskov, and he was now busy filling it in. He became uneasy when she said that she would be keeping his passport for a while, and enquired anxiously when he would get it back, as it still had his travel permit inside it. The signora reassured him that he could have it back after dinner; it was just a matter of routine. When she took his room key down from the board, she paused, fished an envelope out from the back of the drawer and handed it to Leskov. The Olivetti name was printed discreetly in olive green letters in the bottom left-hand corner.

'Signor Angelini asked me to give you this. You'll be seeing him later at dinner.' With the corners of her mouth twitching, she watched Leskov feeling the envelope and then, with the clumsiness that came from embarrassment, putting it in his jacket pocket. She rang the bell for a porter to take his luggage.

The time had come. Perlmann handed the text to Leskov. That movement sealed his fate, and was enfolded in the numbing silence of a nightmare. He didn't utter a single word and their eyes met only fleetingly.

Leskov received the text rather distractedly, because the porter was loading his luggage on to the cart, which he seemed to consider very strange. He bent down to his suitcase and opened the zip of the outside pocket. The piece of rubber band remained stuck in it. *Now he'll notice. Now.*

'Good evening,' said Brian Millar, who had joined them along with Adrian von Levetzov. Leskov glanced up and straightened himself, still holding the text in his hand.

'I assume you're Vassily Leskov,' Millar said in his sonorous voice. 'Pleased to meet you.' He looked at Leskov's hand. 'I see you've been given the text already.'

'What in God's name has happened to you?' von Levetzov cried, interrupting the greeting, and pointing at Perlmann's clothes.

'Philipp had a flow of blood from the nose,' said Leskov as he saw Perlmann standing there like a sleepwalker. It was the first time Perlmann had heard him speaking English. The ungainliness of the sentence and the tight, nasal pronunciation sounded like mockery. It was as if he had just started running the gauntlet.

They wouldn't disturb him any longer, von Levetzov said and pointed to the waiting porter. They would be seeing each other over dinner at half-past eight, after all.

By now the suitcase with the open outside pocket was on the cart as well. 'So, see you very soon,' said Leskov, waving the text significantly and following the porter to the elevator.

Perlmann watched him go. He had never fainted. Now he wished it would happen, so that he wouldn't have to experience that sensation any longer, the sensation of endless falling.

'You're as white as a sheet,' said Signora Morelli. 'Are you not well? Would you like to lie down?'

'It's nothing,' said Perlmann, and looked at her for a long time until she became embarrassed and ran her hand searchingly over her hair. *I've got to tell someone before the others find out. Why not her? But no, that's impossible. What would she do with such a confession? And it wouldn't change anything at all.*

She handed him the key and made a maternal face that he had never seen before. 'It must have been a difficult journey from Genoa to here,' she said. 'There's always a lot of traffic on a Monday, especially trucks.'

'Yes,' Perlmann said, barely audibly. He took his key and went to the elevator.

He sat on the bed and slumped back. A few moments before, when he had closed the door behind him and seen the spacious room in front of him, he had had a moment of relief: after four full hours spent in such close proximity with Leskov, he was alone again at last. Leaning on the door, he had stood there for a while and yielded to that feeling of respite, knowing that it was a stolen emotion, a lie that could be washed away by anxiety at any moment. It wouldn't have been washed away exactly. It was more that the desperate consciousness of his situation had seeped up from below, constant and inexorable, and had colored and replaced all other sensations. He had gone to the wardrobe and pulled a yearned-for cigarette from the hastily torn-open pack. But he had stubbed it out again after two drags.

Now he had room for only a single sensation: the feeling of not knowing what to do with himself. In his mind he could relocate to any place imaginable, any corner of the universe – but he always felt the same thing: *I have no right to be here.* He felt as if he had to wring every last breath from that ruthless, devastating sensation. There was that one point from which all experience emanated and to which everything flowed back, that inner center that he always carried around with him. Again and again Perlmann attempted to withdraw entirely into that center, and find his footing at its midmost point, to put a small bit of difference between him and the overwhelming, overarching feelings of guilt and shame, a distance that would have allowed him to say: *So I am something else, too; you can't judge me in the light of this single offence.* But attempt after attempt failed. Guilt and shame remained hot on his heels; wherever he turned, they followed him into the innermost depths like a shadow. He tried to duck away, and to keep taking a step back and inwards, but there was no escape. He said to himself, pressing his fists to his temples, that he, too, had a past, and that there were things in it that he had done properly. But even that was useless, the feelings that held him as if in a stranglehold refused to accept that appeal, that defense, as valid.

Exhausted by all his vain attempts to assert himself, it seemed simply impossible that he would survive even the next second, which appeared to be taking an infinity to come. And that was something quite different from the prolongation of time that took place in the anxiety and uncertainty before making a decision. Then time was extended towards a goal. You knew that the tension would ease sooner or later, even if the outcome was not a good one, and that you would then return to the normal flow of time, its normal pace. Now, however, there was no goal and no uncertainty, which meant there was no longer any hope, either, that he would soon be able to yield to the natural self-evidence and inconspicuousness of temporal flux. His own private time beyond all present, which had emerged the previous morning from his fatal resolution, had dissolved into nothing somewhere beyond the tunnel, and he yearned to return to ordinary, shared time. But that wasn't possible now, either. Because that ordinary time led into an open future, while his future was no longer open. The discovery of the deception by the others in a sense closed off his time. It walled it up. It brought time to an end as something in the course of which his own experience could develop. Time now was only this: a sequence of weary, extended moments stripped of possibility. Each individual one of those moments was to be awaited in its pure passing, one moment after the other, in all eternity and without any hope. It was hell.

He wished he could fall into a profound unconsciousness that lacked any center of experience, so that there was no longer anyone whose presence was illegitimate. But Leskov could phone him up or knock on his door at any minute. Leskov had been distracted when he had been given the text, but by now he was in his room and no longer had to worry about his luggage. Perhaps he would take a shower first, get changed and then look out on to the bay again. It could also be that he was excited about dinner with all of his colleagues, and would at first simply put aside the text. But it was equally possible that he had immediately unrolled the papers in the elevator and cast a first glance at it. The altered title would have protected Perlmann for an instant, but even then Leskov might not have immediately recognized it as his text. It was in English, after all, and hence estranged from itself. Later, a barrier of disbelief would have formed in Leskov's mind, and then, gradually, dissolved as he went on reading, until the initially vague sense of familiarity would have condensed into certainty. *That could be now. Right now.*

On the way back to the hotel Perlmann had imagined Leskov working out the whole truth in an instant. But, he thought now, that was not the obvious thing to assume. Since Perlmann's name was not on the text, for a moment Leskov would not suspect him of plagiarism. Instead he would assume that Perlmann had arranged the perfect surprise for him: first telling him on the way there that the Russian text had been still far too difficult for him, then handing him, without further comment, the translation that he had, in fact, produced. Leskov could not help but feel flattered – almost overwhelmed, in fact, by the idea that someone like Philipp Perlmann might take all that time to translate such a long text. He would find the work significant, outstanding; there was no other possible explanation. Excited and filled with gratitude, Leskov would pick up the phone or come up to his room. Perlmann could almost hear him knocking at the door already. On the other hand it might have occurred to him what a shame it was that it wasn't a trans-lation of the second, far superior version. He would reach into the outside pocket of his suitcase, and freeze. He would be flummoxed, then rummage around in the whole case, again and again. But he wouldn't suspect anything. On the contrary, once again he would be extrava-gantly grateful for Perlmann's gift, because now he would at least be able to present this version. And again Perlmann felt as if he could already hear Leskov's footsteps in the corridor.

He couldn't stay there. He would have to pretend to be deaf and let each individual ring, every individual knock wash over him. And Leskov would try it for a long time, and again and again, because according to Signora Morelli's information Perlmann hadn't left his room. Perlmann got up and, without really noticing, he was glad that for the time being he had a goal, even if only a vague one.

He took off his shoes, and only now, when the pressure eased, did he become aware that his toes had been hurting for many hours, and that the dull pain had turned them into a single, unfeeling lump. But there was no time to rub them. He was quickly slipping into his other trousers when he noticed that they were the ones with the torn leg. Now the only pair he had were the pale trousers, far too light for a November night, even in the south. No time to put on a belt, Leskov was on the way, pullover and jacket – luckily he hadn't changed the combination lock on the suitcase that morning: money, travellers' checks and credit cards, the cigarettes, a splash of cold water on his face, the pack of sleeping pills – he slipped them into his trouser pocket without a thought; it was like a reflex. It was only in the doorway that he looked at his watch: eight thirty-two. He closed the door. He would have to wait for at least five minutes, otherwise he risked bumping into the others.

So Leskov hadn't read it yet. Or else he planned to thank him for the translation over dinner, loudly, impossible for the others to ignore. When Perlmann walked to the window he saw the piece of paper with Kirsten's address on the desk. It had been moved. And the red lighter was in a different position on the round table from earlier that morning. The chambermaid.

By now they would all be sitting at the table. Leskov would be uneasy and, in spite of his gratitude, a little annoyed that his host hadn't come down to introduce him to everyone. Millar would be furious at Perlmann's repeated social solecisms – he could have been punctual today of all days. Millar would have no hesitation in acting as substitute host – Perlmann could hear him using the English word, self-righteous and accusatory. But perhaps Angelini would have anticipated him and taken control of things with all his skill and charm.

Perlmann shifted Kirsten's lighter slightly, and straightened the piece of paper with her address on it. He had just opened the door when it occurred to him: *the text*. He had to get rid of the text, which he had put under the telephone book that morning. The thought was not the result of a reflection. It wasn't deduced from something else. It was just there all of a sudden, and it involved an irresistible need to get rid of that stack of papers. He took the pile out of the desk drawer. His breathing quickened. Where can it go? He couldn't carry it through the hotel, exposed like that. His suitcase was still in the car. At last he jammed it between the covers of the big hotel folder with the menu, the prospectuses and the writing paper. With his hand on the door handle, he turned round. Whatever happened now, he would never step inside this room again. He had no idea what would become of his things, his clothes, books and papers – where they would be taken to and by whom. He just knew this one thing: here, in this hotel, no one would ever see him again.

When the door shut, the telephone rang inside the room. *They've started looking for me.* Unseen, he made it to the rear entrance.

39

It would soon be very dark behind the rocky outcrop from which the reflection of the city lights could no longer be seen, and the calm, black surface of the water struck Perlmann as quietly menacing. Over by Sestri Levante there flowed an endless stream of light, and far in the distance a ship was just visible, a light blinking rhythmically in its bow. In the long pauses between the cars he listened to the quiet rush of the little waves, and the exhaustion that numbed him helped him to think of nothing. At one point he gave a start, when a young couple walked in a close embrace. And only now, when the hotel folder nearly slipped over the balustrade, did be become aware of how absurd, how utterly nonsensical it had been to smuggle his copy of Leskov's text out of the hotel, when all the others had a copy already. 'Now I'm losing my grip on the simplest things,' he said into the night, and he felt the weird sensation creeping over him that his thoughts were going off the rails and his ability to think was silently disintegrating.

He started shivering. Heading on towards Portofino was out of the question; the cat with the divided face was there, and the landlord in suspenders, knocking at the door. And that way it was dark, dark and cold. Perlmann walked hesitantly back to the rocky outcrop, the folder under his arm, his hands in his pockets. He looked across to the hotels and on to the city and its lights like someone standing on the threshold of a forbidden world.

The Miramare looked like something out of an advertising prospectus, very elegant, the illumination of the porch and the floodlights in the pines made it look mysterious, enticing, seductive, and then there were the white neon letters against a royal blue background – film images, dream images. From here, the front windows of the dining room were concealed by the columns, but through the furthest one back he thought he could make out a chandelier.

He could neither go forwards into that glittering world nor back into the dark. He felt as if he could no longer take a single step in his life, as if he were damned to stand for ever in that one place.

Outside the Regina Elena Hotel a taxi stopped, and the driver helped an old woman out. Perlmann ran as if he had to catch the last taxi in the world. The folder was cumbersome, the covers forced apart by the thickness of the text, he waved and called, and by the time he breathlessly reached it, the driver had already turned on the engine. He got into the back and gave his destination as the Hotel Imperiale. As they drove past the Miramare, he shielded his head with the hotel folder, feeling as if he were in a cheap thriller full of kitsch and clichés. On the hill leading up to the Imperiale it occurred to him that he couldn't enter the hotel with the folder, on which the word MIRAMARE was engraved in big gold letters. He took out the text and quietly slid the folder under the passenger seat.

The chairs by the window, where he had sat with Kirsten, were occupied by a group of elegantly dressed people who were celebrating something, drinking champagne and laughing loudly as Perlmann came in. He sat down in the dark corner, where the light seemed to be broken, and ordered a whisky and a mineral water. Kirsten had been particularly impressed by that: a waiter coming all the way from the bar to serve them. *You feel so important, and rich*, she had said, and he had seen how her enjoyment of this elegant world was in conflict with other, contrary attitudes that she had expressed for a long time, attitudes typical of her generation.

He set Leskov's text face down on the low marble table and lit a cigarette. His lungs felt dirty and sticky after the two packs he had already smoked today, and in the taxi a few moments ago his dry cough had been very painful and seemingly endless. But that was no longer of any importance. He wasn't hungry, but he did feel queasy, and a strange weakness all the way through his body gave him the ridiculous feeling of sitting uncertainly in the high-armed chair. When the waiter brought the drinks, he ordered a sandwich. He would have to force it down. But he did have to eat something.

He had never before found himself in this situation of not having the faintest idea how his thoughts – if he ever had any ever again – might continue. It wasn't blindness. It wasn't like trying to stare through a plank. It was a sensation of hopelessness that settled on the imagination like mildew, coated it with a milky and impenetrable whiteness and completely paralyzed it. Nonetheless, now, at the end, making a mistake out of pure physical weakness – that was something he didn't want to do.

Twenty-five past nine. Now they would all know. Over dinner the conversation would have turned to tomorrow's session, and Leskov would have asked if there was a written text by Perlmann – he'd forgotten to ask him as they drove to the hotel. Millar had looked up in amazement. He himself had put a copy of Perlmann's text in Leskov's pigeonhole, and he, Leskov, had been holding it in his hand when they had greeted him earlier on. No, no, Leskov would have replied, perplexed, that had been something quite different; a surprise that Perlmann had prepared for him: an English translation of a text that he, Leskov, had written. He had been utterly flummoxed to discover how much massive effort Perlmann had taken with it, and he could still scarcely believe it. Such overwhelming kindness! And it seemed to be an excellent translation: it was only with the title that Perlmann had made a curious error. Leskov was also especially grateful for that, because he could now give them all something in writing to hold, particularly since a terrible slip had occurred: he had left another text, which he had planned to talk about here – the new version of the one translated by Perlmann – at home in St Petersburg, although he could have sworn he had packed it. But it wasn't so bad after all. He could explain the changes orally. Tomorrow morning he would ask for copies to be made for all of them, in preparation for the session that he was, as Perlmann had told him, to hold on Thursday.

At first, thought Perlmann, there would be a pause. Evelyn Mistral understood now why Perlmann had wanted to keep his Russian a secret. He saw her laughing face as she spoke of her complicity. The confusion would only set in later on when she had worked out that his secrecy had been illogical: if it was Leskov that he wanted to surprise, why couldn't the others know? And if the game of hide-and-seek was supposed to be part of the surprise prepared for Leskov's arrival, why had he been playing it weeks before the telegram, when he could not have known that Leskov was on his way? But those questions had never been asked.

It would be Achim Ruge, Perlmann imagined, who would ask the crucial, annihilating question. He would pose it quite dryly and – a sign of tense foreboding – savor his Swabian pronunciation: what was the title of Perlmann's translation that he had got so wrong? THE PERSONAL PAST AS LINGUISTIC CREATION, Leskov would say. A crass and somehow incomprehensible error of translation, but still a beautiful title, much more so than his own, and apt. He would ask Perlmann's permission to use it in future, of course with the appropriate reference to him.

It would have gone quiet at the table, Perlmann thought, incredibly quiet. He saw the others pausing as they ate, and staring at their plates. They couldn't believe their ears; what followed on from this information was too monstrous to contemplate. At first they didn't look at each other, each one of them wondered whether there mightn't be another, harmless explanation.

'So you think,' Millar asked after a while, speaking dangerously slowly, 'that the text headed THE PERSONAL PAST AS LINGUISTIC CREATION is a text that you wrote and Perlmann merely translated?'

'Erm . . . yes, that is the case,' Leskov replied uncertainly, confused and alarmed at Millar's tone and the jerky, jabbing movements that he made with his knife.

The renewed silence must have been deafening.

'That is incredible,' murmured Millar, 'simply incredible.' Catching Leskov's quizzical eye he went on: 'You see, Vassily, it is a sad fact that we have all, each individual one of us, been given a copy of this very text. Admittedly, Phil's name isn't on it, but we were led to believe it was his contribution to tomorrow's session. He hasn't handed out any other text, or done anything to rectify the situation. There is also the fact,' he might have added, 'that the text was distributed at a point in time when no one knew of your arrival, not even Phil himself. All of this forces us to assume that Perlmann wanted to deceive us by presenting your text as his own. Plagiarism, then. Unimaginable, but there is no other explanation for it. And now we can no longer be surprised that he hasn't appeared at dinner.'

It took Perlmann for ever to take the first bite of the sandwich. He chewed and chewed; each movement of his jaw was an achievement. The smoked salmon and egg didn't taste of anything, and the obstruction that had formed in his throat could only be overcome by pushing very hard with his eyes closed. Of course, it was Millar who had voiced the thought. Perlmann's old hatred flared, and despair made it even darker than usual. He set the bread back down on the table and started taking small sips of his whisky.

He didn't dare to imagine Leskov's face after the revelation of the truth, which had started working away in him after his first shock. The many curious features of the journey suddenly returned to his mind, and assembled themselves into a pattern: Perlmann's irritation at the airport; his agitation at the wheel and his taciturnity; the strange route; the nausea; the insane driving in the tunnel and the lame explanations afterwards. Leskov couldn't prove anything, even though he had been watching Perlmann like a hawk. There hadn't been a single false move, nothing that would have clearly and irrefutably revealed an intention to commit murder. That someone, at a moment when a wide car had to be driven through a bottleneck, should have taken his hands off the wheel and closed his eyes, was careless, negligent and even more irresponsible than speeding. It wasn't even superficially comprehensible, and pointed to a darkness in the driver's personality. But it wasn't a trace – not a shadow of proof – of premeditated murder. That much was clear to Leskov, too, so he wouldn't tell anyone; such an accusation was too monstrous. Even in confidence he wouldn't be able to accuse him. He couldn't prove that Perlmann's story about nausea and a morbid fear of bulldozers were outright lies. And yet Perlmann was quite sure that this evening – *now, at this moment* – Leskov knew everything. It was completely out of the question for him ever to meet this man, who would regard him as a murderer, ever again.

When Perlmann's hand accidentally brushed the edge of the table, the bandage on his finger came off. It was only now that he noticed that his finger was very swollen. Around the bruised spot it was yellow and green, the skin was tense and hot. And now his head was itchy again as well. He took out the box of sleeping pills, held them under his jacket, looked furtively around and took one from it. After a moment's hesitation he broke it in two and washed one half down with mineral water.

They would all be waiting for him in silence when he stepped into the Marconi Veranda tomorrow morning.

'You've all got this text now,' he would be able to say with a smile. 'I hope you didn't mistake it for my own, even though my name isn't on it. By now I am sure you will know that it is a text by our Russian colleague, which I have translated. I had it distributed because it was to serve as the starting point for an idea I should like to develop now. And it is a happy coincidence that Vassily himself can now be here. I expect a great deal from this.'

It would be an audacious bluff. Perlmann grew quite dizzy at the idea, and that dizziness merged with the start of the effect of the pill. They wouldn't believe a word he said, not a single word. They knew he was a fraud, a con man, and now they were also getting to know him as an ice-cold liar. He would never summon the strength to return each of their contemptuous stares with harsh defiance, forcing them into a state of uncertainty. They would only be uncertain if he now proceeded to deliver a thoroughly original, brilliant lecture. But he had nothing to say, not a single sentence. He would stand up there at the front like someone mutely gasping for air.

Or should he sit up there and in dry words, stony-faced, tell the truth? What words would he use? How many sentences would he need? Where would he look? And when he had said it, what then? Could one, in fact, apologize for such a thing? Was it not almost mockery simply to say, 'I'm terribly sorry' and then get up and go? And where to?

Could one go on living with such ostracism? Really live and inwardly develop, so that you weren't merely crouching and creeping, enduring and surviving, vegetating? You would have to find a possible way of making yourself independent of the judgment of others and of the need for recognition. A way of becoming free, truly free. All of a sudden Perlmann felt calmer. The surge of panic and despair subsided, and he seemed to be standing very close to a crucial, redeeming insight, the most important of his whole life. Why, then, should it not be possible to withdraw entirely from his professional role, his public identity, into his private, authentic person, the identity that was the only thing that counted?

Basically, it had been simply the pleasure of translating – his old love of jumping back and forth between linguistic worlds, his dream of being an interpreter – that had brought him back repeatedly to Leskov's text. That was how he was. There was nothing wrong with it. He could stand by it. No intention to deceive had been involved, either consciously or as a hidden undercurrent. He was absolutely sure of that. It was just how things were. He didn't need to persuade himself. And the rest – the rest had been self-defense. He had held Leskov's text up in front of him as a shield protecting him against the intrusive eyes of the others, against their unchanging, monotonously updated expectations, which they treated as if people developed in an uninterrupted, linear fashion – as if the successful life consisted in making those professional decisions that were taken early, too early, and that hardly ever merited the name in any case, in total identification, with a complete lack of emotional detachment, decade after decade. *What do you want to be? You have to be something. Whatever would become of him?* Those were the principles his parents expressed over lunch and dinner. He had heard them countless times, and they had sunk into his deepest depths, and deeper still. They were sentences that had never been up for discussion. They came along hypnotically, as if they were completely natural, and in their monotonous, thoughtless repetition they became a background noise, so vast and all-consuming in its diabolical self-evidence that afterwards one couldn't imagine what a life without it might be like.

You have to be something, or you're nothing. That was the axiom, in all its perfidious simplicity and obviousness. He would take it, that iron axiom, Perlmann thought, he would summon all his powers, even those at the hindmost corner of his soul, and then use those concentrated powers to bend it until it broke. What he had become – a respected professor with prizes and an invitation to Princeton – he was as of tonight no longer. That was destroyed. But that was a long way from saying he was nothing now. There was a great deal left in him, a very great deal, and the others had no idea about it. He would lodge himself in there, and then it would be a question of making his soul quite spherical and coating it with wax so that everything would slide off it, even the hostile glances of the others. He would walk along the streets quite upright, with his head held high.

It was a liberating train of thought. But it was still new, so it threatened, as soon as it had concluded, to slip away again. He would have to repeat it often and, so to speak, internally perform it, until it was solidly rooted within him. Perlmann took the second half of the pill out of the box and swallowed it, along with what remained of the whisky. His finger didn't hurt any more, and the itch in his scalp had faded away. He ate the sandwich. He had a future again. He felt comfortable in the deep armchair and was pleased that he immediately recognized the melody that reached him from across the bar. The crucial thing was not to lose one's sense of proportion. What did it matter, from the point of view of eternity, whether the thirty-seven pages which were, in the end, quite unimportant, came from his pen or from Leskov's? Who really cared seriously about that? There were milky ways and beyond them more milky ways, without end, and here, on this tiny clump of earth, imprisoned in their insignificant little lives, which would be completely forgotten after a few decades, they made a hell of their lives for a handful of letters. It was laughable, quite simply laughable. Perlmann tried to imagine what people's coexistence would look like if everyone always considered himself and others from the point of view of eternity. But he couldn't quite do it. The question was hard to grasp and kept slipping away again. But that didn't matter. The main thing was not to lose sight of the correct proportions. The corrected proportions. Proportions.

When he – addressed by the waiter – started from his half-sleep, it was five to eleven and the room was empty. He was going to stop serving soon, the waiter said, and asked if Perlmann wanted anything else. Perlmann ordered a mineral water. He had a dry mouth and a thick, furry tongue. He no longer had the faintest idea of what had happened for the past hour. He was shivering. He didn't know where to go from here. Not a single step. He still had four pills. That wasn't enough. He took the text and went outside, without waiting for the waiter and without paying.

The cool night air made him dizzy, but it also felt good. On the way down to the big square he saw a garbage bin in a side street. It seemed to belong to a hotel or a restaurant, because kitchen smells came from the extractor fan above it, and he could hear the clatter of cutlery. Apart from a layer of potato peelings the bin was empty. That was the third time today that Perlmann had got rid of a text. He was good at it, and he felt as if he had been busy doing nothing else for weeks. But this time it was something special. Because this time it was completely pointless. It was as if he were destroying his copy of a newspaper in order to impose a news blackout.

Perlmann rested both arms on the edge of the bin and started laughing quietly. In the hope of relief he tried to keep that laughter going and to spur it on from within, but it was hysterical laughter that soon dried up and turned to retching. The papers fell on top of the rubbish.

At Piazza Vittorio Veneto he caught a taxi to the Regina Elena. He asked the driver to stop in a dark spot near the hotel. He flicked through his banknotes and gave him the biggest one, a 100,000 lire note. 'Keep the change,' he said.

'*Ma no, Signore*,' the driver stammered, 'I can't take that. Can't you see what you've given me?' He held the bill right under the ceiling light.

'It's fine,' Perlmann said irritably and got out.

*

He sat right at the end of the little beach jetty reserved for hotel guests and set the pills down next to him. Walking into the water with his clothes on and swimming out further and further until his strength gave out. Since that day at the public baths it had always been a drama if his head went under water when he was swimming. But the pills helped. He wouldn't feel much, and soon he would lose consciousness.

A wave of pill-weariness washed over him, and then there was a void. He was glad the beach was unlit. He could only think very slowly, and often lost the thread.

It was an undramatic, quiet way of saying goodbye to life. No onlookers, no excitement after a bombshell. Tomorrow a police boat would pull him from the water. That was all. It accorded with his desire to disappear unnoticed from the world. He wished he could also magically ensure that all the traces that he had left in the minds of the others would be erased. As if he had never existed.

A textbook suicide, he thought, practically classic: a man who can see no way of escaping his shame. Forty-eight hours ago, after looking down the hotel facade, he had rejected that way out. It had been the thought of the judgment of the others that had put him off. But back then there had still seemed to be some leeway, a set of other possibilities. He could still plan things that might have prevented his exposure. And that had created a perspective from which something could be pondered and rejected. Now that the only possibility left to him was the black water out there, when he thought about the others he had a new, strange experience. It was actually too complicated for his heavy head, and everything was intermittently suspended as if he were having a blackout. Then he shivered all the more violently in his thin trousers on the cold stone. Nonetheless, he kept returning to that experience. He homed in on it and, in the end, he managed to grasp it more precisely and dependably.

It was the experience of an unexpected inner disengagement. He had to concentrate on one of those feared people, on that person's face, but even more on their atmospheric outlines, on the kind of situation that they created through their presence. The important thing was not to avoid the threatening and almost unbearable feelings which arose when he thought of the judgment that that person up there in their illuminated hotel room had by now formed about him, and to which tomorrow they might, once he had been found, add the thought of cowardice. The important thing was to let these feelings get near him without resisting them, and to stand up to them with disciplined calm. After a while, the person in question lost their threatening, oppressive proximity and began to retreat. His dented soul was able to bulge outwards, the tormenting feelings slowly died away, and he was free. It was an ethereal and fragile freedom that was coming into being, a floating present in which one seemed to be balanced on the point of a needle. He was on a narrow strip of no-man's-land between the life behind him, a life interwoven with the lives of others, and the darkness in front of him, in which life would be no more. Being free like this could have been a form of happiness, had it not been for the black water, which would rise higher with each step he took. And without the water, he sensed with great clarity, that freedom would not exist. If he turned round and returned to the land, it would have fled in a moment, and the others would have buried him beneath their stares.

The one face that refused to go away was Kirsten's. On the contrary, the longer he saw it in his mind's eye, the harder it was to let go of it. He had had no opportunity to explain it to her. The news of his suicide, followed by the news of his deception, would fall on her as if from a clear sky. For her they would stand together dry and mute, those two pieces of information: he had perpetrated a deception, and when the matter came to light, he had walked into the water. He would sound like the little clerk who had taken money from the cash register.

It was so shabby, so shockingly shabby, that familiar story, its short version untrue, even for the little clerk. Somehow Kirsten might sense that it wasn't true for him, either. But she had no way of getting to the true story all by herself, or even getting close to it. He had never talked to her about his profession slipping away. Or about his unsuccessful delimitation from others. Or about the fact that a preoccupation with languages was his attempt to regain a tiny shadow of the fleeting present.

Those weren't things that one could explain to a person of her age. Or at least he had always assumed as much.

But perhaps that was wrong, Perlmann thought, and he started talking to his daughter under his breath. At first the words came out only haltingly. He spoke them into the quiet, dark water, and only occasionally raised his eyes to look into Kirsten's face for signs of understanding. Later the things he had to say came fluently. He began to sound more convincing, even to himself, and Kirsten started nodding. Admittedly, his tongue remained heavy, his lips didn't always obey, and some words were blurred. But Kirsten wasn't repelled. She understood, so he didn't need to be embarrassed and was able to go on talking, more and more, until everything was completely clear, its every impulse comprehensible. So that he could be forgiven.

He put the pills in his pocket, got up stiffly and uncertainly and went back to the street. He couldn't drive himself in this state. But he could persuade a taxi driver to fetch his passport and drive him to Konstanz. If he paid a princely sum, one would certainly be found. He could sleep on the back seat, and by the time they arrived tomorrow morning he would have a clear head again, and clear speech. Then he could tell Kirsten everything, explain everything, just as he had just done a moment ago, only much more thoroughly and much better.

40

In the lobby of the Regina Elena, inebriated wedding guests were rowdily forcing a glass of champagne on the night porter, who was trying to conceal his annoyance behind a sour smile. Under these circumstances Perlmann couldn't possibly ask him to call a cab. He wasn't even a hotel guest. He had no *gettoni*, so phone boxes were of no use to him. He went over to the Miramare and leaned against the wall at the foot of the steps. Dart in quickly, say the few words to Giovanni and then immediately come back here to wait, unseen, for the taxi. He wouldn't be in there for ten seconds. That he would, during that time, meet one of the others, was unlikely. It was already half-past twelve. But it wasn't impossible. Laura Sand, for example, sometimes took another walk at this time.

Perlmann climbed the first few steps until he could see the entrance beyond the edge of the terrace. His heart was thumping, and his breathing, involuntarily, was quite shallow. Giovanni was propped with one elbow on the counter, reading the paper. *Rethink*. Again he leaned against the wall. Otherwise he would have to look for a taxi stand in town. He could drag himself as far as the station. But hardly any trains stopped there in the middle of the night. What would taxis be doing there? And he couldn't remember another rank. He would wander, lead-limbed, through the quiet alleys, each step a form of torture. Again he glanced across to the reception. Giovanni was now leaning against the counter on outstretched arms, reading the page under him. Shadows stirred in the bar, and a moment later a grey-haired man walked through the hall to the elevator. It was too dangerous. Perlmann would have to wait for another hour or two. He closed his eyes. A paralysing irresolution took hold of him.

'*Buona sera, Dottore,*' said Signora Morelli, coming energetically downstairs, her coat flapping behind her. 'Is . . . is something wrong? Are you waiting for someone?'

'No, no . . . nothing,' Perlmann replied, startled, and making a special effort with his pronunciation. And because it seemed impossible not to say anything else, he added: 'You're still here?'

'Yes, sadly,' she said and pulled a face. 'Taxes, we have nothing but problems with taxes. It gets worse by the year. I was working on it until a moment ago.' She smiled. 'Well, yes, and it's mad to run such a hotel without more managerial staff, almost like a family business.'

It was the first time he had heard anything so personal from her, and if he had still belonged to her world, and the world in general, rather than mutely nodding he would have loved to show an interest.

'Oh, by the way,' she said, already turning to go, 'I put the original of your text in your pigeonhole. In my haste on Saturday I left it by the photocopier. I hope you didn't miss it.'

Perlmann didn't understand. And he didn't want to understand. Never again did he want to have to understand a sentence with words in it like *text, original* and *copy*. Never again.

'*Venga,*' the signora said when she saw his blank face, and went back upstairs. It was impossible not to follow her. She shoved aside Giovanni, who looked up in surprise from the newspaper and was saying hello, and took a text out of Perlmann's pigeonhole. '*Eccolo,*' she said. 'But now I really have to go. *Buona notte!*'

Giovanni looked at him quizzically when she had gone.

'A taxi,' he said. 'I need a taxi.' Giovanni reached for the receiver.

Perlmann realized then that he was confused by the fact that he stood there, contrary to his plan, as Giovanni made the call. He held the text limply in his dangling hand, and he held it the way you hold something that you're going to drop in the gutter at the next possible opportunity. Never again did he want to hold a text in his hand. Never again.

The taxi company took its time, and an unpleasant, silent wait began. It was just to do something that Perlmann looked down at his hand that held the text. And it was a moment before he noticed the small, long card stuck under the paperclip that held the pile of papers together. Even before he knew what it said, something in him began to vibrate. He abruptly bent his arm, brought the card up in front of his eyes and read: *6 copie. Per il gruppo di Perlmann. Distribuire, come sempre.* He didn't understand. *I threw away the original a little while ago.* But his breathing quickened, he read again, lifted the card and saw the title: MESTRE NON È BRUTTA. Underneath, his name.

For a few seconds he stood there motionless, blind and deaf to his surroundings, wrapped in the beating of his blood. *Maria. The call from Genoa. She finished typing up my notes. In spite of the people from Fiat.*

It lasted until the thought had found its way to his body. Then Perlmann started running. He collided with the door, twisted his ankle on the steps and lost a shoe, but in spite of the pain and in spite of the cold cobbles he ran as he had never run in his whole life, clutching the rolled-up text in his fist like a relay baton. He got a stitch in his side and started coughing. *Good God! I hope I'm thinking the right thing!* Now he saw the figure of Signora Morelli walking along the marina. He ran with lungs that threatened to burst. There was no breath left to call out and, at last, when his soft knees refused to support him and he began to stumble, he had caught up with her. He couldn't get a word out, just bent down breathlessly and coughed, his hands pressed to his ribs because of the stitch.

'This note here,' he panted at last, and now he no longer cared that his mouth wasn't properly obeying him, 'does this mean that you copied the text six times?'

'*Sì, Dottore,*' she said, and on her face her initial surprise made way for an expression of preparation for self-defense.

'And those were the copies that you put in my colleagues' pigeon-holes on Saturday morning?'

'*Sì.*'

'And you didn't copy and distribute any other text?'

'No, Signor Perlmann,' she said, now visibly annoyed with this breath-less questioning, 'this is the text that Maria gave me. I haven't had another one.'

He held the papers up as closely in front of Signora Morelli's face as if she were half-blind.

'This text here? This one here? No other one?'

Signora Morelli's tone changed when Perlmann lowered the pages and she recognized the harbingers of tears in his face.

'But yes, Dottore,' she said gently, 'it was this text here, this one exactly, and only this one. What have I done wrong?'

'Wrong? Nothing, nothing,' he stammered between the sobs that he could no longer control, 'on the contrary, this is . . . this is my salvation.'

He turned away and searched in vain for a handkerchief. Then he rubbed his eyes with the sleeve of his jacket and looked at her again.

'Many apologies,' he said quietly and vainly resisted his returning tears. 'I can't explain it to you, but I have never felt such relief. It's . . . indescribably great. Indescribably so.'

When he took his hand away from his eyes, she was looking at him as if she were seeing him properly for the first time. She smiled and touched his arm. 'Then you should go and sleep now,' she said. 'You look completely exhausted.'

He watched her go until, without turning round, she disappeared down a side street. It was a moment of presence. A redemptive present that he would not have thought possible.

Then, when he walked back very slowly to savor the precious present, he felt as if he were treading on needles each time he set down his ice-cold foot, and a stinging pain in his lungs pierced him from time to time. But it didn't matter. Nothing mattered any more apart from his over-whelming relief. *No plagiarism. I haven't committed plagiarism. No plagia-rism.* It was like slowly, disbelievingly, emerging from a very great, very dark depth, accompanied by a jumpiness that he thought he could feel in every fibre of his body. Again he read Maria's instruction on the card. And then twice. It was that text that Signora Morelli had copied, exactly this one and only this one. That was what she said. *Did she say it?*

When he turned the corner and saw the crooked pines, which were no longer illuminated at this hour, but only stood out against the night sky with their milky greyish green, his relief blew apart, and he felt as if he were being pressed down into the depths again by an incredibly heavy weight. *Giovanni must have made the copies himself and distributed them. That's why she doesn't know anything about Leskov's text.* An iron claw grabbed him by the chest, and each individual twinge in his foot was genuine torture as he hobbled hastily back, slipped into his lost shoe on the steps and walked, breathing heavily, to the reception desk.

'On Friday night,' he gasped, 'when the football match was on television, I brought you a text. What did you do with it?'

Giovanni glanced down. 'Erm . . . nothing,' he said and took a long drag on his cigarette. Then, when he had expelled all the smoke, he looked at Perlmann uncertainly. 'It was like this . . . I wasn't really concentrating, so to speak, because . . . You see, there was this equalizer in the ninetieth minute, and then the penalty shoot-out . . . and afterwards I couldn't remember exactly what you'd said to me, so I just put the text in your pigeonhole. I'm sorry if that meant something went wrong, but it was so exciting that . . .'

Perlmann closed his eyes for a moment and exhaled in slow motion. Then he rested his hand on Giovanni's. 'You've done the right thing. Exactly the right thing. I'm very glad. *La ringrazio. Mille grazie. Grazie.*'

A stone fell from Giovanni's heart. 'Really? I . . . You know, I had quite a guilty conscience because of it . . . Is there anything else I can do for you?'

'No, nothing,' Perlmann said with a smile, 'and once again, many thanks!'

Giovanni made a clumsy movement with his arm, interrupted halfway, which expressed his admiration better than any word or any facial expression could.

Perlmann walked to the elevator, but didn't wait for it. Instead he started hobbling up the stairs. He took his time. He was too wound up to have been able to turn it into a sentence. But the feeling was there: he could move freely in the hotel again. He wasn't a cheat.

*

When the line started crackling he put the phone down. What had he actually wanted to say to her? And in an alarming call at a quarter to two in the morning. And with that heavy tongue. His hand enclosed the red lighter. Now he didn't need to explain anything to her. He had nothing to apologize for. He could meet his daughter just as he had before. He was back from no-man's-land. *No plagiarism. No plagiarism, and no murder.* He repeated the words again and again, loudly and in his thoughts, who knows how many times, until, hollowed out by fatigue, they were no longer the expression of an emotion, but only a mechanical inner echo that grew increasingly sluggish.

If I hadn't gained self-confidence by writing in that harbor pub, and the courage to stand by my own notes, I wouldn't have called Maria, and the text wouldn't have been finished in time. If I hadn't taken that tour of the harbor, and hadn't got worked up about interpreting, I wouldn't have ended up writing in the harbor bar. So exactly the same inclination that had put him in the greatest danger, had also saved him. Perlmann sighed. That connection made him feel that he didn't just owe the redeeming turn of events to a concatenation of coincidences, but that they had their origin within him, in his way of thinking and feeling.

He went into the shower and washed his hair. The water stung his scratches. But it was a salutary sting, because it meant that the fog of alcohol and pills was beginning to clear. He showered, hot and cold, and then the same again. New life flowed through him, and now he felt sober and clear again.

It wasn't at all true that he had saved himself. Precisely the opposite was the case. *If I hadn't phoned Maria, the pigeonholes would have been empty on Saturday morning. I would have taken Leskov's text again and wouldn't have had to live through that whole nightmare with the tunnel.* His fanatical obsession with the translation had brought him not only to the brink of plagiarism, but also to the brink of murder and suicide. Back in Genoa, the frantic, desperate search for presence in the familiarity of foreign languages had for a moment given him the courage to stand up for himself, not least in front of the others, and because of that same courage he had ended up spending three endless days and nights in a world of fantasies and terror which had absolutely nothing to do with the real world.

All that saved me was coincidences, banal coincidences and inattentions. A sluice opened up in Perlmann's head, and he was deluged by a cascade of if-thens. *If that equalizer hadn't been scored, there wouldn't have been a penalty shoot-out. Giovanni would have been on top of things and would have passed on the instruction to copy Leskov's text. Then on Saturday morning both texts would have been in the pigeonholes, and that would have allowed me to rectify matters without loss of face. If Giovanni had done what he was supposed to, and if Maria hadn't finished because of the people from Fiat, only the fatal text would have made it to the pigeonholes; the disaster would have taken place in the real world and not just in my imagination. If Giovanni had just left Leskov's text on the shelf under the counter, my pigeonhole would have been the only one empty on Saturday morning. I would have checked, learned what had really happened, and there would never have been a murder plan. But perhaps I wouldn't have checked, paralyzed as I was. If Giovanni had left the text on the shelf, then when Signora Morelli was distributing them she would have noticed that my pigeonhole was the only one that was empty, and then she would have looked for the original by the photocopier. If my pigeonhole had been in a row with the pigeonholes of the others, I wouldn't have switched rooms; the signora would have hesitated when distributing the texts, then seen that the text in my pigeonhole was a different one; she would have looked for the original by the photocopier, and when I came back from Portofino I would have had two texts in my pigeonhole, and Maria's card would have resolved the matter. So if I hadn't had this exaggerated need for empty space, I would have been spared the tunnel. If when I returned from Portofino there hadn't been all that noise in the next room, I would have taken Silvestri's copy out of the pigeonhole and discovered the true state of affairs. And if, arriving with Leskov, I had glanced at the feared text in my hand, just a single short glance, I wouldn't have needed to imagine wading out into the dark water.*

Perlmann knew it was absurd, this orgy of unreal conditional clauses, but it also devoured his sense of relief, so that he yearned now for the tears he had shed when he first discovered his redemption. But that knowledge didn't help, the search for more and more connections was like an involuntary addiction. *If Larissa hadn't been plagued by a guilty conscience, she wouldn't have urged Leskov to make a fresh application; there would have been no telegram and no fear of exposure, and what had appeared the night before would not have been a planned suicide, only a nagging feeling of guilt. If the waiter hadn't brought me the telegram just as I was about to talk to Evelyn about Leskov's text, I would have been able to tell by what she said that something was wrong, and even then I would have been spared the bulldozer. If there hadn't been a wedding party at the Regina Elena tonight, I might have asked them to call for a cab, and then I would have told Kirsten in Konstanz about an act of plagiarism that didn't even take place.* Perlmann stopped.

So for days now they had been holding his notes, headed by an Italian sentence that must have seemed mannered and pretentious. He picked up the computer printout. It was fifty-two pages long. *I could have told from the thickness of the pages. Seventy-three pages in my pigeonhole compared to fifty-two in everyone else's; that's a difference that could have been spotted from a mile off. And this evening, when I turned up, I could have felt in my hand that it couldn't be Leskov's text: that the sheaf of papers was too thin.*

He let the pages slip through his fingers and weighed the pile in his hand. He didn't dare flick through it properly and tentatively read it, and he took care to ensure that his eye didn't get caught on the top page. Now that he felt like the survivor of a disaster, he didn't want to alarm himself on top of everything else – with trashy metaphors or a maudlin tone, for example. And he didn't want to encounter his written English right now, either – English that was seldom exactly wrong, and yet never had the effortless precision that he would have wished for. He slipped the papers into the desk drawer.

Angelini's remark on Sunday evening, he thought, now appeared in a new light. *Un lavoro insolito*, he had called the text. And it was no wonder, either, that no one else had wasted a word about the text. That they had basically pretended it had never existed.

In six and a half hours he would have to go up the three steps to the veranda and sit down at the front. All the people sitting there looking at him would have his text in front of them, from the first page to the last. *Only I and I alone don't know what's in it.* That was a plainly incorrect, nonsensical thought, Perlmann knew. Even on Friday, on the ship, he had gone through the notes in his head. But the thought wouldn't go away. In fact, it swelled still further. They knew more about him than he knew himself. They were waiting, and he couldn't think of anything to say. They delivered their criticisms, and he had no response to give.

It couldn't be the case that the unimaginable relief that had filled him even just an hour before was already being stifled by a new anxiety. It just couldn't be. *I didn't become a fraud and I didn't become a murderer. What other reason can there be for being anxious now?* Perlmann clutched that thought and then tried with a single lurch to wrest away the inner freedom that would make him invulnerable to everything the others might or might not say, to their faces and their stares, and also to the stares which, in the awkward silence, fell on the gleaming table top.

He phoned Giovanni. He could do him a favor right now, and sort him out with two pots of strong coffee. He still had six hours. That wasn't enough for a complete lecture. But he could write a memo that could be further developed orally. The thing was to develop something in the abstract and draw up the outlines of a conception. Then the discussion would focus on that. He could say, off-handedly, that the distributed text was incidental; he had only wanted to provide a small insight into the observations that he had used as his starting point.

Perlmann's heart was thumping as he sat down at the desk. Until now, sitting here had meant translating Leskov's text. Hour after hour, day after day, he had removed himself further and further from reality. Each translated sentence had brought him a little closer to the deadly silence of the tunnel. A quiet feeling of vertigo took hold of him as he carefully straightened the chair, lit a cigarette and reached for his ballpoint pen. For four weeks he had avoided that moment. His hands were sticky, and the stickiness transferred itself to the pen. He got to his feet, washed his hands in the bathroom and wiped the pen. Giovanni brought the coffee. Perlmann put it first on the right of the desk, then the left.

He threw the piece of paper with Kirsten's address into the waste-paper basket. He prepared a back-up pack of cigarettes and fetched the red lighter from the bedside table. Wearing only his dressing gown he would soon start shivering. He dressed completely. His light-colored trousers were too cool by now. But the tear on the other pair bothered him. Then there were the dark flannel trousers, the ones with the bloodstains. And it would be better to put on the lighter pullover. And turn up the heating a bit instead. Again he straightened his chair. He would have to be close to the desk. But not too close.

Why hadn't he tried it much sooner? The sentences came in spite of everything. They actually came, one after the other. At first he was anxious before each period, for fear that everything might dry up after it. But when the first page was full, this anxiety melted away; feeling in general faded into the background, and the calm logic of the sentences themselves took charge. For months, almost years, he had struggled to force out each individual sentence; it had seemed as if, in future, he would only be able to think in very small units. And now all of a sudden each sentence led quite naturally on to the next. Something started building up. He was writing a text, a real text. *So I can still do it after all. Now everything's fine.*

His pen went flying over the pages and the thoughts came one after another so quickly that he could barely capture them on the paper. At last his block had gone. Again he had something to say. He only lifted the pen from the paper to light another cigarette or pour himself the next cup of coffee. He held his cigarette in his left hand, and with the same hand he brought the cup to his mouth – it was unusual, but his right hand must not be interrupted while writing. *Not a memo; it's turning into a lecture, a complete lecture.* The unfamiliar way of holding the cigarette meant that smoke kept getting in his eyes; it stung, but his right hand wrote on and on. He was amazed and cheered at how good, how apt were the phrases that flowed so naturally on to the paper; some of them, he thought, practically had a poetic force. He hoped he had enough paper; otherwise he would have to start writing on both sides. Eventually, he would run out of coffee. It was lucky that he had even more cigarettes in the wardrobe. He hoped the lighter wouldn't suddenly pack up on him. At one point he paused and closed his eyes. *The present. This is it. Now I'm experiencing it at last. It took all these traumas to break through to it.*

At five o'clock he opened the window. Billows of smoke drifted out into the night. He took a deep breath of the cool air. He felt dizzy, and had to hold on to the window catch. He felt as if he were moving on dangerously thin ice at breakneck speed. The strip of light beyond the bay was quite even, narrow and still. When his eye fell on the beach jetty by the Regina Elena, he quickly shut the window. He wanted to believe that all those things happened a very long time ago.

Perlmann didn't immediately know how the next paragraph should begin, and started to panic. But then he read the last three pages and found his way back into his writing frenzy. After a while, when all the coffee had gone, his tongue felt furry. Annoyed at the interruption, he went to the bathroom and drank a glass of water. He was used to his pale, anxious face; he had seen it often enough over the last few days. But now he gave a start. His features were sunken and skewed. He thought of pictures of people who had been exposed to enhanced gravity. But that didn't matter now. What mattered were the sentences that had originated behind that face and were flowing into his right hand. It was a complete mystery how it was happening, and for one brief moment Perlmann experienced the fascination of the scholar confronted by a mysterious phenomenon, a fascination that he had lost. *Everything's going to fall back into place.* Even though he didn't have a headache, he took two aspirins from the pack on the mirror shelf and washed them down. Then he walked back to the desk with a glass of water.

Dawn began to break just before seven. Without the darkness of the night Perlmann felt vulnerable and lost his sense of equilibrium. His sentences started to go wrong. He had to cross some of them out, and eventually he reached the last sheet, which he crumpled and threw in the waste-paper basket. The mixture of lamplight and daylight enraged him. As he walked across to turn off the standard lamp, his ankle throbbed violently, and felt as if it could no longer support him. He couldn't quite manage without electric light, and turned the desk lamp back on. His memory began to fail. The simplest English words stopped coming to mind, and all of a sudden he was uncertain about his spelling, too.

A short break. He could lie down for a moment, until it was really light. Just for a few minutes. After that he still had an hour and a half to finish writing his lecture.

41

A wild honking of car horns on the coast road woke him with a start. Perlmann felt disoriented and immediately sank back into leaden weariness. His eyelids seemed paralyzed, and would only open after he had made an extreme effort of will to sit up on the edge of the bed. His head hurt at the slightest movement, and his veins seemed to be far too cramped for his violently pounding blood. The noise of traffic was unbearable. It was seven minutes to nine.

No time for showering and shaving, nor could he order any more coffee. He was relieved to establish that his tongue, although thick and stinging, was under his command again. He shovelled cold water into his face with both hands, evoking the memory of the gas station toilet in Recco. *No murder. No plagiarism.* He hurriedly bundled together the sheets of paper on the desk. There were at least twenty pages, he thought. The last half-page was crossed out. *I'll have to improvise at the end.*

The elevator was busy. Two minutes past nine. Perlmann gritted his teeth and hobbled downstairs. He had forgotten the printout of his notes, and when he went to check that he was at least carrying a pen, he saw that there were two big stripes of dirt running diagonally across his jacket. *The garbage bin by the fan.* He looked at his trousers: bloodstains everywhere. Arriving in the hall, through the glass front door he saw the sea glittering in the morning sun. At some point in the night, he remembered, he had thought he had finally found the present. An illusion, woven from relief, alcohol and pills. The present was further off than ever.

The door to the veranda was open. Perlmann felt no more twinges as he walked through the lounge towards it and took the three steps. The anxiety settled on him like a numbing veil. He wasn't quite in the room before he had seen that they were all there, even Silvestri and Angelini. And at the back, on the right, Leskov with his pipe in his mouth. Perlmann immediately looked away. He didn't want to be wounded by any of those faces. As he had been during the night. He wanted to stay completely closed away in himself, inaccessible to the others.

As always, there was coffee on the table, a special pot for the speaker. Perlmann sat down without a greeting, poured himself a coffee and concentrated on not shivering. The coffee was hot. One could only drink it slowly. He couldn't possibly drain the first cup with everyone staring at him. After taking three sips he set it down. He had planned to say some introductory words of explanation, about the distributed text and his relationship to what he was about to say. But he couldn't have said such words with his eyes lowered, and he couldn't now bring himself to meet the eyes of the others. Not before they had heard last night's text, which would rehabilitate him. He took another sip of coffee, lit a cigarette and began to read.

The introductory sentences were too long-winded. Perlmann noticed it immediately, became impatient and rattled them off hastily so that he could finally get to his first thesis, which, in its originality – he was quite sure of it – would immediately grab the attention of everyone present. He set aside the first page and was glad to see that there were only three lines to go before the crucial paragraph. When they were over with, he took two big swigs of coffee, looked up for a moment, and then plunged into his train of thought.

When he read them the words were so unutterably weak that the sentences literally stuck in his throat. It took a special effort – almost a retch – to read each of them to the end. It was pure kitsch, nothing but sentimental nonsense, cobbled together by someone at the end of his powers and also under the influence of alcohol and pills, so that all critical capacity, all self-censorship, had completely closed down. Perlmann wanted to sink into the floor, and when he went on reading, in a voice that grew quieter and quieter, he only did so because he didn't know how he would bear the silence that would fall if he stopped.

Leskov choked on his pipe smoke and had a coughing fit. His face bright red, he bent double, his coughing so loud that Perlmann's lecture was interrupted. Perlmann looked over at him, and in that moment a thought forced its way into his consciousness that had until then been suppressed by some power or other: *I would have killed him for no good reason whatsoever. It would have been a completely pointless murder. A murder based on an error.* Without his really noticing, the sheets slipped from his hand, his mouth half-opened, and his face went blank. He shivered. He heard the penetrating, high-pitched whistle, and saw the huge shovel of the bulldozer with its side prongs coming towards him. It turned quite silent, as if they were surrounded by cotton wool and snow. Perlmann took his ice-cold, sweat-drenched hands from the wheel. Then there was nothing but weakness and darkness. Perlmann's cigarette fell from his hand and, in a curiously retarded, flowing motion he slipped sideways to the floor.

It was a pleasant, effortless glide up through ever thinner, ever paler layers. At the end there came a faint, quiet start, the world stood quite still, and with a tiny hesitation that he only just noticed, before immediately forgetting it again, it became clear to Perlmann that the impressions forcing their way to him through his open eyes meant that he was awake.

He was lying under the covers in all his clothes except his jacket and shoes. In the red armchair by the open window sat Giorgio Silvestri. His back was turned towards Perlmann and he was reading the newspaper. Perlmann was glad that he was smoking. That made the situation less like a sick-bed visit. He would have liked to look at his watch. But Silvestri would have heard that, and he wanted to be on his own for a little while longer. He closed his eyes and tried to order his thoughts.

His unconsciousness had calmed him, and even if his tiredness slowed everything down, he still had the feeling of being able to think clearly. He could no longer remember the details of what had happened in the veranda. All he remembered was his horror at his embarrassing text, and then the coughing Leskov, who had slipped uninterruptedly into a maelstrom of images from the tunnel. *I have disgraced myself for ever. It couldn't have been more embarrassing. But now it's over. I didn't commit fraud and I didn't commit murder. And never again will I have to sit at the front in the veranda. Never again.*

Two men must have carried him upstairs. Perlmann was glad they hadn't undressed him. Who had it been apart from Silvestri? Apart from those two, had anyone else come into his room? The strong sleeping pills were in his jacket pocket. Had Silvestri found them? Had he seen that he was poisoned, and deliberately looked for them? Or had they perhaps fallen out when he was being carried upstairs?

Leskov's text. For God's sake, I hope they didn't find it here. Perlmann sat up involuntarily. Silvestri turned round, got to his feet and looked at him with a face that strangely combined a warm smile and a professional, medical expression.

'I came back at just the right time,' he said.

'How long was I unconscious for?' Perlmann asked.

Silvestri looked at his watch. 'Just a few minutes. Stay calm. There's no reason to worry.'

Perlmann sank back into the pillow. *A few minutes. That could be ten, or twenty. Enough at any rate to find the text. If they hear Leskov saying practically the same thing as in the text on Thursday, they will know that something's wrong, and put two and two together. It isn't over yet.*

'Was Leskov in here, too?' he asked hoarsely.

'Yes,' Silvestri said with a smile, 'he insisted on helping Brian Millar carry you. He started wheezing terribly. A nice guy.'

Then he saw his text here, and now he'll be thinking back to the tunnel. Perlmann started sweating and asked for a glass of water.

As he drank, Silvestri looked at him thoughtfully. He hesitated at behaving like a doctor, but then he took Perlmann's pulse. 'Has that happened to you many times before?'

'No,' Perlmann said, 'that was the first time.'

'Do you take sleeping pills?' Silvestri made the question sound innocuous, almost incidental.

Perlmann liked and knew straight away that he was being seen through.

After he had folded up the newspaper and lit a Gauloise, Silvestri leaned against the desk and said nothing for a while. Perlmann was about to tell him everything. Just so as not to be alone with his thoughts any more. To have peace at last.

'You know,' Silvestri said slowly, without a hint of an instructive or patronizing tone in his voice. 'You are in a state of profound exhaustion. Not quite dangerous yet. But you should be a bit careful. Take a rest. Get a lot of sleep. And go and see your doctor at home. He should give you a thorough examination, at any rate. If you need anything, just give me a call.' He walked to the door.

'Giorgio,' said Perlmann.

Silvestri turned round.

'I . . . I'm glad you were there. *Grazie.*'

'*Di niente,*' Silvestri smiled and reached for the door. Then he let go of the handle and came two steps back. 'By the way, I find a lot of the observations in your text very interesting. Particularly the things about the freezing of experience through language, and the point that sentences can both inspire and paralyze the imagination.' He grinned. 'Of course, the others expected something slightly different from you. But I wouldn't place too much importance on that. And, generally speaking, you shouldn't take all of this too seriously,' he said with a gesture that took in the whole hotel.

Perlmann nodded mutely.

When the door clicked shut, he threw back the covers and hobbled hastily over to his case. He saw with horror that the lock was set at the correct combination. No text in there now. The veins at his temples seemed about to burst with each pulse beat. He sat down on the edge of the bed, only to jump up again a moment later. *The phone book.* Pressing his hand to his head, he pulled open the desk drawer. There was no text under the phone book either. He knew there was no point, but he checked in the bedside table and the wardrobe as well. So they'd discovered it and taken it away as evidence. Leskov would identify the text. Attempted plagiarism. That was the only explanation for Perlmann so carefully keeping the existence of the text a secret. And seen in that light, what happened in the veranda also became comprehensible. They would go easy on him today. To some extent he was unfit to stand trial. But tomorrow they would call him to account.

Perlmann stubbed out his cigarette and was glad that the nausea subsided when he lay down. Now, he couldn't present the text as a welcome gift. He had learned of Leskov's arrival less than three days before. And why hadn't he given him the present ages ago? He had thought the text was so good that he had planned to send the finished translation to St Petersburg and suggest publication in a relevant journal. Then, when he learned that he was coming, he had prepared the text as a surprise. He planned to hand it to him tonight at dinner. *That's OK. That doesn't sound incredible. At any rate, they can't refute it.* The thumping in his head subsided. *It's over. One or other of them may be left with a feeling of suspicion. Nothing more can happen. It's over.* He turned onto his stomach and let his face sink deep into the pillow.

But the text was no longer here. I threw it away during the night. Perlmann sat up and wrapped his arms around his knees. The big garbage bin under the fan had been empty apart from potato peelings. And the open lid had covered the fan. He conjured up as many details of the situation as possible, to assure himself that these were really memories, and not a trick being played on him by his imagination. He heard once again the dull thud when the stack of paper had landed, and smelled again the kitchen fumes that had passed through the fan. It was an effort to call all that to mind, because it was swathed in fine mist that wouldn't be dissolved even by the utmost effort of concentration, as if it were not merely a veil of the remembered objects, but belonged to their essence. And the images were erratic and hard to hold on to; it was as if the remembered perceptions last night had not really had the opportunity to bury themselves into his brain. Nonetheless, Perlmann's certainty grew that they were real memories. The imagination would not provide images that were so dense and coherent, in spite of the mist. Yesterday evening – he remembered that, too, now – getting rid of the text had struck him as the epitome of senselessness. Now he was glad of this attack of unreason. Loads of refuse, huge great loads of it, had fallen on the dangerous text in the meantime, and buried it.

When he came out of the bathroom wearing his pyjamas, his eye fell on his light-colored jacket, which they had hung on the back of a chair. It wasn't only the two strips of dirt above the chest; both sleeves were dirty on the outside, too, just under the elbow. He had propped himself up on the garbage bin. And the hotel folder was missing. Now it was clear once and for all. There was nothing left – nothing – that could still betray him.

At the back of the desk, with one corner under the foot of the lamp, lay a stack of paper. It was the text that he had written in the night. *The trashy text.* That was where they had put it. In whose hand had it been carried up? Silvestri's? Millar's? His handwriting on the pages was bigger than usual, the lines jauntier, more expansive. On the last few pages much of the writing was unreadable. Perlmann tore each sheet in two several times and let the bits fall into the waste-paper basket.

Then he lay down in bed. He would have liked to sleep for a year. Silvestri hadn't found his notes outrageous. Perlmann saw Silvestri's smile in his mind's eye when he had spoken of the expectation of the others. That mocking detachment, which needed no spite – Perlmann had never envied anyone anything so fiercely. He tried to imagine his way entirely into that smile – to be someone who could smile about the matter like this. As he did so he slipped, for the first time in days, into a deep, dreamless sleep.

42

It was just before three when the phone woke him. As if he had never experienced such a sensation before, he flinched from the ringing as from a physical assault. *But I don't need to hide myself away any more. It's all over.* He picked up the phone and heard Leskov's voice, far too loud. Could he visit him? Only, of course, if it didn't disturb him. Perlmann's head started thumping. His face, still hot with sleep, was filled with a dry, stinging sensation, as if he had been hiking for hours in cold winter air.

'Are you still there?' asked Leskov.

Perlmann said he would be glad of a visit. He didn't know what else he could have said.

The sky was overcast, and a light rain fell from the pale grey. *The second version. The rain falling on the yellow pages.* The journey via Recco and Uscio would take an hour at the most. If he got rid of Leskov quickly, he could be there in time to pick up the pages in daylight. He took the car key out of the pocket of his blazer, and put on his soiled jacket. That way it would be obvious that he was about to leave.

As soon as Leskov had slumped into the red armchair, he took his pipe from his pocket and asked if he could smoke.

'Yes, of course,' said Perlmann. He shouldn't have needed to say it. *I'd rather you didn't,* he could have said instead. From the mouth of someone in need of care that would have been enough. A few short words. He hadn't said them. He hadn't managed to. Now he smelled the sickly sweet tobacco. It would linger everywhere. He would have to smell it for days. He hated this Russian.

He had given them a real fright there, Leskov said. Of course, he hadn't been able to stop thinking of his nausea on the journey and the excitement in the tunnel. The others didn't know anything about it, incidentally. Last night he'd just said something vague about him not being very well, to explain why Perlmann wasn't there at dinner. The details, he said with a smile, were no one's business but his, were they?

The intimacy that Leskov was forcing on him with that remark could not be the intimacy of blackmail, Perlmann knew that, even though his certainty still felt very fresh and slightly unsteady. Nonetheless, it was an unbearable intimacy, and it made Perlmann so furious that he suddenly didn't care that the rain seemed to be getting heavier.

'By the way,' Leskov said, 'I was told about the reception at the town hall.' He smiled. 'So that was your medal and your certificate on the back seat. And now I understand the tie that was lying around as if you'd furiously thrown it into the back. The whole thing must have been incredibly awkward and distasteful to you! We were doubled up with laughter at lunchtime when Achim described the whole scene.'

Leskov was enthusiastic about Perlmann's text. He had stayed up for a long time last night to read it all the way through. He hadn't understood absolutely everything; there were a number of English words and phrases that he didn't know. But both the subjects and the way of addressing them – it had all been surprisingly close to his own work. It was really a shame that Perlmann had found the Russian text too hard. Otherwise he would have recognized how close it was straight away. But he must have understood the title?

Perlmann nodded.

'We should write a text together one day!' said Leskov and touched his knee.

At any rate, Perlmann's text had given Leskov the courage to talk about his own things here. He'd had the jitters a bit. In such illustrious company. He thought it was great that you could be so open here, and there didn't seem to be any kind of academic straitjacket. If only that terrible slip with his text hadn't happened. He hurriedly exhaled great clouds of smoke, which condensed more and more in the room into a solid blanket of blue haze that cleaved the whole room at head height.

'Oh, of course, you couldn't know anything about that,' he interrupted himself and gesticulated animatedly. 'I told you about the second version of my text, and how I nearly left it at home because of that annoying phone call.' Leskov waited until Perlmann nodded. 'And now it seems that that's exactly what happened. Last night, in fact, when I'm coming back from dinner, I reach into the outside pocket of the suitcase, where the text should have been. But there's nothing there. Nothing at all. Empty.' Leskov pressed his fists against his temples. 'It's a complete mystery to me. I could swear that I put it in there at the last moment. It was the open outside pocket that reminded me of it.'

Perlmann opened the window, leaned out and looked to the northwest. It was lighter in that direction. Maybe it had stayed dry up there.

'Does the smoke really not bother you?' Leskov asked.

'Not at all,' Perlmann replied into the rain and glanced furtively at his watch. Twenty-five to four.

He had spent half the night puzzling about it, Leskov went on. And from time to time he had had the feeling that his memory of packing the text had really only been a delusion, whose vividness simply expressed the strong desire to have done so.

'It's very unpleasant,' he said, 'and not only because of the text. It gives me the feeling of no longer being able to rely on myself. Have you ever known anything like that?'

Yes, said Perlmann, awkwardly lighting a cigarette, he did know that feeling.

He was used to reading something whenever he had to wait around, Leskov said thoughtfully. So he had now been wondering whether he might have taken the text out on the journey and left it somewhere. Not in St Petersburg. It had been too hectic for that at the airport. And not on the flight to Moscow, either, where an inebriated war veteran in the next seat had constantly bothered him. At Larissa and Boris's he had been monopolized by the children the whole time. At the airport in Moscow, perhaps. Or on the plane. Or in Frankfurt, when he'd been waiting for his connecting flight. It was crazy: because there wasn't a trace of a memory of such an action. He would now have to think of himself as if he were a stranger, from outside, so to speak. And Leskov ardently hoped that he was wrong. Admittedly, his address was written at the end of the text, he did that quite automatically, even with a manuscript. But he didn't think anyone would take the trouble. Certainly not at Moscow Airport. And in Frankfurt no one would be able to read it. Perhaps Lufthansa would do something if the text were found on the plane. On the other hand: a cleaning crew would simply throw a pile of unreadable pages out with the rest of the rubbish. 'Or what do you think?'

'I . . . I don't know,' Perlmann said tonelessly.

Leskov paused and looked straight ahead with his eyes slightly narrowed. Perlmann knew what was coming next. There was one more small thing, he went on, that he barely dared to mention, however ludicrous it might seem: a little bit of rubber band had got stuck in the zip of the outside pocket. He couldn't get that out of his head, because it could mean that he had taken the text out and broken the rubber band with which it was held together. He tapped his forehead with his knuckles. 'If I only had some kind of memory!' After a while he opened his eyes and looked at Perlmann, who was staring at the floor. 'I'm sorry for bothering you with this. In your condition. But you know how much this text matters to me. I've already tried to phone friends at home to look in my apartment. But I can't get through.' He set his pipe down on the round table and hid his face in his hands. 'I hope to God it's there. Otherwise . . . I can't bring myself to think about it.'

The rain had stopped. Perlmann went to the bathroom and leaned his back against the basin. He was shaking, and his head threatened to explode. *I've got to collect the pages. At all costs.* Five past four. If Leskov went soon, he could still do it. *You can even make out these pages in the gloom.* He flushed the toilet. Then he clenched his fists to keep from shaking and went back into the room.

Leskov was standing up. He would have to do some work. There wasn't much time until his session on Thursday.

'The text is probably just at home. There isn't really any other possibility. Otherwise I'd have some kind of memory. Some kind.'

Perlmann couldn't stand his questioning stare for long, and walked ahead of him to the door. Before he went out, Leskov stopped just in front of him. Perlmann smelled his tobacco breath.

'Do you think a translator might be found for my text?' he asked. 'I'd love you and the others to be able to read it. Especially since I now know your text. Payment would be a problem, I know that.'

'I'll think about it,' said Perlmann. It took him an enormous effort to close the door quietly.

A little while later Perlmann left the room and, after some hesitation, set off through the hall. There he was intercepted by Maria, who came sniffing out of her office, holding a handkerchief. Was he feeling better? She had heard from Signora Morelli that he had been surprised to find that the text she had finished on Friday had been distributed.

'Please forgive me if I've done something wrong. But when you told me on the phone on Friday that it was urgent, I automatically assumed it was the text for your session, which is why I attached the copying instruction to it. And I think I even added your name.'

The people from Fiat?

'Oh, them,' she laughed, and had to blow her nose. 'I didn't have a sense that they got a lot of work done. And when I said something about a research group and an important text, Santini immediately waved it through. He's very patient. He's often been with people here.' She rubbed her reddened eyes. 'They'd said Saturday afternoon would be fine. But then I got the feeling this cold was on the way, and I finished typing the thing on Friday so that I could spend Saturday in bed. Oh, one moment,' she said, gestured to him to wait and disappeared into the office.

If she hadn't had a cold, the pigeonholes would have been empty on Saturday morning, and I would have noticed Giovanni's omission. But if he hadn't made his mistake, her cold would have saved me.

'Here,' Maria said, and handed him the black wax-cloth notebook. 'I like typing your things up. They're not as technical as the others, and not as dry. That was true of the other text, the one about memory. And this one here has such an original title. I like it. So are you sure nothing's gone wrong as far as you're concerned? Should I perhaps have had the other text printed out and copied again?'

'No, no,' Perlmann said, and had to fight down the haste in his voice. 'You did exactly the right thing. *Mille grazie.*'

In daylight, the damage to the Lancia looked very bad. The dark-blue paint was ripped open in several places all along the car. The scrapes went deep into the metal, and the wing had been powerfully crushed next to the headlight on the right-hand side. Perlmann took the tie, medal and certificate from the back seat and put them along with the black notebook in the empty suitcase. Then he set off.

He hadn't even reached the big jetty when it was clear to him that he wouldn't manage to do it now. He was shivering with weakness, and his reactions were grotesquely delayed, as if his brain were working in slow motion. Under the stare of a policeman he stopped in a no-parking zone and wiped the sweat from his cold hands.

Just as he was about to turn and drive back, his eye fell on the Hotel Imperiale on the hill. There was something about it. Again his brain made an eerily long pause. *The waiter. I didn't wait for him. And I didn't pay. That means bilking on top of everything else.* Compared to everything else this was so preposterous that Perlmann pulled his face into a grin. Very slowly he drove up to the hotel and waited for several minutes outside the gate until even the most distant oncoming traffic had passed.

It was the same waiter. He assessed Perlmann with a dismissive glance. The pale, unshaven face. The soiled jacket. The blood-stained trousers. The unpolished shoes.

'I forgot to pay yesterday,' Perlmann said and took a handful of cash from his pocket.

'We aren't used to guests like that here,' the waiter said stiffly.

'And it isn't a habit of mine,' Perlmann said with a weary smile. 'I think it was a sandwich, a whisky and a mineral water.'

'*Two* waters,' the waiter said abruptly.

'I'm sorry. Yesterday I was a bit . . . a bit under the weather.'

'I can see that. And I'd also say that we could do without a second visit from you,' the waiter said and simply stuffed the three 10,000 lire notes in the pocket of his red jacket.

The two things – being barred and that movement – assembled themselves in Perlmann's feelings into something strangely liberating. He looked the waiter in the eyes with undisguised contempt. 'Do you know what you are? *Uno stronzo.*' And because he wasn't sure whether the insult was strong enough, he added his own translation, 'An asshole. A great big asshole.' The waiter's face colored. '*Stronzo*,' Perlmann said again and went outside.

On the way back he felt more confident and, all of a sudden, he felt properly hungry – a sensation that he had almost forgotten over the past few days. At a stand-up bar he ate several slices of pizza. The five o'clock news was just coming to an end on the television behind the bar, and a weather map appeared. Perlmann stared at the clouds to the east of Genoa. They were white, not grey. But then the clouds on maps like that always were. Weren't they?

'Do you know the road from Genoa via Lumarzo to Chiávari?' he asked the man in the vest who was taking the pizza out of the oven with a long shovel.

'Of course,' said the man, without interrupting what he was doing.

'Do you think it's going to rain there tonight? Up by the tunnel, I mean.'

The man paused abruptly, left the shovel half inside the oven and turned round.

'Are you kidding?'

'No, no,' Perlmann said quickly, 'I really need to know. It's very important.'

The man in the vest took a drag on his cigarette and looked at him as if he were someone very simple, perhaps even disturbed.

'How on earth am I supposed to know that?' he said mildly.

'Yes,' Perlmann said quietly and left far too big a tip.

*

'That conversation last night,' Perlmann said to Signora Morelli when she set Frau Hartwig's yellow envelope and another little one for him on the reception counter, 'I . . .'

She folded her hands and looked at him. He wasn't sure, but he thought he saw a tiny twitch in the corner of her mouth.

'What conversation?'

Perlmann gulped and shifted the two envelopes until they were exactly parallel at the edge of the counter. '*Grazie*,' he said quietly and looked at her.

She gave only the hint of a nod.

The room smelled of Leskov's sickly tobacco. The haze had escaped, but the open window hadn't been able to do anything about the penetrating smell. Except it was cold now. Perlmann tipped a mountain of pipe ash and charred tobacco into the toilet and shut the window.

Frau Hartwig's envelope contained two letters. One was his invitation to Princeton, written on expensive paper that looked like parchment, and signed by the President. The invitation had been issued because of his *outstanding academic achievements*, it said. And the President assured him that it would be *a great honor* to have him as a guest for a while. Perlmann didn't read the letter twice, but immediately put it back in the envelope and threw it in the suitcase.

The other was an invitation to give a guest lecture. He was to open a series of lectures, and it was very important to the organizer that Perlmann should be the first speaker. The letter talked about works that he had finished three years ago, but which had only appeared in print at the beginning of the year. Back then, he thought, everything had still seemed all right. Except that he had been getting increasingly bored with his things. And every now and again he had woken up in the middle of the night and hadn't known where to go from here. He hadn't had long conversations with himself when that had happened; few thoughts came to him on such occasions. He listened to music, and he usually stood at the big window as he did so. Then Agnes was surprised to find him at his desk so early.

In the other envelope there was a note from Angelini. Unfortunately, he had to go back to Ivrea that afternoon. He wished Perlmann a speedy recovery, and hoped it was nothing serious. He would try to come to the last dinner on Friday, although he couldn't yet promise anything. At the end was his private telephone number.

The words were friendly, if conventional. Perlmann read them several times. He thought back to their first meeting and the enthusiastic phone calls that had followed. You couldn't say that these words gave off a sense of disappointment. Not at all. And not detachment or coldness. But he sensed them. He, Philipp Perlmann, had revealed himself to be a bad investment.

He turned on the six o'clock news. But on that channel they only had a schematic weather map that was no use to him. No big change to be expected tomorrow. A little while before, the roads had been almost dry again. He walked over to the window. There was no point now in staring up into the starless night sky.

He took a long shower and then lay down in bed. The pillow smelled of Leskov's tobacco. He fetched another one from the wardrobe. The sheets and the wool blanket smelled too. He pulled off the sheet and covered himself with replacement blankets from the wardrobe. The heating intensified the smell. He turned it off and opened the window. His body was vibrating with exhaustion, but sleep wouldn't come. He didn't take any pills. On the seven o'clock news the clouds around Genoa looked denser than they had done two hours before. Outside it was still dry. He was shivering, and fetched the last blanket from the wardrobe. It was too noisy on the coast road, and he closed the window. If he set off at half-past five, he would be there by first light. He set his alarm for five. He went to sleep at about eight.

He saw no bulldozer, no tunnel walls. In fact, he saw nothing at all. No seeing took place. It was simply the case that he hadn't the strength to take his hands off the wheel. He held it tightly and turned it to the left, further and further to the left. It could be that he was the one who turned it. Or else it was something inside him, a force, a will, but it was alien to him and not really his. And perhaps the wheel had gained its autonomy, and was guiding his hand against his will. He no longer knew what was going on; the impressions piled up on top of each other and he didn't know what – of all of it – he was most afraid of. He was completely paralyzed by fear, and he had the feeling of losing control of his bodily functions, particularly his abdomen. That took half an eternity, in which he expected a collision at every moment, and then he woke up with a twitch of his whole body that had something terrible about it, something uncanny, because it too completely escaped his control; it was an animal, a biological twitch that seemed to come from a very deep region of his brain.

Perlmann leapt up and examined the mattress. It was clean. Then he sat down on the edge of the bed and smoked. From time to time he felt the physical echo of a turn to the left. Later he took off his wet pyjamas and went into the shower. It was just after midnight. The coast road was wet. But now it wasn't raining any more.

Over the next few hours he kept waking from the same dream at brief intervals, before dozing off again. This time it wasn't a nightmare, but a bothersome and ridiculous combination of things that were completely unconnected as far as the dreamer was concerned. There was the name *Pian dei Ratti*, which returned with such frequency that it was like a constant background noise, an incessant echo that filled every last corner. And the name smelled. It was enveloped in a smell of sickly tobacco and mist; it was as if that smell stuck to the name, so that without the smell the name had no meaning whatsoever. The fact that the name was always there, ringing out, made one shiver and, sniffing, look for coins, which kept slipping with a painful rub through your fingers. Your shoes tipped over, and women laughed. Then everything was full of yellow sheets, and there was no point making yourself very small in the trunk.

Perlmann changed the bandage on his finger. The inflammation was beginning to ease. Every time he woke up he opened the widow. Only a few drops were falling outside. The dream had the dependability and monotony of a record that always sticks at the same place. At half-past four he showered, shaved and dressed.

'*Buon giorno*,' said Giovanni, rubbing his eyes and looking at his watch.

Perlmann turned round again in the doorway. 'That equalizer that led to the penalty shoot-out. Who scored it?'

Giovanni was almost struck dumb. 'Baggio,' he said at last, with a grin.

'From which club?'

Giovanni looked at him as if he had asked him what country Rome was the capital of.

'Juve. Juventus Turin.'

'*Grazie*,' said Perlmann. He felt Giovanni's startled eyes watching after him.

He had become a weirdo.

43

The coast road was so quiet and deserted that Perlmann instantly forgot the three or four cars that came towards him, in their brief, eerie presence. Rapallo was a night-time silhouette with motionless lights that called to mind paper cuts and engravings. The flashing traffic lights in the dead streets of Recco gave him the feeling of driving through a ghost town, and the two old men who were creeping along close to the houses further intensified that impression. Lots of lights were on already in the farmhouses along the road to Uscio. The crowing of the omnipresent cocks drowned out the quiet sound of the engine. Perlmann tried not to think back to Monday. The main thing was that it plainly hadn't rained here in the past few hours. Past Lumarzo, however, the gear stick was suddenly damp with sweat, and he had to swallow more and more often. On the climb towards the tunnel he drove with his arms outstretched on the wheel, and decided not to look and to think about nothing.

He braked. Over on the light-grey crash barrier: dark strips. He put his foot down – only to put the car out of gear again straight away. *Here, exactly here is where I took my hands off the wheel.* He sat up. There was nothing to see. It was idiotic. He furiously screeched his tires and then stepped hard on the brake as if to prevent a pile-up in the empty tunnel.

Most of the pale mud had been covered up with a tarpaulin, which had been weighed down with bricks. By the wall there stood an empty wheelbarrow, with an untidily rolled-up rope underneath it. He had never worked out what happened at this passing-place, and this latest change made no sense to him at all. He knew it was nonsense, bordering on paranoia, but he couldn't shake off the impression that he – he in particular, he alone – was being played for a fool – that someone was constantly rearranging things at this spot, with the sole intention of confusing him, goading his useless thoughts and stoking his apprehension. He bit his lips and drove out of the tunnel. The toothless old woman's shop was in darkness, and looked like a discarded dream backdrop. It was a quarter past six, and still the darkest night.

It could only be two kilometers, or three at the most. Only a few bends. But it wasn't behind this one, or the next. Seen from this direction everything looked very different. Suddenly, so quickly that he couldn't believe it, he was at the gas station where he had made the first attempt to *disappear* Leskov's text. Yes, that was the word. He stopped outside the dark cottage and tried to imagine what had happened afterwards. His memory was sluggish; nothing came back of its own accord. It was hot and stuffy in the car. He had been driving the whole time with the heating turned up full. But the air from outside made him cold, and he whirred the window back up. The skin of his face tensed and felt like paper.

What was he actually doing here? In the end he would be holding a pile of dirty, ragged pages in his hand. Then what? What in the world would he tell Leskov when he handed him the papers? It would, that was clear, have to be the story of an oversight, an ineptitude, an unintended stupidity. And the story would also have to explain why he had discovered his stupidity only today, of all days. Perlmann felt his head emptying, and felt that emptiness filling with a paralysing weariness. With the best will in the world, even calling on the furthest reaches of his wildest imaginings, he couldn't possibly explain how the text had made it out of the closed suitcase and the closed trunk into the mud, without anyone having had a deliberate hand in it.

A first shimmer of diffuse, grey light lit up the solid cloud cover. A car passed now every few minutes. If he simply kept on driving to Genoa, he would be at the airport just before eight, and soon after that the Avis counter would open up. *But I can't just let the sheets of paper lie here and rot. That's out of the question. He has to get his text back. Somehow.*

Perlmann set off slowly, even more slowly than on Monday. It was up there on the bend that the truck with the full-beam headlights had appeared, the one he had allowed to pass him. And, sure enough, the first pale sheet lay there in the roadside ditch. The sight of it electrified him and all of a sudden he was wide awake. Hurriedly, as if the paper might escape his clutches at the last minute, he got out and bent down. It was a piece of half-transparent, crumpled grease-proof paper. He couldn't halt his hand, he had to touch it. Now he had mayonnaise on his fingers. Disgusted, he rubbed them on his trousers and got back into the car.

It couldn't have been the next bend; there was no paper to be seen far and wide. It was the next but one. Perlmann could see all the pale sheets in the ditch from far away, and accelerated as if on a home straight. He came to a standstill with both wheels in the ditch, climbed out of his crookedly parked car and ran breathlessly over. The pages were often far apart, but in two places several had fallen on top of each other and formed irregular little piles. Perlmann laid them on the hood. The sun must have been shining here yesterday, the two top sheets were both dry. The pale yellow had faded almost completely, the sheets were curling, and it looked as if they had blisters. Then came a few that were still damp, and under those several that hadn't been touched by rain at all, at least in the middle. Only at the edges were they all wet and grey with dirt. The ink on the top sheets had run. The first two were hard to read, but it got better after that.

So far there were seventeen sheets, including page 77. Now it was the turn of the individual, widely scattered sheets in the ditch. When Perlmann was bending down for the first one, a car drove past and its wake blew three pages down from the hood. He hurried back and gathered them up. One page had fallen under the wheels and been ripped. Annoyed, he laid the whole pile on the mat in front of the passenger seat. Half of them were completely smudged, but Leskov would still be able to reconstitute the text. The others, which had been lying face down, were in a better condition. There, too, the round letters of Leskov's careful handwriting had often dissolved at the edges, and flowed outwards.

At those points the background was no longer yellow, but a washed-out pale blue shimmering into green. But the text was still legible. The sheets that had lain among the trees had been dried by the sun and had warped; the others had softened and were unpleasant to the touch.

After that, Perlmann often had to climb the steep embankment to fetch the next sheet. Many were sticky with mud, some were crumpled and torn. At one point he slipped on the damp soil, the pain from his ankle shot through him like knives and he nearly fell. At the very last moment he was able to cling to a tuft of grass. Now he had earth under his fingernails. From here he managed to gather fourteen pages together, including page 79, which had a space at the bottom, but which still couldn't be the last, as there was no address on it. So at least twenty-five pages were still missing. He leaned, exhausted, against the hood and smoked.

By now it was twenty to eight and broad daylight. The traffic was building up, and now the last truck was coming towards him. Its bumper was far too narrow, its gas tank unprotected. When it had passed, Perlmann, who was standing in the middle of a black cloud of smoke, became aware – to his amazement and relief – that his heart wasn't pounding. Only his cigarette had fallen into the road without his noticing. It was, he thought, as if a first thin dividing wall had formed between him and the trucks; a first protecting distance which would get bigger and bigger over time until one day he would also be able to forget the red mist. *As long as Leskov has his text back.*

Astonishingly, large numbers of sheets had been blown on to the embankment that sloped downwards on the other side of the road. The ground there was soft and damp, and at one point Perlmann sank beyond the edge of his shoes into the quagmire. The sheets had been resting on the tips of the grass, and weren't very dirty. With two exceptions, they had been lying writing-side down, and were still legible. Now he had rescued a total of sixty-seven pages. He looked around a wider area, methodically, patch by patch, the whole thing three times. The rising sun pierced the cloud cover and Perlmann looked up, blinking. There were sheets in the tops of two tall bushes, one in each. It took a desperately long time before they finally came floating down, and with his furious shaking he must have presented a comical sight, because the school bus drove unusually slowly, and the children laughed and pointed at him.

One sheet was the first page with the title. There was no name underneath. It was creased and had a hole in it from a branch, but reading it wasn't a problem. At least eight pages were missing now. Perlmann looked at the wheels of the passing cars and imagined the sheets getting stuck to tires like those and then being pressed rhythmically between rubber and tarmac, before ending up lying in rags somewhere.

When the road was empty for a little while, his eye fell on a brown rectangle, which hid part of the white marking in the middle of the road. It was a page of Leskov's text, drenched with rain and dirt and driven over countless times. He lifted it by one corner, but the paper was fragile and tore immediately. A bottom layer. Puzzled, he opened the glove compartment and saw the map that Signora Morelli had lent him on Saturday night. He half-unfolded it and pushed it carefully, centimeter by centimeter, under the soggy sheet. On the lid of the trunk he started carefully dabbing the page down with his handkerchief as if it were an archaeological find.

It was page 58. In the middle, Leskov had written a subheading. All that could still be made out was that it had consisted of two quite long words, preceded by the number 4. But the ink had run almost completely; it had mixed with the dirt, and all that remained was a smear. Perlmann wiped the words again with another tip of his handkerchief. Perhaps something of the old ink traces that had been put on paper in St Petersburg would be revealed if one dabbed away the diluted and running ink that now lay over it. And some clues did become visible. But they weren't enough to make out an unambiguous sequence of words. He lit a cigarette. The last word, he was more and more certain of it, must be *proshloe: the past*. But he could imagine at least three variants: *iskazhennoe proshloe: the distorted past; pridiumannoe proshloe: the invented past; obmanchivoe proshloe: the deceptive past*. And even a fourth: *zastyvshee proshloe: the coagulated past*. That he knew *zastyvat', to coagulate*, he owed to a viewer of Agnes's photographs, who had dared to compare her particular way of capturing the living present in images with the process of coagulation. Her fury had been boundless, because *coagulation* was her name for the process in which people rigidified into lifeless figures because of their conventions. And to keep from suffocating on her fury, afterwards she had done something that was usually Perlmann's own habit: she had looked up the word in every available dictionary.

Smoking hastily, Perlmann repeatedly compared the words he tried out with the thin traces of ink. But the vague lines simply made any decision impossible. He measured his conjectures against what he had of Leskov's thoughts in his head, and against the vocabulary that he had appropriated from Leskov's text. But even that didn't yield complete clarity. The intervention of language in the events of memory could, according to the first version, be characterized in all four ways. And besides, the text that he knew was not a reliable standard, since Leskov, as he had said, had thoroughly reworked it for the second version.

What was it that he had said about the new version on the drive on Monday? In the middle of traffic that was now becoming increasingly dense, and in which the trucks were beginning to accumulate, Perlmann tried to call Leskov's words to mind. He had perceived them, he remembered that. And something had passed through his head as he did so. He closed his eyes. On his face he felt the heat of exhaust fumes. A truck's gears clashed. He saw the beam from its left headlight in front of him, with nothing matching it on the right. Otherwise, he had no memory. And for a short and terrible moment he had the impression that he no longer knew how it was done: remembering. Then he put the card with the sheet on the rest of the pile and got in the car.

He would have liked to arrange the sheets to see how big the gaps were between the missing pages – whether they were all gaps of one or two pages, which it would be relatively easy for Leskov to fill, or whether there were bigger breaks in the text that would take him weeks, because a whole train of thought would have to be reworked. But in the state in which the pages were, that could not be accomplished without further damage.

He was sure that 79 was the highest page number he had read. It was the first thing he had paid attention to, and the page lay separately beside the pile. He picked it up and laboriously translated the last line that Leskov had squashed in tiny letters between two crossed-out lines: *But that would be a false conclusion. Instead one must . . .*

It wasn't inconceivable that the text finished on the next page, which meant that there were only ten pages missing. Naming the correct conclusion could be the rhetorical culmination and climax of the work as a whole, and that could easily be done on a single page. But of course, it was equally possible that Leskov had taken a breath here, and introduced a new thought that it would take five or ten or even more pages to develop.

A great many tires had driven over the bottom-most papers. It hadn't rained on Monday. Even so, the dirt from tires and the road had acted as glue, with the result that a whole pack of pages had been stuck to a tire all at the same time. Not twenty – some of the ones at the bottom would have come away, and he would have had to find those now. Ten? Five? Three? Perlmann turned and drove to Genoa, slowly and with both hands firmly clutching the wheel.

44

In the first big department store he went into the stationery department and demanded 320 sheets of blotting paper. The salesgirl incredulously repeated the number before she went to the store room. Perlmann put the four packs in the car and then walked helplessly, hesitantly, along the street. He imagined a bright library, empty and silent, with long tables on which he could peacefully clean each individual sheet of Leskov's text and lay it between two sheets of blotting paper. He aimlessly crossed the road and turned down a quieter side street. From the end of it came the break-time cries from a school. Ten o'clock. He stopped for a moment and rocked on his heels. Then he walked on, avoided the scuffling children in the playground and stepped inside the schoolhouse.

A woman came towards him in the corridor, dressed in white like a doctor. Did she by any chance have a classroom for him? Perlmann asked. Or another room with long tables. Just for about half an hour. He had to dry some important papers. 'I . . . I know it's an unusual request,' he added when he saw her lower lip beginning to jut.

She took off her glasses and rubbed her eyes, as if to dispel a hallucination. Then she studied him from top to bottom, from his bleary-eyed face to his shoes, which were completely covered with mud.

'What do you think this place is?' she asked coldly. 'A Salvation Army hostel?' With that she left him standing there and closed an office door behind her.

In the next alley but one he passed a little carpenter's workshop. In the middle of the room there were two long, empty tables. A man in an armchair was reading the newspaper. Perlmann braced himself for a fresh rebuff and went down the two steps. Could he use the two tables for a few minutes to . . . arrange some important papers? He would also pay to . . . rent the tables, so to speak, he added, when the man's face darkened.

'*Chiuso*,' the man said gruffly and held his newspaper up in front of his face.

The lunatic with the important, wet papers. *The madman of Genoa with the thousand sheets of blotting paper.* Perlmann went and stood in the hallway of a building and waited until the rain shower had passed.

He could send Leskov the text anonymously in St Petersburg. Frau Hartwig had the address in the office. But how would the unknown sender know the address, when the last page was missing? That didn't work. He would bring suspicion on himself. He could neither give him nor send him the text. So what was he doing here with hundreds of sheets of blotting paper? *The madman with the blotting paper.*

In a side street not far from the car he came upon a bar with wide shelves along the walls. After ordering a coffee and a sandwich, he asked if they would mind if he spread some papers out on the shelf for a moment.

'As long as you don't drive my customers away,' was the reply.

'*Mamma mia*,' said the proprietor when he saw Perlmann coming back with the stack of papers, hanging down at the sides, and two packs of blotting paper.

Perlmann started very carefully separating each sheet from the pile and laying it between two sheets of blotting paper. Now he would need one more sheet of paper to note something down, he said to the proprietor.

'Anything else?' the landlord replied wryly, and handed him an order pad exactly like the one in the harbor bar on Friday. 'Would sir like a pen with that?'

Perlmann grinned and took his own pen from his jacket. He noted down the page numbers and made corresponding piles. The blotting paper turned blue and brown. The proprietor came out from behind the bar and glanced curiously at the yellow papers.

'What language is that?'

'Russian,' said Perlmann.

'So you can speak Russian?'

'No,' Perlmann replied.

'Now I don't understand anything any more,' said the proprietor. 'And all the dirt on the pages! *Mamma mia!*'

The madman with the dirty Russian text that he can't read.

Among the page numbers in the thirties there was a gap of three pages, and towards the end two pages in a row were missing. Otherwise, there were gaps of only one page. On page 3 came the first subheading: *1. Vspomishchesya stseny: Remembered scenes.* Subheadings 2 and 3 must be on the missing sheets. And probably towards the end there was also a section called *Appropriation* or something like it.

It could have been much worse, thought Perlmann as he laid the packed pages on top of one another. As long as a lengthy and crucial piece wasn't missing at the end, Leskov would manage.

'*Mamma mia!*' cried the proprietor, throwing his hands in the air with ironic staginess, when Perlmann now asked him for a piece of twine. He watched him carefully tying the whole thing up. 'So what are you going to do with it now?'

'No idea,' said Perlmann and ate his bread.

'*Buona fortuna!*' the proprietor called after him, and it sounded as if he was releasing some hopelessly confused and extremely vulnerable person into the harsh world outside.

Perlmann put the bound package in the trunk along with the rest of the blotting paper. Then he drove to the airport. The man with the red cap stood next to his cabin and smoked. Perlmann didn't know why, but this man – the sight of whom made him feel suddenly hot – reminded him that there was something else he had wanted to do, a secret thing. He turned and drove a little way back until he was behind a hedge. Exhaustion blocked his memory. Only when he glanced at the bandage on his finger did it come back to him. He took the screwdriver and the wrench out of the trunk. Then he looked quickly around and inserted the screwdriver at the exact spot where the two coins touched. With the third powerful blow, the black box creaked, and the coins fell on to the rest of the money. The belt scraped a little, but otherwise it ran impeccably. As he closed the door he noticed the paint that had come off the bottom corner. That hadn't been from the crash barriers in the tunnel. It must have happened when Leskov had heaved himself out of the car at the gas station, and the door had bumped against the concrete plinth with the air-pressure metre. *When he nearly caught me.*

Perlmann took the suitcase off the back seat, locked the car and glanced again at the driver's seat. The bloodstains on the pale leather looked almost black.

'We've been waiting for this car for almost two days, Signore,' said the lady from Avis. She recognized him now, and her tone turned frosty. 'Why didn't you contact us? We have our job to do, too.'

Perlmann hadn't given his rental period a thought until that moment. He was startled to notice that he was grateful for the reproach. Being reminded of a contract meant being fetched back into the normal world, into normal life, in which things resumed their regular course. It was as if he were being granted permission to leave the private time of his nightmare with its frantic lack of present, and return to public time, which flowed at its normal pace.

'I couldn't do anything about it,' he said and attempted a smile. 'I'm sorry, but I really couldn't do anything about it.'

'Any accidents?' the woman asked in an unforgiving tone and straightened her fashionable glasses.

Perlmann took a deep breath. 'Yes,' he said, 'I was forced off the road and drove into a crash barrier. The right side of the car is damaged.'

'Were the police called?'

'No,' he said, and quickly cut off her next question, 'the other car had disappeared even before I stopped.'

'You should have called the police anyway,' she said curtly and took a form out of the drawer. 'Where was that?'

He gave the correct details and signed.

'Half a million excess,' she said, glancing at the insurance details. 'It will come off your card, along with the rest.'

Perlmann picked up the suitcase and went up to the bar. There was a different waiter there today, and otherwise only a girl in sneakers eating an ice-cream sundae and glancing often at her watch. Only gradually did he realize how relieved he was to be rid of the car. The sky had darkened, and the airport hall was bathed in a gloomy November light. He liked the sobriety that lay in that light. He grew calmer and, as he took slow, long drags on his cigarette, he kept thinking: *It's over. Over.* On Saturday they would all be leaving: Leskov on Sunday morning. In four days' time, at this hour of day, he himself would be on his flight home, and in the evening he would be in his familiar apartment. Exhaustion made way for quiet confidence. He paid and, hands in his trouser pockets, strolled over to the stairs that led up to the viewing area. He wanted to see the runway by the water and imagine his plane flying in a great loop out over the sea as it rose to ever higher altitudes.

'Your case, Signore.' The girl in the sneakers had come running. Perlmann took the suitcase from her, and struggled to hide his feelings.

'Oh, yes, thank you very much, that's very kind of you.'

The girl returned to her ice cream. He was filled with helpless fury, and stopped on the stairs with a blank expression on his face. A few moments ago, with his hands in his pockets, he had felt strangely light and free, unreally free, in fact. But he hadn't tried to know why that should be; with no plan in mind, he had simply, thoughtlessly pursued the impulse of leaving everything that had happened over the last few days, everything that was part of it, behind him along with the car. It had been like the first unimpeded breath of air after a near-suffocation. And now the suitcase holding Leskov's text, a ludicrous amount of blotting paper, the black notebook and the ridiculous props from the town hall hung leaden from his arm. He felt as if the whole nightmare of the past few days were contained in compact form in that suitcase, engraved with his initials.

He stepped on to the terrace and leaned against the balustrade. A Lufthansa plane was heading for take-off. He looked at his watch. *My plane.* As it roared into the air, just at the moment when the back tires lost contact with the runway he had the feeling that he could bear it no longer. That must be the end of notes and texts and translations and copies and lies and false leads and secrecy. It had to stop now. It had to stop. Right now. *Now.*

His foot brushed the suitcase. As if in a trance he stuck both hands in his jacket pockets, lowered his head and strode to the door, trousers flapping. He almost collided with the girl in sneakers. *'Mio padre!'* Then she slipped past him through the door and started running to the parapet. Perlmann gave up. Slowly he followed her. When she turned round and, with a laugh, pointed to the case, he raised a hand in thanks. The Lufthansa plane disappeared into the low cloud.

Leskov's address, which the anonymous sender couldn't possibly know, wasn't the only problem, Perlmann thought on the train. There were, for Leskov, only three places where he could have left the text: Moscow, Frankfurt or the plane. And there was simply no way to explain how the sheets might have ended up in that condition in an airport building or an aeroplane. And how so many of them should have vanished without trace.

If you added these two points together, Leskov was left with only a single hypothesis: someone who knew his address independently of the text had done something strange with the pages under the open sky, and was now sending them to him out of a guilty conscience. And on that day there was only one person who had been outside with him, and who could have had access to his suitcase: Philipp Perlmann, who had known his address for a long time. When Leskov ran through the drive in his mind, he would quickly see that there were, in fact, two places where it could have happened: the gas station and the roadside stop shortly afterwards. The shortness of the time in both cases could mean only one thing: Perlmann hadn't done anything unknown or inexplicable with the text – he had simply thrown it away.

But why, for God's sake? What harm could it do him? What did he have to fear from a text that he didn't even know? He had the first version, and possibly he'd just read it. Then there was . . . yes, exactly, then there was only one condition under which the second version could have constituted a threat to him: if he had presented the first version, in translated form, of course, as his own text.

At this point Leskov's thoughts would become very, very wary, and he would ensure that they came slowly. It was irrational to throw away the menacing text, when its author, who could reveal his act of plagiarism much more quickly and directly, was sitting next to him in the car. That was only rational if – the tunnel.

There was no question of Perlmann sending the text to St Petersburg. There was only one thing for it: to throw it away a second time. Throw the carefully preserved, 'restored' text, into a garbage bin, like before. Or quietly let it somehow lose itself. Perlmann glanced at the initials beside the lock on the suitcase. Then, when Santa Margherita was announced over the loudspeaker, he took out the certificate, the medal and the black notebook. He left the suitcase on the seat in the empty compartment and quickly walked to the front, to the carriage door. The wheels squeaked on the rails. Someone beside him opened the door. *You know what this text means to me. The blacklists still exist, and I'm on several of them.* Perlmann ran back, picked up the case and got out.

Leskov would be sitting beside Maria in the office, leaning forward and staring, his hands between his knees, at the screen. Perlmann wouldn't immediately know what it was about this sight that alarmed him. Only in the elevator would he understand: his translation, the fraudulent text, was still stored downstairs in the computer. Certainly, Maria had no reason to put it on the screen in Leskov's presence. But such a thing could easily happen inadvertently. In all likelihood she'd given the group their own folder. A couple of mistyped keys and Leskov would read: THE PERSONAL PAST AS LINGUISTIC CREATION. The title would electrify him, and he would lean still further forward to read the first few sentences. *Who's this text by?* would be his excited question. Maria might be distracted, or tired, or scattered, and already it would have happened. There would no longer be an innocuous explanation to give Leskov. Now, a full three days after his arrival – not to mention the conversation about the missing text – his mind would start working.

A curse, Perlmann thought. Leskov's text weighed on him like a curse that he wouldn't be able to shake off, wherever he went. The suitcase that he hadn't got rid of. And now the clues in the computer that could give everything away if Maria made just one tiny, innocent slip. He set down the suitcase in the wardrobe, closed the wardrobe and put the key in the bedside table drawer. He had just pulled the heavy curtains closed and lain down on the bed when he got up and took the suitcase out of the wardrobe. Working as carefully as a picture restorer, he replaced the old, stained sheets of blotting paper with new ones. The treatment had helped. The bits of ink had been absorbed where they had run, and the original lines now stood out more clearly. The dirt had dried, and turned paler. Perlmann put the suitcase with the text back in the wardrobe and crept under the covers. If Maria was working with Leskov now, she would have set up a new data file for him. Then there would be no reason to call up another. There was no opportunity for a mistake. When she went home at five or six, she simply turned off the computer.

Later. Sometime later he would gain access to the office and erase the dangerous file himself. It wasn't impossible. He relaxed.

The girl in sneakers had swung the suitcase over her head as if it were as light as a feather. When he had tried to lift it himself, however, it was like a piece of lead, fastened to the floor by a magnet. Around him, a sea of blotting paper darkened and ended up looking like a huge slab of rust. Did he think this was an ironmonger's shop? the white teacher had asked him, pulling her Salvation Army hat down over her face. *No!* he cried, his voice failing, and tugged on the suitcase, which was wedged in the carriage door. On the platform, as he tried to keep pace with the accelerating train, he saw the black tunnel coming ever closer.

45

It was pitch-dark when Perlmann was finally woken by the stubborn buzz of the telephone. He wanted to apologize for not coming to dinner, Leskov said. Maria had said she was ready to spend some more time working with him at the computer, so that his written submission would be ready for tomorrow's session.

'I don't know what I would do otherwise,' he said. 'I've only just finished, even though I worked nearly all night. And all because I forgot the damned text like an idiot!'

Perlmann fetched the text from the wardrobe. The fresh sheets of blotting paper were only very slightly stained. Most of the pages were dry by now. The biggest problem was the page from the middle of the road, the one with the fourth subheading. And the one from the ditch was difficult, too, the one that had been so wet that it must have been under a dripping tree. He packed these two between fresh sheets of blotting paper again. He closed the valise in the wardrobe and stuck the key in his blazer pocket when he went down to dinner. For the first time in weeks he was punctual.

How was he to explain the friendliness, the warmth, even, that they all showed him when he stepped to the table? There was nothing fake about it, and nothing obtrusive either, he thought, as he ate his soup. And yet it was hard to bear. Because it had something of the friendliness, the zealous humanity, that you would show towards a patient – someone who was being granted a breathing space, a period of convalescence. For a while lots of otherwise quite natural expectations and demands were put in parentheses. And that meant: temporarily he wasn't taken entirely seriously. Perlmann was glad when Silvestri asked him across the table, in quite a matter-of-fact manner, whether it would be all right for him to deliver a brief talk on Friday.

The perception that began to preoccupy him when he listened to the conversation at the table took time to assume a clear substance. While he had been enclosed within his delirium and his anxiety, the others had been getting on with their lives. And they had done that together, as a group in which all kinds of relationships had formed. There were constant hints, allusions and shared memories. There was irony, a knowledge of the forgivable weaknesses of the others; there was a playing with criticism and self-assertion, a delight in intellectual and personal banter. And there were shared experiences involving this town, its restaurants, churches, the post office – experiences that the others had been having while he had been sitting in a courtyard with his chronicle, trying to find the present through the past. He felt a pang, and remembered school journeys on which he had often come in last.

Achim Ruge – and Perlmann noticed this with astonishment, as if he had only just got here – had in the meantime plainly become something like the secret star of the group. His chuckle regularly set the others off, and with each new subject it seemed to Perlmann as if they were all waiting for one of his dry remarks. When they had been discussing Laura Sand's film, a personal aspect of Ruge had come to light. Otherwise, Perlmann didn't actually know anything at all about this man Achim Ruge.

I never gave the others a chance to get to know me better. Perlmann had never shown anything of himself but his purely professional side. From the very outset, his anxiety had reduced the others to one-dimensional, schematic figures. They were adversaries first and foremost. That applied even, in the end, to Evelyn Mistral. He had been constantly trying to work out the others. Inside, he had delivered harsh judgments about them. At the same time he knew – outward appearances aside – as good as nothing about them. His panic at the idea of being exposed had frozen his perception at a terrifyingly superficial level. Another two days, then they would be leaving. He had found out nothing about them, learned nothing from them, and the only relationship that he had developed with them lay in his attempts to close himself off and protect himself from them.

But Leskov was really unlucky to have left his text behind, von Levetzov said. He'd taken that long journey, it was his first time in the West, and now he'd been sitting nonstop in his room since yesterday afternoon preparing himself. And he had to go back on Sunday.

'Sometimes,' he added, 'he seems to be anxious that the text has been lost somewhere en route. He hinted as much to me this afternoon. He looked really distraught. Something professional seems to depend on it, too.'

Perlmann left his dessert and went out to Maria's office. When Leskov saw him through the glass door, he came up to him with a bleary-eyed face, red with excitement.

'We'll be finished soon. Unbelievable what a computer like that can do! Calling a text up to the screen just with a click on a key! Just one click! You just have to move the cursor to the right place!'

Perlmann went out on to the terrace and smoked a cigarette. In his mind's eye he saw Maria's hands with the red fingernails and the two silver rings. She would be careful with the name of the file. She wouldn't be scattered. She would pay attention. Before he turned to the door, he couldn't help looking up to his room. The only row of windows without a balcony.

Over coffee, Laura Sand asked him if his father was still alive.

'He was completely mistaken, in fact. There are wonderful corners of Mestre. If you know how to look. I always feel that modest, hard-working town is a relief after spectacular and somehow unreal Venice. I always stay in a hotel in Mestre, never in Venice. David thinks it's a fad of mine. But I like it. Quite apart from the price.'

'While I think Mestre is quite dreadful,' said Millar, looking at Perlmann with a grin that was filled with conciliatory mockery. 'I had to stay there once because there was something wrong with the causeway to Venice. The evening seemed to go on for ever.'

Perlmann was grateful for the remark: Millar wasn't condemning him for yesterday. *He's lifted me up.* Their eyes met. He, too, seemed to be thinking of the moment in the town hall.

'I knew a girl in Mestre once,' said Silvestri, expressionlessly. 'Great town.'

'Well,' said Millar, frowning satirically.

'*Ecco!*' said Silvestri, blowing smoke towards him.

'I'm going to take my next holiday in Mestre,' chuckled Ruge as they broke up after dinner, 'and I'm not going across to Venice once!'

The two most badly damaged pages had once again transferred moisture to the fresh sheets of blotting paper. But they were still far from dry and Perlmann laid them on the radiator along with a few others. Then he cleared the round table, fetched his toothbrush and started removing the dirt from the dry pages.

A lot of brownish stains remained, some of them speckled, which couldn't be got rid of, and where fat drops of water had fallen, the paper had been warped when it had dried. But even if it was faded, the text was legible again, and Leskov himself would soon know, even with the shapeless ink stains. Perlmann became quite practiced with his toothbrush. He now had a feeling for the correct angle of the bristles, and knew how to remove damp bits of soil. He kept blowing the dust away, and every now and again he fetched a towel from the bathroom to clean the toothbrush. As he worked, he rocked his torso slightly back and forth, and tapped out a rhythmic beat with his foot.

He had just started on page 49, and it was half-past eleven, when there was a knock on the door.

'It's me,' said Leskov. 'Can I come in for a moment? I need to talk to you.'

I need to talk to you. Perlmann froze, and suddenly felt as if he had been sitting in icy cold for hours. *She made a mistake with the file name. He's seen the text. He knows everything.*

'Philipp?' Leskov knocked again.

'Just a moment, please,' Perlmann called, unable to keep a hysterical squeak out of his voice. 'I've got to get dressed!'

He feverishly packed the finished pile on top of the others and collected the pages on the radiator. As he did so, the problem page with the subheading slipped from the sheets of blotting paper, fell to the floor and ripped as he picked it up. Valuable seconds elapsed. Perlmann looked frantically around, and then shoved the whole stack under the bed. On the way to the door he threw his towel and toothbrush on to the bathroom floor. Before he opened the door, he looked back. The wire waste-paper basket was full of stained blotting paper. The powder-blue carpet covered with pale dust. The table unnaturally empty. *Too late. The time has come. He's caught up with me after all.*

'Sorry for disturbing you so late at night,' Leskov said, hastily blowing big clouds of smoke into the room. He set a computer printout down on the table. It was his submission for tomorrow. Reading it through, he had suddenly been unsure if it would work – if one could present such a thing at all. He had a sense that it contained some contradictions, some inconsistencies. 'But I no longer trust my tired mind. Having to do the whole thing in such a short time and without my text: it was simply too much. Would you read it through for me?'

Perlmann picked up the six pages and held them in front of his nose. He wasn't in a state to read a single word with any understanding. The blood pounded all the way to his cold fingertips. The only sounds in the room were Leskov's wheezing and the gurgling of the radiator. Perlmann estimated the time for a single page and turned to the next one. When it was time for the third page, he felt he urgently had to go to the toilet. For a moment he looked over the edge of the page. Leskov looked at him uncertainly. Could he quickly use the bathroom?

Perlmann threw the counterpane over the bed and pulled it up until it touched the carpet on the side of the window. Then he leaned back with his eyes closed, Leskov's pages read in his lap. Maria had been careful with the file name. Maria wasn't scattered. And Leskov's text, a summary of which lay in his lap, was under the bed. It was hidden, even if Leskov were to bend down. Nonetheless, his anxiety didn't go away. Perlmann felt twinges in the region of his heart. Fine smoke rose from Leskov's pipe in the ashtray. Once again, it would smell sickly sweet all night. He hated Leskov. No, that wasn't true. He just wanted him to disappear. Everything to disappear: his smell, his text, the man himself. That all of it would disappear without a trace. For ever.

'So you really think it will be all right?' In Leskov's relieved face there were traces of anxiety and doubt.

Perlmann nodded.

'And the contradictions? You know, the thing that annoys me most is that I can no longer bring together the complicated business of invention and appropriation. And it's all there, in black and white. In Petersburg. I hope.'

'These theses here can be defended, I'm sure of it,' said Perlmann, handing him the sheets with a gesture so resolute that it seemed almost violent. He watched his own movement with astonishment, and was amazed at how loud and firm his voice sounded. It was the voice, he thought a moment later, with which one makes a promise.

The doubts vanished from Leskov's face, and he held a match vertically to his pipe. Could Perlmann now see the similarity between the two texts?

Perlmann nodded mutely.

Leskov was about to start talking about that similarity when he broke off. 'I'd better let you sleep now. You still look exhausted.' At the door, he surprisingly gave Perlmann his hand. 'That was very important for me,' he said with a grateful smile. He slowly reached for the door handle behind him. 'You know, over in my room, at the desk, the thought came to me over and over again: *The text is lost. All I have in my hand is these few lines.* The more tired I got, the more often that thought got in the way.' He smiled. 'High time for me to get a good night's sleep.'

Perlmann looked at the coarse hand that gripped the smoking pipe bowl, and nodded. The moment when the door clicked shut took an eternity to come.

*

With the window wide open, Perlmann set about cleaning the rest of the text. Tomorrow morning, when he saw Leskov stepping into the veranda and sitting down at the front, he wanted to be able to think that the manuscript was upstairs in the room – ready to be given back at any moment. But all of a sudden all the dexterity that he had acquired over the past few hours seemed to vanish. He rubbed either too gently or too hard, and in his patience he forgot that dry-looking crumbs of earth could still be damp inside. More and more often the cleaning became a smudging, and now he also discovered that moisture had entrenched itself at the top of the bristles of the toothbrush; it must have come from the bathroom floor, and was now increasingly forcing its way to the tips of the bristles and into the proximity of the paper. At the bottom of page 57 he gave up, and when he set the page aside he saw that his hand was trembling.

Now it was the turn of the problematic page 58, which he had previously put back between fresh blotters, and set on the radiator again. Perlmann went and got it and looked at the remaining traces of the subheading. The mixture of ink and dirt had by now dried completely, and could be wiped away with his handkerchief. *Pridumannoe proshloe: the invented past*, he thought, was the most likely reading of the pale fragment of the line. He took off his glasses and held the lenses as a magnifying glass over the paper. Now he discovered that before the first word there was a pencil marking for an insertion. Of the insertion, also written in pencil, the only letters that could be made out were *n* and *o*, which seemed to belong to the beginning and end of a single word. *Nevol'no pridumannoe proshloe: the involuntarily invented past*, he thought. In which case Leskov had extended his theme in the second version: apart from the linguistic impression of memories, it was also about truth and volitional control.

Once again Perlmann cast a sober glance at the few clues: nothing that could be made out there really supported this over-hasty assumption. Disgruntled, he covered the page with the blotter. When he pulled it away again and started to read, he felt the trepidation of the addict.

His reading proceeded only slowly, as he had no experience of Russian handwriting. But, eyes stinging, he continued until there were three words in a row that he didn't know at the bottom of the page. He lit a cigarette and, as his eyes remained focused on the line, his hand reached with mounting impatience for the dictionary. The sensation of emptiness had to be repeated a number of times before it dawned on him that there couldn't possibly be any dictionaries there now. He gave a start, as if from a forbidden daydream. His face stung. He quickly closed the text in the wardrobe and, shivering, walked to the window.

'I need to use the computer for a moment,' he said a few minutes later to Giovanni at reception. 'Check something about my text. For tomorrow.' A spasm ran from the back of his neck and down his back, and he had the feeling that he could barely turn his head.

Giovanni reached towards a drawer and then paused. Hesitantly, he raised his head and looked uncertainly at Perlmann. 'The office . . . no one . . . I have instructions . . .' He lowered his eye and rubbed awkwardly at the handle of the drawer.

'I understand,' said Perlmann and prepared to go.

Then Giovanni suddenly looked at him with a grin. 'Oh, come on, I'll make an exception for you.' He took a key from the drawer, walked ahead of him and opened the door. 'I'm sure you know how to use the computer already,' he said as he turned on the light, 'because I . . .'

'Of course,' Perlmann said quickly, 'thanks very much.'

He hoped Giovanni would retreat into the back room. But he stayed standing at the counter, nodded and smiled and raised his hand slightly. Perlmann cursed the glass door of the office. Now he would have to do it right in front of Giovanni's eyes. He straightened the chair in front of the screen and reached for the switch at the back of the computer. Nothing happened. He rocked the switch back and forth several times. No effect of any kind. He walked around the table and took a look at the switch. It was the right one. Giovanni raised quizzical eyebrows and made as if to come over. Perlmann hastily gestured to him to stay where he was: *Tutto bene!* Perlmann's hands were damp, and the spasm at the back of his neck was becoming stronger and stronger. He stared blankly straight ahead. *The plug.* He slowly rolled his chair back and looked under the table. All the plugs were in their sockets. He avoided glancing over at the counter. Only now did he notice the round lock without a key. *Finished. Of course, the business documents.* He turned to the side table with the drawers and screened his hands from Giovanni's eyes with his back. The open drawers contained only office material, he could see that as soon as he opened them a crack. The key for the computer would be in the narrow top drawer, from whose lock the key had also been removed. In the only box on the desk there were just paperclips.

Perlmann breathed in twice, slowly. His back relaxed. Relief was mixed with tiredness. The fact that he noticed the transparent box of disks when he stood up had something to do with the fact that the plexiglass reflected the fluorescent light from the ceiling. He slid the chair to the tray at the side and opened the box. The disk with his name on it was the second from the front. Under the name it said on the label: PERSONAL PAST. MESTRE.

Perlmann took care that his movements were easy for Giovanni to make out as he rolled himself back to the computer and put the disk in the drive. Then he sat down in a pose of concentration in front of the dark screen and simulated typing movements. He could at least remove the disk. Perhaps Maria had only worked with it, and the text wasn't even on the hard drive. He grew calmer. With a pen from the desk he tapped the edge of his nose a few times and then stuck the tip between his lips while, leaning back with legs outstretched, he pretended to gaze into an imaginary distance. Then he made a few more typing motions, took the disk from the drive and pressed the switch. With his back to Giovanni he stuck the disk in the belt under his pullover, ostentatiously snapped the box shut and left.

'That's it,' he said. 'Many thanks.'

Giovanni caught up with him in the portico.

'You were asking about Baggio yesterday.'

'Yes?'

'He scored another goal tonight. Against Bayern Munich!'

'He's plainly a great striker,' said Perlmann, and an emotion that was hard to distinguish from pure tiredness brought tears to his eyes.

'*E come!*' said Giovanni.

'*Ciao*,' said Perlmann and touched him fleetingly on the shoulder.

'*Ciao*,' Giovanni said, too. He said it hesitantly and slowly, and it sounded like an incredulous echo.

When Perlmann looked down at the beach jetty by the Regina Elena, a group of young people stood applauding because a lanky boy was kissing a girl who, in spite of her piled-up hair, barely came up to his chest. That wasn't his jetty, not the one that led out into the black water. It was as if the jetty of two days ago had been extinguished by the young people, or rather: expelled from the world.

He went on walking beyond the rocky spur until it was quite dark. Then he slung the disk far out into the sea. The movement came from his wrist and shoulder at the same time, the little disk turned quickly on its own axis, rose for a while in a low curve, then fell spinning and chipped almost vertically into the water. Perlmann heard quiet applause, but couldn't tell if it was only his imagination.

From the rocky spur he looked across to the Miramare. A letter seemed to be flickering in the middle of the neon writing. Somewhere in the dark hills over there were the garbage bins into which he had thrown the first version of Leskov's text. Tomorrow, immediately after the session, he would finish cleaning the second version. He certainly couldn't send it from Italy. Nor from Frankfurt. But the very thought was pointless. He couldn't possibly send the text to Leskov.

The young people had moved on. The beach jetty was empty. His jetty was back in the world, washed around by black water. Perlmann felt himself beginning to crumble. There were delicate, treacherous cracks within his inner structure. He quickly went back to the hotel.

The air in the room was cold, and it still smelled sickly sweet, even though this time Leskov had only used the ashtray for a match. Perlmann washed out his toothbrush several times. But it was as if the dirt had practically eaten its way into the bristles. The foam when he brushed his teeth had a brownish tint.

In the morning, he thought in the dark, Leskov would be sitting at the head of the table in the veranda, anxiously and with almost nothing in his hands. He didn't know it, but Perlmann had promised to defend his theme, which he didn't know in the new version.

It was an antediluvian screen, bright bilious green on dull dark green, and it flickered so wildly that it made the eyes stream straight away. A nauseating, sickly sweet smell flowed from it. That couldn't be, but it was, and when he sniffed at the ventilation slits smoke was emerging from there as well; a treacherous smoke that couldn't at first be seen, but then suddenly formed a dense, suffocating cloud. A flood of incomprehensible Italian orders and file names swam across the screen. At last he somehow got hold of the right one, but Leskov's text simply wouldn't be erased, he pressed the key over and over again, hundreds of times, until nothing remained of the key, but Leskov's text with Perlmann's name went on flickering under the title. At last he clicked the on-off switch, but nothing happened; even pulling out the plug had no effect: Leskov's text went on flickering and flickering, and now Perlmann's name was suddenly there in capital letters. Then he gripped the huge sledgehammer in both hands. But it wasn't so easy. You had to take a run-up with lateral, rhythmically swinging movements before lifting the hammer high above your head to deliver the crucial blow. At last the time had come, the hammer rose up, it passed the apex, but then all of a sudden it had no substance and no weight, and rather than bringing it down with a crash into the computer, as he woke up Perlmann found himself on the bedcover, his hand clenched convulsively into a fist.

46

Nonetheless, he had the feeling of having had a proper night's sleep for the first time in ages. As he got dressed he established that he had no fresh underwear, and saw in his mind's eye the full plastic bag falling on the stinking cabbage. The wound in his finger was no longer damp, the bruise and the swelling had subsided. At the smallest pressure, admittedly, his fingertip still hurt so much that it brought tears to his eyes. He put his last bandage on it.

At exactly eight o'clock he went down to breakfast. If they thought he was finally eating humble pie in the wake of his disgrace, that was their business. Signora Morelli had just stepped out through the portico, and was straightening one of the round tables. Unnoticed, he bent over the reception desk and shoved the stained map, which had been on the radiator all night, between other papers on the shelf.

The dining room was completely empty. Not a single place had been used at the group's table. The waiter who brought him his coffee and egg was plainly embarrassed. With each minute that passed without anyone appearing, Perlmann felt more and more that he was being ridiculed. Asking the waiter whether the breakfast habits of his – yes, his – group had changed was impossible.

Adrian von Levetzov came at a quarter past eight. It was the first time that Perlmann had seen him without a waistcoat and even without a tie. His pale, wrinkled neck made him look old.

'Oh, Perlmann, good morning,' he said more flatly than usual, and rubbed his eyes. 'We all stayed out very late last night. There's a feeling that it's all coming to an end.'

Perlmann nodded and took another roll. And then another. The silence was unbearable. The tablecloth was stained. The waiter's movements were affected.

'I didn't know about your wife's accident,' said von Levetzov, holding his coffee cup, 'until Leskov told us about it on Tuesday. Terrible. That must have brought you very low.'

Leskov: the man who explains my breakdown to other people. 'Yes,' said Perlmann, topping up his coffee.

Someone had put a damp spoon in the sugar; there were brown lumps in the bowl. In the fresh ashtray there was a tiny bit of chewing gum, with a drop of water on it.

Perlmann wanted to make an effort with Adrian von Levetzov, but he had no idea how to do it.

'Yep, it'll be back to the rat race,' smiled von Levetzov. 'What will you be teaching?'

As he gave a vague description of his lecture series, something quiet and dramatic happened in Perlmann: he made the decision to abandon his professorship.

What was happening inside him was not an internal action. There was nothing active about it. It was more like the process of a little gear wheel that has long been moving with his pen, slowly and inexorably towards a lock, finally snapping in place and thus setting in motion something bigger, something revolutionary. He hadn't known that the time had come. And yet it seemed quite natural that it should have happened right now – at a time when the empty dining room emphasized his alienation from his colleagues and their world quite as self-evidently as if it had been a scene from a film.

Von Levetzov got up with a glance at his watch. 'I have to make a phone call,' he said apologetically. 'See you later.'

Perlmann took in the empty room. He would think back time and again to this room and this moment. It was hazy over the bay, impossible to say whether the sun would part the clouds. He slowly finished his cigarette and ran his hand along the edges of the tables on his way to the door.

Then someone pushed the door open with his shoulder. It was Millar. He had taken off his glasses and was running a hand over his face. After that Ruge came in. 'A bucket of coffee!' he called to the waiter. Evelyn Mistral, who was walking behind him, laughed her pearly laugh. She had piled her hair up, and was carrying her writing pad with the shield of Salamanca under her arm.

'See you later,' Perlmann said, escaping from their startled stares.

'Signor Perlmann!' Maria had left the office door open, and now came out from behind her desk. 'Giovanni told me you wanted to use the computer last night. Is something wrong? I always close up in the evening. A safety measure. If I'd known . . .'

Perlmann looked at her hands – those hands that couldn't make any mistakes, that couldn't under any circumstances hit the wrong key.

'It wasn't all that important,' he said with forced equanimity, 'I just wanted to try something out with my text – something, erm . . . that you can't do with the printout.'

'I know, people always say that.'

She ran her hand through her hair, and again Perlmann wondered mechanically whether her fingers wouldn't be sticky with hairspray afterwards. *You've been living under a rock. Like way, way out.*

'Which of the two texts was it, then?' she asked with a smile. 'The one about memory?'

'No, the other one,' Perlmann said and gulped.

'And it occurs to me,' she exclaimed and turned towards the office, 'that I still have to give you the disk!'

As she opened up the box and started searching, Perlmann leaned against the doorframe with his arms folded. *She'll never find out.*

'I don't understand this,' she murmured, sat down and went through the disks again, slowly, one at a time. 'It was in here, and now it's gone.' She looked through everything on the desk, smiling at him awkwardly from time to time. 'I'm not usually as scattered as this.' Distracted and incredulous, she went through the drawers, and you could tell by the wrinkles on her nose that she was battling against irritation with herself.

Suddenly, she made a dismissive gesture. 'It doesn't matter. I'll just copy both texts for you quickly again.' She turned on the computer and put a new disk in the drive.

At that moment Perlmann heard Leskov's voice behind him. 'Are we starting on time?' He turned round. Leskov was wearing his bilious green shirt with a brown tie and a grey waistcoat stretched over his belly.

'*Ecco!*' Maria was saying, 'so first we've got the text about memory . . . what abbreviation did I give it . . . oh, yes, that's it.'

He doesn't understand Italian. The sound of copying began. Perlmann looked at his watch for an unnecessarily long time. 'Yes, we'll have to be there in a minute,' he said.

Leskov walked up to Maria and held out his hand.

'*Un momento,*' she smiled. 'Now the other one. That was . . . yes, just *Mestre.*' Her fingers flew over the keys. '*Ecco!*' The sound again. Now she shook hands with Leskov, who was looking at the screen. 'Good morning,' she said in English.

'Incredible how little time it takes,' Leskov said raptly. Then he showed Maria the stack of copies that he was carrying under his arm. 'The text from yesterday. Thank you very much, once again.'

As Leskov was leaving, Maria took the disk out of the drive and stuck a label on it.

'Erm . . . you don't need to do that,' Perlmann said hastily as she reached for her pen. He slipped the disk into his jacket pocket. 'Now you can delete the texts.' His hoarseness and the quiver in his voice made it, he thought, the caricature of a casual remark.

'I will at some point,' she said and turned off the computer. 'But there's no rush. The computer has a huge hard drive!' She got up and looked down at her folded hands. 'You know, I hate erasing documents that I've typed up. All that work, and then one click of the keys – and poof!' She threw her hands in the air and looked at him with a shy smile that he had never seen before. 'I know it doesn't make any sense really, because nothing happens to the documents in there once the people have gone . . . It's just how I am.'

Perlmann nodded. 'Thank you,' he said, and tapped his jacket pocket.

*

Leskov had already distributed his handwritten submission, and was now sitting at the front moving his papers back and forth. He gripped his pipe bowl with both hands as he began to speak. He had already talked about the mishap with his text, he said. His tone revealed the fact that he had firmly resolved not to start talking about it again. But then, from one second to the next, his facial expression went blank, he rubbed his pipe absently with his index finger, and you could actually feel him being sucked into the pool of his attempts at remembering.

As he had done so often in this room, Perlmann hid his face behind his clasped hands as Leskov told parts of his story again. Quickly, and even though he didn't try fully to understand the reasons why, Perlmann's sense of guilt turned to fury: it had been a crazy, unforgivable act of recklessness to take such an important text, a text on which Leskov's advancement depended, on a journey without making a copy before-hand! How could he do such a thing?

Even when Leskov was already some way into his lecture, Perlmann was still quarrelling with him. Until he suddenly stopped abruptly: *What would have happened if he had told me about such a copy just before the tunnel?* He took his hands from his face and tried to listen.

The others, with their sleepy faces, weren't taking the Russian seri-ously. The contrast between the tie cutting into Leskov's neck and Adrian von Levetzov's unaccustomedly open collar was so vivid that Perlmann succumbed to fury once more. But this time it was a fury on behalf of Leskov, even going so far as to defend that horrible green shirt. Millar, who had never appeared in the veranda without his blazer, was wearing a windbreaker, and there was a camera on the table in front of him. And Evelyn Mistral, who had always listened to the others with her pen at the ready, was drawing circles with her folded glasses on her unopened pad. The only curious face belonged to Giorgio Silvestri.

In the discussion, Leskov was spared at first, and a patronizing benev-olence was apparent. But by now Leskov had shed his self-conscious-ness, and surprised everyone with his doggedness. He stood by what he had said, and to Perlmann's alarm he quickly went on the attack. There was nothing now of the anxiety with which he had sat facing Perlmann in his room the previous evening, like a student before his first presentation. Leskov's attacks, in spite of their factual harshness, were prevented from being insulting or wounding, largely because his flawed English had a unique charm. Many of his turns of phrase, which weren't quite accurate, had an involuntary comedy about them, which he only noticed when he saw himself reflected in the faces of the others. Then he laughed loudest of all. The victims of his attacks were often uncertain: had he meant it seriously? Or did he perhaps not know exactly what he had just said? Above all Achim Ruge, who seemed to have no sense of humor at all today, seemed bothered by this uncertainty, and when he took out a pack of aspirin, Laura Sand burst out laughing.

Leskov noticed the hesitancy on the part of the others more and more often, and more and more quickly. Then he repeated his reservation in different words, and in most cases the variation in expression showed that he actually had meant exactly what he had said. After some time the doubts of the others fled. His initial phrasing was taken seriously and the fact that linguistic expression as a theme in its own right had disappeared made the discussion more tart and direct. Evelyn Mistral was writing now, and Millar hung his camera over the back of his chair. The sickly sweet tobacco smell filled the whole veranda. Von Levetzov opened a window.

He, Philipp Perlmann, had been prepared, in cold blood, to murder that person up there at the front, who was now, brazenly and without the slightest vanity, keeping to the point. As he scribbled on the back of Leskov's submission by way of self-disguise, Perlmann desperately sought a posture – an internal maneuver – that might save him from being totally suffocated by the feelings of shame and guilt that engulfed everything else. He tried to see Leskov only externally, as just a body, so to speak, and to concentrate on the things that repelled him: the sweat on his bald head, the bulges of his bull's neck, his sausage fingers. It was a cheap, vulgar trick, and afterwards Perlmann's shame was all the greater for it.

He, too, had to say something. And he couldn't wait much longer. He shivered. The draught from the open window was suddenly icy. An athlete, he thought, must feel rather like that at his first competition after an injury. Over the bay the sun seemed to be falling against the low, milky cloud. The morning light grew softer. John Smith stood irresolutely at the edge of the pool. Millar pulled a mocking face at the sight of him.

What had happened in the empty dining room had left behind a sensation of something crucial and definitive; the impression of a release of tension. The feeling of liberation that he had longed for, however, had not arrived. Perhaps it was only a matter of time. His decision was only about an hour old, after all. But, basically, Perlmann knew better. It was quite different from the time when, coming out of the director's office, he had stepped into the street outside the Conservatoire. In spite of the rain he had walked through the city for a long time, without an umbrella, his briefcase full of the things from his emptied drawer. Then he had driven to the sea. That time the defining feeling had been one of great liberation. He knew that behind it, still temporarily concealed, there lurked other feelings, more complicated and less pleasant. But for the moment he enjoyed being released from the iron discipline of practising. It was a relief that his battle with self-doubt had come to an end, and at the age of just twenty-one he felt incredibly grown up. Admittedly, a feeling of emptiness had set in soon afterwards, after getting up he didn't know quite what to do with all the time ahead of him, and was glad that his term at Hamburg University would soon be beginning. But he was left with a mood of liberating insight, of finishing one thing and emerging into something new. Now, a good thirty years later, it was also an insight that guided him. At any rate he hoped so. But it was embedded in a different, darker experience: in alienation, weariness and guilt. The only thing missing was anxiety. He would find something. Something or other. *Kirsten is taken care of.* Perlmann was amazed that there was no anxiety. He barely dared to trust that perception. Something had changed within him. A development had been set in motion. All of a sudden he felt light, almost cheerful.

There was a moment's silence. Perlmann gave a start. 'So that's my train of thought,' said Leskov and reached for another pipe.

When Perlmann took the floor he had no idea what he was going to say. He had been far too preoccupied with himself to listen to Leskov elucidating his paper again. Just to have something to talk about, he started by explaining how he had worked out Leskov's train of thought over all. They listened to him with emphatically benevolent attention. Their determination not to condemn him for Tuesday, and to go on taking him seriously in spite of everything, to be scrupulously fair – he thought he could almost physically hear it, as a particularly intense kind of silence that fell when he started speaking. He deliberately chose sober, plain phrases, and used components of the academic rhetoric that he despised. Just to show that he could do that, too. At first he gave a start when he noticed that he was moving through his translation, section by section. He came close to breaking off and simply falling silent. But he was no longer in control. The text, which he knew almost off by heart from the effort of translating it twice, pulled him along with it and, all of a sudden, he realized that he was enjoying the danger like a gambler. His presentation, which had already extended far beyond the length of a contribution to a discussion, became ever more sophisticated, fluent and engaged. He closed gaps in Leskov's train of thought, produced additional references, identified possible misunderstandings and swept them aside. Evelyn Mistral's feet played with her red shoes as she wrote down what he said. Laura Sand slowly rubbed her forehead. Ruge and Millar picked up their pens almost instantaneously. *I'm rehabilitated. Thanks to Leskov's text.*

It would have appeared unnatural – revealing, in fact – if he had not looked several times in Leskov's direction. He helped himself by staring at the ridiculous tassels fixed to the wall, which lay at eye level. As he did so, the image of Kirsten appeared in front of him, tugging on the tassels and laughing at the clouds of dust. He started to falter and only found his thread after he had closed his eyes with a grimace and opened them again, which must have looked to the others like an epileptic twitch. Sometimes, when he couldn't do anything else, he did look at Leskov, but to a certain extent removed himself from his gaze and soon turned his head away again. Only after Perlmann had finished did he turn to face him and look at him quizzically.

All the while, Leskov had sat leaning back in the armchair, his massive thighs crossed. At regular intervals, little clouds of smoke had escaped from the corners of his mouth. Now, when he leaned forward and rested his elbows on the table, his face bore an expression that alternated between joy and disbelief. He thanked Perlmann extravagantly for his summary. It was more or less precisely – no, *precisely* – the way his ideas had originally developed. He paused, looked thoughtfully at Perlmann, and then let his eye linger on the table for a moment as he tamped down the tobacco with his thumb. *He's sure I've read the text. Completely sure. But he will never be able to prove it.* Meanwhile, of course, his considerations had developed further, he said and pointed to his paper. And he ran through the new points once again, checking that Perlmann, who was taking notes, could keep up with him.

As he drew a thick line under his earlier scribbles, Perlmann started thinking. He was working. It was as if something had just come crashing in; something that had been left unused for a long time and had, in its uselessness, created nothing but friction. He hadn't been so alert for ages. He and Leskov were the only people in the room. He asked questions, recapitulated, suggested additions, to test his understanding. From the corner of his eye he saw writing hands and surprised, curious faces. They hadn't seen him like this before. He enjoyed his concentration, his synoptic view and his presence of mind, and every now and again, when he was able to pay attention to himself because Leskov was speaking, Perlmann thought he sensed that now, slowly and inconspicuously, an inner liberation was starting to gleam through, and that his new alertness, so unlike Monday night's, wasn't overwrought in the slightest and was connected to that morning's decision.

And then, when Leskov's new train of thought was quite clear to him, he started defending the earlier Leskov against the later one. It could have been a game, and at first he suspected himself of playing games, as if he had taken leave of his senses. But soon he worked out that he actually believed what he was defending. *In which case there would, in fact, have been no plagiarism.* He started getting carried away by his own words. Leskov smiled to himself like someone who is only too familiar with these reflections. From time to time he hesitated, frowned, took his pipe out of his mouth and wrote something down. Evelyn Mistral's face revealed how pleased she was that Perlmann had obviously recovered. She nodded often, and for the first time Perlmann ceased to be afraid of her glasses.

Once when Leskov said something to defend his new thought, Perlmann forgot himself. 'But here your earlier argument is much more convincing!' he explained.

Adrian von Levetzov pushed his glasses back along his nose with his index finger and gave him a questioning look. At first Leskov smiled understandingly, before he suddenly jerked his head and looked at him with his eyes narrowed. He meant the argument they had discussed in St Petersburg, Perlmann said after a second of terror, and assumed an expression that felt opaque and impregnable. For a while Leskov stared, blinking, into the void. Then he started nodding. His face bore a look of astonishment. Never before had anyone remembered something he had said after such a long time. His thought had never been so important to anyone. He almost seemed to be embarrassed in front of the others. Perlmann looked for signs of suspicion. It was impossible to decide whether something was shimmering there, or whether it was only incredulous astonishment that gave Leskov's face that expression.

Having grown impatient, the others began to express their doubts about Leskov's method. Perlmann thought that Leskov didn't put up a good defense on this point. For the first time he became aware that during the weeks that he had spent translating, he had anticipated all of these reservations and even a large number of others, and come up with possible defenses for them. *Which means that I have been working the whole time. Then I'm still on top of things after all.* He intervened in the discussion. As he did so he argued with a calm lack of agitation, and at one point he even managed an ironic remark. And then, as he coolly – one might even have said icily – fired off a series of rhetorical questions, looking at all the others in turn, the whole liberating effect of his decision finally unfolded. It happened with the momentum of a physically perceptible thrust. Last of all he looked at Silvestri. The unshaven Italian responded with an expression of clinical curiosity. That expression, Perlmann thought, was the only thing he didn't like about the man.

One thing he hadn't touched upon, said Leskov, was the idea that one can appropriate one's past through narrative memory. For someone like him – who liked to stress the inventing, creating character of memory – that was, of course, a problematic thought. And there wasn't time for more than a hint in that direction. He cast a glance at Perlmann: 'Above all, one must clearly understand that the narrating self is none other than the narrated stories. Apart from the stories there is nothing. Or rather, no one.' He smiled. 'Most people find that a shocking assertion. I've never understood why. I find it quite pleasant that that's how it is. Somehow . . . liberating.'

'One question, Vassily,' said Millar. 'Do you really mean *creating* and *inventing* when you talk about remembering? I assume you mean *creative* and *inventive*. I could go along with that.'

Leskov looked over at Perlmann. 'What would be the difference in German?'

'*Erschaffend* and *erdichtend* as opposed to *schöpferisch* and *erfinderisch*,' said Perlmann.

Leskov smiled. 'I see. No, Brian, I'm afraid I mean the former.'

Millar looked at his watch. Ruge gathered his papers together and started playing with his pencil. But Laura Sand had another question. Did he mean in the end that that which we take to be an actually experienced past is merely an invention?

Leskov pursed his lips and nodded, his eyes laughing. One of the subheadings of his new text was: *Neizbezhno vydumannoe proshloe*, the inevitably invented past, he said.

'One moment.' Ruge jutted his bottom lip and leaned far over the table on both elbows. 'In that case *is* there such a thing as a true story about the experienced past?'

Silvestri audibly inhaled his smoke. Laura Sand playfully pulled a strand of hair over her face. You could see that Leskov would have loved to capture this moment for ever. Never, it appeared, had this man enjoyed a moment so much. Perlmann wouldn't have thought him capable of that face. It was the unbuttoned face of someone who has shed all anxiety and is now entirely at home with himself. Perlmann liked it.

'No, there is no such thing as a true story about the experienced past,' said Leskov with the stem of his pipe to his lips. 'Of course not. Klim Samgin.' His grey eyes were very bright and very clear, and their challenge consisted entirely in that brightness and clarity.

The pencil in Ruge's hands broke in two with a loud crack. Millar took a film from the pocket of his windbreaker and picked up his camera. Von Levetzov smiled appreciatively when he saw that.

As he got to his feet, Silvestri stepped up and invited Leskov for a drink in the bar. Laura Sand wanted to know if she could come, too. She wanted to find out more about this cheeky thesis.

47

The paces that Perlmann later took as he walked up and down in his room were both exaggeratedly cautious and aimless. Often he interrupted his restless walking, folded his arms and lowered his head on his chest. How did one do it? How did one abandon a professorship? What did one write in the requisite letters? They would have to be laconic. He sat down at his desk and wrote some drafts. The texts grew shorter and shorter. Even words that seemed at first to be the bare minimum struck him, on rereading, as superfluous. Ideally, he would just have written: *I've had enough and request my dismissal.* An explanation would be demanded. After a while he noticed that in his thoughts he was sitting opposite the dean, a small, pale man with a crooked mouth, a ramrod-straight head and faultless creases in his trousers. *You would like to know why? Very simple: I've just discovered my professional incapacity.* That was the explanation he liked best. Especially if he managed to deliver it with a laugh. He couldn't see enough of the dean's uncomprehending expression. But suddenly the whole scene collapsed, and he felt as exhausted as if he had been talking for hours. He tore the pages with the drafts on them into tiny scraps. All of a sudden he was anxious after all.

He had left the toothbrush unused in the morning. He took Leskov's text from the wardrobe. In many places, where yesterday there had still been a hint of damp, the dirt could now be blown away after a light touch with the bristles. But that wasn't the only reason why the work was different today. Suddenly, Perlmann was no longer interested in the yellow sheets. No, of course that wasn't quite true. He was resolutely determined to give the text back. He just needed to think about how

Leskov had savored his punchline a little while before: the man must have his text back, regardless of the matter about the position. No, it was something different. All of a sudden he didn't care that he didn't know the Russian words for *inevitable* and *invented*, which Leskov had pronounced so quickly and indistinctly, and couldn't fit them in his mind into the inky traces that remained of the subheading. That it was a Russian text at all – he didn't even care about that. He didn't understand the connection, but it had something to do, he thought, with the fact that they had talked about the text in the veranda. It was as if the others had stolen the text from him by learning of its content – but without freeing him of it.

Perlmann rang Frau Hartwig.

'You are missed,' she said. 'Everyone's asking when you're coming.'

He asked her to give him Leskov's home address, the only one she had. He wanted to bring the conversation to an end as quickly as possible, and sensed how hurt Frau Hartwig was that he was so abrupt.

'When shall I tell the others you're coming?'

'Don't tell them anything.'

'I'm just saying,' Frau Hartwig said stiffly.

Perlmann studied the sheet of hotel paper with the jotted address. It had been on a street corner with mountains of swept-up, dirty snow. Leskov had rested on his briefcase and scribbled his address on a piece of paper that fluttered in the wind.

'I'm sorry, my handwriting's a disaster,' he had said when he noticed how much difficulty Perlmann was having in reading it. He took out another, crumpled piece of paper and wrote down the address again, this time in Latin capitals. 'When you write to me, please use this address,' he had said. 'It's safer.' Perlmann remembered his embarrassed facial expression, because it was that expression that had kept Perlmann from asking whether it was because of the secret police or because he didn't have an office at the university.

What use was that address to him? An envelope would arrive at Leskov's house, containing the text which would turn out to be missing, among other things, the final page with the address. After his first, massive relief Leskov would start brooding. How had the stranger who must have found these sheets somewhere on his travels obtained his address? It had been sent from the West. Who in the West apart from Perlmann knew this address?

Perlmann had thought the same thing yesterday. But was it really inevitable that Leskov should suspect him? It wasn't the first thing that came to mind. You had to think about it for a while. But there was also another possible explanation: whoever had collected and dispatched the text had been distracted or otherwise diverted, and had – after writing down the address – forgotten to put the last page in the envelope with the rest. An act of carelessness, of negligence. Thoroughly within the realms of the normal; by no means impossible. And was that not much more likely than a monstrous suspicion of Perlmann?

Perhaps Leskov's embarrassment had been caused by the idea that he would need a home address even for a text like this. But perhaps that wasn't it. After all, he taught at the university and he would want to signal that, even if he didn't have his own office there. And the subject was politically neutral, at least in the eyes of the thugs in the secret police. And besides: didn't colleagues from the East sometimes say that their work address was the politically safer one to use? But if Leskov had written his work address on the last page, it would be a complete mystery to him why the unknown person had used not that address, but his private one, which they couldn't possibly have known. Now the suspicion could no longer be averted: Perlmann had lost the last page and picked up the only address available to him. Leskov would remember how the two of them had stood on the street corner.

But what was Perlmann supposed to do? He didn't even know the name of the university in St Petersburg, let alone the name of the institute or the street. And writing something vague on it was too unsafe. Who could say where the text would end up? Let alone the fact that this was incompatible with the innocuous explanation: either the unknown person had the address, in which case he had it exactly. Or else he didn't have it, in which case he couldn't even know that it was St Petersburg.

What about simply asking Leskov for his work address? But why would he ask that, when their correspondence had hitherto been sent via his home address, at Leskov's express wishes? Eventually, when the text arrived, Leskov would remember that question, and he would remember finding it a bit surprising. And if it turned out that his home address *had* been at the end of the text . . .

Did he usually write his private or his work address at the end of his academic texts? A casual question among colleagues. It could also be asked in a more generalized form: what was the usual practice in Russia? A question asked out of harmless curiosity about the foreign country that was now edging closer. But Leskov would remember even that when he was puzzling about the envelope with the western stamp. And if Perlmann got the answer that the work address was usually the one given, he would look even more stupid than before: if he asked what that address was, that conversation would be the first thing that sprang to Leskov's mind when he opened the envelope.

A steadfast will was of no use whatsoever. It was simply impossible to put into practice. Not, at any rate, without giving oneself away.

There was a knock at the door. While he was still bundling the sheets together and blowing the dust from the table top, Perlmann noticed to his surprise that he wasn't panicking. Without hesitation, almost with a feeling of routine, he pushed the pile of papers under the counterpane and slipped his toothbrush into his trouser pocket.

It was the new chambermaid, bringing him a hotel folder. She had meant to bring one for ages, but it had kept slipping from her mind. Had there never been one? 'There was,' Perlmann said and bit his lip. The chambermaid looked at him in surprise for a moment and plucked at the duster in her apron pocket. Then she asked if everything else was all right, and left.

There were another dozen pages to be cleaned. It was surprising that the pages with numbers in the seventies didn't look worse. Lots of tires must have passed over them. Did that mean that there had been a thicker clump underneath? Or did it mean the opposite?

*

In the midst of these inconclusive reflections the phone rang.

'I've been trying to get hold of you in the evening for ages,' said Kirsten. 'So I thought I'd try during the day. Although it's going to be really, really expensive. Is everything all right?' And she asked if his turn had come to make a contribution. 'Did it go well?'

Perlmann sat down on the edge of the bed and gulped convulsively. The receiver grew damp.

'I'm sorry. What sort of question is that?' Kirsten said, laughing with embarrassment. 'Of course it went well. Things like that always go well for you. It's just, the day before yesterday, Astrid – my friend from the shared apartment, I told you about her – made a complete flop with her presentation. Lasker obviously doesn't like her, and he really tore her off a strip. Afterwards I had shivers up and down my spine.'

He would be coming home on Sunday, Perlmann said in response to her question.

'You sound tired. You're glad it'll soon be over, aren't you?'

Perlmann sat down on the edge of the bed until he was dazzled by the sun, which had found a gap in the low cloud. Then he pulled over a corner of curtain and wiped down the last two pages, which were only dirty at the edges. He slowly flicked through the whole pile before at last precisely aligning them. Leskov would manage. When he typed out the whole thing he would be able to fill the gaps from his memory. Unless there was a big chunk missing at the end. *The thing that annoys me most, you know, is that I can't get the complicated business of invention and appropriation to come together. And yet it's all there, in black and white. In St Petersburg. I hope.*

Perlmann picked up the last page. If he fought his way through the battlefield of deletions and additions, he might be able to estimate if there were lots of pages still to come. But at the top on the left there were two words that he couldn't make out, and he didn't know the one after that. A paralysing fatigue set in. *Never again.* He pushed the sheet under the pile.

The envelope in which he sent Leskov the text would have to be especially tough. Practically weatherproof. Perlmann saw it lying on an open mail car. It was at an abandoned Russian station, night was falling, and the snow was coming down in thick flakes. There was no point telling oneself that it was nonsense, because the consignment would go by plane, straight to St Petersburg. All the way to the stationer's shop and also in the moment when he rested his hand on the shop door handle, he saw the deserted platform and the snow falling on the envelope.

The shop was still shut. Forgetting the siesta and then standing stupidly outside a closed shop – suddenly that felt like the theme of his whole stay. Ashamed, he looked round to see if anyone had noticed him. But apart from one bent old man, who was almost being whirled round by his dog, there was no one to be seen. In the shop window where the chronicle had been, a Christmas crib had been set up. Perlmann slowly began to walk around the block. When someone pushed up the iron shutter of a pharmacy with a pole, he waited and then bought a new toothbrush.

Leskov had said nothing about the deadline by which the text had to be presented if he were to have a chance for the job. But regardless of that, Perlmann really wanted to take the text to the post office that afternoon. It couldn't possibly be there by Sunday evening, when Leskov excitedly stepped into his apartment. But the thought of the days that Leskov would have to spend assuming that the text was irrevocably lost was unbearable, and Perlmann didn't want this nightmare to last an hour, a minute longer than necessary.

But sending it from here, with the Santa Margherita postmark, was out of the question. Should he drive to Genoa later on and send it from there? The day before yesterday, when he was listing the places where he might have left the text, Leskov had stopped at Frankfurt. It didn't seem possible that he could have left it on the Alitalia plane. Or was it just a coincidence that he hadn't mentioned it? If there was a reason for it, though, and he was sure that it couldn't have happened on the flight to Genoa, the Genoa postmark would hardly be any more revealing than the postmark from Santa Margherita. No, Perlmann absolutely couldn't send the text from Italy. He would have to do it in Frankfurt.

But he wouldn't be there until Sunday lunchtime, and that meant three more days of despair for Leskov.

Perlmann looked at his watch. There was still the evening flight at six. But he wouldn't get back today, and after everything that had happened he couldn't possibly miss Silvestri's session tomorrow. Tomorrow afternoon and evening were also out of the question: they were the last few hours that the group was able to spend together, and it would be far too outrageous of him suddenly to disappear. Which left Saturday, if everyone but Leskov had left in the morning. Leskov could spend the afternoon alone, and he would be back so that they could have dinner together. Anyway, it was one less day of despair.

Perlmann quickened his pace and went to the travel agent's in another part of the town. Here, too, he had to wait another ten minutes, during which he paced uneasily up and down. How long would it take for an airmail package to travel from Frankfurt to St Petersburg? And how secure was the mail? He couldn't have the text couriered – airline company employees wouldn't think a manuscript worth sending with any great urgency. Was it possible to imagine them sending it registered post?

The computer for flight reservations was on strike, and he was told to come back later. Perlmann was glad that the stationer's was quite a long way away; the walking helped to combat his helpless anger. Apart from the fat woman, there was a lanky boy with a pimply face behind the counter. At the woman's request the boy silently spread out a selection of envelopes. Perlmann immediately discarded the ordinary ones without reinforcement and padding. Then he took the one with the cardboard backing and bent it back and forth until the cardboard nearly snapped. He liked its firmness, but the paper was nothing special, and he wasn't sure whether the envelope was big enough for the unusual format of the yellow sheets. He moistened his index finger with his tongue and rubbed the saliva on the paper, which turned dark brown and dissolved layer by layer.

'Don't worry. Of course I'll pay for it,' he said to the woman, who was furiously gasping for air.

The two padded envelopes that struck him as exactly the right size were made of matte paper, less tightly pressed than the other, shiny paper, which his saliva dissolved worryingly quickly. A revolting-looking, grey wadding came out of it; the other one was padded with transparent plastic. The corrugated foil would keep the moisture out. But what happened if the address disappeared under the snow along with the disintegrating paper? Perlmann set this envelope aside as well. As the boy stared at him, mesmerized, the woman sniffed agitatedly and made a face as if he were busy pulling the shop apart.

'You really don't need to worry,' Perlmann reassured her and took some cash out of his jacket pocket. 'I'll pay for everything.'

The last envelope was made of well-glued, shiny paper, but the padding was much thinner than it was in the others, and it was far too big. The pages would slip back and forth inside it, and be damaged even further. He asked the boy, who was glancing anxiously at the woman and still hadn't said a word, to give him a pile of typing paper, and tried it out, shaking the envelope wildly back and forth. The result wasn't quite as bad as he expected, but some of the pages were already slightly crushed. He asked them to show him various staplers, but none of them was capable of producing a line of staples that would have reduced the envelope to the right size. The paper survived the saliva test very well. Perlmann turned the envelope inconclusively back and forth, then suddenly asked for a glass of water.

He had to repeat the request. As the boy was going into the back, the woman resignedly lit a cigarette, and when a man came into the shop on crutches, with his foot in a cast, and greeted her like an old friend, she gave him a significant look. Perlmann walked to the door with his water and poured it over the envelope. For two or three seconds it looked as if the water would drip off the shiny paper without leaving a trace. But then the envelope was covered with dark patches that quickly got bigger and came together to form a single damp patch. Perlmann reached into the envelope and tested the dampness. The image of the Russian station platform appeared, and this time the dripping was melting snow. When he turned round he saw the three faces just behind the window. *The madman with the water on the envelopes.*

Mutely, and with the face of someone who is pleased to have had a bright idea, the boy gestured to him to wait and went to the back. The man with the crutches put his wallet in his pocket and left the shop, shaking his head. Perlmann paid and wedged the damaged envelopes under his arm. He was reading the chronicle a lot, he said to the woman, who smoked as she stared at the floor in front of her. But she didn't seem to remember, and Perlmann was glad when the boy broke the awkward silence.

The envelope he handed to him was ideal; Perlmann saw it straight away. It was a used envelope with an address and an American sender. The boy, he read from his gestures, had taken off the stamps. The envelope was made of thick yellow cardboard that felt waxy. It had plastic padding and reinforced corners and it was exactly the right size.

'*Perfetto*,' Perlmann said to the boy, who beamed at him and indignantly waved away his offer of money.

'Three thousand,' the woman said, looking up from the floor for one brief moment.

As Perlmann gave her the money, the boy furiously grabbed the envelope, looked in a drawer and finally stuck fresh labels over the address and the sender's details. Without deigning to look at the woman he handed Perlmann the envelope and gave him a jokey salute.

On the next corner Perlmann threw all the other envelopes into a garbage bin. When he crossed the street, he saw the man with the crutches, who seemed to have been watching him the whole time. *The lunatic throwing away envelopes.* At a school drinking fountain Perlmann splashed water over the yellow envelope. Spherical droplets formed, and disappeared completely when shaken and blown on. Suddenly, the Russian platform couldn't have mattered less.

In the travel agent's they booked Perlmann a flight to Frankfurt for lunchtime on Saturday. For the return flight at five they could only put him on the waiting list. Then Perlmann walked slowly towards the hotel and wondered how he could disguise his handwriting when he wrote Leskov's address on the label – and *which* address?

48

A hand grabbed him by the sleeve from below, and when he turned round, startled, he found himself looking into the laughing face of Evelyn Mistral, who was sitting at a café table. She pulled him down on to a chair and waved to the waiter. Perlmann hesitantly laid the yellow envelope on the table. *It's not dangerous. She can't possibly know what it's for.* As he waited for his coffee and they talked about how warm it still was, even though the sun was setting and the lights were being lit at the tables, he frantically wondered what he could say if she started talking about the envelope. Then, when he was stirring his coffee, she rested her hand on his other arm for a moment. What had been up with him over the past few days? She wanted to know. They'd hardly seen him, and when they did he had been so strange. '*Reservado,*' she smiled. And then fainting like that. They'd all been rather puzzled, and concerned.

Perlmann took another spoonful of sugar. He didn't know what to do with his hands, and when he put them in his jacket pocket, he touched the disk, which he had forgotten in the meantime. As if he had touched something burning hot or particularly disgusting, he immediately took his hands out of his pockets and lit a cigarette. Then, for a while, he looked across at the moored yachts, rocking on the wake from a motorboat.

'I don't even know myself,' he said at last, and avoided looking at her. 'I . . . I've just somehow lost my equilibrium.'

'And you really didn't want to deliver any kind of lecture, did you?' she asked softly and brushed the hair out of her face, which rested on her open hand. Perlmann looked at the levelling waves and nodded. He really wanted to leave, but at the same time he wished she would go on asking him questions.

'Can I say something? But you must promise not to take it amiss.'

Perlmann attempted a smile and nodded.

'If I may put it this way: I think you've made a mistake. You should have explained at the outset that everything's a bit difficult for you at the moment, and you could also just have said that you didn't want to give a lecture. Your wife's death – everyone would have understood straight away. As things stand, everything that happened – dinner and everything – was interpreted as arrogance. Until Vassily put us right. The rest of us were completely in the dark.'

So it was a good idea to tell Leskov about Agnes at the fortress back then. It meant that he was able to provide a redeeming interpretation. The man I was inches away from murdering.

In their seductive simplicity, Evelyn Mistral's words had been an enticing offer of self-deception, which Perlmann was unable at that moment to resist. He had committed a social solecism. He had made a very simple error. He wanted to enjoy the peace that lay within that insight. It could happen to anyone. You could avoid it in future. And in three days, at this time, he would be at home.

'You're completely right,' he said, 'it was a mistake. Nothing more to be said.' It sounded shallow, almost insincere. So, after a pause, he added, 'Sometimes it's so hard.' He hoped he wasn't overdoing it with his tortured face.

Ruge, Millar and von Levetzov slumped on to their chairs with feigned exhaustion and put their shopping bags full of presents under the empty table next to them. Perlmann had been able to see them coming from a long way off and, with a movement that looked like a reflex, he had taken the envelope off the table and rested it against the leg of the chair.

'At exactly the usual time,' Evelyn Mistral smiled, glancing at her watch.

'Yes,' said Millar with a nostalgic sigh. 'The first time we came here, a month ago, it was still light at this time of day. I'll miss these daily meetings.' He looked at Perlmann. 'Just a shame you were never there.'

The others nodded. Perlmann felt cold, and when he buttoned up his jacket, the disk bumped, with a quiet, dull sound, against the arm of the chair.

'But if I imagine,' Millar went on, 'the same thing happening to me as happened to you – I don't think I'd feel like doing anything. Except sailing,' he added with a grin.

The remark took Perlmann's breath away for a moment, and he felt himself welling up. Achim Ruge must have seen that something was happening in his face. With an expression and a voice that Perlmann wouldn't have thought possible, he started talking about his younger sister, whom he had loved very much. He couldn't even have imagined her taking drugs. Until she was found dead.

'You know,' he said to Perlmann in German, and his bright green eyes seemed to be even more watery than usual, 'I basically dropped out for almost a year after that. Things went up and down in the lab. I had to cancel lectures, and my irritability towards my colleagues became legendary. Nothing seemed to have a point any more.'

Superficial, thought Perlmann, *my fear of them has made me terribly superficial.* So superficial that he couldn't even imagine them capable of the most elementary, the most natural impulses and reactions. Otherwise he wouldn't have been so flabbergasted. Fear made other people bigger and stronger than they were, and at the same time they became smaller and more primitive. Couldn't he have gone to them on Saturday morning and explained his irrational actions? And wouldn't that still have been possible at a later time?

'I could imagine,' von Levetzov said, 'that your invitation to Princeton hasn't come at exactly the right time.'

Perlmann nodded, and again he was surprised by the sympathy that he was suddenly encountering. Was it, perhaps, not only fear that had made him superficial, but also that fear had come about because his view of things had been superficial from the outset – because he hadn't thought the others capable of sympathy, and hence of depth?

'Things like that can be postponed,' confirmed Millar, when Perlmann looked at him quizzically.

He was actually considering that, Perlmann said, and tried to look at von Levetzov with a particularly open and personal expression, as a way of apologizing for his abruptness over breakfast. A personal relationship with Adrian von Levetzov would be more easily achieved in the presence of the others than in private. When Perlmann realized that, he became very confused. All of a sudden he had a sense that he didn't know the slightest thing about people and their relationships with each other.

The others seemed not to see Leskov, who was waddling and flailing his way towards town. Perlmann hadn't recognized him at first, because tonight he was wearing a peaked cap that lay on the bulges of his neck and, as a result, looked too small. *If only he would walk more quickly.*

'Hang on, that's Vassily!' called von Levetzov, jumping to his feet and running after him.

Perlmann reached for the envelope beside the leg of the chair. No, it would attract less attention down here than on the next table.

Leskov liked the jokes about his cap. He showed it around and acted the clown. Later, when the conversation turned to the session, he touched Perlmann on the shoulder and said he hadn't been able to get over his amazement when listening to him.

'I would have bet my head that you'd read my text,' he laughed, 'and very carefully, too. I sent him,' he said, turning to the others, 'the earlier version. But he denies it. Apparently, my Russian's still too hard for him.'

'Didn't you say you didn't speak Russian?' von Levetzov asked with a face in which irritation and admiration balanced one another.

Perlmann avoided Evelyn Mistral's eyes, took off his glasses and rubbed his eyes. *It doesn't matter. I haven't committed plagiarism. No plagiarism.* 'Just a few words,' he said.

He couldn't bear the pause that followed for very long, and went inside with an apology. At the end of the corridor where the toilets were,

a door was open, leading to the other side of the quay wall. He walked
to the water. Kitchen waste floated below him. He took the disk out of
his jacket pocket and looked round. When he let go of it, it was caught
by a gust of wind and fell with a clatter on the wall. He looked round
again, and then kicked it out.

'We're just talking about this amazing envelope,' said Leskov, and
rested it on the table. 'It fell over a moment ago when you stood up.
Brian knows this kind from home. I wish we had things like that.'

'Anything important I send in those envelopes,' said Millar, 'especially manuscripts.' He rubbed the cardboard with his thumb and forefinger. 'The things are practically watertight.'

Perlmann felt as if all the strength were suddenly draining from him,
so much so that lifting his coffee cup seemed too much. He was filled
with an overwhelming sense of pointlessness. Unable to think of an
answer, he waited to be asked where he had got hold of the envelope.
But the question didn't come.

The conversation now turned to dinner. Just for once, the others
didn't want to eat at the Miramare. Suddenly, Millar, who had folded
his hands behind his head and was looking over towards the hill on the
other side of the bay, said, 'Why don't we go to that white hotel up
there? What's it called?'

'Imperiale,' said von Levetzov. 'I had a drink there. The restaurant
looked good.'

It was agreed that Silvestri and Laura Sand would have to be told,
and Signora Morelli as well. Perlmann nodded. On the way to the hotel
Leskov joined him and, with a smile, handed him the yellow envelope.

The lamp in the corner of the lounge where Perlmann had sat on
Monday night was on again today. On the chair, two children were
practising gymnastics, while their grandmother struggled to keep them
under control. It made everything look very ordinary, even banal. *The
viewpoint of eternity*, that was what Perlmann had thought about in that
corner. The fear that he had been using that idea to defend himself
against had been terrible. But it had given the thought a weight and a

depth that were now lost. Now, surrounded by his good-humored colleagues, who were studying their menus, the thought seemed shallow and dull; it was little more than a sequence of words.

Perlmann was also generally bothered by the others, and he had to take care that his irritation, which had made him tear off two shirt buttons when he was changing earlier, didn't intensify still further. This was the place where Kirsten had asked him whether he'd been happy with Agnes. And it was where he had experienced an extreme despair. It was his hotel. The others had no business here.

Through the swing door of the kitchen came the waiter that Perlmann had called an arsehole. He was wearing the same red jacket as on Tuesday, and now he whipped out his order pad and stepped up to their table. Standing at an angle, he didn't see Perlmann at first, and took Ruge's and Silvestri's orders. Then, as Laura Sand was speaking, his eye wandered one chair along. Perlmann waited with his eyes half-closed, annoyed at the pounding of his heart. The waiter wrote something in his pad, then paused. His eyes narrowed and, after a further motionless moment, he turned his head sharply and looked at Perlmann, who was pressing his hands together under the table. The waiter jutted his lower lip, looked slowly away and then it seemed as if he would go on writing. But then he slipped pad and pen into his jacket pocket, turned round abruptly and walked quickly through the swing door.

'What's up with him?' Laura Sand asked irritably, tapping the back of her menu rhythmically against the edge of the table.

'No idea,' said Perlmann, when she looked at him quizzically.

The maître d' in the black tuxedo stood, arms folded, by the swing door and watched furiously as the waiter came back to their table. The waiter turned to Laura Sand.

'*Scusi, signora,*' he said tightly, 'would you please repeat your order?'

Then he turned the page of his pad and, without deigning to glance at Perlmann, looked at Millar. Surprised by the silence, Millar looked up, glanced sideways at Perlmann, who was sitting next to him, and said in a cool voice which Perlmann envied him, 'You seem to have forgotten someone.'

The waiter didn't move, but just raised the pad over Millar's head
and looked into the room. The maître d' was about to move, when
Perlmann gave his order, in dry, clipped words. The waiter brought the
pen to the pad, but didn't write. Then he looked again at Millar, who,
after a brief hesitation and with raised eyebrows, dictated his wishes.

She had had no idea about his wife's accident, Laura Sand said. Why
hadn't he said anything? It would have made a lot of things easier to
understand.

'She's right,' said Millar, and in his mouth it sounded yet again like
a reproof.

'I don't know,' said Perlmann, and was glad that his voice revealed
nothing of the anger that was starting to rise up in him. Now, after
they had experienced his breakdown, and he had been dropped as a
rival and an adversary in the academic game – now they were all speaking
so sympathetically, they were full of generosity and didn't seem to have
the faintest sense of how repellent moral complacency could be. Would
they have thought and spoken like that if nothing so dramatic had
happened to him, nothing that came so close to an illness? Superficiality
as an effect and a cause of fear; that was right. On the other hand: how
exactly should he have said it? Where were the individual words of which
his explanation would have consisted? And when exactly would he have
made it? Perlmann was furious at the shallowness of their generosity, at
their lack of precise imagination. With each question about details that
passed through his head, his fury intensified still further, he became
blind and deaf to his environment and didn't notice that a long piece
of his ash was falling on the freshly starched, blossom-white tablecloth.

The others had been served ages before, but Perlmann still had nothing.
The waiter, who had treated him as if he didn't exist when he was serving,
let the long minutes pass, and an awkward silence fell in which the others
cast puzzled glances at his empty plate. Perlmann had just pushed back
his chair to go in search of the maître d', when the waiter, with a face
like ice, brought him a *piccata alla Milanese* and slammed the dish down
on the bottom plate with a loud clatter, ensuring, with deliberate negligence, that it landed at an angle. The others resumed their conversation.

With his first bite, Perlmann knew: after it had been prepared, the dish had been put in the fridge for a while. Inside it was still warm, but its surface was chilled, and the coldness felt artificial to the tongue. The tomato sauce was particularly cold, and the outermost layer by the cheese was like rubber. He kept an eye out for the maître d', then got up and walked to the swing door. The waiter, as far as one could make out, had stood watching through the little window in the door. Now he kicked the door open and stepped defiantly out towards Perlmann.

'My dinner is cold,' Perlmann said, so loudly that the people at the other tables turned round. The waiter chewed on his lip and looked at him with a hate-filled, contemptuous grin. Then he walked at a pointedly sluggish pace to Perlmann's place, took the plate and disappeared with an eloquent shake of the head, designed to accuse Perlmann of grouchiness, into the kitchen. When the food was put in front of Perlmann again, it tasted warmed-up and stale, and after a few bites he left it.

It wasn't just that they were making things look far too simple by reproaching him – in what was intended as a friendly way – for having said nothing and for not having made use of their sympathy. Much worse was that he couldn't count on their sympathy at all if he told them the truth: that the academic world and its lifestyle had long ago slipped away from him and become something quite alien. To keep from drawing attention to himself, every now and again he poked around at his food, which he could only see now as a disgusting orangey paste, and as he did so it became clear to him that the rage that seethed in him was actually directed far more at the simplistic chatter about his missed explanation than it was at his personal situation.

Before, in the café, he had allowed himself to yield for a moment to the thought that his distress had been caused by the commotion that had resulted from Agnes's death. *That could happen*, he thought with amazement: you fled into a thought that you had several times exposed as deceptive, and you did so and opted for blindness because you wanted peace, peace from the flickering questions that oppressed you if you admitted the truth. And, of course, what had happened had had something to do with the fact that it was Evelyn Mistral, of all people, who had suggested that old and seductive thought. But now, as he looked with revulsion at his plate and waited to be able to smoke again at last, Perlmann was once again filled with rage at the idea that they were forcing him, through their lack of sympathy, to leave the excuse about Agnes uncontested, and to distort his pain still further with a lie.

What did that lack of sympathy really mean? At last he could light a cigarette, and his concentration on the question helped him ignore the waiter, who deliberately brushed his sleeve with the plate as he cleared the table. He ran through his colleagues one by one, glancing furtively at each as their turn came. No, in this matter he didn't underestimate the others out of fear. He couldn't allow himself to be deceived even by Evelyn Mistral's face, red with wine and laughter. If he closed her eyes, her head with her piled-up hair and glasses superimposed itself over the image that he had just seen. The only one he thought capable of understanding was Giorgio Silvestri. But he didn't represent the hated academic world anyway. And besides: could he really understand how someone could have fallen victim to an incurable indifference towards all desire for knowledge? Perlmann doubted it, looking at him now, leaning tensely forward and making the gesture of precision with his thumb and forefinger.

Over coffee the talk turned to the teaching duties that awaited his colleagues when they returned home. As he listened, it suddenly occurred to Perlmann that at breakfast that morning, when von Levetzov had asked him, he had described not his impending lecture series but last year's. And as his smoking grew increasingly frantic, he realized with growing apprehension, almost panic, that the lectures that began next week had been blocked from his memory: he had their subjects on the tip of his tongue; they were present to him in the form of a vague sensation, but every attempt to bring them into the focus of his attention failed; the titles and the precise questions refused and refused to come. *When will my resignation take effect? Can I simply stay away? Nothing more can happen to me now. Nothing.*

This term, Ruge sighed, it was his turn to give the introductory lecture. As Millar and von Levetzov responded with sympathetic words,

Perlmann saw himself at the last session in Frankfurt, at which the teaching program had been discussed. The others had found it extraordinarily collegial of him to give the introductory lecture for the third time in a row. But there had been a momentary pause, and their astonishment was tangible. Was it only thoughtfulness that had appeared in their faces, or was it already suspicion? *I find it increasingly important,* he had said. *I like working with beginners. Their minds are unspoiled.* It was an explanation that they could not dispute. And even so, the director of the institute had had to give himself a visible jolt before carrying on.

Perlmann delivered the introductory lecture slightly differently every year, and the new thing was his increasingly unconcealed detachment from the material. More and more often he wove in remarks like: 'At this point one might ask the question . . . One doesn't *need* to ask it, perhaps, but *if* one asks it, then . . .' or 'Now there is this distinction . . .' and then he made a pause of ostentatious thoughtfulness that would inevitably create the impression in his audience that he thought this distinction unnecessary or even nonsensical. He was in danger of exaggerating and giving the whole thing a comedic note. Particularly on days when he felt out of sorts. The students enjoyed it. But while they laughed, he hated himself for his play-acting. Because he didn't like play-acting. He was deadly earnest about this detachment from his subject, which affected him like an inexorable process of growth, and which he observed with mounting despair.

Leskov had been busy with his pipe, and had sipped quietly at his coffee. He wished, he said now into a pause in the conversation, he too could complain like that. From one term to the next, he was unsure whether he would receive a teaching job or not. He said it quite matter-of-factly, and without a trace of self-pity.

'But if I hand in the new text now, that might change,' he smiled, and glanced across at Perlmann. 'Provided it turns up again,' he added with a face in which intense humor imperfectly masked lurking panic.

Perlmann made a helpless gesture with his hand, and had no idea whether what he was trying to do with his facial muscles was leading to a smile or to a grimace. *To which address?* he thought frantically. *To which address?* And the envelope. And the waiting list for the flight.

While the others were leaving tips, Perlmann paid the sum precisely, and pushed the notes slightly towards the middle of the table, so that the waiter would have to lean a long way forwards to reach them. But again the waiter treated him as if he wasn't there, and simply left Perlmann's money where it was. Laura Sand pointed at it, and touched Perlmann's arm with a questioning expression. He pretended not to have noticed. He let the others walk ahead and waited in the hall until the waiter, who had now picked up his money, came out of the dining room.

'You know,' he said and tried to stare him into the ground, 'I was right: you really are one. And how.'

'*Stronzo!*' the waiter hissed back, his lips seeming not to move a millimeter.

Perlmann left him standing and walked outside to join the others, who were waiting for taxis.

49

When he woke up at about seven o'clock the next morning, Perlmann's first thought was that his sore throat came from his furious roaring in the dean's office. It became clear to him only very gradually that the dry scratching must have come from breathing with his mouth open, as his rage had clearly been directed at a figure in a dream. At the end it had been the dean. But he gradually remembered that that figure had had its original source in the waiter. He had bawled him out in the presence of the others. He had got up, tipped his cold food on the immaculate tablecloth and had, accompanying each word with a slicing movement of his hand, repeated his small and awkward repertoire of Italian insults again and again, the perception of his narrow linguistic boundaries adding to his fury. The longer it lasted, the more formless the waiter became, and the figure had become increasingly similar to Leskov. In a room that was no longer a dining room, Perlmann had reproached him for not having made a copy of his text, his accusations growing louder and louder, while Leskov looked as if he wasn't even listening. The silent and unreachable Leskov had then become a pale, almost faceless figure, but one which in spite of its vagueness was unambiguously the dean. Perlmann had dealt with him more ruthlessly and thoroughly than he had ever treated a person before. With his heart hammering, he had screamed accusation after accusation until his voice failed. He held the rector responsible for everything papery and dead in the world of the university. He blamed him for the mistrust, the resentment and anxiety that prevailed in that world. He insulted him as the source of all pomposity, and finally held him responsible for the decades of his life that he had lost to his job. Just as he was hurling at him the question of why he had prevented him from being an interpreter, he noticed that there was no one in the room, and that his hoarse words were echoing in a ghostly void. He had finally woken up surrounded by the resultant feeling of impotence.

Perlmann ordered coffee and, after showering, sat down at his desk. If yesterday his letters to the dean had become shorter and shorter, today the opposite happened, although he powerfully resisted the bitterness and agitation that rang out within him even now. He didn't want his letter of resignation to be defined by such feelings – he didn't want it to be an epilogue to his dream. He immediately crossed out every harsh word and replaced it with an expression of pointed neutrality and sobriety. In this way he produced increasingly official-sounding texts. And yet he couldn't prevent them from turning into bills of indictment, long and ever longer explanations in which evidence was piled on evidence for the claim that a life determined by academic study and its pursuit must inevitably become an alienated life, a life missed. Like an addict, he went on writing more and more, and each new outline was even longer and more expansive than the one before.

It was already after half-past eight when he paused, exhausted and trembling. For a while he stood at the window and stared into the streaming rain. Another two days. In fifty hours he was at the airport, waiting for his flight home. And tomorrow he would be travelling for half a day, and time would go much faster. Hitherto he had always been lucky with waiting lists for flights.

He scanned through the last page that he had written. Then he brought all the pages together and threw the whole pile into the waste-paper basket. It wasn't a general problem of academics, or even of academia generally. It was a problem of his very particular life story. That was all. To turn it into an ideology was mischievous nonsense. Basically, that had always been clear to him. In the end, all his writing that morning had become an extension of the dream. And now he had cheated himself out of his breakfast, to which, he reflected with surprise, he would have liked to go today.

*

Giorgio Silvestri's session was sheer chaos. It started with him leaving half of his documents in his room, and having to go back and get them. Then, when he had found his way through the chaos, he began a lecture that had no structure and for a long time also seemed to have no destination. He talked about typical linguistic disturbances among schizophrenics, which were expressive of mental disturbances. His technical vocabulary sounded cobbled-together and eccentric, and he made no effort to introduce it. Admittedly, after some time it was fairly easy to recognize how it could be translated into familiar concepts. But it was irritating that one had to discover them for oneself. There was also the fact that Silvestri's English pronunciation was much worse than usual that morning; somehow his mouth didn't really seem to be obeying him. That was particularly unsettling in the case of the example sentences, which Silvestri had only in Italian, and of which he gave impromptu translations. Often one didn't know how much of their strange sound could really be traced back to the mental patients, what came from Silvestri's halting delivery, and whether additional distortions were not produced by the translation of difficult linguistic material. Soon his colleagues started drawing decorative doodles in their notebooks, and even Evelyn Mistral, who had at first been smiling with sympathy for Silvestri over the chaotic nature of his lecture, became impatient.

Again the time has come, Perlmann thought: he felt abandoned by someone he had internally clung to. Silvestri – the man with the important and honest profession, which gave him the necessary inner distance to be able to sit on the lounger with a newspaper over his head and rock back and forth on his chair during the sessions; the man who had advised Perlmann not to take the whole thing so seriously; and, in the end, also the man who had been able to get to grips with his notes. And now he was sitting up there at the front, turning over the empty coffee pot for the second time, and darting increasingly insecure glances at the group. All of a sudden his stubble was no longer the expression of independence and incorruptibility; it just looked scruffy. His skin struck Perlmann as even paler than usual, and now for the first time he spotted a small boil on Silvestri's chin. *You do get through your heroes,* he heard Agnes saying, and he didn't know who he should be more annoyed with: her, or this Italian who seemed, once more, to prove her right.

Now Silvestri pushed his papers aside, lit a new cigarette and started explaining the basic points of his investigation. He was no orator, and it wasn't a fluent, suggestive lecture. Nonetheless, Perlmann noticed with growing relief that the man had something to say. Leskov, who had looked unhappy and had several times sighed quietly, also relaxed, and Laura Sand had begun to take notes. There were many years of work with schizophrenics behind the ideas that Silvestri was developing, and an inexhaustible patience when it came to listening to them. His dark-eyed, white face now showed great concentration, and when he spoke with admiration of Gaetano Benedetti, whom he saw as the most important researcher into schizophrenia, one could tell how much passion he had devoted to his work.

The sounds of tearing paper broke the silence that had fallen when Silvestri looked for a quotation from Benedetti. Millar had torn a page from his notebook. He now wrote something and with a flippant gesture passed it to Ruge, who was today sitting slightly further away from him than usual. At the last moment Millar must have sensed that he was being impolite, because his arm twitched, as if he wanted to undo the gesture, but it was too late: the page slipped to the edge of the table and sailed to the floor, where it stopped in front of Silvestri's eyes. Perlmann had to crane his neck slightly, and then he could read it: *De Benedetti?!*

Silvestri, who had found the quotation at last, followed the eyes of the others and read the note. He froze for a moment, his face colored, and he closed his eyes. No one moved. Millar stared at the table top in front of him. In fact, Perlmann thought, it was just chitchat; a piece of schoolboy mischief. But at that particular moment, it must have felt like a slap in the face to Silvestri: recently Carlo De Benedetti, the President of Olivetti, had been in court because of his previous involvement in the bankruptcy of a bank. If one knew that, the reddish sheet of paper on the gleaming parquet called to mind the world of money, power and corruption. It was only a joke, and not remotely malicious. That was certainly apparent to Silvestri as well. But at that moment it was already too much for him that while Gaetano Benedetti's self-sacrificing labours, his great life's work, was under discussion, someone else's thoughts were wandering in another, ugly world, even though the association came about in the simplest, most innocuous way imaginable. Obviously, Silvestri experienced it as practically a personal attack – as if his own commitment were being indirectly disparaged or even ridiculed.

Silvestri hadn't seen where the piece of paper came from. He must, Perlmann reflected, have recognized Millar's handwriting, because when he looked up now, Millar was the first person he looked at. He stared at him for a few seconds, and the vertical wrinkles above his nose gave his gaunt, hollow-cheeked face an angry, unforgiving expression. As Silvestri directed his gaze, which now assumed a rather downcast quality, back to the piece of paper, he took out his ballpoint pen and clicked the tip in and out. He did it several times, the rhythm stretching as if on a slow-motion soundtrack, and the individual clicks seemed to whip their apprehensive silence like gunshots. Perlmann involuntarily held his breath. Now Silvestri leaned back, rolled his hands on his head and, as he took a breath, looked Millar full in the face. Although the look was not meant for him, Perlmann shrank from the harshness of his dark stare. Silvestri's voice would be piercing when it came.

At that moment the door opened, and Signora Morelli stepped inside the veranda with a piece of paper in her hand. The silence in the room must have struck her as strange, because she hesitated and left her hand on the handle before she gave a start, said, '*Scusatemi*' and walked up to Perlmann.

'I thought you should know this straight away,' she said as she bent down to him and gave him a note.

She had said it quietly, and yet the Italian sentence had been audible throughout the whole room. *Phone call travel agent: flight Frankfurt–Genoa confirmed tomorrow 5 p.m.* the note said.

'*Grazie*,' Perlmann said hoarsely, folded the note and slipped it into his jacket pocket. He didn't dare to look at Leskov beside him, so he didn't know if it was his imagination or whether Leskov turned his head away only now.

Only when the door clicked shut did Perlmann notice that Silvestri had risen to his feet, and had plainly been walking up and down. Now the Italian stubbed out his cigarette, hesitated for a moment and then, sitting on the table top, swung himself into the middle of the horseshoe. With a jerky movement he lifted the reddish piece of paper, stood in front of Millar and, without looking at him, silently and carefully let the paper float on to the table. Then he swung back over the table, meticulously straightened his chair and went on with his lecture. After a few sentences his breath became normal again. Laura Sand exhaled audibly.

When the discussion began, Millar at first cleaned his glasses for several minutes. Later, as Silvestri was battling with Leskov's questions, which were much less clear today than they usually were, Millar stared with blank concentration at the swimming pool, where the heavy raindrops were splashing the water high into the air. Now and again Silvestri darted him quick glances from the corner of his eye. But his agitation seemed to have subsided, and here, once again, he proved to be a good listener, who encouraged his interlocutor, with a brief nod and the hint of a smile, to go on spinning out the thought that he had just embarked upon.

What Perlmann particularly envied was the amount of time that Silvestri took before answering a question. He wouldn't, it seemed, allow any question in the world to put pressure on him. Questions weren't something he felt coerced by. They were primarily an opportunity to think, regardless of how long it took. *No wonder Kirsten took to him immediately.* Again Perlmann hid his face between his folded hands and tried inwardly to imagine what it must feel like to be someone with so little fear of other people and their questions. He almost felt dizzy when he concentrated intensely on the notional point of experience that could be achieved were he to succeed in dismantling the structure of his anxiety piece by piece and transfer it into another way of feeling.

It was Ruge's chuckling laughter that tore him from his reflections.

It was plainly inspired by the way in which Silvestri defended himself against doubts about his method. He had dealt at such length and so devotedly with his patients that he had the unshakeable assurance of having achieved a profound understanding of the pattern of their linguistic and mental disturbances. What made Silvestri assailable was his refusal to have anyone look over his shoulder and check what he was doing. *There is no theoretical context*, Perlmann thought, but somehow that refusal could surprise no one who knew the dangerous gleam that appeared in Silvestri's eyes when the discussion turned to the issue of bolted asylum doors. The man was a maverick and a fanatical defender of liberty, who must have seemed, in his clinic, like an anarchist, albeit an anarchist in whose office the light still burned even when his team had gone home long ago. *Your hero-addicted imagination.* Agnes had been proud of her verbal creation.

'I have listened to many of these people for years,' Silvestri said with unshakeable calm. 'I know how they speak and think. I know it precisely. Really precisely.'

Ruge gave up with a sigh, and an uncomfortable pause settled, so that Silvestri began to get his things together. Then Millar ostentatiously sat up in his chair, rested both elbows on the table and waited until Silvestri met his eye.

'Look, Giorgio . . . ' he began, and the use of Silvestri's first name sounded like mockery. And then he lectured Silvestri on the safeguarding and evaluation of data, about sources of error and the danger of arte-facts, about multiple verification procedures, and finally about the idea of objectivity. More and more he slipped into the tone of someone explaining, in a course for first-term freshmen, the ABC of academic work, and assuming no more than an average intelligence among his listeners.

Silvestri looked out over the edge of the table to the parquet – to where the piece of paper had been a few moments before. There was a lot going on in his facial expression. The initial look of anger and indig-nation gave way to various shades of amusement and arrogance, but also of irony and contempt, which moved into one another uninterruptedly and without any fixed arrangement. Then, when he noticed that Millar had nearly finished, Silvestri withdrew completely from his face, straightened his papers again and sat down on the very edge of the chair. His long, white fingers were trembling slightly when he brought the lighter to his cigarette. Evelyn Mistral threw her hands to her face like someone trying to flee an inescapable disaster.

'I believe, Professor Millar,' he said gently, his pronunciation now impeccable, 'that I have understood you perfectly. You want repeatable experiments. Laboratory conditions with calm, stable objects. Controllable variables. Am I wrong, or would you also really like to strap these people to chairs?' He stubbed out his half-smoked cigarette, took his belongings and a few steps later he was outside.

Millar had red patches on his face, and for a moment he looked almost numb. 'Well,' he said with artificial cheerfulness, and got to his feet. His rubber soles squeaked loudly on the parquet as he stepped vigorously outside.

Only then did the others stir.

50

The rain had stopped, and the clouds were moving. Perlmann stood at the window and tried to apologize for Silvestri's gaffe without being unfair to Millar. It didn't work. He went from one extreme to the other, without finding a resting point. In his memory, Silvestri's voice had become a hiss, and it wasn't hard for Perlmann to sense the hatred behind that hiss. It was particularly easy to understand when one remembered Millar's unbearably didactic tone. And at such a moment no one could have demanded that Silvestri take account of the plain fact that Millar had been trying to erase the memory of his faux pas with the piece of paper by childishly going on the attack. But then Perlmann saw, again and again, Millar's face with its red patches; the face of someone reeling inwardly from a completely unexpected slap. He had looked very vulnerable, this man Brian Millar, not at all like the monster described by Silvestri's unfortunate remark. All right, Millar supported the death penalty, which already made him very odd. But that evening, which Silvestri would probably never forget, Millar hadn't advocated it with any bigoted, missionary zeal. Silvestri was right: there was a certain lack of imagination at play, a kind of naivety. But did not this very lack of imagination, this naivety, mean that one couldn't possibly attribute to Millar the perverse and inhuman desires that resounded in Silvestri's perfidious question? Or was it exactly the opposite?

Perlmann tried to remember all of the things he still had to do today. But he couldn't keep his thoughts together, so he sat down at his desk and made a list. It took ages, and he had to overcome a paralysing reluctance to write down each individual point. *Travel agent.* It was urgent that he buy his ticket straight away. *Stationery shop.* Going back to that mute boy was out of the question. There must be another shop that sold envelopes. *Trattoria.* The bright courtyard now struck him as remote and alien. But he couldn't bring himself simply to leave the chronicle there and vanish without a word. Not least because of Sandra. *Maria.* He would have to say goodbye to her today; she wasn't in the office tomorrow. And then there was something else. That was it: *Angelini.* Perlmann's stomach lurched. Should he simply wait and see whether he appeared for dinner? But then if he didn't come, Perlmann would have to call him on his private number, which was in his recent note. Perlmann bridled at the idea. After all that had happened, he wanted to thank Angelini and say goodbye in a very formal and businesslike fashion.

He was about to ask Olivetti for Angelini's number when Silvestri came to say goodbye. Instead of a suitcase he was carrying a kind of duffel bag over his shoulder.

'I'm leaving now,' he said simply and held out his hand to Perlmann. 'Thank you for the invitation. Give me a call if you're ever in Bologna. And if you have a text like that last one again, I'll read it.'

He had half-turned away when he paused, looked at the floor and described a semi-circle on the carpet with his foot.

'With that particular subject I always lose control. Old sickness,' he said in a cautious, muted voice. Then he looked at Perlmann with a smile in which embarrassment, defiant self-assertion and roguery merged, and added, 'Incurable.'

But, as he absorbed this, Perlmann knew that he would never forget the image of the Italian with the duffel bag, the face turned crookedly upwards and the ambiguous smile, at once vigorous and fragile. It sank inside him like the frozen image at the end of a film.

'Oh, yes, please pass on my greetings to your daughter,' Silvestri said in the doorway. 'Providing that she's willing to accept them,' he added with a grin. 'And really, go to the doctor when you get home. You still look ill.' Then he raised his free hand slightly and was gone.

When Perlmann saw Silvestri coming out of the hotel down below, Evelyn Mistral was walking beside him and nodding. They walked slowly, as if on a deserted platform. Just before they reached the steps, Silvestri let the duffel bag slide to the ground and stretched out both arms to pull her to him. She took half a step backwards and threw out a hand. He automatically grabbed it and, after a brief hesitation, clumsily laid his other hand on her shoulder. He didn't seem to be looking at her any more, but bent down, threw the duffel bag over his shoulder with a forceful and possibly angry movement, and quickly walked down the steps. He was already quite far down when Evelyn Mistral's lips formed a word that must have been *Ciao*. She grabbed her hair with both hands and pressed it together as if to make a ponytail. Then she let it fall again and, holding her wrist behind her back, turned slowly to the door.

When Perlmann was about to close the window, he saw Silvestri driving past in his old Fiat. He was flicking a cigarette butt out of the sunroof, and then be bent down to turn the knobs of the radio. What would have happened if he had confided to this man, whom he was going to miss, and would never see again?

The phone rang. Angelini said that sadly he wouldn't be able to come to the farewell dinner. Something unexpected had come up: trouble with a translator whom he had recommended to the firm, and who had revealed himself to be a bit of a dolt. Perlmann gripped the receiver more tightly than necessary, and listened very carefully: no, Angelini wasn't telling him this in so much detail in order to conceal the fact that it was an excuse. On the contrary, in an almost friendly way he seemed really to want to share his concern with him. Quite as if there had been no trashy text, as if he hadn't fainted, and as if the whole thing hadn't been a terrible disappointment.

'*Senti, Carlo,*' Perlmann said, suddenly inspired, and it felt like a liberating leap into the unknown, 'there's something I'd like to discuss with you. Something personal. Could I pay you a visit up there in Ivrea?'

He would be delighted, Angelini said immediately. But Sunday . . . no, Sunday was impossible, with the best will in the world. Either tomorrow afternoon or Monday morning.

Perlmann hesitated. Leskov's text would have been dispatched long since, and they would have to wait another day for him at the university. That was no longer of any importance.

'Monday morning,' he said at last. 'At nine?'

'For God's sake, no,' laughed Angelini, 'they'll faint if I get there as early as that.' The pause sounded as if he was biting his lip. 'Shall we say, shortly after ten? And should I book a hotel for you for Sunday night?'

Perlmann said no.

'Just tell the driver, "Olivetti, main entrance". They'll help you at reception,' said Angelini.

I'll ask Angelini if I can have this job as a translator. Or something like it. Perlmann puffed away on his cigarette as he walked up and down. Yesterday morning's decision was one thing, the idea of a concrete alternative something else entirely. A hot, intoxicating feeling of liberation took hold of him. Soon it turned into a feeling that the ground was swaying beneath him. And then, from one moment to the next, he despaired. How would he get a work permit for Italy? And what qualifications did he have? No language exams, no diplomas, nothing. Would Angelini override that? Could he just do it? Even if Perlmann didn't have to work directly under him, somehow, in the future, he would be dependent on this smartly dressed man with the well-cut suits and loose-fitting ties. Suddenly, Perlmann saw Angelini's boss-face in front of him, the one he had worn when that business at the town hall had got too lively for him. At the time that face hadn't permeated through to Perlmann; it had belonged to a world that was edging further away with every minute. Now that Perlmann imagined a life haunted by that face it struck him as hard, brutal and abhorrent. And then there was the age difference, which wouldn't even be an easy matter on Monday: the older man petitioning the younger. *I could still call it all off,* Perlmann thought. A phone call would do it. And he would simply leave his flight reservation for Sunday as it was.

At the travel agent's Perlmann was the last one before lunch. He bought his ticket for the following day and paid a horrendous price, because he was booking at such short notice. For Monday, he booked himself a seat on the afternoon flight from Turin to Frankfurt. *Perhaps by the time I'm sitting on that plane I'll have a new job.* And, last of all, that hotel in Ivrea. The young man with the long hair and all those silver rings on his hands began to get impatient with all the phone calls, and kept looking at the clock on the wall. Perlmann didn't dare to refuse when at last a room was found at an exorbitant price. To get out, Perlmann had to turn a bunch of keys that the other employee had left in the door when he went out.

The wind had got stronger. The clouds drifted across the city from the sea, and every few moments the sun bathed everything in a strangely cold, glassy light. Perlmann felt slight and a little shivery, like someone who has just taken a long-overdue step into a new future. An appointment for a discussion, a hotel reservation, a reserved flight: it was nothing, and at the same time it was a great deal. As he studied the clean, sharp shadow that he cast in this extraordinary light, he felt surprised with himself – at the fact that he had actually begun to turn a decision that was barely thirty hours old into action. He also felt a quiet pride. And after a while it became clear to him that he had never had such an experience before: knowing almost to the minute when he had started really believing in a decision. He immediately saw himself in an office filled with southern light, immersed in the thing he liked doing best since he had stopped playing the piano: immersing himself in words and phrases and circling within himself to test whether the expression in the foreign language precisely captured the nuance required. The images and feelings that rose up in him now were so precise and so powerful that, without really noticing, he kept stopping after a few steps and, motionless, stared blankly into space. Startled again by his unbridled, overheated imagination, which was actually trying to compel a dreamed future into existence, he rubbed his eyes and then walked on with a disciplined step, looking – to distract himself – more closely at the window displays than he usually did.

Even as he parted the glass-bead curtain he realized that the trattoria was alien to him now. For a moment he considered whether it might be the unusual light falling through the glass roof of the courtyard. But it wasn't that. The restaurant was now as strange to him as a place where one had lived so long ago that it's hard to believe that that life was once one's own.

'*Professore!*' called the proprietress. 'We thought something had happened to you!'

Perlmann was relieved that she didn't try to hug him, as she seemed at first to be about to do. With the delighted zeal with which she would have served a long-lost relative, she and her husband, who was wearing the inevitable white apron, set Perlmann's food in front of him and insisted that he have a second portion.

'You look so overworked. You must eat!'

Although the pasta lay heavy on his stomach, Perlmann continued eating, glad that chewing excused his silence. The familiar atmosphere that had previously prevailed now struck him as a sentimental, tacky lie, and he feared the coffee, when it would inevitably become clear that he had absolutely nothing to say to these people, whose gabbling cordiality struck him today as inappropriate and actually quite peculiar. The situation was then saved by Sandra, who hurled her schoolbag in the corner when she came in and, weeping, reported on a failed dictation in English.

When the proprietor brought Perlmann the chronicle and, lowering his voice, urged Sandra to stop bothering the *professore*, one might have imagined it was a sacred book. Today Perlmann felt that the pictures on the gleaming cover were noisy and repellent. Tired, and with a full feeling in his stomach, he sat over the unopened book in such a way that the proprietor, before he disappeared into the kitchen, gave him a concerned look. Perlmann listlessly flicked a few pages. But the history of the world that had accompanied his life story no longer held the slightest interest for him, and the whole idea of appropriating his past present by remembering the course of events in the faraway world struck him as mystical nonsense.

Now the images of the bright office entered the foreground once more and, behind his closed lids, Perlmann drew various silhouettes of the town of Ivrea, which he would look down on from his high window.

Interrupting his translation work and looking at this unspectacular, perhaps even ugly Italian town: that, he was quite sure of it, could be his new present – the first one that he had properly achieved.

With sudden haste he began to translate the page of the chronicle that he had opened at random. In the office, it would have to be done quickly. It was a business operation. There was money at stake. Would his Italian be good enough? In the text in front of him there were several words that he didn't know. And what about business Italian? He saw himself sitting in an attic room until the small hours, filling the gaps in his vocabulary. At this new image, his high spirits faded to make way for the feeling of trepidation that you feel when relapsing into an experience you thought was firmly in the past. But only later, in the street, did he become aware that the image of the attic room had been modelled on his time as a schoolboy and a student, informed by nothing but the feeling that the present still lay far in the future.

When the proprietors heard that this was his last visit, they refused to take any money for the food. Their extravagant gestures and assurances contrasted starkly with his tense haste to leave. Sandra's thoughts were plainly still on her muffed dictation. Nonetheless, Perlmann was upset that she only briefly shook his hand and then disappeared again. For a moment he saw her lying on the bed with her knee socks pulled down. His original impulse to give her the chronicle had suddenly been blown away. He took the heavy book under his arm. With his free hand he parted the curtain one last time. He let the cool, smooth glass beads slide slowly over the back of his hand. He felt something break as he did so, something precious and intangible.

Perlmann laid the chronicle on the step in front of the stationery shop to which the proprietor had directed him. He formed a funnel with his hands and stared tensely inside the shop, which was still dark. *But it's nonsense*, he thought, *of course you can't tell what selection of envelopes they have just by looking.* Next to the shop there was another, with tablecloths, napkins and that sort of thing in the window. As Perlmann waited for the siesta to come to an end, he looked absently at the display. The third or fourth time he did so, the solution leapt out at him. In the corner, right at the back, packed in a plastic jacket with a zip, was a set of handkerchiefs. Involuntarily, his attention had leapt from the content to the packaging, and now, in his mind, he was excitedly comparing the size of the jacket with the format of Leskov's text. The yellow pages, he estimated, would slip back and forth a little in transit. But otherwise, this actually was the solution: if the whole thing was also put in a padded envelope, the snow and rain could do nothing to the text.

Unless the water forces its way through the zip. Perlmann was glad when the shopkeeper appeared, and proved to be so chatty that she kept this troubling thought from taking root. Perlmann bought the handkerchiefs and, next door, the biggest padded envelope into which the plastic jacket would fit. To write the address later on, he chose the most expensive felt-tip pen in the shop. Then, having reached the street corner, he turned round again to ask for a plastic bag. There were thousands of envelopes like his. But he didn't want anyone to see this one when he entered the hotel.

51

Adrian von Levetzov waved so energetically that Perlmann couldn't help crossing the hotel terrace to the table where the others were all sitting.

'We're betting on when the first drop will fall,' von Levetzov said, pointing at the threateningly dark wall of cloud that was piling up in the mountains and loomed far over the bay. 'The nearest one gets 10,000 lire from each of us.' He straightened a chair for Perlmann. 'Join in!'

Perlmann hesitantly set the chronicle down on the table. There was no room for it anywhere else. He rested the plastic bag against the leg of the chair. He was glad that Leskov was sitting far away. As he waited for his heartbeat to settle, he looked with great concentration at the sky, as if he were carefully considering his contribution to the bet.

'It isn't going to rain,' he said at last, to his own great surprise. He felt as if he had just defied the whole world with that sentence.

Millar tilted his head, and his face twisted into a wide grin. 'I like that, Phil,' he said, and his voice expressed regret that he hadn't thought of this ploy himself.

'May I?' asked von Levetzov and picked up the chronicle. He opened a few pages at random and then flicked on until he found some pictures. 'Aha,' he said suddenly, straightened the book and held it further away from himself with an appreciative expression. Then he turned the book round and let the others look at the picture. It showed Christine Keeler, the prostitute who had brought about the fall of the British war minister John Profumo in 1963. She was straddling a chair and completely naked.

Ruge's and Leskov's laughter sounded unself-conscious, while there was something embarrassed about Millar's grin.

'The style's a bit like something out of the *Sun*,' said Laura Sand, as Levetzov went on flicking through the book. Perlmann felt as if they had just caught him with a copy of *Bild-Zeitung* or a men's magazine. *Now, on top of everything else, the man who has failed in academia is buying tabloid books.*

'There's better to come!' cried von Levetzov, and turned the book round again. A quarter of the big page was taken up by a photograph showing Cicciolina, the Italian porn star, who had been elected to parliament. She was naked and was lolling in a provocative pose. Millar blushed and straightened his glasses. The two other men only looked for a second. Evelyn Mistral, straight-faced, pouted and brushed the hair from her brow.

'The photographer is only moderately talented,' Laura Sand said dryly. Grateful for the remark, the others exploded in laughter that was slightly too loud and too long.

In his mind's eye, Perlmann saw Cicciolina entering the polling station in her fur coat and dropping her envelope coquettishly into the ballot box. *Don't turn it off!* Agnes had said when he reached for the remote control. *I think she's great. Simply fantastic.* Her face wore an expression he had never seen before. *You're mouth is hanging open, isn't it?* she had laughed.

'At the last elections she founded the Love Party, *Il Partito d'Amore*,' said Perlmann and knew immediately that he couldn't have said anything clumsier at that moment. The others looked at him with surprise. *He knows that kind of thing.*

'I wouldn't have had you down as an expert in such things,' said Laura Sand, raising another laugh.

Perlmann closed his eyes for a moment. *Agnes's photographs are better than hers. A lot better.* He picked up the plastic bag and got to his feet. The laughter died under the loud scrape of his chair. The faces that he saw out of the corner of his eye were puzzled. After a few steps he turned round again and nodded to the sky. 'Still not a drop.' He attempted a smile. No one returned it. He walked quickly to the entrance and up to his room.

There he immediately walked to the window and looked down on the terrace. Evelyn Mistral had the open chronicle in front of her, and was reading from it with the vague and searching gestures of someone delivering an impromptu translation. The others were doubled up with laughter.

They were laughing at the book with which he had embarked on the search for his present. The book that had seduced him and kept him from his work. But also the book that had kept his head above water. A mass-market, noisy, superficial book entirely alien to his nature. And also a book that had repelled and bored him before, in the trattoria. And yet a book that he was very fond of. An intimate book. His quite personal book. And they were laughing at it.

He went into the shower.

It hadn't rained, and the others were still sitting outside when he went down to say goodbye to Maria. She was busy tidying the office.

'Can I help you at all?' she asked.

'No, thanks,' he said. Then he took the Bach CD out of his jacket pocket and gave it to her. 'You can have this. You helped me find it.'

'*Mille grazie*,' she stammered, 'but don't you need it any more?'

He just shook his head. He couldn't find the words he had composed in his head. She looked at him quizzically, and when the pause lasted too long she picked up her cigarettes.

'Somehow I'm going to miss your group,' she said, and as always she exhaled the smoke as she spoke.

Now he knew what he was afraid of: that his rage with the others might make him turn this farewell into something unnecessarily emotional and sentimental. *It wouldn't be the first time.* He gulped and looked at the floor.

'By the way,' she said with a smile, 'I have relatives in Mestre. Of course, you can't call it a beautiful town. But ugly – no, it isn't ugly at all. A bit cramped, perhaps. But it's also a nice place.'

'Yes, that was my experience,' said Perlmann, grateful for the subject. 'I particularly liked Piazza Ferretto. And the little galleria next to it.'

'So you've really been there?'

'For two days.'

'Professionally?'

Perlmann just shook his head and looked at her. Her eyes glittered strangely, and her mouth twitched.

'Not because of that one sentence?'

Perlmann nodded, and now he managed a smile.

'You mean you travelled specially from Germany to Mestre just because of that one sentence?'

He nodded.

She tilted her head slightly and took a long drag on her cigarette.

'Of course, if I can put it like this, that's a bit . . . mad. But knowing your text . . . OK, it isn't all that surprising. Your fury with that sentence leapt off the page. I couldn't help laughing when I was typing out that section. So was that sentence eventually . . . defeated?'

'Yes,' said Perlmann. 'But there are lots of others.'

Laughing, she stubbed out her cigarette and looked at her watch. 'I've got to go. Your texts are stored safely away,' she added and tapped the computer. 'Maybe I'll read them again in peace.' Then she shook his hand. '*Buona fortuna!*'

'You too,' said Perlmann, 'and thanks for everything.'

A few minutes later, from his room, he saw her standing with the others. Leskov hugged her when he said goodbye. Shortly before Perlmann lost sight of her, he saw her running her hand through her shining hair. Passé. So passé.

Leskov's text fitted even more exactly into the plastic jacket than Perlmann had expected. The pages had only a small amount of clearance from the edge. Perlmann took his ruler and measured: 1.6 cm wide and 1.9 cm high. But the zip was hard to open. It was a cheap one, and two of the teeth seemed already to be a bit loose. At any rate, it couldn't be opened and shut too often. Why hadn't he done the water test straight away? Annoyed with himself, Perlmann took the pages back out. As he pulled, he almost had to use force, and was startled when the tab suddenly glided swiftly over the loose teeth before jamming again, and could only be moved to the end stop with great difficulty. Perlmann carefully dipped the top edge of the jacket in the full washbasin. Bubbles formed on the outside of the zip. They were tiny and, in fact, barely visible. But still: the zip wasn't airtight. Perlmann left it in the water for a good minute before carefully drying it off. As he opened it, one of the loose teeth seemed to have been further damaged, and right at the end one of them was remarkably crooked. Just pull it shut once – the zip wouldn't take more than that. Perlmann ran his finger along the inside of the zip. Was what he felt only the cool of the metal, or was there moisture in there as well? He looked at his finger and rubbed at it to check: dry. But what if the envelope were left in the rain for hours? The zip wasn't completely airtight, that much was clear.

Perlmann held his face in the water. After that he felt better. He checked in the suitcase to see if he had forgotten a page. Then he counted the sheets and flattened the particularly worn sheets smooth again. At last he pushed the pile carefully into the jacket and tormented himself with the zip one last time. Leskov would be amazed at the effort Lufthansa had taken with this jacket. He would have to get hold of a Lufthansa sticker for the jacket as well as for the envelope. Then it would look more like a routine package.

Now he laid out the envelope and took out the piece of paper with Leskov's home address. *I've just got to risk it.* Leskov would doubt his memory anyway. If he had indeed put his work address at the end of the text, in his general uncertainty he would mistake his correct memory for another error. Perlmann set the specially purchased felt-tip pen down on the envelope and, horrified, immediately drew it back, as if he had almost set something on fire by accident. He hadn't practiced disguising his handwriting. It took several pages before he had finally decided on a backwards-sloping, stiff script, which, of all the variants he had tried, seemed the furthest removed from his own. He practically painted the letters on the envelope, so that they ended up looking like a grotesque form of calligraphy. His hand had shaken when writing two of the letters. But the address was clear. The envelope would get there.

Exhausted, he pushed the jacket with the text into the envelope and applied the staples. Then he tore the test pages into little scraps. When he threw them in the waste-paper basket, he felt like a forger clearing his workshop.

It was still dry on the terrace. The only people sitting there now were Leskov and Laura Sand, who had clearly fetched her warm jacket in the meantime. Leskov seemed to be smoking one of her cigarettes. The chronicle lay open on the table. *Before he suspects me, Leskov will doubt his memory.*

Perlmann looked at the address. There was something about it that bothered him. That was it: the Latin letters. For the German postal service that was essential, of course. But what about Russian postmen? Could they read it? He turned over the envelope. He could repeat the address in Cyrillic letters on the back. Yes, that was the solution. He took the lid off the felt-tip pen. No disguise was necessary for the Cyrillic letters. But was it really a good idea? They might mistake the address in Russian letters for the sender, since no sender was specified.

Perlmann put the lid back on and stepped to the window. Now Leskov was alone on the terrace, and the chronicle was no longer on the table. *But in that case it would get to him anyway.* He gave a start: it had taken the duration of a whole cigarette to work that out.

Uncertainly, he sat down and picked up the felt-tip pen. How likely was it that a Lufthansa employee dealing with lost objects would be able to write an address in Russian? Again he felt as if his thoughts were having to fight their way through an invisible medium of insidious tenacity. Of course: if someone could read the address on the text and identify it as such, then he was also capable of writing it or, at least, copying it out stroke for stroke. Perlmann began to write.

In the middle of Leskov's surname he paused. There were various conventions of transcription. Particularly with the sibilants, with which the address was swarming, and that was particularly aggravating. What system had Leskov used when he had written his address out again for Perlmann on that draughty street corner? If he made a mistake now, he would end up with a sequence of Russian letters that was different from the ones Leskov had written under his text. The postal service would probably manage anyway. But for Leskov it would be one more incongruity: why had the Russian-reading employee in Frankfurt made so many mistakes when all he had to do was copy out the address? And if he thought about it for long enough . . .

Perlmann wrote over the line with the felt-tip pen until all that could be seen was a block of opaque black. Then he put the envelope in the suitcase and set it out ready for tomorrow.

52

Laura Sand was holding the chronicle as she waited for him in the hall. Her face lacked its usual shadow of rage.

'I'm sorry about what I said,' she said. 'It was completely superfluous. And that *Love Party* thing is actually quite witty.'

'Don't worry,' said Perlmann, but wished it hadn't sounded so irritable. You would have to consider someone unstable, even vulnerable, to apologize for such a harmless joke. Without another word, he took the chronicle from her and asked Signora Morelli, who was staring at the envelope with great curiosity, to look after it until afterwards.

Was he mistaken, or were the others treating him indulgently and attentively as one might treat a convalescent – just as they had two evenings before? It was striking how quickly Evelyn Mistral drew back her hand when they both reached for the salt at the same time. And was there not a new veil of self-consciousness over her smile?

'Maybe it's not a bad idea to give a chronicle this sort of packaging,' said von Levetzov as their eyes met. 'And actually these are the things you really remember.'

'And no one reads serious stuff anyway – far too dry,' grinned Ruge.

Again Perlmann saw the others, doubled up with laughter when he wasn't there. He looked at his plate and choked down his food, even though his lunch from the trattoria still lay heavy in his stomach. *Just this one hour. It could be even less. And tomorrow the goodbyes. It will be quite different in Ivrea. Freer. Much freer.*

When the waiter had served dessert, Brian Millar tapped his glass. Perlmann gave a start. A speech to which he would have to react. It caught him entirely unawares. As if he had never before experienced such a thing. He thought back to the first session in the veranda, when he had feverishly thought about what his subject should be.

They had been wonderful weeks, said Millar. The intense exchange of ideas. The collegial, even friendly atmosphere. The excellent hotel. The magical town.

'On behalf of us all, I would like to thank you, Phil.' He raised his glass. 'You did a great job. And we all know how much work it was for you. We hope you got something out of it yourself – in spite of your difficult situation.'

Just don't say anything that might sound like an apology, thought Perlmann as he lit a cigarette to occupy his hands during the prolonged applause. He pushed back his chair, crossed his legs and was about to start his answer, when Leskov got to his feet with a groan.

Unfortunately, he hadn't been able to be here for long, Leskov said solemnly, but they had been unforgettable days for him. He had never made so many friends all at once, or learned so much in such a short time. He was an outsider, not to say an eccentric, he smiled. All the more because of that he wanted to thank them for their kindness and the consideration they had shown him. He looked at Ruge. 'Even if I have made some assertions that must have sounded quite crazy.' Ruge grinned. But most of all he would like to thank his friend Philipp. 'He invited me without knowing much about me. After a conversation in the course of which he – as I have discovered here – understood my train of thought better than anyone else before – almost better than I do myself. It was fantastic to experience this trust and sympathy. I will never forget them.' He pressed his hands together and made the gesture of thanks.

He, too, had got a lot out of his stay, Perlmann began. Much more than he had been able to show. A very great deal more. To some people it must sometimes have seemed as if he were engaged in a feud with his subject. But precisely the opposite was the case.

Perlmann realized with horror that he could no longer stop what was about to come. He spoke very calmly and even slipped into a thoughtful pose. But at the same time he clutched with his left hand, which was threatening to tremble, the wrist of his right, which lay on his knee.

Recently, in fact, he said, he had been writing a book on the principles of linguistics. Millar and von Levetzov raised their eyebrows at almost the same time, and Ruge reached for the mended arm of his glasses. His work on it had brought him to increasingly fundamental issues such as this: how the central questions of the discipline had come about in the first place; how one could distinguish questions that could open something up from erroneous questions; what it was that linguistics really wanted to understand about language, and in what sense. And so on.

Leskov's fist was clamped, unmoving, on his unlit pipe. He smiled conspiratorially. The ice cream in the glass bowl in front of him melted.

And one question, Perlmann went on, preoccupied him particularly: whether the subject, as it was currently pursued, could do justice to the eminently important role that language played in the diverse and multi-faceted development of experience. Much of what he had said here had concerned that question, he concluded. And he had often played devil's advocate. To learn from the others.

'It has advanced my own work greatly. And for that I should like to thank you all.'

It was still too early to light a cigarette. His hand might tremble. It hadn't sounded too bad. Even quite convincing. But within the heads of each of those sitting at the table, the same question must have been forming: *Then why didn't he deliver anything from that book, rather than inflicting that other, weird stuff on us?* With a hasty movement that was supposed to mask the trembling that he feared, Perlmann reached for his cigarettes and then, so that his hands could keep one another calm, he held his lighter as if a storm were sweeping through the dining room. The smoke tasted unfamiliar, as if it wasn't his brand. He tried frantically to think of the bright office in Ivrea, and even managed to conjure a precise image of the desk. In spite of this he felt ill.

When could one expect the publication of this interesting book, asked von Levetzov, thus seeming to take the words out of Millar's mouth.

He wanted to give himself time, Perlmann answered, and let the ash fall past his knee to the carpet so that he didn't have to bring his hand to the ashtray. Might the publication of the work discussed here not be the ideal place to introduce his first ideas? von Levetzov asked. When he saw Perlmann's hesitation, a shadow of suspicion flitted across his face.

'That publication is firmly planned, isn't it?'

'Of course,' Perlmann heard himself saying. 'But you know how these things are: sounding out the publishing companies, negotiating – the usual. And I will have to talk to Angelini about finance. Then you will all be hearing from me.'

'I could imagine my publisher in New York being interested,' said Millar. 'Especially in a book like yours. Shall I talk to him?'

Perlmann nodded silently. He had no idea what else he could have done. His cigarette burned his fingers. He dropped it and trod it out on the pale carpet. Leskov drew lines on the table cloth with the handle of his spoon. *He's thinking about a translation of his text. He'll ask me again tomorrow.*

Signora Morelli appeared and offered them coffee and cognac in the lounge. '*L'ultima serata!*' In the hall, Perlmann turned round and went back to the dining room. He picked up his cigarette butt and wiped the spot with his napkin. It had left a big, black stain. There was only one couple left in the room. They were preoccupied with themselves, and only glanced at him fleetingly.

'I went outside for a moment,' said Millar as Perlmann sat down in one of the armchairs in the lounge. 'Still dry. Now the money can only go to you or Vassily, who guessed it would take an hour.' He took a 10,000 lire note from his pocket. 'We could get the jackpot ready now.' He weighed down the resulting bundle of notes with the ashtray. 'How long should we keep the bet going on for? Shall we say till midnight?'

53

Perlmann hadn't known he was going to do it. He only realized at the moment when Millar rested his arms on the arms of the chair and pressed himself backwards in preparation for standing up. It was almost as if Perlmann were being pushed by an invisible force that knew more about him than he did about himself. With a single movement he was on his feet, and walked quickly to the grand piano. Before he sat down, he screened his hands with his body and pulled the bandage from his finger. As he lifted up the lid, from the corner of his eye he saw Millar slipping back from the edge of his chair.

Perlmann didn't need to think. Nocturnes were the only thing that he thought himself capable of playing after almost a year without playing a single note. Anything apart from Chopin was technically too difficult; the danger of disgrace was too great. And in the Nocturnes there was no problem with memory. He had grown up with these pieces. He had heard and played them hundreds of times.

If only there weren't that damned problem with the rhythm. He had a very precise and effortless sense of rhythm. But it was always a while before it settled in and his internal metronome started ticking. He played the first few bars like someone walking after being roughly woken from sleep, Bela Szabo had always said. And he was right. But when his sense of rhythm kicked in it was like an awakening; there was a liberating security in his head and hands, and every time it happened Perlmann had the impression of never having been really awake, as awake as he was now. He had learned to put those brief phases of uncertainty behind him before playing to anyone. But now they would all hear.

He started Opus 9, Number 1 in B minor. Without a bandage, the ring finger of his left hand felt cooler than the others, and when he touched the keys he didn't feel, as expected, pain, but a fine, sticky film. Nonetheless, the attack was good, he felt, the feared strangeness of touch had faded after a few notes. He had slipped into the first run, and was concentrating on the strange mixture of protraction and acceleration, when with a deafening crash it began to thunder. The first crack hadn't yet faded away when the cold light of a flash of lightning lit up the lounge, mixing unpleasantly with the warm, golden light of the chandeliers. Immediately afterwards a new, even louder crash made everything tremble. Perlmann took his hands from the keys. All heads were now turned towards the window, through which a quick succession of lightning flashes could be seen, bright ramifications of spookily brief duration. Perlmann took out his handkerchief, moistened it and cleaned his ring finger. A moment later he felt a sting along the scar.

When the natural spectacle seemed to be over, and everything was calm but for a distant rumble, Perlmann started over again. Now his sense of rhythm was there immediately. He had the whole piece clearly in front of his eyes and grew calm. Yes, he could still do them, his soft yet glass-clear Chopin notes – the only thing that Szabo had always acknowledged, and even slightly envied him for. It was with a similar touch, Perlmann imagined, that Glenn Gould had played Chopin. *Glass clarity with velvet edges.* He was also pleased with the pearly runs. But it didn't sound dreamy. And that wasn't due to the fact that his left ring finger, now that the accompaniment was growing louder, was really starting to hurt, just as the two fingers of his right hand, which had previously been holding his cigarette, stung when they rubbed against one another. What was that about?

To prevent any applause, Perlmann seamlessly moved on to the second Nocturne from the same Opus. Again it thundered, but this time the crash was no longer directly over the hotel, and he went on playing.

'Now I've got to see if it's raining,' Millar said sotto voce and got to his feet. Evelyn Mistral put her finger to her lips. Millar stepped outside.

That was it, Perlmann thought: he had always compared his sound with Millar's Bach, and that acted as a block that prevented him from finding his way into the right state of mind. He closed his eyes, yielded more to the notes and tried to forget. The third Nocturne was more successful. Only his sore fingers were gradually becoming a problem.

Towards the end of the piece Millar came back, unmistakeably clearing his throat.

Next Perlmann chose Number 1 in F major from Opus 16. He only noticed that this one contained a danger when he was in the middle of a theme. Suddenly, he felt that he had a face. It started to sting behind his closed eyelids. *For God's sake.* He involuntarily stretched his back and closed his eyes tight in a violent grimace. Seconds of horrified waiting. No. Once again it had been fine. At the very last moment he had managed to force back the tears. *So I can't play the piece in D flat minor. Under no circumstances.*

A moment before, he had played two wrong notes, but the relief made him forget that, and now came the dramatic, technically difficult passage. He no longer had any time to be afraid of it, and suddenly it exploded in his hands, and he played the passage all the way through without a mistake as if he had been practising it only that morning. A massive feeling of relief, almost of arrogance, took hold of him. The pain in his fingers was unimportant now, and as he played the piece to the end he was suddenly sure of it: *then I'll do the Polonaise as well.*

But before he did that he needed time to gather himself. The best thing for that was the third, technically easy piece from Opus 15, which was also easy on the fingers. He wasn't quite on top of things. He had started to become agitated. So the first third was a flat, lackluster sequence of notes. But then came the 'Debussy passages', as Szabo had called them when they were going through the piece. The melodic structure became weaker, the notes seemed to flow aimlessly, and developed an irresolute, hesitant, almost random quality. *Perlmann*, Szabo used to say with an irritated sigh, *you can't play that as if it's Debussy. There's still a clear melody, a clear logic in it. It sounds almost as if you are advocating a melancholy of dissolution. Gloom, fair enough. But Chopin!* Perlmann made the notes sound as vague as possible. *To hell with Szabo.* It was a declaration of war on Millar and his obsession with structure, and Perlmann had to struggle against the temptation to look across at him. He felt something in him breaking free. He was asserting himself against this man Brian Millar, and standing up for himself in front of everyone else. And now he did something he would have considered unthinkable during his public performance: later in the work he repeated two of the passages in which this self-liberation seemed most successful. He had needed a jolt to get beyond Szabo's internal presence, and now defiance and a bad conscience held each other in balance.

To plunge straight into the A flat major Polonaise – no, that was too risky. First he needed something more technically demanding than what he had done so far. Because of his self-confidence. He wasn't entirely sure. The A flat major Waltz from Opus 34. A piece that he had played on many solemn occasions, almost ad nauseam. Now, once again, it would have to be impeccable. It contained some chord runs like the ones in the Polonaise. And after that he would be attuned to the key.

At first he made two pedal errors, and once he played one key too many. But otherwise it was impeccable. When it started thundering again and the storm seemed to be approaching once more, he effortlessly stayed in time. He started shivering slightly, but now it wasn't, as it had been so often over the past few days, an expression of anxiety, but of tense expectation. He could play the Polonaise. He would play it. His arms and hands, which felt very safe and strong, told him that.

He hadn't given a thought to the scar, when a needle-sharp pain ran through him. He had to leave out three notes with his left ring finger, lost his concentration and messed up the next run of chords in his right hand. He did regain his equilibrium, but his confidence had gone. The mighty chords of the Polonaise, on which everything depended, loomed up in front of him like enormous hurdles, and now the sore fingers of his right hand were stinging much more than before. The sharp pains had gone, but his playing was hesitant now, with a ritardando that the waltz couldn't take. *It's impossible. I'll stop after this one.* When the end of the piece came within sight, he speeded up again. The twinge that came now wasn't quite as keen as it had been a moment before, but it was enough to spoil the closing run completely, so that he merely slid into the final chord.

It was shaming, having to stop like that, and Perlmann was full of rage with himself when he reflected that with his murder plan, completely unnecessary as it was, he had also ruined this attempt at self-assertion. Nonetheless, he would have got up and walked over to his armchair had Millar not at that point started waving the cash from the bet. As the rain lashed the windows, he held them up to Leskov with a smile, undeterred by the fact that Leskov irritably waved them away, and by the equally irritable faces of the others. First his attempt to disturb Perlmann's playing a few moments ago, and now this. It was too much. Amidst the beginning applause Perlmann started in on Opus 53, the A flat major Polonaise that Chopin had called the 'Heroic'.

From the first bar he could hear the frightening passage. But there were still almost seven minutes before he got there. Even the first chords and runs required much more pressure than anything that had gone before, and Perlmann bit his lips with pain. But soon the pain could touch him no longer. As ever, he was overwhelmed by this music; it enfolded him and gave him the feeling that he could effortlessly keep the world at a distance. After half a minute the run-up began for the big theme, dressed up in powerful chords that came cascading down from above. The last bars before the first of these expansive chords had to be played at a slightly slower tempo to provide a proper setting for the beginning of the theme. Szabo himself had acknowledged that. But Perlmann – and this had been his constant reproach – overdid it to an unjustifiable extent. He was inclined to delay the entry of the topmost chord by more than a second. That, he found, was what made the tension properly palpable, and intensified the subsequent liberation. And that liberation was what truly counted – the idea that for the moment when one touched the keys with both hands and with one's full strength, one was master of things. *You abuse these passages*, Szabo had said. *You're supposed to be playing Chopin, not yourself. Take Alfred Cortot as your model.*

Szabo fell silent, and Perlmann played himself into a genuine state of intoxication. With a sure touch, he hammered the redeeming chords into the keys, rising from his chair with ever greater frequency to launch his attack. Unrestrainedly, he slowed down the introductory beats so that each chord had the significance – more than ever – of a liberation from chains. Then, when the storm broke out again, it fitted what he was doing perfectly. Because right now – three minutes in – came the first of the two passages in which the same dark chord was to be played seven times in a row. Never before, it seemed to him, had he played chords with such force. Trampling over what little remained of his restraint, Perlmann thundered all of his fury into the keys, his fury with Millar and all the others who beleaguered him; his fury with Szabo; his fury with the storm that he had to drown out; and above all his impotent fury with himself, with his insecurity, fear and mendacity, which had driven him into the murderous silence of the tunnel.

Afterwards, his sore fingers hurt so much it brought tears to his eyes. The thought came to him that if he brought his finger down on the keys the scar on his finger would burst, the blood would run over the white keys and seep into the gaps, and his fingers would lose their hold in the red smear. But the image was too fleeting to survive and, during the next, fourth minute, Perlmann devoted himself entirely to the effort of playing so seamlessly and compellingly as he had at the Conservatoire, when he had reaped such praise. His left hand mostly contributed to the climaxes, and he was glad that the intense pain in his finger had now become something constant that he could adjust to, something that no longer appeared in the form of unpredictable episodes. The whole passage flowed once again into a thundering repeat of a single chord. Then the same thing was repeated once again, but this time it was followed by a surprising dissolve into a sequence of bright, blithe bars. They made way for a lyrical passage, which, as Perlmann played it, was intended to remind the audience of the dreamlike mood of the Nocturnes.

He was now in the sixth minute of the piece. As the notes grew softer and quieter, Perlmann broke out in a frightened sweat, and his fingers seemed to have grown damp from one second to the next. Soon would come the run-up to the final repetition of the theme and, starting with its first chord – he remembered quite precisely, even today – it was forty seconds to the terrifying passage. Forty-three, perhaps forty-four if, out of panic-fuelled calculation, he slowed down again. The passage itself lasted less than ten seconds. Then came a speeded-up and shortened version of the theme with seven clearly articulated chords, and then it was over.

Perlmann drew out the last lyrical notes until he could no longer avoid speeding up and descending to the low chords in preparation for the theme. Then, summoning up all his defiance to defeat his anxiety, when he attacked the first chord of the theme he felt like someone who – after a series of devastating losses – has staked everything on a single card, knowing that his chances of winning are vanishingly small. *It's grotesque to hope for a crash of thunder during those crucial seconds.* He tried to imagine himself back in the bare practice room at the Conservatoire – he was someone who played entirely for himself. That exercise worked, but he had started it too late, soon the long run from the low notes would be on him, and then the time would have come. Later, he couldn't remember how he had done it, but suddenly he was back in the middle of the theme, repeating two lengthy passages from the beginning. Confused by his own maneuver, he concentrated again on the idea of playing in the empty room. He couldn't chicken out again. He heard the two frenzied runs, which darted so rapidly through the structure of the other notes that you only really became aware of them when the last, bright note flashed. The rest of the runs had actually gone flawlessly. So it wasn't impossible, even though the two critical sequences belonged to a quite different category of difficulty.

For the very last time, the complete theme. The long run from below, which still had a human tempo. A series of familiar, light chords. *Now.* Perlmann couldn't feel a thing any more, as his fingers slid over the keys. His anxiety had subsided, too. For just ten seconds he experienced a present full of numb tension, in which he was nothing but hands and ears. And then, with the bright conclusion of the second run, he knew it, even though he still couldn't believe it: *no mistakes. Not a single one. Not one.* The rest was child's play.

He sat where he was for a moment, as if completely dazed. A shudder of exhaustion ran through him, and at first his legs refused to obey him when he got up. A precious moment of presence. He would have given anything to be able to capture it for ever.

The applause, with which even the other hotel guests joined in, was loud and sustained. The loudest clapping came from the corridor, where Perlmann now spotted Giovanni and Signora Morelli. When their eyes met, Giovanni raised his thumb in a sign of congratulations. It was as if he were congratulating Perlmann for successfully scoring a goal. At that moment Giovanni's gesture meant more than all the applause. But even more important was the expression on Signora Morelli's face. It was the same one with which she had looked at him on Monday night, when he had spoken of his relief with tears in his eyes. Now she smiled at him, and set the applause off again with her clapping. It was as if that mute encounter across the whole room made him immune to the opinions of the others. It almost didn't matter what they thought.

Leskov was the last to stop clapping. 'I had no idea . . . ,' he began, and the others nodded in agreement.

Perlmann was sparing with his information, but savored each item. So why hadn't he . . . ?

'I don't like performing,' he said, and glanced straight past Millar. 'I prefer to be alone with music.'

The way the others looked at him had changed over the past half hour. At any rate that was what Perlmann fervently wanted to believe. And the pause in the conversation that occurred now, which seemed to echo with surprise, seemed to bear it out.

Millar played with the rolled-up cash. 'I remembered the Polonaise as being shorter,' he said, and straightened his glasses so slowly that it looked as if he was doing it in slow motion. 'But that was a long time ago, and I'm not a Chopin connoisseur.'

For a moment Perlmann saw only the reflection of the chandelier in Millar's glasses. The expression that he saw a moment later contained no suspicion. But there was a glittering thoughtfulness in it, which, it seemed, was actually waiting to turn into mistrust. Perlmann gave a non-committal smile.

'I like the insistent way the theme keeps returning,' he said.

When Millar immediately got up and sat down at the piano, no one expected anything but Bach. What he played, however, could hardly have been further removed from Bach. It was the *Allegro agitato molto* from the *Études d'exécution transcendante* by Franz Liszt. Perlmann didn't know the piece, but identified it straight away as Liszt. Millar made the occasional mistake as he played, and from time to time he had to bring the tempo back down a little. Nonetheless, his playing was a brilliant achievement for an amateur, and Perlmann felt a stabbing pain when he heard him overcoming technical difficulties that put everything in the A flat major Polonaise in the shade.

He himself had always steered clear of Liszt. There was something about his particular form of effusiveness that repelled him. And if anyone mentioned Chopin and Liszt in the same breath, it made him furious. Liszt reminded him more clearly than any other composer of the limits of his technical gifts, and his dislike was mixed with fear. But he had never wanted to analyse it in any greater detail.

When the piece was over, Millar took off his blazer and threw it on to the nearest armchair. There was sweat on his face. No one clapped: his energetic movements announced far too clearly that he was about to play an encore. It was *La leggierezza* that he played now, one of Liszt's *Trois études de Concert*. The piece seemed familiar to Perlmann, even though he couldn't remember the title. Again he felt envious, particularly of certain runs and trills. All the same, it was comforting when Millar stumbled in the incredibly long run that rippled down with glassy brightness, and cursed quietly.

It was shortly after this run that Perlmann noticed. *They aren't waves, Philipp,* he heard Hanna saying, *they're ribbons – bright, billowing ribbons like the ones that girls pull behind them when doing floor exercises.* From then on, he had always had that image in his head when he heard or played Chopin's F minor Étude from Opus 25, in which the right hand had to run through an almost uninterrupted sequence of regular quavers, when the charm of the piece lay in the fact that one could imagine no better medium for the theme than in precisely that regularity. And now he was hearing the same kind of ribbons in the piece by Liszt. They weren't quite so long or quite so regular, and sometimes the left hand was involved as well. But it was the same musical idea. And while Perlmann inwardly made the comparison, he became clearly aware of something that had hitherto only touched him in the form of a vague, fleeting stumble: there was a thematic similarity between the first piece by Liszt that Millar had played and Chopin's F minor Étude. Even the key was the same. With growing agitation, he tried to lay his memory of Chopin's Étude over the notes by Liszt that he had just heard, like a pause the precision of which one wants to check. The piece that was being played interfered with that, and he tried to blank it out. Did that thematic kinship really exist? In one second he was quite sure of it; in the next he mistrusted his impression. If only he had a few minutes to hear the two pieces one after the other.

Perlmann didn't stir from his concentration until he heard the applause and saw Millar putting his blazer over his shoulders, before slumping in the armchair.

'Liszt?' asked von Levetzov.

'Yes,' smiled Millar, 'the only two pieces I can play. And I've always thought they somehow belong together.'

Perlmann pounced on the last remark as you might pounce on an opponent's error in chess, if you saw straight away that it could decide the whole game.

'That's true,' he heard himself saying. 'Liszt cribbed them both. From Chopin. From the same piece, the F minor Étude from Opus 25.'

When Millar heard the word 'crib', the blood rushed to his face, as if the word had been applied to him. For a while he sat there numbly.

'Cribbed?' asked Leskov. 'What does that mean?'

'*Spisyvat*,' said Perlmann without hesitation.

Leskov grinned with surprise and improved his emphasis. 'There you are. You even know a word like that . . .'

Perlmann reached for his cigarettes.

In the meantime, Millar had recovered himself. 'I think, Phil,' he said with controlled calm, 'you will agree with me that a man like Franz List didn't need to copy anything. Certainly not from Chopin, who isn't a patch on him.'

Perlmann was seething, and he felt that his fingers, which were all painful now, had gone cold. It was, he thought, idiotic to provoke this confrontation now, less than twelve hours before Millar's departure. And yet there was also something that he enjoyed: his fear of open conflict didn't – as he had expected – discompose him. He felt a solidity that was new to him.

'Whether he needed or didn't need to imitate Chopin all the way down to his individual figures, I don't know,' Perlmann said on the way to the piano. 'The fact is that in this case he did.'

He played in a lighter and more liberated way than he had expected, given his trembling fury, and he managed the brief Étude, which contained no particularly great technical difficulties, flawlessly. It only sounded a little too gentle, as he balked at a harder attack.

'Encore!' cried Giovanni, who had sat down a little way off, with Signora Morelli. Perlmann didn't outwardly respond to the exclamation, and went back to his chair. But inwardly, Giovanni, his fan on the edge of the playing field, had performed a small miracle: the conflict with Millar, which Perlmann had just got so wound up in, suddenly lost its power over him, and assumed a playful tinge. He casually lit a cigarette and, as Silvestri had sometimes done, blew the smoke in the direction of Millar's armchair. Evelyn Mistral tilted her head and nodded slightly.

'I can't hear a trace of plagiarism,' said Millar, and his East Coast accent sounded even stronger than usual.

Ruge took off his glasses and ran his hand over his head. 'I'm a terrible philistine. But I did have a sense, Brian, that there's actually something to Philipp's assertion.'

'Me too . . . ,' von Levetzov began.

'Nonsense,' Millar interrupted him irritably, visibly aggrieved that his two allies had left him in the lurch at the last minute. 'Those two bars of Chopin's are just thrown down haphazardly. A piece that's been roughly hand-crafted. Practically ingenuous. Liszt's things, on the other hand, are always very refined.'

Perlmann felt his face getting hot. Giovanni was forgotten. He looked at Millar. 'You might also say deliberate or calculated or overblown or stilted or affected.' It was like a breathless obsession, always adding another *or*, at the risk of not having another word to hand. He didn't know he knew all those English words, and he had the strange, spooky feeling that they had come to mind only for this occasion, and that they would soon vanish from his vocabulary again without a trace.

Millar took off his glasses, closed his eyes and rubbed the top of his nose. Then he set his glasses on as carefully as if he were at the opticians, closed his eyes, folded his arms and said: 'Remarkable vocabulary. But acquired. You can always tell the foreigner. And, of course, the words don't have the slightest thing to do with Franz Liszt.'

Laura Sand quickly laid her hand on Perlmann's arm. 'I liked your Chopin. Particularly those lyrical pieces. It's a shame you didn't play them before.'

As he left, Leskov put the money from the bet in his pocket. Then he rested a heavy hand on Perlmann's shoulder. 'You are a one. You play like a professional and don't say a word about it. And you know the most obscure Russian words!' He laughed. 'Do you know what your problem is? You keep too much to yourself. But you see: it all comes out in the end!'

Perlmann lay awake for most of the night. The storm clouds had passed. A shimmer of moonlight lay over the bay. It was quieter than usual. For hours he didn't hear a single car. The five weeks were over; the mountains of time without present had faded at last. They had read his notes and heard his Chopin. Now they knew who he was. He had always thought that could never happen. He was confused that the disaster failed to materialize. He waited. Perhaps it would come after some delay, and all the more violently when it did. But it didn't just begin like that. Very gradually he started to sense that for decades he had been living with an error. It wasn't true that delineation meant screening oneself off and walling oneself away, as if in an internal fortress. What it came down to was something quite different: that if the others found out, one should stand calmly and fearlessly by what one was in one's innermost depths. And Perlmann felt as if this insight was also the key to that present that he so longed for, which had always remained as intangible and fleeting as a mirage.

Now and again he dozed off . . . *Not a trace of plagiarism*, he heard Millar saying. In reply he slung unfamiliar English words at him, until he noticed at last that it was always one and the same word: *spisyvat'*. *It's all coming out!* laughed Leskov, and in his mouth there was just a single tooth stump, because he was the old woman by the tunnel. *Like in a film!* She said. '*As if!*' And then she threw the chronicle at the others, who were doubled up with laughter.

At one point Perlmann turned on the light and looked in the suitcase to see if the envelope with Leskov's text was still inside.

The moon had disappeared. A fog bank blurred the silent lights of Sestri Levante. Luckily, he had resisted the temptation to play the Nocturne in D flat minor. *Why in the world don't you want to play that piece?* Szabo had asked. *Because*, Perlmann had replied, staring at the keys. Now he could hear it, bar for bar. Her golden hair with the dark strand.

54

When the two taxi drivers stepped into the lobby, everything suddenly went so fast that Perlmann, who had been counting the hours, felt quite unprepared.

'Don't worry,' said Ruge, after thanking him for everything. 'Worse things happen!'

Perlmann felt these words tearing open a wound. They assumed something had happened that someone could take amiss – a failure, a disgrace, even a transgression. And he had merely given a weaker presentation than usual. One time in his glittering career. Accompanied by a fainting fit, certainly. But who can do anything about their body? Otherwise, from the vantage point of the others, nothing had happened. So why this sentence that cut and burned, made even more unbearable by the terribly respectable, Swabian cadence? *What*, he called inaudibly after Ruge, *what am I not supposed to worry about?* Von Levetzov was already shaking his hand and saying something about a conference at which they would certainly see one another again, while Perlmann still wrestled with Ruge's words. Was he referring to his fainting? Or the notes? Or that dreadful text? Why did he have to say that? And why at that precise moment, which gave what was said – whatever it might be – a particular weight? He tried to call to mind Ruge's face and the tone of his voice when talking about the death of his sister. But the more he struggled to remember those things, the more they eluded him. Had they really existed?

Laura Sand didn't know where to put her cigarette and finally jammed it between her fingers, which were holding her travel bag. 'I'll send you a few pictures,' she said, tapping her camera bag. 'Pictures that Chopin would have liked,' she added with her mocking smile. In the doorway she tripped over her long black coat. For a moment Perlmann closed his eyes to make sure that the inner picture of her mocking face would always be available to him.

What came next was something that he had tried several times to imagine during the night, but his fantasies had got him nowhere.

'Thanks for everything,' said Millar, shaking his hand firmly. He said it in a workmanlike manner. That was how he would always say goodbye. And yet he wasn't just acting in line with convention. There had been a twitch in his face, leaving yesterday evening behind. 'And about your book: I'll talk to my publisher next week. I'll entrust it to him quite specifically.'

Perlmann nodded mutely, and felt as if for those whole five weeks he had given the same response to everything anyone had said to him: a silent nod of the head.

Millar pulled up the zip of his windbreaker and picked up his case. Two steps later he set it down again and turned round. 'By the way: your Chopin – it sounded pretty good. And Liszt isn't all that better. No comparison with Bach,' he grinned.

Perlmann thought about Sheila and the balloon. 'I've never heard Bach like yours,' he said. 'A very distinct style.'

Millar blushed. 'Oh, thanks. Many thanks. No one's ever said that to me before. We should have . . .'

Perlmann nodded mutely. Before Millar got into the taxi, he looked back up at Perlmann and raised his hand. When the taxi disappeared, Perlmann was filled with a feeling of emptiness and loss.

Leskov was sitting on the terrace in the sun when Perlmann and Evelyn Mistral came outside half an hour later. Her train left Genoa at eleven, she said in reply to Leskov's question.

'Then you'll easily be back here by one,' said Leskov to Perlmann. 'Because that's when our ship sails,' he added, seeing Perlmann's incomprehension. On such a beautiful day Leskov wanted to invite him on a boat trip to Genoa, harbor tour included. Especially when the coast road had just been closed. 'I'll pay with this!' he said with a laugh, and pulled his crumpled winnings from his trouser pocket.

Perlmann felt the handle of the suitcase getting damp. Motionless, he looked down at Evelyn Mistral's red shoes.

'You can't possibly refuse him that,' she said to him in Spanish, lowering her voice.

Two more days of despair for him. Unless he scrubbed the idea of Ivrea. Then it's just one.

'Don't you want to?' Leskov asked. The disappointment in his voice and his anxious face were unbearable.

'No, of course I do,' Perlmann said hoarsely, 'and I'll be back by one whatever happens.' He was glad when the taxi hooted down below.

It was a silent train journey. Perlmann fought unsuccessfully against the trepidation that was choking him. He had to extract each individual word from himself, and didn't know how to make it clear to Evelyn Mistral that his silence had nothing to do with her. As she began, out of embarrassment, to talk about the book she was just reading, he wondered again and again whether he should give her Leskov's text, so that she could hand it to him in Geneva. *Two days. One, at any rate.* No suspicion could fall on her. She had never been anywhere near Leskov's suitcase. Perhaps Leskov would assume that his plane had flown on from Frankfurt to Geneva, where the text had been found at last. But how in the world was he to explain to her that the envelope had to reach St Petersburg as quickly as possible, when they had both stood facing its recipient half an hour before?

'You'd rather have had the afternoon to yourself, wouldn't you?' she asked as the train arrived at Genoa Station.

Perlmann nodded.

'But he seemed to be looking forward to the boat trip as excitedly as a child.'

Again he nodded mutely.

The big suitcase with the red elephant on the middle of the lid bumped against the steps of the carriage as she got in. Perlmann took the case from her, and let her hold his suitcase. When they stood facing one another in the empty, musty-smelling compartment, he ran his hand over her freshly washed, straw-like hair. After a brief hesitation, during which she tried to read his face, she put her arms around his neck and leaned playfully back.

'*¡No te pierdas!*'

He nodded, picked up the valise and a few steps later he was outside. When he turned round she was standing at the open carriage door.

'That earlier text of Vassily's: you read it didn't you?'

Perlmann took a deep breath and looked at her. 'Yes. But it would be too long a story.' He looked at the floor for a moment, and then raised his head again. 'Our secret?'

Her radiant smile crossed her face.

'I like secrets like that. And I'm the soul of discretion.'

The conductor walked along the train and closed the doors. She stood at the compartment window. She was plainly thinking away. Her curiosity got the better of her.

'Was it the text you had with you on the terrace when I arrived?'

Perlmann nodded.

'And that's why you didn't want the others . . .'

'Yes,' he said.

The train set off.

'You could make up various stories about that,' she laughed. 'I'll try that on my journey. As a way of passing the time!'

Perlmann was glad that instead of talking he was able to wave. He went on mechanically doing so until her carriage was out of sight. Only when he lowered his arm did he notice that he was clutching the handle of the valise so tightly that it cut into his hand.

He ordered a coffee in the station bar. According to the hands of the clock on the wall, behind its cracked glass, it was just after eleven. The plane he had planned to take left at a quarter past twelve. Now Leskov was keeping him from atoning for his action as quickly as possible. It was only with difficulty that Perlmann managed to keep his impotent rage within bounds, and the young woman next to him looked with alarm at his fist with its white knuckles holding the long sugar spoon, rather than putting it back in the bowl. *You can't refuse him that.* But she couldn't have known. Disappointment over a boat trip, as against two more days of despair, that was the calculation. And it wasn't just despair. Perhaps those were precisely the two days that would cost Leskov his job, because they were the two that would have let him copy out and rephrase the missing pages in time.

Perlmann took the bus to the airport. He closed his mind's eye to those memories and, without looking round, he immediately went to the check-in counter and on to security control. On the x-ray screen Leskov's text was only a vague shadow. He sat impatiently in the waiting room and looked out at the plane that was just taking the food container on board. The water beyond the runway lay in gleaming light. What had Leskov called the southern light? *Siyayushchy. I've hardly seen anything of this area. When the coast road was closed, on top of everything.* Perlmann started pacing back and forth. Then he would have to fly tomorrow, as originally planned. His reservation was still valid. Just one more day that Leskov would have to wait for the text. That would mean scrubbing Ivrea. Or at least postponing it. He imagined the bright office. Or else he could fly back here tomorrow afternoon and take a later train to Ivrea. He studied his boarding pass. *Yes.* He crumpled up the green piece of cardboard, threw it in the bin and pushed his way, amidst cries of protest from the security officials, past the queuing people and out into the hall.

There were no seats on the flight from Frankfurt to Genoa tomorrow afternoon, and the waiting list was already long. Perlmann still felt the pressure of the crumpled boarding pass in the palm of his hand. What about flights from Frankfurt to Turin? The hostess listlessly consulted the computer, and mistyped several times. All flights were booked, but there was just one name on the waiting list. Perlmann asked her to add his to it.

Ten past twelve. With the check that he had planned to cash in Frankfurt, he went to the bank in the arrivals hall. As he waited in the line, Perlmann couldn't help going through Leskov's arrival all over again. *I like to have my own money.* Then he ran, with all his cash in his hand, out to a taxi and asked the driver to take him to Santa Margherita as quickly as possible.

55

Leskov was standing by the edge of the road, opposite the landing stage for the boats, attentively studying the traffic. He had one leg in the road and the other, strangely bent at the knee, lightly touched the pavement. His torso was leaning forwards expectantly, and he tried to hold his head upright, clutching his big glasses with one hand. When the taxi a little way in front of Perlmann's came towards him, Leskov bent down to get a better view of the passenger. He maintained this posture when he saw Perlmann's taxi. He jerked his back, tipped his glasses slightly to check what he had seen, and then walked, with swinging arms that crossed above his head, into the middle of the carriageway, as if to stop the only car on a lonely stretch of road at night.

The driver stopped with a cry of alarm. From the moment when he glimpsed Leskov, Perlmann had been unable to think about anything. He had just gripped the handle of the suitcase even tighter. Now he gave the driver a large bill and got out.

'I thought you weren't coming,' said Leskov, immediately trying to keep the reproachful tone out of his voice. 'The boat's here already!'

For the first half hour of the trip it wasn't especially striking that Perlmann said hardly anything. Leskov enjoyed standing at the front of the almost deserted ship, looking out at the still, dazzling water. After a while he took a map out of his jacket. Signora Morelli had lent it to him. Perlmann recognized the traces of dirt straight away: it was the same map that he had used when planning his crime, and which he had used, when collecting the yellow sheets of paper, as an underlay for the fragile page with the subheading. No, he said, when Leskov pointed to

Portofino, he had never been there. And he didn't know Genoa harbour, either.

Later, when Leskov came back from the toilet, he sat down on the bench next to Perlmann, and as he lit his pipe, he studied the suitcase. Every time he had seen a suitcase over the past few days, he said, he hadn't been able to keep from thinking of his missing text. And the piece of rubber band in the zip of the outside pocket.

'Do you think it's most likely that I left it at home? I mean, after all the things I've told you?'

Perlmann nodded and picked up his cigarettes. 'At any rate, I don't think the text is simply lost,' Perlmann said, relieved at the firmness in his voice. 'Lufthansa is famous for its care with lost objects.'

'So you really think they'd send my text back?'

Perlmann nodded.

'But the address is written in Russian, and by hand,' Leskov said. His eyes were unnaturally large behind their thick glasses, and that made the anxiety behind them seem enlarged as well.

Perlmann glanced quickly away. 'Lufthansa is one of the biggest international airlines, and they fly to Russia. I'm sure they have people who speak Russian.'

Leskov sighed. 'Maybe you're right. If I could only be sure that I really did write the address on it. The night before last I suddenly started having doubts.'

Perlmann closed his eyes. His heart pounded. He braced himself. 'What address do you usually write at the end of a text like that?'

'What? Oh, my work address.' He looked at Perlmann. 'You mean because I asked you only to use my home address? No, because it's different in cases like that.'

Perlmann excused himself and went inside, where he leaned against the wall next to the toilet. The pounding in his chest subsided only gradually. No, it was too dangerous to ask him for his address, quite apart from the fact that he had no convincing reason to do so. Perlmann would have to ask him to write it down, and the whole thing would thus become an action that would linger vividly in Leskov's memory.

Perlmann slowly walked back, avoiding a sailor on the way, and stepped out on deck.

His heart stopped. Leskov was holding the suitcase on his knees, and was just snapping both locks shut. Now he set the suitcase back on the floor. Perlmann took a few steps to the side. No, Leskov wasn't holding the envelope, and he stood up now and filled a pipe by the railing. Perlmann walked slowly up to him and touched the back of each individual bench as if seeking reassurance that he could use them to support himself.

'You people in the West have lovely things,' said Leskov, indicating the suitcase with the stem of his pipe. 'That leather. And those refined and elegant locks. It would really make a person envious.'

Perlmann clutched the railing until his knees started obeying him again.

When they stepped out on land in Genoa, Leskov suddenly stopped. 'Let's assume I left it on the plane. Do you know what I'm most afraid of? The cleaning crew. If they found something like that, how would those people know it was precious?'

There was no other option. Perlmann had to find out, and this was his chance.

'Anyone would hesitate if faced with such a thick stack of papers. If they're typed, they're going to be important. And it's half a book. Isn't it?'

Leskov nodded. 'You could be right. It's eighty-seven pages long.'

That means there are seventeen pages that Leskov will have to rewrite. The length of a whole lecture. But he still has it all in his head. You keep things like that in your head for a long time.

Perlmann avoided the harbor bar from which he had called Maria a week before. But it was hard to find anything else nearby, and in the end they sat down at the only table by a snack bar that smelled of fish and burnt oil. Perlmann was glad of the noise in the street and the children sliding right past them on their skateboards. These things would give a casual sound to the question that he couldn't hold back for much longer.

'When do you need to hand the text in? For that job, I mean.'

'Two weeks' time.'

Perlmann couldn't stop himself. 'That gives you exactly fourteen days.'

Leskov looked at him with distracted surprise. 'Thirteen,' he said with a smile. 'Saturday doesn't count.'

'What would happen if you didn't turn up with the text until the following Monday?'

The puzzlement in Leskov's face was more alert now than it had been a moment before.

'I just wondered how fussy they are in your country,' Perlmann said quickly.

'They would probably acknowledge me anyway,' he said thoughtfully. 'But you never know. They're bureaucrats. It's better not to give them a formal excuse. And the date isn't a problem either,' he added calmly as the waiter set their food down in front of them. 'I really just need to type up the text, and I'm quick at that. For the notes I would need half a day at the most.'

Perlmann choked down his sheep's cheese and felt his stomach tightening. *He won't have the text before Friday. Then he has a week. That could be enough. But what if he only gets it the following Monday, or even Tuesday?*

'Incidentally, how long did it take my letter to get there?' Perlmann asked.

Leskov doesn't understand at first. 'Oh, I see,' he said. 'You're thinking about what will happen if Lufthansa send it. I can't remember exactly; about a week, I think.' He poked around absently at his salad. 'Good that you ask. That means, in fact, that the text might still be on its way if I don't find it tomorrow evening. It could even take one or two days before the business about the Russian address is sorted out. So I can't give up hope straight away. Particularly as the post doesn't usually come on Monday. But if there's still nothing there by Wednesday or even Thursday . . . Oh, it's all nonsense,' he said with a forced smile, filling his fork. 'The text is there on my desk, in the middle of all that chaos, I can see the yellow sheets right in front of me.'

That year's harbor tours had stopped the previous day. They wouldn't start again until the beginning of March. Leskov read the English text of the notice three times under his breath. Suddenly, his enthusiasm for his surroundings and the southern light seemed to collapse in on itself, and all his confidence vanished.

'Now I myself have destroyed my only hope of a secure post and a bit of calm,' he said as a taxi took them to the upper edge of the city, to get as good a view as possible. And then, on a terrace with a heavenly vista, Leskov talked about the power struggles and intrigues at the institute, and about his insecure position. It wasn't true to say that the others didn't think much of him. Quite the reverse, in fact: they feared and envied his independent mind. And then there was his time in prison, he said with bitter mockery. It gave him a degree of moral authority that he didn't like because it created a circle of grudging and uneasy respect around him, so that certain conversations regularly stopped when he entered the room.

And then this new post had recently become available.

'I'm the logical candidate. But you can imagine that for all these reasons they don't want me.' And there was an argument: he hadn't published very much. Leskov rested one leg against the edge of the railing, gripped his knee with both hands and looked down at the sea, where the light had already lost some of its glow. His face twitched and trembled. 'First you're thrown in prison, then you're accused of not having published enough. You see, that's why the text is so important. Would have been so important. The argument they advanced against me would have lost validity. "If only we had a longer, more recent text!" I've heard that often. And now the text is on a garbage dump somewhere. Gone. If only I had been able to make a copy of it! But after waiting around in the travel agent's and at the telegram office it was too late: having photocopies made in Russia is still terribly difficult.'

Perlmann turned sideways, and touched the suitcase with his foot. He covered his face with his hand. *I just need to take it out. But no, it's impossible. There simply isn't an innocent explanation. At some point he would bump into the truth. Inevitably.*

Leskov touched him on the arm. 'Let's walk down a little way. And now let's stop talking about me!'

The sea was the color of copper when they stood side by side by the railing on the way back. They hadn't spoken for a while, and it seemed to Perlmann that every further moment of silence, as in the tunnel, would produce an undesirable intimacy. Soon Leskov would start talking about Agnes.

'At the end of the session,' Perlmann said, when Leskov turned towards him, 'you made the surprising assertion that there is no true story about our experienced past.'

Leskov grinned. 'The assertion that cost Achim a pencil.'

'And then you added two words – Russian, I think – that I didn't understand. What was that about?'

'So someone noticed,' Leskov laughed. 'I thought everyone would have thought it was simply Russian babbling. But you, of course, noticed.'

Perlmann felt as if he were being presented as a prize pupil in a school class.

'The two words were *Klim Samgin*. It's the name of the central character in Maxim Gorky's last novel, a four-volume work, over two thousand pages long, with the title: *Zhizn' Klima Samgina: The Life of Klim Samgin*. With this character Gorky creates a narrative perspective for the description of forty years of Russian history. One important motif is that Samgin has a self-conscious, one might say a broken relationship with reality, into which radical doubts about the narratives of others, as well as his own perceptions, often creep. In this way Gorky allowed the little boy Klim to discover that the invention of things is an important component of life, something without which we cannot exist. There are wonderful sentences like . . . wait . . . yes: *I vsegda nuzhno chto-nibut' vydumyvat', inache nikto iz vzroslych ne budet zamechat' tebya i budesh zhit' tak, kak budto tebya net ili kak budto ty ne Klim.* Did you understand?

'One moment,' said Leskov. He closed his eyes and murmured the Russian sentence to himself again. 'In English it would be something like: *You must always be inventing something, otherwise the adults won't pay attention to you, and you will live as if you aren't there, or as if you aren't Klim.* Or another sentence . . .' As he said the words to himself, Leskov mutely moved his lips. 'Something like this: *Klim couldn't remember when he had actually noticed that he was invented, and he himself had begun to invent himself.* Gorky always uses the same word: *vydumyvat':* to invent or fabricate. And in the subheading of my new text, which I mentioned in the session, I use this word in the special sense that it has in Gorky.'

In his mind's eye, Perlmann saw the sheet covered with road dirt, lying on the map that now peeped from Leskov's jacket pocket.

'A hint of plagiarism,' Leskov smiled, 'but really only a hint.'

Perlmann experimentally took the hand holding the cigarette off the railing: no, outwardly it wasn't shaking; it only felt as if it was. He inhaled deeply, and from the bottom of his burning lungs he wished he had the power suddenly to extinguish that most terrible of all words – PLAGIARISM – from the minds of all human beings, so that he would never, never again, have to hear it. To do so, he thought, he would be prepared to enter any – really any – pact with the devil.

'The theme associated with this word,' Leskov continued, 'assumes a particularly dramatic form in Gorky's work when it is linked with the idea of a trauma.' He saw Perlmann turning his head away. 'Am I boring you?'

Perlmann glanced at him and shook his head.

'One day Klim Samgin sees another boy, a boy he hates, falling into the river while skating, and disappearing into a hole in the ice along with his female companion, whereupon the girl clings to him and drags him down. He sees the boy's red hands clinging to the edge of the ice, and his glistening head with its bloody face emerging every now and again from the black water and shouting for help. Klim, who is lying on the ice, throws him one end of his belt. But when he feels himself being pulled closer and closer to the water, he lets the belt slip from his hand, and shrinks away from the red hands which are breaking off more and more ice as they come towards him. And all of a sudden there's just the boy's cap floating on the water.'

Leskov paused and sought Perlmann's eye. The red hands coming closer and closer: wasn't that an image that could be pursued?

Perlmann nodded. He was glad it was quickly darkening.

'Gorky doesn't just call the hands *red*. He uses an expression that is stronger, more insistent. But I can't think of it right now,' said Leskov. 'Anyway, at the end of that scene he has someone say: *Da – byl li mal'chik-to, mozhet, mal'chika-to i ne bylo?*'

Perlmann, who had understood straight away, responded to his questioning gaze with a shake of the head.

'*Yes – was there a boy there at all, perhaps there was no boy there?* That's how you would have to translate it,' said Leskov. 'And you see: this question, which returns in later passages like a leitmotiv, picks up the theme of invention.'

The lights of Portofino were already coming into view when Leskov started talking about prison. They had locked him up for just three years. No, no torture, and no solitary confinement, either. Quite normal imprisonment. Four of them in a cell at first, later alone. Not being able to read anything, that had initially been the worst thing. After six months they had allowed – it was a miracle – his mother to bring him Gorky's novel. She had no idea of its content. She had come across it in a junk shop, and had bought it just for its length. Two thousand pages for so little money!

'What it meant for me back then to hold those volumes in my hands and feel their weight – it's impossible to capture that in words,' Leskov said quietly. Throughout his remaining time in prison, he had read it fourteen times. He knew hundreds of scenes off by heart.

'The theme of invention grabbed me straight away. But it took a long time before it assumed the form that it now has in my text. Gorky is primarily concerned with the invention of objects and events outside in the world or – when Klim Samgin talks about the invention of himself – of episodes in his external life story. And one slightly disappointing aspect of the novel is that Gorky effectively throws the theme down at your feet without really developing it. Although the story with the hole in the ice is ideally suited for that. There is, in fact, a moment, as Gorky

says, where Klim enjoys seeing his enemy, normally so arrogant, in that
desperate state. And this yields the question of whether he lets go of
the belt out of pure fear, or whether hatred is also involved. Because it
is a traumatic experience, Klim will have to invent something about it,
too, and this time it's an invention of the inner world. He will narrate
his inner past. And there is nothing, nothing at all, that he could cling
to when he wonders which of the various stories is the true one.'

Leskov held the flame to his unlit pipe. He was now standing with
his back to the water, staring, it seemed, at the numbers on the hull of
a lifeboat, and when he went on, it sounded as if he were a long way
away.

'Then something strange happened to me. When week after week
passed in this terrible, grey monotony, which is worse than any kind
of bullying, I gradually lost all sense of my own internal past. After a
certain amount of time you simply no longer know what your experience was like before you came along. It must sound insane to an
outsider, but you lose a certainty that was previously so much taken
for granted that you knew nothing about it. It's a silent, creeping, inexorable loss of your inner identity. You fight against it as you have never
fought before. You narrate your inner past to yourself over and over
again to keep it from slipping away. But the more often you do that,
the more intrusive the doubt becomes: is that really true, or am I merely
inventing this past experience for myself? And I'm sure you can imagine
how Gorky's theme and his own experience increasingly merged until
the name Klim Samgin became a symbol within me for that abyss of
lost identity.'

Leskov left the ship as though in a trance and stopped a few steps
later. 'And yet I hadn't yet got to my crazy thesis. That is only reached
when one accepts the thought that experience is not formed by narration, but in a sense created by it – the idea, then, that you know from
my earlier text.'

Perlmann noticed too late that he had been nodding. Horrified, he
turned his head towards Leskov. But he hadn't noticed anything, and
went on talking.

'You know, it's hard to describe, but the inner formulation and defense of my thesis were a great help to me in surviving my remaining time in prison. Why that should have been so I still don't quite know. But I suspect that it had less to do with the content of the thesis than with the feeling of having made an exciting discovery. That gave me a piece of inner freedom, and made me invulnerable to many things.'

Leskov stopped again on the steps leading up to the hotel. 'When I was out, and had regained my ability to work, I had lost the courage of my most important thesis, so in my first version I settled for observations about the creative role of language for experience. In that text I touch upon the radical idea only now and again. I think I was afraid of discovering that I had temporarily lost my mind in prison. Only in the course of that summer did I start fumbling around at the subject within myself. And when I then wrote the whole thing up, that was a process in which even imprisonment was addressed and, I hope, dealt with. A kind of healing process.' By the portico, Leskov took his glasses and rubbed his eyes. 'That's why I've got to find the text when I get home. I simply must. It's not just because of the post. That text – it's a piece of my soul.'

'Did you have a good flight?' asked Signora Morelli.

'Yes, thank you,' said Perlmann like someone who has just been woken up.

'She asked you that because of the note yesterday morning, didn't she?' Leskov said in the elevator.

Perlmann nodded. 'A misunderstanding.'

Up in the room he threw himself on the bed. He did it without first setting down the suitcase – as if it had grown onto him. When he did finally let go, he saw that the leather handle was black from the sweat of his hand.

There was nothing more to think about. Now it was just a question of will power. Trembling, he waited for the feelings of guilt and his own shabbiness, with which he was attempting to forge an alliance, to emerge victorious over fear. Only then could time start flowing again and carry him forward, wherever that might be.

Before five minutes had passed, he sat up. He slowly took the envelope out of the suitcase, removed the staples and drew out the plastic jacket. He no longer had to be careful with the teeth of the zip fastener. With one single jerk – into which he put all of his despair – he pulled open the zip. One of the loose teeth was torn out and fell between the pages. Perlmann forced himself to inhale slowly a few times and cautiously pulled out the text. He ran the back of his hand several times over the top, curling page. The hole with the ragged, brownish edges, where the twig had gone through, was bigger than he remembered.

He washed his face and combed away a ridiculously prominent tuft of hair. A fresh shirt. Yes, and the jacket, too. The warm water wouldn't do much for his cold hands, but he went back into the bathroom anyway. He pulled the door to his room closed behind him as softly as if someone were sleeping in there.

When he turned into the corridor that led to Leskov's room, Perlmann's pace slowed. Two doors before Leskov's he turned round, walked to the elevator and sat in the big wicker chair. There was nothing more to consider. If he gave Leskov the text, then he would have to admit everything. If he didn't give him the text, then Leskov wouldn't get the post, and it was Perlmann's fault. It was all quite clear. Crystal clear. There was no reason to sit here in the wicker chair. No amount of waiting could make it any clearer.

Perlmann waited. He would have liked to smoke. John Smith from Carson City, Nevada, who was coming out of the elevator in his tracksuit, showed Perlmann the headline of a newspaper and shook his head disapprovingly. Two French businessmen with briefcases came out of the corridor and walked, chatting, down the stairs. A chambermaid with bedlinen over her arm slipped past.

Perlmann walked back along the corridor. The blue nylon carpet was exaggeratedly thick; he felt as if he were wading. Next to Leskov's door he leaned against the wall. Then he held his ear to the door and heard Leskov coughing. Perlmann rolled up the text and hid it behind his back with his left hand. One last hesitation before his crooked finger, an ugly, repellent finger, touched the wood. He knocked twice. Leskov seemed not to have heard. Perlmann's nose started running. He took a few steps back, wedged the roll under his arm and blew his nose. After he had knocked again, he heard Leskov coming to the door. A short cough before the door opened.

'Oh, Philipp, it's you,' said Leskov. 'Come in.'

It was impossible to do it. Impossible. It wasn't an insight. It wasn't knowledge or a decision. It wasn't even a thought. It didn't even really have anything to do with the will. It wasn't anything that Perlmann remembered; nothing that he had at his command. Afterwards he felt as if he hadn't even been there. His body simply couldn't put the plan into action. The intention was confronted with powerful, unshakeable forces that wouldn't move. The resolution slipped off those forces like something laughably feeble. The system went on strike. A white, completely emotionless panic overrode everything.

'Come in, please,' Leskov repeated with a cordial but slightly puzzled smile.

'No, no,' Perlmann heard himself saying. 'I just wanted to check when your flight leaves tomorrow morning. So that I can tell Angelini.'

'Oh, I see. Wait, I'll take a look. But please, do come in for a moment.'

While Leskov fetched his ticket from his suitcase, Perlmann stayed with his back against the door, which he had left ajar. Where his hand gripped the pages, they were wet.

'At five past nine,' said Leskov. He pointed to the armchair. 'Time to have a cigarette?'

'Not really, no. I promised Angelini I would call him back. He's waiting.'

Perlmann took a step to the side, pulled the door open with his right hand and walked out backwards. Leskov stopped in the doorway and watched him go. Perlmann took a few more steps backwards. Then he quickly turned left on his own axis and, in a contrary motion, swung the rolled-up text in front of his chest. After a few quick steps he was on the stairs.

In his room he sat motionless on the bed for several minutes, staring straight ahead. Then he fetched his big suitcase. In it, partly telescoped in on itself, was an unopened envelope full of mail from Frau Hartwig, as well as the invitation to Princeton, the black wax-cloth notebook, the little volume of Robert Walser, the certificate and the medal. Perlmann couldn't remember when he had thrown all these things in. He stared at the chaotic pile. It felt like a sedimentation of failure, guilt and dereliction. He didn't know what to do with it. He wearily laid his torn and bloodstained pairs of trousers over it, then his dirty, pale jacket. It would look idiotic if he stepped into Olivetti headquarters in a blazer and far too pale trousers.

He put the chronicle in the other drawer. Then he packed the books – none of which he had opened in the course of the whole five weeks – in the suitcase. The zip of the plastic jacket would only close halfway. He no longer had the strength to think about it. He put Leskov's text back in the envelope and placed it between the books. In the bathroom he got his sponge bag ready and took a whole sleeping pill. From the desk drawer he took the printout of his notes. He tore the sheets in half and threw them in the waste-paper basket.

Before he turned out the light he called Leskov and made his apologies for dinner. When he set the alarm, he felt the effect of the tablet in his fingertips.

56

Leskov's stained suitcase was standing beside the reception desk when Perlmann came downstairs. On the gleaming marble floor of the elegant hall it looked like a remnant of another era. It was just after seven, and Giovanni was waiting for Signora Morelli so that he could go home.

'*Buona fortuna!*' said Perlmann as he shook his hand.

'You too!' replied Giovanni, and went on shaking. 'And then . . . erm . . . I just wanted to say: you play the piano really well. Really brilliant!'

'Thank you,' said Perlmann and exchanged an awkward glance with him. 'Is there a cup competition coming up where I could see Baggio on our television at home?'

'Juventus are playing Stuttgart soon. I could check . . .'

'Don't worry,' said Perlmann, 'I'll keep an eye out. What's his first name, by the way?'

'Roberto.'

Outside the door to the dining room Perlmann turned round again and raised his hand: '*Ciao.*'

Giovanni said the same word back, and it came out of his lips more lightly and surely than it had on Wednesday evening. It sounded almost as natural as if they were two old friends.

Leskov had put his suitcase on a chair next to him. Perlmann flinched when he saw him now, and immediately his eye looked for the little piece of rubber band in the zip of the outside pocket. It had gone.

'Rather shabby compared to yours, isn't it?' said Leskov when he saw Perlmann staring at the case.

Perlmann gestured vaguely and picked up the coffee pot.

'If I understood correctly the other evening, you'll be talking to Angelini about the question of publication,' Leskov said hesitantly as he folded up the napkin.

Perlmann nodded. He had seen it coming. *But in a good hour it'll be over. Once and for all.*

'It's about a translation of my text . . . Do you think . . . ?'

'I'll talk to him,' said Perlmann and pushed back the chair. 'I'll let you know.'

Perlmann would have liked to say goodbye to Signora Morelli, who was just taking her coat off, on his own. Leskov's presence disturbed him, and when he heard the Russian's extravagant words of thanks he went to the toilet.

But Leskov was still standing next to her afterwards. Today she was wearing a black scarf with a fine white edge, and above it her still rather sleepy face looked paler than usual.

Perlmann gave her his hand and was glad that Leskov now bent towards his case. 'Thank you,' he said simply, 'and all the best.'

'You too,' she said. Then for a moment she rested her other hand on his. 'Have a rest. You look completely exhausted.'

Leskov gave the taxi driver a sign and walked laboriously down the stairs. Perlmann set down his luggage and went back into the hall. He looked at Signora Morelli and had no idea what he had wanted to say.

'Is there anything else?' she asked with a smile.

'No, no. I . . . erm . . . I just wanted to say it was good to have you here for those few weeks.' And then, when her hand awkwardly reached for her scarf, he added quickly: 'Have you sorted out your taxes?'

'Yes,' she laughed. 'Thank God.'

'See you then.'

'Yes. Have a good trip.'

Perlmann was relieved that Leskov had chosen to sit beside the driver. Behind him, Perlmann leaned into the upholstery and closed his eyes. The after-effect of the sleeping pills pressed against his eyes. Contrary to his habit, when the taxi came round the corner he hadn't turned back to face the hotel. Now he saw it in his mind's eye, in all its details, and he even climbed the steps to the Marconi Veranda once more. It was over. *Over.*

'For publication I could make a shorter version,' said Leskov. 'What do you think?' In spite of several groaning attempts Leskov hadn't managed to turn round completely, and now he was looking at the window past the back of the driver's head.

Perlmann jammed his fists into the seat. He would have to run the whole publication business properly through his mind, he said.

After a lengthy pause, in which he had slipped into a half-sleep, the back of the front seat struck his knees. Leskov had loosened his seatbelt and rolled on to his right side, and was trying, once again in vain, to turn all the way towards Perlmann.

'I barely dare to broach the subject,' he said submissively, 'but I don't suppose you would be willing to translate my text?'

Perlmann froze and was glad that the driver was suddenly forced to overtake at that point, cursing as he did so.

'I just thought that because you know my thoughts so well, and have responded to them with such interest,' Leskov added hesitantly, almost guiltily, when he received no answer.

Only now did Perlmann manage to shake off his torpor. 'Just from the point of view of time, it's not going to work,' he heard himself say in a hollow voice. 'We've got the term coming up . . .'

'I know,' Leskov said quickly, 'and I'm sure you're going to want to go on working on your book. Incidentally, I wanted to ask you if I could read what you've written already. You can imagine how intensely interested I am.'

Perlmann felt as if a ton weight on his chest was keeping him from breathing. 'Later,' he said at last, when Leskov had long since clicked his seatbelt shut again.

'The man with the cap is working today again,' Leskov laughed when the taxi drove past the parking cabin to the airport entrance. 'I won't forget him again in a hurry. Such stubbornness!'

Then, as they stood in line at check-in, Leskov suddenly said that he
hoped the plane wasn't as full as it had been on the inbound flight, when
he hadn't known where to put his feet because of the suitcase. In the
end the stewardess had saved him by stowing it somewhere at the back.

'At least this way I can be sure that I haven't left the text somewhere
along this route,' he said with a crooked smile. 'You must knock on
wood very firmly that I find it, when I step into my apartment in . . .
wait . . . in fifteen hours.'

They slowly walked towards passport control. *Another two, three minutes.*

Leskov set down his suitcase. 'When you step into your apartment,
I'm sure it seems empty to you, even today. Doesn't it?'

For one brief moment Perlmann experienced the same rage as he had
felt in the silent tunnel; it was as if it had ceased only for a few minutes,
not for several days.

'Kirsten will be there,' he lied. And then, contrary to his intentions,
he asked the question: 'Klim Samgin – how does he come to terms with
his trauma? Or doesn't he?'

Leskov made the face of someone normally unnoticed who learns,
completely unexpectedly, that someone is interested in him, in him
personally.

'I've thought a lot about that. But it's strange: Gorky doesn't answer
the question. On the one hand the memory of the hole in the ice keeps
flashing up; on the other hand you don't learn anything about how
Klim feels about it. If you ask me: you can't really come to terms with
a trauma of that kind. It isn't so much that something terrible happened
to him that he couldn't do anything about. Like me with prison. He
lets go of the belt; that is, he does something, he performs an action.
And also there's this hatred within him. If there's any chance of something that might be a real reconciliation with oneself, and not just a
frantic self-reassurance. I doubt it. The red hands will never have let
him go again. Or what do you think?'

Perlmann didn't say anything, and just shrugged. Leskov took a step
towards him, and put his arms around him. As stiff as a mannequin,
Perlmann let him do it.

'I'll write to you straight away about the text!' called Leskov, as the official flicked through his passport. 'And, of course, I'll send you a copy as soon as it's typed out!'

Incapable of reacting, Perlmann watched Leskov waving his passport before he disappeared. With his head completely empty, Perlmann stood on the same spot. For several minutes he noticed nothing of the bustle going on around him. Only when a running child bumped into his case did he really come to his senses. *Over.* Again and again he said the word, only inwardly at first, then under his voice. It had no effect. The relief he longed for didn't materialize. He took a few sluggish steps and leaned against a column. Fifteen hours, then for Leskov days of despair would begin, of impotent fury with himself and his increasingly faint hope of a dispatch from Lufthansa. Perlmann involuntarily hunched his shoulders and folded his arms in front of his chest.

Nothing had changed in the waiting list for the afternoon flight from Frankfurt to Turin. There was still that one man in front of him. Perlmann walked over to the bar. But even before he was served his coffee, he left some money on the bar and went up to the viewing terrace. He set down his luggage as far as possible from the place where, long ago, he would have left the suitcase, had it not been for the girl in sneakers. The pilots were already sitting in the cockpit, and now two cleaning women with big garbage bags were leaving the plane. *Do you know what I'm most afraid of? The cleaning crew.*

Leskov was one of the first to leave the bus, which had driven out to the plane in a big loop. With his heavy gait he climbed the gangway and, at one point, he seemed to have trodden on a flap of his loden coat. Having reached the top, he looked as if he wanted to turn round, but was forced in by the others.

Perlmann wanted to go. He stayed where he was. Behind which window might Leskov be sitting? The plane rolled painfully slowly to the start of the runway, and time seemed to stretch to tearing point. After it had turned, the plane stood there as if it couldn't be moved again, waiting in the pale morning light that seeped through a fine veil of clouds. Otherwise, nothing moved on the empty tarmac. Perlmann held his breath and felt his blood thumping. He felt as if this silence and inertia had been staged specifically for him, even though he couldn't have said why, or what its message might have been. For several minutes the whole world seemed to him to have been frozen in an unintelligible act of waiting. Only the revving of the engine set time in motion once more. Without knowing why, and caught up in his blind tension, Perlmann concentrated on the precise moment when the tires lost contact with the runway. Then, when the plane flew out in a lazy loop over the sea, he saw in his mind's eye the view that Leskov had now. *That's how I imagined the Riviera, exactly like that,* he heard Leskov saying. Perlmann only bent for his luggage when the low cloud had swallowed up the last flash of the wings.

He checked in his case and collected his boarding card for the eleven o'clock flight to Frankfurt. He would – he thought in the bar – have to wait five long hours at Frankfurt Airport for the flight to Turin, not knowing whether he would be able to find a seat. If not, he could always drive to Ivrea. He could get there by ten o'clock tomorrow. Admittedly, that would mean he wouldn't be at the university before Wednesday. But with the prospect of his new job in the bright office Perlmann was invulnerable to reproachful glances.

In the hall he sat down in a corner and unpacked his books. He picked up each individual one and examined it with puzzled thoroughness, as if it were a document from a very distant, very alien culture. He ran through the contents lists and, although he was familiar with all the topics, he was amazed at all the things that were in there. He opened a few pages at random and read. They were brand-new textbooks, hailed as revolutionary on the blurb, but he had the feeling of reading the same thing as always. The spine of the book snapped when he moved on to the next random sample. The shiny pages with the illustrations and tables smelled particularly intensely of fresh print.

At last he packed them all away again, leaving out only Leskov's text. No, the engraved initials on the case couldn't give him away. Suddenly, he was repelled by the dark sweat-stains on the handle. On the way to the restroom he carried the case in his arms like a shapeless package. He hid it behind the garbage bin under the washbasin and then walked quickly to security control, where the envelope containing Leskov's text was suspiciously examined.

Sven Berghoff was sitting with his back to him when Perlmann stepped into the waiting room. Perlmann recognized Berghoff immediately by his unkempt red hair, the raised collar of his jacket and his long ivory cigarette holder, which protruded from the side of his mouth. Berghoff was the only one who had caused Perlmann any difficulties over his leave. It had been his revenge for the fact that Perlmann, whose lectures were always full to capacity, had recently burst in to one of Berghoff's lectures in search of chalk and had found only six people listening. Berghoff had turned red, claimed there was no chalk there, when there was a great mountain of the stuff beside the sponge and, even though Perlmann, to keep from embarrassing him, had left without any chalk, Berghoff had cut him ever since.

The sight of Berghoff put Perlmann in a complete panic. All of a sudden there was no Leskov any more, and no text that had to get to the mail. There was only the dark corridor of the institute, the lecture halls and seminar rooms, the grouchy and unctuous remarks of colleagues. He turned round, swung over a barrier and ran – with Leskov's text pressed firmly to his chest – out to a taxi in which he asked to be driven to the station. Perlmann only calmed down when the train set off for Ivrea.

57

It was cold when Perlmann stepped out on to the station forecourt. An icy wind drove sand from an abandoned building site into his eyes. Even though it was just before four, lots of cars were already driving with their lights on. There didn't seem to be a taxi stand. Holding the hand with Leskov's text under his coat, Perlmann walked towards the center.

In the hotel they asked him, perplexed, if he had any luggage. The room he had booked – more expensive than the price originally agreed – seemed shabby after the luxury of the Miramare. When he had showered, he put his clothes back on and went to the window. There was snow on the mountaintops of the Valle d'Aosta. The remaining light in the west was cold and forbidding.

There were lockers at reception, but they were too small for Leskov's text. They would keep the envelope somewhere else. 'Nothing'll happen to it,' the man behind the counter said with a smile when Perlmann turned round again at the door.

The way to Olivetti headquarters led down a long, straight road leading out of the town. The massive building was dark, and the black glass facade, broken at an obtuse angle, looked menacing. There was a single car in the parking lot. Perlmann walked a little way around the star-shaped complex and tried to make out something inside. Behind a side door, a uniformed watchman sat at a faintly lit desk. When he saw Perlmann, he got up and shone his inspection lamp outside. Perlmann turned round and went back to the hotel. On the way the toast that he had eaten on the train kept repeating on him.

As soon as he had lain down on the bed and covered himself with a blanket from the wardrobe, he fell into a dull sleep, haunted by the priest with the pointed, malevolent face who had sat opposite him on the journey and looked at him disapprovingly every time he smoked a cigarette.

It was half-past eleven when Perlmann woke up, his limbs stiff. It had been half-past eight when Leskov had spoken of the fifteen hours. So now, when it must have been half-past one in Russia, he was entering his apartment in St Petersburg. He would be dashing to the desk and rummaging among the chaos: nothing. He would be looking in every possible and impossible place, still in his loden coat. In the end he would give up, fall silent and stare into the distance. Gradually, Leskov would start hoping that the text would come by post, perhaps even tomorrow, but certainly on Tuesday. By Wednesday at the latest. He would go into the institute every morning at mail delivery time to receive the dispatch. And every morning he would experience the same disappointment.

Perlmann went down to reception and asked the grumpy night porter to fetch him the envelope with Leskov's text. He put it beside his pillow when he crept into bed afterwards, and also laid his coat on the blankets.

Now Kirsten would be phoning Frankfurt to ask if he had got home all right. He was glad he didn't have to talk to her. He thought about Giovanni sitting in front of the television. And about Signora Morelli. He didn't even know what street she lived on. Once again he saw himself standing in the train compartment with Evelyn Mistral, and felt her hands on the back of his neck. She hadn't said a single word about his notes. Perhaps that was the reason why his thoughts didn't stay with her any longer than they did. Instead he now kept seeing Brian Millar, just before he got into the taxi, turning towards him once more and raising his hand. *No one told me. We should have . . .* Perlmann buried his head in the pillow.

The morning light here was quite different from the light by the sea, harsher and more featureless, without magic and promise. Perlmann showered for a long time and brushed his teeth with the wet corner of his towel. His stubble reminded him of the morning when he had fainted. Before he went to breakfast he checked that Leskov's text was still in the envelope.

Afterwards, when he sat on the edge of his bed with the receiver in his hand, the number of Frau Hartwig's office refused to come to him. A strange weakness, like that caused by a rising fever, kept him from remembering. In the end it was his motor memory when dialling that helped.

'There's an important meeting at four o'clock today,' said Frau Hartwig. 'I just wanted to make sure I'd mentioned it.'

It was as if her irritability continued straight on from the end of their last conversation – an irritability that had not existed in the last seven years.

Perlmann held the receiver away from him and exhaled slowly and with great concentration. 'As I said,' he said calmly, 'I'll be in the office tomorrow morning. At about ten, I would say. And send out those notices as we discussed.'

He handed in Leskov's text at reception again, for safe keeping. Yes, he had needed it during the night, he said in reply to their puzzled question. Outside the streets were beginning to fill with commuter traffic. In the future he, too, would go to work in the morning in a stream of others. Or stand in a crowded bus and read the paper. A sandwich in a bar at lunchtime, followed by coffee. In the bar he would see the same people every day, and those wonderfully light, floating acquaintance-ships would come into being. Home in the evening to a simple, prob-ably noisy apartment. It would be a while before he got used to the noise, the shouting of children through the thin walls. But on the other hand he would be free, and like everyone else he could lean out of the window in the evening or sit in front of the television. Books – he would allow himself some time for those. And then only Italian books, fiction. After a while he might risk translating a novel. If he wasn't too tired in the evening. Because he would now – for the first time in his life – be a person who had evenings. A person with a proper job. Honest toil. A person with a present.

Perlmann stopped outside a shop selling toiletries and waited for it to open at nine. He imagined Kirsten stepping into his apartment, still inadequately furnished, after walking down a shabby corridor with damp walls. She was already slightly embarrassed, he thought, but also impressed, and eventually she would say she thought it was great to have a father who did something so unusual.

He bought the most basic toiletries. Then he went back to the hotel to shave and brush his teeth. The same underwear for a week. He took his tie out of his blazer pocket and put it on. His shirt collar was dirty, and the bloodstain on the lapel of his blazer was impossible to ignore.

The closer he got to the Olivetti building, the more his confidence faded. After an unfamiliar shave, the wind felt bitter on his cheeks, and that sensation passed into a feeling of general vulnerability. What did he actually want to say to Angelini? How was he to formulate his question? How to explain, so that the whole thing didn't sound like romantic eccentricity, like a twenty year old's fantasy of running away? And how could Perlmann avoid revealing a connection with his fainting fit? It would, he thought, have to sound light and undramatic, almost playful. But not capricious. In spite of everything, there would have to be a sense of mature serenity behind the lightness of his words.

The parking lot was almost full, and people were still streaming into the huge building. Perlmann counted seven floors. The windows of the main facade had a coppery sheen. Behind them, in big, neon-bright offices, nothing but men in suits. He imagined they had a wonderful view of the mountains. On sunny days those spaces would be flooded with light from dawn till dusk.

It was a quarter to ten. The door behind which the watchman had been sitting yesterday was the exit, through which the employees left the building. As they did so, they stuck a card in a machine. *An electronic time clock.* Perlmann gave a start. Maybe it was just some sort of security measure. On the other hand: anyone could stroll in unimpeded through the main entrance. He would find out. He, too, would get a card.

Already in the doorway, he glanced once more across the street. Not a bar to be seen. What he was stepping into now was a kind of ghetto in an open field. On the other hand, he was sure there would be a first-class caféteria. That had its advantages, too.

Angelini's office was on the fourth floor of a side wing, and had an anteroom with two more doors leading off it. The secretary brushed the long blonde hair from her brow as she looked in the diary. There was no sign of his name, she said, and looked at him with cool regret from her freckly face. The appointment was more of a private one, said Perlmann, and tried not to be intimidated by her pointed nose and narrow mouth. She looked at his pale trousers, and her eye also lingered for a moment on the lapel of his blazer. Then, with a shrug, she pointed to a chair and returned to the screen.

Angelini appeared at about half-past ten. His temple still bore the impressions of the pillow. Unasked, the secretary handed him a cup of coffee, which he took into the office. The way he apologized for his lateness and pointed Perlmann to the armchair next to the desk, was so slick it bordered on caricature. He let a stack of letters slip through his fingers, flicked backwards and fished out an envelope that he slit open with a decorated letter opener. As he scanned the text with a frown, he took the occasional sip of coffee. 'Just one second,' he said and disappeared into the anteroom.

The only thing Perlmann liked about the room was the Miró and Matisse prints. But they, too, hung over the conventionally elegant furniture, as if that was just how things were supposed to be. The burgundy leather chair behind the black desk was too flashy and didn't match it, but it was the only thing that emanated a little individuality. There was no point looking out of the window. It gave a view of a hill with trees and bushes, from which only a few brightly colored leaves still hung. It was only if you stood right off to the left that you could get a view of the mountains.

Angelini apologized again as he leaned back in the armchair and lit a cigarette. His face was relaxed now, and full of friendly curiosity. 'What can I do for you?'

Perlmann looked at the crossed feet under the desk, dangling just above the floor, and below the ankle of Angelini's right foot he saw a hole in his sock. All of a sudden he felt safe, and the impulse to laugh, which he struggled to suppress, gave his voice the requisite jauntiness.

'I wanted to ask you if the company might have a job for me. As a translator, for example. Something like that.'

It was the last thing Angelini had expected. His feet stopped dangling. Without looking at Perlmann he picked up his coffee cup and drank it down in a series of slow sips. He took his time. Yet again he ran his cigarette along the inner rim of the ashtray. Then he looked up.

'You mean . . . ?'

'Yes,' said Perlmann, 'I'm giving up my professorship.'

Angelini stubbed out his cigarette. His face now looked as if he didn't know what expression to decide upon.

'Can I ask why? Has it got something to do with . . . ?'

'No, not at all,' Perlmann said quickly. 'I've been planning it for ages. I'd just like to try something new. In a new country.'

Angelini took a cigarette and walked to the window. When he turned to Perlmann, his face was full of baffled admiration. It was the most personal expression that Perlmann had ever seen him wear.

'You know,' he said slowly, 'I'm completely bowled over by this. A man of your academic status, your reputation . . .' He walked to the door. 'It will take a moment. I also want to ask them about the likelihood of a work permit.'

The secretary brought Perlmann coffee. Now, all of a sudden, everything was going far too quickly for him. He felt all a-flutter, as if before an exam. In conversation with Angelini he had not, to his knowledge, made any mistakes in Italian. But they would inevitably come. From one minute to the next, even though nothing had happened, he felt clumsier, slow and dim-witted. He wasn't really talented, that was as true when it came to languages as it was with music. He had a good memory, and he was a hard worker. That was it. He was no Luc Sonntag.

Angelini was smiling contentedly as he came back. 'In your case the probationary period would only last a month. Just a question of form. And the legal department sees no problems with your work permit. Where languages are concerned, you're always at an advantage.' His expression revealed that he was missing something in Perlmann's face. 'And you're quite sure you want this? Forgive the question. It's just . . . it's simply so unusual.'

'I know,' said Perlmann.

Even now, Angelini had expected more of a reaction. But after a brief hesitation he made a special effort. 'Could you start on the second of January? The company will make you an offer over the next few days. And we'll try and help you with a apartment as well.'

Perlmann nodded repeatedly.

'While you're here,' said Angelini, 'I can show you your office.'

It was a cramped office with two desks opposite one another. The window faced backwards, towards the east. It looked down on a low building connected to the main block by a walkway. Beyond it, on the slope, an electricity cabin. In the months when the sun managed to peep over the hill, there might be two or three hours of morning sun.

The woman at the other desk had turned on the light. 'This is Signora Medici,' said Angelini. 'Our chief translator. She comes from Tyrol and speaks five languages. Or how many is it?'

'Six,' the woman said, shaking Perlmann's hand firmly.

The contrast between name and appearance was so great that he could barely keep from laughing. She was a plump matron in knee socks and sandals, and a pair of horn-rimmed glasses sat on her nose, with lenses as thick as magnifying glasses.

'Don't worry, we can speak German,' she said as Perlmann made one mistake after another.

After that remark he felt dazed, and later he remembered only that he had stared at the wall with all the holiday postcards, which looked exactly like the wall in Frau Hartwig's office.

Yes, he said later in Angelini's office, his work with the group had been a great success. He would contact him shortly about publication.

'You know,' Angelini said as they parted, 'I still can't imagine why you would want to give all that up. Well, anyway, you can think about it for a while now that you know more about it. And tell Carla out there what your expenses are. She'll write you a check. This was a job interview, in a way!'

The secretary was on the phone. Perlmann nodded to her and went outside. On the way to the hotel he accidentally bumped into two people. The man at reception who brought him the envelope containing Leskov's text, pointed to the address.

'St Petersburg. Will something like that really arrive? I mean, does the mail to Russia actually work? With all the chaos over there?'

While Perlmann was dozing in the train to Turin, that question pursued him like a stubborn echo. For the whole journey he held the envelope so tightly that there were sweat stains on it afterwards. He kept hearing Signora Medici's Tyrolean accent, when she had suddenly spoken German.

At the airport check-in desk he pretended not to speak a word of Italian. He bought two German newspapers, even though he was more interested in the Italian headlines. German, that was the language he knew. The only one. To imagine anything else was conceited nonsense.

When the plane rose, he saw the grounds of the Fiat works. *The people from Fiat. Santini.* He closed his eyes. When flying, he had often noticed, thoughts formed that you forgot later when you stepped inside the airport, as if they had never happened, so that it remained unclear for ever whether they had really been thoughts at all. *Finding a perspective outside oneself, to live from there in greater freedom within oneself.* It could be a goal, he thought, an ideal. But perhaps it was also a chimera, the expression of his fatigue. He picked up both newspapers and read them from the first page to the last. He immediately forgot every article that he had read. So he didn't need to think, either about what had been or what was yet to come.

Only once he interrupted his reading and looked down at the snowy mountains. *The perspective of eternity.* If one did everything from that perspective, wouldn't that mean losing the present completely – so completely that one wouldn't even miss it? Was it not, to put it this way, a precondition for the experience of the present that the plane would eventually sink below the clouds and touch the ground?

58

The rain was pelting down in Frankfurt, and the wind whipped the water so violently against the aeroplane that Perlmann involuntarily flinched behind the window. All the while, Leskov's text had been in the net on the back of the seat. It was in such a net, Leskov would think, that he had forgotten the text. As he was going, Perlmann clamped the envelope under his left arm and also held it tightly with his right hand.

His calculation was correct. As the counter where he had to ask for his suitcase, there was a stack of Lufthansa stickers. As the man at the desk fetched his case, Perlmann slipped three of them into his pocket. He sat down near the post office counter, opened the envelope and stuck one of the labels on the plastic jacket. He stuck the other two on the envelope, one on the top left, the other on the bottom right. He held the envelope at arm's length: it looked good, business-like. The home address. *An address that no one here could know but me.* Perlmann felt the whole mechanism of his tormented reflections beginning to set itself in motion. For a moment he pressed his fingers against his brow, got up and walked to the counter.

As the post office clerk was sticking the stamps and the label for express delivery on the envelope, Perlmann asked him how long, in his view, it would take to arrive. The clerk shrugged.

'Three days, a week. No idea.'

Why should it take a week? Perlmann asked irritably. The man threw the envelope into a basket, counted the money and then looked at Perlmann in silence for a second or two.

'As I said: no idea.'

So why are you worrying me, then? Perlmann yelled at him inwardly. Out loud he said, 'I'm sorry. It's . . . so much depends upon it. Do you perhaps know . . . I mean, can you estimate how great the danger is of the package going missing?'

The expression that now appeared on the clerk's face reminded Perlmann of the pizza chef in Santa Margherita whom he had asked about rain near the tunnel.

'Nothing gets lost here. As to the Russian post – no idea.'

Slowly, as if he needed to free himself of another internal obstacle, Perlmann walked towards the exit. He avoided looking over at the book display where, almost three weeks before, Nikolai Leskov's book had leapt out at him. Just as he stepped through the light barrier and the sliding door slid sideways, it occurred to him. *A copy. For safety's sake I've got to copy the text.* He practically ran to the post office counter and, at one point, his case, which was on wheels, tipped over. Now there was a line. Perlmann stood on tiptoes: his envelope was covered up by others, but the basket with the blue label was still there.

'As if we didn't have anything else to do,' murmured the clerk as he sought out the envelope a little while later.

Was there a photocopier anywhere in this building? It was already dark outside when Perlmann was finally allowed into the back room of a newsagent's in a completely different part of the building. The half-closed zip of the plastic jacket could only be opened fully by a violent tug. Now six of the teeth weren't working, and there was no point even thinking about pulling it closed again. After sixty-five pages the machine ran out of paper, and Perlmann had to wait a quarter of an hour until the staff could take the time to come and fill it up. Two copied pages fell on the dusty floor. When he cleaned them with his handkerchief he had a feeling that he would never, ever be done with Leskov's text, and he started breathing with difficulty. The metal of the staples on the envelope had become far too soft from all that bending, he thought. He hoped they wouldn't break on the journey.

As he left, he handed the flustered staff a fifty mark note and then walked the long way back to the post office. He asked the clerk, who stared silently into the distance after recognizing him, whether it was a good idea to register the package, or whether that might slow everything down.

'What now?' was the only reaction he got.

And then he won't be at home, and they'll take the envelope away again. 'Don't register it,' he said.

The taxi progressed slowly through the city traffic. Perlmann had closed his eyes, and was trying to use his exhaustion to keep all thoughts at bay. The rolled-up copy in his hand was getting sticky. *There's no point in it whatsoever. I could never give it to him without exposing myself.* He gave up, and at that moment he had the feeling that he had just relinquished absolutely everything he had, and that it was a more complete surrender than he had ever experienced before. As the wall of rain lashed the taxi, he saw the black lines of the felt-tip pen running and the address on the envelope blurring to illegibility. When the taxi had driven off and he was looking for his front-door key, drips fell, unnoticed by him, on to Leskov's text.

III

The Message

59

On the first night Perlmann had a heart attack and was taken to the hospital in an ambulance. But the doctor on duty saw no reason to keep him in. All his readings were normal. He diagnosed complete exhaustion, gave Perlmann a tranquillizing injection and signed him off work until the end of the year.

Perlmann spent the rest of the night sleeplessly in an armchair, looking out at the garden, where it started snowing towards morning. Every now and again he wrapped himself up even more tightly in the blanket, and enjoyed the fact that the injection slowed everything down and kept his thoughts away.

Shortly after eight he told Frau Hartwig. His voice sounded so flat that she didn't ask a single question. Later, he stepped out into the dense snowstorm, and walked slowly to the bank, where he put the copy of Leskov's text, now blistered and browned by the rain, in a safe deposit box. He bought the barest necessities, put the chain on the door and, after disconnecting the phone, went to bed.

He spent most of that day, and the two next days, sleeping. When he was awake for one or two hours he thought about Leskov waiting for the post. Each time he was unable to bear the idea for long, and was soon glad to feel exhaustion pulling him back into sleep. At four o'clock on Thursday morning he was woken by hunger pangs. He found that he had lost eight kilos, and forced himself to prepare a proper meal. After a few bites he couldn't go on, and left it. While he stared at an old late-night western without following the plot, he slowly ate half a loaf of bread and drank camomile tea that reminded him of the time of his childhood illnesses. He hadn't smoked a cigarette since Turin, and he didn't feel like one now.

On Thursday afternoon he stayed awake for longer. As it went on snowing outside, Perlmann sat on the sofa and stared blankly at the coffee stain on the living-room carpet. He felt as if he had, silently and without really noticing, shattered apart, and was now lying around in vague pieces somewhere outside, far removed from himself, and as if all those scattered pieces now had to be drawn together on invisible threads from some imaginary middle point, and carefully reassembled until his inner essence was complete once more, seamless and unbroken.

As he walked from room to room looking at Agnes's photographs, he moved cautiously and with deliberate slowness, like an invalid. The post office clerk had clearly thought it possible that the text would only take three days to arrive. The information had just been flung out like that. But he had still been given a time limit. If that was so, the text would arrive in St Petersburg today. The courier could bring it to Leskov tonight. At any rate, it would be delivered tomorrow morning. *Will something like that really arrive? With all the chaos over there?*

That night he dreamed about Signora Medici, who lived in Pian dei Ratti. She spent the whole day leaning in the window, watching him, with Leskov next to him as a driving instructor, practising driving straight ahead in front of the slate-grinder's, and having to fight against the steering wheel's constant pull to the left. *Don't worry, you can speak German!* she kept shouting. *That will make things easier!*

Perlmann woke drenched in sweat and made coffee. Six languages. If you included Russian, he had the same number. He lit a cigarette. Wrapped in the feeling of dizziness that began after the first drag, he got to work on the signora. He chased her through all the languages he spoke, and ruthlessly set her up for the most obvious traps. It was already past eight and broad daylight when he was finally able to free himself from that hate-drenched compulsion.

Now the courier could ring Leskov's doorbell at any moment. The Russian's despair would be at an end. He could immediately start copying it out and filling in the gaps. He still had exactly a week. Hopefully, when the courier came, he wouldn't already be on his way to the university to wait. Most letter boxes were too small for an envelope of that size, and who knew what might happen if it were simply left outside the door?

Now the time had come to phone Kirsten. He got her out of bed. She had called every evening at the usual time. Where had he been hiding himself? Perlmann dodged the question, saying something about tedious professional dinners. He didn't mention the hospital, or the fact that he had been signed off work. Kirsten hemmed and hawed for a while before saying that she probably wouldn't be coming home before Christmas. She had to deliver two more presentations, and she also wanted to help Martin move house. Perlmann concealed his relief, and said magnanimously that that was all perfectly fine.

In the afternoon he unpacked his case. The phone rang as he was stuffing the blood-stained and the torn trousers into a bag, which he fastened tightly. He suddenly dropped it and ran to the corridor. *That might be him!* But the ringing had already stopped. Perlmann carried the bag outside and threw it in the bin. He laid out the pale jacket with the strips of dirt ready for dry-cleaning. The blazer, which hung on a hanger from the wardrobe door, had fine, white traces of sweat on the back. He saw that only now. He put it with his jacket. As he did so he discovered a strip of dried tomato sauce on his sleeve. *Stronzo.*

The chronicle had plainly slipped around in the suitcase, and the cover was torn. He threw the cover away and set the volume down on his empty desk. Next to it were the unopened envelope from Frau Hartwig, the invitation to Princeton, his notes. He opened a page of *Jakob von Gunten* at random and read a few sentences. Then he put the book back on the shelf. He would never read it again.

He fetched a new bag for the medal and the certificate. It was the first time he had unrolled the certificate. It referred to one FILIP PEREMAN, who was henceforth an honorary citizen of Santa Margherita Ligure. On the way to the bin Perlmann couldn't help grinning. The last things he unpacked were the new handkerchiefs from the plastic jacket. He held them indecisively in his hand, then set them down on the chest of drawers in the corridor.

Later he collected his private post from two streets down. While he was still in the post office, he tore Hanna's letter in two. She had been delighted by his phone call out of the blue, she wrote, but also unsettled. Could he call her when he was home again? And could they see each other again? It would take a few days, he thought, as he stamped through the slush, before he was ready to make that call.

He saw on the television news that the match Giovanni had mentioned – the one between Stuttgart and Juventus Turin – took place today. It was already half an hour in. Roberto Baggio was playing; his name kept being mentioned. *If he hadn't scored, I would have been guilty of plagiarism.* Perlmann waited for a throw-in that provided a close-up of Baggio's face. A strange face, he thought, and turned off the television. *But it would only have been a disaster if Maria had finished typing up the text on Friday. If she hadn't had a cold. Or if Santini had had something that urgently needed typing.*

The woman at international directory enquiries was very helpful. They had only a few numbers of major companies in St Petersburg to hand, but they could call information there to ask for a private number. However, that could take a long time – up to a day. Should she call him back? Perlmann gave her Leskov's name and address and said that the time of day didn't matter; it could be the middle of the night.

While looking for the piece of paper with Leskov's address on it, Perlmann had come across the two unused plane tickets: the original one for his flight home, Genoa–Frankfurt, and the horrendously expensive one for the flight to Frankfurt on Saturday. Together they were worth more than 1,000 marks. He tore them up. It was like an expiatory sacrifice.

Then he started cleaning the apartment. He had never cleaned it like that before. He had never cleaned anything like that before, with such furious, fanatical thoroughness. Every last nook and cranny was scoured till it shone. Every now and again, shivering with exhaustion, he sat down on a stool and wiped the cold sweat from his brow with a kitchen towel. When he had finished his study, he stood at the window for a long time and looked out into the night. Then he took Agnes's picture from the windowsill and put it on the little table in the corner. Last of all came her room, where he still hadn't changed anything. On a stack of books on the floor he found her copy of the Russian grammar. Her underlinings were rougher, her notes more carelessly scribbled than in his copy, but there weren't as many. He walked back and forth with the book in his hand. In his mind's eye he saw the dark-brown cabbage and smelled the warm, stinking fumes that had come out of the container. Breathing with difficulty, he took the Langenscheidt and the two-volume German-Russian dictionary out of the shelf. He put everything on the chest of drawers in the corridor and then assembled the few Russian books that they had both – always with a sense of imposture – brought home from some specialist bookshop or other. It would be hardest for him to part with the volume of Chekhov short stories, a particularly beautiful book bound in black leather, which he had come across in a side street behind the British Museum when he had spent a few days in London with Agnes and Kirsten.

Later, when he lay in bed, exhausted and shivering, and imagined Leskov sitting at his desk now and brooding over the gaps in his text, Perlmann's heart started racing. Neither conscious breathing nor reading did any good; only the tranquil landscape pictures on late-night television helped. He moved the phone still closer to his bed and checked that it was set to the loudest volume.

That night, for the first time, he had the tunnel dream that would haunt him at regular intervals over the coming weeks. He was driving – pressed back into his seat by the acceleration – along the vibrating floor of the tunnel, which described an endlessly long loop to the left, and fell away to the left like a cycle-racing track, so that there was always a danger of slipping into the opposite carriageway. The headlights coming from the opposite direction were like huge waves of dazzling light that sloshed over the car and obliterated his vision. At the start of the journey he was holding a steering wheel, but later his cold hands simply clutched the air, and now he could only wait, with a feeling of boundless impotence, for the impact, his ears full of that terrible whistling that gave way, after a time, to a rattling, ringing noise with regular interruptions, and dragged him from sleep.

'You registered for a call to St Petersburg?' asked a dark female voice.
'Yes,' he said and looked at his alarm clock: twenty past four.

'Just a moment, I'll put you through.' There were two clicks followed
by a hiss, and then, through a filter of background noises, he heard
Leskov's voice.

'Da? Ya slushayu . . . Kto tam?'

Perlmann put down the phone. He got dressed, packed the stack of
Russian books in an old bag and dragged them through deserted streets
to the big supermarket garbage bins.

At the weekend Perlmann started his training in slowness. He wouldn't
have imagined that it would be so difficult. Again and again he made
hasty movements, abrupt changes of intention. Then he forced himself
to repeat the whole thing so slowly that a slow-motion calm was produced.
After some time he came up with a ritual: before any lengthy sequence
of actions he went into the living room and listened to the ticking of
the big clock for half a minute. All that Saturday he waged a stubborn
battle against his unfounded haste, and often felt as if he would never
learn to do it. But by Sunday he had already managed to slow some
things down all by himself, and he felt his nervous exhaustion turning
every now and again into a natural, redeeming tiredness. Now each time
he spent a good minute listening to the big clock.

Late on Sunday afternoon he sat down at his desk for the first time.
He thought of the many books that he had left in Genoa in the airport
restroom. Would he buy new ones? He managed to push his tiredness
like a buffer between himself and that question and, for a while, he span
out that thought still further: the important thing was to take that tiredness, which was too deep-rooted ever to disappear entirely, and turn it
into a protecting shell – a substitute for serenity.

The envelope from Frau Hartwig, which he opened now, contained
only requests and demands with deadlines that had already passed. He
threw everything into the waste-paper basket. He hid the letter from Princeton
in his desk drawer. Then he put the chronicle, along with the old wax-
cloth notebook, in the kitchen along with the out-of-date newspapers.

Then he sat for a long time at his completely empty desk. From time to time he ran his hand over the gleaming surface. For the next little while the important thing was not to think too much, and even then to think slowly. Above all, he didn't want to think in sentences, in articulate, properly formulated sentences that he heard internally. For a long, very long time, he didn't want to look for words, weigh words, compare words. His thoughts should be entirely concerned with doing certain things rather than others, going to the left rather than to the right, into this room rather than that one, taking that path rather than that one. His thoughts should be apparent in the fact that he did things in their logical sequence, that there was order in his movements, a meaning in his behavior. Beyond that, his thoughts should go unnoticed, even by himself, without conscious traces, and above all without an internal linguistic echo. Even if he wrote one sentence rather than another, silence was to prevail inside his head. The pen was to pursue its path across the page, leaving its trace, without the sentence produced by that trace possessing an internal present. In the end Perlmann would send the trace to wherever it was that they were waiting for a text from him.

Something else that he had to carefully avoid was trying to work out what other people were thinking. Henceforth, he didn't want to think about what other people might think or do if he did one thing or another. He would do what he did, and the others would do what they did. There would be nothing else there. And he also had to silence his obsessively detailed imagination. He would complement his slowness training with lack-of-imagination training.

The first thing he saw later on, when he turned on the television, was a close-up of hands gliding over piano keys. Someone was playing Bach. He immediately switched to another channel. Here, a Russian physicist was being interviewed, and someone was simultaneously translating. Perlmann kept his finger on the button of the remote, he would soon switch this channel, too, but then he stayed with it, one more sentence, and then another. He felt himself being sucked into a vortex that summoned up everything again. Now the interpreter was losing the crucial balance between the old sentence and the new. *No, now you've got to skip the old sentence and concentrate on the new one!* Perlmann silently yelled at him, and slipped to the edge of the sofa. It was only when the tension turned into a stomach-cramp that he tore himself away.

Then he took a long walk through the dark park and paid attention to the emptiness in his head. When he took his glasses off to go to bed, he thought about the tunnel. Perlmann slept better than he had done for the first few days. Only once did he start awake: he had taken on Signora Medici in Russian, and then worked out that he himself didn't know the words, and had forgotten his own questions like a senile old man.

60

Perlmann spent the next week waiting for Leskov's letter. If the text had arrived on Friday, the letter could already be here by Tuesday. But it would arrive by Saturday at the latest. He stood at the window for hours and waited for the postman. Why didn't Leskov call him? Or send a telegram? Recently, not a single half hour had passed without Perlmann thinking about Leskov and the promised letter. But no letter came. The postal clerk at the airport had probably been right, and it would take a whole week. *The post doesn't usually come on Monday*, he heard Leskov saying. So Perlmann couldn't expect the letter before next Tuesday.

The offer from Olivetti came in the middle of the week. Now they were talking about a three-month probationary period. His tasks: translating business correspondence with German, English and American partners; overseeing the German and English edition of a large advertising brochure that was to be produced next summer; occasional interpreting at trade fairs. Signor Angelini had mentioned that Perlmann also spoke Russian; they would bear that in mind in the future. And, lastly, it would be nice if he could support Signor Angelini in his collaboration with the universities. They offered him four million lire per month – just half of what he currently earned. They would speak about pensions, insurance and the like when he had fundamentally agreed. For those things they would need a raft of documents.

Who had told Angelini anything about his Russian? Evelyn Mistral had kept mum, he was sure of that. It must have been Leskov, at the dinner after he arrived, when Angelini was there. He had told him how they had met, how they had walked together through the Hermitage

. . . But why, then, had Adrian von Levetzov been so unsettled in the café, when Leskov had talked about sending his first version to Perlmann? It must have been like this: over dinner Leskov had told only Angelini, who had been sitting next to him . . . Perlmann struck his knuckles against his forehead. He must stop trying to work out other people!

He had just set the letter aside when Frau Hartwig called him and passed on a message that Brian Millar had sent by email. His publisher was extremely interested in Perlmann's book. Could he suggest a delivery date? He missed Italy, Millar had added, and: 'How's your Chopin?'

Was he still there? Frau Hartwig asked after a long pause.

The book would take a while yet. Perlmann asked her to write and thank Millar for his trouble. And in conclusion: 'How's your Bach?'

'I knew nothing about a book,' Frau Hartwig said, piqued.

'Later,' he replied.

The sun was shining, and everything was thawing as he walked along the river. But he didn't notice much. He was too busy trying out letters with which he could return the prize he had recently been awarded. At last he had a text with the right tone. But when – his shoes still soaking – he had sat at his desk and written it down, he found it melodramatic and threw it away.

During the night Perlmann had pains in his heart and came close to calling the doctor. Early the next morning he went to see him at the hospital. The doctor, whom he had known for many years, didn't say much, and made long pauses that Perlmann found uncomfortable. At last he hesitantly prescribed him some new sleeping pills and told him not to smoke.

On the way home Perlmann walked past the familiar bookshop. He wished he knew more about meditation, the technique for reaching inner peace. For a long time he stood by the shelf with the books on the subject. But each excerpt that he read contained something that repelled him, something sectarian or proselytizing, an emotionalism that he didn't like. He didn't buy anything.

Friday. Today, Leskov had to hand in his text. And still no letter.

Of course, he had had to work day and night; there had been no time left for a letter. And anyway, it probably wouldn't arrive until the weekend. That meant another week of waiting. But that was actually a good sign: it proved that the text had arrived. Otherwise, Leskov would have had any amount of time for a letter. Unless he was in such a bad condition that it was out of the question.

At the time when she had usually come back from lunch, Perlmann called Maria. She sounded spontaneous and sincere when she said how pleased she was to hear from him. Nonetheless, the conversation was something of a struggle. Those two weeks had been enough to move everything far into the past, and each sentence sounded like a frantic attempt to warm up something obsolete. He had done a lot of preparation for the question of whether she had deleted the files in the meantime; it was supposed to sound quite casual, like a joke at the end of a flirtation. When he asked it now, it seemed to come completely out of nowhere. She had just cleared up her hard drive, said Maria; but right now she couldn't remember whether his files had been among the deleted ones. Did he want her to check?

'No, no,' he said, trying to make it sound light and playful. 'It really doesn't matter!'

'Even if they aren't in the computer any more, I still remember those texts very clearly!' said Maria, laughing.

It would be impossible to call her again, he thought as he hung up.

His credit-card bill arrived on Saturday. They had deducted the sums for the rental car, including the excess for the repairs, and for the two dictionaries from the bookshop in Genoa. That day Perlmann had wanted to start on a book that he had been offered for review. Now he just sat around and kept hopping from channel to channel.

He had been worried that he would dream about the tunnel again. Instead, he spent half the night – it seemed to him – battling with a computer, which, when he tried to delete a file produced a back-up copy instead. Brian Millar watched over his shoulder, so closely that Perlmann could feel his breath. All at once Millár's arm was thrown in front of Perlmann's face, holding out a plate piled high with ice-cold food. Perlmann turned to him and, when he recognized the waiter, he threw the food so hard in his face that half of it splashed on Evelyn Mistral's hair and her snow-white blouse.

On Sunday Perlmann started taking down some of Agnes's photographs and clearing them away. Only a few were to remain – not necessarily the best ones, but the ones with a personal history. For example, the one with little Kirsten in the beach chair on the island of Sylt. It was hard work, and more than once he got chest pains. In the end he had a sense of having gone too far, and hung a series of pictures back up, whereupon the plaster started crumbling as the nail was hammered in for the second time.

Evelyn Mistral rang in the early evening. It was a conversation with a lot of pauses. Perlmann wished she was sitting opposite him. Had he heard anything about Leskov and his text? No, he said, nothing.

'You know the phone call I suddenly remembered after the reception at the town hall?' she said towards the end of their conversation. 'It was a good thing I called. Once again, everything that could go wrong did go wrong. And the coast road was closed anyway!' she laughed.

Over the following week Perlmann sat down to write his review. He saw the author in his mind's eye, a glittering Berliner with a French wife and a house on the Côte d'Azur. Perlmann had to take a lot of breaks and, sometimes, when his reluctance became too violent, his chest felt like concrete. Then he reached for a cigarette.

The key chapter of the book presented as new discoveries things with which Perlmann had long been familiar from the work of a little-known French writer. He knew exactly where he should have looked: the book was on the top shelf on the right. He waited for a feeling of triumph or at least of calm satisfaction. When it failed to materialize, he was at first disappointed, but then glad. He left the French book on the shelf, and in his review, which was objective, fair and positive on the whole, he didn't mention the matter at all.

In the middle of the week he sat back down behind the wheel for the first time. He was surprised at how close the handbrake of his car was to the passenger seat. He drove to a carpet dealer he knew and bought a light-colored Tibetan runner to cover up the coffee stain at long last. On the way back, in the early twilight, several trucks came towards him, one of them with its headlights on full beam. Each time a truck appeared, Perlmann braked to a walking pace and drove on to the grass. He decided not to drive in the near future, and wondered whether he should give the car to Kirsten.

As he was taking out the ignition key in the garage, he remembered that moment at the gas station next to the hotel, where he had thought he had understood that the problem of inner delineation from other people and the lack of a presence were one and the same problem deep down. He clearly remembered that this had struck him as the most important insight of his whole life. On the way to his front door Perlmann had rephrased that insight over and over again. But now it was just a sentence. A sentence, admittedly, that sounded right, and one that he agreed with, but only a sentence now, not an experienced insight. At the front door he turned round, opened the garage and sat down at the wheel again with his hand on the ignition. Afterwards it seemed ridiculous to assume that an experienced insight could be poured into a particular physical posture.

There was still no letter from Leskov on Friday. No wonder, in fact, because it must have taken him the past weekend to recover, and a letter could – as that veteran postal clerk had estimated – be en route for a whole week. Leaving from his mailbox, Perlmann finally put away the new handkerchiefs, saving one for his pocket. Then he wrote a letter to Olivetti turning down their offer, and a second letter to Angelini. He cited his reason as unforeseen family difficulties that would keep him in Frankfurt for the time being. He wrote both letters quickly and effortlessly. He tried to exploit that momentum, and started on the letter to Princeton. But he couldn't get beyond the salutation, and then took a long walk through the familiar city, which seemed alien to him in the gloomy December light.

Laura Sand's photographs, which arrived on Saturday, disappointed him. He didn't know why. They were dreamy landscape shots. Some of them must have been taken on the misty morning when he had completed the translation of Leskov's text. In a separate envelope were several shots of colleagues, which, to judge by the unselfconsciousness of posture and expression, must have been taken unnoticed. On the accompanying slip of paper were the words: *There are exceptions to every rule!* The pictures showing him with Leskov he immediately threw away, and the other shots of colleagues ended up in the waste-paper basket as well. He kept only a single snapshot of Evelyn Mistral. Her laugh, her skewed T-shirt, her red shoes. He put the landscape shots in a drawer, then walked through the rooms for a while and looked at Agnes's photographs.

He should really, in fact, have chosen her best shots, not the most personal. He swapped them round.

After the Sunday night concert on television he sat down at the grand piano. He played the Nocturnes that he had chosen in the lounge. There was a vacuum between him and the notes, a thin hiatus, which didn't even disappear the second time. He couldn't understand what was wrong, and played the A flat minor Polonaise. It didn't matter at all that he got snarled up in the frightening passage. What was worse was that everything, even the liberating chords, sounded as if it had been dunked in fine sand.

There was no point even thinking about sleep. In the middle of the night he sat down at the piano in his pyjamas and played other Nocturnes. They sounded as they had before, and now he understood: what he had played in the lounge had shifted away from him because he had abused it, abused it as a weapon in his battle with Millar. That was an abuse different from the one that Szabo had meant. Music couldn't be used as an instrument like that, or you lost it.

Towards morning Perlmann took a sleeping pill. When it started to take effect, a thought passed through his head, even though he hadn't been thinking about the tunnel: Leskov had never asked him why he hadn't just stopped in the passing bay to let the bulldozer through. Why not? It would have been a quite simple question, the most natural, in fact. And Perlmann couldn't have told him the answer.

61

The bundle that the postman held in his hand on Tuesday contained Leskov's letter. Perlmann could tell from the brownish paper of the envelope, which he knew from his earlier letter. Still in the hall, he tore open the envelope and looked, with thumping heart and feverish brain, for sentences that could immediately reassure him . . . *there was no text there when I entered the apatment . . . I slipped, without really noticing, into a state of apathy . . . a state of dull endurance, of wordless resignation . . . desire to end it all . . .* And then came the words that let him breathe again for the first time: . . . *if the text hadn't turned up after all . . .* He closed his eyes and hung on to the chest of drawers for a moment before he went on reading, his eyes still burning: . . . *the envelope just lying by the front door . . . the two yellow stickers . . . The state of the text was a shock . . . Seventeen pages!* Perlmann had to skip through five endless paragraphs until it came at last: . . . *I had, contrary to my custom, written my home address, that's all . . .* He pressed his hand to his stomach and breathed out, before dashing on to the next bit of redemption: . . . *typing errors. But just after eight o'clock on Friday morning the thing was finished . . .* And, at last, in the next paragraph but one, came the sentence that his eye really devoured: . . . *the decision was to be made at around midday: they simply couldn't do anything other than give me the post.*

Perlmann leaned against the door frame, the sheets slipped from his hand, he started silently sobbing and went on sobbing, on and on, for several minutes. He only paused to blow his nose. With trembling hands he collected the sheets, sat on the sofa and started from the beginning:

St Petersburg, December

Dear Philipp.

I feel very guilty about writing to you only now. I had promised to tell you about the text straight away. But if I tell you how it all came about, you will, I hope, understand.

I reached home very late, because Moscow Airport was chaotic as well, and the plane here set off only after an hour's delay, it was already the middle of the night. The passengers were delighted that there was still a bus into the city, even if its heating didn't work and it was an icy-cold journey. The deepest winter had set in here in the meantime, in fact, and even though I somehow like the curiously cold, almost unearthly light that a fall of snow emanates even in the darkest night, I found myself longing for the glowing, yet transparent light of the south, from which I was coming. I will never forget how that light overwhelmed me when I stepped out of the airport with you and then stood next to the parking cabin (with that stubborn man in the red cap!). I feel as if months have passed since then!

And it's just two weeks. They were, however, a nightmare. Because there was no text there when I entered the apartment. Throughout the whole journey it was as if I was sitting on coals, and I was so furious about the delay in Moscow that I snapped at everyone I came across. When the plane prepared to land here, something strange and almost paradoxical happened to me: out of pure fear that the text mightn't be there, suddenly I didn't want to go home. The state of uncertainty that spoiled some aspects of my stay with you all, and which became all the more unbearable the closer we got to St Petersburg (which is somehow strange in itself), that state suddenly seemed the lesser evil, compared with the feared discovery. But of course I then walked from the bus stop to the flat as quickly as my suitcase allowed me, and my hands – albeit from cold – were shaking when I opened the door.

As I have said: when I dashed to the desk, the text wasn't there, I saw it straight away, because I had written that text on yellow paper. Of course I looked around the whole room, and also in the corridor, from where I had phoned before I set off. But fundamentally I was under no illusions. Even less so since now, since now, when I was back where it happened, my

*memory of packing the text was quite clear and unambiguous. I could actu-
ally feel the hasty movements with which I had put the pages in the outside
pocket of the suitcase. I knew immediately: you must have taken it out and
left it somewhere on the way. Hence the piece of rubber band in the zip.*

*I had actually expected to be assailed by intense despair, mixed with
impotent fury about my scattiness. And that that would stop over the next
few days of waiting for a package from Lufthansa. (It was a very good thing,
by the way, that you addressed the subject of postal duration, I immediately
thought of it and cautioned myself.) But it was quite different, and even
now I don't know whether I should think of it as better or worse than the
natural reaction. As soon as I had sat down to rest, without really noticing
I slipped into a state of apathy. I was glad of the inner quiet that that
involved, because I had feared the agitation, the sleeplessness and everything
bound up with it. But soon it became clear to me that I had, quite automatically, let myself fall back into the state into which I had settled in prison
– a state of dull endurance, of wordless resignation, which, as you soon learn
there, saves your strength. And I'm very shocked by that, because I had
thought that that experience was a thing of the past.*

*I wasn't able to free myself from my apathy over the days that followed,
and perhaps I didn't want to, even though the state seemed dangerous to
me, because there was also something increasingly self-destructive about it.
For example, I started to wonder whether there might be deeper reasons for
my oversight: that I didn't actually want the post, or that I was trying to
distance myself from the content of the text. My uncertainty became so great
that I couldn't tell Larissa anything about it, even though she sensed on the
telephone that something wasn't quite right with me.*

*Every day I went into the institute and waited for the post. And when
nothing came, I didn't know how I would get through the next twenty-four
hours. It was impossible to start a letter. It was impossible to start anything,
in fact. I spent a lot of time standing on the banks of the Neva. The apathy
I'm talking about: it's shot through with grey, waiting for everything to pass
without the slightest idea of what should be good about its passing. Part of
this is the – how can I put it – mild desire to end it all. I hadn't felt that
desire for a long time, quite the contrary, now it made its presence felt again*

and merged with the suddenly resurfacing grief over Mother's death. Where that would have led if the text hadn't reappeared, I don't know.

Of course, I wondered whether I shouldn't at least present the first version under these circumstances. But after a few attempted readings I rejected the idea. The text is simply too feeble, and so confused as to be repellent to me. How is one supposed to present a text that is far below the level one has attained on the subject in the meantime? It's an emotional impossibility. Sooner no text at all!

On Wednesday, when still nothing had come, I summoned all my courage, sat down and tried to reconstruct everything from memory. I felt a bit as I had in Santa Margherita when I was preparing myself for my session. I must have spent close to twenty hours sitting tight at my desk, and there was so much smoke in the apartment afterwards that it was too much even for me. Then I gave up, and when I crept half-dead from my bed on Thursday I had buried all hope of the post and started looking around for part-time work. (You do it even if it seems pointless.)

For that reason I called in at the institute again on Friday, since I was in the area anyway. From the way the conversations fell silent as I appeared, I had to conclude that my never-arriving package had already become a talking point. Vassily Sergeevich's imaginary package! And then it happened: as I got home from the institute, having abandoned all hope, there was the envelope just lying by the front door! Just imagine all the things that could have happened! I concluded from a long way off that it must be my text (quite apart from wishful thinking) from the two yellow stickers, because the Lufthansa address labels that I saw on items of luggage on my journey were the same color. And then I also saw the red express delivery label that looks different to the ones we have here. As I ran the last few meters I nearly fell on the ice, and I opened the envelope while I was still on the doorstep.

The envelope itself was nothing special (not to be compared to the one you had with you that time in the café!), but just imagine: Lufthansa had taken the trouble to put the text in a plastic jacket! When I thought about it later, that struck me as slightly grotesque, as the jacket couldn't be closed because of a defective zip, so that some feared moisture (if that was what it was for — but what else, if not?) had seeped into the paper anyway. But for the first moment I was quite astonished. Such care. 'German thorough-ness', I thought at first; but then I remembered the sour face you pulled when Brian used that cliché.

The state of the text was a shock. As if it had been in a ditch for days! First of all, most of the pages were dirty, in places to the point of illegi-bility. Others are torn, and the first page has a hole in it as if it's been shot. But that was all fine. What left me completely paralyzed for a while was the discovery that seventeen pages were missing! Seventeen pages! And the last eight, of all things, the ones in which I show what appropriation can mean in my conception of narrating, inventing memory! At first I thought: I'll never do that in a week. And again I felt that apathy that had all at once dissolved to nothing at the sight of the yellow stickers. But then my memory came into play. I realized that much that was lost was coming back to me, and then I pulled myself together and went to my desk.

You will probably think this mad, but I couldn't really start work before I had found an explanation for the state of the pages. And that wasn't easy.

The package had been dispatched from Frankfurt. So I had left the text in the waiting room when changing planes. (Not on the plane – you know my theory about cleaning crews.) Even now I can't remember taking it out. (Or rather the opposite: I have remembered in the meantime that, hidden by a newspaper that someone had left behind, I spent ages staring at a fantastic-looking woman two rows ahead of me.) But it must simply have been the case. But where did the dirt come from, and the blisters in the paper that seemed to have been caused by water? Only that night in bed did it occur to me: at some point – by being touched by a coat, or a child – the pages fell on the floor; there are lots of things on the floor in waiting rooms like that at the end of the day. I have never seen such a machine myself, but there must be huge vacuum cleaners or at any rate automatic cleaning machines that tidy the place up. And then it's quite clear: the pages must have ended up in a thing like that. That would explain the dirt and the tears, and since you can't clean without water, the blisters and waves in the paper can't come as a surprise.

That no one noticed the many yellow sheets of paper: somehow I imagine two chatting cleaning women, heedlessly running the vacuum cleaner tube along the floor. Then, when the dirt-container is being emptied, they discover the paper. Seventeen pages have been hopelessly destroyed; all you can do is shrug. The rest they pass on to the lost and found, if there is such a thing. You see: this one cleaning crew is the exception to my theory. As befits a deus ex machina!

It was an unsettled night, because every time I was about to fall asleep, another mystery occurred to me. One hard nut was the business with the address. I can't remember if I told you: I always write the address on the last page. But it was missing! I got as excited as if it were a chess puzzle. In the end I had three hypotheses, which I can't choose between even today: either the last sheet was so badly damaged that they just copied out the address and then threw it away; or else the person who prepared the envelope kept the last page out to copy down the address and then forgot to put it in the envelope (perhaps he was distracted by something); or finally, as I often use old envelopes as notepaper, an envelope with my address on it had slipped between the pages. That was where they got the address from, not my text.

I got up again and looked at the postmark once more: why had it taken Lufthansa a whole week to send the package? For a while I was furious with those people: how much they could have spared me if they had been a little faster! But then my gratitude prevailed, particularly when I became aware that the address was in Russian on the text. They must have fetched someone specially who could read Russian, and handwritten Russian at that! All right, then, I thought, Lufthansa is Lufthansa. In the meantime, I've written a thank you letter, and I will also provide a recommendation. (As if Lufthansa needed my recommendations!)

The last incongruity occurred to me only the next morning when I was shaving: how did Lufthansa know my home address, when it was my work address that was on the text? No one in Germany knows where I live. (Apart from you, of course.) That ran through my head again and again over the course of the day, and struck me as the one insoluble mystery. Of course, there's the possibility of an envelope with the home address on it. But there's something artificial about that (another deus ex machina!). And besides, wouldn't they have sent that portentous envelope as well? That's what I would have done. An open envelope in someone's hands doesn't necessarily mean that that person is also the addressee. And if someone receives a name-less text, he's more likely to make sense of things if an envelope addressed to him arrives with it, than if there are no clues at all. (If he hasn't just fished it out of a waste-paper basket, the current owner of the envelope will be one of the acquaintances of the addressee, and the author of the text will eventually be found among them.)

Whatever. The more natural story, I finally and reluctantly admitted, is that I didn't write my work address on it at all: if my memory deceives me over the question of whether I took the text out of my case – why couldn't it deceive me here, too? Contrary to my usual habit, I wrote my private address on it, simple as that. It unsettles me to find that I plainly can't rely on my memory. That used not to be the case. An experience which, of course, fits Gorky's subject and my thesis (even though that connection, as you know, is more complicated than it might superficially appear). If the experience were not so awkward . . .

In spite of all these explanations: a hint of strangeness, of mystery, still remains. As if a drama had been played out around this text, of which its actors have no notion . . . If that had happened to Gorky – he would have made something of it!

What happened outside the world during the six days that followed – I haven't the faintest idea. I can't even remember the weather. I was typing things out, filling gaps, going on typing, reconstructing the next missing thought, and so on. As long as I hadn't finished the day's workload, I simply didn't stop, regardless of how late it was getting and how much my back hurt. The tension was so great that I even brought myself to ask a hated neighbor to do some food shopping for me. (She couldn't believe her ears. Since then our relationship has been excellent!)

Between Wednesday night and Friday morning I rewrote the lost conclu-sion. The text isn't nearly as good as the original one. In fact, it's even rather shoddy. Somehow I was so exhausted that I couldn't really keep my thoughts together. And temporarily I felt as if my earlier impression of having found a coherent solution for the problem of appropriation was pure delusion, a Fata Morgana. I didn't go to bed. I just dozed for half an hour on the sofa every now and again. I think there are a few typing errors. But shortly after eight on Friday morning the thing was finished.

I walked slowly through a thick, fairy-tale snowstorm to the institute, and made several copies there. I savored the moment when I laid the manuscript on the table in front of the Chair of the Commission. He had given up expecting it, and you could see that he was distressed. I could swear that he had already made promises to someone else (I don't know to whom) which he would now have to revoke. I think he really hated me at that moment.

All that weekend I just slept, ate, slept. The Commission's meeting, I discovered later, was that Monday morning, and the decision was to be made at around midday: they simply couldn't do anything other than give me the post. (Of course, in that short time no one had read the text. Once again they were concerned only with externals such as length.) But they kept me waiting. No one informed me. Then, when I called on them yesterday, I was informed of the result in an insultingly casual manner. And I also discovered that the conditions for the post are worse than expected. Still, though, it's a permanent post, so I can breathe for the first time. I would have liked to celebrate with someone: but the only possible person would have been Yuri (the one with the fifty dollars) and he wasn't there. I tried to call you, but those endlessly engaged phone lines are hopeless, so I started this letter, which I had to interrupt because my exhaustion caught up with me.

I think a lot about that wonderful week with you all. I will send you a copy of the text under separate cover. (You will probably be annoyed if I say this, but still: I don't think it will be too difficult for you.) I would really like to send all the other colleagues a copy – so that they can see that this portentous text really exists! Because it's a nightmare typical of our profession: being invited to give a lecture somewhere – and you have no text! How easy it is to feel that the others think you're a fraud! But perhaps it will end up being translated and published. Can you envisage that any more clearly now?

I hope to hear from you soon. You struck us all as seriously exhausted, and I hope you will soon recover. I felt that you didn't want us to mention Agnes, so I just want to assure you that there was a lot of sympathy for your difficult situation in the group.

And let me add one thing in conclusion: even when you were here, I had the feeling I had a friend in you. After my week with you I am now sure of it. You showed an interest in my work that no one has ever shown before. And the way you were interested in Klim Samgin showed me that we have much else in common. I don't need to stress how much I look forward to seeing you again soon.

Do svidaniya. Yours Vassily

That last paragraph brought tears to Perlmann's eyes once more. But now they were no longer tears of relief, but of shame, and he hid his face in the cushion. When he went to the bathroom afterwards, to wash his tear-drenched face, he felt a weight lifting from him, one so powerful that he had had to turn his emotions away from it all the time, to be able to bear it at all. He lay down, exhausted, on the sofa, and after a while he read the letter again.

The worst passages, he found, were the ones about the prison and the parenthetical remark about Perlmann's knowledge of his private address. Then came the passage about the drama and the unknown actors, and it was also unbearable that Leskov, because he had no one to celebrate with, had tried to call him – him, of all people, when he had been a hair's breadth away from murdering him. Only in the course of the day did Perlmann manage to smile about one passage or an other, which he read several times, and it was always an endangered smile that didn't dare to go too far for fear of subsiding into tears once more. When evening began to fall, he went to the piano and played the Nocturne in D flat major. Blind with tears, he kept hitting wrong notes.

62

In mid-December Perlmann went to Hamburg to see Hanna Liebig. Her golden hair had developed a silvery sheen, and under the dark strand that she combed emphatically over her forehead there was a long scar, which, as she said with embarrassment, was the result of a car accident. She was still energetic. But there was, he thought, something washed-out and disappointed in her face. He liked her apartment, but an overly ornate clock and some ceramic knick-knacks bothered him, because they struck him as whimsical – as if they were signs that Hanna's finely honed sense of elegant design was deserting her.

Over dinner he told her about the research group, about Millar and their rivalry. He also mentioned that he had played the A flat minor Polonaise. Afterwards she had some idea of why he had phoned her. But without the tunnel, the fear and the despair the whole thing sounded hollow and childish. When she ran her hand playfully over his hair on the way to the kitchen, as she had done in the past, he was about to start over from the beginning and tell her the whole story. But something in her face, something new that he couldn't have described, seemed strange to him, and then the feeling was over. They talked again for a while about Liszt, but it was mere shop talk, which soon bored him, because it had no connection with Millar and the ochre-colored armchairs in the lounge. Afterwards in the street he reflected that they had been closer to one another recently on the phone than during the whole of their meeting that evening.

They had arranged to meet for lunch the following day. Perlmann didn't go. As he heard her playing through a run and explaining something, he slipped a note under the door of her apartment and then took the bus to the Conservatoire. The sound of Mozart came from the room where he had always practiced in the past. After a while he opened the door a crack. At the piano sat a man with curly hair and an oriental face, playing with unimaginable lightness. The room had different wallpaper now, and the painting by Klee was no longer on the wall. He carefully closed the door. He had planned to seek out the street where he had grown up. But when he saw the black iron fences in his mind's eye, and felt his arm hopping from one fence post to the next, he abandoned the plan and took the next train to Frankfurt.

In his mailbox there was a message from the post office about a package. He could see straight away that it was from Leskov, when the clerk took it from the shelf the following morning. He wished it hadn't come, whatever it might contain. Leskov's letter was what he had needed, and he had had to endure it. He had found its thoroughness oppressive, but it was hard to admit this to himself. It had been the most extreme thing he could bear, and it was the last he wanted to hear from Vassily Leskov. Fine, he would have to give him some kind of reply. But that could be done in a conventional tone. There were moods in which Perlmann scribbled down such things without any inner involvement. And then he never wanted to hear from Leskov again. Never again.

Inside the parcel was the promised copy of Leskov's text. Underneath it, four volumes in Russian, bound in light-brown artificial leather: *Maxim Gorky, Zhisn' Klima Samgina*. On the first page of the first volume it said in shaky handwriting: *Moemu syno Vasiliyu*. The dedication was written in black ink, and the pen had sprayed, there was a sprinkle of black dots around the words. The leather was worn, stained and in two places torn. It was the volumes that Leskov had read in prison – fourteen times.

Perlmann knew that he was supposed to feel touched, but all he felt was fury, a fury that grew every time he looked at the books. Through those brown volumes with their gold inscriptions, Leskov had managed to make contact with his flat, and Leskov was now present in a way that was almost even more oppressive and paralysing than his physical presence. Now Perlmann also smelled the hint of sickly sweet tobacco that lingered between the pages. He felt that he might be about to lose his head and hurl the books outside into the mud, so he put his coat back on and walked slowly to his block.

Later he set the volumes on the shelf in the broom cupboard and covered them with a dishcloth. Then, when he reluctantly flicked through the typed text, he discovered that Leskov thanked him extravagantly at the start of his acknowledgements for his discussion of an earlier version and his constructive criticism in four footnotes. The burden that had been lifted from him by Leskov's letter seemed to sink down upon him once more, even though he didn't understand how that could be, now that Leskov had managed to get the position he wanted.

Perlmann defended himself against the books in the broom cupboard by finishing his review and preparing his course of lectures. When Adrian von Levetzov rang and asked about publication, Perlmann sent off a round letter to his colleagues, claiming that some participants in the group had other plans for their contributions, so that he had abandoned the plan of a special publication. The same day he rang the school authorities and asked about the possibility of taking on a job as a teacher. Not without the proper qualifications, the shrill voice at the other end informed him, and not in the current job market. That night he dreamed of Signora Medici, standing in front of an audience in a tartan skirt and hiking boots, reading sentences in an unknown language from light-brown books, as he looked excitedly in his desk for his crib sheet.

Perlmann's training in slowness was starting to work. Usually, it was no longer necessary to go to the living room to look at the clock; he simply paused and imagined the ticking. He started thinking about that ticking when he was on the phone, as well, and gradually understood that slowness in reacting could be the physical expression of a lack of subservience. He was so happy about this discovery that he overdid it, and had to fight once more against his tendency to fanaticism.

Now and again, when he sat in this living room late at night and heard the clock ticking, he tried to think about why he had taken his hands off the wheel. Because of Leskov? Because of himself? But it was always the same thing: the thoughts dried up before they had really begun. In his mind, he had been ready to die. Out of despair, admittedly, not out of stoical serenity. Nonetheless, the experience of imminent death had changed something within him. Of course, it had been an error to believe that this change, whose contours were still in the dark, would develop all by themselves into greater confidence and a piece of inner freedom. It wasn't as easy as that. But what exactly was it that he had to do about it?

One evening, while watching a silly comedy on television, Perlmann laughed again for the first time. Then he remembered the man with the long white scarf from the airport bar, and gulped. But by the next joke he had started laughing again.

The next day he bought the German translation of Gorky's novel and read it until he came to the passage about the hole in the ice. *Gleaming red*, Gorky called the hands that clutched the edge of the ice, which broke off. Perlmann went into Agnes's room, to look up the second word. Only when he saw the gap on the shelf did he remember the books he had thrown away. He was startled, as if he had only just found out about it.

Perlmann found the novel heavy going, and the countless philosophical dialogues got on his nerves. He really wanted to put it down. But that day he read another hundred pages, and worked out that he would have to get through at least 120 pages if he was to finish it that year. Often he succumbed to the temptation to ease his attention and just let his eye slip over the pages without really reading. But he never overindulged himself, instead flicking back and reading everything over again with reluctant but embittered precision, knowing that he would immediately forget most of it again. In the first days he told himself that it was a matter of becoming acquainted with part of the mental world in which Leskov had taken refuge in prison. He owed him that, he thought, and each time he did so he stumbled over the vague feeling of not knowing what he thought. Only after a few days did he understand that that wasn't what drove him to torment himself again by reading it each evening. It was more the vague desire to pay off his debt to Leskov, and atone for his planned murder. After that discovery he felt ridiculous every time he opened the book again. But he kept on with it.

Late in December he rang Maria again. He wished her a Merry Christmas and hoped she would be able to tell him something about the deletion of his text. But nothing more came of it than a friendly exchange of good wishes, which they soon had to bring to an end to avoid embarrassment. He would never find out when the dangerous text was finally destroyed, or whether indeed it had been.

Kirsten came on the second day of the Christmas holidays. As soon as she stepped inside the apartment, she pounced on the new carpet, looked at it from all sides and, finally, lifted it up to look at the label. When she saw the coffee stain, she burst into peals of laughter and gave Perlmann a boisterous kiss. He still didn't let her wheedle the carpet out of him.

Later she came into the kitchen so quietly that, preoccupied with cooking, he didn't notice her for a long time.

'You put away some pictures,' she said.

'Yes,' he replied, and looked at her for a moment, the salt cellar in his hand.

'But you're leaving these, aren't you?'

'Yes,' he said, 'definitely.'

'Does this Ms. Sand take good pictures?'

'They're OK,' he said.

'Black and white?'

'Color.'

'Oh, I see,' she said, relieved, and took a piece of salmon from the plate.

When they were eating, she suddenly lowered her knife and fork, and stared at his hand.

'You've taken off your ring.'

Perlmann blushed intensely. He didn't say anything.

'I'm sorry,' she said quietly, 'of course that's your business.'

Later, when they were clearing away the plates, she asked in a pointedly casual way, 'The blonde in the group, what was her name again? Evelyn . . .'

'Mistral,' he said, and put away the coffee cups.

He was standing in his study when Kirsten handed him his Christmas present: a navy blue sailor's jersey, the kind he had always wanted. Inside the package there was something else, a book. Nikolai Leskov, *Short Stories.* He was speechless and turned the book around mutely in his hand.

'A really important writer,' said Kirsten. 'Martin's writing a dissertation on him. Unfortunately, I didn't manage to find a Russian edition. Don't you like it?'

'No, I do,' he said hoarsely, and walked, moist-eyed, to the window.

She wrapped her arms around him from behind. 'It's really hard for you right now, isn't it?' He nodded.

As always, she walked curiously along his bookshelves. 'You've done some tidying.'

He looked at her questioningly.

'I don't see the Russian books.'

Perlmann poked his nose into a desk drawer. 'I . . . cleared them away. Temporarily.'

'And the big dictionary I saw in Italy? The one with the revolting paper?'

He nodded.

'And the volume of Chekhov? I told Martin about it.'

'I . . . I had a kind of impulse.'

For a while she looked in silence at the wall of books. 'Then perhaps Leskov wasn't such a great idea.'

Perlmann gave a start when he heard the name in her mouth.

'No, no,' he said quickly, 'that's completely different.' It sounded tired and implausible.

They didn't talk much as they did the washing-up.

'Dad,' she asked into the silence, 'did something happen down there? In Italy, I mean.'

All of a sudden the hands with which he was cleaning the frying pan were quite numb. He ran the dishcloth over the edge. 'What do you mean – happen?'

'I don't know. Since then you've been somehow . . . different.'

He looked at the crumbs floating in the dishwater. An answer was required. 'I . . . I lost my equilibrium. But it has nothing to do with Italy.'

When their eyes met he saw that she didn't believe him.

'Do you remember,' she asked in a cheerful voice that was supposed to make him forget the subject, 'when we sat in that white hotel and the waiter came all that way from the bar with the drinks?'

When Kirsten had gone to bed, Perlmann fetched the suitcase from the wardrobe. The wedding ring had slipped right into the corner of the tie compartment. He locked it in his desk drawer. After that he couldn't get to sleep. Even so, he didn't take a pill. Eventually he went to the broom cupboard and took out the key.

In the morning it snowed, so he had an excuse not to get the car out of the garage. He was glad there were lots of practical matters to talk about in the taxi and on the platform. As they were saying goodbye Kirsten looked at him as if she wanted to ask her question again. He pretended not to notice, and lifted her gloved hand. He turned it into a sober farewell that hurt him so much he spent several minutes afterwards wandering aimlessly through the station.

That day he had the feeling that he had to start his slowness training again from the beginning, and spent a lot of time in front of the ticking clock. He wrote half a dozen drafts of his letter to Princeton, with various white lies. He constantly had to fight against his tendency to confess the truth, and only defeated it when he gave it free rein and then threw the text away with revulsion. After that he made a point of being as laconic as possible, until he realized that they would sense his fury, which would betray him in a different way. In the end it was a bland and formal letter of refusal, which he left on the chest of drawers in the corridor.

The tunnel dream, which had left him in peace for a while, now assailed him again, many times, and when he woke up, it was always with the sentence: *The red hands will never let him go.* He never found out whether these words were being uttered by Leskov, sitting next to him, or whether they only came to mind after the dream ended. He became used to getting up straight away and listening to some music over a cup of tea.

The ring finger on his left hand bore a fine white scar.

Once Perlmann dreamed he was playing the A flat minor Polonaise. Everything went smoothly, even the frightening passage, and he didn't understand why he awoke as if from a nightmare. Only in the course of the day did it become clear to him: he had been bored while playing. Unsettled, he took a long walk past shops in which the Christmas decorations were being taken down. He felt as if someone had broken a great piece out of him. He heard the chords quite loudly in his head, and now he thought again of Brian Millar. He hated him.

He wrote his letter to Leskov on the last day of the year. That day he couldn't eat anything, and the letter was stiff. He had, he wrote towards the end, bought himself a copy of Gorky's novel immediately upon his return. For that reason he was returning his, Leskov's, copy, because the books were so very precious to him. He fine-tuned those sentences for ages. He wanted to create a sense of distance, without hurting Leskov. It was an insoluble task. At last he decided that the practical tone he had given the whole thing was quite clear enough.

The day after New Year's Day Perlmann took everything to the post office. When he bought a newspaper on his way back to the kiosk, he met the institute librarian. As they laughed about the latest gossip, Perlmann was tempted to put his arm around her shoulder. He felt the anticipated movement in his arm, but managed inwardly to halt it, and his hand stayed in his pocket.

In the paper he came upon an advertisement looking for a teacher at the German School in Managua. He set off and had the required photograph taken. On the way he reflected that he could have taken the job with Olivetti that very day. When he had finished his application, it occurred to him that he had forgotten to go shopping. Perlmann stepped inside a crowded bar with trashy Christmas decorations on the walls. When he was greeted with the loud laughter of a large group sitting around a table he turned on his heel and walked along deserted streets to the station, where he stood at a snack bar and ate a burnt sausage and a roll that tasted like sawdust.

On Monday morning Perlmann put his application for Managua in the post box opposite the university. On the way to the lecture hall he slipped and fell. After he had brushed the snow from his coat, he stood still for a moment and closed his eyes. He thought about the ticking clock as he stepped inside the hall and slowly walked towards the auditorium.

Nothing had happened.